For you,
Flather and
amigo,

Jim
Strasioux

THE MOONDEAD

A SACRISTAN MYSTERY

A Novel

L. A. MASCONE

A SACRISTAN Book

Llyndragon Publishing LLC
Phoenix, AZ

SACRIS✝AN

This book is a work of fiction. Names, characters, places and situations are
products of the author's imagination or used fictitiously.
Any resemblance to actual events, locales or persons,
living and dead, is entirely coincidental.

Manufactured in the United States of America

Library of Congress Control Number: 2014921650

ISBN: 978-0-578-15409-1

In memory of my mother,
Mabel Williams Herdman
1906 - 1942
Requiescat in pace

For Christopher, Maren,
Scotlyn and Siena

...and for all those looking for a little redemption

INTRODUCTION

If you thought you were choosing a cozy mystery, *The Moondead* is not of that genre nor is our nun even close to the character played by Ingrid Bergman in "The Bells of Saint Mary's" though L. A. Mascone liked the movie. Touched by the supernatural, our mystery is a modern-day crime drama; a medieval morality tale reinvented. The detectives duck under crime tape to discover grim scenes they can't understand. Their words may sometimes offend; the narrative, heavy with dialogue. The nun, who will give an assist, often whispers: "Everyone's looking for a little redemption."

But not all will find it in a remote desert city several hours north of the Border. In a fictitious locale in the Arizona Sonoran, one is confronted by contrasts. The clamor of a First Precinct squad room cannot compare to the calm, daily ritual behind convent walls. The sun-bleached desert is far removed from the dark of a Cathedral with secrets and a graveyard hidden beneath the home of its bishop.

The Moondead is Book One in a series entitled the Sacristan Mysteries; its content supposedly taken from the journal of a bishop's sacristan, a nun, whose notes cover years of sleuthing by the side of a fiery Irish detective. Paraphrasing other resources and search engines, at the end of each chapter, Mascone provides author's notes consisting of commentary and even translations of non-English words and expressions. In the Addendum, more definition concerning the characters and a Glossary will hopefully assist the reader.

Newly arrived to the parish of San Miguel, the archaeologist-turned-nun, Sister Magdalen, is restless and would welcome some *convent noir.*

Things are not what they seem in L'Arroyo.

TABLE OF CONTENTS

INTROIT

Belfast-born Lt. John Padric would always remember where he was the night it came over the wire; the Jameson was smooth and he was drinking alone at the Bog & Mudd, a dive as dank as the name implied. Early on, the case of the moondead had been handed off to the First Precinct; the investigation alone almost buried him. Lead night detective for Major Crimes, Padric had traded blows with the city's underbelly for eighteen years on the force and often, waxed eloquent over a bottle of ale: "What we've got here, *bhoyos*, is Wild West-medieval." Once an academic and serious scholar, he was still a devotee of the Bard and F. Scott Fitzgerald and known to quote them at crime scenes. The man spoke with style and revealed another John Padric

Earlier that night, they'd been called out to a derelict house that hung like a cobweb between two walls in an alley near the Cathedral. There'd been some complaints: odd noises, vehicles coming and going. They found nothing and Martinez muttered: "For old time sake, Johnny, quote me some Effin' Scott Fitzgerald." Padric had barely whispered: "Show me a hero…" when the floorboards in the kitchen gave way and in seconds, both were picking themselves up off the rough cement in a makeshift mortuary under the house. They cursed and he offered some Shakespeare as well: "All that lives must die, my man; we got dead people. Get CSI over here."

Alleys all over L'Arroyo had been dubbed the Underground Railroad, networks of travel so complex the law could hardly contain them. Criminals used them for nefarious reasons and the skeletal remains they had found would be probed for weeks. Back in the hummer, the two men, closer than brothers, cruised through the dark. The whole city was on alert…a priest had been slain in the street. Padric glanced up at the moon. "Something's coming our way, Alex, I can feel it."

"Ah, *si, la luna muerta…*"

1 A DEATH IN THE STREET

Wednesday, close to midnight, February 6

It was late and a half moon, high in the sky, offered little light to the two walking into the dark. Laughing, they shadowboxed with each other on their way home from a late shift; they were young, but talked like they were older. An overhang of olive trees carved even stranger shapes into the sidewalk; two streetlights were out. The boys hastened their steps but something was wrong up ahead; a shaft of light from the open door of San Paolo's church revealed a struggle…two men, one fell to the ground. Ramos looked at his friend…did they want some of this? Both broke into a run when they heard Father Villa cry out.

Closer now, they could better see the assailant; the hood of a monk's robe hiding his eyes and he, bending over his victim and wielding a zip blade. They were too late…the stranger was slitting his throat. Stones all over the street told of more than a knife fight. There was ritual here; in some archaic way, someone had tried to stone Father Villa to death. The two skidded to a halt and later admitted they'd no idea why they froze.

The stranger raised his head and with menacing eyes glared through an unusual half mask of gold…it was elegant, shimmering, something one might see at a Mardi Gras Ball or on *Dia de los Muertos*, but certainly not for a killing. More sinister now, he slowly rose to his feet as if growing out of the pavement. Acting like he'd time to spare, the man wiped the blade on his sleeve then pointed at them like they were next.

Carlos backed off. *"Demonio!"*

"No, he's not." Ramos lunged at him. "*Oye, vato, estas muertos!* You're dead!"

But the man lashed out with his knife then with almost supernatural agility, posed his victim in the form of a cross and bolted into the alley. Someone was waiting, gunning an engine; a truck spun its wheels in the gravel and sped off, but the killer clung to the door, laughing as he struggled to crawl through the window.

It was Carlos who heard the hard, shrill laugh of the driver...a woman. "*Bruja...ay Dios mio!*" With no headlights on, the vehicle vanished into the dark but the boys caught sight of it under a streetlight. "That's one tricked-out red Mercedes, damn! Who's got wheels like that around here?" He punched in 9-1-1 on his cell, knowing too well the Fifth Precinct's slow response in this part of town.

Ramos shouted into the night: "*Asesinato! Ayuda!* Our padre's dead!"

But on these streets, families heard cries like this in the night all the time. Shaken, the two stood over their priest like not so brave guardian angels. Carlos stared up at the sky and looked for the moon...an unusual mist had passed over it. He sank to his knees, closed the priest's eyes; he'd seen it done in the movies.

"*La luna muerta*...padre's one of them now."

It was happening more often. Elders only whispered about it; talk in the street was all about the *moondead*. Hadn't they all heard the story since they were little: there was no such thing as a man in the moon but a woman with night eyes who watched all they did, even when it wasn't her turn to be up there. Truth be told, it was said she was the one killing holy ones, the nuns and priests in their city.

The full moon was a *bruja* looking for trouble when she dipped low over the city and lately, she'd found it; people were dying below when she was looking her loveliest...*si*, Carlos was thinking, *la luna muerta*. And all those nuns and priests his *abuela* had been whispering about, the moondead, good souls, she said, and there would be more going to God.

It had begun. In hushed voices, old women, shucking their corn or washing their green *tomatellos* warned everyone...those who died with a full moon overhead would be blessed in the next life but, not in this one. With the sign of the cross, they had whispered: "Beware to the rest of us…" Their spirits, they said, would walk the streets of L'Arroyo on every full moon thereafter and especially on *Dia de los Muertos*.

Still no one…Carlos again pulled out his cell; the boy called his mother. And then, from a humble *casita*, crept an old woman, howling like a *lobo* at the moon when she saw her priest, bloodied and still. The sound of it set off the neighbors who poured from their homes; the wail so loud, it drowned out the sirens. In an eerie contradiction, men stood like sentinels in a circle around the body. Though they'd been called in to help, the police weren't welcome and thought to be outsiders trampling on something sacred. And there was that ever-present reality of who would be blamed and swept up in a van. This was gang turf; certain things understood.

But…this time the Fifth Precinct was rattled as well. Father Villa, well known for his wisdom and holiness here in the barrio, was down; an EMV on two wheels turned the corner with a fire truck close behind it. Those guarding the fallen priest finally stepped back when paramedics pushed through the crowd with a gurney; the low murmur of women whispering frantically made the scene even more ominous. Some ran to the church, the door still wide open. Father had apparently rushed from his prayers when someone called out his name in the street. His breviary still lay open on the communion rail; a woman kissed it then placed it on the main altar. Ramos and Carlos had followed them and silently watched from the back of the church. They'd often sat with their priest alone in the night; it had been his custom to remain in the church to listen to all those in need. Briefly, matter-of-factly, the police had already questioned them; taking their names and half-listening, saying they'd be in touch.

The two were on edge. It was Ash Wednesday.

Thursday, near two in the morning, February 7

In the convent of San Miguel in downtown L'Arroyo, a nun, unable to sleep, sat by her window, looking into the garden below. Moments ago in the shadows, she'd seen a hooded figure in a flowing monk's robe kneel briefly by an altar of stone; oddly, a tall cross of wood covered in thorns seemed to grow from its center. She thought it beautiful and her eyes traced the dirt path up the slope to the rear wall of the Cathedral. White blossoms in a moon-garden glowed eerily in the night. But dearest to her were a dozen angels of marble, rising like standing stones from the lush, well-watered undergrowth at their feet; one was more beautiful than the other. They too silently contemplated the darkness. On the other side of the bishop's private retreat was his imposing three-story residence; still now, as if watching and waiting for night to end.

Glancing up at a waxing moon, Sister Magdalen smiled a little; new to the parish of San Miguel, she was more curious than apprehensive about the unspoken mystery here. Within days of her arrival, the enigmatic Bishop Santo Cantera had appointed her sacristan of his Cathedral. Tasked with the care of holy vessels and vestments, altars and liturgies, she'd make the sacristy her second home.

But what a strange place this was. Wasn't it yesterday, she'd overheard something curious, some intrigue? She liked intrigue. Her altar servers had been trading tales of urban legend and lore about an unseen L'Arroyo, a silent, shadowy network of tunnels under the city, some going nowhere, others leading from beneath the Cathedral itself to below the Plaza and beyond to the archaeological museum's receiving bays for new acquisitions. Rumor had it...an unusual shipment had arrived from Egypt; her art history students had mentioned as much only last week: they'd watched, kept out of sight but had seen several large pods and just knew they were from Cairo. But how would they know all this...and what, in God's name, were they doing down there?

She'd learn soon enough the more adventurous were taking some chances, poking about in the tunnels at night just for the thrill of it. But Magdalen loved the night and dark places, too, and secretly envied them yet not fearing any less for their safety; she had chided them but later pondered how she could investigate all this on her own. She had recently told them the moon tides intrigued her. They'd been discussing Van Gogh's "Starry Night", how he'd painted it while in the asylum of Saint Remy-de-Provence and kindly stated the man had some personal problems. "See how erratic and frenzied the brush strokes hit the canvas?"

They'd only showed some curiosity about the ear he'd cut off… but what about Egypt, they'd asked. The boys were remembering that other discussion they'd started yesterday; forget this crazy, old red haired Impressionist. The girls had hushed Ben and his cohort and said Van Gogh had been brilliant.

What about Egypt…they wanted more.

Magdalen had quickly said it might bore them but they insisted. She walked to the window of her second-floor classroom overlooking the Plaza. "You've told me you love that obelisk in the middle of the square over there. People who started this city must have liked Egypt, too. Look at the public buildings, the architecture is magnificent…they call it Egyptian Revival. The wall surfaces are covered in scarabs and lotus." She paused, said nothing as if suddenly somewhere else.

Ben drew her back in. "Sister?"

Magdalen smiled: "Yes, there's a crescent moon in our painting…but the moons in Egypt were huge and full of all kinds of mystery, the night sky larger, stars brighter." She turned to them. "You have the same here in the Sonoran." They smiled. "The moon over the desert is stunning." And the nun spoke more of her studies.

"Sister, what's up with all that death and mummies and stuff?"

"Stuff. Antonio, you know better. Be more specific." They laughed.

The boy shook his head. "I can't. I don't know enough. You tell us, Sister."

"We don't say *can't* in my classroom…you must try; give me something, anything!"

A quiet girl in the front seat raised her hand. "King Tut was young like us when he was murdered." Others joined in with what they had learned from fourth grade and the Discovery Channel; forget freshman year and World History class.

Ben said Julie was right: "King Tut got offed, plain and simple;

he was too young to die. He got punked big-time." Some laughed though Magdalen stated the cause of the young pharoah's demise was still up for debate. Everyone, shouting over each other, joined in. She pushed on. Wired on carbs and not wanting to be there, the class after lunch had always proved problematic. But she'd reeled them in; Van Gogh could take second chair to King Tutankhamen at least for a day. She pointed to a topical map, places that spoke to death and dying, entombment and ritual. Mortuary archaeology had brought her to Egypt for graduate studies and she spoke to them of the necropolis in which she had spent researching for days and the many unusual passage tombs. It all sounded thrilling; there were actually people called Egyptologists and they all wanted to be one.

"Your English teacher, Miss Howard, told me you're reading F. Scott Fitzgerald's *Berenice Bobs Her Hair*." The girls smiled, the boys didn't. "Did you know the Egyptian Queen Berenice inspired him?"

The girls were ecstatic, the boys not so much but Ben surprised everyone. "I'd never have left Egypt."

Their nun had a faraway look. "Well, Ben, I almost didn't, but life calls…you know all about that; you're upperclassmen and know everything." The boys hooted; Magdalen hushed them, describing how the work had consumed her, leaving her forever curious.

"About what?" someone asked.

"Things hidden. Mysteries are everywhere if you have the sight to see them."

They glanced at each other. "You've come to the right place, Sister." Ben again. "You've got all that here in L'Arroyo."

Some rolled their eyes, shook their heads. Others said it was so when Danny suggested: "You got to come with us; there's something you need to see." Magdalen pondered all they were saying; yes, she'd need to investigate Danny's ossuary church of Saint Rita's; he'd called it *the Church of Bones*. She surmised from their description, there was a cavern of sorts, a reliquary beneath the now defunct church condemned by the city and soon to be torn down and demolished. She'd seen it, was curious about such a holy place left in a state of such disrepair; it looked haunted and lost. Would she come with them? *In a heartbeat…yes.*

"I'd like to hear about some of your adventures."

"No, you don't. You don't know Danny Bellati." They laughed; he looked annoyed but was used to it and no, she did not know Danny, but had been keeping her eye on him.

"No matter. Danny, your Church of Bones…I'm interested. Will you take me there soon?" They all spoke at once. Danny was pleased…this was a first; a nun was taking an interest in someone like him from a family who had history with the police; his father, a local bookmaker with a reputation and betting parlor not far from the Cathedral. "Make a list of what you want me to see in the city and let's talk! But it must have something to do with the making of art, a studio or museum, a gallery, some sculpture or architecture or even a graveyard full of carved tombstones, and definitely something about the past and maybe…a mystery."

That was a lot to cover, they said. The bell rang for change of class and they groaned…and that, too, was a first. But how curious…Ben, a boy who loved football and monster trucks, had said here in L'Arroyo, she had all the mystery she needed and Danny was warming up to her finally. Then Julie, a junior, who sat in the front of the class looking up at her every day had asked: "May I do a report on Queen Berenice?" Why did the one's who had straight A's always ask to do extra credit?

Magdalen smiled…Egypt works. It was a start. Her students had sensed the same; she wondered if there would be more mystery than ministry here. She had replaced the Sahara with the Sonoran, perhaps one culture of death for another…*muertos.* And there would be more when an unexpected and overheard conversation between two older nuns would confirm this. Magdalen's curiosity was even more set afire with whispers concerning a graveyard hidden under the bishop's residence?

She needed answers now, this minute.

Sister Patrice in her kitchen was always good for a chat about things not to be said. "Ay, the Garden of Gethsemane cemetery, now defunct, as they say. You'll find out soon enough; our good Father Peña's the one who hid it from view when he built his house

over the top of it, if you can believe it. And that happened only after he tried to exorcise it of demons." She paused in the telling and
lowered her voice. "There'd been a desecration there, luv." Sister
put her finger to her lips. "Something to do with that Patti Devlin,
the rich lass from Darby Hill. The dear man was never sure he'd
quite done it."

*Demons, a graveyard, a rich girl…*Magdalen would try to keep up.
"Done what?"

"Father was never quite certain he'd scared the *bejeezus* out of
the Devil's minions, and so off he went performing an exorcism,
he did…or tried to." She made the sign of the cross.

Minions, exorcism…what? "And the interred?"

"Some say a few of the dead may be resting there still…" She
hurried about the kitchen. "But no, I'm almost certain all were
exhumed and re-interred elsewhere." *How macabre was that?* "And
the bishop's family mausoleum is still intact down there; it's
a stunner, I'm told. Heard it was grand; the Canteras had it all."

And this lay under the bishop's house? Perhaps L'Arroyo's first cemetery was waiting for someone to go there and listen, just listen; it
had a story. Her thoughts were racing. Magdalen could do this;
she liked stories. But she wondered how Bishop Cantera could live
happily above such a place. It was time and a mystery to solve
would suit her just fine; she'd been too long without one.

The archaeologist-turned-nun could do with some convent noir.

But she'd let it go for tonight and gazed at a mist-covered
moon high in the sky. Magdalen would have much to unwrap in
L'Arroyo but for now, she'd let the earth go its way with her prayers.
Across the garden, a lamp still glowed in the bishop's study, its light
dusting the mesquite and acacia below; but the night-blooming cereus stood poised, as if waiting. Magdalen shuttered…it was back,
that seventh sense, a gift of knowing she'd possessed longer than
she could remember, pointing to something amiss, an unholy act.
A soft knock at the door made her jump; no one had ever done this
before in the night. Her visitor was pale; Sister Petra wasn't herself.

The woman was generally placid, contained, but not now.
She rushed to the window. "Did you see it?"

Magdalen smiled. *Ah, good, something to wonder about.* "The monk?"

"Is that what I'm seeing? What do you think we have here?"

"I assumed you'd know...someone who lives with the bishop maybe."

"Oh, no. Only His grace and the monsignor are there. They don't do that."

"Do what?" Silence. "Never mind...you're upset; let's put you to bed. I'll do this."

"You'll figure this out for me?"

"Trust me...I love a good mystery."

The convent director smiled weakly. "You've come to the right place." Hadn't her students said that? "May I sit?" Magdalen pointed to a chair by her table covered with books and manuscripts. Petra hesitated, glanced out the window again. "I've wanted to speak to you about...about things not spoken of here at San Miguel." She had Magdalen's attention. "You'll understand soon enough." Had Patrice not said the same?

"That sounds ominous...what is it?"

In a rush of words, she said all that Patrice had told her as well and then abruptly asked: "Tell me about this gift you possess."

"It goes back to Egypt but at the time, I didn't get it." She described an observant professor who told her she had the gift. "He insisted I use it."

But Petra explained she had the same sense of things...a gift of knowing as well, an uncanny understanding and ability to discern the heart of a person. She studied Magdalen for a moment. "You're missing all that, I mean Egypt, your research, aren't you, Sister."

"Yes, but mostly no, though I admit to being restless sometimes. Truly though, the Life means more to me than all that." For years, she said, she'd suffered from unusual forebodings, the knowledge of dark deeds happening at that very moment somewhere. "I agonize over what I can't stop and it's more than what the Jesuits call *discernment of spirits*. It's nothing like that. I just know. It happens."

"Surely you're not responsible; don't even think it."

This was no comfort. "After Cairo and a few digs in Italy, I returned to the states and worked for my uncle, a sheriff." She described how a year before entering religious life, she'd consulted on a case; a dozen monks had been murdered. "I had been a student of mortuary archaeology and didn't work random crimes but consulted on those that revealed premeditation and religious obsession…ritual."

"And you're thinking something as horrible as that has happened here in our city."

"Why, yes…I believe so." She felt silent, feeling powerless.

"My dear…we will see. My gift allows me to read people's thoughts, discerning the anguish or goodness inside them. I hear other things in the words they say, the tone of their voice. I…I simply know things, too." She was silent for a moment. "Your training however could be helpful. The Life doesn't always give us space to run a hunch as you've done in the past, but I need you to do some of that here." The archaeologist-nun assured her she was no miracle-worker. Regardless Petra lowered her voice as if they weren't alone, proposing she play detective without shirking her duties or neglecting her prayer. "Nothing desperate or alarming now; there's no time tonight to share my list of intrigues but I trust you will assist me, Magdalen." And before saying good night, Petra surprised her. "I'm so glad you're my second assistant. God has brought you to me."

"Sister Agnes though is your first and she is so conscientious; I'm not always that."

They walked to the door. "Conscientious is good and so is Sister Agnes. I need her, but the dear woman thinks only in black and white. To survive San Miguel, one must perceive things in pastels with a much broader palette." Petra had her own way of saying things. "As for me, you must know I'm not always well and still suffer some weakness from a bout of polio I endured as a child though…" And she smiled. "I made the final cut in the city ballet after high school, thank you very much." They laughed. "I trust you will be there for me. And that other thing; investigate a bit, but only with caution." Magdalen said that she would but then…that "other thing" would allow her to snoop around a bit. "You're here for a reason! Forgive my intrusion but it's to bed now."

Magdalen returned to the window and looked again into the garden. She smiled a little. Petra's proposal had stirred a fire inside her. Her Welsh-born uncle, Sheriff Wilem John Williams, liked to call it Sherlockian, then *viola*! Cause and effect, dilemma, solution; all would be neatly tied in a bundle. But she sensed Petra had not told her everything. When she had asked about a former convent director, Sister Viviana, she had paled, fallen silent. Apparently some mysteries were off limits and that, too, was a mystery.

She seated herself at the table and set to work, arranging her papers and pens...not wanting to sleep. Finally weary, she gazed one more time at her beloved angels of stone who stood silent and watchful as if waiting for something to happen. Magdalen prayed her last prayer of the day and eyed the old altar, covered in cat's claw and jasmine. Patrice had mentioned a door cut into the side of it, within it, the gardener's tool shed with another door that gave access to a tunnel within the north wall.

This posed a serious problem for Magdalen: where would such a passageway take the curious or someone with darker intent? Had the shadowy figure disappeared under the altar? Undoing the braid at the nape of her neck, she leaned back in her chair and considered who it might be. There were several possibilities, most likely the bishop himself. Santo Cantera was an eccentric man, charismatic nonetheless; ah well, it's his garden; this should be interesting.

She finally reclined on her narrow bed with the simple, brown coverlet. At least for the moment, what more did she need than this humble room with its desk and chair and old wooden bookshelf overflowing with theology books and bound studies on art history and archaeology. On a worktable by the door was her basket of Saint Brigid's crosses; replicating the medieval saint's handcraft from centuries ago, she had a talent for weaving strips of fabric and reeds together. The Cathedral gift shop had even taken an interest; parishioners were requesting the archaeology nun's Saint Brigid's crosses now. *Tomorrow I will make more.*

She closed her eyes content, that after years of searching, she'd chosen this uncluttered life. The nun fell asleep; but what she'd seen in the garden, would change forever the lives of the Sisters asleep in their beds.

The following day heads turned when she passed through security; a female detention officer approached. "Your students have not been charged, Sister."

Magdalen brushed passed her. "How could this happen?"

Yesterday before the last bell of the day, she'd pointed to the handcuffs the police had placed on two of her students. "You couldn't have waited until you were off campus?"

The detective, an arrogant man, had entered her classroom with two officers to remove Carlos Guerrera and Ramos Robles; they had been hustled out to a waiting police van. Magdalen demanded to know the detective's name. "Dan Mason, at your service; Sister." With obviously no sense of boundaries, he had leered at her. "I'm giving an assist to the Fifth Precinct. They're swamped these days with this kind of kid."

This kind of what…what had he said? She wanted to pounce on his remark; the boys in her class took offense. Ben had stood up and pushed back his desk.

The detective glared at him but extended his hand to Magdalen; she declined. After he left, her students voiced their upset at his way with their nun. "We'll kick his ass for you, Sister." Dear Ben.

"Language please; there will be no kicking of anything…but thank you for being so gallant." They had grinned then rushed to the windows and stared down at their friends. Carlos and Ramos had endeared themselves to the nun with their humor and stories, coming often to her for help with their studies. Now they were being whisked away and trying to be stoic.

After school, Petra gave Magdalen the keys to the convent SUV and she was gone. A throw back to the early fifties, the juvenile detention center was huge, dark and Dickens-like; it looked out-of place in the Sonoran and stood in sharp contrast beside the new Palm Street City Jail. The setting seemed fitting: one of her students had taken his life, ended it.

Carlos Guerrera was dead.

Walking the yard, he'd suddenly bolted and thrown himself onto an electric fence; Ramos, unable to stop him, had witnessed his friend's self-execution. Believing he'd sinned in not saving the life of his priest, he'd believed he was deserving of hell. The boy, urged on by his own guilt, was gone.

Sadly, neither boy knew they had been cleared and, as the officer would admit, through an administrative error, they had been placed in the yard with more hardened youth and been threatened. Word spread quickly: they'd killed a priest…even in their prison mates' world there were limits. Ramos made it clear: "Gangsta' or not, that's something you don't do, Sister."

She understood and a devastated Magdalen sat down, finding some relief in the empathy of an officer overseeing the visiting area. Sgt. Jesús Marcus whispered he was even more frustrated than she and that happily, this was his last day on the job; he'd been re-assigned to Lt. John Padric's unit, as if she should know who he was. She would learn later Marcus had studied for the priesthood, been in the seminary; they would become lasting friends within weeks.

Author's Notes

Dia de los Muertos – Day of the Dead celebrated during the first week of November.

Demonio – Spanish, for devil.

Oye, vato, estas muertos! – Spanish, for "Hey, fool, you're dead!"

Bruja – Spanish, for witch.

Dios mio – my God.

OMG – on social media, meaning oh, my God.

Asesinato! Ayuda! – Spanish, for murder, help.

Abuela – Spanish, for grandmother.

Casita – Spanish, for small house or enclosure.

lobo – Spanish, for wolf.

EMV – emergency medical vehicle.

breviary – see Addendum: Glossary.

Ash Wednesday – first day of Lent on which Catholics attend special liturgies and receive the sign of the cross on their foreheads with ashes as a sign of penitence and resolve to do better.

Sacristy, sacristan – see Glossary.

urban legend – legends, part myth, some based in reality but often with macabre overtones and kept alive in the minds of the locals.

Van Gogh – *19th C. Dutch post-Impressionist painter and his "Starry Night."*

Saint Rémy-de-Provence – *French city in which Van Gogh admitted himself into Saint Paul Asylum during a time of extreme depression.*

Egyptian Revival – *an architectural style mirroring ancient Egyptian imagery and motifs; it was popular during the Napoleonic Age and thereafter in Europe and the United States. In our novel, Egyptian anthropologist, early town father and city planner built and curated the city's anthro-archaeology museum on the Plaza.*

King Tut – *refers to the boy pharaoh, Tutankhamen, born circa 341 B.C.E.*

Necropolie – *plural for necropolis, consisting of countless passage tombs and burial spaces; defined generally as a city of the dead found in Egypt.*

Berenice Bobs Her Hair – *F. Scott Fitzgerald's 1920 short story of a young woman's liberating experience of cutting her hair. Fitzgerald's choice of the name, Berenice, likely refers to the wife of Ptolemy III, Egyptian Queen Berenice, who sacrifices her hair so he is victorious in battle.*

Ossuary – *used for the final resting place of skeletal remains, a vault perhaps, a chest or receptacle, a building for this purpose.*

Reliquary – *a container, a space, even a vault, for the preservation of holy relics.*

Bookmaker – *bookie or turf accountant who takes bets on sporting and other events.*

muertos – *Spanish, for death.*

Sherlockian – *reference to Sherlock Holmes and his sleuthing.*

convent noir – *author's play on words, referencing the French term film noir, a 1944- 1954 Hollywood movie genre of crime drama and detective stories with cynical, hard characters and often beautiful woman, good and bad.*

cereus – *short-lived, night blooming cacti.*

mausoleum – *funerary building enclosing the burial chamber of the deceased.*

Garden of Gethsemane – *garden at the foot of the Mount of Olives in Jerusalem where Jesus prayed before taken by his enemies and put to death; first cemetery in L'Arroyo.*

viola – *musical instrument, member of the violin family.*

Saint Brigid's cross – *see Glossary .*

Dickens-like – *a reference to Charles Dickens, famed fictional author of the Victorian Era; his depictions of places often dark and dismal.*

2 THE NUN

"My name is Magdalen, Sister Magdalen. Thank you for speaking with me but when might Mrs. Guerrera see her son's body, take him home?"

The female officer overheard and, already annoyed at the nun, retorted: "Sister Magdalen, is it?" The two women locked eyes but Magdalen did not respond. "You can't see we're short-staffed, too busy and overcrowded? Those boys were not the only two who walked through our doors yesterday. Please remember that."

"And one of those boys, my boy, will never walk out." Silence. But Magdalen would continue, tell her she resided in the convent of San Miguel and was a teacher at Cathedral High School." Visitors turned their heads, looked at the two, when the detention officer told her she did not like her tone.

And then oddly it happened: Magdalen lowered her head like a wolf and rose slowly from where she was seated. Marcus would never forget it: the other began to stammer and turned to walk away but Magdalen could read the woman's own pain and would ameliorate things. "I more than understand the pressures you bear in your work. God be with you and all you are doing here."

The woman turned slowly. Would Marcus have to break up a girl fight? But the woman rushed to Carlos' mother and embraced her, explaining she too had lost a son and was bitter. When she withdrew, Mrs. Guerrero looked at Magdalen.

"Who are you, *hermana*?" More silence.

But Ramos had heard nothing and was somewhere else in his

head: "Me and my boys…we'll get this *diablo*. My man Carlos' life is worth something, isn't it? That monk-creep freaked him out. He saw something in him…his eyes were black like the devil's. I'll find the fool…he's a dead man."

"*Mijo, mijo*, no more!" His mother, a hard woman and tired of trouble, slapped him on the side of his head. "Not in front of the Sister."

"Don't call me *mijo*, ma. I'm a man!" It had all been quite sad. Magdalen would always remember his chilling words: "I'm tired of seeing dead people." Upon his release, he'd disappear and never return to her classroom.

She would leave moments later.

Magdalen parked the SUV in the courtyard beside the Cathedral. It was Lent and on Friday nights the Cathedral was open for prayer. Rushing up the sacristy steps, she found the bishop vesting for Benediction of the Blessed Sacrament. He was grateful she'd prepared things, but his eyes were brooding and sad and she ventured a comforting word; one never knew how such things might be received. "Your grace, I'm sorry for the loss of your friend, Father Villa. I know of your deep regard for him."

He reassured her the good priest's work would continue. "Stefano wears the robe of a martyr for all eternity; his dying sheds grace on us all. Now I must tend to the living." And there it was again: the bishop's obsession with martyrdom. Martyrs of the early Church would be the recurring theme of his Lenten homilies. He entered the sanctuary.

Monsignor Steed had busied himself in the vestry but overheard his remarks. "It takes time to understand the man, Sister; he's holy and good but a complicated sort."

Magdalen smiled. "Well, I like him; he's progressive enough, even liberationist in his theology but his liturgies speak to the old traditions."

"And he allows his priests in their parishes to do the same. Our churches are filled with the devout from Haiti and Brazil, Sonora, Chiapas, even Guatemala, Sister. He's from El Salvador; his father brought him here when he was a boy. And look at our Borders now…they overflow with their children."

"Our Sisters have opened two Border missions within the past month."

"And he's already visited them several times. But…Santo is not always in line with the latest Vatican imperatives." Both knew there had been the occasional letter of inquiry from Rome…Santo Cantera did things his way. "You know, Sister, he appreciates how efficient you are. The last sacristan wasn't." Sister Anna.

What else could he tell her? But like her Sisters, he would say nothing about the nun who, one Saturday morning, had removed her veil and holy habit and simply walked out of the convent and into a waiting red Maserati.

And there was that other matter about which the Monsignor was silent: the bishop's disappearing for long periods of time without explanation; it was becoming more frequent and noticeable. Would he do it again tonight?

With the Lenten liturgy over, the Cathedral emptied. It was quiet now; incense from a thurible still lingered in the air as Magdalen hurried from vestry to altar. But, at one point, she turned slowly, searching the shadows in the nave of the church. Bishop Cantera had made it his own…the exterior, resembling the old mission church of Santa Maria Magdalena in Sonora, Mexico; it was known he often made pilgrimage there.

The interior of the church was another matter: European medieval with strange twists and turns, niches and narrow doors, perhaps filled with mysteries for Magdalen. She loved it and smiled a little. Silence. Sconces high on the walls draped soft light over the pews; light from the flickering votive candles in side chapels danced in the aisles. She liked working here in the evening but the shadows were longer now; she glanced around one more time before leaving. Despite her never fearing the dark, she was apprehensive of late; from her first week in the sacristy, she'd sensed someone was watching her. She paused…a sound. It was woefully sad, a sob, someone weeping, but from where?

She left quickly, the moon watching as she hurried down the

sacristy steps and on to the convent but Magdalen looked up; the elder was waving at her from her usual spot at a second-floor window overlooking the courtyard and Plaza across the street. The revered Sister Monica was her special charge; she'd said earlier a late supper would be fine and thank God for that. Magdalen was late…it was almost six-thirty. This holy woman of God, now ninety-one and the Order's treasure, was the only living member from the "first days" when, during the Depression, she and four nuns on their way to a mission in California, had lost their way in a dust storm. Unable to go any further, they'd laid down roots among the arroyos in a remote desert valley.

The sacristan/high-school teacher was decidedly busy; Magdalen's duties of caregiver to several retired nuns and second assistant to the convent director, Sister Petra, made for a full schedule. But it was Monica she loved most and tonight, the old woman patted her hand when she sat down beside her in the window seat. If anyone could enlighten her on San Miguel's secrets she could, but it would not be tonight. "Some supper please, dear." And off they went to the refectory.

Later with Monica finally tucked in her bed and after a long conversation with Sister Maryjohn, the old one she called "wizard", Magdalen slipped into her space near the kitchen; once an old tool room and gardener's shed…it was shaping up nicely. Assistants to the director each had their own office, but Sister Agnes' was nicer, more proper like she was. At one time, Magdalen's had been filled with clay pots and seed bags; it still smelled like a greenhouse, but some renovation had turned it into a workable office and copy room for the nuns.

Her desk, an old wooden potting bench with a smooth writing surface, sufficed and, at the moment, was covered like the one upstairs by her bed, with manuscripts and all kinds of research. But this one had a section carved out for her students' papers and art history class projects. Air-conditioning but no heat and a tiled floor made it decent.

Now, from her retreat, Magdalen gazed through the large window in front of her desk into the convent garden brimming over with bougainvillea. She sank into her swivel chair, observing with pleasure the Sisters enjoying their final conversations of the day, only to have the eccentric Sister Amata, recently retired and not liking it, ask for a moment.

Expecting to be heard, she was often intrusive, asked too many questions and now stood in the doorway. "I am upset about things, child." Magdalen wanted to tell her she wasn't a child like Ramos had told his mother he wasn't a *mijo*. A tense conversation evolved over the sudden death of Father Villa; she wanted answers, curious about all Magdalen knew, but Sister Dolorosa appeared at the door. Amata withdrew. Magdalen smiled, her new friend a welcome sight. Now here was dynamite wrapped up in one petite woman; she was Cathedral High's dean of students and often sounded like one. She "got things done" and in Magdalen's presence occasionally uttered the F-word. Tonight they spoke of the boys, one cold in a morgue; Ramos, angry and looking for vengeance.

Dolorosa could see Magdalen was distracted. "You're not with me tonight."

"I overhear conversations, you know, the bishop and the way he says things to people."

Immediately Dolorosa reacted. "What did he say…not unkind I hope."

"Oh, no, just the opposite. He's charming to me." Dolorosa rolled her eyes…she knew him differently; her family had worked for his family. "He told a group of women…you know how they huddle around him…that demons roam the edge of the city at night."

"And what else? All of us growing up here have heard that a thousand times."

"That we, our Sisters, keep them at bay with our lives? Tell me this isn't so."

The nun drew her chair closer. "Maggie…" She only called her this when they were alone. "There are things you don't know about this place and, believe me, I know L'Arroyo. You're looking at a girl, who was born and raised on legend and lore and with six older brothers who only believed half of it. There's an evil here though and the man in the moon is no man at all but a woman, a *bruja*, who sees all we do. But…around the convent, some say there's a halo of angels, like gargoyles, who set us apart and watch over us. These walls are our sanctuary, not to be breached."

It sounds like Grimm's Fairy Tales…oh, dear. "I've seen the looks on faces when I'm out and about. I think I'm beginning to understand. We Sisters have history here."

"That's right but I'll let our elder tell you more and we'll talk. In this city some mock the Life because we've gone back to our first traditions, wearing the original holy habit again. Even other orders of nuns think we're *old school*, praying in common, taking our meals together, living the Rule…it sets some of them off."

"The bishop said it's all or nothing with the Sisters of the Crucified…I like that."

"And you'll learn soon enough Sister Monica's thinking on this." Dolorosa imitated the elder, tilting her head wisely and looking sage. "Not all are called to our way of loving the Lord. We ask for a stricter observance." They laughed, knowing well the old nun and her ways.

But Sister Gabriela was ringing her hand bell for evening prayer; the observance of silence until morning would begin. Following the others into the chapel, Dolorosa whispered a reminder to Magdalen…tomorrow was an important one. She would be visiting her childhood home in south L'Arroyo to attend her parents' *anniversario de boda*, their wedding day long ago. Another nun, Sister Cecelia, her friend since they were three, would join her with her own family as well, she said. "And you're invited. Sister Petra wants you to come with me."

Magdalen laughed softly. Amata glared at them to be silent… they smiled.

But the sacristan would ponder all she had seen and heard that day as the chanting began. Regardless of skeptics, the Sisters' attire made heads turn in a city with an edgy reputation and encircled by demons…or so it seemed. But for now, she would give herself over to Compline, the evening prayer of the Church.

Out in the night, two detectives drove slowly passed the Cathedral; the streets were suddenly darker and Lt. John Padric looked up at the moon...*la luna*. He'd forgotten; there was talk of a lunar eclipse sometime after midnight, closer to three in the morning. Martinez, his partner, too, was uneasy.

Both were unaware of a tricked-out red Mercedes truck, the same Ramos and Carlos had seen, swerving onto the I-10 and speeding toward L'Arroyo. The hooded one in the passenger seat was chanting a medieval dirge for the dead...*Dies irae, dies illa*.

Day of mourning; day of doom...

Author's Notes

hermana – Spanish, for sister.

diablo – Spanish, for devil.

mijo – Spanish, for son, a contraction of *mi hijo*; may be used to speak to others with affectionate.

Benediction of the Blessed Sacrament – brief liturgy/devotion to the Eucharist.

liberationist in his theology – refers to Liberation Theology, a movement within the Church specifically addressing the poor and oppressed through involvement in political and civic affairs. Not always well received by the Church establishment, its activity is found more often in South American countries.

martyrs of the early Church – refers to the Apostles and early Christians (1st-3rd C. AD), executed for their belief in Christ.

Church of Santa Maria Magdalena in Sonora – old mission church in Mexico.

Grimm's Fairy Tales – collection of German fairy tales intended for children but initially not well received by their parents due to dark content, violence and sexual innuendo. The stories were truly "grim" and went through many editions and variations.

old school – refers to past trends generally associated with fond memories.

anniversario de boda – Spanish, for wedding anniversary.

fiesta – Spanish, for party.

3 BLOOD MOON

Saturday, near two in the evening, February 9

Magdalen sat up in bed. A dog was howling in the street at the moon. She smiled sleepily...*this must be the one Sister Cecelia loves so much; he waits for her to come home every night.* She rose quickly...a lunar eclipse was in progress; its strange light, hypnotic, drawing her in; she gazed up at it, thinking there must be some holy lesson in this.

Across town, a nun stepped into the moonlight; a charge nurse at Meadow. Tonight the good Sister was finally going home and waved to the orderlies enjoying their break. One even offered to walk her to her car. No worries. She was happy...tomorrow it would be *fiesta* with family at the de Torros. Sister Cecelia pondered the last twenty-four. This high-security medical facility for crime victims and first-responders had been unusually busy tonight; was it the moon?

She looked up; it was blood-brown and she frowned. It wasn't that time of year for a harvest moon if that's what it was but she smiled at the sight of a red Mercedes truck with dark tinted windows parked at the edge of the hospital grounds. *Waiting for someone coming off shift...it would be nice to be chauffeured home in something like that* and she recalled once stealing the keys for a joyride in her brother's Dakota with her childhood friend, Melissa de Torro aka Dolorosa. A small woman, she stood on tiptoe as she climbed into the convent SUV, unaware of the Mercedes gliding up quickly behind her. Monk-like and silent, a hooded figure slid from the passenger side, grabbing her from behind. Duct tape and swift moves confused her; she swooned from fear. Darkness.

Minutes later, Cecelia opened her eyes; her body, slamming back and forth into the sides of the truck bed as the driver sped away. She sobbed aloud through the tape cutting into her face. Intermittent lights overhead told her she was on Interstate 10.

"I'm dying; I'm dead." She was cold as the moon but it was blood red and on fire now in an unholy glow. Her heart pounded when she heard monks chanting a requiem.

Dies irae, dies illa.

Saturday, ten in the morning, February 9

Scrambling up the incline, some of it flat, two detectives slipped and stumbled as they made their way up a high rise of rock off a dirt access road surrounded by cotton fields.

The new CSI greeted them at the top. "Did you eat yet?" They stopped...it's that bad? He turned around. "See for yourself. Not pretty." The men followed Jon-Gabriel Milleau. "I'm liking the sick bastard who did the priest for this one." The young man never cursed; but this one had left him aghast; he said he'd get back to them soon enough.

"Thanks, lad, work your magic." John Padric was only in his mid-forties but always spoke to the young ones in L'Arroyo PD like he was their father. "Give it your best!"

"Will do, Lieutenant. Miller and some of the others are still working the canal...that's probably the primary. Check it out. The deed wasn't done here."

Coming off nightshift, they'd stopped in a diner for coffee when they were called out again. They'd sped through the streets to get to a scene so horrific it would send the city into a tailspin. Padric surveyed the vast acreage of land owned by the Aguilar-Murphy Partnership, two men, two dynasties, a pot of gold at the end of their respective rainbows. David Aguilar had called in a 9-1-1 from his hacienda two fields away and said he'd noticed them twice: headlights disappearing and reappearing between nine and ten the previous evening and again around three the following morning. At the first hint of dawn his workers had arrived for the day, eating breakfast in the back of their trucks. One, who often sat on the hill of rock close to the road, had climbed to the top then fled into the fields before he could be persuaded to stop.

Jesse, Aguilar's older son, had arrived just as the man stumbled away; the black and gray of the nun's garments draped over the rocks drew him to the top of the ledge. He'd called out for his father and Aguilar himself was distraught. "My wife says it's a curse on our land."

Looking down, Martinez drew a sharp breath. "Ritual…body posed, same as the priest." Another servant of God, a nun this time, lay very dead and alone on a hill.

"Bloody hell." Padric stared down at the sacrilege and made the sign of the cross. At their feet, lay a nun, fully clothed, arms outstretched in the form of a cross on matted thorns and cacti spilling out over the ledge. It appeared her head was simply turned to the side, but further examination revealed it was barely attached at the nape of the neck; the victim had been decapitated…almost.

Martinez, a devout man, could only whisper: "*Dulce Jesús*, cartel maybe, *nada*; most of them would never do this! Looks like the killer tried a few hits and gave up. This is sick. I'm hating my job."

But Padric was having his own encounter and said nothing. It was already mid-morning and the cadaver had attracted a stunning bird eerily perched atop a mesquite by the side of the road; it had been eyeing the scene for some time. The detective knew birds, this one, a golden eagle and illegal to own in Arizona. He glanced at it curiously then looked down at the body…moments passed; he looked back. Transfigured, the bird had unfolded its wings, slowly evolving into a seraph-like creature. *Holy Mary, what am I seeing? This doesn't happen in my world.* The night detective, already into three hours overtime, chalked it up to weariness.

But now tall and graceful, some kind of supernatural or maybe an angel emerged. It bowed its head as if grateful. But Padric was a cynical man and not easily persuaded, yet what if such a creature had stood guard over the victim's remains until someone arrived to gather them up? He said nothing to his partner who by now was wiping his face with a handkerchief.

"She's fully dressed, robes arranged carefully, doesn't look like a sex crime; they'll do a rape kit." But for Padric such things and nuns didn't go together. Growing up with the Sisters of Mercy in Belfast, the sight of it shook him to the core and here was a man who never looked shaken or, for that matter, stirred; he kept it inside…but long ago, he'd been one of those well-meaning altar boys and this wasn't right. Time for him had turned the nuns' teachings into a life of carousing and disbelief.

He examined the nun's clothing more carefully. "Alex, this one's from Cathedral."

The school was his alma mater; he glanced up at the sky and wanted some angels. They needed to take her home…all of her, body and soul. Martinez shook his head. "The Crucifieds! *Santo madre*, my boy's a freshman there. Strange, animals didn't get to her." He stood up and noted some clouds forming over the sun. "God takes care of his own."

"Not here, He didn't…He was out to lunch on this one. You call this cared for?"

Martinez ignored him; he was all too familiar with his partner's cynicism. "Okay then, what's this looking like, Johnny? It's not the same MO but the same…"

"Choice of victim. What was the priest's name?"

"Padre Villa…Stefano Villa. Loved him; he knew me better than I knew me."

"There's minimal blood. Like Milleau said, she was cut somewhere else; died here. We've got two crime scenes and a third, where they grabbed her." He pulled back the bloody sleeve of the nun's garment. "Damn, her hand's gone. We'll wait on the coroner's take. Rubin will flip; you can bet on it."

"How much?"

"*Kema sabe*, I'm not a betting man. I'm into other things."

"And there's more than a few women who'll agree to that."

"And none of them are talking, fool; forget the personal." He looked sadly down at the nun. "Her face, man…she looks like an angel." He gently closed her eyes. "I'm calling the Captain…priests and nuns dying, sufferin' Jesus."

"Better you than me; there'll be hell to pay with O'Manion, no pun intended."

Unaware of the shroud soon to cover them, the nuns in the convent of San Miguel were smiling, the mood light even joyous. An early morning sun streamed through the kitchen windows as the Sisters came from their Hour of Lauds and Holy Mass in the chapel. This was Sister Patrice's domain. She laughed and drew them into her world and a well-laden table.

"We have rosemary *faccacia* and cranberry scones for the taking." But wasn't it Lent? The older nuns pointed to the Brie in a wreath of decadent jams; Camembert in a wooden box, a huge golden wedge of Livarot tucked among apples and pears. Quiches with leeks and ham were tucked beside the bialys covered with onions and breadcrumbs. Amata smiled at a sideboard of *tarte tatin* and *charlotte aux pommel*. "Is it a holy day?" Their meals were often quite meager.

Petra smiled. "This will last us till Easter; the bishop is good to us so please, Sisters, come round the table."

"He always does this at report card time. It's end of school quarter." Agnes was predictable. "Remember, teachers, your grades are due on Monday." Leave it to Agnes.

But Dolorosa had her own take. "He does this just to keep us around." They laughed.

Petra too wondered if there might be some hidden agenda in this grand cornucopia. "Come, let's ask for a blessing. Enjoy!"

Magdalen could not; her sense of things had filled her with dread when she awoke at dawn...*where was Cecelia?* Dolorosa too asked where she was. Patrice assured her she'd be home shortly and pointed to a basket of well-floured *blaas*, a warm reminder of her childhood in Waterford. "Eat now...enjoy. As my good mother would say: *bain taitneamh as do bhéile!*" But after a repast of Camembert and *faccacia* and the strongest roast coffee she could find, Magdalen slipped into her office and attacked her desk covered in paperwork. But she could not sit still...something was off, very wrong.

At noon, the Angelus rang out from the campanile of the Cathedral like an omen; Gabriela appeared in the doorway; two detectives were here. *Ramos, yes, Ramos perhaps*…he had never returned to her classroom. *It must be Ramos; he is alive.*

"Good morning." They turned, the men's faces grim; Petra drew them into the parlor.

But Padric was tired and needed a drink; besides, convents made him uneasy. He was a sinner and sinful, as he often said to his partner. But for now he'd do his job.

"Detectives Padric and Martinez have come to speak with us about…" Slowly, she sat down; Magdalen rushed to her. "I wanted you here before they gave me the details. Sister Agnes is unavailable at the moment." The care they showed each other only made it worse for Padric, who had done this a hundred times; no death notification was easy, but with nuns?

"We regret to inform you we found one of your Sisters; she has died. Her body was discovered earlier today." Silence. "The medical examiner puts her death at around three or three-thirty in the AM; we're calling it a homicide pending investigation."

Petra gasped; Magdalen had sensed it. "Who?" One word. One question. He eyed the nun…this was different.

"The name tag sewn into her clothing ID'd her as Sister Cecelia Ramondo." Petra reached for Magdalen; she'd not been herself; the death of her friend, Father Villa, and the sensational suicide of their student had shaken her.

Martinez frowned. "Didn't you miss her when she didn't come home?" Cecelia's heavy workload, they said, often forced her to keep unusual hours; she'd often slept at the hospital. Magdalen asked where her body was found.

"West of the city in the Aguilar-Murphy fields."

"What was she doing out there? Where is she now?"

"With the coroner; family members ID'd the body. It looks like she was abducted from the hospital parking lot where she works after shift…your SUV is still there."

"The Ramondos know then; I must call them." Petra looked at Magdalen. "Stay here and do this. You are familiar with this kind of thing."

"How so?" Padric looked at her…unusual, composed, not falling apart, green eyes.

"I assisted my uncle, a sheriff, on several homicide cases back home." He asked her background. "Interpreting crime scenes, finding the dead; looking for what's underneath; my last case was quite convoluted, a dozen bodies, all monks. I…I am by profession a mortuary archaeologist." She forced a smile. "Or at least I was all that…"

He sensed her wistfulness…the woman had given up a lot and was missing it. "Burned alive in the monastery incinerator…the Crematory Murders; that was you?"

She couldn't resist. "Why, no, the killer did that." They smiled. "It was many people working very hard." They liked her.

The men glanced at each other. "And you are modest. I'd like to talk with you more about that case. But I'm wondering if you could look at something for us. You did this as a nun?"

"No, sir, before joining our Sisters after returning from graduate research in Egypt."

Egypt. She'd seen the world. "This brings me to the second reason why we are here. We need a nun or a priest, someone who can put an interpretation on what we're dealing with. We've got victims dying in unusual ways; looks like some delusion and religious obsession."

Martinez asked: "Would you help us, Sister, take a look at what we've got?"

Petra stood up. "Yes, she will."

Magdalen stared at her. "Sister, just a moment. I…" The detectives were amused.

"Is there a problem?" Who could refuse Petra? Magdalen knew how this worked. She looked through the lace curtain out into the school quad on the other side of the high wrought iron gate of the convent. *Life will never be the same again…but yes.*

"Of course, if I can take care of our elder, teach and care for the sacristy."

Padric had to say it: "The good Sister's doing all that? Are you sure you're not working her too hard? Sister, you'll let us know what you can and can't do."

Petra gripped Magdalen's hand. "Carefully now. Do this for

us…for these good gentlemen." She turned to them. "Detectives, I must leave you…so much to do." But she glared at Padric. "You have us to think of now. I trust you will give this matter your utmost attention." Her adamant tone brought back memories of Belfast and his seventh grade nun, Sister Moira. The woman had taught him everything about God and the world.

He was stammering. "Your safety is…is my personal concern."

"That's not good enough. I want specifics." *Sister Moira.* "What will you do for my Sisters right now?" Years had passed since a nun had backed Johnny Padric into a corner; he assured her there were patrols already walking the perimeter of the Cathedral complex; Commander Ramirez of the First Precinct had heightened security around every church in the city. "Ah, yes. His children attended our high school…good."

"And Captain O'Manion is with the bishop, as we speak." He worried; the two men were not a good mix; the Cap' would be cranky for a week.

Magdalen waited for Petra to leave. "Tell me what you didn't say to my Sister." She was sharper than Padric expected, but looking at him like she knew every sin he'd ever committed. She told them to sit; nuns always did that and, in the months ahead, the parlor table would become a familiar place for the three.

But now he would say it: her Sister had been almost decapitated. "Sister was mutilated, posed; displayed fully clothed on top of some rocks." Nothing. No reaction…she could ride with them. "Better yet, come with us. Give us something we don't have. We're going there now."

Magdalen looked from one to the other, both weary. They were concerned with this one, wanting it solved, determined to stop whoever was doing it. "One moment." She turned to leave but looked back at Padric. "I'm sorry you had to see this today."

He nodded his thanks…no one ever said this to them; they felt like garbage men, picking up human trash, dead bodies left in a field, behind buildings, somewhere forsaken. "I'm sorry I had to bring the bad news, Sister." He glanced at Martinez after she left. "Those eyes, man…she looked right through me."

"Johnny, she's a nun. Remember that; know your place."

"She's vowed to God, man. I'm married, Al, for Christ's sake."

"Does the front desk at the Nile know that?" *Ah, the Nile Hotel.* His partner knew he had something going on with a beauty there. Padric sighed: "No worries with this one; no chance in hell."

Crime tape surrounded the rise of rocks. She stepped out of the car and without hesitation walked toward the hill. *God, help me.* Magdalen took one step then another. Padric eyed her curiously. *Nuns are cold creatures, giving away so little about themselves, but this one…* he wondered and had no idea she wanted to run and hide. But she'd need to do this; relying on the detectives' confident manner wouldn't be enough. They handed her gloves and shoe covers; she slipped under the tape.

Padric joined her. "Tell us something we're not seeing."

"No pressure, right." They bleakly looked up at the ledge. "Nuns as victims don't make it a hate crime or religious obsession, you know this, Detective." Without emotion, she stated her Sister might simply have been in the wrong place at the wrong time.

*Realistic, not spooky…*he liked that. "Point taken, Sister, but fresh eyes help. I'll show you where we found the body." *The body…she was my Sister; how cold the language of forensics.* Magdalen eyed the ledge above and he offered to take her hand, but she had already started up the incline. Lifting her robe above her ankles, she moved carefully from rock to rock.

The men nodded their heads; this one could stand on her own, not too fragile. Reaching the top, Magdalen quickly sensed the dread covering the vast fields spread before her, the stark desert beyond. Her Sister had to have seen the eclipse and a blood red moon or had she mercifully passed on to her Lord by then? "The moon then…it must have been the last thing she saw." The men looked at her curiously. "There was a lunar eclipse…for a brief time, it was red, so red." This was staggering to even contemplate.

"The ME said it was around three-twenty, three-twenty-five in the AM."

It had been years since she'd visited a crime scene. She'd put all her archaeology training aside and go with her gut, the life of one of her own gone, now on a slab. Or maybe she lay on an autopsy table or gurney in a cold hallway waiting in line; there were others ahead of her. Magdalen studied the smooth ledge where the victim had been posed in the form of a cross. "She bled out somewhere else, but you know that." She pointed to the lavender ash in the rock. "I'm sensing your killer has access to this like I have in the sacristy."

She strained to look as far as she could passed arroyos and clusters of chaparral, tall, soaring palms edging the cotton fields. "There is peace, at least on this side of the canal, though something's very wrong on the other. And here she is placed on an altar, the lamb is slain, given to God. But how is a near-decapitation moved from point A to point B without detaching the head?" It sounded crude…almost comical. No one smiled.

"I'm hoping that's a rhetorical question…I don't know yet."

She peered through chaparral and clusters of bottlebrush beyond the canal where *Chato's* bar sign blinked even in daylight. "Tell me please, what is that over there?"

Then she saw it…almost lost in the overgrown fields where the desert came up to meet it. Alone and neglected, a graveyard lay desolate under a tall, gnarled tree; it looked like the movie set of an old Western movie. Magdalen could barely distinguish the wooden crosses and broken headstones protruding through the dry grass. She was at home now. A graveyard…this was her cup of tea.

Later she would learn the dead were carelessly tossed to their rest here. She would return on her own without the detectives, but how strange this world beyond the canal. Intrigued she would go there when all this was over, she promised herself. Then Magdalen would hear dark tales of lives lost…even children discarded there and now silent; their souls still crying out for remembrance. A sense of finality pervaded the field and spread over the land like a pall even to the rise of rocks where she stood. *And what of those dried fields over there, the houses scattered far apart and silent, not a man or woman in sight…what was it called? The Edge, that's it.* Dolorosa had mentioned it. "What goes on over there after dark; would you tell me?"

"The Sonoran sun has no mercy, Sister. Don't let it fool you; see that club over there." He pointed. "You're looking at a real toilet come sundown. Darkness hides ugly in what's known as the Edge. We're standing at the city line where the desert runs up to the edge of it…thus, the name. There's a lawless wind that blows in these parts and it's hard to grab hold of. What's done between consenting adults can't always be labeled a crime, but people get hurt and die just the same." His words sounded like something Willie Nelson would sing.

"They're real clubs then, bars with no names."

"Exactly…and that's what they're called, no-names. At night the air's black and roads so dark, they say the devil camps out on the white line down the middle."

"Anything goes then. Is there a link…do our killers live there?"

"No one lives there; if you work in the Edge, you live somewhere else, but it sees a lot of traffic from as far as southern Cali and Mexico even Vegas; hell, it's included in some alternative, low-end travel packages. There's a runway just passed those trees for leer jets. People come to the Edge like locust on Egypt; it's always Saturday night. Chato's owner runs Chato II, another one with the same rep on the other side of the Border. The town's called Poco… never had the pleasure, but they say the bar's so long it stretches the length of the town. Is there a link between what's here and what you've got over there, I have no answer." But that was a long explanation for having no answer.

"It looks like free enterprise in the Edge pays off."

That sounded like something he'd say. "Certain people of influence don't want it gone; judges and other law-types fight it." He hesitated. "They can be pleasured out here and hide easy, but we wait for their fall from grace."

Falling from grace…he knew about that; she'd done that, too. Yet how articulate this hard-nosed cop; she studied his face for a moment…working with him would prove interesting if she could keep up. "It's so different here on this side of the canal…peaceful."

"The land you're standing on is well-tended and belongs to honest, hard working men. The canal's pretty deep, making what's here inaccessible to what's over there; but this dirt road coming off the I-10 leaves it open for visitors…welcome or not."

"The canal…may we go there. It's linked to whatever we have right here. I am sure of it."

"I was about to suggest that." Padric offered his hand and guided her down the rocky incline; his confident ways were a comfort and she whispered her thanks. Padric smiled a little; he could read women, but wasn't sure about this one. *Damn, I'm holding the hand of a nun with green eyes…this was a first*; Belfast's Sisters of Mercy weren't into that, but for the moment, he'd felt the touch of someone good and the peace that came with it. "Come with me!"

He winked at Martinez who was shaking his head. But Dave Aguilar approached. Padric wasn't in the mood. "He looks pissed." Martinez would speak with him.

The two continued on to the canal. He wasn't sure he heard her correctly when Magdalen whispered: "It's us they're after."

"Sister, we'll take care of you. I've got this."

She wanted to believe him. "You must know that, with or without you, I must stop this." She stared at the canal ahead, determined to end this.

Padric's eyes narrowed…he heard some rogue in the woman; she'd be a challenge. "No, I'll do this. Sister, I'll make it my only case but need your help. We don't expect you to ride around in a squad car or solve the bloody thing, though our Captain would probably like that. This type of victim, we don't see everyday. We hate the delusion; it spooks the public and throws us off our game. Here in L'Arroyo, we've got religion dark and religion lite. The first one we worry about." He thought for a moment. "I remember some talk about an incident in the forties; some of your Sisters ended up in that graveyard over there."

She stopped and looked at him. "Tell me."

"They got themselves in some trouble; it ended badly." Padric eyed her, watching the wheels and conveyor belts turn in her head. "But that's for another day."

Yes, a mystery to solve…he had her thinking. "I understand."

"No, you don't. I have a feeling you'll be on that nugget of information like a fly on honey." She smiled. "Am I right, Miss Marple?" Magdalen loved Agatha Christie's self-appointed detective and yes, she'd never rest until she knew every detail. They moved on; his knowing her thoughts made her uneasy. "We had cadaver dogs out here earlier to see if there were more bodies. Nothing." A shout from the team hastened their steps. "Or not...let's go."

But something had not gone unnoticed by Magdalen...the field crew was still at the site. Detained for so long, some slept while others ate the food Aguilar's wife brought them. Some were undocumented; Padric knew it, but he chose his own battles and few questioned his politics; he too was an immigrant.

The nun's presence and the sight of her robes made the men bare their heads. Magdalen touched their hands, asked them their names; they told her about their families and were grateful. But others not so much; they were uneasy, even spooked. The murdered woman was a nun; the sight of another walking among them was more than a bad omen. A few cursed...give us some work or let us go home. There were still others, newly arrived from a cartel-ravaged Mexico, who said they'd seen worse; a dead body was of little concern.

Magdalen approached Aguilar. "Could you not compensate them in some additional way...*por favor*? My Sisters and I, we can bring food for them and their families, so your wife is not burdened."

He reassured her it was taken care of; no need.

Martinez was back. "How's she doing?"

The lieutenant eyed Magdalen. "She's working the crowd like a union rep." When she rejoined them, he yelled to the search team: "Whatta you got?"

"How you keeping, John?" Cunningham from the K-9 unit was one of his countrymen, both from the North, County Antrim. He approached. "Nevel's got something for us. You better take a look." The police dog looked pleased; he'd made a discovery under a bottlebrush and was seated beside it. Nevel.

Padric chuckled. "You never disappoint, *bhoyo*. Nevel, is it? What did the royal beast find for us and the good Sister?" The sergeant pointed to a gold ring, bloodied and embedded in pebbles. Padric moved closer to the dog and whispered some niceties. Nevel ignored him. He was muttering: "No way. Milleau didn't see this?"

Magdalen paled. Cunningham noticed. "Sister?"

"It's ours. I'm sure this was my Sister's…it's the ring she was given when she took her final vows." She held up her hand and showed them her own. "May I look at it, Sergeant?"

Cunningham nodded. Nevel was eyeing Magdalen. "Thank you, my friend." The dog bowed its head and lay down at her feet. Cunningham was astounded, would allow it. Dog and nun looked intently into each other's eyes. A chill passed through Padric. He looked at the ring, now catching the afternoon sunlight.

"There." Magdalen said. "The small engraved cross etched into the top…we are the Sisters of the Crucified." She thought for a moment. "Yes, we truly are, especially today. My Sister suffered so."

"Are you okay, Sister?" Cunningham saw a sadness in her.

"Oh, yes…you see, we all have one. It's painful to see this, but thank you." Years later, he would tell the story of the ring, his dog, and a nun, to whomever would listen. Nevel and Magdalen would meet again and Padric would tell that story. But now he was livid… evidence had been overlooked. Detective John Padric was done with being low-key for the nun's sake; he'd been nice up to now and was done with it. On a rant, he walked into the field.

Padric hated sloppiness, was surprised his best CSI hadn't seen this. "Fucking son of a…" The officers glanced at the nun and looked down at the ground. He'll come back, one of them whispered, not to worry. But she sensed he'd be more himself if she weren't there. "I think I might be cramping your style. I can leave."

He stopped pacing…yes, he supposed he did have some style to cramp; there was some truth in that. Right now he needed her like a hole in the head, at least that's what he told Martinez later when he admitted how badly he'd acted.

Her words had startled him. "Forget it…I'm not cutting you loose." Did he say that? Nevel emitted a whine. Cunningham was relieved when the nun looked amused. Padric had embarrassed himself. "Sister, you'll need to cover your ears from here on in or be shocked…apologies up front. I work things my way, but this one's going steadily south." He barked orders and snapped pictures of the ring where it lay. "Get Milleau out here again!"

The detective side-eyed the nun who had stepped aside and made her way to the edge of the canal...she knelt down and listened; the water, balm to her soul. She was surprised when he joined her; she didn't look up. "They beheaded her here...almost."

"Both holding Sister's body over the water...there were two maybe more."

"One attempted to remove the head."

"And the other steadying the body."

"Removing a head can get clumsy." She heard herself saying this almost casually.

It had no effect on Padric but he saw her pain. "This is a tough business we're in, Sister...are you all right?"

"I'm all right." Magdalen continued to study the water. "They needed the canal to expedite the head if it detached itself. The script required otherwise."

"That's cold. What script? This is fucked up, apologies...my language is bad and that's not going to change any time soon!"

"I'm thinking the same...say what you must. I've worked around men most of my life until I entered the convent."

"Welcome back then." Sister Moira would have slapped him.

"Thank you. Sister died instantly with the first blow. She was small, a lightweight, easy to lift and carry about. Displaying her on those rocks prolonged the act; it was pleasurable for him but not in the way you might think. He lingered over the body...he'd made a martyr. The choice of a remote location speaks to the need for time to perform ritual."

"Ritual on the nun came into play postmortem. But a martyr, you say?"

"Yes, and they went to a lot of trouble to do it. A gun would have been easier if they simply wanted my Sister dead. So why didn't they use one?" He wasn't seeing what she was. "Detective, the killers are replicating the deaths of first and second century Christians in the early Church. There was no gunpowder until alchemists employed it in the ninth century. The Chinese of course took it further."

He knew such things but then...he even knew martyrs...seventh grade, *Sister Moira.*

"This is a reenactment and what they cannot imitate to the letter, they finish with knives, but those are invasive and personal. Forgive me, but he, they…they probably get off doing it this way."

"Now you're talking; this I get." He had not expected the conversation to go here. "What if the dominant is impotent, not sexually active; it helps him do what he can't?"

"That's not part of his agenda, Detective. He's delusional but pure of heart. Getting some kind of physical pleasure from all this is the farthest thing from his mind." Magdalen was feeling uncomfortable around this man of the world but he was calm and respectful. Unmoved, he listened to all she was saying. "She was not found disheveled?"

"Not at all…she looked like she was laid out for a funeral."

"Not stripped and re-clothed; no signs of sexual assault?"

"On the contrary…great care was shown to the victim after a very violent end. At first, we saw a severed neck then realized it was barely attached to the spine by some tissue; one hand was removed and I have no idea where it is. Her clothing was arranged."

He looked away; Magdalen asked him his thoughts.

"The memory of her face will stay with me the rest of my life, Sister." She was curious to know what would touch him like this. He looked down at his shoes. "She was a beautiful woman. I can't erase the look on her face from my mind. It was peaceful, not part of this world…she was gone, free, yet the violence here was over the top." He surprised her when he sighed deeply and said: "*But Lancelot mused a little space, she has a lovely face…*"

"And *God in his mercy give her grace.*" He looked at her…she had finished it for him.

With a grateful nod, he regarded the nun, she got it…she was getting him. "I see terror on faces, eyes open; mouths left frozen in screams. But not with Sister; it was…holy."

She studied him: his hair long enough to be tied at the neck, he looked like a pirate; his tanned face and solid jaw, dark, haunted eyes told her he'd seen things.

"God bless you for telling me this. I pray you can recover from all you see." He studied her: strong face and brow framed in linen, her eyes deep and green like the glens of Antrim, but there was a sadness, a secret in them…she'd had a life somewhere else but was now living a life few understood in a grim, discontent town with a dark side. But what had she said?

"Ah, yes, recover…I do that a lot but not with much class, sometimes I need a pint or a few shots of Jameson. But thanks for knowing some Tennyson…*that* was a comfort."

For a moment, they'd stepped out of a reality that was calling them back. Padric would need to put closure on this but he was distracted. Cunningham had followed Nevel down the canal road and the animal kept looking back at Magdalen.

Allowed to return to the nun, he sniffed the rosary that hung from her waist and ran away. "Nevel, show her!"

Padric and Martinez looked on. With veil dancing around her, she followed him quickly. "I hope he's not playing."

Padric grinned. "Go for it, Sister…I'm with you."

All were amazed when Nevel stopped at a small rise of boulders and rocks much farther away. At its edge of the canal, the dog sat down staring into some low hanging mesquite bending over the water. Cecelia's killers had thrown her beads to the wind; a long, white rosary swayed back and forth, waiting.

Magdalen knelt down beside Nevel. "You are my friend, now and forever." He hesitated like he was thinking it over then licked her face.

Cunningham ordered the dog to behave. "My apologies…he's trained not to do that."

Padric approached. "Ah, cut him some slack; he likes her. She might need him some day, God forbid." And he would be right. They wondered why Cecelia's attackers would not have taken the beads or the ring for trophies…had they become flustered, in a panic? Magdalen pleaded with the men that these items be returned at some point to the convent of San Miguel and bid her farewells to Cunningham. She whispered something to Nevel; his eyes followed her as she walked away. Padric pointed to a CSI tent.

Martinez smiled. "So, Sister, you like dogs?" They laughed and sat down, but the men wondered if she'd seen too much on her first day working with them. Regardless they laid out their thoughts as if they'd been together for years. Padric pulled out the signature journal and pen he brought everywhere; this team might work…*but a nun?* The ever-irascible Captain O'Manion had doubted it. Who was this archaeologist-nun anyway and what the hell was she doing in a remote place like sun-baked L'Arroyo? "Most Arizonans don't even know where this God-forsaken town is!" Padric wondered the same. The reason his family had settled here came out of a decision his father had made to join a gaggle of miners from County Antrim on their way to the States to work in the mines during the Troubles. But today the detective didn't need another mystery.

He'd need to clean up his act with a nun working beside him. It had nothing to do with his eye for a beautiful woman; he'd strayed down that path too many times. This was different, that odd feeling he had holding her hand…*what was that?* His women had no place even near her. *Bloody hell. Was it guilt?* He had plenty of that and she wasn't part of his cop world and other things.

And now here she was proposing a scenario neither detective expected. "The killers are replicating the deaths of first and second century Christian martyrs. This is what I meant by a script but the victims meet a certain criteria. It's essential to what motivates them." Magdalen would need to be more specific.

"What…eye color, height, weight, and race?" She said it was none of that…simply put, the victims had to be good, live holy lives. The men looked at her in disbelief.

Magdalen would need to explain. "You've heard the expression 'it's all in a name; our victims die like their name-saint.'" She spoke of the martyrologies and ancient texts the killer might have referenced before killing. "The Scriptures tell us Saint Stephen died from lapidation. Someone tried to stone Father Stefano Villa to death; that was impractical, didn't work. He was stabbed to death."

"And now we have Cecelia, a Roman woman, living in the age of martyrdom and the persecution of Christians. She had converted her husband-to-be and his brother and they were killed for it, dying as Christians professing their faith. A prefect came to convince her to renounce her faith and she scorned him…that's all it took. The executioner attempted to behead her with three strikes of a sword, which was as much as the law would allow and he left her for dead. But she lived for three days and while dying, she gave all she had to the poor and her house to the bishop. So you see, she was beheaded…almost. And we have here a near-decapitation."

Padric stared at her. *Someone could think this stuff up?* He'd seen it all…dark things, but he wanted this simple. "So, Saint Cecelia."

"Wanting it done to the letter, our executioner beheaded his victim…almost. He could have struck off her head and allowed it to drop and float down the canal, a precaution they planned to use just in case. He's young I think, idealistic, brilliant maybe, probably OCD. This drives him to certain victims, no one else will do. His pathology has dragged him under…he might have been one of the good guys."

Padric was seeing the light. "Nuns and priests…supposedly good; and you are that?"

"I fear I am very flawed but God is merciful and lets me rise each day to try once again. But we're getting off track…the killer seeks a pure heart; this makes the target worthy for martyrdom."

"This reminds me of the Nicole Simpson case in '94."

"And I'm thinking Saint Cecelia's, second century."

"Good one…we'll help you get justice." The joker in him was gone. She was silent on the drive back to the convent. "What is it, Sister?" They were nearing the Cathedral.

"There will be more. What do we do about all those vowed souls with the names of martyrs? They are potential victims. How do we keep them safe?"

"We'll access diocesan records, ascertain where they live and work in L'Arroyo." Martinez promised added security. "We'll go to them, talk to them personally and may ask your help with that." He was a hard man, but religion and God and holy ones thrown into the mix were something different.

"I'm sure there are two, but only one is the architect; he will challenge himself by mimicking the most gruesome martyrdoms he can find in his research; his list of victims is growing." The detectives glanced at each other. "His working knowledge of early

Church History and access to books of this nature fuels his pathology; all this empowers him. He has time on his hands, is alone, I think.
It is dark where he lives, where he spends his days and nights."

They were standing now in the Cathedral courtyard; the men,
in no hurry to leave. Padric surprised both of them. "Your vocation, the life you live, gives you the insight for this and we're grateful." She studied him…so intelligent and articulate, educated, his
eyes, so intense, but there's a searching; he's struggling with his own
demons. *Dear man, I will pray for him.*

But he was doing the same…*brilliant woman, good eyes, some intensity there. She's at peace with her life but there's more, a fire, something left over
from another time and, damn it, I wish I'd been there.* From that moment,
this brash, Irish detective would be her guardian from a distance
for the rest of her life if she needed him, but, with heavy heart, he
feared she'd see the mess in his soul.

The detectives walked her to the door of the convent and she
invited them in for some beverage. They declined but Padric needed to know: "Saint Mary Magdalene…what about her? You know
what I'm asking."

She smiled a little. "She wasn't a martyr. My name-saint's history lies elsewhere; forget Brown's conspiracy theories and all those
new discoveries with texts posing doubt and empty debate."

"What then? She's your saint, tell me."

Magdalen looked away and thought for a moment, then told
them of a holy woman, who'd borne in her soul many things.
"She'd seen too much and was there when Christ died, the first
to go to his grave, His body gone. She discovered this and later
becomes known as the Tomb Woman." Little did they know Magdalen herself would become known by this name the longer she
stayed in L'Arroyo. "I felt like one when I studied in Cairo, moving
from one grave to the next. Horror surrounded the woman and she
had a deep insight into why Jesus did what He did. She understood
men; she'd been with enough of them."

"You're not speaking autobiographically, are you, Sister?"

Martinez glared at his partner. "Johnny, watch yourself. Sister,
forgive my partner; he gives everyone grief. It's good to know you're
not in the killer's crosshairs; but we'll keep you safe, too."

"Not to worry, Detective. But is autobiographically, a word?" They laughed. She said she would pray to her Sister. "Our Cecelia will do this for me...she'll help us."

No one had ever said that to them about one of their victims. Martinez was moved and said he'd never prayed to any of the dead he'd found. "Begin" she whispered and looked at them kindly. "You're tired, your families are waiting."

They said their goodbyes and the two said nothing as Martinez drove back to the Precinct. Padric looked out the window; *families of our own.* He and his wife no longer spoke. Later, not wanting to go home, he stepped into the street. *Christ, I need a drink.* But it would be coffee from Cuppa and later, alone, he worked out downstairs in the weight room. Falling asleep in the dorm, he thought of his two wee girls and whispered to them in their dreams."

Author's Notes

"Dios mio...por favor, por favor." – *Spanish, for My God, please, please.*

Dulce Jesús – *Spanish, for sweet Jesus.*

Nada – *Spanish, for nothing.*

Dies irae, dies illa – *Latin, for day of death and dying, day of wrath; refrain from medieval funeral dirge.*

alma mater – *Latin, for our mother, referring to one's school.*

"The Crucifieds!" – *refers to Sister Magdalen's religious community, the Sisters of the Crucified, who maintain Cathedral High and live in the convent of San Miguel.*

Santa madre – *Spanish, for Holy Mother.*

"Kemo sabe" – *Native American term of endearment, catch-phrase used in the radio/television show "The Lone Ranger" who calls his sidekick, Tonto, kemosabe ; Padric and Martinez often address each other with this.*

Hour of Lauds – *morning prayer of the Church as part of the Liturgy of the Hours prayed by nuns and priests and the devout.*

Faccacia – *oven-baked Italian flatbread.*

Brie, Camembert, Livarot – *types of French cheese.*

tarte tatin – *French upside down pastry in which fruit is caramelized.*

charlotte aux pommel – *French for popular Normandy dessert cake with apricot or custard sauce.*

blaas – *doughy, white flour bun associated with Waterford, Ireland.*

bain taitneamh as do bhéile – *Irish, for "Enjoy the food."*

mortuary archeologist – *scientist who studies burial sites and the remains.*

arroyos – *stream beds, dry washes or gulches edging the city of L'Arroyo; thus, the name.*

chaparral – *desert vegetation of thorny and tangled bushes and small trees.*

bottlebrush – *heat-tolerant tree with red 5-inch blooms resembling a cleaning brush.*

The Edge – *a dark, lawless side of L'Arroyo where vice reigns; a thorn in the side of the city's law enforcement.*

Miss Marple – *fictional sleuth and character in works by Agatha Christie, British crime writer.*

"But Lancelot mused a little space, she has a lovely face…And God in his mercy give her grace." – *Lines from Tennyson's Lady of Shalott. This small moment reveals another side of the hard-nosed Detective John Padric who, in fact, is an academic, well read, sensitive and probably more content if he were an English Lit prof.*

The Troubles – *refers to thirty-year conflict and sectarian strife in the six counties of N. Ireland (1968-1999); Irish nationalists, favoring a united Ireland; a violent campaign against Britain army and Loyalist paramilitaries who enforced British rule. Detective Padric grew up in Belfast with his father, Guinness Padric, a patriot of the times.*

Martyrologies – *see Glossary.*

OCD – *obsessive-compulsive disorder displaying symptoms of uncontrolled recurring thoughts and behaviors.*

"Nicole Simpson case in '94" – *reference to highly publicized murder case involving once popular athlete, O. J. Simpson, accused and later found guilty in a civil suit of the murder of wife, Nicole, and her friend, Ron Goldman. She was nearly decapitated as was the nun, Sister Cecelia.*

Saint Mary Magdalene – *saint affiliated with the apostles who followed Jesus, said to have been a courtesan but this has been disputed.*

Cuppa – *Irish, for a cup of tea; name of a fictitious franchise in L'Arroyo.*

4 THE NILE HOTEL

Saturday, one in the morning, March 15

Tonight, she was unable to sleep and gazed out at the city from the window seat in the hall. The obelisk in the center of the tree-lined Plaza was flooded with light and Magdalen wondered if L'Arroyo had been designed just for her. As she'd pointed out to her students, its founding fathers had voted into law Egyptian Revival architectural design be reflected in all public buildings.

After all, the first city planner was Dr. Jameson, an Egyptian anthropologist-archaeologist *par excellence*; his premier museum on the Plaza, brimming over with treasure from Cairo. Covered in lotus and papyrus motifs, the slanted slab walls rose into the night sky. Beside the museum, the Nile's facade in artful scarabs and hieroglyphics, stood silent.

The nun smiled, wondering where her new detective friends were tonight? *What good men they are, but that self-assured Irish lieutenant with secrets of his own…he's a hard read, complicated.* She whispered a prayer for him. Dimly, she observed a lone figure leaning comfortably on the ledge of a balcony looking out at the night…*how nice, just to be there.* The man thought so too. This was his city.

Padric gazed up at the moon. "That's all you got for me?"

It ignored him. Major Crimes lead night detective, a husband and father of two, was as usual taking a risk just standing there. A hotel towel wrapped round his loins was the only thing between him and the night; again he spoke to the moon, *la luna.* They were friends.

"Beware the Ides of March and all that."

His partner, Martinez, liked to gamble, but he took risks of a different kind and now had some decisions to make. He'd been careless with this one, hadn't known much about her. In his business there were rules of engagement for situations like this and he had a situation; Johnny Padric had done no background check. Behind him she lay naked, waiting for him to come back to bed. They'd met before the holidays in the lobby downstairs; he looking for a suspect; she eluding an annoying ex-lover. Looks turned into words then something else and they took it upstairs to the fourth floor. It was customary for Padric to allow himself a little adultery.

Though he didn't indulge all the time, his drug of choice was a beautiful woman who wasn't his wife; she'd need to be exceptional, smart and very discreet, have all the physical attributes and moves he required. But they would never be Lara. He'd been told his father had struggled with the same demons, but neither had needed to chase the ladies; the two drew them like moths to a flame.

For a moment, Padric was lost in thoughts of the man, wondering if talk of an empty coffin returning to Belfast for burial was true; he lived with the dread of unanswered family secrets re-surfacing, fearing they'd be too painful to resolve. Recently, an older, very beautiful woman had stopped him in the street, thinking he was her "own dear Guin Padric; the love of my life, come back to me...ah, how he loved me."

But John Padric could only think of his mother and how it would hurt her to know this; besides, he was doing the same to his wife. He said in a clipped tone she must be mistaken and bid her good afternoon. But he understood, even felt sorry for her; his father had fed her a line, some fantasy to live on; but then, who knows...maybe he loved her. But Darragh Padric, his mother, was beautiful, his father's Maureen O'Hara.

Her eyes often flickered with an eternal sadness he couldn't fix; sometimes it was all he thought about, hating his father then wanting him back in his life. Someday when he had time he'd look for him up in the hills, down into the mines, the one where they had found him. His younger sisters, Mary and Fiona, said his mom was quieter now. She'd insisted the two return with her to Belfast when she brought back her husband's body for burial in Milltown Ceme-

tery. They told him she kept things inside her with a far away look
in her beautiful eyes and rarely spoke of their da'. They said she
talked all the time about *him*, her John the copper. And there was
her oldest daughter, Mairead, the newspaperwoman, who'd stayed
behind in L'Arroyo to keep an eye on her rascal of a brother. He,
with his dark eyes and hair slicked back in a short ponytail like a
pirate, looked like his da'. John James Connelly Padric worried his
mother but his brother Liam the priest, light haired and blue-eyed,
could do no wrong.

Padric wondered if his father, living and breathing, was walking around somewhere else. He ached for the man and closed his
eyes, remembering the Irish patriot on fire with idealistic rhetoric;
but where was he? In his gut, he knew his da' was alive. On nights
like this with a woman, he'd give himself the standard, hackneyed
excuse he was trying to forget the death and darkness he found every night on the job. But he knew: John Padric was trying to silence
his little boy cries for his father…abandonment was a bitch.

Padric glanced back at the woman who eyed him expectant-
ly…she was a package wrapped up and waiting. He'd never wanted
to know her last name, though she'd said it was Cruz and the less he
knew the better. He'd become over-confidant, relying on his usual
good read on a person…it went with his job, but he was off. The
detective didn't know she was a collector, and had plans for him;
he'd never be rid of her. Johnny was in for a world of hurt.

Joanna was cut from a different cloth. She liked racking up
men; discarding or keeping a few, tucking this or that one away in
her web. She'd let them dangle. Ms. Cruz, if that was her name,
played with powerful, judges and magistrates, the occasional attorney or OG, a gangster bad boy…they all had her silence.

After all, she had her own brand of bedroom ethics. But Padric believed he was in charge of whatever they had and thought
he had set down the parameters. He'd made it clear; he'd give her
some of himself with no promises. If she wasn't satisfied with room
service and his bedside manner, oh well. There'd be no phone calls,
texting or emails, no out on the town or in public. "It is what it is,"
he had said and she was hooked; no man had shown her that much

nonchalance. He wasn't like all the others; she'd take whatever he wanted to give…no strings, knots or tangles.

What they had was cold and hypnotic. But, for a man who was known for his dedication to detail and duty, he'd tossed caution aside. His choice of a lover…*who was she?* It would be his undoing.

Earlier Padric had taken the backstairs two at a time to her suite in the Nile, but he'd been doing some introspection; tonight he was done, ending it. The woman was proving to be cumbersome… good word, cumbersome; she had questioned him about someone else. *For God's sake, she was the other woman* and worse, her point of contention, a nun; she'd seen them talking. *She'd never voiced any concern about Lara, so why the Q&A over Magdalen?*

Game over. This romp had been an escape and the Nile was good for that; known for its opulence, the hotel was peopled with none other than the Big Five, a select group of families with influence. The Jamesons owned a whole floor, as did the Whittons and Zalconi's, the Devlins, too, and so did hers, but Padric didn't know that. Then there were the secrets. The Nile was known to have many; discretion, its hallmark and a code of silence clause written into every staff member's contract. No one under age thirty need apply to work at the Nile and not any guest walked its thick carpet.

Tonight Joanna had been more creative than usual; she was calling his name now, wanting him back. He looked once more at the city lights and north toward the red tile roof of the convent. He wondered if the nun was asleep, dreaming good things. The lass was different and lovely, and the one woman he couldn't have, so why was he thinking of her when a beauty ten feet away was waiting? He sighed, thinking of Magdalen, and withdrew from the night air.

Even farther north, on a quiet street in the suburbs, another beautiful woman lay asleep on her couch. Upstairs in their beds, her two little girls lay peaceful, content with their dreams. But she quickly sat up; a commercial lit up the screen. She clicked the remote and tossed it aside, hoping he'd come home soon…she wanted to talk, had something to tell him. Lara Padric stared into the dark.

Two blocks from the Nile, the security guard at the gate looked up at the moon still dangling over the city. He warned Brother James to be careful as he pushed his cart up the street to the Nile Hotel's service entrance. He didn't drive and never asked for a ride, but he kept his homeless shelter afloat. Its pantries near empty, he hoped for a good offering.

Back at the hotel, Padric had drifted off; when he awoke, Joanna was gone. That was a switch: he'd always left first. He propped up the pillows and stared out through the open balcony door into a starry night and frowned. *She's jamming me up over a nun and I'm fucking married? That's not how this works.* Trouble…he could feel it. Guilt was Padric's not so imaginary friend; it followed him everywhere; it had many names: Irish guilt, Catholic school guilt or what-he-knew-was-right-in-his-gut guilt. He burrowed deeper into the pillows… only to have his dream world suddenly shattered.

It wasn't real, a figment of his imagination. Scrooge had called it "a bit of undigested meat? A piece of cheese?" *Ah, Dickens…you'd love L'Arroyo!* But he'd heard it, a cry full of terror; the out-of-control laugh of a woman. His feet hit the floor running the length of the suite. From behind heavy drapes, Padric peered from the open rear window overlooking the hotel courtyard and parking garage. *Why now, why me…*a body had floated by and collided with an awning below, catapulted into the courtyard and certain death. With a thud, it hit the hard, cold tile. Bones cracked…a skull exploded all over the pavement.

Padric was not sure what devastated him more: the death of a man or the fact he was in the wrong place at the wrong time. With heart racing and nauseous, Padric lowered himself to the floor, unaccustomed to feeling this way; he couldn't move, had never been in this situation. John Padric was always a first-responder…now he was frozen, stuck, his back glued to the wall.

The screech of tires in the parking garage stunned him into reality. Padric flipped onto his feet. In seconds, half dressed he leaped from one stairwell to another, cell phone to his ear. O'Manion grunted: "Aren't you off the clock, free to be with the wife for once? What, may I ask, are you doing there at this hour?"

"First, you may not ask. Christ, Cap', you're not my da'. Long story. Second, I'll stay till the uniforms and ME get here." He hung up. Martinez was home, hadn't seen his kids in awhile; he wouldn't bother him.

"N-double-A-C-P, Tarkington." Tark liked giving Padric heat. Major Crimes' tech wizard, in front of his screen, had seen several anonymous calls pop up in dispatch. Someone, they said, had thrown a guy off the top ledge of the parking garage. "It landed like a watermelon…pow, splat!" There were even more vivid descriptions called in. Tark was behind the Nile Hotel in minutes.

"Johnny, I'm here, man!"

Padric looked around. No Tark. "Where are you?"

"Walking toward you, eyeballing you…damn, you're looking shit-faced." In the academy together, both had lived a lifetime of crime fighting through bad times and good; Padric loved Tark, the best crime-tech on the force. "Yeah, I'm fucked." But he couldn't say why. Tark could see Padric better now. "Whatta ya' need?"

"You. Get your tight ass over here. Looks like a jumper, but I think he was dropped, thrown long and hard from the top of the parking garage. It's Bro James."

"Ah, shit…I'm there." Both men knew this one. Brother James was their friend. Padric, kneeling now by the mangled body, checked his pulse. *Not again…Christ; another one of God's own, done and dusted. This is sinful…I am, I am, too.*

Uniforms from the First Precinct swarmed the area. He stood up, scanned the rooftops. It was back. A golden eagle, high on a ledge near the roof of the Nile, waited, but this time the detective had arrived quickly; its transformation from bird to seraph took place in seconds then nodding, it soared away. He watched it until it disappeared. "Star-gazing isn't gonna do it, man." Tark.

Two hours later, Padric drove home. Feeling old, he was looking for something, anything, maybe that red Mercedes, the one that kid who'd witnessed the death of that priest, had mentioned…it was a ghost and he felt like one. Last night had been surely a bad omen. He needed his woman, his beautiful wife, who made heads turned when she walked in a room.

But that ghost he was looking for had disappeared. Already a tricked-out, red Mercedes truck was putting some distance between itself and the Plaza. The driver was laughing. Riding shotgun, her hooded companion chanted an old Latin dirge: *Dies irae, dies illa…*

The moon receded and light poured over the city and the convent alive with the usual Saturday bustle. It was noon when Padric came to the door and Petra drew him into the parlor.

"We knew you would come…we heard about this earlier today." The man had no desire to be here, but he'd come alone, half hoping Magdalen would be there, and not knowing why. "It's Brother James from the homeless shelter."

He gave Petra few details. Magdalen joined them…what a comfort to see her. But she was asking him things, wanting to know how they knew the deceased had collided with an awning before hitting the pavement. He abruptly left, wishing he'd asked someone else to deliver the news. He glanced into his rear view mirror; and there she was, standing on the front steps of the convent, watching him drive away. She had sensed something was off, knew he was troubled. He cursed in Gaelic, hating himself.

Author's Notes

anthropologist-archaeologist – relying on socio-biological sciences, one trained in the study of humans, their culture past and present; their ancient and recent human history through material remains. Archaeology is a subfield of anthropology.

Ides of March – a reference to March 15 and days preceding, marked by religious observance to honor the God Jupiter but the date was made notorious by the assassination of Julius Caesar in 44 BC. The term is famously used by Shakespeare in his Julius Caesar, Act Three, Scene One.

Milltown Cemetery – in Irish, Reilig Bhaile an Mhuilin, a large cemetery in west Belfast, Northern Ireland very familiar to John Padric, and to which his mother and he returned his father's coffin to be buried there after his death. Over 200,000 rest in Milltown, most Irish Catholic. 80,000 are buried in the cemetery's poor grounds, many dying from the flu pandemic of 1919. Located in the heart of West Belfast, it is linked deeply to Irish republicanism since many famed patriots from the conflict are buried there. In total, 77 IRA volunteers have been laid to rest in what is called the 'New Republican Plot', 34 in the County Antrim Memorial Plot used between 1969 and 1972 at the height of the Troubles. Throughout the grounds, many more IRA volunteers are buried with family, among them supposedly Guinness Padric, our protagonist's father.

Big Five – *see Addendum. 472: City of L'Arroyo for delineation of five families.*

"...a bit of undigested meat, a piece of cheese?" – *reference to Scrooge's words in Charles Dicken's "A Christmas Carol."*

"N-double-A-C-P, Tarkington!" – *Jace Tarkington spoofs on the acronym NAACP, the National Association for the Advancement of Colored People, founded in 1909; he's one of a few black detectives (most are Latino/Latina) in the L'Arroyo P.D; his parents, strong public advocates for civil rights back in the day.*

5 THE SACRISTAN

Magdalen smiled when she heard the familiar voice. "It's time for the *secretarium!*" Sister Monica liked using the old Latin reference for the sacristy; Magdalen would nod and off they would go. It was Saturday ritual. Together they would hasten to the Cathedral, Magdalen pushing the elder's wheelchair through the side door and up the ramp into the sanctuary. It was silent and waiting for them.

The *sacristia* or sacristy housed sacred vessels and vestments for Holy Mass and other liturgies. Cruets, ciboriums, chalices and patens, each had their place and there was much to be done; tomorrow, Palm Sunday. Holy Week loomed and she set to work, giving the vessels an extra rub, checking the linen corporals and purificators. The used, she would wash in the *sacrarium,* a basin set aside for the cleansing of holy things; its water, diverted into the Bishop's garden instead of a septic tank.

And there was the vestry, a huge walk-in closet filled with liturgical garments. With the slight push of a button, Monica moved about in her wheelchair and followed Magdalen into the room. It was a veritable museum, at least for the bishop, its shelves stacked with tomes on liturgical practice, worn lectionaries, psalters and a very old antiphonary to which the bishop referred on occasion.

But front and center, were his precious martyrologies stacked on shelves next to his reading table. Santo Cantera was a student of martyrdom in the early Church, *circa* first and second century. Glass cabinets showcased artifacts from his travels. *Birettas* and *zuchettos,* head coverings no longer used, sat safely on shelves and part of his memories from his studies in Rome. His pectoral cross and miter were on display...the man was a collector.

The elder was smiling today. Sister Monica had been San Miguel's first sacristan and now she gazed through the glass door of a narrow case at a single threadbare cassock worn by the first priest, Father Aloysius. But the old nun would move on with certain procedures to be observed. "I will take care of things, dear."

Not missing a stitch out of place, her fingertips moved over the fabrics and embroidery of each vestment as Magdalen moved quickly about but pointed now to the table where the bishop often sat reading. "He has a huge study and shelves full of research at home; what is it about this room and these texts that consume him? He sits here quite often...the man loves this room. Odd, he makes this his retreat when he has a huge residence and all of Cantera."

She was referring to his father Arturo's sprawling ranch, his lands all over Arizona and on the other side of the Border. But in this humble sacristy, nothing had escaped Santo Cantera's touch. When a young priest in the newly built Cathedral, he had artfully inscribed in Latin the names for the ancient vestments; they were mystical sounding: *omophorion, phelonion, polystaorion,* and *slicharion.* He'd set to work on it after returning from Greece, recreating what he had seen in an old 14th century fresco in Mistras.

Today however, something was out of place in his world. "That book is not where it should be." Monica pointed to a copy of the precious *Martyrologium Hieronymianum.* "See, it's been left open on the counter." Magdalen smoothed down its vellum cover and glanced within at the text, detailing the lives of the early martyrs, listing each by name and their manner of dying; how odd that such a book should lay open here at this time when all of L'Arroyo was paralyzed in fear by three shocking modern-day martyrdoms.

A page had been bookmarked; like Padric, she saw nothing as random...why would she now come upon something like this? There was purpose here: an unusual holy card of Saint Mary Magdalene, embracing the feet of Christ, lay on the page as if waiting for her. She scrutinized each word in the text and drew a deep breath…here was a detailed narrative of the death of Saint Cecelia. Had not her Sister, with the same name, died in similar fashion?

"Who would bring this to my attention now?"

"Ah, yes," the elder whispered. "Though there are those who still question her existence, this book contains the oldest historical account to be found on holy Cecelia's passing. A coincidence then or more?"

"And you would say the bishop is versed in all this?"

"He is a student of it; the early Church and its martyrs, his passion. So yes. He constantly reads the old wisdom. This book was Father Antonio's; he was the pastor who built this Cathedral with a very young priest assistant who is now our Bishop. Father came to us with some very old treasured manuscripts and this book; it's a copy of the original, of course. Back then we had very few books of our own. I was permitted to read each from cover to cover. But you're looking at this for another reason and thinking there is a connection." It wasn't a question. Magdalen asked if anyone else might have access to all these books, to the sacristy.

"They might." And who else but the monsignor and bishop? "Put it up for now. Ask Santo if he will allow you to borrow it." *Santo.* Magdalen smiled. Monica's status and age allowed her the freedom to call the bishop anything she wanted. Yes, she would do it and watch his face when she asked.

"Watch his face when you ask him. You'll get your answer." Magdalen shook her head…*she knows what I'm thinking.* Again her fingers smoothed down the cover of the book. She wondered if it was too far-fetched to assume someone might have consulted the text before taking the life of Sister Cecilia. *And worse, might they have referenced here in this very room the details of the death of Saint Stephen before killing Father Stefano?*

Brother James. Had he not, less than twenty-four hours ago, met a tragic end? Who would be next? She felt suddenly cold…a section detailing the martyrdom of the apostle, Saint James the Less, had been bookmarked as well. *Was the bishop…no*, she could never imagine him a delusional killer…*no, absolutely not.* Quickly she returned the book to its place, but not before skimming through the traditional narrative of Saint Cecelia's martyrdom. "She is buried in the Catacomb of

Callistus. I've been to this site."

"That was after Cairo, eh? It would seem you had a charmed life, but not always."

"I endured some things there that almost did me in, but I'm here now." Monica knew she would tell her some day.

"Good answer. We do what we must and now you are safe with us." *But how safe am I, are we, the priests and nuns of the city?* Magdalen was frowning again, lost in her thoughts. Monica eyed her caregiver closely. "No fears now. His light will reveal what is beneath."

"Beneath what?" Monica drew her closer and whispered things. She was describing another place, a world of shadows below the city, "a labyrinth of ways", she said, where she thought there might some answers. She knew things, had been here longer than most, describing a maze of passageways under the Plaza, winding their way further, passed the archaeological museum and beyond the First Precinct to Saint Rita's, the Church of Bones. She reminded Magdalen she was still an archaeologist and must investigate things…there was much to do, she insisted but gently added: "Now, within reason, dear, and not without help from your detectives." What had she said…*her* detectives?

"You must join us then…say you will!"

Monica winked: "You betcha! But hurry. I'm getting old." Magdalen laughed. And yes, that Church of Bones…she had promised her students, soon.

They noted the time and quickly finished their tasks. Passiontide. In the bishop's Cathedral, crosses and statues were draped in purple, a custom no longer observed in many churches. Admittedly, there was something haunting and ominous in the Lenten mourning cloths. And today, Monica sensed even more; she paused and looked up at a long wooden cross, covered in purple and suspended over a side altar in the sanctuary. It bore no corpus, but was simply two sturdy planks of polished wood hung by a heavy chain.

"I'd like to pray here if I might. There is much pain in this place." *Our elder knows things and how odd for her to say this now when there is death all around us. What next?*

Magdalen looked to where Monica pointed. A small bird was

gliding through the nave of the church, but this was not uncommon; there had been several who had gained entry through an opening in the belfry. This one flew noiselessly toward them and alighted on the cross above them.

"It's a sign…the sudden sighting of a bird speaks of death, my Magdalen. Someone will die…one of us, more; it will be so!" Her words were unnerving.

"Sister, it will find its way out just as it came in." But as Magdalen spoke, the bird fell to the sanctuary floor; it fluttered and expired. "Or not…" She hurried to scoop it up in a cloth she quickly retrieved from the sacristy. *How strange this should happen now?*

"I will bury it in the garden, dear. I know how to bury things." Her words would haunt Magdalen but the day would become even more singular. As they came down the ramp, Petra was walking toward them with the parent of one of their students. Timothy Whitton, successful CEO of Whitton Corporation was one of Cathedral's alumni and another of Padric's classmates.

He too was pushing a wheelchair bearing a precious burden, his grandfather, the founder of Whitton Corporation; recently the old gentleman had finally returned to L'Arroyo to spend the rest of his days. Monica raised her hands to her face in surprise; her smile full of delight. Magdalen quickly knelt down beside her and asked if she knew the dear man.

"Why of course, dear…it's Jack!" Magdalen turned quickly to look at his worn handsome face. Monica knew him at once.

Tim grinned. He too knelt down beside her. "Sister, you knew my grandfather a very long time ago." The aging scion of the Whitton family, as bright eyed and sharp as Monica, reached out to her.

Both clung to each other with tears in their eyes. "You left me here in the Sonoran, Jack, what was that about, you old coot?" Petra and Magdalen glanced at each other.

"Well, I'm here now, don't you know. My apologies, Sister, I needed to take care of my mother and sister who insisted on leaving; a dilemma to be sure, my dear." He leaned closer. "I kept turning around searching for one last glimpse of you. I will never forget it." Monica patted his hand, whispering quiet words and understanding. Magdalen was pleased and studied their faces: so this was the lad who had helped Monica bury the bones from the side of the hill so long ago. Here is the man who had caught a glimpse of L'Arroyo before it would become a city of intrigue.

Petra said softly: "You, sir, are the dear young man who left the shovels for our Sister Monica and we are forever grateful." All the nuns knew the tale from beginning to end. Tim drew the two into a side chapel and joined the nuns nearby. They were silent, watching the elders share their stories. Petra smiled at Timothy. "You are a generous man and busy, Mr. Whitton, how did you find the time?"

"Sister, this means more than any corporate merger in some cold board room...I try to escape as much as possible without losing my shirt." They laughed and he asked about his son Larry to whom he had given little attention...the boy had done well in his studies at Cathedral High and would be off to West Point after graduation, but the man had rarely visited the school. Magdalen knew Larry well, he was one of her altar servers and she wondered: *is every Whitton assigned his destiny?*

She watched the family patriarch talking to Monica...how final it seemed; he had come back to L'Arroyo to die. The two old friends would stay in touch, meet again. Jack would dine with Monica in the convent parlor; she'd show him the glass case in the vestibule. He'd gaze for a long time at the three shovels Monica had faithfully kept...and beside them Sister Mara's precious stoneware pitcher, all symbolic of "the first days" in L'Arroyo.

Later alone in her room, Magdalen carefully wrote down all that she heard...this very night she would compile the many notes from her observations thus far on the case of the moondead. Tonight she would begin preserving all that befell her and the convent of San Miguel in a journal.

On the cover, in her signature Celtic Hand font, she would inscribe the curious title: *The Sacristan Mysteries.*

Author's Notes

secretarium − Latin, for what is now the sacristy.

sacristia − Spanish, for sacristy; See Glossary, for detailed description of the sacristy and sacred objects, the vestry and sacred vestments.

"the first days" − reference to L'Arroyo's beginnings when the elder, Sister Monica, a young novice then and a small band of Sisters of the Crucified found themselves lost in the Sonoran and set down roots in what would become L'Arroyo.

omophorion, phelonion, polystaorion, and sticharion − ancient Greek orthodox names for holy vestments worn by the priests during liturgies.

14th century fresco in Mistras − Bishop Cantera has knowledge of many things but is widely traveled especially as a young priest when he discovered this art.

Martyrologium Hieronymianum − see Glossary.

Vellum − derived from the Latin for vitrilinum, meaning made from calf.

Catacomb of Callixtus − cemeteries in Rome where many popes and early martyrs were entombed. Saint Cecelia is buried here. In her archaeological pursuits, Magdalen has spent much of her time in Egypt, Italy and the Holy Land.

Passiontide − the last two weeks of Lent.

BACKSTORY

Anno domini AD 1933

They were lost. A dust storm of burning sand had set off course a band of displaced persons during the early Depression. On their way to California, they had hid themselves under their broken-down produce truck against a hill and waited. When the roar of the wind had stopped, there was a great stillness and one by one they emerged from under the vehicle and some canvas coverings. The desert lay quiet but, among the group, were seven nuns with a very young novice, Sister Monica, who noticed it first. On the slope of the hill, exposed to the now searing light of the sun, was a cache of human bones, churned up by the storm and strewn across the incline. Fear rippled through the rest of the travelers.

But it was Monica who asked for a shovel from the truck and began to dig a long, shallow grave. Her Sister companions knelt down and pushed the gravel and sand aside for the remains to be given their proper rest, regardless of the grumbling that spread through the camp. During all this, a young man, who had watched and listened to the youngest nun, stepped forward, unable to stand silent any longer. He offered to gather the bones with the nuns and together they laid them carefully in the narrow mass grave. It was growing dark and with no help from the older, stronger men who had turned their backs, they continued their work of mercy. A man, wearing a red bandana, called out obscenities and mocked them, until a woman hit him in the face with her fist. The others laughed, but grew silent when the nuns turned slowly and looked at them.

The young novice, Monica, would not cease her efforts and the handsome youth would not leave her side. In later years, Jack Whitton would speak of her beauty and courage and how he had wanted to stay with the Sisters to protect them or simply take the novice with him for her own protection. At his mother and sisters' insistence however, he had been forced to leave her and the others behind. A silent departure took place at the first light of dawn when, without a word, the other travelers, no longer able to use their truck, had moved out over the flat desert terrain before them. They left without waking the sleeping nuns.

It was Monica who woke first and discovered the betrayal. She allowed the others to remain at peace in their sleep and climbed up a large mound that rose from the desert floor. There, shielding her eyes from some dust in the wind, she looked in all four directions. Far off to the west, a glint of metal, perhaps from a rifle one of the men had been carrying, caught her attention. It would be insane *to attempt to catch up with people who had shown such hostility and left them to fend for themselves in harm's way. She thought of green Ireland from where she had sailed less than two years ago. Sean Noonan would not be happy with his daughter and where she stood at the moment. Bit he'd expect her to survive.*

The Sisters' initial intent had been to reach the Pacific Coast where refugees from the hard-hit Midwest and Dust Bowl of a Depression had immobilized the nation. Many would find their living and a meal as pickers in the orange groves of southern California. There the nuns had hoped to minister to the unfortunate. They smiled when Monica said: "That would have been too easy."

"We will settle here," their superior, Sister Mara, had said. "Run, Sister Monica, to the top of the hill and find for us the greenest spot you can see."

Within seconds she'd called out: "It's here, Mother; you're standing on it."

They had looked about and discovered several arroyos; some deeper than others that could prove dangerous if they suddenly filled with waters from the high country. The washes were shallow and dry at the moment, but would eventually receive the run-off of melting snows in the mountains to the north; it was already early September. Chaparrals of mesquite and acacia would provide them with cover and, within days, their sprawling branches would be draped with fabric from their own holy habits and robes. With their small store of sewing supplies, their veils were turned into smocks and bandanas for their heads and they laughed at how much they had made with so little.

A lighter moment in their desperation came when Monica discovered the travelers had left not one, but several shovels behind. "It was Jack. He did this for us…so sad that he could not have stayed. We will build things."

Since there had been no rain to damage their matches, they were able to light small bonfires each evening as darkness approached. "We must focus on keeping one flame alive," Mara had warned. They kept it apart from the wind in a stoneware pitcher that would become in their small community, the symbol of all they had left and lost. It would be their beginning.

Each day they scavenged the land anew, along with a coyote eyeing them curiously, but who never came closer. And each night, while two Sisters kept guard with hands on their shovels, they could see the eyes of desert nocturnals peering at them. Eventually the animals would move farther away out of respect.

The days grew colder and in mid-November, it snowed in the high country. One gray day, in an unusual show of nature, it rained all afternoon and into the night. They scooped up what they could from the flowing stream in the few containers they had. But they kept one flame aglow in the stone pitcher safely lit beneath some tarp the travelers had left on the opposite side of the hill. There was also the truck they were unable to move. Monica said she would drive it someday.

One early morning, they rose to discover a priest and several men, one from El Salvador with his very small boy and some women; all lay sleeping close to their dwellings, but far enough away as not to alarm them if they awoke. They had said they could go no further, and asked if they might stay, contributing what little they had and praising the Sisters for all they had done. Close to where the bones had been found Father Aloysius and the men, with the shovels the young man had left, dug out a small enclosure in the side of the hill where an altar was built for the Eucharistic liturgy. Happily while doing so, they discovered a spring…there would always be water.

The nuns were surprised when the priest described how at quite a distance east of their settlement, Tucson and Phoenix had become growing towns. Regardless they would build their lives here and close beside them, eager to help, the boy called Arturo would grow stronger each day. He was a Cantera and his name would be forever linked to L'Arroyo.

And so began life in the small town around a mound where some bones had been buried and the nuns and priest saw their remnant of land as a blessed place, calling it simply L'Arroyo after all that surrounded them. It welcomed all those with good intent who drifted into their midst but Monica continued to wonder if any misfortune had befallen Jack at the hands of the men with whom he and his family had disappeared.

In the months that followed, others came on foot, since there were no roads guiding them to the remote desert place. They'd often leave again, making the long trek to California or hitching a ride to faraway Phoenix or Tucson or Yuma. Most were never heard from again; but it was hoped they had reached their destination. A hushed silence fell on the group one night as they sat near the fire, when a newcomer told them of the remains of some travelers who were found near the edge of Death Valley. Around the skull of one of the corpses was a faded red bandana. On hearing the news, Monica had secretly wept, wondering if among them were Jack and his family.

Later that evening she had slowly walked back and forth beside the arroyo while the coyotes lay at a careful distance and watched her in silence.

It was she they knew best, often sitting beside them and whispering to them, but this night she had tears in her voice and they sensed the change in her...some moving closer. Her favorite drew even nearer and lay down with head lowered beside her; he would be named simply Brother. That night when Monica had finished her prayers, the coyotes had risen to their feet and stood with heads bowed until she disappeared among the shelters and tents. Many years later, another nun would come, not realizing at first her purpose and she too would have a way with animals and an almost wolf-like quality in her read on people.

She would realize she lived half in this world and half in the next but that is another story. And so it was that a town grew, people living and dying there. When yet another priest happened through, they welcomed him. With bricks molded from clay in the arroyo beds, he built the small adobe Church of San Miguel to honor the Archangel Michael, their defense against demons for not only coyotes paced back and forth in the dark.

Sinister spirits would appear to rise from the desert floor and circle the town...at least that's what Father Murphy had said in a whisper.

And Monica kept all these things in her soul.

Author's Notes

anno domini – Latin, for "In the year of our Lord."

Dust Bowl of a Depression – name given to the Great Plains region devastated by drought in the '30's.

Death Valley – in California, a desert of extremes, record heat, steady drought.

6 MANO A MANO

Monday, ten in the morning, March 17

Today a Q&A would throw the spotlight on Major Crimes and Captain Brendan O'Manion; he was grumpy and hungry and muttered something about "it's way passed my bedtime." Night shift ended at seven. With no clear-cut answers to offer, he hated being at the receiving end and here he was with Commander Ramirez doing just that. The First Precinct was holding a press conference on the bishop's turf in the Diocesan Center next to the Cathedral.

A nun and a priest had been murdered, a brother of God slain; for now, he could only make assumptions and he rarely assumed anything. O'Manion, a man of faith, was not accustomed to crimes of this nature; he'd rely on his lead night detective, cynic and sinner, to figure it out, explain things to the media. John Padric was theater; reporters loved him, hell, what lawman in this town had ever studied Shakespeare at Belfast's Queens University?

They flocked to press conferences with him at the mic; the man was articulate, made for good press, but O'Manion would mutter to Commander Ramirez that the lad had a way of making them think he gave them an answer and he'd given them nothing. The two would smile and watch their lieutenant, handsome and swashbuckling, sell everyone in the room a story. John Padric was all a good cop should be…it would seem.

But today explanations were cryptic; there was a killer or killers out there. Priests and nuns in the city were left feeling vulnerable and the bishop, with all his power, could do nothing to fix this one. Reporters and clergy pelted him, wanted to know; he pelted back with his usual rapid-fire, in-your-face answers; divulging little, but with the flair they expected. The city knew Johnny Padric and trusted him; he was their Batman.

Petra was there; he'd hoped to speak with her, tell her how much they'd appreciated Magdalen. He had to admit he liked how he felt when he was around the nuns and the convent of San Miguel. But so did Bishop Santo Cantera; he too had seen Petra and caught up with her in front of the Cathedral after the public briefing was over. He had a special place in his heart for the Sisters of the Crucified; good women, God's own, he was blessed.

But today, he'd be scolded by one of them. At first the two exchanged pleasantries until Petra told him to cease and desist. "Your grace, you must consider more carefully what you impart in your Lenten homilies, this dying for Christ and martyrdom. Your words are sadly being misinterpreted by someone." *How dare she critique me.* "The killer wants us dead." *What was this nonsense?* He had expected more of her; insisted the recent killings bordered on something apocalyptic, a time of glory.

His words didn't silence her. "You are not listening to me." The bishop stared at her. "Our situation is grave. Be silent for us; we've lost our Sister; you've lost your friend, Father Villa, and good Brother James. Who is next?" He asked her to lower her voice; Petra persisted. "I understand we are sanctified in our sufferings, and what we endure redemptive but…"

"You lay this on me?" *How dare this snip of a woman speak to me like this?* The bishop told her he would think on all she had said.

Petra frowned. *Is he dismissing me?* Again she insisted his homilies and what he encouraged were being taken out of context. "Obviously, you do not wish to hear what is true. We will speak further, good day, Your grace."

The nerve of the woman telling me what we will do and when we will do it; he glanced at his watch. Men did that; his episcopal ego bruised, the bishop rushed up the sacristy steps.

Petra glanced back when she heard the door slam. *What does he do in there?*

Padric had smiled a little as he walked to his hummer. The

bishop's people had demanded he solve these dreadful murders immediately, this afternoon or, at the latest, by dawn tomorrow. But his thoughts were of Magdalen…if she'd be consulting for Major Crimes, he'd need to put his extra-curricular activities on hold.

The detective had been playing it fast and loose with his lover and excelled at covering his moves; his job and the night had a way of hiding a lifestyle he wanted this nun to know nothing about. He looked up at the campanile. He'd been one of those good Catholic boys and even considered the priesthood like his brother, Liam, newly ordained and missioned in San Francisco.

Turning the corner onto L'Arroyo Boulevard, he slowed down. Petra and the bishop were engaged in some verbal combat; *trouble in paradise…interesting.*

☩

Later that night, all eyes in the squad room were fixed on monitors or glued to their iPhones. "Betty, baby!" Martinez laughed. "The divine Ms. Branston in your face."

"She's foaming at the mouth," someone said. And indeed, the woman had the curiosity and body language of a ferret. The shapely, well-dressed redhead moved in close, pushing a microphone into Petra's face and asked what she was thinking.

The nun gazed into the crowd converging on the convent steps. "As you can imagine, sadness and anger, questions unanswered. I don't fault our First Precinct…they're hard at work and we wait." The men smiled.

"But doesn't that say Major Crimes isn't doing their job?"

"Shame on you, Ms. Branston…do not put words in my mouth." Padric grinned. "We will stop this interview if you do not behave." The detectives doubled over in laughter. They were pleased…they needed a nun on their side.

Branston pushed the microphone closer. "I've heard evidence of a ritual slaying."

"Speak to those who processed the scene." More questions, faster now, found Petra ducking and weaving. She countered finally with "Let's wrap this up, Ms. Branston. Get to the point."

Padric was surprised…she was feisty. Hard realities did that to people. The camera zoomed in on Magdalen, calmly scanning the crowd, studying the faces. He smiled a little. "She's working it for us…reading the crowd. Nice."

"Some say the bishop encouraged the killings by his glorification of martyrdom."

"No comment. Ms. Branston, you are hiding in that old cliché, 'some say'!" The men hooted. The whole squad room was glued to the monitors now. "You allege these recent deaths and our bishop are some how connected…nonsense."

Branson was furious. "Well, you've listened to his sermons… what do you think?"

Rarely did a Sister of the Crucified go public with anything. She thought for a moment; the crowd silent. "Regardless of how well intentioned our words, they are subject to misinterpretation; conclusions are drawn on one's own perceptions." *What? Too articulate.* Branston liked throwing her interviewee off balance; she'd underestimated the nun. Petra would seize the moment: "To those here tonight and watching at home, we thank you for your concern. Be assured we will abide regardless of threat. If you can help, go to the detectives working the case." She stepped closer to the camera. "Speak with good Detective John Padric." A rousing shout went up in the squad room; he was Batman.

Somewhere else in the city, a beautiful woman tossed back her long, black hair and rolled over. She flipped on the late night news. "Damn, what kind of name is Petra?" She sat up. And that other one…she'd seen that one twice this week with her man. *They looked intense; he's into her.* "Watch it, bitch."

There were others watching the coverage as well; they had deeper concerns and had been left to pick up the emotional pieces of dealing with the death of a nun on their land. Wanting to feel good again, Nina Aguilar was upset, goading her husband, needing answers.

"What really happened out there two weeks ago, husband? I've held my tongue long enough. I've heard things. Tell me. You must."

"You don't want to know." But Nina said that she did.

His son insisted: "Yeah, Dad, mom needs to know." Jesse put his arm around her.

"A nun was murdered on our land." But she already knew that…what else? Aguilar looked at the younger ones playing and laughing nearby. "I don't want to say it."

"Dad. I saw what I saw; it was bad."

"And I'm sorry, *mijo*." He motioned them into his office. "*Madre*, watch the children for a moment, *por favor*." Pilar stepped into the hall. Aguilar glanced at her altar covered with statues and candles, remembering wistfully how he'd tiptoed passed her room when he was a child. Things were different then.

"When you tell your mother to watch the kids I always need to sit." Nina was on edge.

He'd tell her a Sister of the Crucified was nearly decapitated. "She was laid out on those rocks by the road. Adolfo, the youngest in my crew, found her. There, Nina, I said it."

No one spoke until his son could no longer be silent: "I saw it. Not cool, totally rude."

"Oh, quiet, Jesse." Nina hated the way he talked. "You sound like a white boy."

"What's wrong with that?" It was Aguilar's business partner. "I'm a white boy and never talked that way."

"*Dios mio*, Paulo, how long have you been standing there?"

Paul Murphy laughed and shook Aguilar's hand. "How's everyone holding up?" They all talked at once. Jesse said he couldn't believe it had happened here on their land. "Why not? Stranger things have occurred in these parts."

David and Nina glanced at each other. Left for dead within feet of the derelict cemetery Magdalen had seen in the Edge, Paul's father had been torn apart by wolves, some said they were demons… more urban legend. "How were the men today?"

"Confused, scared. They're more superstitious then I use to be. But the nun who came out to the fields with the detectives calmed them down." *A nun was here?*

"The Cathedral. She teaches at the high school and works for the bishop…nice, had a way about her. Nina said she blessed the land just walking on it." His wife wept. "She was helping the detectives, you know, consulting on the case. Heard she was an archaeologist, worked in forensics and such, before being a nun. I was glad she was there; our men were spooked though."

Nina sobbed even louder. Paul put his arm around her. "You can't do this, Nina; think of all the good years we've had here. Look at your beautiful kids, even this one." Paul punched Jesse's arm. They smiled. "What happened on our land didn't come from us. Our lives have been formed from these fields." Don't go making this something it isn't." Paul had a way with words. "Evil touched us for a moment…we're not cursed."

"Mom's just freaked. She'll get over it." Jesse put his arm around Nina.

"*Mijo*, don't talk about me like I'm not here."

Jesse turned to Paul. "You don't come into L'Arroyo much, do you, Mr. Murphy?"

"No, lad. I make a point to stay away as much as possible."

"Considering what happened to your father out here, I get it."

"Ah, son, life goes on. I was small and he was a good man."

Nina smiled. "And you have his gift; speaking so well like you just did to us. I was told his sermons touched everyone."

Paul's father had been one of the early priests in L'Arroyo, the pastor of San Miguel when Patti Devlin went missing in the church graveyard one night; she'd been partying there and, in the eyes of the people, the cemetery, forever cursed. But the good priest had been indiscreet and committed a pubic sin; he'd fallen in love with a good woman who bore him a son. They named him Paul but Paul would change the subject.

"Jesse, lad, school will be over soon. Will you give me a hand?" The young man asked if the horses would still be there. "I'll be taking them up to cool country in a month, Flagstaff, this year." The young man said he would help and disappeared down the hall.

His mother asked him where he was going tonight.

"Chill. I'm…"

"She should do what? What kind of word is that?"

"Sorry, *madre*. I'm meeting Ramos. Don't worry so much."

"Ramos. Now there's a kid who's seen too much." David looked at Paul. "Enough...we need to talk. *Vamanos.*" The men strode from the hacienda. "One of your countryman, that Irish detective from Major Crimes, was here with his partner."

Paul knew him, he said. "He's a tough one, that kid, but he had to be. I knew his dad before he died or, at least before they said he did; the truth still needs to be told. They came here to escape the Troubles, probably a wanted man in the Six." Aguilar frowned... the six. "Ah, what do you know, you're not Irish. Northern Ireland, I'm talking about...the other six counties that should be part of the Republic, damn it. His old man was I.R.A., I'm sure of it. The Padric boy gets his balls and grit from him; but the lad's a cultured sort, educated, and not connected to the movement. Captain O'Manion swears by him. Johnny, his name is." Aguilar asked what happened to Guin Padric. "He died...an accident at the old Shelton mines but his mining pals living in Nugget just over Horsehoof Hill. I swear the widow went back with an empty coffin."

He put his finger to his lips.

Later that night on the other side of the canal, a car sped down a dark road to the Edge. "Ramos, slow down. Where are you taking us? It's friggin' dark out here." Jesse wasn't happy, ready to explode. "Look, you can see my house from here."

Ramos laughed. "And your old man's fields...stop whining."

"This is the Edge...no one in their right mind comes here."

"A lot of people come here at night."

A third boy in the back seat was smoking some weed. He was happy but worried. Jesse glared at him. "Throw that shit out, Carmine. My parents will fuckin' explode if they smell it on me."

"I'm not tossing my blunt, man." Jesse rolled down the window but Ramos wanted it open and he cursed...his boys were acting like babies. The window stayed down. At the end of a long dirt road, he slowed down in front of a house; they could hear music inside. "Damn, old-school, Santana, but I dig it." Lights tucked into the landscaping threw shadows onto the walls of a sprawling white adobe. Set back behind a no-name bar, there was no other house like it for miles.

"Let's go, Ram…we need to get out of here."

"*Chiquita* at quarter to six!" chirped the boy in the back seat between puffs. "Damn." A beautiful woman with long black hair suddenly emerged from the house. Ramos watched as she stepped onto a veranda covered in vines and small, twinkling lights.

He was smitten. "Shut up, Carmine." Now she was gazing back at them. They waited as she walked slowly down the path toward them.

She was purring like velvet. "What can I do for you, gentlemen?" They were awestruck…*gentlemen.*

Jesse wasn't buying it. "Let's go, man…we don't belong here."

Ramos glared at him. "Stop acting like a pussy. Grow up!"

She smiled. "Shouldn't you be home? It's a school night."

"No, we're good. What's your name?"

"My name? Call me anything you want. My name's Joanna."

"Joanna then…what do you want to do for us?" Ramos was growing bolder.

She threw her head back and laughed. "*Mijo,* you can do something for me. *Mijo* again…he didn't care.

"Yeah? Whatta ya' need, beautiful lady?"

"Oh, I've got a long list, sweety. Come inside and we'll talk." With hips saying 'come get me', she moved back up the path.

"All of us?"

She glanced back over her shoulder. "No, just you, baby!"

They looked at each other. "Ram', come on, let's leave."

"Shit, I'd go for it." Carmine was laughing. "Get you some!"

"Shut up, fool." Jesses grabbed Ramos' arm and he laughed. "You two are going home…now. I'll find a way back into town." He glanced up. A Hunger Moon hung low in the sky. He followed the woman into her house. The stars were gone.

Monday in Holy Week, March 17, the holy day of Saint Patrick

Though Padric had tipped back a pint at lunch there'd be no Guinness tonight. With shots fired in two separate arrests, they'd dragged a few unlikely suspects and some of the usual into the Precincts. Pubs all over the city were spilling out into the streets. The holding tank down the hall from O'Manion's office was "filling up nicely" as Hildred, the Major Crimes secretary, remarked.

There would be no good times for Padric and Martinez though they talked more that night, *mano a mano*, as they cruised through side streets taking them deeper into south L'Arroyo. They stopped in front of Father Stefano's old church where he'd died in the street and even drove down the alley where the killers had exited the crime scene. The church was locked now, a way of life for the people, gone. Their priest would no longer be there for them with his prayers and kind words all through the night.

Still the two men were looking for a tricked-out red Mercedes truck spotted only briefly cruising the bar scene. At some point they rounded the corner on School Street behind the convent and saw a light in the gym, students laughing and talking. Padric loved his old school; it had been his first taste of America. He heard a fiddle. Martinez slowed down. "Come on."

Mr. Dave Helmstone, music director/school drama coach, was enjoying a rousing band rehearsal; his students, playing their hearts out, on authentic instruments from Ireland.

"Where in bloody hell did you get these, Mr. H.?" The man smiled when he saw Padric...the lad had been one of his thespians.

"Well, Detective, I brought them back one by one on my travels to Ireland doing harp competitions." Harp competitions...Padric was ecstatic. He would escape from the streets for a moment and stared with delight at the *feadan* and *buinne;* Martinez would get a music lesson and Helmstone was pleased, remembering his football playing lead in a stage play or two and introduced him all around to his students. They were impressed and all spoke at once.

Macbeth was to be Mr. Helmstone's *pièce de résistance* next fall... would he give them some pointers; after all, he knew all about tragedy, death and dying. And might he play the role of the ghost of Hamlet's father in the spring...they would need someone older. Padric laughed out loud but Helmstone looked hopeful. Padric said yes, but was distracted. What was this he was seeing?

Magdalen, Patrice and Petra at the other end of the gym were drawing students onto the floor as the fiddles struck up a jig and a reel. They had lifted their skirts "just a bit", as Padric said later, and were stepdancing with astounding skill and precision. And there was their nun…*what a beauty; where'd she learn to do this?*

She twirled around and suddenly saw the men watching. "Come do this with us!" she called out and he did.

The whole building echoed with clapping and music but it ended as quickly as it had begun, Martinez pulling his partner away and into the street. Granted, it wasn't Brigid Brady's Pub and a pint, but it made their night. Good Mr. Helmstone was happy but unaware he and the detective would become allies under a much darker venue in the months to come…Macbeth and Hamlet could do that. There would be more than a bit of "toil and trouble" for both men; the world at Cathedral High and the Ankh Theater, would become a stage.

But nearby in the bishop's residence, His grace had set a bottle down on the table. "You wanted to talk, good man. Come, we'll have some wine. I'd offer you a Guinness if I thought you were Irish." He motioned for permission to smoke a pipe. The monsignor nodded and opened a window. Monday in Holy Week was always set aside for the blessing of holy oils used in liturgies and the giving of sacraments throughout the year. They had been busy today with the Mass of Anointing and visiting the sick and glad to sit down, but the monsignor wanted a serious word.

"What is it, Theo? Have I not done all you have asked?"

"More than you should, Santo, and thank you, but we must talk, *mano a mano*."

"You wish a duel with me. What burdens you? Say it then."

Steed swooped in with a few choice words: the bishop would need to desist with his highly charged homilies concerning the glories of martyrdom. Santo Cantera stared at the picture of Our Lady of Guadalupe over the fireplace and blew smoke rings at it; the monsignor, not sure how respectful that was, demanded the man cease his personal crusade on the glory of dying for Christ. The city had been turned upside down by the demise of those known as the moondead. Again the bishop blew a ring of smoke in the air.

"You are not pleased with me."

"Not at the moment."

"But should we not encourage the sacrifice of one's life to Christ, Theo?" Of course, Theo had answered, but wondered if the recent deaths were not linked to his Lenten homilies. "My God, man." He sat quickly up in his chair. "There is someone running around martyring people because I said so? This is ridiculous." He resumed smoking.

"I'm asking you to stop with the mention of these so-called martyrdoms in your homilies from the pulpit."

"You will conclude shortly, I assume."

"Why, do I bore you…please. Terrible things are happening to our people…these are not good times to be voicing such things. We are targets…my God, I spoke with Dave Aguilar. Paul Murphy called me. They are in agony over what happened to a nun on their land…a beheading? I've seen you at night pouring over those old martyrologies. You're looking for answers just like that Irish detective you don't like." The bishop stared for sometime into the fireplace where no fire burned that night.

Miles away two other men spoke with the same intensity, *mano a mano*. "Jesse, get in here." The young man asked what was up. "Don't 'what up' me. Whose car were you in? When was that, Nina?" Aguilar was upset with his son. "I want details."

"March 6th. Thursday. Tia Ana saw you on Old Division."

Jesse paled. *Shit.* He couldn't lie to his old man. "It was Ramos' car, Dad. Chill."

"What'd you say to me? Nina. I don't like him with that boy."

"Ramos met this really hot woman…scratch that." His father said that was more like it. "She asked him to come inside her place. She was hot and wanted him and Ramos liked what he saw…like I said, she was hot."

"I get it, *mijo*, she was hot…you don't know hot!"

"Not like you maybe, but…"

"I'm feeling old…make it quick or I'll upside you."

"I drove his car to his mom's house so I could get my car and come home."

"He came home before midnight, David."

Nina always took her son's side. But David was reading his boy; he was not going to be played by the likes of his own. "Hot women, Jesse? You're a boy; where was this *chica*? Where were you?"

Armageddon. "Over there." He pointed toward the canal.

"Over where, fool? You're pointing at the wall!"

"Don't call your son a fool, David?"

He sighed…*woman, shut up.* "Where, Jesse?"

"Over there…you know, in the Edge."

David stared at his son. "*No me jodas!*"

"Dad, I wouldn't fuck with you…I was there. Ramos wanted us to stay. I said 'no'. I knew you'd be pissed. You're pissed, right?"

"'Us' who?"

"Carmine was with me."

David rolled his eyes. "That *cabron*…he's a meatball, that one."

"Dad, whatever."

"Don't 'whatever' me, *mijo*…you're lucky to be alive."

"I know that. Dad, I'm worried." The man said he should be. "No, I mean it…it's about Ramos. He never came back; he…he never came home." Aguilar's face changed.

He walked to the window. "We should call the police, that Irish detective. Your *amigo* could still be there, getting hurt. He's in over his head. I'll call John Padric."

But Jesse said Ramos' mom didn't want him to do that. Her daughters were Edge *putas*; "their friggin' pimp's a nutcase, man."

"I'm not your man, *mijo*. Friggin' and nutcase? Who are you?"

Aguilar left the room and walked down the hall; Jesse stared after him. "So what now?"

"You're grounded for the rest of your life. Go to your room."

Below in the dark under the city, the hooded one pondered his next move: "I'll need you in two days…Good Friday, we have a full moon." She said that would be perfect…there was something she'd like to get done as well. The dim light of the candles touched the rim of her wine glass. "Where, this time?" He laughed and she smiled. "You will surprise me then."

She left and he returned to the martyrology spread out before him but later, he took his nightly walk through the passageways under the city; light from the street grates, his guide. A huge man with a billy club walked beside him. They made their way to the ossuary under Saint Rita's Church of Bones and undetected by the watchman above, added the acid-bathed, de-fleshed hand of the nun to the collection of bones. It was beautiful.

Tuesday in Holy Week, early morning, March 18

She had dressed more slowly than usual; were things catching up with her? After prayer and Holy Mass in the Sisters' chapel, Magdalen stepped into Patrice's kitchen before going to the sacristy and on to her classroom. "Sister, I'm not at my best."

Patrice looked surprised. "Come, drink some of my breakfast tea and have a poached egg. It does it for me. I'm surprised you're up and walking, Sister. I could never do what you do…going out to the crime scenes and such. These are strange times."

"You can't tell me you don't see and hear a good deal from your kitchen."

Patrice hesitated, looked away. "I do. I've been at my post here for twenty years on. Many things have been said right where you're sitting. Food and a wee bit of tea will do that. What I hear is often about the past. The nuns here don't complain about each other. I wouldn't abide that." Patrice was saying all the right things, wondering if Magdalen had another agenda in coming to see her. "It wouldn't be right to listen to gossip. It's personal but sometimes it's hard to suffer alone. The Life isn't easy."

Magdalen thought for a moment…she'd ask: "Did Sister Anna ever sit with you?"

Patrice walked quickly to the sink and silently fussed with some pots and pans. Magdalen asked if she'd heard what she asked. "I did." Her voice had changed.

"Is there a reason why no one will speak of her to me?"

"Get out."

"What?" *Did she say that?* Patrice stared blankly out the window into the bishop's garden. "I am her replacement, have been assigned to her former position in the sacristy; why all the hush-hush and how wrong can it be for me to ask about her?" She brought her dishes to the sink; in silence she washed and dried them. "I won't speak to you of such things again. Thank you."

She left, not looking back. Patrice rushed into the hall. "Wait!" But Magdalen gave it no heed. *I'm told to get out? I see now…there are certain mysteries not to be questioned like not asking about the former convent director. Who was she, this Sister Viviana?*

When school ended, Magdalen slipped into Sister Lucy's art studio; her classroom smelled of clay and acrylics, oils, and linseed. Huge canvases, half covered in paint; others awash in color, leaned against walls and windows. Several pottery wheels were surrounded with clay works, most leather-hard and covered with plastic, others were bisqued, some already glazed. The art room covered a third of the high school's second floor and faced west into the afternoon sun. The room was like Lucy, bright and intuitive, warm and embracing. They had met under less than gracious circumstances only a day after Christmas and Magdalen's arrival when she had bumped into Lucy, sending her paint pots in every direction and splashing color all over the school lobby. Forced to spend several days during their holiday break cleaning it up, they had laughed most of the time. The two were a team: Lucy, sculptor, potter, and painter; Magdalen, art historian and master calligrapher.

But she would learn Lucy's parents were "connected", a subtle reference brimming with innuendo in both Italy and the Sonoran; her father, Bruto Genova had close ties to the powerful Angus Zalconi, well-known restaurateur and purveyor of things in L'Arroyo.

"You know he is one of the Five." Magdalen wondered what that was. "My sources tell me it's a custard of families…that my family is part of all that. It gives me *agida*."

"You have sources? And custard and indigestion? Too much information…I think you mean a *cluster* of families."

"That too…they are the quintessential makers and shakers in the city. Papa, not so much…he stays out of the moonlight."

"The *spotlight*, Lucy…he stays out of the spotlight. And, from what you've said, understandably so." Though Lucy meant to say *movers* and shakers, Magdalen would make no further effort to edit the conversation. The young girl in Lucy had never quite mastered her English in a country new to her ten years ago. Lucy, the daughter of Italian entrepreneur, Bruto Genova, on a visit to relatives in Boston, had met the charismatic Mother Thérèse, superior general of the Sisters of the Crucified, She had been immediately swept up by what she saw in the Life, had entered the Order and would never return to her father's Tuscan *estancia.*

Lucy was funny; attempting often to comment on American politics and the President whom she called *the Obama*. It suggested the man was some kind of art object or species of dinosaur; critically describing his first term in office as on-the-job training and hoped he'd get it right this time with his second term very much underway. She would not expound on this but Lucy was worried. Magdalen had doubled over in laughter when she observed the President's hair had turned gray much too fast, though she thought he looked quite distinguished. And what of those whining, complaining Tea Party people who hated him so. *Mama mia,* they should be sipping Sambuca and eating tiramisu.

Today, the art teacher was busy; the fundraiser of all fundraisers, a spring student art show and dinner, was just weeks away. Since her arrival, five years ago, it had been one of the highlights of the year for the high school. The mother of every art student wanted in, wishing to be part of the planning…the night itself, an extravaganza. Coaches and booster clubs were jealous. Sister Lucy had it down…the art of wooing her backers.

This year, Magdalen would assist. Today however there were sacristy duties as well…she must step up the pace. But Lucy was admitting she'd been indiscreet.

"Oh, good!" Magdalen grinned.

"*Cara mia,* I overheard you with Sister Patrice today."

"Oh, she apologized, a dear woman…but refused to explain her behavior. I know now what I can and cannot ask here at San Miguel…something is very wrong."

"Ah, you are a detective. The car though…Italian, a Maserati!"

"What car?" Lucy gave some additional details. It seemed young Sister Anna, disillusioned with the Life, had one day walked away. Recently released from the County Jail where Anna had served in the Sisters' prison ministry, Isaac Rojas was waiting for her in his showy red sports car. With promises of taking her to her parents in Santa Barbara, he had whisked her away, her family still waiting. She never arrived.

"It was red, *bellissimo*! But these are dark San Miguel questions we do not discuss." *Dark San Miguel questions…the place is full of them.* Lucy had nailed it. Her eyes burned a hole in Magdalen. "Do this for us; help us. She was young but a good girl!"

"You take me for some kind of savior. I can't rescue the past."

Their talk turned to other things. "So what kind of trouble found you in Italia?" Magdalen smiled a little.

"I'll admit to nothing, but for you I will break my silence. I was confronted only once by the *Polizia Municipale* in Compagnia. It was late and we'd been dancing, all of us from the dig were there and then I was suddenly in the middle of the street with a man who had more affection for me than I, him; I sang "*O sole mio*" at the top of my voice and he kissed me to keep me quiet when the *polizia* came out of nowhere. They told me to go back to America…they said they didn't like noisy Americans."

"But did he kiss you again after the *polizia* left?"

"Oh, yes. I had two glasses of wine and kissed him much more than I should have. He was handsome and smart, but I wouldn't remember him now if I saw him." Lucy laughed and whirled around, thrilled to know at least one of Magdalen's secrets. But Magdalen looked down at the street from the open window.

"What have I walked into here in L'Arroyo?"

"Purgatory, *Magdalena*…it will prepare you for heaven. But what will you do with what I have told you? Wouldn't it be wonderful if you could play under the covers in your holy habit, looking proper and solving mysteries?"

"Undercover, Lucy, undercover! The Lord will tell me when it is time. I must go."

Lucy looked at her curiously. "Our Lord is telling you that?"

Magdalen laughed but she felt nauseous, weak. Below in the street, a tricked-out red Mercedes truck stopped under the window; a hooded male figure in the passenger's side leaned from the vehicle, looked up, an eerie half-mask hiding most of his face. Then in a surprisingly gracious gesture, he nodded as if wishing Magdalen well. As the truck moved slowly away from the curb, he raised his hand in farewell and the Mercedes disappeared into the early evening to the lingering tone of *"Dies irae, dies illa…*

She said nothing and rushed from the room leaving Lucy to wonder. She would find Magdalen later that afternoon, kneeling in prayer at the bottom step of the main altar.

"Cara mia, something has frightened you…I'm not leaving and will sit very still while you do what you must; please let me help."

But Magdalen had turned at the familiar sound of the old caretaker's slippers. Someone else was joining them. Bent over with age and deformity, Guadalupe approached, whispering her name. She was beautiful, a diminutive woman with worn face, luminous brown eyes and smelling of cilantro and cloves; her long, silver hair pulled back in a bun.

"Hola, hola, Hermana, sit with me." She pulled Magdalen down beside her on a bench by the wall. She was hiding her troubles but the nun knew.

"You're upset…what is it?" She spoke of her seven brothers, in and out of prison most of their life, the one who had taken Anna away. So where was she? *Nada.* Her eyes betrayed other things, her care for the young Sister she had adopted in her heart as she had done with other souls like the once young priest, Santo Cantera. She had devoted her life to his service and then to her God. "It is time to talk of things."

"I am always here for you, Lupe. On Saturday then after the Easter Vigil."The old woman was relieved.*"Gracias, gracias!"* And she was gone.

Lucy whispered: "The woman is heavy with secrets…she has lived here in the Cathedral under the belfry forever. Some call her the Hunchback of San Miguel…it is cruel."

Even at this moment, many miles way in a rocking Border town bar, Shakira's *"La Tortura"* shook the platform under the pole dancer's red stilettos. The establishment was owned and managed by two of Lupe's brothers and Constanzio Chato; everyone knew and feared Chato. Men were ogling the woman and asked: *"Amigo, we want her. We came here for her, ese."*

The club owner glared at the men. "I'm not your *amigo* and don't call me *ese*; the *chica* dances, that's it." She'd been crudely advertised as the Virgin Mary; her long hair swinging wildly about; bare breasted, she slid down the pole and thought of her Sisters at San Miguel. *"Dios mio,* someone find me."

But Magdalen heard footsteps again, this time a heavier tread. "Sister?" She turned and smiled; she knew this good man, had spoken with him at the crime scene in his own cotton field.

"Mr. Aguilar?" She drew him into a side chapel.

"We have met…this is my son, Jesse." A tall, handsome, young man, he smiled at her; but not sure he wanted to be there. They spoke quietly of what had occurred on his land, the man empathizing over the loss of her Sister; she, expressing a thousand concerns for his family and workers.

But he said he was here on another matter…two, in fact. "When do you want the lambs?" *The lambs…there are lambs?* "No one has told you?" The two men grinned at each other. "It's tradition… in January on Saint Agnes' Day, the bishop comes out to our farm and picks two of our best looking sheep for Holy Thursday. But this year he picked up the lamb before Christmas…you weren't living here yet. We put them aside, tend them well then they're brought up to the altar and shorn during Mass."

"During Mass in the sanctuary?" *This was new; the logistics alone overwhelming.* "This happens during the liturgy with all assembled? How do I…what?"

Unperturbed, Aguilar explained: "The Sisters of Saint Uriel spin the wool and knit blankets for babies left at their gate…it happens. The nuns care for them and find them good homes. It's done differently in Rome, you know. No one told you?"

About Rome…no, but yes, she knew things were done differently in Rome, and no, she knew nothing about lambs. She smiled. "Obviously not. I look forward to it." The three laughed. Jesse liked her…*so this was Carmine's and Ramos' nun. She was nice.* "But, Mr. Aguilar, right here in the sanctuary?" They laughed again and assured her, the shearing took place in the courtyard after the bishop's blessing. She was relieved.

"And what else, Mr. Aguilar…there were two matters."

He pointed at Jesse. "You're looking at him, Sister. I'm registering him for next year in the fall…he'll be a senior and he's going to be an altar boy like I was."

This would require some delicacy; she looked at the young man. "And you, Jesse, what would you like?"

"I better do what he says, Sister."

"Then, shall we say, you are playing your cards right?"

The men smiled. "Talk to Sister…I need to speak with the Bishop. I'll be back." Aguilar disappeared.

"I…I'm friends with Ramos and he liked you." She was stunned. *Ramos.*

She invited him to sit with her in a pew. "If he's in trouble, take me to him. You must."

Jesse hesitated; could he say it? "I can't…you can't. You can never go where he is, where I *think* he is. He's in…sorry, but he's in deep shit, Sister." *The detectives.* She knew a few men whose job it was to get people out of that. In fact, they would be stopping by, said they had things to discuss. Did she have time, they had asked.

*Do I…*Magdalen's heart beat even faster. *And the hooded one in the tricked out red Mercedes…now that was something to talk about.*

Author's Notes

Vamanos – Spanish, for "Let's go, move it."

Hacienda – Spanish, for an estate, often linked to an agricultural complex, a ranch.

the Republic – the sovereign and independent state of Ireland.

I.R.A. – acronym for the Irish Republican Army.

Shelton mines – mines west of L'Arroyo in which Padric's father, Guinness, worked with other immigrants. Rumored that gold was discovered here, the mines were curiously shut down by the state. They will figure more dramatically in Book Three: The Church of the Bones.

"Nugget, just over Horse Hoof Hill" – reference to fictitious old mining town.

Santana – reference to legendary late sixties musician Carlos Santana and his American Latin rock band.

chiquita – Spanish, for young woman.

thespians – actors, theatrical performers.

feadan and buinne – Irish, for a fife and a flute or oboe.

pièce de résistance – French, for creative piece of remarkable quality.

Ankh Theater – fictitious theater and center for the arts in L'Arroyo.

Holy Week – week preceding Easter beginning with Palm Sunday.

Sacraments and Mass of Anointing – see Glossary.

Our Lady of Guadalupe – title of the Blessed Mother associated with devotion surrounding the 1531 vision witnessed by Mexican peasant, Juan Diego, on the Hill of Tepeyac in Mexico City.

chica – Spanish, for girl or young woman.

No me jodas – Spanish, for "Don't fuck with me."

cabron – Spanish, for dumbass.

amigo/amiga – Spanish, for friend, male, female.

puta – Spanish, for prostitute, hooker.

The Life – term used by the nuns when referring to their vowed way of living in the Order.

agida – Italian, for heartburn.

estancia – Italian, for estate.

Tea Party people – in U.S., a 2009 movement of conservatives protesting government.

mama mia – Italian, for my mother.

bellissimo – Italian, for most beautiful.

Polizia Municipale in Compagnia – Italian, for police in Compagnia, Italy.

"O sole mio" – Italian, for my sun or my sunshine; a Neapolitan song written by Eduardo di Capua in 1898; made popular in U.S. by vocal artists Mario Lanza, Sergio Franchi,

Luciano Pavarotti, Tony Bennett with a Big Band arrangement and Tony Martin who recorded his famed "There's No Tomorrow" with the same melody.

cara mia — Italian, for my love or dear one, dear friend.

hola — Spanish, for hello.

Easter Vigil — liturgy observed on the eve of Easter.

gracias — Spanish, for thank you.

Shakira's "La Tortura" — 2005 Latin pop song written by Columbian singer Shakira.

esé — Spanish, for street greeting loosely translated to mean fool or dog; in 2007, it became associated with gang members, particularly the Mexican Mafia or surenos; but was used in the forties by Pachucos or zoot suiters.

Saint Agnes' Day — observance of holy day of Saint Agnes, martyr, January 21.

Sisters of Saint Uriel — fictitious order of cloistered nuns, originally, from France but now living in an abbey west of L'Arroyo.

7 REVELATIONS

Tuesday, four in the afternoon, March 18

In the convent of San Miguel, Sister Patrice had been busy all day; it was Wednesday in Holy Week and the feast of Saint Joseph. Her Irish *brack*, twisted loaves of challah and hot-cross buns sent an aroma heavenward and drew the detectives more quickly into the convent. They glanced at each other as Gabriela ushered them into the parlor.

Martinez was weary and sank into a chair. "I'm hungry... damn, it smells good."

Padric laughed. "Wait, you'll see." He'd been a recipient of the Sisters' pantry. "What did I tell you?" He spied bowls of chicken and *cavatappi,* a basket of warm bread. It was raining today and the food looked inviting...but was the sudden spring storm a sign? It had not rained for months in L'Arroyo and Good Friday would mark the first day of spring but it had been unusually cold.

When Magdalen returned, they stood up. "Come on...sit with us, Sister." Padric drew a chair up between them; the nun was one of them now. They poured out their frustration. Still with no evidence to target the killers, no weapon, no DNA, they'd come to reconnect. They'd dragged in the usual suspects and Ramos, their one known witness, was off the grid. Magdalen confessed she'd gone to the crime scene behind the hotel on her own.

"You did, did you?" He remembered. Padric, frustrated and feeling guilty, had not offered to take her there; he'd left her standing on the front steps of the convent watching him drive away. Like angel's wings, her veil had been caught up in a breeze and whirled around her head…he'd never forget the sight of her, even years later. But now she was telling them Brother James' death too was a replication. *Bloody hell.*

"Another James, an apostle of Jesus, was thrown from the roof of the Temple by the Pharisees." *Sister Moira.* Padric knew about this one…he knew his religion inside and out. He just couldn't abide with what it asked him to do and the hypocrisy he'd witnessed in some of those doing the asking. But he wouldn't say that.

"I'm sure he tried to reason with them."

"I know Bro James…he probably pissed them off."

"I'm surprised there was no indication of blunt force trauma over and above what he suffered in the fall." Padric assured her the ME had said there was nothing postmortem. Besides he had been there almost immediately…*postmortem.*

"Keeping in mind how literal these killers are, how obsessed with detail in copying manner of death, I would look for such injuries since in Saint James' case, after he fell to the ground, he still tried to get to his knees, but was finally clubbed to death."

This didn't happen…he'd seen the whole thing. Padric was miserable. "No one reported this. Surveillance cameras picked up no one around his body. But we were able to view the footage from the cameras in the parking garage…two people, monks' robes and hoods, freaky masks, lotta glitter, bright red, covering part of their faces. Tapes show that damn Mercedes truck leaving the scene."

But she'd seen it, too, she explained; they stared at her. She explained what she had seen in the street below Lucy's studio window. "We're next."

"You knew that might be the case the day you stood on that hill of rocks." It was harsh.

But Martinez was on to something; he always thought long and hard about motive…this is something he liked to do. "What if the killer's trying to prove something to someone, to show off what he knows; gain favor…staging each kill, going for some drama. They're trying too hard; who's he trying to please, show off for? That's more important than any script."

"Of course…that's it. We have three deaths obviously very pre-meditated. The obsessive pathology is coming from somewhere, a toxic family situation. Those involved are related, intertwined in each other somehow, though I see them as total opposites."

Martinez again. "That kid Ramos said he and his homey heard a woman laugh. What if it's a Bonnie and Clyde, some wicked attraction?" Magdalen agreed.

He'd been eyeing her. "What aren't you saying?"

Magdalen reminded them of the bishop's homilies. "On the first day of Lent, Father Villa is murdered." Padric realized her dilemma; Martinez frowned…he didn't like it.

"We're looking at the bishop." Martinez' *abuela* loved him…*no.*

Padric didn't buy it. "Sister, I've never liked the man and, as much as I'd like to nail him for something, I don't think he'd go down that road."

But Magdalen heard herself making a case against Santo Cantera, telling them of his martyrologies. "They're books of lists, names of martyrs their bios and deaths."

"Like hagiographies." Padric knew about this. *Sister Moira, seventh grade.* Magdalen was pleased.

Martinez was adamant. "It's got to be someone who's delusional enough to believe they're helping him out, giving him martyrs. He's not the doer; it's being done for him."

Padric agreed, a Cantera, one of his own. "Did the woman tell Jesse her name?"

"She said her name was Joanna." Joanna, he knew one.

They left, grateful for the food and conversation. Later that night, Padric poured over the case with O'Manion, not wanting to put any of his team in the Edge. But they had little to go on…they needed Ramos. He'd been within feet of the killer and the nun had asked them to find him. Reasons enough.

Author's Notes

brack or Irish brambrack – Irish, for yeasted bread with sultanas and raisins.

challah – Jewish term for braided bread eaten on Sabbath and Jewish holidays.

cavatappi – Italian, for corkscrew; macaroni formed in this shape.

abuela – Spanish, for grandmother.

tia – Spanish, for aunt.

8 HOLY THURSDAY

Holy Thursday, three in the afternoon, March 20

The following day Magdalen rose with renewed energy. Wednesday was behind her; tonight at seven, the bishop and his people would celebrate the liturgy of the Lord's Supper. Steed found her in the sacristy at her worktable. "Monsignor, do you think the bishop's Lenten homilies could be a call to action for a delusional mind?"

Of course, I do. "Christ, Sister! Call me Theo." Steed was glad to sit down for a moment. He liked Magdalen…she was easy to talk with but what was this about the bishop?

"Theo, then…his obsessive pouring over the ancient martyrologies, it worries me."

"The bishop is more mystic than mystery. His nature would never allow it." But he didn't want this conversation. "Granted, Santo has a side I'm unable to reach and he struggles with his own nature and arrogance. He has bouts with dark thoughts…priests are the worst to be set upon by such things. We hear every possible suffering, are told every dark deed and we carry this inside us, give it to God. He's got a lot on his mind. Pray for him." He left.

Well rested now, Monica had insisted on working beside Magdalen despite her protests. Petra would be joining them shortly. "A last look at everything then! We'll do it together, dear."

She waved when she saw Eduardo changing the purple veil on the crucifix to white. Magdalen nodded. "Eduardo, *com esta*"

"*Bueno, bueno!* How are you? I am ready to work." Eduardo had served the bishop for nearly forty years. He and Lupe were fixtures in the Cathedral and knew more than the priests about what must be done. As always, the elder would make a fuss over him.

"You know what to do, *mi amigo, gracias*."

He'd grown up working beside her. "Ay, for you anything, Madre!" But the elder was on to Magdalen and what she must do. Had she not ordered the flowers? She had not.

Monica laughed. "You, with your elegant style, Magdalen, will make it beautiful. Eduardo will get the flowers for us. Ah, better yet…you need to begin snooping about, eh?"

Unbelievable. The elder was clever. "Well, Sister, what do you have in mind?

"Pick a few from the bishop's garden; that's where Eduardo gets them." *Ah, the garden.*

"Santo doesn't like store-bought. You've wanted to go there since the day you laid eyes on it." She thumped Magdalen's arm. "Do this! It will whisper to you." *Whisper. It whispers?* "The garden speaks to some souls, surely it will to you." But Magdalen said no one was allowed to enter. "Nonsense. I've been there hundreds of times…at least, before this." She patted the arm of her wheelchair. "I'll ask him."

Magdalen glanced at the clock; the altar servers would be coming soon, but the door suddenly opened and in burst the students. Mario Martinez, a freshman, slipped in between two senior boys and grinned proudly; he was the detective's son.

They immediately crowded around the elder, a frequent visitor to the school quad during the lunch hour. Her stories fascinated them and she knew at least one member of most of their families. "Now, my friends, you must listen to Sister. What you will do today is important…an honor indeed."

The students scattered; remembering all they had done last year and eager to show Magdalen. Under her sharp eye, preparations were underway. Having served at the altar the longest, Larry Whitton, off to West Point after graduation, honed in on the incense and thurible and ordered the others about. Ellie Thomas was special to Magdalen, a perceptive, bright girl who lived in the Hook, a notorious part of the city, but she'd been awarded the Bishop's Scholarship for her essay on first century martyrs.

How did she know Santo Cantera would be impressed? She covered the processional cross with a violet cloth while Sam was on a hunt for the *crotalus*, a wooden clapper used instead of the bells during the liturgy.

Magdalen reminded him to keep it 'low-key'. "Gently now, Sam…no rock and roll." The others laughed. Maya, never saying too much, set to work with her cousin Beatrice, covering the credence table and thirteen chairs with white linen then gathered basins of water, towels, and even aprons for the washing of the feet. The bishop himself would do this as the Pope would do this somewhere in Rome on this day.

And now, unnoticed, he with Petra had entered the sacristy and stood watching them. He finally spoke: "Bravo, Sister…"

"The students were pleased. Sam grinned. "How long have you been here, Your grace?"

"As long as it took me to see how much enthusiasm you have." Everyone laughed. "I'm glad you're on board tonight, young man." The bishop saw a potential priest in every boy.

But Magdalen hustled Sam away. "How are you, Your grace?"

He said he was always happy on these days. "And you will celebrate your community holy day later tomorrow?"

"Why, yes…Good Friday is a special observance for all Sisters of the Crucified." Monica reached out her hand to him. "We are grateful that you remember us." The bishop knelt down beside her so they could speak face to face. She had known him when he was a young, handsome priest full of zeal, but he'd always carried a burden within.

He turned to Magdalen. "Lay out another vestment for someone you will be seeing more often. Thank you. I'm welcoming a new priest to the Cathedral. The monsignor could use the help; God knows I keep him too busy." She smiled and asked his name. "Why, Father Michelantonia Sebastiano who goes by simply Sebastian…a glorious name! He's ex-Marine, a former league soccer player and public accountant…what a prize! He will reshape our diocesan accounting system; oversee our youth ministries and be our offensive coordinator for Coyote football in the fall. We must win the state championship in our division this year."

"He will be busy…my goodness, Santo." The students glanced at each other. Monica had used the bishop's first name; a look from Magdalen sent them away.

But even she wanted to know. "How will he find time?"

"Like the rest of us." He looked at Monica. "You wanted to ask me a question."

"May my Sister gather flowers from your garden for the Altar of Repose?" The Holy Sacrament would remain in a niche adorned with flowers on a side altar during Good Friday. It was the bishop's wish there be nothing to give the appearance that Jesus had risen; the altars stripped bare, the ever-glowing sanctuary lamp removed until a new flame was struck at the Easter Vigil on Holy Saturday.

Magdalen glanced at him. He had hesitated; but quickly composed himself then he asked: "Eduardo will help you…it's his garden. He will do this for us."

"The students know what they must do. Thank you!" But Magdalen noted his demeanor had changed, a fear of discovery perhaps; regardless she was delighted to be led through a dimly lit passageway she'd never seen. She smiled even more when guided through a door under the bishop's vestibule staircase. At the end of a ramp, Eduardo opened a door onto the garden and stepped back. Wonderland.

At last…wide eyed, Magdalen gazed at the beauty around her; it took her breath away. Angels of stone gazed down on her; they seemed amused, grateful she'd come.

She glanced at her watch; the Supper of Our Lord would begin at seven…there would be time. Eduardo told her she was standing in a burial field, "But burial fields have no grave markers… where were the dead laid to rest?"

He pointed. "Count the angels." There were a dozen or more. She had been gazing at tombstones every night from her window and now she was hearing of more Sisters who had died. He asked her to follow him to the altar at the lower end of the garden, telling her that someday, with the elder's permission, he would give her to read the crumbling, vellum bound journal he drew from a stone box at the foot of the altar. On its cover were scrawled the words: *Ledger of Buried Souls.* But what Eduardo said next left her cold…the souls buried here were her own Sisters who had died violently one afternoon while Monica had gone to a ranchers' market.

"It's common knowledge, *hermana*…the Sonoran has not always been gracious to your Sisters. May it treat you better."

He'd let the elder explain, he said, but later would apologize for perhaps frightening her. Regardless, the garden seemed darker now, less beautiful, weighing her down, its secrets pulling her under. Branches of mesquite and acacia cast longer shadows over the flora. But she thanked him and moved slowly up the incline toward a winged sculpture of the Archangel Michael. Among waves of blue desert flowers, a delicate pelotazo branch pulled at her sleeve. Soothing green vines and well-watered, lush violet undergrowth carpeted every inch of the garden.

Eduardo smiled. "You like, *hermana*? This is my work." He looked with pride at the desert honeysuckle and tuber anemones… they were his children.

"*Muy bonita*! You are an artist. I could stay here forever."

"Me, too, *gracias*, much respect." She smiled at the clusters of poor man's weatherglass, rock cress and seaside petunias surrounding her favorite angel. There were iris and snapdragons everywhere. "Please, those will do and lots of green vines to tuck round them perhaps. *Gracias*, Eduardo, *gracias*."

She was lost in her surroundings and Eduardo took pleasure in the nun's delight. "I'll do the gathering. If you see something, take it." He gave her a pair of cutting shears. "You have wanted to come here, *si*?" This dear old man, like a *santos* whittled from wood, smiled kindly at her and returned to his flowers, but he worried. The archaeologist-nun was asking questions, wanting the truth as she should, but he had some concerns. He watched her move up the terrace, stopping to look at each angel; did they approve of her being there?

Like the monoliths she'd studied in other places, they rose like standing stones. Those in her research often stood over burial chambers filled with bones and pottery and precious things, but the treasures here were her Sisters' remains. She paused to look into the face of one of those she had admired from her window, but was forced to step back…an audible sigh came from within the fold of its marble garment, or so she thought.

She glanced back at Eduardo and was even more startled. He had leaned down to pluck some vines, and above him, a pair of eyes were watching them. Curiously, they peered out from a crack in an old broken door held shut by a pile of rocks. Dizzy with discovery, Magdalen was face to face with what she'd sensed from the beginning: someone was living below the bishop's house in the graveyard once called Gethsemane. She could only stare back…the eyes were gone. Distracted now, she backed up and felt the cold stone wings of the most exquisite angel she'd ever seen. It was her favorite and now she was standing beside it. It was believed by most scholars that all angels were male, but this one appeared to be female, a maiden, her wings curled round her; hands hiding her face. It reflected everything she had felt in her soul since her coming here.

Magdalen impulsively pressed her cheek to the rose colored marble; a ribbon carved elegantly across her breast revealed a single word *amabilis.* "Latin…*amabilis,* most loving." Magdalen whispered it several times. More angels bore the names of other virtues: *patientia, humilitas, prudentes,* and *misericordia.*

She knew she must leave. "Rest in peace, my *amabilis.*" Kissing the hand of the angel, Magdalen hurried back down the path, not daring to look into the dark of the old basement door. But before she withdrew, she looked up; the bishop must have returned to his study and was now, with dark somber eyes, gazing down on her. She smiled…Santo Cantera did not.

But there were some in L'Arroyo unmoved by Holy Week and its sobering reminders; they preferred more the comfort of earth. A lieutenant at his desk buried in paperwork called his wife.

No answer. Padric stared at the family photos on the bookcase, his wife's large eyes and fragrant, long hair; *she's a beauty…my Lara.* Last week, she had said she was letting him go, needing to make plans of her own. He'd looked for the right words to say…that ship had sailed. For once he was speechless, fell silent and left the house.

He'd need to turn it around; the detective was in a black hole. He shut the door of his office and walked down the hall to the parking garage.

Across the Plaza, light from the open doors of the Cathedral and its worshipers streamed into the street. Martinez had attended the liturgy and introduced Magdalen to his wife. *How lovely, but what of his partner?* He was a mystery like the bishop who was hard at work stripping the altars for tomorrow's somber liturgies of the Sufferings of the Lord. Later, he entered the vestry and closed the door. Emerging later, he knelt down near the altar and wept.

Though the Cathedral may have been for many a beacon of light or even a pit-stop to "drop off one's sins and pick up some peace of mind", as Dolorosa would say, Zalconi's Ristorante offered its own form of salvation from the cares of the world five blocks away. It exuded warm camaraderie from the marble foyer to the *bocce* ball court in the back; the First Precinct often found a good meal in a back bar they'd made their own. Lara called it *simpatico…* she always knew what to say.

And, as Martinez once said, it didn't hurt that the owner's daughter was a detective with Major Crimes. They loved Jana. Padric locked the door to his office and walked to his car…they'd been told to work their own hours on the case. He'd drop by Zalconi's.

Author's Notes

credence table – small side table, covered with linen, in sanctuary of a church.

washing of the feet – liturgical rite on Holy Thursday in imitation of Jesus at Last Supper who washed the feet of the Apostles.

community holy day – in religious orders, a special day of celebration to honor the founder; with the Sisters of the Crucified, it is Jesus Crucified and their day of remembrance, Good Friday.

Altar of Repose – decorated with flowers and candlelight, an altar where consecrated hosts are reserved or placed in a small tabernacle to be distributed to the faithful the following day, Good Friday, since the celebration of the Eucharist does not occur on this day.

sanctuary lamp – in the sanctuary of a Catholic church, a candle continually lit to indicate the presence of God in the Eucharist reserved in the tabernacle on the altar.

Supper of Our Lord – reference to the Eucharistic liturgy on Holy Thursday.

Ledger of Buried Souls – old journal hidden beside the stone altar in the bishop's garden;

its contents, written by the elder, Sister Monica, list the names of her Sisters, murdered long ago by a cohort of men, unusually large, giants said to live deep in the hills surrounding the city. Revealing the deceased are buried beneath the angels in the bishop's garden, the ledger describes how they died, tells even more, regarding three more nuns who later endured a horrible death under equally dark circumstances under the city. Though mentioned in Books One and Two, the Ledger will be of some importance to Magdalen in Book Three: The Church of Bones.

mesquite and acacia – trees found in abundance in the Southwest Sonoran.

Archangel Michael – chief among the archangels who rank highest among the nine choirs of angels; the Cathedral and convent bear his name, San Miguel, and angels, especially arch-angels, are a presence throughout the Sacristan Mysteries. Other archangels most commonly revered are Gabriel and Raphael but also Uriel, the name of an abbey of cloistered nuns.

Muy bonita! – Spanish, for "How beautiful."

santos – Spanish reference to wooden statue of a saint or holy one. Santero refers to the wood-carver who makes such devotional art pieces. The word Santos has many other mean-ings outside The Moondead narrative.

liturgy of the Sufferings of the Lord – refers to Good Friday devotions in church.

bocce ball – or Anglicized bocci, refers to ancient strategic but relaxed ball throwing game often associated with Italian enthusiasts.

Simpatico – Italian, for nice, pleasing but in Spanish, sympathizing.

ossa buco – Italian reference to Milanese dish of veal shanks braised with vegetables, white wine and broth.

9 RISTORANTE

Holy Thursday, nine-thirty in the evening, March 20

O*regano* and *parmesana* paired with the usual garlic and basil drew Padric into the back room where dark walls covered in black and white glossies of *film noir* gangsters and gun molls. It was far removed from the elegant, Italianate main dining room. Here it was bare bones with no fuss, a First Precinct hideaway, often growing too loud when an off night turned into morning. Even the Captain would join them; he liked the *ossa buco*. Padric sat down, others showed up, his close friend, Ducci, and a few detectives from Homicide. Jace Tarkington was lost in his sax; his jazz like butter melting into a softly-lit room where a late night dinner crowd turned to watch him do what he loved to do best.

But no one knew he was playing his heart out on orders from none other than Padric and the Captain. His gig was more than a night of smooth sounds; the crowd at Zalconi's overflowed with the usual suspects. What better view could a cop undercover have than working it from a band platform? Who better to portray the disinterested third party, while observing who talked to who or what passed between them? He had an air about him…smooth, on fire but there was a quiet inside him. With eyes half closed, he had a popular supper club on his radar.

Marcus arrived in time for the cheer that went up when the waiters appeared with large plates of *calamari* and clams *oreganata*, *antipasto*, and baskets of bread. Lt. Jana Zalconi, playing *maitre'de* on her nights off in her dad's *ristorante*, had sent their favorites to the table and she waved to them from the bar. Her real job found her undercover every night in the Hook and was far less elegant; a call girl in the street talking up cronies for *intel* on all manner of crimes.

The restaurant was a family affair: the owner and family patriarch, Angus Zalconi's children managed it. He liked the detectives, but the Irish one…he'd been aloof with Johnny Padric; he knew his Jana had history with him. In high school they'd kissed under the bleachers after games before she'd been whisked away in her father's limo; she'd loved him her whole life, loved him now; but Johnny Padric was long gone; he'd moved on.

The wait-staff was always ecstatic when the Precinct arrived; they were hungry and fun, told a good story and tipped well. Martinez had joined them and was eyeing the appetizers. "Did our baby girl do this?" He slipped into a seat next to Padric, who was feeling relaxed despite his personal life.

But like every night, he waited for the inevitable. Clubs and bars stayed open till dawn; the city, one of Phoenix' watering holes after hours, a place to engage in darker pursuits; the Edge did that for them. L'Arroyo was a party town, the music, hotter; venues more exciting…the women both. Nor was it outdone with its reputation for having the most beautiful women in western Arizona and a calendar to prove it. Obviously this did not bode well with the more gentile and created more than a few problems for law enforcement. It disturbed the bishop to no end…this was his town.

Tark's set was over and the banter continued. Martinez told Padric he'd been a proud father tonight. "My son was an altar boy with the bishop and a bunch of priests; there's a new one. He's different; looks like an athlete." Padric wished he had what his partner had at home; "Where you headed after, Johnny?"

"Home." It made him feel better to say it. "Let's enjoy!"

But gradually talk turned to murder and mayhem, religion and ritual. Someone mentioned the nun who was consulting with them; an archaeologist. How'd we get one of those? When martyrologies and martyrs were mentioned, it drew everyone in; they had a serial killer and it sounded like malice murder. Marcus would punctuate their remarks when he said he expected a repeat and more moondead; tomorrow was Good Friday with a full moon overhead. An uncomfortable silence had them staring into their drinks.

Padric toyed with his food…he wasn't hungry. "Nothing like the thought of another kill to shut us up." They agreed, but the nun…what about her? With all the women out there and ripe for the picking, he wondered why he was thinking of her more than he should. She wasn't available, not on the market, wouldn't be; this one breathed air in a different atmosphere. It was obvious… Magdalen was committed, solid in what she had chosen, was into something he understood, but hoped his daughters would never choose. He'd several aunts who'd received the veil; one who'd even come to the states. No one knew where she was but he'd kept her picture in his wallet for luck. His dad had insisted. Their nun though…she was easy to be around and he half-wished she was sitting there with them now. Padric even felt guilty when, for one nanosecond, he imagined what she might look like in street clothes and four-inch heels; *she must have been…never mind.* But her kind ways and his visits to the convent of San Miguel had him thinking about making a change. Women generally didn't do that for him and she did. He'd behave and get Lara back.

Tonight he'd be content to be with his comrades and feast on *salmone in crosta.* The Captain moved from his seat at the bar to their table. "What are you thinking about?" He'd been concerned about his favorite detective. But Tark had the answer.

"A woman…it's gotta be a woman." *If they only knew…*Padric laughed and pulled up a chair for O'Manion…they sipped *espresso* and talked. Finally the crew paid up and headed for the parking lot. A black Escalade with dark tinted windows and motor running was parked in the shadows. Padric had seen it before, even one night when they were leaving the convent.

*Forget it…*he was feeling the wine and called Lara; she still wasn't picking up. But Martinez knew his partner had something in play at the Nile. "You're scaring me."

"Shut up, fool. I'm changing my ways, renouncing the 'extra-curricular'. No more fucking around, too old for this shit. Need to be at the top of my game."

"And by a miracle, you are, Johnny, but why the change-of-heart all of a sudden?"

"The truth?"

"No, lie to me."

"Our nun's eyes." They talked about Magdalen like she was one of them.

"Christ, now you're hot for a nun?"

"Don't even say something like that...ever, man." He opened his car door. "I'm in enough shit to ever go near the likes of her. I respect what she's into; I grew up around that. But I'm thinking she did some serious living before she took the vows." Martinez sighed...only Johnny.

Padric returned to the Precinct and worked at his desk for over an hour but he needed Lara. It was colder now and a full moon high in the sky was watching him as he drove away. Across the Plaza, the Nile Hotel was aglow but the same black Escalade was blinking its lights. *Bloody hell.* He approached and pulled up behind it. A woman's wrist, heavy with bracelets, waved him closer. *Joanna. Damn, she's looking fine.* He heard his partner's last words for the night: "Who would have thought Johnny would change for a nun?"

But this was not so...not yet, *just one more time; this'll be it.*

The moon shook her head.

Several hours later, a beautiful woman sat up in bed and tossed back her long, black hair. Padric had drifted off. She'd lost track of time, dressed quickly and, for a moment, stepped onto the balcony and gazed up at the stars...she'd be keeping this one. He looked vulnerable, his watch on the elegant night table, his clothes on the chair. She'd buy him new things; he was her man. He could trust her; ripping someone off or taking a lover's wallet while he slept wasn't her thing. Joanna was beyond rich and had never stolen anything except women's husbands.

She stepped onto the elevator. A couple were into each other as it made its descent. She wanted more from this guy...she'd kill for it. The two exited at the lobby and when the door opened again on the lower level, she laughed. A young man was waiting,. "Hey, Sis!" He looked at his bodyguard. "Bruno, take the Escalade."

Author's Notes

calamari – *Mediterranean cuisine, fried squid served with lemon and salt.*

clams oreganata – *Italian-American dish, usually an appetizer, of baked clams with bread crumbs and oregano.*

antipasto – *Italian dish, often an appetizer, of cured meats, olives, pepperoncini, mushrooms, anchovies, artichoke hearts, provolone or mozzarella), pickled meats, vegetables in oil or vinegar.*

ristorante – *Italian restaurant.*

10 THE DETECTIVE

Good Friday, three in the morning, March 21

Upstairs in the Nile, Padric rolled over and slipped on his watch then leaned back on the pillows. She was gone; he closed his eyes. But this had been the scenario several weeks ago when Brother James was pushed to his death. Coldly, he had returned again to the Nile and now he was sick inside. *Home.* He threw on his clothes and once in the unmarked car in the parking garage, sat very still, staring into the shadows, alone. He should never have come here tonight…but he had not been able to walk away, not yet, *damn, maybe never.*

He'd skip going home, get some coffee, a few eggs; go back to the Precinct and shower. It was five in the morning when he walked into the Quarter to Three; the diner, a throwback to the fifties and sixties with Sinatra all over its walls and crooning twentyfourseven. A block south of the Precinct, the small, non-descript eatery was the daily haunt of on-and-off duty First Precinct cops and the cities heroes of Firehouse No. 4. It had stood on the same corner for ages; its name, a tribute to a song crooned by Ol' Blue Eyes himself. The owners, Doug and Gordon Black, were retired firemen, two brothers, two Scots from Glasgow, their establishment, a landmark for bagpipe-playing firefighters and footballing cops. They had their favorites and Padric was one of them. But at the moment, their lad was staring hopelessly into a cold cup of coffee.

Christ, what time is it? Padric had thrown himself onto a stool at the end of a long empty counter and was peering into the mirror behind the coffee machines. Someone bumped his arm.

"Are you leavin' or stayin'?" Tark.

"I'm in between."

"That's called purgatory, my friend, at least that's what Brother James told me once." *Brother James…don't say it; don't say his name.* Padric and Tark had seen a lot of 'bad' in their day, saved each other's lives more than once. There'd been crazy good times and one too many parties and there were the ladies they never discussed.

"You sounded good tonight, Jace." Padric tried to be upbeat.

"Thanks, but who talks to themselves in the mirror in public?"

"I'm fucked." He went to the men's room and threw cold water on his face. When he returned, Tark pulled him into their favorite booth. Padric said he needed to leave but would give him five minutes, said he had something for him. It would require some risk-taking. "You've been there, done that."

"Sweet Jesus, you're setting me up…hit me."

"The Edge."

Tark's eyes narrowed, the brief flicker of memories still smoldering under the surface; they were quickly dismissed. He'd gone down some dark roads on and off duty, working VICE, DEA, ATF. Jace Tarkington joined Major Crimes well prepared. The Edge had been his 'on again, off again' stomping ground…it would prove useful to Padric.

"Who are we looking at?"

"Good to hear you say 'we'…how's your new partner doing?"

"Good, J's quick, knows the law, smart in the street."

"So we're not calling him Jesús." They laughed.

"It's J-Dog; he's good with it."

"I won't lower myself to call him that, damn." Padric liked J-Dog; there'd been something on his application when he transferred into Major Crimes. Jesús Marcus had studied for the priesthood, been in the seminary; it shone through at the oddest times when he took a more serious stance. Marcus would make an effort to quell a firestorm and did it with grace; he'd reason with perps who others disdained. He could get just about anyone to tell him their problems, spill the unpleasant details. He was their "priest" now, Padric said.

"The lad's uncanny. He shuts down the freaks. Jana calls him an *old soul*."

"So who is it, Johnny…what do you need?"

"Robles. Ramos Robles. He saw it happen to the priest and I know now where he is."

"On whose *intel*?"

"Our nun's, damn it; get this: Dave Aguilar wants to put his kid in school at Cathedral…the kid talks to Sister. Evidently he's the last one to see Ramos." Padric gave him the details. "Tonight at the latest. It's Friday; do the Edge. I'm told he looks older, was invited into some woman's house; her name's Joanna…no last name. So, eyes and ears, my friend! You said you had something…what?" Tark told him he'd seen a face looking out of place after Padric had left the crime scene behind the Nile. "Who?"

"She has an entourage, a rep in the clubs, known for liking it kinky. She's a Cantera."

"The bishop's a Cantera, related? A cousin…so what?"

"His sister…the woman was driving a smokin' red truck, a Mercedes, with a dude sitting on the passenger side in a hood."

"That truck is a ghost and we're seeing it now? So this *chica*…"

"*Caliente…mucho, mucho.* Latina, long black hair, always the bright red lipstick, a lot of bling, but the real stuff; she's beautiful but a cobra."

"We've gotta lotta those, Jace. So you're liking her for what… these kills, all of this?"

"What did that kid tell the cops in the Fifth? It was tricked-out, red, a Mercedes…a truck like that in the *barrio* stands out. Now I'm seeing her in it at the Nile after another kill?"

"So we've officially got ourselves a serial killer; we knew that… describe her again." But what was he hearing? A diamond in the nail of each pinky, great eyes, small mole under the left one and there was more. "Some body, everything where it should be and more." *Bloody hell. Who was this sounding like? Impossible…wait just one minute. Johnny Padric could spot a monster, knew a killer when he saw one. Sufferin' Jesus.*

Tark eyed him curiously; he'd struck a chord.

"Damn, you look like shit." *Damn is right*; he'd been had. "I mean it. Where's the First Precinct's boy-wonder?" No answer. *Nada.* "Watch yourself, *amigo.* You look the way I used to."

"Yeah, how was that?"

"Like horse poop. I was fucking around on my wife, a beautiful woman and lost her; and worse, she took my boy with her. You got that look. Run away from it; move your ass."

He thought he'd been hiding things better. "I want to heave."

"Yeah, I do that to people." Jace said his wife had disappeared. "I got nothing. I live at my job. We're the most ripped boys in the LPD we work out so much. I play the hell out of my sax; you bury your head in F. Scott or Shakespeare."

"And Batman comics, you forget." But Tark was right...they more than most lived at the Precinct, slept and worked out, showered there; eating bar food and dogs from a vendor. They'd slip into Tark's favorite, the Dirty Rice, a Cajun food-jazz bar down the street. "I won't even side-eye a woman, not anywhere, not even playing at Bugsy's or the Merengue. It's 'get away from me, bitch'."

"Even at the Merengue? There's good pickin's over there." They laughed. Padric looked into his coffee cup. "I'm not a good person." His self-effacing tone startled Tark; his man had done a three-sixty. "Trust me...I'm no good to anyone anymore, anywhere, and now, this one case, this moondead thing, has me chasing my tail. I...I gotta get out of here...my wife." He needed Lara. He stood up, dizzy with what he had done, with whom he had done it.

Tark eyed him. "Hey, don't wait; you could lose everything."

Padric sat down again. "I have...I already have." Tark saw how broken he was and trying to hide it. "This red Mercedes...our nun saw it."

"Where...near the school?" Padric nodded. "So did I. It skidded, left rubber in the street behind the hotel...we have CSI printing it. I thought I was seeing things; she's hard to miss." Padric asked him to repeat her name. "Joanna. I've seen her in action. She's definitely "Edge" material, hard-core, not to be trusted, a spooky broad. Heard she has a place out there, does some business on the side, co-owns one of those no-names. Rumor has it that she parties with high rollers; has a tat of a heart with a knife through it on her…" *The tat.* Padric knew where it was; his lips knew. He wasn't sitting there anymore. Tark's voice seemed far away when he said: "There's only one Joanna."

But Padric needed two. There must be a Joanna Cruz if the one in the truck was Joanna Cantera. He stood up…the color gone from his face; his hands shaking. He was off center like he'd been slammed with a stungun. He'd leave, hide, vomit in the alley; hell, sit down by a dumpster, stay there for a few hours, commune with the street. Hadn't their nun said a Joanna invited Ramos into her house in the Edge and now Tark's saying this one has a place there?

He told Tark to stop talking. "Joanna Cantera has Ramos." Boom. Tark eyed his friend. "And who else does she have, Johnny?"

Padric stood up, said the java was on him. Tark could feel a vibe coming off a man and watched the metamorphosis in his friend; he followed him to the door. *Damn, she got to my boy. He's had her. Fuck.* Their eyes met; Padric's, full of pain.

Tark put his finger to his lips. "Not a word, my man, not a word. Go, make it right." He'd do what he'd asked, he said. "I'm in the Edge…you say when." A booth of detectives called out to him. Padric faked a grin; he'd see them tonight.

Out in the street, he was gasping for air. Tark's words had flattened him. He'd go home; they'd make love, a lot of it. That always worked… at least he thought so. Ahead of him, the Cathedral stood silent, judging him. He couldn't look at it, but an early morning Mass would mean she'd be in the sacristy; the nun would say something, make him feel right about himself, but what was he thinking? How could he be in the same room with her when he just fucked Joanna what's-her-name?

Lara. Jaysus, she'll be pissed; he went over in his mind what he'd say. Padric looked at himself in the rear view; had he just crawled out of a toilet? He sped away, his mind spinning out of control, the case looking even more complicated; the Cantera name alone, enough to bring down anyone who got too close and he had. Funny. Their prime suspect was right there in front of him, underneath him, on top of him. He knew every curve in her body and had no idea who she was. *Hell, a head doctor would have a field day with both of us.* He stared straight ahead, heart beating out of his chest A moth had fluttered too close to the flame and singed its wings.

Home at last. Knowing Lara would be there was already a comfort. He'd lie to her; she'd listen, maybe even believe him.

But…Christ Jesus! What the…? Padric pulled into his driveway and clicked the remote; the garage door slowly lifted but he was little prepared for the exhaust fumes billowing onto the lawn. The adrenaline he felt on the job kicked in. Stumbling from his car, Padric called dispatch, speed dialed Martinez, yelled to his neighbor mowing his lawn. A postal truck screeched to the curb.

His personal hell had arrived. Years later, he'd have nightmares and wake up, remembering. With no seat belt in place, Lara was slumped toward the window; bruised cheek pressed to the glass, eyes closed. Blouse ripped, breasts exposed, hands clenched in terror…this had just happened. A woman walking her dog and two runners joined in the rescue; had anyone seen the assailants? A red truck was in front of the house then left like a bat out of hell, someone said. It careened down the street passing one of the joggers.

The detective was exceptionally strong, but later, had no memory of how he'd roared like a lion when, with sledgehammer and one of his neighbors, ripped the door from its hinges when the remote didn't work.

He carried Lara into the cool morning air onto the lawn, and searched for a pulse. "Stay with me, lass! Lara! Don't leave me, girl." *Son-of-a-bitch…*he was losing her.

Author's Notes

Quarter to Three – reference to the first line in Frank Sinatra's bluesy number, "One for My Baby"; diner/favorite hangout for the First Precinct and Firehouse No. 4 in L'Arroyo.

VICE – division enforcing laws pertaining to gambling, narcotics and prostitution.

DEA – Drug Enforcement Administration.

ATF – bureau enforcing laws to alcohol, tobacco, firearms and explosives.

barrio – Spanish, for neighborhood.

nada – Spanish, for nothing.

11 THE WIFE

Good Friday, seven-thirty in the morning, March 21

Neighbors arrived; some helpful, others annoyed he'd brought this kind of trouble into their quiet lives. When "officer's wife down" went out over the wire, fire trucks, squad cars, EMVs wailed like banshees through the streets in seconds. The Quarter to Three emptied out. Pistasio and Tark in the lead sped toward Padric's house. Some pulled up on the lawn, swarming the house and back-yard. They fanned out down the street, into alleys, over walls and fences. One, two and three fire trucks moved quickly into place.

Padric turned another shade of pale...*wee Kara and Kate!*

As EMTs hovered over Lara, he shouted to Pistasio and Tark, who took the stairs to the second floor...his girls were gone. *God, not that; not them...punish me, kill me, send me to hell. School. Would they be in their classrooms*...he was home so seldom he didn't even know their schedule. The attendance office, horrified by the call, reassured Padric his girls were with their teachers; their day had begun. It had been a neighbor's turn to drive them to school and she'd arrived early. Stunned at the upheaval and with guns drawn, the three men moved quickly through the rooms. His house had been trashed, but a chilling thought gnawed at Padric...what if this was no home invasion at all and Lara had staged it to take her own life?

No, never; not my girl. Lara wouldn't go all passive-aggressive, sending a message like this. She'd just say it. His wife was strong, more than of sound mind and body; he couldn't have driven her to it. Was he that narcissistic to think she'd simply fold on his account? She'd never leave her daughters to the likes of him. Closer examination caused him more agony…what had they done to his woman? Tark and Pistasio stepped back out of respect; there were signs of molestation, a huge, angry bite mark on Lara's breast, bra torn, her hands covered in defensive wounds, blood everywhere. He tried to cover her. This didn't happen to the wife of John Padric; there'd be a reckoning. He hoped his wife fought like a she-wolf; someone wanted her hurt and humiliated.

Moments later in the medical van, he looked more closely at the bite on her breast then at the attendant. "Do a swab…we'll get it to the lab." But he didn't need a lab. Out of his mind with guilt, he knew. "The bitch had her way with my wife."

The EMT listened but said not a word. Never had Padric felt this much anger. He studied the victim's contusions, broken nails, bloodied knuckles, scraped knees; her legs covered in drag marks, she'd resisted. His eyes narrowed. *She's knocked unconscious after a struggle; they want the exhaust to finish her. They're sure of themselves. They don't belt her in, thinking why should they; she's down for the count. And if they're wrong and she lives, who cares? She'll suffer from fear, be out of her mind for the rest of her life. But no, one of them wanted her dead and out of the way. This was attempted murder.*

"Who do I fuckin' kill?" Martinez. He leaned into the van.

"*Kema sabe,* leave that to me. I know who it is." Padric left Lara to the care of the paramedic and drew his partner aside, quickly telling him things, admitting to an affair and only learning the real ID of his lover just hours ago. She was getting obsessive, questioning him, wanting all of him.

But there was no sympathy. Martinez slammed him with a few choice words; had he not warned him about this? "What does it take for you to stop, fool? If she dies it's on you. Go, get out of my sight; be with your woman. We'll deal with it here." He'd finally said it to the man he loved more than a brother. "Fuck you, Johnny! Fuck you!" Martinez walked away leaving Padric standing alone on his lawn. Years later, he'd remember this as one of the lowest points in his life.

The man had suddenly lost his way and, for the rest of his life, he'd never be sure he'd found it again. He slowly returned to the van, cursing to himself, muttering: "You bitch...*God has given you one face and you give yourself another.* Damn you." But quoting Shakespeare wouldn't do it for him; his head would be clouded with plans on how to rid himself of Joanna Cantera.

The EMT placed an oxygen mask over Lara's face, hooked up IVs; trying to stabilize her. Both men were alarmed when she suddenly opened her eyes; dazed, she pulled at the mask and cried out for her children. She sobbed for her husband, not seeing him there, whispered his name, sending him into even deeper agony. "Please come home, Johnny, come home..." Then she saw him...he would never forget the look of relief in her eyes. He had not seen this in her for a long time and leaned very close, whispering his love and regret, vowing devotion. She closed her eyes.

The attendant pounded his fist on the cab wall. "Roll this mother. Move it out!" The van shuttered, lurched forward and Padric looked back at his house; half the Precinct was on his front lawn. Martinez and his team, CSIs Milleau and Miller, were already processing the crime scene. But as the van turned the corner, he spotted a detective for whom he'd little respect and was now pulling up in front of his house. A wily, annoying man, Dan Mason was a bad cop who wore too much cologne; a small-minded clown and Padric's nemesis for his entire career in law enforcement. *What is he doing here?* But he looked at his iPhone...the Captain had texted him. Mason would be lead on Lara's near death; it was his case. This would leave no conflict of interest for John Padric or his other detectives...but there was. He'd slept with their prime suspect.

Padric shouted: "This one's going to Meadow!"

He was surprised when a voice sounding like Ireland fired back: "And where else would I be taking your lass, sir?"

Padric looked at the paramedic. "Ay, that's good Billy Kelly... he drives this thing like a jet." He too had a brogue and Padric asked him his name. "Brady, sir, Declan Brady. My dad owns the pub with my mum's name, Brigid Brady's, God rest her. He was tight with your da' when me and my brother, Pat, were curtain climbers."

And that sounded like Derry talking. "Ah, good Mr. Colin

Brady himself and Pat…he's a fine one, playing that hot guitar with style all over the state. He can tear up a place. Thank you, lad, but I think my girl might be leaving me in more ways than one. This is on me, all of it. And now I'll be walking the line a bit tighter; my wee girls need to be safe. I'm a cop."

And not a very good one, he was thinking. He'd allowed someone dangerous and unpredictable into his life but he'd liked dangerous and unpredictable…once. When Padric asked if his wife was going to make it, Declan gave no assurances but posed a theory that offered some hope. "Your perps got in and out pretty quick, not leaving much time to do that much damage, and that's brilliant when you think about it, sir."

"They knew my schedule, when I came home in the morning; time was tight. They didn't arrive earlier because one of them was preoccupied…" She'd been with him but he didn't say that. "But why take the time to trash the place?" But he knew. "She knew that house was Lara's castle…this was all done to hurt *her*."

"Ay and apologies…your wife was targeted, plain and simple, by a woman at her worst. As you say, that house was your lass's making, her creation, and this she-devil ruined it for her. But for now, her pulse is strong and it's not to the morgue we'll be taking her. Hate seeing this happen to one of your kin."

For both men, the ride to Meadow would prove interesting when again Lara opened her eyes. Always in control, always together, she was hanging on to her dignity for dear life. When she asked the attendant how he knew her name and he said he was a fan of her husband's, she snapped: "He's no rock star, believe me!" It left the men wondering if they should laugh or not.

Padric waited until she was calmer then leaned forward. "Lara, it's me, the rock star." She unloaded on him and finished with a flourish: "Is this what it takes to get you back?" Martinez had asked the same. "Was it worth it?" *Round one*…the next one would come soon enough. She'd been saving an arsenal of words for him,

But Padric had more on his mind. "It was two. They tag-teamed it maybe, but one was making it personal."

"Who'd want to hurt her unless they wanted to get to you, sir?"

He leaned back but Lara, disoriented and trying to focus,

motioned to Brady. "I must speak to my husband. He's a detective…he'll want to know." Padric wondered if she could give him anything credible but all would become painfully clear. "The backyard…the wall," she was saying.

"They came over the wall?" Was it one, two, how many?

Lara frowned…trying to remember. "Two. My face…the second one punched me." Her left eye was swollen. "I gave them some fight-back like you told me to do, but it did me in."

"And I love you for that, lass, but, son-of-a-bitch; I'll kill him."

"Her…" *What? Damn.* "A woman punched me hard with her fist." *And there it is.* "She was angry; it was personal I think…but why? I passed out and came to in the car." Lara described the smoke, the fumes. "I died…I think I died." The two men glanced at each other; she tried to sit up. "It's Good Friday, Johnny. I'm scared…I want my girls. Where are my babies…my baby?" Declan nodded…good, she knew what day it was.

"They're safe in school…I've got it covered."

"You always do, Johnny…you always do, damn you."

Ah, woman. "What did they look like?"

"Half-masks, beautiful like the ones we saw when we were in Venice." He closed his eyes, remembering…Venice, magical. They were beyond in love. "Hoods pulled down over their eyes though, monks' robes, odd. I…I was afraid." She closed her eyes.

"How did you know one was a woman?"

"Red, bright red…" *Shut up, woman.* "Lipstick…she laughed at me…perfume, very expensive, Chanel No. 5." His heart was racing…*do I really want to hear this?* "She was talking the whole time; she hit me, the other one was quiet."

Dare he ask? "What was she saying, Lara?" *Don't say it.*

"Your name, your fucking name…Johnny this, Johnny that,"

Joanna. Damn it, Joanna. She'd been following him, showing up where he was, checking his moves, making plans for the two of them. But Lara was still talking, looking for answers. "She…she pulled at my blouse, ripped it…the one you gave me for Christmas; she enjoyed what she did to me, wanting me like a man, like you." *I'll fuckin' kill the bitch.* "She…she bit me, did things." She wept, thrashed about, tore at her clothes and tried to cover herself.

"God, she was touching me. Johnny, she…hurt me."

Joanna Cruz, Cantera, whatever. Padric could stand it no longer; despite Declan's protests and the IV's in her arm, Padric gathered Lara up in his arms, holding her close, kissing her face, whispering his love for her over and over until Declan pulled them apart.

"That fucking bitch…" He buried his head in his hands.

Lara turned into stone. "You know her; you fucked her…" She clutched her stomach and cried out. "Help me, help us…save us." Silence came when Declan's drugs drew her under. Padric hoped she'd forget and tucked the blankets around her. *Save us…odd. Who does she mean?*

Sensing defeat at every level, Padric could only muster: "How'd they get passed my security; it's like Fort fucking Knox."

They were nearing Meadow now with staff on alert and waiting; the victim wasn't just anyone. Bay doors glided open; Padric stepped aside, eyeing the usual ER choreography. Meadow had an unusual staff, its nurses and orderlies, even some doctors, were law enforcement; the Head Physician, Chief of Medicine, had insisted on it. Physician's assistant, Sgt. Gina Chavez, moved about quickly. She'd been a co-worker with the nun who was almost beheaded and had loved Cecelia; now she was taking her friend's wife away. She and Padric had cruised the streets in a patrol car together; even been more than partners, had crossed the line with each other. It didn't last…they were friends now and she said she'd handle it.

Lara cried out: "My babies, my girls, my…"

He shouted over the heads of the medics. "Our girls, luv!" Could he win her back? His cell phone lit up. Kate and Kara knew their Aunt Jana and would go with her to Auntie Mairead's. Assistant newspaper editor at *The L'Arroyo Moon,* she'd been following the story. Lara and she were best friends; she'd care for them.

He slipped behind the curtain where Lara lay as the staff prepped her for surgery. "We're never going back to that house."

Her voice softened, telling him not to worry…she'd never liked it anyway. *She didn't?* He bought it for her. He watched her now as a team of medics hurried her onto an elevator and up to the O.R.

Brady appeared. "She's safe now. No one can get to her."

Padric doubted that. "Lad, if someone wants her bad enough, they can." He stood up. "My apologies for the family drama." The man was feeling embarrassed.

"Detective, I hear a lot; will you be improving things then?"

"And now you're a priest? Ay, if she'll let me. Do you still think I'm a rock star?"

"I'm giving it second thoughts after that chat with your wife."

BOLOs were out for a tricked out red Mercedes, long gone from the city and for Joanna Cantera and the other nobody knew.

Cutting it close and now in a heated discussion, they'd made it to high ground, the untraveled roads in the hills. This hadn't been on his to-do-list; it had been her idea. She'd make the usual car swap with Bruno.

The desert was in bloom, a nice day for a drive.

Good Friday, five-thirty in the morning, March 21

In the early dawn, a nun, troubled and not herself, moved about in a cloud with heart pounding. She'd heard sirens, common in downtown L'Arroyo, but she'd rushed to the window and surveyed the garden as if it held every answer she'd ever need. A dark, unseemly deed had been done…*the killers perhaps, stirring the pot, brewing more mayhem.* Would there ever be a time when she'd be free of such premonitions…a woman this time but not like before, someone loved and forgotten, brutally treated; the other, beautiful, dark, demon-like. A faint outline of the moon was still visible on this early Good Friday morning…*la luna muerta.*

She gazed thoughtfully at the stone altar; its cross, entwined with thorns. "My Saviour, my Lord, there are dark times ahead… but today is your day." Her morning prayer would be filled with night dreams and marked with an unusual sunrise, given the holy day; the horizon was crimson. *Red sky in morning, sailor's warning; red sky at night, sailor's delight.*

"There was a full moon last night and so it will be again," whispered Sister Barbara as they entered the refectory. It was she who had spoken to Magdalen of the recent lunar eclipse. Chairperson/

teacher for the high school's sci/chem/physics department, Barbara was a woman conversant with moon tides and theologies of the universe; the two were friends and Barbara, though kind, made few close friends. She had observed Magdalen after her arrival and decided she liked her; they often spoke, both researchers sharing their theories and ideas with each other. For Magdalen, it was a comfort since so few around her were so inclined and had no passionate curiosity. Barbara was an academic; she liked that.

"Sister B," as Magdalen preferred to call her, "you are just the one I need to speak with."

"You look concerned. You've been pale of late."

In whispered conversation, they withdrew to the convent garden with their small repast of bread, cheese, and coffee. The nuns would observe the austerities of Good Friday with unbroken silence and fasting until later that evening when they'd share a simple but celebratory dinner on their community holy day as Sisters of the Crucified. Again the bishop had made sure it would be memorable with several baskets of food to be enjoyed at their leisure; an invitation for him and the monsignor to join them was declined.

Today would be a challenge for Magdalen; she was on edge. "I can't say this to too many people. It would spook them, but I've a bad feeling about tonight."

Barbara sighed: "And you're speaking to someone who thinks scientifically. I don't assume very much but the few assumptions I have are not based on a feeling...you know that."

"And you know I allow things, not seen under a microscope, into my thinking. I think in with words like: maybe, perhaps, there might be" because my former research ended very often in a twist or turn or even more uncertainty. I can't say simply "yes or no" to questions on a number of issues...there are other considerations, what if's. Our human nature allows for this...there are things that can't be analyzed with a template."

Barbara nodded. "Point taken, but enough with our mindsets, what's troubling you?"

"There will be a full moon tonight and my sense of things tells me something's terribly wrong. I wanted to say, it does not bode well, but I'd sound like Charles Dickens." They laughed. "I dread another martyr murder, given the past scenarios." Magdalen was surprised: Barbara had reacted with no incredulity. "The medical examiner puts our Sister's death almost down to the exact time the lunar eclipse completed its course. If the killers are aligning their crimes with the phases of the moon, how pre-meditated was that? Our victims are called the moondead by the media for a reason. I can't forget what I was doing then."

"And that was…?"

"I no longer sleep as well as I'd like. That night, a dog howled in the street; it woke me and I saw the eclipse; the moon brown, turning red. It was chilling…so awesome."

"What have I asked you before, Sister?"

"Ah, awesome…a deplorable word in your way of thinking."

"Exactly…God alone is awesome. He fills us with awe. I have students who will tell me Lady Gaga is awesome as are the Arizona Cardinals or Phoenix Suns when and if they score, which I understand is not always as it should be. A bug with an orange back was awesome for two girls in the sophomore biology class on Wednesday…but my God, let us refrain from using this word."

If anyone else had said this to Magdalen she would have told them to take 'a flying leap'; she would not do it now…besides, a flying leap would have posed a whole new set of theories and criteria for Barbara to ponder and that might take hours.

"It was blood red; later when I heard Sister had died close to that time, I couldn't forget what I'd seen. I decided, then and there, I'd observe every change in the moon until this case was closed, and now here we are on Good Friday about to see it again."

"And what are you asking?"

"Are people really affected by the moon? I'm not talking werewolves but plain, ordinary people's reactions to things in nature."

"Well, if the moon is affecting someone to any great degree then we'd have to say they're not quite plain and ordinary, do we agree on that?"

"Why, yes. But in light of what we've experienced lately, I'm freaked, bottom-line."

"Freaked...now there is a term I..."

"Don't even go there. I'm not up for another etymological cross-reference. But to quote Lieutenant Padric, lay it on me."

Barbara laughed. "Science says there's nothing to substantiate the moon's adverse effect on human beings. Psychologists conjure up their own hypothesis; then we have folklore and recorded instances of unusual happenings. But we also know there are those who would do the same strange things regardless...no moon necessary."

"What do you feel in your gut, Sister?"

"I'm apprehensive and I hate myself for saying so. I admit I'm coldly scientific and am even vain about it, but the Life, my vows, my faith in things unseen, speaks to me as well. I struggle with this dichotomy inside me."

"I appreciate your honesty and am frankly humbled that you'd even share that with me, Sister. But what's your bottom-line then?"

"I will spend the day in prayer."

"Your bottom-line."

"As you are, so am I."

"Oh, for God's sake...what's that?"

"Freaked."

Close to noon, she watched from the sacristy as the nave of the Cathedral filled with worshipers; Magdalen and Petra had laid out the vestments for the many priests attending the *Tre Ore*, an Italian reference to the three hours Christ hung on the cross. And so it would be, as only the bishop could express in his liturgies. Steed and the new priest were there at his side, looking like archangels, tall and solemn; they gave an assist when, in a stunning gesture, the bishop himself chose to carry a huge cross down the center aisle for the faithful to venerate with a kiss on the steps of the main altar.

Magdalen had smiled when Mario Martinez had offered to help after the liturgy. Marisol, his mother, had waved from the door, but not without telling her of Lara's assault. The nun, having hours before been filled with premonitions, wanted to hide in the vestry, anywhere. She quickly recovered and managed to be gracious.

Mario and Petra too had set to work…she'd taken a special interest in him. "I think I shall be calling you Father Martinez one day; you are doing a wonderful job." But he shook his head and said he wasn't good enough. When his father appeared in the doorway, Magdalen told him of his son's remark.

He was stunned, looked down at the floor, smiled. "For my son to be a priest would be the highest moment of my life. I would be out of my mind with happiness, Sister." He said he would say nothing. "He plays a lot of sports but could help around here, give you a hand, spend time with you here. You know how much I admire you and Sister Petra." It was then he too commented on what had happened to Padric's wife. "I think he'll want to speak with you."

She would wait for his call. "This is the work of the same who killed our Sister?"

"I can't say, but my gut tells me 'yes' though…"

"Lara doesn't fit the victim profile."

Petra was listening, when the nuns were alone, she wept.

Magdalen embraced her, only offering empty reassurances; she too was bewildered but hiding it better. Petra rallied, apologized. "Come, Sister. It's home for us now to be with our Sisters!" Her face brightened. "They're sitting down to celebrate our feast day. It's time." But Magdalen had more on her mind.

It was close to seven in the evening when she and Petra took their places beside Monica in the refectory; she was pale, her hands trembling when she pointed to Petra and shook her head. What was this holy one seeing? She asked that they visit her later tonight.

Magdalen could eat nothing. Later she disappeared for a moment of quiet into the chapel before returning with Petra to the sacristy with mended vestments and freshly pressed linens. Though the Cathedral had been sealed like Christ's tomb, each had their own set of sacristy keys; it would be quiet tonight. Contemplating the great mysteries of the day and the circumstances surrounding Lara, she prayed. Silence.

But Gabriela was gently tapping her shoulder…phone call.

Good Friday, eight in the evening, March 21

"*Benedicite,* how can I help?"

Padric never sounded like this. Calm at first, his voice finally cracked; he tried to go on. Only Lara had ever heard him like this.

"Detective, our humble home is yours." She begged him to come. "If you wish to stop for some beverage or conversation, I am here." When she asked about his children, he told her about Mairead...she realized he'd never spoken of family. Now he'd be living two blocks away with his sister and said he'd never return to his house, the horror too much to bear. "You will be our neighbor; I feel safer already and relieved you have family here. Come for a cuppa before you go to your little ones."

Tea or coffee would not be his choice, but he was glad for the invite. "I'll be there in ten...or maybe not. It's Good Friday."

Magdalen insisted. Distraught and trying to hide it, he was surprised to see the sandwiches and even more taken back when Gabriela appeared with a pint. "Sufferin' Lord, is that a Guinness I'm seeing?" Gabriela was delighted she had surprised him.

"Ah, Detective, we save it for special people like yourself even on a Good Friday evening. Enjoy." The three smiled in spite of the circumstances.

Ignoring the food, Padric drank slowly, blurting out what had happened, how he had found Lara. He confessed to Magdalen his indiscretions, his careless treatment of family, how he had trampled all over his wife's patience, her love for him. She was a beauty, he unworthy of her. "She's a sensitive lass, brilliant; the woman has been devoted to me and my girls." So great was his pain, she wanted to rush to him. Under different circumstances, she would have done so, held him close; this was her way. But she said not a word as he poured out his soul.

Occasionally she nodded her understanding then he stood up and walked to the window, revealing his adulterous ways with a woman who was now a potential suspect. He couldn't utter her name. It was maddening...Joanna Cruz was Joanna Cantera; he could only imagine what the bishop's sacristan might do if he said her last name. "I've placed this whole case and my unit's rep in jeopardy." He was mumbling to himself; Padric never mumbled.

Had Magdalen heard correctly? "This woman then is a suspect in the martyr murders?"

He said he wasn't sure then said yes, that he thought so. "Which is it then, Detective?"

"Lara was out of it, she wasn't herself but I know her; she's got a mind like a steel trap…what she told me has me convinced." His own wife was a victim now.

"Sit down." It was an order; nuns did that. He sank wearily into a chair. "I can't imagine how difficult this is for you." She leaned toward him. "But we, you and I, do not fall on our sword so easily." Had he said nothing that shocked her?

But Magdalen was thinking other things…there was something wrong with this scenario. "If these are the killers in the martyr murders, they've changed their MO; there's no martyr's name, no martyr's death to replicate." Padric agreed…it was vengeful; an act fueled by jealousy. She hesitated: "I'm seeing a very bad case of delusion and erotomania, a psychosexual hunger, satisfied only by the actions you describe, the intimate nature of where the victim is bitten and so on." She hesitated, uncomfortable saying such things to the likes of John Padric. "But you know these things."

Yes, he did, but she was sounding like a woman with an understanding of more than just incense and whispered prayers. "Talk to me, Sister…you can say it."

"I see two people wrapped up in themselves, what they want; a woman who can't have a wife in the picture and a man who can't get enough of what he thought was just a little something on the side…forgive me if I offend, but you asked me. She will bury you." A nun was saying these things…their nun, his nun.

"Damn, Sister…"

But she'd never reveal she couldn't have shared him either. "The other one…the male, he doesn't engage in such behavior; he operates on a higher level." She waited for this to register.

He frowned. "Explain."

"He's on a mission, compelled by inner demons and delusion."

"I get that, he's the dominant, designing the kills but not this time. She called the shots, made the move on my wife for reasons that had nothing to do with martyrs and nuns." He stood up, walked around, sat down again. "This one's on me…it's my fault all of it."

"You'll have no mental clarity if you wallow in regret; you're doomed if you do. You'll have time later to ponder your place in hell." She had hoped she could jolt him into reality but he was already considering his place there and wanted to wallow. Padric finally looked up. She hesitated. "You fear this woman will expose you, I think."

"And if she does, my wife will never look at me again. Plus…all we've done on the case will be tainted, if a judge thinks I colluded in this or attempted to off my wife. I'll need to recuse myself."

Magdalen was stunned by his words. "But your lover may say nothing." He studied her for a moment. *What kind of nun thinks like this?* "You're a woman, what about it? I'm listening."

He was surprised by her insight when she calmly suggested the woman would never expose their affair or bring him public disgrace. "She knows you would despise her for it and she wants to keep you. In fact, she may already believe she has lost you, if she thinks you suspect her of hurting your wife. She may be frantic, knowing she's gone too far."

He stared at her. "Are you sure you're a nun?"

"Every inch of me."

"But you know the love of a woman for a man…" He was curious…his focus had changed to the nun with green eyes.

"Some other time, Detective."

He smiled a little, wishing he'd been on the receiving end of whatever she wasn't saying, but she wouldn't allow him to go there and he understood. Still…he wanted it his way and such thoughts would be shattered. She leaned forward and looked quite sternly at him. "When will you change your roguish ways?" *Sister Moira.*

He was too tired to laugh…a rogue now, he was. Achieving such status might have been dashing years ago, but now? It was Shakespearean at best. Queens University and his theater/lit classes had allowed him to play a few of the Bard's villains back in Belfast; but such memories were quickly dismissed; he smiled a little.

The nun had, kindly put, told him to stop fucking around and now she would show him no mercy, assail him in a whisper that it was time to grow up, get a grip; again...*Sister Moira.*

He was silent and listened but she could see he wanted to say something else...unrelated perhaps. "I've assumed too much, coming here, laying this on you. I'm sorry, but...but you've grown on me. I knew you were different the day I met you here in this room."

"I think we're friends, yes."

He wanted more but said he'd made a living putting people's mistakes under a microscope and now the roles had been reversed. "I needed to tell you, before I go to my Commander with this but I'm sorry I laid it on you. You're..." He stopped, looked down.

She was startled at the personal tone the conversation had taken. No man had shared things like this with her, said such words, in years. She would say it...regardless. "I...your feelings touch me, but I cannot tell you my own. We both have our own lives and are wed to another, you to a beautiful woman; I to my Lord."

He'd said too much. "I'll honor that always."

"Please know that I'm not judging you...I can't. I wasn't always a nun and also suffered for choosing unwisely. I get it. I came face to face with dark times, loved too much; it's not easy getting back up." He wished he'd been the one she had loved too much.

"It's hard to believe you've had any problems at all. So you didn't drop out of heaven?"

She smiled. "Some of us are more damaged than you might like to believe or we wish to admit. But God has picked us up and dusted us off. He has embraced us."

Damn. Who says this shit? "And you're happy, Sister?"

"Oh, yes...I thought long and hard before I chose to live in His service." Magdalen had not hesitated; he'd been trained to notice such things. Her heart was embedded here in the Life, but what kind of existence did this gifted, beautiful woman have, for God's sake, but he knew and understood, Catholic boy that he was.

"We're all looking for a little redemption, John Padric."

"And you've found it?"

"Sometimes I think not, but yes, here in the Life, as we call it;

there have been times I felt like bolting out the front door and running as fast as I could into the desert, not looking back, not once,
not ever." But she stopped, shook her head…he probably expected
more of her; she apologized.

He leaned closer and told her to let him know when she did.

"I'll rescue you."

"But that would defeat my purpose in running." She gave him
no satisfaction. *God, who is she?* He wouldn't tell her he'd resolved
once before to watch over her from a distance as long as he lived.
But he frowned when she said: "I shouldn't have revealed such
things. Our rule discourages this with outsiders…"

"Your Rule I get, but me an outsider, after all the times I've sat
here with you, talked of your Sisters, come to your door and had
to deliver bad news?" She smiled. "I ate your food, argued with
you and questioned that sense of things you've got? After all I've
admitted to you tonight? Hey, I'm a little more than an outsider.
The Precinct says I have a responsibility to protect you, so I'm in."
He lowered his voice. "I've got you inside me and that's all I'll say."
Silence. He'd said it. *Damn.*

Magdalen moved in her chair, stunned. *My God, my God…what
have I done? Am I guilty of too much familiarity with this man? But no, perhaps yes, but it was bound to happen, revealing to each other one's thoughts.
He knows what is right, what I'm about. I'll be careful.* The detective was
reading the nun…he'd put her in an awkward position. But she,
for one moment, she allowed herself to be comforted…she looked
down at the table and finally whispered: "And I cannot respond."

"Ouch! And here I thought I had charmed you." She smiled a
little but said nothing. This was his way…it seemed flirtatious and
he wasn't trying to be, but what he was doing was subtle, his feelings
sincere. Though tempted to play, she would not.

"If I were younger and had a different past, you might have.
But sadly I've seen too much in my life and hold my own story close
to my heart. You are very…you are…" She stopped and looked
down at her hands.

"I'm what?" He wanted to do a John Garfield and leap over
the table, hold her, tell her everything would be fine, promise her
undying devotion.

But she was saying things: "You're quite a challenge; as for me, I cannot dwell on these things." She was struggling...he was suddenly ashamed. Padric had overstepped even with all that had befallen his wife. He'd played it loose with a beautiful nun and would have liked to pursue this game of words further. He felt miserable all over again.

It was inappropriate; no more, not with her. "I shouldn't have gone there...I'm sorry."

"We're trying to save the world, you and I. Some day I may need you and I know you will be there."

"Never forget you said that to me."

"I...I won't. I'm so grateful to you for the way you and your partner have shown your concern." They regarded each other in silence.

The nun asked no further questions; had she said too much? She'd need to distance herself; this intense, intelligent Celt warrior-sleuth had said things that pleased her...and he was beautiful. Nuns shouldn't have the likes of a Johnny Padric saying such things, but she was realistic, understood: the rush of emotion, a word spoken...the moment would pass. But the detective, with his story, had awakened memories in her of another time in a strange, exotic place, where she too had loved and been loved. No matter, she'd chosen the Life, with no turning back or taking another path; with no voice strong enough to dissuade her...not even that of a handsome Irish detective.

Padric said he must go. "Thanks for the beer. Never thought I'd be saying that to a nun, but I said a lot of things tonight. Did I tell you my brother's a priest?"

"When do I meet him?" He said very soon, but there was a knock, Petra on the way to the sacristy with fresh linens and mended vestments; though Magdalen offered to accompany her, she insisted she stay. Their smiles and words...were they angels? He was so undeserving. But he must go.

A voice called out his name as he walked to the door: He eyed the older nun walking toward him. "Wait...are you who I think you are?"

Gabriela put her hands on her hips. "Why yes, if I am who you think I am." They laughed and she regaled them with her memories of the student John Padric. As time slipped away, he glanced at Magdalen, her eyes. He knew her ways; she was on to something. Petra! The two quickly left; Magdalen to the sacristy, he on his cell watching her, but there was good news: Lara looking better, his girls, safe in their beds at Mairead's. He needed to go, be with them but the nun…something was off. "Sister?"

Magdalen, finding the sacristy door bolted, no light within, rushed to the side door under the colonnade. "She's been gone too long…we would have seen her if she came home!"

His inner cop kicked in. "What was Sister thinking going there by herself?"

"We do it all the time…I've come here many a night alone."

"And you'll be doing no more of it…my orders."

Ominously, the full moon, *la luna*, dipped low over the Cathedral, as if to warn them. Padric surveyed the courtyard, scanned the rooftops. On schedule, a squad car arrived, he snapped a mic onto his shoulder and the two slipped into the Cathedral.

Author's Notes

"God has given you one face and you give yourself another" – Padric quotes a line from Hamlet, Act 3, Scene 1.

Meadow – a high-security medical facility exclusively for victims in protective custody, injured officers of the law and their families; its staff is unusual, its nurses and orderlies, even some doctors, are law enforcement with physician's assistant, Sgt. Gina Chavez, a central character in the narrative.

The L'Arroyo Moon – the city's only newspaper; Padric's sister, Mairead, is the assistant editor.

"Red sky in morning, sailor's warning; red sky at night, sailor's delight" – common phrase used as a rule of thumb for weather forecasting but also a line from an ancient rhyme used by mariners. Jesus is quoted in Matthew 16: 2-3 as saying: "When it is evening, you say, 'It will be fair weather; for the sky is red' And in the morning, 'It will be stormy today, for the sky is red and threatening.' Shakespeare remarks in his Venus and Adonis (1593): "Like a red morn that ever yet betokened, Wreck to the seaman, tempest to the field, Sorrow to the shepherds, woe unto the birds, Gusts and foul flaws to herdmen and to herds."

"Are people really affected by the moon?" – Magdalen asks this of Sister Barbara, scientist and in-house genius at San Miguel. The nun gives a good enough answer but many question this. If the moon influences the tides and we are considered to be 75 percent water, would there not be, at such times, something at work within us?

12 A BAD GOOD FRIDAY

"Sister's here." Magdalen would remember later she'd said this. "You'll see, she's in the vestry…all is quiet." In Padric's line of work, quiet and dark were not always a good thing, *but it's a church, for God's sake, what could happen?* His eyes searched the shadows…*nothing. She may be right.* Magdalen smiled. "Stay…you must say a prayer for your Lara and the girls, then go straight home." *Sister Moira, telling me what to do.*

He wasn't leaving.

A hint of incense still lingered. Peaceful. A change was stirring inside him, but the altar peered back, drawing him in, pleading for him to come closer. Though the detective hadn't set foot in its shadows for years, he knew this church. Was it needing him now? Padric stood up. Following Magdalen with his eyes, he walked down the side aisle. She was approaching the sacristy door but before he could warn her, she'd glanced back and saw what he saw.

The detective had been an altar boy here. What were the chances he'd be walking around in the dark and facing off with some undefined evil twenty years later. This didn't happen in the Cathedral of San Miguel.

But it was…a sinister, grotesque, unseemly sight; Padric was oddly searching his mind for more words to describe it…a dark shape swayed back and forth above the side altar where earlier Magdalen and the elder had observed a bird fall to its death. Now she was walking slowly toward it. There was no time for Padric to shield her eyes; she cried out.

The lieutenant leaped over the communion rail. Before them, hung an image so macabre it would never be erased from their memory. "Padric to dispatch…I need a bus now at the fucking Cathedral. I need everything!" For the second time in one day, he coded Martinez. Uniforms in the courtyard, hearing his call, burst through the door. Someone had tampered with the panel and circuit breakers; with no light, he drew his 9mm and swept the sacristy, kicking open the vestry door. Nothing. The officers were already clearing the nave of the Cathedral; soon the clamor of back up heightened the tension.

Pistasio and his squad came out of nowhere; as Padric reentered the sanctuary he could smell it. Every cop knew what it was; he was stepping in it; blood oozed from the side altar onto the marble floor. What he saw was not possible, too horrific. "Holy Mary!" He glanced at Magdalen; so very still, motionless, eyes fixed.

She found her voice: "Not like this! Get her down!"

"Step back, Sister!" Padric was face to face with a first.

The cross, with no corpus of Christ affixed to it, was suspended by a single huge chain; back and forth, it swung like a pendulum. The body of a nun, arms at her side, her holy habit wrapped tightly around her with duct tape, hung bound to it like a cocoon…upside down. Though wounds appeared shallow, blood oozed from her bindings and the gashes in her feet…long narrow nails protruded from them, others were scattered all over the floor.

Someone had tried to crucify Petra.

Lack of time had apparently thwarted their plan. Nothing, no hammer or mallet, knives, rolls of tape, could be found. The sacrilege of it all stunned Padric. Petra's white coif was still wrapped loosely round her head, now soaked in blood; her long, black veil trailing slowly back and forth in the blood on the altar as the cross swayed from side to side. The nun's eyes and mouth had been covered in tape.

And there it was…that signature bite mark; Petra's bodice ripped open, breasts partially exposed like Lara's. "One and the same," Padric muttered aloud. *Joanna.* He tried to cover the nun but the weight of her body suddenly forced the cross to slip in its chain dangerously close to the altar, the crown of her head almost grazing it now. Magdalen, frustrated, reached up but slipped and fell back on the marble floor. It was too hard to bear…she doubled over in pain, wept aloud, but when the cross jerked and slipped lower, she rose to her feet.

"She can't die. Is she dead? Lord, take me, not her!"

Padric leaped onto the altar, struggling to steady the still swaying cross, his strength no match for the weight of the wood as it swung away and returned. He checked the nun's pulse. "She's bleeding out…we're losing her. She may be gone already." But again Magdalen was lost to him; she sank to the floor but Padric barked: "Get your ass over here, Sister…your nun needs you! Up, woman! Talk to her…let her hear you!"

His voice brought her back and Magdalen straightened. He leaped from the altar allowing others to detach and lower the cross with Petra still on it to the cold, marble floor. But he had no time to stop an out-of-control Magdalen who, lost in her grief, was suddenly beating on his chest with her fists.

"You should have made an arrest by now; none of this would have happened! Damn you, Detective! She was my Sister. I promised her! I told her I'd keep her safe." With all her strength, Magdalen slapped him hard in the face. Stunned, Padric visualized arresting the good Sister for striking a police officer. But she was still talking: "What's the matter with you; do your fucking job! I promised her…I promised."

She sobbed aloud as more detectives arrived from Homicide and a criminal apprehension team entered the Cathedral; uniforms flooded the complex; fire trucks, already lining the Plaza, were blocking the streets in downtown L'Arroyo…no exit, no entrance. Padric would risk it and threw his arms around Magdalen, tightening his grip, not letting her move, until she relaxed. "Quiet now, lass…" He waited. "I'm letting you go now…easy."

She fell silent, her heart pounding against his; suddenly feeling the beat of his heart, she stepped back, shocked at herself, the way she had acted. "I…I'm sorry, my God. Yes, of course; I must help."

She withdrew, disappearing into the sacristy where she scooped up boxes of candles and matches and hurried up the altar steps; soon the sanctuary was ablaze with an eerie glow. Padric resumed his efforts; others arrived; grim-faced, eyes saying things they could not utter aloud...most had responded that morning to the Padric residence and now here they were again; some, visibly shaken. A nun on a cross...this was worse; many made the sign of the cross. Some were former students of Petra's...they were Cathedral.

Two in one day...Lara, now this, Padric could hardly breathe. This was more than disturbing...he'd not been there to stop such disrespect to a woman like her.

Magdalen became quickly absorbed into the macabre as Petra was slowly removed from the cross but EMTs allowed her access. She bent over the body, her face almost touching her Sister's...if she could just will her back, breath her own life into her friend. The nuns' veils became oddly entwined, their blood co-mingling on each other's clothing. She would live...she must; *my Sister will live.* But how...she was blue, not a breath from her lips. And now someone had joined her and was kneeling beside her...the young sergeant she'd met at the juvenile detention center, whispering encouragement. Like a priest might do, he urged her to be strong and whispered a prayer over Petra.

"Jesús...Jesús Marcus, I remember. You are needed here."

He agreed. Magdalen stepped aside, receding into the wall, disappearing inside her soul, wanting it to be yesterday. She considered how unforgivable her conduct had been toward the detective; but such feelings had been simmering beneath her nun-façade for days. There had been no progress in the case of the moondead and now, it was no longer one of her mysteries, her own little romp; she should have been more in charge of her emotions; the Life demanded it.

But again the Cathedral doors opened. O'Manion was in the house. Statues in their niches challenged him; their eyes pleading for reverence; he would defy them and bellowed Padric's name for an update. A female officer sprinted up the sanctuary steps and made the sign of cross; she spotted Magdalen, alone, looking vulnerable, the First Precinct swarming around her.

"Officer Duran here. I was Cathedral once." Magdalen had heard this mantra at basketball games...code for school pride: "I am Cathedral! We are Cathedral!" She hadn't witnessed football under Friday-night-lights yet and could only imagine the spirit and uproar. She wondered if she might "be Cathedral" someday, but didn't her being the Cathedral's sacristan count for something?

"What a good Catholic girl you are, coming to a nun's rescue."

"You bet, Sister, but the hell of it is, she was my favorite teacher."

"And I'm sorry you have to see such things. Go, you can be of more help than I."

"Stay put...I'll return." *Stay put...*she hated staying put and wanted to wail like a waif in a war zone when the paramedics, attempting to stabilize Petra, found it futile and gradually began the slow process of bagging her body.

Martinez was suddenly there, having worked the crime scene at the Padric residence most of the day. She watched him make the sign of the cross and heard him say: "*Dios mio!* What happened?"

Padric's response was inaudible. Martinez turned. Magdalen. Their nun was standing in the shadows, clothes covered in blood, eyes full of pain and trying to hide it. He was horrified, hesitated; Padric nodded. "Go, man, she's pissed at me."

"She'll get over it." He slowly walked toward her and she rushed to him, both reassuring each other of prayers. Padric smiled a little; his partner did that better than he did. His call to the convent brought Agnes and Dolorosa, Patrice and Lucy, floating like angels into the Cathedral. None were strangers to suffering; but they stared in horror at their fallen Sister, at first hesitating then running to her, only to be gently pulled back by Duran. They were grateful she was there and embraced her, a Cathedral girl, class of 2008. She quickly gave them assurances. Lieutenant Padric would end this, she said; he'd speak with them soon. But Padric overheard what she said and wanted to run like a mountain lion into the hills.

When they saw Magdalen, disheveled and pale, they encircled her, allowing no one to come closer, but the quiet strength they knew and saw each day in her was back...they hadn't seen her at her worst. Now she was calming them. Both detectives witnessed the deference shown Magdalen and were relieved, even awed at their sense of community. But O'Manion, grumpy and out of sorts, wouldn't allow her to return home; she was the sacristan, first on the scene with Padric. There would be questions.

The detectives needed to do something Johnny Padric-style. Where was the bishop? Had his residence been compromised? A shout brought Martinez into the sacristy. a thud, the sound of splintering wood, a crash told him Padric was kicking in a door to the narrow hall Eduardo and Magdalen had used yesterday.

O'Manion fell in behind him. "There are keys for this kind of thing, dipshit!"

Once in the bishop's vestibule, Padric with Martinez ordered every exit secured but would not go to the infamous graveyard; he saw no need and wished later he had. Padric glanced up. At the top of a long staircase stood the bishop.

"Easy now, son," The Captain hated "conflagration", a word he used on occasion to describe the aftermath Padric would leave getting things done.

Santo Cantera was mildly appalled. "What is the First Precinct doing in my house?"

Steed appeared then Sebastian, the new priest. They'd heard the sirens, thrown on jeans and tee shirts. The new priest wasted no time, slipped passed the two and ran down the stairs; he nodded his thanks and bolted into the passageway. Padric smiled; a practical man. The other two now stood face to face with the detective. He'd omit telling them Marcus and Tark were slipping over the wall into his precious garden. "Your Cathedral is officially a crime scene…a homicide has occurred here, the victim now being prepped for removal." Silence. "We're here to execute a sweep of your house for your own safety." This was not a request.

Without a word, Padric pointed to the stairs; Martinez took them two at a time with some uniforms. Still trying to process the news, the bishop was amazed; the men had only needed the lieutenant's mere gesture. Only yesterday Santo Cantera had complained to Ramirez about his Precinct still "snooping about" his Cathedral. It was annoying, a nuisance, he' d said, but now he was confused now, what had this obnoxious detective said?

It was clear neither man liked each other. Done with the posturing, Steed disappeared into the Cathedral and the bishop continued to look with disdain at the over-zealous detective. These things happen…no need for the drama, he was saying. Surely one of the homeless dying before his time; an old woman down on her luck…this wasn't the first time they'd discovered an unfortunate in the Cathedral at dawn. "Where was this one found?"

This one. Padric walked away. "On a cross."

"*Dios mio.*" The bishop stared after him then followed him. At the sacristy door, he peered into the sanctuary, hesitating, unable to go any further…*my beautiful marble floor!* He eyed a silent, disheveled Magdalen, the blood spatter. "My Cathedral and, God in heaven, my sacristan…"

Now she was his? Padric was furious…*she's ours; the First Precinct's…my nun.* Magdalen would choose her own battles from this point and did not respond. The bishop walked quickly to the open body bag and fell to his knees, face ashen, shocked, but he immediately administered Last Rites and remained with Petra.

Sebastian had already hurled himself over the communion rail as Padric had done earlier; the detective spotted him…so this is the new boy. *Damn, he's looking like us.* Not trusting outside eyes and wanting his own answers, the priest moved from pillar to wall, alcove to niche, peering into the shadows and places most knew nothing about; he kicked open doors Padric never knew existed. He watched as Sebastian scaled a narrow staircase to a walkway circling the edge of the high ceiling above him. *How'd he do that?* Not sure what the police had done, the priest was determined to do something. He'd seen Petra's body.

When Tark and Marcus returned from a sweep of the garden and rooftops, he even questioned them like a battalion chief; they took no offense. Tark said he had *chutzpah* and could walk with them. The three joined Pistasio's squad already widening its search on foot, emptying Church Street of the curious, pulling others aside. Throwing the priest a bulletproof vest and some night goggles, the sergeant saw him as one of them but insisted he "hang back", explaining later to an irate O'Manion that a man of God might prove helpful if a talk-down was necessary besides, he had street cred'…he'd heard he fought in Fallujah. Padric had laughed out loud.

Back in the Cathedral, Bishop Cantera stood silent, thrown off balance by the assault on his kingdom; his fortress now bound up in crime tape. He finally disappeared into his comfort zone in the vestry and sat down at his table. No book, no martyrology, could comfort him. He snapped: "What is it now?" When Padric found him there.

The detective unloaded a list of "must dos"; the Cathedral and high school even the sports complex would be crime taped until further notice. Closed. The Precinct would be calling the shots now, he said, and ended with a volley of words, infuriating the man. "This happened on your watch…what do you know about this? Who might have had the balls and lack of respect to think they could do this in a Cathedral and to a nun no less?" Silence. "You know something, maybe not everything. But damn it, you know." Perhaps the final blow came when he said: "There will be a subsequent search of the cemetery below your residence."

The bishop paled. Padric had waited for this, taking note of the change when he mentioned the graveyard below, but the bishop said nothing and the detective's words would fester inside him.

How dare this arrogant know-it-all. He'd speak with the Commander about this pushy detective from Major Crimes.

But O'Manion and Padric had more to consider: the convent would need to be cleared; it would need a respectful man. Within seconds Martinez was dispatched to the Sister's home and Padric returned to the sanctuary where Magdalen paced back and forth, lost in her thoughts. He pointed to the pews.

"Sit down." She said no. "Say what?"

"I said no…I don't want to sit down. I'm not a child."

"Sister, I'm in charge. Remove yourself from the crime scene."

She backed down. "My apologies…you're right."

Padric generally got what he wanted from people and Magdalen knew it; now they were looking at yet another martyr murder. Petra had died like Saint Peter…he knew that much. *Sister Moira.*

"Talk to me." He said that a lot. Padric was now standing in the aisle beside her; though calm, she was looking uncomfortable, her clothes bloodied. He'd fix that. "Duran, front and center. Take the good Sister to bag her clothing for the lab and bring her back ASAP." Magdalen was furious all over again...she was being taken somewhere and brought back like a piece of baggage?

Duran was there in an instant. "Step aside, Lieutenant. You may talk to her when we return."

He wanted to laugh. Duran had a reputation for effectively controlling the moment; she was often impatient with what she called the inefficiency of the human male, even if they had more rank than she did. Within a half-hour, the two returned with evidence bag in hand; the nun in fresh garments.

They'd taken too long, Padric said. Annoyed, Duran shook her head...men needed to get it. She pointed to a pew. "You may sit down, Sister. Lieutenant, I am aware Sister is consulting on the case. At your command, I request to serve as her personal security detail since she's putting her ass on the line, would you agree?"

Magdalen hid her amusement but winced; they were discussing "her ass" like she wasn't there. The detective stared down at his shoes; the man never stared down at anything. *Why is it always these tiny women...Dolorosa now Duran, and there was his seventh grade nun, Sister Moira, all of them four-foot-five, hell-bent on keeping me in line?*

"Much appreciated, Officer. But keep it at a distance for at least fifteen minutes."

"Certainly, sir. I will stand by."

But the man was showing signs of wear; the knee-breaking shock of his wife's attack, his home in chaos. Magdalen motioned him closer. "Come...sit for a moment."

He ventured to speak: "What happened with this one, Sister?"

"They're getting bolder, acting out with such violence here in a church, using it like a theater, but this time, they did a clumsy job replicating the death of Saint Peter. Sister's name's from the Greek, *Petros*, means "the rock", and refers to the apostle, as you know."

"Right...he was crucified upside down." *Sister Moira.* "He believed he wasn't worthy to die like Christ; he wanted it this way."

"Exactly…some will dispute the motives and his manner of dying but that's one of the more common traditions. But do you need me? The intent is quite clear here." She waited; he said nothing, thinking other things. "I'm sorry…you are not looking well."

From the pew, he studied the crime scene. "I'm dead inside and trying to act like something matters."

Magdalen whispered: "This has been a difficult day for you all around…but if I could. In the small window of opportunity they had, how did our Sister's attackers do all they did? Hoisting a body up on a cross, binding the victim…how?"

"It was in and out, skillfully pre-meditated. And now you challenge our efficiency. You don't think this was not one of our first questions? We get it. They have access; gain entrance from the inside when we are surrounding them on the outside. Is the bishop himself letting them in through the sacristy door and saying: "Hi, and how the hell are you?" I don't know that…yet. Do they enter in a way I'm not seeing? Is it from below or are they dropping down from above through a hole used by owls? I'm not sure. There's a tunnel from that fucking graveyard to the old gravedigger's house in the alley, Sister. Maybe that's it and we're on it. I wait for reports. We breakdown crime scenes in five minutes for a living! This will take longer."

She had pushed…he had silenced her. Duran returned, looking from one to the other. *Jesus, what's up with them?* Magdalen's eyes asked her to wait. She withdrew.

The nun would be careful. "You are seeing things more clearly."

"You mean the way you want me to see them."

She told him what she had seen in the garden…the eyes peering back at her. Upset, he said if she'd called him, he could have…

"Please…could have done what, in what year and with what search warrant?" It was cold; she didn't care. "Protocol, you will say. My Sisters are relentless with questions, never letting me rest and God forgive me for complaining; but they look to me to somehow settle this; do I not grieve as well. I am so angry." They glared at each other but her voice softened. "I've been thinking…"

And suddenly O'Manion was having a tantrum. Padric ignored

him. "The bite marks, more than one, on our Sister's breast, the hypersexual component."

"Yes, the same I found on my wife."

"This is so over the top; yet great effort has been taken to keep Sister modest; tape binds her holy habit around her, when she could have been very exposed."

"The two approach the same victim differently. I know this. They offset each other."

"One neurosis dovetails the other; and they are related, close."

He stared at her. "You may be right. We've discussed this before though…our dominant male, delusional, idealistic…"

"But the roles are reversed in your wife's assault…the male wants nothing to do with it, the female vents; it is unscripted. His intent is cerebral; her's emotional."

Joanna. He was sure of it now…but the other? *Someone close, another Cantera; I'll kill them both.* She tried to tell him again of the bookmarked martyrology linked to each killing, the presence she sensed in the sacristy…he wasn't listening. O'Manion was louder, more adamant. Padric stood up. "I don't want you to be afraid anymore." He walked away, sounding like he was somewhere else. But he turned and looked at her. "It goes to show you what a little religion can do to some people." He didn't wait for a response.

Magdalen closed her eyes. *Go, go, do what you must, John Padric. Let me hear bells; the bells have been silent today; Good Friday, yes, I know, but my Savior, let them toll for my Sister. Holy angels, be with us tonight and with my Petra.* But whispers and a sound at the side door made her turn; her students stood, staring, in awe. Ben and Danny with several girls, even small, quiet Julie moved closer; they were horrified, the boys trying hard not to show it.

What time was it…what were they doing? Magdalen confronted them. "This is a crime scene. Please go. Leave at once."

Ben was adamant. "Then what are *you* doing here…are you okay?" The students crowded around her; girls hugged her. One of them stroked her veil like she would a friend's hair, her eyes full of concern. "We will help…what can we do?"

My God, they want to help…the death of innocence.

"Who's dead…it's one of our nuns, isn't it?" *Our nuns.*

Magdalen hesitated; such news would be too harsh. "I cannot say; you will know soon enough. The school will be closed for several days with all that has happened; perhaps we can talk then… I'm sorry." They were stunned; their nun had seen horrible things.

"Look at the time. What are you doing out in the street?"

"We went to a late movie at Esplano Mall and had pizza." *So much for Good Friday*…she looked from one to the other.

Danny asked how all this could happen in a church. "Are you sure you're okay? I'm just saying, Sister, this town is different… things happen here." Again…would she come with them to see the Church of Bones.

That's all I need. "Soon, Danny, soon." But she thought for a moment. "When?"

The boys grinned. "There's no school next week, let's do it."

"Let me think; now get out of here, all of you."

"Later…we'll check in on you to see how you're doing." *To see how I'm doing. Goodness.* But one of the girls gasped. "Look, Ben, there's your hero!"

Magdalen turned…*and who would that be? There are still heroes alive and well in L'Arroyo?* Only Padric was standing in the center aisle talking with Duran. *Ah, yes, and why not?* "Students, wait!"

But they were already standing in front of him, one begging to interview him for the school newspaper. Even Julie forgot her usual decorum. "Sir, are you truly our city's Batman?" She reminded him of his oldest daughter and he smiled a little.

Duran however would step in and speak for the man. "He is, young lady, but the winged one is busy." She pointed to the side door and politely told them to get lost.

But Ben was bursting to speak. Padric needed a little distraction. "What is it, lad?"

"I play safety like you did. I'm a Coyote."

Padric shook his hand. "So you're good at disrupting the pass then." Ben was ecstatic. "Like you were…I run it back; we score. I'm all over. Coach showed us film of you…all the old guys." Padric chuckled. The boy realized what he said; Julie, horrified.

Ben pushed on: "Would you come to one of our games?"

The detective would learn Ben's father had left hearth and home years ago. He said he would…he could do with some old time school spirit, but hoped his new fan would never learn of his sins. Magdalen thanked him with her eyes and hustled them through the side door; they backtracked and blended into the crowd edging the crime tape around the Cathedral.

Gazing sadly down at the convent of San Miguel, a Good Friday moon in mourning bowed to the elder who had not moved from the window. She knew; her lips moved silently: *Petra, my Petra…mercy, sweet Jesus. Magdalen, come to me soon.* She has seen her only briefly when she, bloodied and tired, had returned to change. But now Monica's prayers resonated deep in the sacristan's soul…*I must go to her soon; tell her everything, let her know another bird has fallen to the cold marble floor in the sanctuary.* But like a sentinel, she would not leave the side of her Sister and whispered to her in her soul.

Milleau arrived. Padric launched into a rant…where the hell had he been? With his usual calm, the young CSI said he'd been at the Drambuie. Padric exploded…out on the town when he needed him most. Milleau was expressionless when he explained what had gone down at the upscale establishment. While enjoying cocktails together, Judge Sanville and his stripper-mistress were offed by his wife, plain and simple. A fitting end, some had said. Processing the scene had been a challenge, took a while. Padric rolled his eyes; damn his and her Honor. "Mr. Milleau; are you with me?"

The handsome, young man with dark eyes slid his glasses to the end of his nose and surveyed the scene. "Always, sir." He looked around. "Very interesting."

What did he say? "*Bhoyo*, this is not interesting…it's not an archaeological dig." He insisted the young man give it his best 'go'. "Harvest everything!"

Milleau smiled. "Good word…harvest. As you wish, oh, great One. Though you know everyone's sloshed their way through the crime scene by now."

"Good word…sloshed; regardless, on your way!" Milleau pushed his glasses back on his nose and walked off, gloves in one hand, forensic case in the other. Padric liked him; he could multitask like an ant, according to his father, himself an anthropologist and son-in-law of the famous Dr. Jameson, archaeologist-turned-city planner and founder of early L'Arroyo. It was all in the family. Padric thought of Magdalen...she'd like Jon-Gabriel Milleau.

But now Dolorosa had returned to remain with Magdalen; they withdrew into the shrine of Saint Michael the Archangel, finding rest under his huge sculpted wings and surprised when the new priest approached. He was tall and athletic with dark hair and eyes...a serious man, not flustered by what he saw. Magdalen tried to explain: "It's not one of our better moments, Father Michelantonio." She said he had come at a terrible time.

"Then it's the right time and I'm glad to be here...call me Sebastian." The nuns glanced at each other. The three would be friends. "Tell me what this is about." The nuns spoke of each victim; his eyes darker now, thinking: what language is this...*martyr murders* and *moondead*? He stared at the body bag; they told him of their love for Petra, who she was.

Padric joined them, was introduced. He knew Sebastian had been more than a priest somewhere else. "Marines."

"You're good, Detective. 1st Regiment, infantry, urban combat; Fullujah. And ISIS, as we speak, makes me think it was all for nothing...friends died there. I still hope."

Padric liked him. "You're here now and your Iraq was my Panama. Pendleton, been there, then Panama, Operation Just Cause. Saw most of it from a LAV-25. Looked like you were clearing the street back there. Fallujah was 2005, how'd you make priest so fast?"

"Long story...we'll talk, Detective. We're both from the other side of the pond...Italy for me and is that County Antrim I'm hearing? We need to be doing something greater than this. The violence done to our Sister here was over the top." *Our Sisters*...the two nuns were grateful. Though different in appearance, the two Europeans were alike, perhaps opposite sides of the same playing card. Sebastian stepped away and slowly approached Petra's body, praying over her, making the sign of the cross.

But Padric had spotted the bishop at the Cathedral entrance;

he would be closing the doors and not feeling good about it; his demeanor had changed. Padric would tone down his rhetoric.

"Someone lives in your choir loft?" Uniforms had reported as much to Padric.

The bishop was now more amenable: "Ah…Lupe! Though I've offered her lodging in my residence or anywhere else she wishes, our caretaker lives under the bells, a choice made many years ago; she wouldn't take *no* when I opposed it. Though we men take care of ourselves, she insists on cooking and cleaning for us several times a week; taking her meals with us in my residence or wherever she wishes." Padric knew now…Lupe had witnessed the attack on the nun.

The convent…he wondered how that was going. Agnes had complied when Padric requested access for a sweep of the convent. Uneasy and wanting to show no disrespect, Martinez was directing a room-to-room search. On the second floor, he was deeply moved; in the dark, at the end of the hall, Monica sat at the window seat with Maryjohn beside her…it was past three in the morning.

They had remained there throughout the night, keeping watch and praying their beads. The elder and her companions wished him well through their tears and he respectfully explained what he must do. But he paused when he came upon a room with Magdalen's name in very small print on the door. He thought twice before entering her space; it seemed too invasive.

He placed his hand on the doorknob; he'd give it a quick glance and move on, but once inside, Martinez was astounded at the austerity. He looked slowly around the cell, as the nuns' rooms were called…*nada*, nothing except books, a well-made bed and brown woolen blanket; a small closet with very few garments and chest of drawers which he refused to open. Her books were piled high in a bookcase; a narrow bathroom with shower adjoined the next room; on its door, Dolorosa's name…they were bathroom buddies. He smiled.

He was touched when he saw the picture of Christ crowned with thorns. There was peace here; it was fragrant…a scent of clean linen and soap.

"Suffering Jesus, is this our nun's?" Calm vanished; Padric was standing behind him, noting everything in the room of a nun for whom he had a growing affection. Here was her chair, the table where she sat at when unable to sleep; he walked to the window and looked into the garden then studied the image of a thorn-crowned Jesus over her bed. "How poor she is. I wish I could…"

Martinez hustled him into the hall. "No, you don't Johnny. Let her be…leave it. She chose this; she's at peace here. Do not…I'm telling you this once, do not even mention to her that you and I saw this. So help me God, I'll slam you if you get cozy with her. Don't go telling this woman everything you want to do for her. I know you. Back off."

Padric frowned, stepped back; his man was right. "I feel like I'm sinning just standing here." They finished the sweep. Padric paused to speak with the nuns. And there was the elder. He knelt down beside her, this woman he'd seen from a distance. They spoke briefly but her presence mystified him; she said she was from Ireland. He would return, he said…they would speak more; the elder nodded. "I know." He smiled…just like our nun.

Later, Magdalen would discover the detectives had been in her room. She understood then why they had been so attentive to her when they returned to the Cathedral. It was embarrassing; they had invaded the only personal space she could call her own and that was even on loan. But Petra had suffered far worse and she said nothing. The simplicity had stunned Padric; he knew they had no luxury but damn, there was nothing that spoke to the woman she was…his wee daughters would never be nuns, he'd see to it.

Finally the moment came for their Sister to leave the Cathedral. Magdalen wanted to keep her, take her home, lay her down safe in her bed, sit down beside her and wait for her to awake. As if in a dream, removing Petra's body from the Cathedral turned into a funeral procession. It was Padric who led with the gurney, guiding it out of the Cathedral and through the side door to the medical examiner's van. Activity ceased; first-responders stood at attention, the body moved silently passed them.

Magdalen glanced at Dolorosa. "Her Sisters should take her from the Cathedral."

Both took their places on either side of the gurney, clutching its rails, falling in step with the others; they stared straight ahead. But Magdalen could feel Petra's presence, tugging at her. Dolorosa did, too. Outside, the media was everywhere, calling out to the detectives and nuns. When Padric raised his hand for order…a stillness fell over the crowd and spread like a shroud over the Plaza. Time stopped.

At her window, the elder rose to her feet as the body bag appeared in the moonlight. Padric glanced up…the holy seraph he saw at each crime scene had been replaced; the old nun would watch over the dead tonight. Magdalen and Dolorosa turned and bowed; she acknowledged their gesture, her eyes like two burning coals searing into the detective's soul. He'd taken care of things, no eagle this time; simply a nun. Padric's eyes scanned the rooftops. Nothing.

When he looked back; she was gone from the window and shouts from hard-nosed newsman and unfeeling bystanders resumed; there was no stopping them now until Petra's body was solemnly lifted into the coroner's van. Petra had once taught a dozen or more of the firemen and officers and now they stood silent, hats in their hand. Magdalen stepped forward. "I can't let her leave like this; I must go with her."

"Sister." Padric clasped her cold hands in his. "I don't ride with the deceased as a rule, but tonight I'll be your Sister's personal escort and guardian for the rest of her journey." Unknown to the two, TV cameras were rolling: a photographer captured the nun, up close and personal, with the well-known lieutenant…it would make the front-page of the morning edition.

She reluctantly withdrew her hands. "I'm ashamed at my own weakness and hope I didn't hurt you back there…my apologies."

"That medical wagon came for me, too. My pain's on you, Sister. I'll get myself checked in at Meadow." He winked.

But Magdalen was insistent. "Take care of her, please." Both were weary; Padric's heart heavy…two crime scenes in less than twenty-four hours, his wife, alive; the other, a nun and now she was one of the moondead…*la luna muerta.*

"Hey, rock star!" Declan Brady. Padric tried to smile; his wife's face flashed before him. The weight of all she had endured had been diverted into all that had happened here.

He jumped into the van. But there was a shout. "I'm in! Bishop's orders and my wanting it! Let's roll!" Padric pulled the young priest aboard.

"Declan, lad, meet the new padre, Father Sebastian."

"Men of God are welcome…you talk better, Father, to both living and dead."

"Well, what it is then, Declan? I'll do the praying regardless."

Accompanied by several police vans, they moved into the night looking like a funeral *cortège*. Padric looked at Brady. "Twice in one day, lad. Does this mean we're a couple?"

Declan said he'd rather date his girlfriend's Aunt Maude as he unzipped the body bag.

"No problem." Padric leaned closer.

"I assume nothing…we may have a live one, no disrespect."

"And thank God for that, Mr. Brady…I need some good news."

"Ay, and it'll be a Guinness next time, I'm hoping. I'll check her vitals." Nothing.

The three gazed down at the still face, strangely beautiful. They rode in silence but as they approached the morgue, Declan pressed his fingers against the nun's neck, leaned his ear close to her heart. "Bloody hell! I've got her…she's back!" It was code; banging his fist once on the wall of the cab, he yelled to the driver: "Move it, *bhoyo,* move your arse!" Only Billy Kelly could make his EMV fly; some said the wheels left the ground when no one was looking. Sebastian made the sign of the cross over Petra.

Speechless for several minutes, Padric finally whispered: "Come on, Sister…come on. Show us you want to be with us… come back!" Nothing. "Your girl, Magdalen, needs you."

Petra's eyes opened. He drew back. She turned her head. "Detective?" He was ashen…talking to the dead, not his *forte*. "Tell my Magdalen I will be home soon." He said nothing, but brushed away tears when the nun whispered: "And Lara, your wife, will recover." He smiled until she added: "But not before suffering the pain of knowing." She closed her eyes.

Padric could hardly breathe. "Sister?" *Where'd you go, woman?* "Where'd she go?" The men stared at her then at each other; *the pain of knowing...Joanna.* "Sister, talk to me."

"Shhh, quietly; you must behave now, John Padric." Padric wanted to hide under the gurney...*she comes back from the dead and like that, knows my name, damn.* Sebastian started to laugh but tried to contain himself; Declan chuckled. Padric could only stare at the nun. It was his turn to be dead. *Joanna. My Lara will know soon enough.*

"Where are we taking her then?"

"Here. The ME can do this...he's as good with the living as he is with the dead. They have the equipment then she can go to Meadow." Evidently this happened a lot; they all spoke at once, but were silenced. The nun who had died raised her hand for silence.

"Make a decision, gentlemen, or I will pass on." Petra had spoken. She told them to hush and again closed her eyes. Padric would recover but was ecstatic...something good, a miracle maybe. Surely it was the priest who'd raised the good nun from the dead. He found himself praying but he'd done this too often in the past twenty-four and now he'd been told to shape up by someone thought to be dead. The van rolled to a stop.

Never did a morgue look so inviting. L'Arroyo, though remote, had a huge medical complex of hospitals and research buildings, standing tall and alone on the edge of the desert. It was often the last port of call for those set upon by dark deeds done in the Sonoran; victims once lost but still clinging to life, Padric glanced toward Meadow; his woman was there but he would focus on this one; with Sebastian he accompanied Petra into the receiving room.

Both slipped on scrubs and nodded to Rubin, the Deputy M. E. for Major Crimes. A long-time friend of Padric's; he had often shared with him more than one shot of Jameson at the Dragoon, a notorious hangout for the medical world of L'Arroyo. But this morgue was not the pristine space seen in *CSI: Miami.* The room swarmed with student-interns, eager to work with the renowned doctor; it had been a busy night and he was as always eloquent.

"Ah, the pride of the First Precinct is with us, boys and girls. And God bless us, with a priest no less...a welcome to good Father

Sebastian. Introductions later, I'm afraid. Let's mind our manners, children, and say nothing about how bad the detective looks or where all that blood came from. Not to worry, he cleans up nicely."

Padric gave him a nod. Often after a homicide, Padric would burst through the door asking questions. Rubin was always good for some standup comedy, but tonight, the ME quickly confirmed the nun's resurrection. "Who says it isn't Easter, children! And we'll give a nod to Passover as well." He never barked orders, but quietly murmured his wishes and all was done with light speed. "Get a move on and sing Alleluia! And that was for you, John, a fine Irish Catholic. A miracle then." Again Padric nodded his gratitude.

Granted, most morgues were quiet and sane, but this one had a swinging door with no down time on a Friday night. The staff enjoyed Rubin, a devout Jew spouting the Christian thing and living on hope and serenity. They now moved quickly to stabilize Petra, placing her on life support in an adjacent rose-colored room, set apart for the unexpected. Hovering over the nun like angels, two forensic anthropology students made her their mission.

It was not the first time Rubin had helped raise the dead. But how many times could Padric's heart pound in his chest like this in one day? It had been like no other. Her wounds horrific, the nun would undergo extensive surgery; both she and Lara would heal in protective custody at Meadow for some time and until their killers were caught.

But it was Padric's wife who was in more danger. Late night TV news said she had rallied; surely her attackers knew of this now, but no one would hear a word about Petra. His thoughts on rewind, he reviewed what had gone down in the Cathedral…and there was Magdalen. He'd never held a nun close before, calmed one down like he did several hours ago. He would have preferred to have done a John Garfield and swept her away with a kiss but he knew himself all too well and could understand how she may have had difficulties with more than a few men if they were like him.

He didn't know she'd been detained at the Cathedral when, without the Commander and Captain present, a stone-faced Internal Affairs pitbull had questioned her for over an hour; he'd taken a decided interest in the actions of Lieutenant John Padric then left. Dolorosa, sitting nearby in a pew, would say later, it had been spooky. "I wanted to wail on his uptight ass!" and Martinez had laughed but was furious and let the Commander know it after he accompanied both nuns back to the convent.

But before closing the convent door, the young CSI Jon-Gabriel Milleau, had appeared on the step, with his sympathies. He had moved silently about the sanctuary and occasionally, had glanced at Magdalen with concern. Now they spoke again, sharing some of their history in Egypt, for he had studied there, too. She had smiled and was reluctant to see him leave but they would become friends and become a team in the months to come for the First Precinct.

It was early morning when Magdalen lay her head on the pillow to sleep, unaware an ME's van with a precious treasure was gliding quietly into a receiving bay with staff waiting to hurry Petra up to surgery. Despite his protests and pleading to accompany the nun into the O. R., Padric was stopped at the double doors.

Sebastian pulled him away and the Captain grunted: "Absolutely nothing to the media about this good nun's resurrection." He went off on the assailant they knew nothing about, his insights unique. "The dominant is wacked. He's psycho-bleach, wanting it pure." The good man needed a bagel. When Martinez arrived he complained about Magdalen being questioned and Padric raged all over again.

They waited. Neither detective spoke for some time then motioned for Sebastian to join them. The two asked if he'd be their next Precinct chaplain since Father Santeresa's advanced age was prompting him to step down. The priest said he would with the bishop's okay and they grinned.

When Martinez muttered they needed to nail the killers, Padric agreed.

"Alex…go home. I'll find a way and kill them myself."

The priest said nothing. These men too were victims; he asked how bad a town could L'Arroyo be, to need such a high security hospital. Padric explained. "The FBI has two agents on duty here with an office on the fifth floor. There's no one better than Bobby

Watson…he's our man with the Bureau; we hate the rest of them." Padric apologized and pointed to Gina as she hurried about, concerned as much for them as for the two new patients. "Interesting about Gina, she's law enforcement like us, but loves medicine and good at it. She wears two hats here. Her gangbanger brothers hate that she's on the side of the law…they love her and keep a distance with what they lay down every night in the streets."

When CSI arrived to consult with the ME at the morgue, one of Pistasio's men told them Dr. Rubin would speak with them later but for now, they should stay with the evidence they had. Milleau winked at Miller: "She made it."

His words echoed those of the doctor's as they emerged from the O. R. with Petra. The surgeon had been on the same hurling team with Padric for years; he looked tired but grinned. "She made it off the table."

The detectives were ecstatic. "Doc, you're the man!"

The doctor pointed heavenward. Further discussion revealed the severity of her wounds and what the surgeons had needed to do. The nun would be long in healing and Padric was looking for payback. Father gave her his blessing. When the men were given the nod, Martinez left. Padric could wait no longer. "Father?"

"I know, Detective, your wife…where is she? They'll let me in."

"Damn…you threw that collar and black shirt on pretty fast. How'd you do that?"

"It's a mystical thing with us; a Celt like yourself should know this stuff." They laughed and ran down the backstairs, but Gina was now at her post and not just anyone could walk on the floor…she was a hawk when it came to her patients and Lara was that.

She knew Padric's ways and shook her head. "Father, did he put you up to this?"

"No, ma'am. I don't take orders from the lieutenant." She stared at him. "A simple request then: could the man not be in the same room with his wife for a few minutes…the detective's borne enough for three men today." She protested. "Is he not deserving of some comfort? Surely John can at least look at his wife from the doorway" Silence. "I am anointing his wife. Surely you understand more than most. Give me this." It was not a request.

Damn, he has the art of persuasion down; Padric was no longer the only charmer in town and had found an ally and this was all a bad dream; his wife, aged forty-three, was being anointed; this happened when a person was old.

But he had to smile…Gina for once had been thrown off her game; the priest had taken it to her. She shook her finger at Padric; he winked nevertheless and followed the priest as the other nurses grinned and hid themselves in their medical charts.

He would watch from the door as the priest drew from his pocket, a small case for the sacrament of anointing; on the bed stand, he placed a vial of holy oil, a small cross and candle though it would remain unlit due to the oxygen being administered to Lara. "From now on, I'm carrying this everywhere…looks like I'll need it in this town."

He made the sign of the cross with the oil on Lara's forehead. "Through this holy anointing, may the Lord in his love and mercy help you with the grace of the Holy Spirit." Padric listened to the prayers, every syllable. The priest cross-signed her hands and feet with oil. "May the Lord who frees you from sin; save you and raise you up." He turned and asked Padric to kneel that he might anoint him as well. The detective fell to his knees; he too was sick in his soul and after, shook the priest's hand.

Sebastian could see the turmoil within. "Stay for a while with this woman who loves you. She's the one…not those fifty others."

The priest left; on Padric's orders, a uniform on staff took him home. *Those fifty others…damn.* Alone now, he stared at the machines and blinking lights. Exhausted, he sat down on Lara's bed, hoping with contrite kisses to revive her, pleading with her to come back to him. Later Pistasio, never too far away, came to check on him.

He and Padric would shower at the Precinct; he'd hit a few stores for surprises. It was noon when his two wee girls heard his key in the latch; they squealed with delight as he came through the door with two huge stuffed bears. His sister and he had always been close…he'd dragged her everywhere with him when they were children and now her arms were around him, telling him she knew everything. At the newspaper, she'd gone over the facts again and again. But now there would be wee ones to care for…she could do both, would have two offices now; the huge desk in her bedroom would be put to good use. When he saw her determination, Padric's burdens fell away and he listened. She was in charge now; her home would be his home, his girls had a nest for as long as he liked. They'd need family around them, would bring their mum to the States. Fiona and Mary, their younger sisters, must join them but would there be room?

Of course, Mairead had said, always for family. She explained a fellow journalist, madly in love with a woman in Guadalajara, had unloaded his '3BDRw.loft' on her for a steal. It would work. But Padric would need to explain to his daughters where their mother was. After a discussion on the floor of Mairead's living room and sitting next to an overstuffed Pooh, the girls said *they* would take care of him but laid down a few rules.

They demanded he come home after work; none of "this staying away" like he'd done with their mom. Kate and Kara, ages seven and four respectively, wanted answers: what had he been doing? Did he think they were stupid…*their words?*

He stared at them dumbfounded; John Padric rarely did that. And there was more: they'd look after him while the doctor "took care of mommy"; it was too much and he wept, holding them close for a very long time; his daughters content to stay very still in his arms. Sister and brother looked at each other; he, wondering if his children, because they *were* children, had the power to heal his cold, jaded heart and not even know they were doing it. He would behave, as Petra wished, as his girls had asked him to do. He looked down at their faces full of trust, looking up at him. Lara had brought them up well; they were resilient like she was. How little he'd done for them in their young lives and he wondered how they could even love him at all. But he could not allow them to be burdened with caring for him. "Lasses, your da' can look after himself. I'm taking care of you; Auntie Mairead, too, and granny will come live with us." They shrieked with delight, clapped their hands. But Kate would not let him forget.

"Remember, da'…no staying away. Not with us, you don't."

Padric was ashamed. "How old are you, Kate?" She said nothing. "Answer now, girl."

"Old enough, da'...I'm seven going on eight in a minute."

"Watch your tongue now...old enough for what?"

"To know you don't always behave and you must." *Behave...* again he was hearing it.

"Kara doesn't understand, you know; but I do."

His youngest disagreed. "I do understand stuff. Be good."

How could he argue with that? He held them closer. "I'm sorry...I'm sorry." He ate nothing Mairead set before him and was full of apologies. She said she understood, but what had her older brother been up to...*damn him!*

She knew he'd fess up soon enough and showed him his own space in the loft; warm and inviting like Lara would have done. But no, he said, the girls couldn't sleep in the room at the bottom of the stairs; he needed them near him. They must sleep in wee beds next to his...he'd buy them today.

He eyed the huge pillows and laughing, fell onto the bed. In an instant his eyes were heavy, his body sinking under the weight of all that had happened. His daughters bound up the stairs with their bears and a basket of Lalaloopsies...they knew what to do, having done it so many times with their mother and pulled off his boots. While they played quietly beside him, he drifted off into sleep. Mairead eventually went downstairs and wept by the window; sister and brother had suffered much in their younger years back in Belfast...now this.

Later he awoke; silence...his girls! The past forty-eight had turned him into a monster, protecting his loved ones with his life was all he could think of; he was frantic. He called out. No answer. He looked over the loft rail, Mairead smiled up at him. Her nieces were napping beside her. He glanced at his watch; it was four in the morning in Belfast. His mother would be sitting in front of the teli'...she never slept.

"Mum, apologies. Bad news, I'm afraid." He gave her few details. Upset and already making her plans, Darragh Padric hung up the phone and called out to her daughters who were leaving for work. They were in shock, but they loved Arizona and Johnny. "If we go, mum...we're stayin'."

Darragh Brannigan Padric looked out the window of her small flat on Clonard and wistfully gazed up at the spires of the Redemptorist monastery; she had tears in her eyes. She'd gone to Mass every morning there and now she wondered if she'd ever come back to Falls Road and West Belfast. Padric sent her a "grand sum", as she called it, and an old republican comrade of her husband's made all the arrangements for her to go to her boy in the States; her youngest, Mary and Fiona, would join her later.

She'd leave the only world she had known but not before making a final visit to Milltown Cemetery. The patriots rested here; as a young girl she'd listened to them, as a woman, walking beside them during the Conflict. Darragh paused only briefly at her husband's tombstone and moved on to the patriot graves. She stood watch for thirty minutes at the resting places of Mairead Farrell and Hunger Striker Bobby Sands then knelt down, listening to unseen souls and their whispers. She'd bring them with her into the desert.

Her son with his girls and Mairead waved at her when she arrived at Sky Harbor Airport only to be subjected to a few questions despite her dual citizenship. "My boy's a copper and standing right over there. Jaysus! We're not carryin' Armalite." But the young woman working for Homeland Security didn't know what Armalite was.

Padric called Liam, wanting him to come to L'Arroyo sooner than planned. The priest sensed his conflict, but his studies and ministry were keeping him in the city by the bay. He shook his head and laughed when his brother, Johnny, told him he wanted him to meet Sister Magdalen.

How had a rogue, if ever there was one, made friends with a nun? But his brother was not feeling roguish. He stared into oncoming traffic as he drove to the Precinct with no will to do what he must. He'd say out loud what was smoldering inside him, knowing he could be nailed for complicity. He would recuse himself from the case.

Briefing for Major Crimes would be much later tonight; it was near six in the evening and he'd sooth the ache with an hour of down time and stepped into the street with Detective Tarkington for some food at the Dirty Rice. It smelled and sounded like Bourbon Street. Needing their Saturday night fix, they sat down in their usual corner in the gumbo shop-jazz bar; Tark's home away from home; Padric, the only one invited to share it. Both loved Bayou food, but even more the tunes of an old, gnarled twig of a man, who played a horn like Miles Davis; his sounds, full of bebop and hard bop and a little jazz-fusion. Batiste did it all day and all night like one of God's angels, this old soul knew things like Magdalen and tonight, his seventh sense was in play.

Several months from now, a chain of haunting events would bring the men back to confer more than once with the old Creole. Tonight Tark tipped his chair back and closed his eyes. "We talked about this. Ramos. I'll go with J-Dog tonight."

"Do it…give me a plan in an hour. I gotta do something I don't want to do." Between mouthfuls of Padric's *amandine* fish and Tark's *anduoille* sausage, they talked. Tark wasn't for it, no way, not a recusal…they argued. "What happened to Lara has nothing to do with martyrs and holy mayhem, Johnny. This was about you but…"

Padric said he had sinned, done Lara wrong and the unit a disservice; he needed to pay. But his thoughts were much darker and he wished he wasn't a cop; the man wanted payback for all of the moondead…it would be easier to kill those responsible if he wasn't the law. They spoke for a while with Batiste then told him they would return. "Ah, *mon*, soon I hope. There are things, Jace baby." The detectives glanced at each other, not sure where the man's words would eventually take them. They stepped into the early night air…Padric wanted to walk around town in the dark for an hour, stand on a rooftop like Batman and look out over the city. But it could wait. Padric took the back stairs two at a time.

The Commander looked up; his favorite detective was not himself and he pointed to a chair. If anyone exuded class and wisdom, it was Oliver Ramirez. He listened, said little. Padric poured out his misery and what he must do.

"Thank you, John. And now you will listen. I don't like it…I don't like your thoughtless ways; you do this. *Ay, caballero*, from this moment on, you will stop thinking with that junk between your legs." Padric stared at him, stared at the floor. "Do you know how my recruits look up to you? I have a squad room downstairs that would run through fire for you, follow you anywhere. Knock it off. Lust for the good, John, lust for the good." What had he said? "Do I need to repeat myself? Lust for unselfish choices, *mijo.*" Padric again looked down at the floor. *Was he a priest?* "I can't lose you but so be it, go." The detective was humiliated; he turned to leave. "And John… you will find the woman or she will obliterate you."

Padric left a vacuum in the room like he always did. Ramirez stood at his window looking out at the city. There was much left undone; he'd need his man back. He'd been around long enough for this case to pass but its fallout would rattle around for years in the lives of those it touched.

"Things come to rest…dust settles," he said aloud. Ramirez would pull him back in.

But the detective was suffocating and, on impulse, glanced at his watch. It was passed eight. He left the Precinct and sped through the streets to Meadow. For a while, he watched Lara sleep; a ray of light from a leftover slice of moon fell on her hair. He missed her gaze, the way she said things with her eyes; he needed her smile. It had been good once but he doubted that would ever be so again. Padric was numb…he'd done this.

But there was a breakthrough: Lara opened her eyes and was lucid, aware; her gaze fell on Padric. Finally in whispers they spoke, full of sorrow for letting themselves drift so far apart; he, for what he couldn't say. And she, looking away sometimes, wept then hesitating, wanting to speak. He frowned and was unable to read her this time…there was something she wasn't saying. She knew. *Joanna.* He said nothing.

An older nurse and true cowgirl off-duty entered the room to check Lara's vitals. He asked if he could hold her. "Everything's a go except lovemaking, partner…use your imagination." Padric laughed and leaned over, kissing her face, telling her he loved her over and over; he whispered that the girls were all right, he'd never let anything hurt her again.

13 CONFLICT OF INTEREST

Padric watched the others in the squad room through the blinds in his office. He'd miss working the case, but he was distracted. A dragnet sweeping up meth labs in and around the city had the holding tank full and interview rooms busy. The Precinct was buzzing. Padric's old friends from the Border Drug Task Force he'd worked as a rookie were everywhere. Some had hunkered down in his office and he didn't mind. They had stories to tell but were quick to express hopes for his wife's speedy recovery. A few offered to give an assist. But he had other things, big things, on his mind and a briefing to run; his unit however was scattered throughout the building, running last-minute checks and typing out past due reports. They were in no hurry to meet as long as he wasn't.

When he explained to his friends what they were up against in the moondead case, they fell silent; stone-faced, some shaking their heads...nuns and priests dying? All knew the Canteras; some had come face-to-face with one or the other and if not the family members, those in their employ. They were just as troublesome and very loyal. Dealing with them had always been highly contentious and if any of them were considered suspects...look out.

After they left, he stood at the window and stared down at the street. "It's now or never."

"It's never, 'never'. I taught you better than that."

He whirled around, knew the voice. "Tommy Brown...*kema sabe!*" His old partner from back in the day on the Border Drug Task Force stood in the doorway looking at him. It was Brown, a

Yaqui native, who had taught a lad from Belfast the intricacies of Sonoran justice. From him, he had learned how to read the desert, side by side in a cavalry unit.

They shook hands, embraced. If there was anyone with wisdom to discern things hidden in the martyr murders, it was his partner, Alex Martinez, but Tommy Brown was a scout, a sage and a sleuth...he could find clues when others had gone over and over a scene and found nothing. An enigma, the man could see what most men could not...an overturned leaf meant something. For John Padric, there had not been the likes of him in County Antrim. He would be schooled in the desert and life. "I'm glad you're here. Tommy. I..."

Brown raised his hand. "I know, John."

"What do you know, man?"

"Clouds, a woman, one in a veil, but clouds and I'm not talking monsoon. It's too early for that. *"A woman, but who, which one...he had a long list. And the one with the veil, surely Magdalen, his nun, a good thing, but he knew lots of nuns and his wife wore a veil on their wedding day, but who..."* "Stop, John...she has your back, walks with wings on her soul, knows things I know." *Magdalen.* "The other, deadly and dark, deep waters." Silence.

Tommy was shorter than Padric but carried himself with an air that made him look taller. His eyes were dark coals, full of passion and things not to be said. He was part mystic and Padric had always kept a respectful distance because of it, but now he was searching his face for meaning and answers as he done years ago.

"Don't misunderstand me, Tommy. I would die for my partner. There's no other like him, but I've missed you and have missed you for a very long time. I sometimes regret leaving you when the task force ran out of money and we were told to find work somewhere else. I got swept up."

And indeed, the L'Arroyo Police Department, dealing with a high rise in crime had sought Padric out, a decorated Marine and outstanding lawman who, with Brown by his side, had earned commendations for performance beyond the call of duty.

"How long are you staying, Tommy? I need to wrangle my

unit together for a sit-down and they're waiting for me." They were watching him curiously now from their desks and Marcus was suddenly standing outside his door. Padric told him to enter but he wasn't there for him. "Uncle Tom-Tom?"

Brown searched the young man's face. There was silence then a loud shout and laughter. "*Meecha?*"

The calm, cool exterior Brown had displayed in front of Padric was gone. He was a strong man and picked Marcus up...he was six foot and growing; holding him close, the man whirled him around then set him down. Padric grinned. "Whoa...what am I seeing?"

Brown and Marcus both spoke at once...Marcus was Tommy Brown's nephew. "My father is Yaqui, my mother Sonoran Yaqui. We haven't seen each other since my father died."

"When was that?" Brown was beaming as Marcus poured out his story to Padric. It was Brown who had raised the boy in and out of his life until the military swept him away and later the law on either side of the Border. He was their financial support though Marcus' mother taught school on the reservation near Tucson. Money arrived but the postmarks were different. Padric listened, wanting Brown back in his life, in the life of his nephew. Marcus was committed to policing, lived alone, spoke seldom of family.

"Come back to us, *kema sabe*. We need you here."

And he would, but not yet and Padric knew why. Brown was on his own personal hunt for a killer while he worked the law on either side of the Border. He'd suffered a tragedy, was left a widower only weeks after marrying the love of his life. His bride had been abducted into Mexico but later, it was Padric who found her skeletal remains in the trunk of a car abandoned at a reststop near Yuma; it still haunted him. Tommy Brown would never look at another woman again; he'd devote himself to Yaqui ways, live like a hermit in a small fortress he built in the hills near the wildlife sanctuary south of L'Arroyo.

"Come back. I need you here. I'll help you do what you need to do, you know that."

"There will be time, John." He looked at Marcus. "You...I am proud of you, *Meecha*."

Marcus turned to Padric. "It means moon...my name in Yaqui."

"I know…your uncle gave me tutorials in Yaqui. Ask him what he called me."

The men laughed; his uncle bowed to Padric: "*Ousei!*"

Padric reciprocated: "*Seenu.*"

Number One…Brown had been that for him. Marcus was delighted. He looked at Padric: "And you, mountain lion…why is that?"

"He runs like the wind…there is no one faster, *Meecha*," said Tommy.

"That was then…I need the open desert, the hard, dry earth under my feet."

"Do it…it will free you, *Ousie.*"

"And I'll do as your uncle says and find some desert to run in again. But, *Meecha*…is this why you offered to stand post in the bishop's garden at full moon when the nuns were afraid?" Marcus smiled. Padric grinned at Brown. "Tom-Tom? I'm liking that."

"A small child's name for an old man…but," he looked at Marcus. "You are a man now, part of John Padric's unit."

"I am."

"I can die a happy man" and he put his hand on his heart. "But not yet." The two laughed. "I must go." He looked at his watch. "We will meet again soon. Give yourself to this moment, Meecha…Detective Marcus. There is a grave problem in the deserts to the west and south of here…details later. Let's get our respective jobs done." Spoken like Agent Seenu Brown, Padric was remembering. Again the man hugged his nephew, shook Padric's hand and was gone.

Marcus looked at Padric. "My father's spirit has come back to me…he gave my uncle to me before he died." He told him how his uncle had been there for him and his mother though he'd been in Tehran and all over the Mideast as an Army Ranger. "He got real quiet when I said I was going into the seminary, but when I came home, he'd left the army as well and was in the academy."

"That's where he and I met, son. He was a few years ahead of me in the academy, was older than most but he had the experience. We were partners in that task force operation. He taught me the desert, but you know much more than I do. The desert changes; it grows like we do." Neither realized how much Padric would depend on Marcus' knowledge of the hostile terrain outside the city in the months to come. "I've let go of some things your good uncle taught me. Those were tough, wonderful times, but the telling of that's for another day. I think Tark's discussed what I need you two to do tonight, where you are going. I'm trusting you're up for it."

"I am, sir."

"Then get out there and put some fire under their tails and rustle them into the Bog for me. And, Jesús…" Marcus turned. His face was glowing. "You're a fortunate, young man. I've carried your uncle's words inside me."

"I knew it. I knew there was something inside you."

"What the fuck does that mean?"

"You're Cuchalain, that Celt, the warrior man."

Padric stared at him. "No, son, I've fallen far short of that. Bloody hell! His name was all over my locker in the weight room at Cathedral High. Fuck…he's every lad's hero in Antrim. How do you know about him?"

"I just know. I'll see you in the Bog, sir."

The others hadn't moved and were now asking Marcus about the unusual man in Padric's office. A booming voice broke up the huddle. "Now…into the Bog!"

"What's up, man?" Tark knew the man's voice too well not to know something big was to be said, something he didn't want Padric to say.

"It's a sit-down; we're putting it all on the table." They would learn soon enough. "Now or never, *amigos*…on the double!" They filed into a drab excuse for a briefing room near the door to the parking garage. Padric threw several files down on the conference table and sat down. O'Manion joined them with Chinese take-out; and muttered something about "the shit-green paint" on the walls as he arranged his meal and utensils with precision on the conference table.

"Hey, boys, you wanted me to sit in?" Jana stood in the doorway dressed for the Hook.

Tark pulled back a chair. "Damn, girl, you're looking fine."

"I'm not sitting near you. You're too nice…I'd lead you astray."

"Astray me, woman, but tell me how you would do that."

Feigning an exaggerated bow of respect, Padric stood up when Jana entered the room; everyone laughed. She curtsied and took a seat near the door. Martinez threw himself into a seat next to Padric. Marcus closed the door. They glanced at each other, laughed a little, joked with some affection about the room no longer a once high-level meeting place. It was now called the Bog by Major Crimes for as long as Padric had been in the unit. Grim with peeling green walls and two large dingy windows, it was officially and unofficially Major Crime turf. Near the Precinct's parking garage door at the end of a hall, it was here Padric's team often strategized uninterrupted and took power naps when pulling a double.

Covered with jottings, timelines, and photos, the white boards stared back at them as they laid down what they knew and argued each point with the little they had.

"Okay," Padric said, "we've been sitting on our hands waiting for crumbs from forensics. The only one giving me hope over there is our man Milleau. He'll find something."

"Dragons," Marcus whispered. Everyone chuckled.

"I'll take a few of those if it helps…we have no DNA, no crime scene evidence pointing to the suspects until Milleau tells us differently. We're hungry for a warrant for that cemetery under the bishop's house and the basement under the Cathedral. There's a request for one on Judge Whitton's desk as I speak. Jay may get generous. What else has to happen at San Miguel? Is the convent next? Alex and I have hashed this out over and over; we've brought it to you as you worked other cases. Now we need you to hang with us in this fiasco. Our prime suspect and an unknown are on a roll."

"And who is it now…the suspects again?" Jana had been the least involved with her undercover work on other crimes they'd been working…it had taken her into the Hook. She and her backup were teaming up with Vice, a sting underway close to midnight.

"Our target is Joanna Cantera?"

"And someone else we know nothing about," added Martinez. "And then there's the bishop…we have more questions for him."

"Possible obstruction of justice, an accessory after the fact," commented Marcus.

"Something like that…but there's more." They groaned.

"We need to make a case for the DA that won't fall apart in court. We don't have that."

"And, yes, I need it soon." ADA Dana Milleau, the young CSI's mother, was in the house. Known to do her job and everything else on her iPhone, she seldom made an appearance. "I heard the name Cantera." She laughed, shook her head, told them they were blowing smoke and wanted irrefutable proof a Cantera was involved… that was it. She left but not before looking at Padric. "I'll talk only to you…I don't need a thousand voices telling me things."

The woman had stepped over O'Manion and chose Padric as her liaison. When she was gone Tark said: "You still got it, Johnny!"

Padric was livid and no one was laughing; the Captain took another bite of his take-out. They stared at him. "What? Get 'er done…you heard the woman. She's a wack job…we got a lot of those. Do it or eat dirt."

"So, boys and girls, there it is. I'll give you forty-eight to pull in all the loose ends…witnesses, et cetera. Tonight Tark and Marcus are in the Edge." He explained what Magdalen had given them. "Ramos Robles last seen there; may be hooked up or worse with Joanna Cantera. Guadalupe Rojas, the bishop's right hand at San Miguel, saw what went down with the nun. She's not saying. The bishop won't allow cams inside the Cathedral and surveillance tapes from those in the streets gave us nothing."

Padric glanced at O'Manion…he nodded. "Kids, I have good news…Sister Petra made it. She's alive but I couldn't say it…Cap's orders." The others were amazed, relieved, but all over Padric for not telling them sooner. He silenced them, giving details but then his mood changed. Padric had been upbeat, but now he was noticeably different. The next moments would be pivotal for the morale of the unit. Padric threw the files he held in his hand on the table, looked around, Tark shook his head. Martinez stared down at the table.

He'd say it. "Hear me out: an hour ago, I went to the fifth floor and recused myself from the case. I'm taking myself out for the good of the unit." A small uproar ensued. Martinez was silent, had opposed it, said as much when the two had shouted back and forth at each other in the Precinct parking garage. "The Commander accepted my decision with a publication ban; no reason given. I don't need to give you one either, but you deserve an explanation."

"And you're pissing me off, Johnny, so be quick about it." Jana glared at him.

"Here it is. I haven't addressed my wife's attack openly because it smacks of conflict of interest and my own need for payback, though there are those sitting right here who might understand if I acted on that." They nodded. The Captain remained stone-faced. "We batted around the idea and know now the same suspects in the case of the moondead went after my wife but it didn't fit the MO we'd come to expect. Lara isn't a nun, had no martyr's name."

"But she was the wife of a cop." Marcus was curious, angry. "So why then? Was this a diversionary move, something meant to distract, something else…why her?"

"And in your home…whose list are you on?" Jana asked.

"This was personal, my friends." He took a deep breath.

O'Manion cleared his throat. "This is all still very fresh, John; we can talk about…"

"I've thought it through, Cap. End of discussion, but here's a footnote. Lara's case is now in the hands of Dan Mason, a man not fit to walk through the back door of this Precinct and in fact, was banned from setting foot on the premises, as I recall. Still…he's been handed the case. I feel disrespected but even that's hypocrisy considering why and how this came down." They frowned but no one looked at each other.

The Captain grunted in a voice like gravel. "I don't need to explain anything to you either but I will. I saw a change in the man, heard some good things lately. He came to me, wanting to help, looking for redemption, wanting to do right by you."

"And you fucking believed that line of crap?" The two often went head to head.

"John, I've received new *intel* and all is in flux."

"You'll understand if something in flux doesn't make me feel all trusting and pleased. Sounds like you're running for office, Cap."

Martinez wondered if he'd ever be working with his partner again. Padric was up for a tangle with O'Manion and everyone else. The troubled detective slowly sat down, folded his hands on the files strewn out before him and stared at his wedding ring, debating, ashamed. *Did they know already…they were detectives, for Christ's sake?* He looked at his partner who nodded reluctantly.

"I was fucking our prime suspect, Joanna Cantera, while the crimes played out." Silence. There were a thousand better ways to say this, but it was Johnny. "I'd been doing her since Christmas, did no BGC, no recon on the woman, never knew her ID until after the third kill in the case. At the Cathedral, I saw her signature: bite marks on the breast of the female victim, a nun for God's sake, like the one I saw on my wife. I knew she was the one who went after my Lara from things she was able to tell me. Her description was hazy at first then sharper; she confirmed my suspicions. Joanna wanted Lara out of the way; Joanna Cantera is our prime suspect, no question. The other one's in the wind." More silence.

His actions had been reckless, he said. He'd put all they had done on the case in jeopardy. "That said, I need to redeem our Captain and turn the blame for my wife's pain back on myself. It's more than his choice of an investigator on Lara's case. I've messed up badly, done something I'm not proud of in my private life and am in the process of making rectitude. It's going to be a hard road back. I took risks in a relationship with someone I knew nothing about and who turned what we were doing into an obsession. My family has suffered the consequences and it has nothing to do with the Captain. He's just trying to clean up my mess with someone he thought had turned his life around. He sees something in Dan Mason I can't. Our suspect is one sick, dangerous, unpredictable bitch. We've got Joanna Cantera to chase down."

More silence. He could not look at his team; that the Captain was hearing this, didn't bother him; besides he was sure O'Manion had known for a while, but Padric was worried more about Marcus than anyone else and Jana would be disappointed in him. Yet it was Marcus who spoke: "I think most of us have known for awhile that something was up but I'm saying that only because I was worried and didn't want to lose you. I'll help if you need anything."

He was young, idealistic…they'd allow his remarks but the others had been silent too long. The room exploded; a back and forth of emotions, a volley of words then disbelief, all numb…mummified, as Tark would say later. They loved Johnny but hated the way he handled his personal life. He said he'd defer to his partner; he'd take lead on the case. Everyone agreed except Alex Martinez.

But it was Tark who expressed what everyone was thinking. "Johnny, for God's sake, we can keep doing what we're doing. I get the stand-up thing you're trying to do here, but we want you on point though we're ready to take shit from Alex; he's a master at it but nicer than you." They laughed. "But damn, reconsider. We can wade through it." Martinez however had no heart for what they expected, though he had a few ideas of his own to "work these Cantera fools", Martinez-style.

Padric looked at Jana; they had history. "You knew?"

"Sweetheart, lieutenant, sir…I'm not on the streets for nothing. I work it; see things. You need to come home to us…I can read a man like the Bible." She put her arm around Marcus. "Forgive me, baby…" The others held onto their seats. "Johnny, fuck this bitch. She's down for the count in my book. You got in over your head and the broad wanted all of you. You're damn right it was personal. It's textbook…Fatal Fucking Attraction 101. We can do this; bring closure to everyone. I'll drag her ass in if you can get me a warrant. I'm not judging you, but I get the recusal…it's the integrity of the case I'm worried about."

O'Manion was pleased…his favorite detective, the lad from Belfast, had stepped up; now they were all clawing their way through it. But he would have to keep the man on the straight and narrow…somehow. He remained silent but it was Martinez who was doing a read on the Cap's face; he was protecting his partner, planning already their next move.

Jana had more on her mind. "I know this recusal is probably best but it stinks. You know how things work in this town, Johnny, we never know if we get justice in the cases we work…we hold our breath. Damn, you know how to pick 'em. If there's a hint of anything pointing to the Big Five, my family included, justice in this town shuts down."

Everyone knew she was right. The Canteras were not alone; the Five were off-limits and a less talked-about family, the Genovas, with homes here and in Tuscany, were seemingly untouchable, too; their only daughter, a nun in the convent of San Miguel, Sister Lucy. They had businesses here...some still unclear.

"And that's why I'm out and Alex is in. We don't kiss and hug much, but he's my other half; has had the same eyes on all this and hell, he's one of the good guys. You all know what needs to get done." Martinez wanted his partner to stop talking. Padric walked to the window. "That's it. Hate me. Bite me, whatever. Go...my apologies; you know what you need to do."

No one moved...not yet; the room was a mausoleum. It was hard to breathe. O'Manion knew it...these were his people. "Lad, you've done the work and we have no doubt you would be objective." This would be difficult. "But...if this becomes public knowledge, our ADA will nail us; she's looking for a way out of working with us on this moondead thing anyway...it's all about the Canteras and you fucked one of them nicely. You messed with one and she did a little messing with you. If Dana Milleau finds out, she'll throw the case in the toilet unless...."

"But if we get confessions, it won't land in the toilet," Marcus offered.

O'Manion ignored him; he didn't like 'witty and cheerful' in his detectives. Acting hopeful was 'too kindergarten' for him. "If I may continue but as the youngster has stated, we'll need one, big, fucking slam-dunk, and that means confessions; I'm talking steaming up the windows in interview rooms once we nail them. And you know Ramirez; he'll want it in writing. We're going to nail them with their own words into coffins, lids tight. The DA hates circumstantial anything. You're out, John, for now, but I may ask you to punt. Alejandro quarterbacks; Marcus and Tark run interference. Zalconi..." They waited. He looked around the room. "What... this isn't the Gettysburg Address!"

Jana sighed: "Sir! Tight end, I know." Comic relief.

They laughed but O'Manion was unswayed. "The word *shift* does not exist...you're on twenty-four-seven but when weren't you; grab food, sleep and lovemaking where and when you can find it. John, you didn't hear that. Re-canvass the neighborhoods. And..." They waited. "Everything has to do with the Cathedral and the bishop's residence. It's there...it begins and ends there; something we're not seeing...this is a crapshoot." He said he was going over the ADA's head. "Jay Whitton. That judge owes me big time for saving his ass more than once. We need a warrant to pull out what's underneath over there, damn it. How much more exigency do we need than what happened to that good nun in the Cathedral." He looked down at the table. "And then there's our Lara twenty-four hours ago?" He walked to the door. "I need some fish and chips." Had he not just consumed a *pupu* platter with double ribs? Oxygen returned to the room.

Each stood up slowly, hesitated then left the room, but Padric remained at the window; they were already making plans without him. They'd known something...they had to; his admissions hadn't shocked them but his choice of a lover was a kick to the gut; Jana was miserable.

Padric wanted to howl like a mountain lion and run as fast as *ousei* up into the low mountains surrounding the city; he looked at them now from the window. Finally alone, he was shaken, regretting he'd said a word, spilled his guts. He closed his eyes, pressed his forehead against the glass pane. Finally he turned to gather his files; he wasn't alone. Marcus, like a sentry, stood by the open door.

Padric with head down, walked passed him but stopped. "I need to say something."

"No need, sir...no need."

"Damn it, listen to me, lad. I've disappointed you and I'm sorry." But Marcus said he wasn't judging him...never could. "Don't even say that when I deserve it; I was like you once and now look at me. I hate myself but now you must push on. Stay close to Alex; try to be *me* for him where you can. Tark's good on his own. So are you and again, my apologies." The young man wanted to speak; Padric shook his head...silence. Side by side, they walked down the hall.

Later Martinez found Padric alone in the Precinct parking garage looking out at the city. They argued, shouting so loud, their voices ping-ponged off the walls. Martinez would sit like a gargoyle, his desk facing Padric's closed door; no one permitted to speak to his partner. Only those in the unit gained entry; if there was a knock, it had been cleared by him.

But he'd forgotten the likes of Detective Anzo Ducci from Homicide; he and his boys knew something was up. They stayed away, but Ducci, a passionate man, would not; he loved Padric. They "were Cathedral" like Duran, had played football together; Ducci, linebacker of all linebackers. Defense. A big letter D was on everything…his desk, his computer; his car bumper, even in the tats on his biceps. His six kids' answered to names beginning with D; he'd married a woman named Denise and called her Dee, named his Doberman, Defcon.

When Martinez told him it wasn't a good time, he wouldn't move. "I'll wait." He stood outside Padric's door like a guard dog. Defense. Later the two finally opened the door, the room dark, Padric, eyes closed and alone.

"I'm feelin' sinful." Ducci and Martinez got it; they were Catholic. He needed some Jameson but said he'd wait…they laughed; but they were checking in on a man who'd fallen from grace. He was a fool with no integrity, he said, had hurt his woman and wee girls, burdened his unit. "I threw my trash in your front yard."

One by one, each came to Padric with support and no sympathies; he of all people should have known better. They wouldn't let him off easy. He was all business; there was much to be done, he said, and outlined the plan he'd gone over and over in his head how to move on the Cathedral. He said he agreed with the Cap'…it was ground zero, but didn't mention that other thing rattling around in his brain…if their killer was Joanna Cantera, and he knew it was, he'd step up and take her down on his own. There was more than one way to skin a cat.

But with an elusive prime suspect not even Tark could nail down on his screen, they needed witnesses…the caretaker, Guadalupe, for one, and that kid Ramos, nowhere to be found but alive perhaps in the Edge. But the caretaker at the Cathedral would need some finessing. Lara…uncertain maybe, this would take time. Tomorrow then for the two of them, but tonight Ramos.

Padric had promised the nun he would find Ramos and now wondered why he'd ever said such a thing. He leafed through his journal, pulled open drawers in his file cabinets, scavenged about for every note he had ever scribbled; there were a few in his pants pocket, two more stuffed into his wallet…most of them bar napkins, things he'd discussed with Martinez. Maybe, just maybe, tonight it could happen: a familiar rap on the door punctuated his thoughts. He knew the knock. "Enter!" Tark and Marcus. "Gentlemen?'"

"Damn, man, turn on some lights." Tark threw himself into a chair. Marcus remained standing.

Padric looked squarely at Marcus. "So, son, you're making your bones tonight."

"We've talked. Ramos was a clubber and underage, but now that his friend, Jesse, dropped it on our nun, we have a slim lead that he's in the Edge, dead or alive. I knew Ramos from the youth club in his hood then later in juvi. Tark and I strategized. I know what to expect."

Tark shook his head. "No, you don't; no one goes into the Edge knowing that, I'm telling you, J-Dog, no heroics…" And the back and forth continued until Tark turned to Padric: "Get outta here and go to your wife and kids; stop hiding behind your work."

But he couldn't leave if two of his own were going into the Edge. The two shook Padric's hand and vanished. He stepped into the hall and stared blankly at them as they disappeared into the parking garage. A chill gust of wind blew down the hall and through his soul and moved on to a garden, filled with angels. It lifted the drapes of a second-floor convent window…the nun shuttered.

What a dark time this is…she sensed her friend was in trouble. There'd be no sleep tonight, only unfinished prayers and reoccurring dreams of an almost beheaded nun, another swaying upside down on a cross.

She stared at her angels, contemplated the garden, praying for the souls of the moondead, but knew nothing of two men driving into the unknown.

Author's Notes

Cuchullain - also Cú Chulainn, Cú Chulaind or Cúchulainn and Irish for "Culann's Hound"; one of the greatest heroes of Irish mythology, a warrior in the service of Conchobhar, king of Ulster. Best known for his single-handed defense of Ulster, he is said to have lived in the first century B.C. but his story was only later written down in the 8th C. A.D; his adventures, recorded in a series of narratives known as the Ulster Cycle. Ulster is one of the four ancient Provinces of Ireland.

Antrim – reference to County Antrim, N. Ireland in which Belfast is located.

14 THE EDGE

Holy Saturday, near midnight, March 22

Like a specter, Tark's gunmetal gray jeep sped into the night, its headlights throwing down a path on the well-worn dirt road. It was beyond dark. A splash of red in the black ahead told them they'd entered the Edge; off in the distance, Chato's bar was smoldering like a low, seething corner of hell. Neither spoke; Tark recalling nights spent on the dark side here when he was younger. He'd dabbled in things while undercover and hadn't liked himself much. Marcus was remembering the handsome, happy-go-lucky face of the boy they were trying to find and not liking the vibes he was feeling already.

Tark turned down a road; at the end, a large, sprawling parking lot; cars, bumper to bumper in front of a club. They called them no-names out here; there were no lights and you'd need to find them, know where they were. All was hush-hush in the Edge. Music, desperate and driven, pounded against the covered windows; the roof seemed to bounce up and down, straining to lift itself off the house. The musician in Tark muttered something about too much bass guitar and Marcus laughed.

But set back in the shadows behind the 'no-name', he pointed to a white adobe house, different, with landscape and twinkling lights on the veranda. "This doesn't fit," he said aloud to Marcus. But he knew…Joanna Cantera. "I'll bet you a million this is her crib."

They kept walking toward the main house. Marcus eyed two men he could barely see on either side of the door. "Why this one?"

"I'm hunching it. Eyes open, keep it close."

"Then we're treading on thin ice."

"More like walking the rim of a volcano but enough with the metaphors." He warned Marcus not "to get frisky."

Frisky. "I'm letting you call me J-Dog but you're not exactly taking some little pup to the mall; stop all the warm and fuzzy."

"Johnny would barbecue me if anything happened to you."

"And you don't think he didn't say the same to me about you?" Marcus glanced up at the sky. He needed a moon. His Yaqui roots had urged his mother, who thought him special, to call him *Meecha*... moon; but the one overhead was covered in clouds; it was dark now.

A man in a cheap suit leaned on the door and extended his hand. Tark gave him a ten; he wanted twenty. "Stay loose, my friends."

A shabby exterior belied the surprisingly posh interior but it was filled with smoke and old men; near-naked women leaning on them. From the far end of the bar, a woman wearing more clothes and orange hair slid off a stool and sauntered toward them.

"Gentlemen!" Big-breasted and heavy with bling, she made no effort to hide her gold teeth when she smiled; her welcome was effusive. She offered to show them around.

Fluttering her grotesquely fake eyelashes, she ogled Marcus; Tark's eye's narrowed. "Tell us when you're done grazing." Her laugh was too loud; she said he was jealous. "How'd you know... show us what you've got. We might like what we see."

"And I'm likin' what I see. We love 'em young here. I'm tired of old daddies."

"Old daddies have bucks."

"That they do." She too was considerably older; the black lipstick didn't help. "My name's Ruthless, not Ruth or Ruthie...remember that. Ruthie's too quaint and I'm not. I own this place with somebody else who will remain nameless."

Marcus was listening. "Like everything else around here."

"You got it! So, what's your pleasure or are you just window-shopping? That'll be twenty dollars for the tour...now, up front." This was the second time they were giving up cash and hadn't left the front room. "When you choose from our menu, you pay before being served. One rule of etiquette here: if someone says 'stop', you stop." She glared at them. "It's that or a body bag." Tark sighed...*ah, the memory of a misspent youth.*

Marcus had reflected on her warning. "So you have ethics."

"You bet your ass. Let me take you down to the lower level."

"Figuratively speaking?" He was doing it again. Tark frowned.

Ruthless laughed. "He's bright-eyed and bushy tailed, isn't he…handsome, too."

At the bottom of the stairs, green, florescent and sinister, greeted them. One felt submerged in seaweed and moss; there was evil here. Marcus sensed it at once and fought the claustrophobia. Something deep-seated and wrong pervaded every turn, every corner of the long, narrow hallway. It suddenly grew wider and snaked left and right into blind spots then disappeared. A sign directed patrons to Chato's. The men looked at each other…there was an underground Edge then; one could walk from one venue to another via several subterranean passageways so wide, a car can pass through them. But where did they lead and how far outside the city limits; where did they surface and go under again?

Padric would eat this up, Tark muttered to Marcus; they'd come back with him next time. Rooms with no doors, but covered in heavy drapes, emitted sounds of pleasure and pain; both were sold here…it was good advertising. Some drapes drawn aside revealed women, young ones, some older, waiting for patrons; down the hall, men did the same. Marcus spotted the word *cinema* over a door. He pointed.

Ruthless grinned. "This is for people with special tastes." She opened her palm. "Two Franklins each. Lay it on me."

Earlier the Commander had issued the two a large sum of money as Padric looked on; they laid out two bills and Ruthless escorted them into a small theater. She left; they waited.

"Looks like porn." But Tark said he thought it was more. The two slumped into some seats in the last row; more patrons joined them.

A middle-aged man, slick like a hawker outside an old burlesque, finally took his place at the door and locked it. He was surprisingly gracious. "You may leave any time, my friends. A locked door allows for no interruptions. The film is only ten minutes in length; it's real and it happened; you can believe it or doubt it. Enjoy or don't, if that makes you feel good…that's what we do here.

No cell phones, etc.; put them on quiver." Some patrons chuckled and apparently knew what to expect. "When it's over, leave quickly; we don't care who you are and you don't want to know us."

The room turned pitch black and a dust-filled shaft of projector light pointed to the screen. Marcus frowned. "It's 16 fucking mm...what the hell is this?" The kid rarely cursed. Tark glanced at him; he knew what it was. "It's for effect...gritty, low-down, and illegal by some standards." The film was in color but moody; a nude male with dark hair, his back to the lens; the set murky. Two girls, late teens, pouty and smoky eyed, lips bright red and glossy, also unclothed, entered the frame from either side; they did things, he did things. The music rose to a frenetic crescendo, the three more entwined. But slowly the youth turned, his face pleasured, eyes glazed, looking intently into the camera.

Tark glanced at Marcus; he'd straightened in his seat. "What?"

"We got what we came for."

"You're shittin' me!"

"I don't do that in front of people."

"You know what this is?"

"I'm getting it...talk."

"I'm not seeing what I need to yet." He was forced to say otherwise in seconds. Eyes riveted to the screen, Marcus leaned slowly back in his seat. Ramos. "If it's real, it happened already."

The three were heating up the screen in a montage of torture-porn in ways the men had not expected. And then...there it was, for only an instant, detected only by a trained eye like Tark's, a blip. With no lead up, the camera zoomed in on Ramos' eyes, they had changed, not looking like his; the light inside them fading with pain and surprise. Marcus knew the look; he'd seen it when he'd try to revive victims and they'd died in his arms, that last glimpse into the soul, now gone from the boy.

That the film was too real to be fake was made even clearer in the next footage revealing a hand with a scalpel, incisively, carefully, slitting the throat of the youth end to end; the torso now headless, spurting blood even onto the camera lens. The girls calmly steadied the body then turned and leered at the camera, their hollow eyes, empty with no soul or was it dread?

But Tark had seen more, a technicality; the dead actor was not the same who enjoyed both pleasure and pain in the preceding frames…the detective had seen some trickery, a grand switcheroo. Another had taken his place and Ramos then could still be alive.

The screen faded to black. Silence. It was numbing. The click of a doorknob roused the viewers; they exited quickly, almost falling over each other.

Tark sighed: "Glad this wasn't theater or we'd be having a talk-back with the actors." He eyed each patron and took a step back; the mayor of L'Arroyo was pulling his hat over his eyes as he left. In a greasy voice, the man at the door announced the final re-run in twenty minutes; there would be copies for sale to a select few. They were thanked for *attending*. It was all very civilized. Tark was livid. "What was this, a P.T.A. meeting?"

Marcus was sick inside. "Do you believe what you saw?"

"Let's just say I'm wondering where your boy Ramos is."

"Fuck you, man. He's dead." But Tark explained what he thought he had seen; something a crime tech might notice.

"So what do you want to do?" Marcus was furious.

"I want to cut out this guy's heart for starters."

They'd need to move on this quickly; bring someone or something back, evidence, Ramos, especially Ramos. They could leave and alert Padric and he'd call Bobby Watson, get the FBI out here.

Or Pistasio and his tact squad could take it from here; they were waiting on the road leading into the Edge at this moment. But not Tark; he couldn't live with himself if no chances were taken; he and his boy, Johnny, were cut from the same cloth. He wouldn't leave without something or someone. And that man at the door… he'd take him down; hook him up for just about anything. He'd think of something.

The two stepped into the hall. Goons with eyes like hawks, an unusual breed of Edge security, lurked about…men with no soul, as Marcus would say later.

Tark glanced at his watch. "Stay put…let me do this."

The man stood in the doorway; he was drunk, swaying. "Any questions…what do you need?" It made him feel important when he was asked things. He looked pleased when Tark said he wanted to buy; he liked the word *purchase*. "I'd need your discretion."

The man has no idea. He was locked in Tark's crosshairs. "I want to do a little producing, sir. Who's the guy to talk to?" A playful back and forth between detective and host would begin.

Laughing, he drew Tark aside. "What guy? It's a woman's industry here in the Edge. Everyone knows that."

Bingo. Joanna Cantera. Tark's thoughts were racing.

Schnood would educate these good-looking men, ripe for the picking, on "where it was at out here in the Edge"; no one could touch him or his cronies. What they were doing sat nicely under the First Amendment, protected speech, and all that. The man even offered a reason for why they did what they did: "It's an acquired thing and feels good when it hurts; we charge money for that, even if all you're doing is watching it happen to someone else." He was becoming more loose-lipped. "S and M, bondage, domination… law-types love it. But frankly, I don't see the sense in it except what it does for my bank balance." Schnood held on to his swagger; the men, careful not to look eager…they'd let him spin his own narrative as they followed him through the green down a hall.

Marcus frowned…was Tark making a buy? What was he saying? "I'm not paying a dime, *mi hombre*. We'll string him along and let him unravel. We need more on this fuck…am hunching what we want is all in plain sight."

"Then hunch me something about those young girls…where are they? We have to find them, too."

"We'll see. He's saying women are behind this. My gut says Joanna Cantera's in this up to her tits and it's all going down in that white adobe we saw coming in. I'm not walking away without something or someone tonight." He raised his voice: "Where can we talk, sir?"

Sir. The man smiled; he liked *sir*, said he liked "polite" in a man. "The name's Mick Schnood. Don't laugh. It's a good name. You like what we do here…I can see that. Ah, yes, there's a renewed interest in the genre today."

"That's what they're calling it…a genre? How Sundance and Indie of them!"

Schnood laughed. "Follow." There were fewer people as they

entered a narrow hall; ahead, was a door under a staircase, leading up to an exit. Schnood's huge key ring rattled ominously; it gave them entrance into an upscale, corporate suite with mahogany furniture and thick carpeting; shelves full of books wrapped the walls. Their transaction with no money down would begin and the two were asked to be seated…they refused.

It would go down quickly from here. Maintaining his swagger, Schnood pointed to the artifacts on his executive desk. He said he was a collector. Tark nodded his head. "The Edge has a lot of those. Looks like you made it to the big time; what gives you the right to a corner office like this?"

Schnood preened, said he was the self-appointed mayor here in the Edge; knew how to run things; had been here the longest, put the place on the map. He pointed to shelves full of ledgers and records. "Everything's there, every damn thing I bought or sold and that includes people." Music to Tark's ear…he'd add all that to his shopping cart but needed to move this along.

Pleased with himself, Schnood leaned back in his chair and waxed eloquent on all he had done and was doing. He told Tark he'd seen him, knew him from somewhere, playing his sax, yes, at Bugsy's, a wise guy hang out and supper club, one of the few places where his money was good; the man was spurned by most of L'Arroyo. He smiled to himself…these two were easy, curious, thirsty for knowledge; he'd work them, give them a con, do an exchange and make a transaction if not with money he'd have his goons do a job on them. They wouldn't be leaving any time soon if he didn't get what he wanted.

But Marcus, like Padric was reading the old man, eyeing his fingers as they moved ever so slightly toward the half-open drawer. He was done with the conversation and slammed Schnood's chair into the wall. "Don't even…I'll knock your sorry sick ass into next week!"

Tark leaned over the desk. "On top, fool, and if you toe-tap under that desk for some back up, we'll hammer 'em just like we're gonna do you. We want tapes, films, records, all of it." Schnood wanted to talk. "That ship has sailed and you, the damn Mayor of a stinking landfill like this, grow the fuck up. Get a life."

But the old man said he had a bad heart, called Tark, brutha.

"Brother, my ass. Gimme all l can see...those in that trunk." He kicked back the lid. "It's all in plain sight." Now it was.

But Schnood wouldn't stop talking, said 'that kid', the one they'd just seen in the snuffer, was in a lot of the porn. "She had a thing for him, wouldn't leave him alone."

Marcus lunged at him. "Where the fuck is he, ass wipe?" Tark half-smiled, amused at the ex-seminarian's transformation. Schnood wouldn't say. They pulled out search warrants, slammed them down on the table; the two snatched up guns and money, tossed them on top of the film in the trunk. Marcus hoisted it onto his shoulders. "Bring him!"

Tark grinned...the kid was in. They stepped into the hall; gone was the sound of business as usual. Was everyone taking a breather? A small window of opportunity was cut even shorter by the sound of Ruthless' laugh in the hall. There were others; their voices, coarse and guttural...her posse, a band of Four Horsemen look-alikes. Tark wasn't in the mood for a tangle with fools. He pushed Schnood up the stairs. He was sniveling now, told them they'd get an eyeful: "L'Arroyo's most respected are looking all vulnerable and wanting it...our workers film everything here with or without consent for our protection."

"Shut up!" Marcus kicked open the door and breathed in the night. Women, employees, were taking a break, leaning on cars, some working their trade on the hoods. Men stood around, smoking. But Marcus had come for Ramos; this wasn't his gig, he felt dirty.

By now, Schnood was panting for air, trying to explain. "I'm not the only one pulling the strings." Tark wanted more; who else? "I can't say her name."

"This isn't Lord of the Rings, jerk-off! I'll fucking hurt you." Marcus liked Tolkien, almost laughed. But Schnood would reveal something even more eerie.

"You need to be careful; there's a new breed out here doing things...I'm even bothered by it. They come out in force here at night and take people, keep them."

They keep people...okay. "Who fool? Keep how?"

"Edge-demons...sounds nuts, but they do things to those who

get lost or act stupid and don't want to go home. They're used for things then discarded...you know."

"No, I don't. Used how?" Tark pushed him into the wall.

"Experimentation, fermentation...whatever. They develop, shall we say, 'medicinals', need folks to...to practice on. They're labrats then let out into the fields."

Tark knew the man was perverse and didn't doubt what he said. Just about anything happened here. "You and me alone, we'll sit down with a fucking waterboard, fool. Show me where the broad is who made this film." Schnood pointed to a white adobe, set back, looking upscale and above it all. Tark looked at Marcus. "This is in and out; get behind the wheel and lock up. Be ready to move with or without me, *amigo*. That package has to make it to the Precinct."

Schnood pointed to the trunk. "You're looking at thousands of dollars in there."

"Like that even matters. Fuck off...get out of my sight." This wasn't sounding like Marcus, who laid his 16-inch long arm across his lap, and grabbed his 9mm. Like Jesse had done with Ramos, he watched Tark walk up to the house.

"She holds court here, probably gone for the night."

Tark looked up...there still was no moon. Lighting tucked into the desert scrub cast a glow on the house; it was different than anything else in the Edge. He could hear music, old school: *Santana*. He wished he were playing it somewhere, anywhere.

A housekeeper, looking like she didn't belong there, answered the door. Tark eyed the woman. In modest attire with black pencil skirt and white blouse, she was dressed more like a schoolmarm. Obviously what went on here wasn't her thing or...was how she dressed a charade or something the clientele liked? She explained she was the business assistant for the owner of the house, the frontman or woman if you like.

Schnood leaned in too close. "Dear, where is your boss tonight?"

She stepped back. "I will not divulge that in front of strangers." She refused to look at Schnood but glared at Tark.

He flashed his shield. "Do you know me now?"

"She...she doesn't live here. This is her studio."

"Studio…is that what you're calling this meat grinder?" She's got no clue. "What's your employer's name? Who owns this place?" She stared at him. "Stop fucking with me, woman…I'm asking you nicely to allow me inside."

She opened the door, hoping he'd mellow a little; he was surprised. The interior was high-end and elegant; museum-like, brimming over with antiques and Mexican artifacts, potted palms and rich furnishings. "Your name." She hesitated. "Again…"

She looked down at the floor. "Madonna."

"And I'm Jamie Foxx."

Schnood laughed. "That's really her name, Detective."

"Lt. Jace Tarkington, L'Arroyo PD Madonna what?"

"Thomas, my name is Madonna Thomas."

"Again Ms. Thomas, the name of your employer." She shook her head slowly. "I'm warning you: you won't like my boss, Lieutenant Padric." She looked up quickly. "He's a loose cannon when it comes to the Edge abusing somebody's kids." But she couldn't tell him she too had a kid, a daughter, a student at Cathedral High; Magdalen's innocent, beautiful Ellie who thought her mother worked at a hospital, but this paid more; her employer, a generous woman. And that Irish lieutenant…yes, she knew him once very well, too well; she'd been a nurse in the ER at Good Shepherd, he a young rookie cop…they'd been lovers.

Tark took out his handcuffs; Schnood sneered. "That's not gonna intimidate anyone; everyone's got those out here, right, baby?" Madonna's eyes were screaming for Tark to understand. He wanted an answer. He'd wait and finally…

"Joanna…her name is Joanna Cantera." Boom.

But she'd struck a nerve in Tark, a woman torn between two worlds…she was in a bad place and beautiful. *Later.*

Everything changed in an instant. Shots fired in the parking lot ended the conversation. Tark paled. *J-Dog.* 9mm. He'd heard it pop. But Marcus had already slid from the jeep and, now close to the ground, was eyeing the scuffle, quickly resolved by two bouncers. They'd leave it alone, but not before Tark would cuff Schnood and Madonna to furniture too heavy to move. He apologized to the woman; she, grateful asking to speak with him later. He nodded and slipped from the house; threw himself into the jeep as Marcus rolled into the passenger side. A cryptic call to Pistasio would take care of things, free them up to keep looking for Ramos or leave with what they had.

The tact squad would uncover in an elaborate network of rooms below Joanna's house, a movie set with expensive, high tech equipment, a walk–in freezer and morgue for the human leftovers of ten-minute snuff films costing thousands. A further sweep of the adobe would bring another revelation: photos on Johanna's office wall of Padric's kids probably taken from his residence during her ill-conceived home invasion. He would smolder for days over this… his little ones' faces displayed in a house of horror.

But Ramos…Marcus was silent, frantic; they were leaving without him. As far as Tark could tell, the young man they sought wasn't dead and someone else was. He muttered something about the drive back into town being quicker than the drive in, but he was reluctant to leave with only a trunk full of God-knows-what; it fell short of finding Ramos. He finally floored it and drove down the dirt road away from the no-name; no matter, they'd never rest till they found Ramos dead or alive. But still he was torn, debating… *turn around, damn it*; he slowed down.

Marcus' heart and mind racing. He eyed the edge of the road as Tark finally spun his wheels, leaving a shower of gravel behind them. But Marcus looked back one last time. *Dios mio, what am I seeing? A vision, it must be! Something extraordinary, not possible…but wasn't it Easter?* The ghastly figure of a young man, in what looked like a morgue cloth swirling around his nude body, was attempting to overtake the jeep. Bloodied and bruised, he struggled to keep his balance and stumbled forward on all fours like an animal. He was shouting for Marcus to stop, screaming in terror.

"It's him! Shut it down, Tark…we've got him!" Not waiting for Tark to come to a stop, Marcus rolled out of the jeep onto the side of the road. He leaped to his feet and raced toward the boy, shouting: "God's listening, Tark!"

Tark did a half-donut. "Wish He'd let me in on this shit."

The jeep came to a stop; he quickly lit up the road with his post lights. Ramos was struggling to reach them; but now two of Ruthless' posse emerged from the dark in pursuit. Marcus, younger and faster, reached the boy first and threw him over his shoulder. Tark raced passed him. "Get him on board…I got this!"

Leaping on one of the men, he dropkicked the other and pulled them both down to the gravel. Stunned, they tried to recover their footing, but Tark slammed their heads together and they collapsed like rag dolls onto the road. Sprinting back to the jeep, he speed-dialed Padric who let out a howl; the squad room hoped it was good news; one never quite knew with Johnny. He pulled Martinez into the parking garage and shouted for Ducci.

But back in the Edge, Tark was cursing…the jeep had stalled, the engine sputtering and choking. Marcus made the sign of the cross and, as if moved by the breath of the Holy Spirit, the jeep shot forward. Tark gripped the wheel…he'd need to stay more in touch with this God Marcus loved. Sobbing and thanking them over and over, Ramos, covered in bruises from all kinds of abuse, lay in the back seat with a trunk full of film. The two men looked at each other then saw lights on the road coming toward them out of the city. Padric with the other two was in the lead, speeding west; Old Division Road was lit up like Christmas with an EMV and squad cars popping as they sped into the Edge.

O'Manion grunted: "9-1-1's never come from out there but our man Jace and whatever J-Dog did it." He chuckled. Major Crimes had finally done something without the help of *that dear know-it-all nun from San Miguel's, no offense*. Five floors up, Commander Ramirez watched the river of light winding its way to a place that had caused him nothing but grief since his first days at the Precinct. He hated the Edge, had lost a daughter no one knew about to its darkness.

Tark laughed. His Precinct boys in a halo of light down the road…he'd ride out to meet them. But Marcus saw it first. There were others on Ramos' trail. Eerily, like something out of a horror movie, dark shapes, some men, a few women, probably the Edge-demons the old man had told them about, had moved into play. Unseen at first, they were slowly advancing across the fields toward the road and seemed in no hurry. The word had gone out…

two of their underground colony lay hurt maybe dead in the road.

"What do we got, J-Dog?"

Marcus' answer was drowned out by threats; the sound, haunting. "Nobody takes anyone out of here…give that kid back." Their shouts were sinister; sounding cultist and dangerous. Were those lured in by the Edge, community property? Schnood had been right. Marcus leaned over Ramos' body to protect him. "Stay down, *mijo*, stay down. Move it, Tark, for Christ's sake! There's more than *putas* and pimps in this place…it's much darker than that, something from hell."

Tark sped like NASCAR into the lights ahead until they saw Padric's hummer, a silhouette in the road ahead. Having put enough distance in front of the unknowns, Tark pulled over; he'd let help come to him, but sat with his hand on a sawed-off shotgun he pulled from between the seats. "We're out, Dog. We're good."

But his young partner's eyes were different now, cold…he was a beast. "Fucking gasoline and a match, you and me. We'll light this place up." But then he was calm. "Yeah, I'm good, I'm good."

Tark didn't smile; his boy was okay at least on the outside, but he knew demons would follow him the rest of his days like they did him; he watched his partner make the sign of the cross once again, his lips moved.

The mood changed when Padric rolled up and leaped from hummer to jeep, squeezing in beside Marcus and holding the boy's face in his hands. "Sufferin' Jesus and His Mother, I'm sorry, lad, we didn't get to you sooner." This was the witness Padric had wanted, but the sight of the boy, safe with his men, was more important. He was somebody's son and a worried nun's student. Martinez was elated, but sobered at the sight of the boy's bruises, the pain in his eyes. Shaking and weak, Ramos recognized him, knew he was Mario's father and smiled a little; he said he'd befriended his son at school, even beat up a kid who found out his dad was a cop and was messing with him. The detective was horrified…*at Cathedral High? Where were the nuns? Because he was the law, his son had suffered such things?*

Ramos shocked everyone. "Don't worry about it…he's dead."

"You killed him, *Dios mio.*"

"No, no. She…they killed him."

The men glanced at each other. Martinez frowned. "You're confusing me, *miho, no preocupa ahora*. Where were you?"

He was being called *mijo* again but this time he didn't mind. "In a morgue…her morgue, you know, in her fucking house. I messed up."

"She…who? She's got a morgue? Convenient. What did you do to get her pissed off?"

"The flick…bad things happen when you mess up. I didn't wanna die."

Tark reassured him: "We saw it…how'd you do that?"

"That's what I'm trying to say. She liked me; cut me some slack. Took me out of it right before she had the girls off him."

"Damn, how'd they work that?" Marcus asked. Padric saw how different he was. He was no longer hearing the ex-seminarian.

"Long story…none of us wanted it. The girls were scared shitless. I just got up and ran. The bitch screamed like a *bruja* for Shrek, you know, fuckin' Bruno. He's dead inside, nothing, never speaks. He hauled my ass back and made me watch, her orders, but he wasn't into it either. They…it was the last scene." He started to sob. "I knew him. We hung out since we were kids; they took his head instead of mine, did some film splicing and shit then forced the girls to do their part over and over till they got it the way she wanted. It was like magic; the dude who edits this shit is the best. Fuck, she's got the money." He stopped then whispered: "My homey died in my place."

His homie. Jessie, not Jessie. Hadn't he just spoken with their nun? "Ramos, which homeboy?"

"Carmine…he was with us the night I first met her. Came back the next night."

"For what, to get you out of there?"

"Not Carmine…he wanted to move in on whatever I had, but she thought he was a *pendejo* and kicked him around, used him in bad ways." He broke down. "He was only a kid."

"And you weren't?"

"What…a kid, maybe, but used? No, God, she was all over me and did other things. I liked it but right away, it got to be too much, man. But, yeah, she made me do things…." The men looked closer at the welts; they were hickeys. "She scared me." It hadn't been too much for Padric, but then, he'd never allowed her to do that to him and she never did; again she had ethics; after all, he was a married man. Her upside-down, distorted Ten Commandments dictated she show his wife some respect…*but yeah, she scared me, too.*

"My boy, Carmine, he was a wannabe, acting all down and doing nothing about it. But the girls, they're out there; we took off and were trying to get out of the Edge, laid low, but it was dark… we got separated. I know those babes aren't dead. I am though…I can't pray." It was an odd thing to say for a young man. They studied his face. "I saw things. I saw it…death, too much of it."

Padric pulled some uniforms aside with orders to fan out over the fields, but Marcus told him about the sinister ones who came out of nowhere with threats and the two Tark had left in the dust. The officers grinned; they were up for some *Walking Dead* and took off.

"Do you know how long we've been looking for you, Ramos?" Padric thought of his daughters. "The girls…who were they?"

Ramos smiled a little. "Damn, sir, you don't want to know."

"I'm asking."

"Cathedral High *chicas*…."

One could have knocked the four over with a feather…even Padric was stunned; the kid was right. He didn't want to know… *Magdalen, my God, and Sister Dynamite; can't imagine the reaction.* "Rich girls, but cool, diggin' on Chicanos like me, Darby Hill all the way…parents thought they were in San Diego. It was spring break, man; anything goes with them. J.C. spotted them in a bar with fake IDs and sweet-talked them back to her place, blowing smoke about modeling and shit. Please, look for them."

J.C.…so that's the handle she's running with. Padric leaned closer. "Son, we have our officers on it. But Joanna Cantera. Talk to me." The mere sound of her name triggered something unwanted and painful. He spoke in broken whispers about her enterprise in the Edge. Schnood had said as much.

Paramedics arrived. "What you need?"

"Ruddy…that you?"

"Tarkington, as I live and breath."

"The Royal Scot! Gimme me some living and breathing right over here."

"We got this." Carefully Ruddy Hughes' crew placed the young man on a gurney. "Who's riding with us?" Marcus jumped in beside Ramos. Ruddy grinned at Padric. "What, it's not gonna be Bubby Sands himself?" Famed 1981 hunger-striker and prisoner rights protester, Bobby Sands, was a hero to many in Northern Ireland. Every lad knew about him, but their mums prayed their sons would never die as he did.

Padric shouted: "Up the 'Ra, for Christ sake! Get out of here, you bloody…" They dared not laugh and moved right along. "Take him to Meadow. I don't want anyone near him." Before the paramedics left, he leaned into the van. "Lad; we'll talk. I'm in the business of fixing things and you can help."

"Sir…" Ramos was calmer now. "I wanna help people but I'm not good right now." Padric climbed into the van and Marcus was grateful he'd take the time.

"You're fine and will be even better. You'll heal soon."

"But, sir, I wanna be a cop like Sgt. Marcus."

Padric glanced at Marcus. "That will take a lot of hard work to be as good as he is…rest now. Be well." He fist-pumped Marcus, and told him with his eyes to ask him for more.

But Ramos persisted: "Sister Magdalen, sir." Padric whirled around. "I need to see her if she'll see me." *Been there.* "I never meant to hurt her, not coming back to school and all that…please tell her. We loved her, Carlos and me. *Ay lad, me too.* If she ever finds out what I was doing…"

Know the feeling. "She's very understanding; she'll want to see you." He signaled for Ruddy to move out; the boy, already in deep conversation with Marcus.

The men stood together on a road that twisted its way through the abandoned Chinese flower farms and where no one came or went at this hour, but Chato's sign glared back at them even in early daylight. *Joanna.* Padric was furious. "BOLO her ass again! Drag her in. I can't touch her." Padric was reminding them he was no longer on the case; they were suddenly grim.

Martinez voiced something aloud some had begun to consider and no one wanted to say: "I'm thinking and hating it...one of our own has a role in not letting us find her. Someone in the P.D. is all over this big time." Padric wouldn't allow himself to believe it...*never*.

Tark kicked the dirt. "Well, she's not in the system...no cell, no ping and has probably ripped out any tracking she has in her wheels. You'd think this broad would be carrying two iPhones... *nada*. Throwaways. Nothing online. She's dropped out of her usual activities, gone under and whatever she needs to get done, somebody's doing it for her. Joanna Cantera's got people all over from club owners to the *chica* painting her nails...nobody's saying."

"Then check out that *chica*...get your nails painted! Alex, you've got this; it's moondead related and I'm out." He'd need to back off. "But we need to ID those girls. What parents in Darby Hill didn't hear from their daughters on spring break? They're in high school, for God's sake." But he stopped...it wasn't his case. Forget Ramos the witness; it was Easter.

A young man, thought to be dead, was alive.

They looked east at the dawn.

Padric drove back alone. But he smiled and thought of their nun; his boys had done it; they could tell her but he'd go along for the ride just to see her smile. She'd hug them. She did that.

Insisting Ramos stay under the watchful eyes of Gina Chavez, Marcus hovered over him during intake at Meadow. She knew the boy's family and called his mother, but before the elated woman arrived, Marcus took Ramos' statement on what he had seen the night Father Villa had died. The Joanna he saw there only briefly was the same he'd encountered out there in the Edge. When asked about Joanna's white adobe; he called it a death house and described what went on there. When his mother finally pressed her son close, Marcus left, his heart beating out of his chest. The Edge had gotten inside him; he felt like he'd sinned and needed Father Santeresa.

At the Precinct, Major Crimes turned over what Tark and Marcus had retrieved from the Edge to FBI Agent Bobby Watson.

Padric and he were good friends; he quickly arrived at the Precinct. Carefully he surveyed the contents of the trunk laid out with gloved hands on the long conference table in the Bog. It was clear their prime suspect was even further involved with crimes unrelated but just as horrific; this involved underage prey; she, the predator. Padric could hardly remain in the room…ashamed of ever having desired the likes of Joanna Cantera.

He'd half-watched the films and a brief discussion ensued about snuff, porn and the Sosazuta Cartel dealing in execution and mutilation videos. Tark stepped up, said what he knew, what he'd seen through his years in DEA and VICE.

Watson remarked. "It's kilos for celluloid."

Commander Ramirez and O'Manion were there; after the Chief of Police said a few words and left, they spoke frankly, laid out a tentative plan to rid the land of the Edge. Padric's mind was on overload; he said little but Ramirez had been eyeing him. "All in good time, John."

"Steady now, Batman," growled O'Manion. "Don't let me hear you've done a Thunderdome out in the Edge." They laughed.

"I assure you that's not my style." They roared.

But an ex-lover's involvement in sex and death cinema sent him deeper into a dark place and he eventually vanished downstairs to the weight room where he worked out with Tark for over an hour. He spoke of the woman named Madonna, admitted some interest in her. This was a first. Tark, after a horrid divorce and the loss of his son, had no woman in his life. But he thought he saw some recognition in Padric when he mentioned her name then his face had gone blank.

Damn, another one coming back to haunt me. But he said nothing.

The Commander soon joined them and stated emphatically, they'd be bulldozing the place. "I want the Edge gone but I'm getting nothing but pushback from big names. We'll see…after this, things may change." There was something going on with Ramirez.

Tark was silent. Padric dropped his weights and sat up. "And what else do you want?"

"I want the Canteras and that arrogant son-of-a-bitch, the one we don't know about. I want the brains behind all of it. We know that he's male and I'll bet you a *peso* he's family."

"Yeah," Tark said, "They're blood."

Padric shook his head. "Good luck. I recused myself."

A look passed between Tark and Ramirez who sat down; the three talked for a while, but the good man was showing more passion. It was personal. Padric reminded him. "I think you want me on this but I'll destroy everything we did on this case if it comes out in court that I'm linked to that woman." Martinez appeared in the doorway.

Ramirez asked him to join them and looked squarely at Padric. "It's not going to court if we get them to talk. I'll water-board them myself."

"We have to arrest them first."

"And you want that more than you need food and a Jameson, John. It's come to my attention your unit refuses to accept your recusal, so shut up." The Commander never said shut up. "Here it is: you will resume lead on the martyr murder investigation, effective immediately but very low key."

Low key…obviously he's being droll. But Padric wouldn't say that. Thinking the same, Tark smiled. The Commander continued: "You will un-recuse yourself, as Jace has so eloquently put it…his words." Padric was not sure how to respond; *damn, this is a first, me, with not a sound coming out of my mouth.* "Nor will the esteemed Latino, with whom you spend your nights, stop nagging me. I almost suspended Alejandro yesterday for being a pain in the ass; seems he refuses to go on living unless you return to lead on the case."

"Christ, you don't know what you're asking."

"And I'll let you know when that is the case. Your partner's performance is stellar, does things with less drama. But he'll be a miserable bastard and pose a threat if you're not on board."

"A threat to what, for God's sake?" He'd play along.

"To the morale of the Precinct."

The other two grinned and, true to form, Padric would go "Days of Our Lives" on them and pulled Martinez to him. "When I say it's over, it's over, *kema sabe*. Find someone else." They laughed out loud.

But the Commander would not be upstaged. "John, you will finish what you started. I have my way of doing things and we have your back. Alejandro, speak."

Martinez did not appreciate being ordered about like a dog, but he'd let it go. "You didn't want to jeopardize the investigation having done the deed with the one known suspect we have. Fuck that...I take that back. Don't." Some laughter. "If we get confessions and we will, there's no trial, no need to concern ourselves with the personal. Even if the woman talks about how good you are in the sack, no one would believe it." They laughed; he realized what he had said. "I mean they wouldn't believe it...she's a wack job."

"You had me for a minute; I thought my rep with the ladies was better than that." The others winced...this was not the time to go *bragioso* given the circumstances. "Scratch that; my words are in very poor taste." The men shook their heads.

Ramirez and the others hammered him despite Padric's what-ifs. "You will return, John." He exhorted the three to move with all due haste whether it was by the book or not. "Our prime suspect collects men in high places; their names are on chamber doors in the courthouse. There will be few to cast stones at you, John; they cannot and won't. Don't go righteous on us when we have exigency here. This case is large; there's public outcry."

Tark was adamant. "They'll ignore some conflict of interest if they're part of the conflicting themselves."

Ramirez nodded. "And be assured the judge on the bench for this case is very conflicted." Padric frowned...*not Jay Whitton.*

"We hope that just once here in L'Arroyo, they'll look at the larger pic but watch yourself, all of you. That's it, John, stop with the soul of integrity crap." Silence. But Padric had more to say.

"Stop!" Tark. He never said much in meetings. "Johnny, for Christ's sake; come down off your cross and stop dying. By any means necessary we do this."

Padric thought for a moment, looking like Atlas with the weight of the world on his shoulders. "Fuck it...thanks for spending your time on my bullshit." He wiped his face with a towel. Relieved, Tark and Martinez left. Ramirez and he were alone. The Commander asked Padric how long had he known him. "Since high school when you spoke at Cathedral and I said I wanted to be a cop. You were a sharp, young lieutenant and I liked how shiny your shoes were. Granted I took a detour, joined the Marines, did some schooling back home in Belfast then ASU. But I've been here forever."

The Commander chuckled…but lowered his voice. "The chilling fact of the matter is that I too am familiar with Ms. Cantera; in the past, she's approached me on several occasions; the woman has certain appetites, looks through a man like a *bruja* and knows his needs in the bedroom." *Not my main man, the Commander…not Ramirez.* "The first time she made a move was at my niece's wedding; my wife's family and the Canteras have mutual friends. For several weeks after, she showed up where I was, knew my itinerary. Once at a hotel where I was staying while lecturing at a law conference at ASU and even at that little hole in the wall I like, Casa Mary's, she showed up. Ms. Cantera had her ways, nothing to brash, but wanting with that thing she does with her eyes."

Yes. Padric knew. "I never resisted. And you, if I could, sir?"

"There was no want in me for this woman; have you ever seen my wife?" He stood up and walked to the end of the lockers. "She'll always be Sophia Loren to me."

Deanna Carrera Ramirez was all that with a little Beyoncé thrown in the mix, but the detective wouldn't say that. "You're a good man, sir; I'm not; but you met my beautiful Lara."

"So, what the hell were you thinking?"

He had no good answer. "I'm a narcissistic son-of-a-bitch, wanting it when I want it. I was impulsive and reckless and there weren't too many women I couldn't have; they put it in front of me. European, Irish, a badge and a gun…damn, it does it for some of them. I'm sorry all this happened to you but thank God, you're a better man than I am."

"*Gracias*. But not always, John; you have trusted me with things, private matters. I am doing the same. I was out of the academy less than a year and newly married, when I had an affair. It's haunted me; consumed my whole life as I fear your fling with this woman will do to you." A chill passed through Padric. He asked how he could help. "There was a child. I have a daughter unknown to my wife." Padric showed no reaction, a better man than he was sitting here pouring his heart out. "Her mother is dead; she walked into a vicious attack on her sister and tried to step in." He sat down again. "She was young, *caliente*, a beautiful woman, a teacher…she was everything to me despite the beautiful wife I had but one who does not like deep conversations about life and the world, art and politics…I did; my lover did. I was at her crime scene while others processed it. I didn't recuse myself because I didn't have to… it wasn't my case. But that story we'll leave for another day when I will ask your help."

"Where is the girl?"

"She's lost to me in a different way."

He'd chance it. "She's in the Edge."

Ramirez smiled a little. "And that's s why you're one of my lead detectives; she's there now if not dead already. Find her." Padric nodded. *Joanna. She'd have had something to do with it. She likes to even things up if she doesn't get what she wants.* The last forty-eight had brought much to the surface; Padric was in again. "You will drag that woman in by the hair for me."

And he would.

Author's Notes

torture-porn — *reference to the so-called over-the-top splatter and gore films focusing on extreme graphic violence and use of special effects targeting the vulnerability of victims and the human body. In The Moondead, Joanna Cantera, takes it further, creating something even more disturbing: the snuff film.*

snuff — *reference to a supposed film genre in which actor is murdered or commits suicide on screen though there is debate as to whether such films actually exist and are simply contrived and produced for the sole purpose of financial exploitation.*

NASCAR — *National Association for American Stock Car Racing.*

pendejo — *Spanish, for stupid.*

'Bubby' Sands — *reference to 1981 Irish Protester/ Hunger Striker Bobby Sands who became a symbol for many during the Troubles in Ireland.*

Up the 'RA — *common cry of protest by and for the Irish Republican Army.*

BOLO — *all-points police bulletin for "Be on the look-out."*

bragioso — *Italian, for bragging, boastful with swagger.*

caliente — *Spanish, for hot.*

15 MAIREAD

Easter Sunday, mid-afternoon, March 23

The girls had pulled him down on the floor for a wrestle and hugs when Padric opened the door. He'd remembered bunnies and eggs and Easter surprises. Mairead was delighted her older brother had followed directions and shopped the right places. Weak though she was, Lara had given some input. Both he and Pistasio had hit the stores before coming home that morning; the sargeant had four teenage girls of his own but hinted about strains in his marriage of twenty years. Padric had told him to hold on; fix it, work it out; they'd been like brothers, Pistasio always the quiet, vigilant one watching the detective's every step.

Within the past forty-eight, he'd visited Lara three times, sat silently watching her sleep, bruised, eyes blackened, hooked up to IVs and tubes; he made the rounds standing by the bedside of Petra, alive but drifting in and out of consciousness; her parents grateful to see him. And there was Ramos…discovered to be filled with infection, HIV maybe; Padric punched his fist into the staircase wall when he left, feeling helpless. Now at home, he was happily surprised when Mairead told him two female rookie officers had accompanied her and the girls to Our Lady of Sorrows for Easter Mass.

Padric picked at her beautiful brunch, couldn't say he'd recused himself from the case but was back…he'd tell her everything someday. He glanced at his watch and called Lara; she was awake. Each, in their own touching way, told her they loved her. His daughters crawled up in his lap and would not let him go; he leaned back with one in each arm resting their heads on his shoulders and closed his eyes. Mairead wept; she knew her brother and his ways. He had more than the Precinct on his mind.

Later that night, Martinez was restless, hating his computer, wanting a secretary, preferably Roselyn Sanchez from *Without a Trace* or Leonor Varela, *Blade II*; he pondered a list of Latina beauties with brains. Padric said he'd tell Marisol. Silence. He stood up and cursed in Spanish. "We're off the clock; Casa Mary's, let's get some *enchiladas*."

"Get 'er done!" chimed the two. O'Manion heard them and stepped into the hall.

Padric looked at him. "What?"

"That's copyright infringement, boys, knock it off." He grinned. "Get in here, you two."

O'Manion was putting a twenty-four hour guard on Mairead's condo, his family…they'd monitor Mairead's movements to and from work, the kids back and forth to their school. The pictures found in Joanna's place in the Edge had raised flags. Padric again punched his fist into the wall…this time doing some damage.

He was in pain but he and Martinez left quickly. "That it would come to this…I want weekly visits in prison until I'm put to death, Alex. I'm gonna kill a woman." In seconds, requests for added security near Mairead's condo were set in motion, a patrol car around the clock; an officer posted in the hallway outside her door. Within minutes, Padric was turning his key in the lock.

Silence. He hated quiet in a dark house at night; there were always bodies at the end of the hall…at least in his world. But there was a light in Mairead's room. Up late and working on a lead story for the newspaper, she leaped from her chair and bolted into the hallway. "Feckin' bloody hell, Johnny, if you're coming home early, call me, for God's sake." She stared at him. "What's happened? Why are you here…" She saw Martinez and smiled. "Let me yell at my brother a bit." He winked at her; Padric intense, asked if the girls were all right? "Of course…go look for yourself."

They were sleeping soundly on his bed with smiles on their faces and had refused to sleep anywhere else, Mairead said. He sat down on the loft steps to explain why they needed protecting. "Sis, I've been fucking our prime suspect since Christmas." Her eyes narrowed. Martinez stood silently at the window looking down into the street. He confirmed uniforms would be posted on Mairead's floor and inside the entrances to the building downstairs.

A police presence was not unfamiliar to Mairead; it brought back childhood memories of a seventies-eighties Belfast. But she had a mindset like her brother; he had even said once that she should be out in the streets with a shield and he buried in what he loved best, the written word and a good story. "She stalked you, Johnny, knew when you came home; she was watching your wife, where she went, what she did. And now she's after our girls…I'll break her knees."

He knew she would do it if given the chance. Padric glanced at his watch. "You're right…as usual. I'll handle this personally."

"I don't like when you look at your watch and say you're handling things personally."

Martinez sighed. "She knows her brother."

Padric ignored them. "I'll be back. But they will not be going again to that school where we use to live. I need them closer. And am putting them in the Sister's convent school for wee ones at San Miguel. It's something new; our nun says they're still accepting applications and you'll be checking it out with me. That broad had pics of my girls on her wall for a reason. My boys went nuts when they found them."

"And a feckin' nice address that is with our girls' faces in it."

"The girls and I will be having a sit-down."

Mairead grabbed his face and made him look at her. "They're wee lasses, for God's sake; do you think you should be calling a conversation with children, a sit-down?"

"I'm their father." Nothing could sway him.

"And that counts? I'm picturing this when they're eighteen; there'll be hell to pay, darlin'. Besides, we're good. I've got it covered." She pulled him into her room and reached up to the top shelf of a cabinet full of newspapers.

Carefully Mairead took down a back issue of the Times;

Padric rolled his eyes. "I'm not in the mood to be reading one of your articles now, lass." Rolled up in its pages lay a 45 Smith and Wesson. "Sufferin' Jesus…Alex! Get in here."

But Martinez was hesitant to enter the lady's bedroom; Mairead motioned to him. "You mind's well make yourself at home, *bhoyo;* looks like we're family now."

The men were astounded. "Christ, Readie, it's a Governor with a trace laser."

"I wanted more than six rounds, but that's all it's got."

"*Santa Madre de Dios*! You paid a thou' for that."

"I got a discount. The fella knew you, Johnny."

"Who? And when did you buy it, woman?"

"Don't ya' dare go all Armalite and Symtex on me, Johnny!"

The men laughed. Padric apologized. "Lass, you gotta…ah, hell, keep it, for Christ's sake. You've had a permit since the day you were hired at the paper."

"I'm more upset you were fecking the lady with the hard on for your wife and girls. I know what she did to her; I edit the articles on every one of the moondead. I talk to people. Jaysus, keep your breeches zipped. You'll never learn." Martinez smiled…*yes, she did know her brother*. But she wept, done being strong. "Your Lara's like a sister to me, my God, the dear, poor thing havin' you for a mate." She swatted him again on the head.

"It's over, believe me, luv. I'll fill you in later. We need to go for a bit. But, damn, where the fuck is all this protectin' we're supposed to be getting?" A soft knock answered his question sending Martinez down the hall; both men drew their revolvers.

Mairead grabbed her own, recalling her father doing the same. "Christ, Johnny, no more drama…put those away." The men turned and stared at her…she stood there with both hands on her piece, but lowered it when she saw the First Precinct at the door. She slipped the gun between the Times again and returned it high and out of reach of the girls.

When the woman returned, her face was serene and cordial; she nodded and smiled at the officer. Padric looked from one to the other. "You know each other?"

The sergeant grinned. "You can't put anything over on him, Miss Padric."

Cunningham. Padric smiled. "You two?"

"Oh, for God's sake, Johnny…the only 'you two' I like is the band." The men laughed and she shut the door, but not before smiling at Nevel. He was seated and listening to every word; Cunningham gave a nod and the dog wagged his tail at her.

Padric laughed. "Damn, he likes the ladies." He thought of Magdalen and winked. "I'll let you take my sister out if you do a good job here tonight." They chuckled and talked for a while. His phone lit up; O'Manion confirming all was in place. Ready to duck, he kissed Mairead on the cheek; he'd taken his share of blows in the past.

He'd tell Martinez later, he hadn't been "batting 300" with the ladies; pounded by a nun in the Cathedral, told to behave by another raised from the dead and a wife raining down verbal condemnation. Nor would his girls, wee things, be outdone, when they told him what he could and could not do if he wanted to stay on their good side. He knew what to expect from Mairead; she could do him some real damage.

It was silent when he was gone and Mairead put on the kettle; feeling little eyes watching her, she looked up. Kate was leaning over the loft ledge.

"What's 'fuck' mean, Auntie?"

Author's Notes

Armalite − trademark name for a lightweight, high-velocity rifle of various calibers, capable of automatic and semiautomatic operation.

Symtex − a all-purpose plastic explosive used in demolition and commercial blasting, in the military; used notoriously by terrorists and the IRA…until recently, extremely difficult to detect.

Santa Madre de Dios! − Spanish, for Holy Mother of God.

"batting 300" − reference to an excellent batting statistic in cricket, baseball, and softball.; today an average higher than .400, nearly perfect.

Saint Dysmas or Dismas − one of two thieves in the Scriptures who were crucified beside Jesus. In the Gospels of Mark and Matthew, they mock Him, but in the Gospel of Luke,

Dysmas asks Jesus to "remember him" when He "comes into" His kingdom. The other, known as the Impenitent thief, questions why Jesus cannot save Himself. It is reasonable then why an institute for criminals might be named for the other.

hacienda-ranchero – *Spanish, for ranch house and ranch.*

La Maschera – *Italian, for the mask, the name of nightclub in L'Arroyo.*

16 THE CATHEDRAL

Several days after Easter, March

From her window, Magdalen had gazed at the angels in the garden for several days…she was one of them and would gradually understand her affinity for them. Tonight they looked stunned and in mourning and she was haunted by what Petra had said only last week: "Why should we expect to suffer any less than Christ?" But Magdalen, weary of soul and heart, fell into an unusual slumber for a whole day, a night and into the late afternoon of the next. When Padric knocked on the convent door and wanting to talk, Gabriela made it clear: Sister was indisposed; she could not possibly speak with him.

He was surprised at his feeling of loss with no access to her. Though he wouldn't admit it, she too was his drug of choice like his other women, but she was balm to his soul. Wistfully Magdalen had said nothing when she was told he had called; though she wouldn't admit it, she missed his concern for her, the care in his eyes.

It was Monica who sat by her side and fed her when she awoke. Two days passed and suddenly Magdalen was back; she sat up and smiled, Neither high school nor Cathedral had reopened; both wrapped in garish crime tape, nor had she gone to the sacristy since Easter when the bishop celebrated Mass in the school gym. Eduardo and Guadalupe were allowed entry after CSI left and they saw to her duties.

Even the bishop anxiously awaited her return. But he too had become more remote. While Steed and Sebastian kept the ship afloat, he sat alone in the vestry regardless of what the First

Precinct wanted. He'd even escaped to the Cantera ranch, rode his horse and assisted the men in the stables. The bishop's burdens had taken their toll and God seemed far removed from him; the shepherd was lost and numbers were down in the pews. Santo Cantera rarely spoke; when he did, he no longer referred to the glory of martyrdom.

Several nights later, feeling better but unable to sleep, Magdalen rose from her bed...her shoulders were hurting, a pain she had suffered since arriving at San Miguel. In the garden however, something unexpected awaited; she had a visitor. There, among her angels of stone and seated apart, was an extraordinary creature, its features seraphic with hair parted in the middle, wings curled gently around him. Resting in the branches of a mesquite like a bird, he was praying then turned. For several long moments, he looked at her intuitively as only an angel would, and with no words, communicated to her his concern, urging her to be strong in the Lord, insisting her gifts were desperately needed in this part of the Kingdom, this dark place called San Miguel. And then...he was gone.

But she questioned how she could understand this otherworldly, unless she was like him in nature? *Do I carry some of his angel-spirit inside me...this is too vain to even consider. But who am I...what am I?* She knew things at times when others did not...angels did that, the holy ones practiced discernment of spirit, Saint Ignatius, his Jesuits; *it was fitting for them, their task to do so, but me?* She'd always known she existed in a world between heaven and earth, somewhere in between good and evil. It was like that in Egypt. Now her life was decidedly different; she would leave it to God and peacefully fell asleep.

The next morning Magdalen sensed something had changed; if she'd had any doubts about remaining a nun, these had melted away like candlewax. She belonged here. Later that Saturday morning, the cool and calm of the Cathedral would welcome her back. A degree of normalcy had returned to her world without Petra and a week away had done wonders. Steed had told her the bishop was anxious for her to return. It was His grace then, who had made certain the sanctuary floor was spotless and shining; after the crime cleanup team had departed...he'd called in even other professionals to rid the Cathedral of every cobweb... and blood drop. It was waiting for her.

Agnes, replacing Petra as convent director, had asked if she was not still in danger. Perhaps…but she'd soldier on and was not really alone. Uniforms were posted everywhere, in and outside the Cathedral, a detail not every officer was happy to work. But rookies Tarkington and Tate were "good with it" if it allowed them to meet the archaeologist-nun working for the First Precinct. But consulting for Lt. John Padric…was she Joan of Arc? He was a handful; she could use an assist. Happily he would soon ask them to shadow her.

But today she knew Guadalupe would be there; the old woman waved when she saw her. They embraced but Magdalen wondered how Petra's demise had affected the woman who'd lived her whole life within the Cathedral. Today however, she was avoiding Magdalen's gaze; when they spoke of no bodies being released until the killers were caught, she wept. The morgue was a cold, silent place between heaven and hell.

Magdalen studied her…*what does she know?* Lupe was staring at the place where Petra had suffered. "It is hard. I am too old for this and don't know what to do."

She waited…nothing; she'd change the subject. "How do you live with the bells?"

Lupe smiled: "*Hermana*, the bells are my children and each has a name. They ring on a timer in the bishop's study. They are *familia*, waking at seven then back to their beds at seven. When they ring I am up and about my business here or cleaning the hacienda at the Cantera ranch, you know." *No, I don't…interesting. How close to the Canteras, is she?* "I am grateful for everything Santo does for me. He wants me to live in his house, two nice rooms next to the kitchen, but I prefer it here. You see, *hermana*, the Cathedral belongs to me." They laughed and the nun asked now she had accomplished this. "It's only in my head; Father Antonio made this holy place what it is. Before he retired to the desert, he told me to watch over it and I have." She looked away. "I have tried." Her eyes filled with tears. "Santo, *sacro senor*, he is a little brother to me." That the bishop could be anyone's little brother was beyond imagining for Magdalen. "Yes, my home is under the bells. I sleep when they sleep."

But Magdalen would remind her: "You had wanted to speak with me last week."

Lupe hesitated. "No, it can wait," she whispered then stood up and abruptly hurried away. Clearly she had seen what had happened that Good Friday night.

Magdalen re-entered the sacristy, startled to find the bishop emerging from the vestry. He was taken off guard as well, but quickly recovered, smiling warmly at Magdalen. "How good to see you at last, Sister."

He left quickly. *Everyone's running away today.* Later, she returned to the Cathedral with Monica; the shrine of Saint Michael the Archangel was getting a "re-do", as Dolorosa put it; she'd shadowed Magdalen all week, but today was Monica's turn and Magdalen sat at her feet in the glow of the votive candles, replacing the used with the new.

The new priest had come upon them and chuckled. "So this is where you spend your weekends." They smiled and the elder beckoned him toward her. Like a young boy, he sat down beside her on the marble step edging the shrine.

Delighted, Monica whispered:."I've wanted to meet you."

"And I you, Sister. I understand you can pray me into heaven."

"I can." And they laughed. "Now tell me. You are a soldier."

"Yes, I guess I always will be. I was military for four years and now here I am."

He glanced at those who were beginning to fill the back pews, seeking a priest to hear their sins. "They're early and looking for a little redemption...will hear confessions shortly." Magdalen wondered what he and the detectives had shared in the ME's van on the way to the morgue with Petra. She thanked him. "I did what I should. The bishop told me I must be out there taking care of the details and assist where he can't, if that's possible." Magdalen was already worried for him.

"So you are learning then. You will be busy."

"San Miguel has its challenges," the elder whispered. But she wanted to know everything about this young man, from his days at Notre Dame to his call to the seminary which he said was cut short by the tragic, sudden loss of his parents, shot dead in a restaurant in Gesualdo, their birthplace, on a return visit to Italy. He was angry, he said, wanted to shoot up things; withdrew from the seminary and joined the Marines.

His eyes were filled with the pain of remembering and Monica would not disappoint. "And you met no beautiful women?"

Only Monica. Magdalen shook her head and could not look at the priest. "I met more than a few. But that's in the past."

"Your seminary obviously took you back then." But they had not, he said; it was the bishop who himself had attended the same seminary, had heard what had happened to Sebastian then arranged that he be ordained with the monks *up the road.*

"Ah, the holy one of the Order of Saint Dysmas. Santo ordained you then."

"Yes…all seven of us; six monks and me. We're good friends now. They operate Saint Dysmas Institute for the Criminally Insane and I'll be visiting their facility weekly. It's quite a place."

"Well, then my boy, Santo Cantera is Church law in the Sonoran. You are in." They laughed but he glanced at Magdalen… was she the archaeologist?

"The cemetery your parents are buried in…" *Ah, there it is.* "Where were they laid to rest, Father?"

Who else would be interested in a graveyard? "I heard you liked cemeteries and understand you're an archaeologist and have dug up half my *Italia.* Theo's been singing your praises. And there was Egypt as well for you." She nodded. "My parents are interred in a private mausoleum on the Tuscan estate of a generous relative. It was their wish, his wish, not mine. But I am here now." He glanced at his watch. "I must pray before I go into the box." He was a breath of fresh air. "And you too are new to San Miguel; not everything's easy here, is it." She only smiled.

He walked away and knelt down on a prie-dieu to pray. But Sebastian knew her…Italy. He'd met her one night; he was sure of it. A prudent man, he would say nothing.

Unknown to either of them, 'a re-do' of a different kind was taking place somewhere else. Padric would have the painful task of putting his own life in order…he had help. After CSI had concluded their findings, Pistasio and Jana descended on the Padric home, sending clothing to the cleaners and huge pods to a storage facility near the First Precinct. When all was accomplished, a For Sale sign sadly appeared on the front lawn. Done and dusted.

Padric was numb through it all but telling no one, he visited the Nile, this time flashing his badge, taking the backstairs two at a time with the assistant hotel manager. He'd arrest her ass. *Nada.* Ms. Cantera hadn't been there in a while. He was nauseous, suddenly needing to see his wee girls...he'd go home, listen to the sound of their voices.

Ms. Cantera was on her way home as well; there was no better place to hide herself than at her father's *hacienda-ranchero,* a place where the LPD would hardly set foot...or so she thought. Joanna knew every alley in L'Arroyo; they belonged to her. Tonight she slipped in and out of them, until she turned into the back road winding through brush and mesquite up to the house. She skidded to a stop at the last barn. A ranchhand grinned when he saw her.

"How'd it do for you, Ms. Cantera, running okay?" She'd switched cars again, purchasing the young man's 1997 Sentra; when she learned his little girl was in the hospital again, she stuffed more bills in his hand.

He refused them; she whispered: "Not another word. Little girls need every break they can get." Later she sat alone on the balcony looking out at her father's land. This would all be hers someday...Arturo had reassured her the other night when they had spoken of many things. Soon she would go with him to a tower house he'd built years ago in the mountains west of the city...*una casa de seguridad,* she liked to say; their safe-house.

But last night, the man had asked her to be careful; he could only shield her just for so long, using who and what he knew to protect her. The Cantera scion had not allowed a search of the *hacienda,* demanded a warrant and no judge would give one. He could do that...his bishop-son, not so easily. Arturo knew his beloved Joanna could handle herself but she perplexed him, gave him nightmares. He refused to believe what he heard about her; he knew she loved drama. Still…his Joanna would always have the option to disappear with him into Mexico, if it got worse or, God forbid, all this was true. Early that day Arturo had left for Sinaloa on business.

Tonight, she'd take her chances. Joanna was restless and risk-hungry; she'd hit up a club or two, where she could hide, her favorite…*La Maschera.* The Masquerade required its patrons wear stylish half-masks, its venue, darker than most and very exclusive to those who could pay the price of a steep cover charge. Tucked away in the theater district behind the museum and only blocks from the First Precinct, it had been built into the walls of an old condemned city morgue…strange things were rumored to happen here. Masked ne'er-do-wells doing nefarious things frustrated the law to no end.

She'd give her wannabe entourage some of her time. Boring. As she touched up her make-up and changed into something red, she turned on the late night news. A documentary and vivid montage/chronology of the martyr murders flashed on the screen. Her face grew somber, eyes darker. There was Johnny, man in charge; she smiled. "Hey, baby!" Surely he wanted her…it had been a while, over a week. Things would soon settle down again…that thing with his wife, nothing to worry about.

She'd seen the coverage night after night and now on the screen there he was again, comforting that nun; even holding her hand. *Damn her.* A wine glass hit the wall. She'd explain a few things to her man…lay down some rules. But one didn't do that to Johnny Padric.

That man was having his own difficulties and a family matter to settle. Mairead had mentioned Kate's asking about the F-word and there was something else. He'd need to take care of this, start acting like the father he hadn't been; he'd call for a…sit-down. But they'd pounced on him as soon as he walked through the door.

Moments later Mairead drew him into her bedroom. Could he speak to Kate about the F-word. Like he needed this, Padric muttered and frowned. He'd take care of it.

"I'm missing your wife, Johnny. I want to see her. My God, this is horrible, but the girls are dealing with it better than I thought."

"Thanks to you, sis. I owe you big time. I'll get you into Meadow this week. Lara needs you, lass. How much time off did the newspaper give you?" The assistant editor for the L'Arroyo Moon would work from her desk at home for as long as it took.

They spoke of many things and of family, his mum, his two younger sisters, but were interrupted by his daughters who crawled up into his lap and would not let him go. He leaned back with one in each arm resting their heads on his shoulders and closed his eyes. They grew very still as if understanding the turmoil inside their father. Kate listened to his heartbeat under his shirt.

"I love your heart, da'?"

"Do you now. Why's that, luv?"

"You're good." He was shocked; tears came easy to his eyes. Mairead turned away. Her brother was carrying a burden and she'd like a moment with the woman who was tearing him up.

"How do you know?"

"You work all the time, but you love us, you're brave like Batman and help people and you're being nice to Mommy now." *Now*...he was being nice *now*.

"I'm happy," interjected little Kara. "She won't cry anymore."

Padric kissed his youngest. "You saw your mum cry?"

"Yup."

"I'm sorry you had to be seeing that, luv." But his concerns about opening up a discussion with Kate about the F-word lay heavy upon him. This was more ominous than an interrogation down at the Precinct.

"So da', do you fuck...what's fucking again, Auntie?" Mairead rolled her eyes and turned away laughing quietly to herself despite the seriousness of the matter.

Kara giggled. "Fuck's a funny word." She waddled around and flapped her arms like a duck. "Fuck, fuck, fuck...fuck, fuck, fuck. Don't worry, da', about us. We won't say it in school Fuck, fuck, fuck...fuck, fuck, fuck."

Never would he conduct such an interview. One subject was acting like a duck; the other had turned it around and was asking him if he's ever done it. He glanced at Mairead and she whispered: "So you were going to have a sit-down with your oldest daughter?"

This was new. Where was his wife when he needed her? He would welcome a spray of bullets, a smack-down in the street. "Where did you get this word, Kate?"

"You, da' and Joey Burns."

"Me? Who the f…" He stopped. "Who's Joey Burns, girl?"

"He's actually very bad."

"A cute boy Katey likes." Kate swatted Kara; they giggled.

"Actually? Where did you get that word, Kate?"

"I heard it around."

"And this Mr. Burns…what am I to think of him?"

"Nothing really, da'…don't worry about it." He had visions of her saying this to him when she was eighteen. Unmanned drones… he would employ them to keep an eye on the two of them. He'd heard the President say he had the same plan for his daughters. He sighed and looked up at the ceiling.

"But da', you're changing the subject. You said you were fucking. I heard it."

He was being told by an eight year old he was changing the subject and had fucked. "When?"

"You thought we were sleeping the other night, but not me; I played like I was, when you came upstairs then I heard you talking to Auntie."

"I'm sorry you had to hear that, Kate."

"Why, what's wrong with fucking? What's it mean?"

Jaysus…Lara, what do I say? Alex…he'd know what to say. Had his kids after asked him this? Probably not…he didn't fuck around. Padric thought for a while. The girls were still waiting. "It's called the F-word because it should never be said. Grown ups say it when they're mad. I was wrong and angry when I said it. You can't say it ever again. Never." The two girls continued to stare at him.

Kara began to flap her arms and dance around again. "Fuck, fuck, fuck…fuck, fuck, fuck." Padric grabbed her up in his arms. She giggled, but Kate persisted. "But what's it mean?"

"It means doing something you shouldn't."

"But you did."

"I did. I was wrong. I did something I feel bad about."

Kara whispered: "Cause you got caught?" *Damn, she's brilliant.* "But what do you do when you fuck...oops. I mean F?"

"Very good, Kara...you're learning, lass. I forget what you do, cause it isn't important." He realized there was more truth to this than they would ever understand. But he'd not engaged in this activity for some time with his wife and was feeling the absence of it. He wanted their mother. "And that's all there is to it; now we'll not speak of it again. Little girls don't need to think about it. I want you to be polite, nice lasses who don't use words like that. And...you'll never speak of this to your mom. She's sick now.' *God, what do I do if they tell their mother I was fucking somebody?* "This is for only grown ups to talk about." He was getting in deeper.

"But we can say fuck, I mean F, when we grow up, right, da'?" Kate wouldn't give up.

"No....never." They wouldn't be growing up if he could help it. *No, they could not think about fucking. This needed to end.* "Now, enough with the F-word!" The girls became silent, waiting...he looked like he had more to say. But Padric suddenly roared like a lion and grabbed them up in his arms. "But I have good news for my lasses. Your granny and aunties are coming to live with us for a while." They screamed and jumped up and down.

"For a long time...please say yes!" They ran away chattering like squirrels but Padric was concerned. His Kate was growing up too fast. Mairead said it was true and called Kate back into the kitchen. Padric pulled her up on his lap. "Come 'ere, girl. Why are you asking so many questions...wanting to know things?"

"I just want to know all about stuff. We have no mum, no house, nothing except..." *My God, it's come to this.* The two adults in the room stared at each other. Padric shook his head slowly; *my kids are causalities of war, collateral damage.* Kara danced back into his arms.

"You've got mum...she's just sick for a little bit. She'll be coming home right away now...just wait. And I'm taking you to see her in the hospital very soon. Auntie and me and granny; we love you."

"And we'll be good if you be good. No more F-word either."

"I'll be good." But he was not sure he could live without saying the F-word. He was tired beyond tired and leaned back in his chair. He needed sleep. The girls ran upstairs to the loft and dragged out their toys.

Mairead hugged her brother. "You've got your walking orders, *bhoyo.*" He avoided her eyes so she wouldn't see his pain, even the fear. She needed his strength; he was weary of being strong but embraced her and held her tight.

He embraced her and held her tight. Grateful for each other, they felt very alone and vulnerable with a watchman and a dog outside their door. He looked out the window into the street below and pulled out his cell phone.

"Yo." Pistasio.

"Anything?"

"*Nada*…what do you want me to do?"

"Find her and hold on to her. I'll come to you."

"I'm on it." The two worked in tandem; it was their way of dealing with things off the books Martinez excluded. Nothing could touch him; he was too good a man.

"Da', Kara wants to ask you something."

"Say it, luv…come here, wee girl."

She ran into his arms. "Can little kids say shit?"

17 EXORCIST

Two weeks passed; in the late evening, a night breeze cooler than usual made the priest shiver. Father Santeresa looked up. A waning moon, almost touching the eaves of the rectory, still gave its light. In mid-afternoon, he'd been graced with a visit from a distraught bishop. They shared a light lunch; as usual, Santo was being mysterious and finally left.

"It's complicated," he'd said. Santeresa had smiled; everyone says that nowadays.

Later, the priest picked up his breviary to pray on the vine-covered porch of the rectory. It was close to the street and passersby often stopped to speak with the priest who held court at dusk and even into the night. Earlier he'd chatted with the young man who was always there to assist. He liked Jesús Marcus, who lived in the condominium next to the church. Since the murders, he'd often sat by the rectory door with him when not at the Precinct. Father Santeresa had never been afraid of the shadows; the dark of night and the moon were his friends. He listened; it told him things, but tonight, the stillness was broken by the mournful strains of a Medieval funeral dirge. *Dies irae and dies illa.*

Down the street in an alley, a tricked-out red Mercedes truck rolled down the ramp of a small, unmarked moving van and rolled slowly out into the night. Lights from the vehicle lit up the street…it was out of place, didn't fit. But Santeresa knew the chant and stood up, eyeing the truck as it slowed to a crawl then stopped in front of his house. *So here they are. My God, it's the Canteras.*

Sitting high in the cab, two hooded figures stared down at him. They were surprised...he appeared unperturbed. Santeresa walked toward them. They both had the bishop's eyes; he'd known them when they were children; *now look at them...always the drama.*

Since the death of his friend, Father Villa, he'd sensed it, knew they were the killers. "If you want me, get out of that ridiculous set of wheels and come get me."

He extended his arms in the form of a cross; his lack of caution, throwing them off their game; this was unexpected. The priest knew it. "You heard me...I'm waiting."

His dramatic gesture appealed to the young man, who leaned forward, revealing the macabre but beautiful half skull of a mask he wore under his hood. In a sinister move, he slowly made a sweeping sign of the cross, but the exorcist-priest didn't flinch; he'd cast demons from the souls of cartel in his Border ministry...this was elementary. He pondered the hooded one's voice, did a read on his spirit; he'd need work...this soul had let evil in.

The priest studied his soul, touched its dark center with his holiness but the unseen pushback from what lived within made him step back, yet he still stood his ground.

"If you persist in stopping by of an evening, I might have to work a good thing on your soul." The young man before him cried out, his hands raised to his face; there was the distinct smell of burning flesh then it was over. Glowing like coals, the eyes of the hooded one peered through singed eyebrows and lashes, a side of his face raw and burned now by fire. Momentarily subdued, his demons only slightly diminished, he spoke in a rasp: "Not this time, *padre*. You're redeemed for tonight...*benedicite.*"

They vanished into the night. *Dies irae, dies illa.*

Two hours later and not far from the rectory, a knock at the door of the bishop's home brought Sebastian down to the vestibule. Steed, up late in his office, opened the door.

"I'll get it, Michael. I know who it is."

An unmarked moving van had stopped near the curb and sped

quickly away. Dressed to the nines, the bishop's sister stood in the doorway. "My...where'd you get this one?"

It was obvious she was undressing the Cathedral's newest addition with her eyes. "I'll leave this one to you, Theo." The priest knew the look and turned his back on Joanna Cantera and disappeared up the stairs. It made his blood boil...women with no boundaries assuming they could do this, objectifying him because of his looks, preying on men of God. No more, nevermore, he muttered; those days of liking such things were behind him. Even Santo Cantera had warned him, wanting him free of what he himself had endured. Unfortunately no one had explained Joanna Cantera to Sebastian. He'd shown none of the usual interest she expected and he would pay.

"What's his problem, Monsignor? Not too friendly." She'd need to do something about him in more ways than one. "What did you say his name was?" Later Joanna would tell her older brother how the young priest had snubbed her; the bishop had silenced her, knowing her ways. Steed too had ignored the drama.

"How are you, Ms. Cantera?"

She smiled graciously at him as she always did. "May I?"

"Go right ahead." She quietly stepped into the kitchen and he returned to his office.

Interesting how she never visits Santo during the day but makes herself at home when she does; the woman knows every nook and niche in this house. Steed shrugged it off...he wanted no part of it.

Author's Notes

"The priest eyed his soul, touched its dark center with his holiness but the unseen pushback from what lived within made him step back, but he still stood his ground" – in these lines, it is implied the old priest has been, for years, an exorcist appointed by the Vatican to cast out demons from souls; particularly in precarious situations close to the Border.

.

18 THE PRIEST

Monday, after midnight, March 31

L ater, a fading moon watched as the same moving van returned and parked near the bishop's front entrance. Minutes later, a cry for help in the street below Sebastian's window caused him to leap from his bed. He could barely see the figure, distraught, its belongings scattered about, the victim of some kind of attack. Or had it been staged...stranger things had happened on Church Street.

Steed and the bishop, asleep in their beds and their windows facing the garden, would not have heard it. He'd check it out and in tee shirt and jeans, ran down the staircase. The officer generally on guard in the kitchen since Petra's attack was no longer there, pulled off his post at the request of the bishop who refused to allow the Precinct to snoop about.

Santo Cantera believed like his family...he was untouchable, his fortress secure. Had he forgotten so soon the tragic demise of the nun in his Cathedral? Oddly, the vestibule was dark as Sebastian felt his way forward; fumbling with the lamp on the sideboard, he realized there was no bulb. He frowned...an eerie silence had settled on the bishop's house as the priest cautiously unlatched the front door, but someone was waiting and slammed it into his face. Thrust backward, Sebastian stumbled and recovered his stance but he hadn't seen the hooded one waiting under the staircase. He counted two and went 'Marine' on them, using a few of his old moves; within seconds, he took a hit to the back of the head with what felt like a frying pan.

Falling forward, he caught himself and rolled over; Though

stunned, Sebastian assessed what he had…masked assailants in monks' robes. They were angry; none of their other victims had fought back and they weren't up for this. One launched a kick to his face. Sebastian was flattened, breathless; he struggled to clear his head, now even more confused…someone was on top of him in a way he hadn't expected.

Desperately he tried to push away the hands caressing his body, unzipping his jeans…perfume, a woman. She laughed, said things. He wanted her off him and so did the other attacker who hissed his disdain and delivered a blow so hard to her face, she cried out. Now Sebastian knew who she was; he'd met her earlier. But who was the male, the side of his face was painfully burned, a fresh lightning shaped gash from right eye to left jaw line. He was hurting but managed to scold the woman…something about not following the script, but all became clear when he mentioned the martyr, San Sebastiano…was he to be one of the moondead? *Never; not this way*…stunned, but with all his strength, he drew his knees up and shoved his running shoes into the woman's face. She groaned and fell backward. Sebastian flipped himself up onto his feet. It would prove useless…a third assailant appeared, his massive frame filling the doorway; he backhanded the priest and tossed him, like a towel, over his shoulder.

Carrying the priest with no effort, the stranger walked down the bishop's front steps. There was little time. Sebastian stunned by the heavy hand of the newcomer in one last ditch effort whirled his body over the man's head, *I can do this*. With his feet, he slammed the other two into each other; they tumbled onto the pavement, *score. I could use John Padric…come find me, damnit.*

But the Hulk, unperturbed; gripped the priest by the neck and dragged him like a dead animal toward the van, *lamb to the slaughter, Lord*. He was receding into the shadows with killers sought by everyone in L'Arroyo. *Lord, save me, don't leave me.* Darkness… the lights were fading on Church Street. The moon hid her face. *Don't leave me.*

A nun rose from her bed. Again it was happening, closer this time, voices floating over the bishop's roof and into the garden. Magdalen stepped into the hall and prayed to the angels…they had walked by her side at San Miguel since her arrival. *Save us this night, holy ones.* Then she saw Lucy returning from chapel where she often prayed late at night. Magdalen had feared for her friend…Santa Lucia too was a martyr. They'd never discussed this, though each knew. "Thank God, you are safe."

"Of course, I am." Magdalen pulled her into her room.

"It's happening again. My God, I thought it was you."

They rushed to the window in time to hear shouting…young voices this time. As they hurried down School Street adjusting their holy habits and veils, Magdalen glanced up at the moon; it was huge and ominous, shouting and silent. She could almost touch it but how troubled it looked…*you are sad tonight, friend. La luna, help me.*

Two old men sipping early morning Coronas and sprawled on the sidewalk, looked up and smiled. Lucy stepped over them. *"Buona sera!"*

They bellowed back: *"Via con Dios, hermana!"* Lucy smiled… she'd never done this before. Being with her friend was exciting; they were nearing the street corner now.

Magdalen froze. "My God, Lucy, look! It's Ben and his friends! Not again…when will they learn?" Her students, throwing caution aside, were swarming like spiders over a huge individual. Ben however was in the center of things; he had managed to climb into the back of the van attempting to pull someone away from two hooded figures. The nuns rushed forward, Magdalen hurriedly did a read on the pair dressed in monk's robes. *My God, here they are.* Those they had sought were just yards from her.

One of them…male, tall and thin, turned when a student shouted her name. But how had he known it was she, there were two of them. She studied every detail; his height, his moves, the macabre half-mask of a skull. In an odd twist, he removed it; here was the architect of the martyr murders. But he was hurt…was that a scar? Part of his face had been burned. *Here you are…the one the First Precinct calls "the other", the one I've wondered about!*

Their eyes met; there was no anger in his; no threat, perhaps
curiosity. He was the same who had looked up from the red Mercedes truck under the art room window. It frightened the nun but
she was mesmerized. She glanced from one to the other; their features similar. *They could be twins, my God.*

They were throwing a body into the van; the doors closing.
"Sister! Sister Magdalen!" Again someone called her name. Lit-
tle Julie was on her cell punching in 9-1-1. "It's Father, our priest.
They've hurt him…they've got him!"

The priest, her new friend, why? *Not him, not him.*

The abductor turned his head, looked at her one last time, his
eyes so intense, she gasped. Beside him, Joanna Cantera, unfocused
and laughing, unperturbed by the students, looked amused; she was
high on what they were doing, confident she could drive away with
her new acquisition without consequence.

But just as frightening for Magdalen, was the sight of Ben now
hanging on the back of the huge one. The man was shouting obscenities until, wrestling free of the boy he threw himself behind
the wheel. Ben hung on to the door as the van lurched forward.

Magdalen could hear herself shouting as if she were somewhere else, crying out to him as the van pulled away, tires squealing.
Losing his grip, he was thrown into the street, rolling literally into
the nun's arms as she rushed forward and knelt down on the pavement. With students descending like crows beside a fallen one, they
hovered over the two. Magdalen, with some of the boys, scooped
him up and dragged him away, scolding Ben, scolding all of them,
ordering everyone onto the sidewalk. "Why were you here? Look at
the hour."

The usual…they'd been walking back to a public parking garage after a late movie and pizza. *Again?* They were silent and angry,
wanting to help. Ben saw the tears in her eyes, said he was sorry;
they all did. But he said they needed their priest back…spring football started next week. Life was simple for Ben. Girls clung to the
nuns. Lucy would whisper later only at San Miguel could such *agatazione* or commotion happen like this.

At the Precinct, dispatch erupted. Bishop Cantera himself was demanding to speak directly to Padric, but the detectives were coming in off the street from an unrelated homicide with Ducci and Pistasio. O'Manion pointed to a phone. "Be nice...act Catholic. He's asking for you!"

Padric cursed; he wasn't in the mood but Santo Cantera was frantic. "We need you. There's blood everywhere..."

"I'm on my way; are you safe at the moment?"

"Yes, damn it. I need you, sir." Well, that must have been difficult, asking for help from the *brash and irreverent Irish lieutenant*. Padric smiled. "Cap, he called me *sir*!"

"You've made it to the Big Leagues, so what? You're back in and on this; get your ass over there and go do your job. Just don't make any headlines or get yourself noticed." Those within earshot muttered something about lots of luck.

This one they'd never forget but they'd said that the last time. Martinez and Padric were gone. Confusion and chaos would greet them on Church Street; a dozen students and two nuns stood helplessly in the street; their eyes wide when they spotted the black Precinct hummer with lights flashing turn the corner on two wheels. Behind it, like dominoes, two EMV's and three fire trucks fell one by one into place. The hummer bounced to a halt and Martinez ran up the bishop's front steps. Padric emerged slowly. *What the fuck was their nun doing out here at this hour?*

He walked toward them. In an instant, Ben was beside him, feeding him *intel*. Padric repeating all that he said to Tark at the Precinct, he muttered: "I need birds in the air...it's that van again."

Sirens already had shattered the night and made every nun sit up in her bed and whisper a prayer. The elder carefully lowered herself into her wheelchair then took her place by the window.

The detective wasn't happy. "You young people have a bad habit of roaming the city at night. What's that about? It's dangerous. You could have died." They paled. "Ben, is it? You did good but don't ever do it again...and all of you, thank you for trying to save your priest but stay off the streets, for God's sake. Where are your parents...do they know you are out here?" And he railed at them for another ten minutes, silencing anyone who attempted to speak.

He shouted for medics to treat those who were hurt. Parents slowly appeared, shocked and embarrassed, some not knowing their child had left the house, others angry at Magdalen for perhaps urging them on in their heroics. This in turn so angered the students and Padric, the parents backed off; she was allowed to explain and made the students own up to their mischief.

Fingers stopped pointing when the adults realized the new priest had been abducted. Shocking, a scandal indeed; they would do all they could to help. Their children would answer any questions the First Precinct might ask. What was going on at the Cathedral?

Again Pistasio's men and a criminal apprehension team fanned out over the city looking for a small, unmarked moving van and Padric was immediately face to face with the bishop.

"So where do you think Father is?"

"Lieutenant, we're asking the same…I'm at a loss." Martinez shook his head…*nada*. Steed explained they had risen early when they came upon a vestibule in disarray with chairs overturned and pictures askew on the walls. Shocked to hear sirens, to see nuns with their students standing alone in the dark, the two men were embarrassed; they'd seen nothing, heard nothing. "And at no time did you see Father last night?"

The bishop had said good night to them at eleven. "This was the last time I saw him."

But Steed had more. "No, it was later than that. A visitor arrived after midnight and Michael came down to answer the door. He didn't know I was in my office…it's right here."

"Who would come here at that hour? The name please."

There was some hesitation. "It was my sister, Joanna, Detective." *Son-of-a-bitch…under our fucking noses, the balls on this woman; I'll kill her.* "She often comes here to see me. You didn't know that?"

The bishop was deliberately, slowly, making a point, measuring Padric's reaction; the detective would not play his game and gave him a blank stare. "And what else, bishop?"

There was no answer; the bishop annoyed, wanting some fluster, a little guilt-ridden behavior. *He knows I was fucking his sister and now she's on the prowl, slinking around like an alley cat spraying her territory; the bitch couldn't keep her hands off the priest.* He'd rage later. "How long did Ms. Cantera stay?" They didn't know. The bishop explained she often fell asleep on the couch in his office. She'd leave on her own. *Yeah, can't imagine it...the fool's lying; she didn't come to see him; it's somebody else.* They knew the other was male; if he could find him, he'd find the brains behind all the kills. But where was Joanna going once she walked through the door?

The monsignor dropped a bombshell. "Father's name-saint was Sebastian the martyr...he died a terrible death. Bishop Cantera doesn't know this, but a bloody arrow was left in the vestry several days ago on top of one of the martyrologies, the page left open to the martyrdom of the saint, shot through with arrows, Emperor's orders. Sister Magdalen knows nothing about this since she hadn't been near the sacristy for several days...we cleaned it up. She'd seen enough...this would have been the last straw."

Damn. "And you said nothing to us?" The two were silent, embarrassed; he fumed, told them to leave, go somewhere safe. They would retreat to Father Santeresa's rectory at Our Lady of Sorrows parish. "We're sweeping this house for the second time in a month; I'm now even more concerned for your safety."

But where had they gone with the priest? Squad cars had taken off after the assailants. Were there holes in the ground that just swallowed them up? He stepped out the door and onto the portico. The students had disappeared. Magdalen and Lucy were standing on the other side of the street, watching and waiting. He approached, searching Magdalen's face. "You've got ten minutes. The good monsignor tells me I have a possible martyr murder in progress."

"Saint Sebastian was a martyr of the Church, yes."

He looked at Lucy. "Sister, you shouldn't be here."

"I'm not leaving my Sister." He'd spoken with her in the past, was familiar with the Genova legacy, her father's reputation. He remembered the Mediterranean lilt in her voice. Padric had enough problems, but still, he needed to make himself clear: "Sister, you'll leave if I say so." Lucy was surprised and looked at Magdalen.

"My Sister will leave momentarily. May I speak further about this with you?"

"Of course, that's why I'm standing here; we need your help on this if you're up for it. I've heard you've not been well; I tried to see you." They walked to the other side of the street. "I was more than concerned, Sister." He glanced at her; she understood.

"And I thank you for that, Detective…what can I do?" Padric needed no melodrama and was relieved at her resilience. "But know Sister Agnes will never let me ride shotgun." He smiled. "They'll stage it like Saint Sebastian's martyrdom. There are several versions, but the general consensus among early writers he was shot full of arrows by his executioners. Sister Lucy knows even more; Sebastiano is honored in her Italia. Tell them, Lucy."

"*Patriarchi* say he resembled a sea urchin he was so covered in arrows. *Investigatore*, you must find him; he may still be alive, I feel it…I do. *Tradizione*, and that's what these killers are into, says he was healed by a holy woman then later martyred again and then died; he is called the saint who was martyred twice."

Investigatore…he liked that. *But what had she said? Arrows.* "Who even owns that shit? Excuse me, Sisters. Bows and arrows?"

"Maybe not…but something like that. They will replicate almost to the letter."

"Ah, yes," he sighed. "Our killers do it by the book."

Magdalen said she had finally seen the other they sought. He was here at the scene, had looked at her directly. Padric turned into stone, asked for more details, but Magdalen could no longer stand there. "Please, I must go to the sacristy; the martyrologies, they can be helpful." A statement like this no longer surprised the detective; there was some kind of magic or mysticism in these holy books where one could find every answer…at least for this case. He'd have to buy himself one.

Padric told her about the bloody arrow left in the vestry. She was shocked, angry the monsignor and priest had not told her. "You will get back to us; think on this. Call me." Padric rushed back up the steps. The nuns left. But no, Magdalen wouldn't call this time; she'd solve this on her own.

It was early morning now; the two nuns entered the sacristy and found Steed vesting for Mass with no one in the church to participate. Again the Cathedral was cordoned off in crime tape and surrounded by uniforms. As it had been the previous Sunday; people, frustrated and nervous, were again turned away from the seven o'clock Sunday Mass.

The monsignor leveled a look at her. "Sister, we can't lose this priest; he's a blessing to us. Find him. Stop them as only you can."

Magdalen stared after him as he entered the sanctuary. *He knows.* Steed was aware of her gift; but did he know what he was giving her license to do? Lucy hid a smile, said nothing as she quickly paged through the martyrology the bishop read most.

It was hard to discern between fact and legend about Saint Sebastian but there was one recurring narrative. The martyr had been tied to a stake in a field to be put to death by a firing squad of bows and arrows. The killer was obsessive about detail. Her thoughts raced: *he'd pick up on something like this, but where would that be in L'Arroyo?* It was full of desert and known for its rocky terrain and arroyos. "They're taking him to a field or near one."

Lucy frowned. "And where do we find those, Magdalena?"

Dolorosa appeared in the doorway. "What do you need?"

"Fields…where would they be in L'Arroyo?"

"L'Arroyo is rock and most of the arroyos have been converted into canals. But if you travel west on Old Division Road where my parents live, there are more than a hundred acres of dried up weeds where the Chinese flower farms were." *Why yes, in the Edge.* She had seen them. Unused and silent, they lay withered and dry in sharp contrast to the abundant green of the Aguilar-Murphy farmlands. *And that graveyard, it too was surrounded by fields on the edge of the desert.*

"Yes, a remote location like the Edge would be a good place for a killing." *He's there now, our priest.* Her eyes were on fire. "They won't waste any time."

Magdalen was fixated now; she was on to something, but arrows…*if not them, what would they use in their place?* Lucy was looking tired and worried; she had more on her mind. *Agnes isn't Petra…she will be furious.* They'd need to explain to her where they had been.

The three quickly returned to the convent and ran up the stairs to her office.

She wasn't happy regardless of how clear and desperate the explanation; she delivered a proper reprimand to Magdalen; Lucy escaped nothing less. What had Magdalen been thinking, impulsively running about on a hunch and even dragging poor Lucy with her; she wasn't Nancy Drew and should stop acting like her.

What am I thirteen, but the woman was right; one didn't run from the convent on impulse to find the origin of a noise in the street. But Nancy Drew… Nancy Drew? She couldn't have called me Miss Marple or Olivia from Law and Order: SVU? Though not the custom for nuns to watch primetime but only the news, Magdalen knew only of Olivia Benson through little Julie and her friends who were always talking about her.

Later, Magdalen apologized to Lucy. "I shouldn't have dragged you out into the night."

Lucy grinned. "But you didn't…I liked it." *Only Lucy.* "No, really, *cara mia*, I want to help you from now on when there are murders." *When there are murders…was a killing in L'Arroyo that commonplace now? Well, they hadn't gone away, had they? I must stop this.*

All they could think of was Father Sebastian. Throughout the day, media vans, cameramen, journalists with microphones assailed anyone entering or leaving the Cathedral complex. They positioned themselves like territorial squatters in front of the bishop's house regardless of what the LPD demanded; they had history together; a tug of war always in play. Media types were determined to camp out in the courtyard under Monica's window. She instead sat quietly on the landing at the top of the stairs or was invited into Magdalen's room to look out the garden. Finally Duran showed up in a huff and banished everyone from the premises; Padric had expected no less from her; there was no need for him to do anything. "If you would back off, sir, I will handle this," she had said and when a special detail arrived to protect the Sisters, she ordered them about like tin soldiers.

She then calmly and firmly posted herself in the convent vestibule: O'Manion's orders. The Sisters were relieved and with her there, Magdalen found peace in the chapel; for now, she would need to talk this over with God.

"Surely, You can help me find your good servant, our priest…" She would need to discern how to get from point A to point B and asked for a blessing.

The old martyrology was with CSI after it had been bloodied. But happily a copy of the *Martyrologium Usuardi* was in its place, courtesy of the monsignor. She had paged through it before and found the commentary on the martyr Sebastian. As she read, dread returned; it was clear now. With access to the sacristy, the killers were flaunting what they did in her face; a bloody arrow said enough. It was "the other", masterminding all of this, reading the ancient works, doing the planning.

Odd though…they had pounced quickly this time. Father Sebastian was new to the parish; what had provided the impetus to target him *or was it all in his name? Did he set someone off?* She knew nothing of the snub he had laid on Joanna. But she'd seen her too, the detective's ex-lover, hooded and dressed in a monk's robe.

Perhaps with the martyrology so bookmarked, they were pulling her into their game; toying with her? *Or is it someone else giving me clues, a heads up? How are they gaining access and was it a nightly thing, slipping into the sacristy undetected? Or is it someone whom no one would question at all for being there?* She hadn't slept; now alone in the chapel, she tried to pray but could see only the priest. *What could he be suffering?* She wept.

Padric and Martinez had returned to the Precinct and rushed to the fifth floor. Ramirez was furious, done with these martyr murders or whatever the hell they were calling them now…end it, he ordered. Enough! On the way down the back stairs, Padric was cursing, shackled by knowing who was doing all this; his gut told him by now she'd worked over the priest in ways that sickened him. This holy young man, wise of soul for his years, was his friend, his confidante; Padric would rid the earth of her and work this on his own; but then…he knew their nun would be doing the same.

Marcus was waiting at the bottom of the stairs. "Why would Joanna Cantera be at the bishop's that late? He says she's doing this often…what's he got that a party girl would be hanging with him?" Exactly. What would compel the bitch to show up at her brother's house so late and so often; what was the draw?

Magdalen was thinking the same.

"Sister." Dolorosa. Her brothers were coming to take her away from this madness if only for a few hours; she was going home, her family elated since Cecelia's death had canceled her last efforts to do so. "Please come…you must."

A mild argument ensued; Magdalen not wanting to leave, Dolorosa insisting she didn't belong to the Precinct. She told her to get a life, "our Life, the one we have here, the one you are vowed to, sistah-girl…your days can't be filled every waking hour with murder and mayhem, for God's sake."

They stared at each other; *what were they doing?* Grappling with her sense of knowing and the need to end the violence, Magdalen had become blind to everything else and she had promised Petra this would not happen. And then there were her friends, the detectives, God love them, not moving fast enough; protocol they would say. Dolorosa watched the wheels turning, bolts clicking. "I'll go!"

Magdalen's eyes lit up…what a beauty. The old rambling house, shaded by trees and filled for years with the sound of young voices, was no different today. Dolorosa had offered a gentle bribe…if she joined them, her brothers would provide transportation to just about anywhere she wanted to go, but the petite nun was immediately swept into the arms of her family.

Magdalen, drawn into a circle of laughter and hugs from little ones, pulling her into their playhouse. Alysia de Torro watched her *familia*, the many grandchildren, her sons and their wives, but her eyes always came back to daughter, Issa, and friend, Magdalena. How wonderful to have them sitting among the bougainvillea and lilac vines in the gazebo her husband had built thirty years ago. Her camera clicked over and over; she always had one in her hand…it captured her world; her photography covered the walls of her *casa*. The Sisters were blessing her home simply by being there; but if she'd heard what they were saying, she might have thought otherwise or…perhaps even told her husband to help them. She watched.

What was absorbing them so…on what was her daughter-nun so intent?

She asked her husband; he only smiled; his Issa could do whatever she wanted.

Here Magdalen had found respite, a refuge, and leaned back in a huge wicker chair. For the earlier part of the afternoon, she would never be without a de Torro baby, interchangeable, differing in size and shape like an assembly line on her lap. But after babies and toddlers had been held more than once, Dolorosa cried out: "*Dios mio!* Enough! Let Maggie rest!" *Familia* had gathered early that day and said their goodbyes, leaving the nuns' conversation to turn to more urgent matters. Dolorosa's two favorite brothers had lingered, curious to know what was so important. They knew their sister, read her eyes; they wanted in. Bright and articulate, handsome and single, both men were very eligible bachelors. Dolorosa made that clear…she was their self-appointed guardian angel, telling all who would listen about them. ASU graduates, one a teacher, the other a businessman, the two came home with girlfriends, referred to as the flavor of the week by their only sister.

After explaining Magdalen's involvement with the martyr murders, she told them their priest was missing. They were outraged… how long was this to continue, they asked. What could they do to help? It was music to Magdalen's ears; she quickly removed Padric from the equation…*he will know soon enough*. Besides, Agnes had finally signed off on what she wanted to do, and that was enough, but in truth, the woman was petrified, angry at all that had occurred and had whispered: "My name is Agnes, my name-saint a martyr and I am very afraid."

There, she had said it…they embraced. Magdalen comforted her. Petra, God rest her soul, would have wanted this.

But it was near four in the afternoon; they'd need to move quickly and agreed it was time. It was not that far by Tomas' driving standards; he and his brother helped the two nuns into his massive Ford Ram and were soon cruising west on Old Division Road. It divided ranches and farms from the barrio and city proper. Magdalen took mental notes as the road gradually gave way to the open grange; they were nearing the sprawling dried fields in the Edge. "Would either of you tell me if you'd ever been out here?"

"Not in front of our sister." Everyone laughed.

"Maggie, what is it we're looking for...how do we find him?" Dolorosa was into this.

Magdalen kept her eyes on the changing landscape; she was worried. Shadows were longer now and she needed daylight in such a strange place. "I know our priest will be tied to something in or near a field...they will not take the time to use bow and arrows but something like them. I dread what he must be suffering if he's not dead already..."

"Damn, we've gotta stop these fools."

"Thank you, Jonah...I can no longer wait for Major Crimes to get it done." But she felt she had betrayed the detectives...*never mind, later*. She would explain.

Dolorosa was doubtful. "They could be in Cali by now."

"We'll see. Tomas, you know where the graveyard is out there."

"You mean out here...look to your right." He slowed down. The sun was still high enough in the west to give them several hours of light before it dropped behind the last hill.

Then she saw it...the old, gnarled tree sprawling eerily over the graves. "I understand if you want to turn back." Down the road and even in daylight, Chato's bar sign eerily blinked at them, but the graves were calling to Magdalen.

Dolorosa wanted this over. "We're here and we're checking it out. Look at this tank Tomas is driving. The National Guard had nothing on us. We're good."

"Then let me get out for a moment...I want a closer look at the graveyard."

Dolorosa punched her arm. "Now you're pushing it."

Magdalen heard nothing they said...the desert lay still, but the fields came up to the edge of it. "Tomas, Jonah...tell me what you are seeing? Stay with me on this."

Then suddenly from beyond the graves, came a black Escalade...it swerved but the driver recovered and brought it back onto the narrow dirt road. Tomas slowed down but refused to budge. His Ram was bigger than anything the other driver thought he had. Again the vehicle veered off the road as it passed; a woman's laugh! Magdalen turned. She was hearing what all the moon-dead had heard, the sound of it, chilling and gut-wrenching…

The darker than legal tint on the windows revealed nothing. But the driver had seen her…the vehicle screeched to a stop. It did nothing, waiting. The four stared back at it. "Come on, come on," muttered Tomas. "Give me a reason, fool."

Dolorosa's old self kicked in. "Tommy…sistah-bitch girl isn't happy. Let me at her."

The driver suddenly was backing up; Tomas did the same. Whispering a desperate prayer, Magdalen stared through the back window. *My God, help us…angels be with me. John Padric will have a fit.* Again the vehicle stopped, but Tomas kept backing up, moving closer. Again there was a defiant laugh. "You bitch! You hung-up, hypocritical excuse for a woman!" shrieked the driver. "You'll never have him…"

Magdalen turned slowly…*is she talking to me?* She could see her now. Through the tinted glass, Dolorosa, too, peered at the woman. They watched in horror as a hooded, shadowy figure on the passenger side shoved the driver so hard her face slammed into the window; her features pressed to the glass…oddly, they were now face to face. But Dolorosa was seeing someone else, a childhood friend she once knew. *There she is, yes, Dios mio. Ah, si, si…it is as I thought.*

The brothers peered through the glass. "Sis, who does she look like? Damn, that's crazy Joanna Cantera, isn't it? Issa, are you seeing this?" Dolorosa said nothing. On the other side of the glass, the woman recovered and glared at Magdalen; the Escalade bolted forward and, in a cloud of dust, disappeared. Tomas looked disappointed; he'd wanted some action.

"Gentlemen." They looked at Dolorosa. "I need to pee." They laughed. "*Maldita sea,* you scared the shit out of me, doing the tango with this thing."

"So, you weren't afraid of that woman?"

"Hell, no. I would've flattened her." Her brothers laughed but she said nothing else.

"Who do you think she was calling a bitch?"

Magdalen closed her eyes. "Me."

Tomas stopped the truck; the men turned completely around, staring at her. Jonah concerned, whispered: "Sounds like she wants bad things for you, Sister. Not a problem...we've got you."

Tomas drove the truck slowly across the dry field. "Does she know you?"

"She hates me because a man over whom she's obsessed was kind to me and my Sisters." *How could I explain?* Magdalen's voice was reduced to a whisper. "No more now. This man is well-known in the city and sadly this woman you call crazy, is one of two prime suspects in the moondead case. I shouldn't even be saying this but it's your safety that concerns me."

Dolorosa patted her hand. She knew now, her own fears confirmed. She would speak with the detectives, to Padric, as he had asked, not wait any longer.

But the mood changed. Magdalen leaned forward. "We're in the right place." The men asked how she knew. "If those two here, then our priest is, too; he's been left behind. You just heard the woman. I saw them abduct Father Sebastian. Come now, Tomas, help me."

"Tommy, do what she says!" Dolorosa was adamant.

Tomas fired up. "Say where and when. This is getting' good, damn."

"But I cannot put you in danger." They smiled, said it was too late for that. "But what will you do if she returns?"

"What I was about to do before they took off? We'll kick their ass..." Tomas held up a long gun, something she didn't expect, but why not...wasn't this Arizona territory?

Jonah showed her another, this one of similar magnitude. "My God, what are you ding with a muskatoon?"

The men looked at each other. "You know guns?"

"I'm no expert."

Dolorosa would explain: "Boys, she was a profiler, studied grave sites in Egypt." They were impressed.

"This is no time to discuss resumes, Sister...what's that?"

She had fixed her eyes on a spot passed the graveyard where the desert began and the fields in the Edge ended. Before them, spread a magnificent forest of saguaro…the tall elegant cacti seemed to go on forever. "There, that crested one, the one with no arms. Tomas, please can you get us out there?"

The wheels of the truck spun in the weeds and covered the uneven ground with ease. Dolorosa cried out: "It's our *padre*! Fuck this! Tomas, move it!"

Magdalen placed her hand on his shoulder. "We'll need a blanket, something to cover him." The sight was gruesome and unholy. "Jonah, you have an iPhone or something. Kindly call the detective at this number."

She handed him Padric's business card.

Sunday, five-thirty in the evening, March 30

"Where's the beast, *kema sabe*?"

"In my driveway…where to?"

"The Edge…long story. We've got him…the good padre's alive, damn it." His partner hooted.

Padric was wired. "Come get me, *amigo*!"

The two had not slept for the past forty-eight hours and tried to steal a few, but this would not be. Martinez strapped on some hardware and kissed his kids. Marisol made the sign of the cross on his forehead. "Come back to me." She always said that.

And he would always respond the same way: "With arms open and wanting you, babe." It was ritual.

Padric alerted Ramirez and rolled off the bed; his girls playing beside him, looked up. "But da', you'll take us to school tomorrow?" He had enrolled them at the Sister's primary school in the convent garden and rectory of San Miguel…Petra had wanted it and now, with the older Sisters, Dolorosa and Magdalen had created a learning center for those who had suffered an "upset in life", or as Lucy called it, a *grande tristezza* or great sadness.

"I will…I must." He struggled with his Doc Marten three-ties. "Are you happy, lasses?"

"Oh, yeah."

"Say 'yes', not yeah, Kate, you sound like a ruffian."

"What's that?"

"A bad one, luv, now no questions."

"You mean a gangsta."

He pulled her close to him. "Where are you hearing that, girl?"

"Mikey O'Malley…he wants to be one. Now, da', stop your worrying." *Fucking little Mikey O'Malley.* "But yes then, I love it. I made three new friends and Kara made four."

His youngest bounced into his arms. "Five. Papa will watch Scooby Doo with us when he comes back, so no bothering him now, Kate." Kara was easy, always would be, even later in life.

"Ah, you're a good one, lass."

"We'll be waiting for you, but if you need to stay longer, go ahead." Kate gave him a matronly pat on the head as she watched him fuss with his boots.

He smiled…*they're running my life.* "Thank you for that, Kate, you're brilliant." He stood up and pulled a First Precinct tee over his head but Kara refused to let go of his leg as he walked down the hall to the door.

"And me, too, papa!"

"Specially you, wee girl." With a kiss to his mum, he was gone. He spoke briefly to Cunningham outside Mairead's door. Each day, Nevel had patiently stood post with his partner for several hours and now raised his head; he wanted to go with Padric.

The sargeant grinned. "Donny Mann will be here to relieve me in thirty minutes. He can have the tea and scones your mum brings me. Where you headed?"

"Nevel'd like this one; his lady's at the scene."

"The nun…ay, my boy needs a good run."

"The woman does that for all of us. It's out in the Edge near that graveyard."

Cunnningham paled. "What the fuck is she doing out there at Bad End?" The derelict cemetery had been called this for years. But Padric told him the priest had been found and he disappeared down the backstairs…he hated elevators. Slipping into the shadows, he saw a patrol car pass; it would do so again in twenty minutes. There were corners and blind spots Padric used often to avoid detection when leaving his home; he saw the hummer rounding the corner and climbed aboard while it was still moving. It shot quickly into an alley.

Back at the Precinct, Marcus told the Captain the nun, with an unusual sense of knowing, had played a hunch. O'Manion would not respond…he hated clairvoyance, but she was much more than that, Marcus said. Still, the woman had done it; the cap' smiled… this would keep his team on their toes.

Padric called Declan Brady, already on the road. "Tell me Billy Kelly's at the wheel."

"Ay, and which nun are we saving this time?"

"It's a priest, *bhoyo*! We've got some rough terrain out there."

"Holy Saint Brendan, we'll dust up the road gettin' there, sir."

Padric stared into his side mirror; squad cars and vans were following Pistasio's tact squad into the Edge. "Christ, it's looking like the Third rolling into Baghdad." Stone-faced, he was horrified that a priest should be found in such a forbidding place.

The graveyard came into view. Martinez sped passed the tombstones into the desert and spotted the Ram 1500. The shadows were longer now. A wind had kicked up and whipped through the terrain like some kind of omen; the veils of the nuns fluttering around them like angels low to the ground. Two men with somber faces were looking about as if guarding the women then the detectives saw what they feared. Padric leaped from the hummer before it came to a stop…*what the fuck? Not him, not my priest.*

Magdalen was attending to someone at the bottom of the tallest crested saguaro he'd ever seen. It was huge and thick and covered with long, hard spikes. *Damn. Arrows.* The killers had used their imagination. Though unnerved at the sight of the priest, the two grimly assessed the scene.

Martinez touched Magdalen's shoulder. "Sister…*Dios mio. Gracias!* Are you all right? Let us take it from here."

She stepped aside reluctantly. But Padric whispered: "If you have it in you, stay near him; he'll respond to you. But later we'll talk, woman…putting yourself in danger like this."

As both men had done when they saw the nun dead on a hill

of rocks, they made the sign of the cross and knelt down beside the nude and bleeding priest whom Magdalen had gently covered. Padric thought the sight of Petra upside down on a cross was horrific, but a priest lashed mercilessly with ropes to a saguaro; his back pressed cruelly into the spike-covered trunk was too much… he was seething. Badly bludgeoned and bruised, his face disfigured; he appeared to be dead. Martinez checked for vitals. "We still have him."

They eyed the other saguaro nearby…some had been hacked; their arms cut off to inflict further pain on the priest, their spikes pressed into the victim's torso. Fragmented and bloody, they were strewn about the desert floor. "They came prepared, heavy gloves, large cutting devices; these low-lifes know how to work it." Magdalen drew close; adjusting the blanket, telling them how she had tried to remove some of the spikes, hoping she hadn't destroyed any evidence. Both men were grateful.

Padric leaned very close to Sebastian. "Talk to me, Father. I know you're alive; apologies for your pain but you're stronger than this…come on now." There was no response. "We're getting you out of here."

The EMV pulled up beside them; Padric shouted for a gurney. In a torrent of words, he snapped orders at the uniforms now swarming the desert around him. At the sound of his voice, they spread out like ants; processing the crime scene. All who arrived were stunned; these were the same who had witnessed the horror of Petra's attack in the Cathedral; they were unsure which was worse, more macabre. Tied to a saguaro, the weight of Sebastian's body had forced him to slump to the ground, half kneeling, half sitting; his face, covered with contusions and spikes.

Slowly he spoke…it was only a whisper over and over. "My Jesus, I love you, My Lord, forgive me my sins."

Padric's eyes welled up with tears. *He had sins? Christ Jaysus, help me.* Magdalen whispered the name of Jesus as well. The detective could stand it no longer and rose, his own sins too many to bear. He withdrew and approached Dolorosa, her brothers. "Tell me everything."

Dolorosa looked at Tomas. "The ride...a black one. It came flying out of here and almost slammed into us out on the road by the graveyard. You didn't see it coming in? It had to have passed you, Detective. A black Escalade." Bingo.

"But there was more than one road out of here; they may never have left the Edge." *Pistasio.* Padric rattled off Joanna Cantera's license plate number into his mic.

Tomas stared at him. "You know who it is? How?"

"I do it for a living. We've got this one memorized." He knew everything about Joanna.

Tomas and Jonah glanced at each other. "Damn, you're good."

"No. I'm not or we wouldn't be standing here doing this." *Damn, if they knew the truth.*

"But that plate...you know who it is."

"I'm counting on it. Now please talk to Sgt. Marcus." He was standing beside them now. "Find out what these people saw."

He returned to Magdalen. "Sister, what have I got?"

"I heard the same thing Carlos did."

He frowned at her. "The laugh...a woman's laugh." She nodded. "And what else?"

"What do you mean?"

"The driver, our suspect, if it is who I think it is, she'd never let you off that easy. She said something to you, didn't she?"

"She called me a bitch, a hung up, hypocritical excuse for a woman."

His eyes narrowed...he hesitated.

"God forgive me, but you're all woman and beautiful."

There, that sounded like John Garfield. She was use to him now but tried not to show her surprise; he looked away...he'd overstepped. "My apologies...I'm sorry for all of this shit. Sister, when you took your vows you weren't expecting something like this."

She disagreed. *Here it comes...she's going to say something mystical like she always does.* "On the contrary, Detective, we were assured there would be hard times; we would suffer like Christ for the vows we had made to Him. We knew this going into the Life...I know this now. But about Joanna...the last person she expected was a nun unintentionally coming between her and her man…it's almost macabre that I would get caught up in this and be hated so. She is clawing at anything to get what she wants."

Padric heard the calm in her voice but he was not calm at all. Later he'd tell his partner it was the nun and her ways at the crime scene that had quieted the guilt and the fear in him and Martinez had said: "Thank God for that."

He asked how her sense of things had brought her to this seemingly God-forsaken place and there it was again…the martyrology. He was amazed at the simplicity of her thinking, an almost naive way of dealing with this. She was an academic relying on lore and oral tradition some of which had found its way into Catholic devotion and practice. But then, she had God on her side…he, not so much lately or so he thought. But he was worried: this was the closest Joanna had ever been to Magdalen; their nun was in danger.

Marcus listened carefully to Jonah. "Out of a horror movie, sir. It came from the driver's side. We'll help. Whatever Sister Magdalen needs from now on, we're in."

Marcus was not sure this was such a good idea…*Dios mio. The woman has a support system to take off on her own and the lieutenant will explode when he catches wind of it.* But he thanked the men for their efforts and returned to the forest of cacti where officers had fanned out. Then from a police van, Cunningham and Nevel appeared; the dog spotted Magdalen and she him.

On Cunningham's command, the animal ran to her side where he would remain until she departed. Padric and Marcus scoured the desert floor for evidence, making it their duty to bag with gloved hands, Sebastian's underwear and jeans, his tee shirt.

Magdalen was beside him again; suddenly Father stirred. "We have you, Father, we have you safe with us now."

Padric would move this along: "Mr. Brady. Mr. Kelly, let's get him aboard. Keep him covered…give the man some respect. "

Brady spoke to the priest: "Father, sir, I'm about to move you onto the gurney then into the van; this will be painful." Martinez and Kelly, several uniforms, all were there in an instant. "Now, lads, he can't take a bump, so we're lifting this feckin' thing off the ground; it has to be smooth. In one effort now!" They hoisted it up to their shoulders, holding it like a precious burden; they glided rather than walked. Carefully the gurney was eased into the van and suddenly to everyone's delight, Father raised his thumb. They cheered but Sebastian was trying to say something.

Brady looked around. "Where is she? Where'd she go?"

"Who?"

"The Sister."

"Which one?"

"The digger, she was just here, you know, the archaeologist-nun...Magdalen, is it?"

Padric smiled a little. *The woman's a digger now?* "Then, fuck, get her over here." The nun, standing alone, had been watching their every move. "He's asking for you, Sister! Come work your magic!" She rushed to the priest.

"Michelantonio, what can I do for you?" Sebastian was trying to form the words...*thank you, thank you.* He reached for her hand. He was back, determined to live, to raise himself up. "Father...no words now. I'll stay with you. I knew you would be here." He closed his eyes; tears rolled down his cheeks. "May I, Mr. Brady?"

There were small towels in packs near the gurney. Gently she wiped his face. Brady smiled a little. "Keep talking to him, Sister." Nuns and priests in his truck...he'd never get use to it...had not that holy one, Petra, resurrected herself in his van, but the priest's pulse came and went; his breathing shallow then stronger, then not at all.

Magdalen gazed at Sebastian, willing him back to life as she had tried to do with Petra. Seeing his dark hair and features, the thorns protruding from his head and a day's beard framing his face...she could think only of Christ crowned with thorns and saw the face of the Savior in his.

Padric joined her; they talked quietly until CSI arrived and Milleau spotted Magdalen. After he looked carefully at Father's wounds, they spoke briefly. Both agreed, whatever this case had yet to offer, they would find all their answers below the bishop's house and under the Cathedral. Was sharing his thoughts an offer to team up in some private sleuthing…and why not? Both were of like minds, archaeologists. But how would he know her intent in such matters unless Padric had complained about her? It didn't change anything.

Now Billy Kelly was gunning the engine. Padric would ride with the priest to Meadow; he took a last look into the dusk as it blanketed the desert…his own Celtic sight was in play, something he was rediscovering of late. "Bad End indeed," he muttered and scanned the saguaro-studded terrain then turned to study the grave-yard. Perched on the highest branch of the old, gnarled tree, his golden eagle was back, observing all that transpired. It transformed as before from bird into seraph, its mere presence having fended off the black vulture not far away, waiting for death to come to the priest but the guardian too had waited. It bowed as always then disappeared. Padric wanted to call out that the nun, who scared him sometimes, had found this one.

But suddenly Dolorosa's voice broke the spell: "*Vamonos, Magdalena!* Will you stay or come with us?"

Magdalen smiled. "I'm going with Father; follow us then!" She had invited herself back into the van. Padric pulled her in beside him; *hell, she's part of the team.*

Martinez thanked the de Torros. "Sister, thank you for your support, if that's what you will allow us to call it."

"My Sister and I, my brothers, are at your service, Detective."

He grinned. "I hear that. And you, gentlemen…" He turned to Tomas and Jonah. "*Gracias, amigos.* You are an excellent posse but please do not make a habit of chauffeuring Sister Magdalen to crime scenes." Her brothers lifted their *'manita* into the truck.

"Mr. Kelly!" Padric would leave CSI to their work; uniforms would be posted here. This was the Edge and he worried.

"Ay, sir, and how are you keepin'?"

"Better than I was on the way in. If you would, we must transport our good *padre* to Meadow with all due haste, my good man! You will do this for us…light her up!"

"On your command, sir." With a wreath of flashing lights, the medical van moved slowly over the rough terrain with a care for the patient and would soon burn up the road with sirens popping.

Father was conscious enough to know what was being done for him as they attempted to remove some of the cactus spikes with the sterilized hair combs Declan produced. He was stoic but cried out several times then humbly apologized. Magdalen would not forget…what had been done to him was more depraved than killing him; the priest had been left on display. *Sacrilege.*

With the speed of angels, they arrived at Meadow with yet another; now there were three almost-moondead sequestered here. And there was Ramos. Padric had a decision to make. Magdalen didn't know Petra was safe in her bed upstairs…so was Ramos. He wanted to say so; he could not. But Magdalen remembered Lara was there and gently suggested: "Let others handle this…go see your wife, Detective."

"Thanks for remembering I have a life, Sister."

"Of course, you need to take care of each other."

"And you…who takes care of you?"

"I'm good, now go." Magdalen stepped aside. The gurney was set carefully down on the pavement; Sebastian turned his head slowly toward Padric who was feeling nothing but grief. "Father, our nun did this…she saved you. What can I do?"

"Pray for me and keep yourself safe. I've suffered more today than my four years in Iraq. I thought I'd die there; just hours ago, I was sure of it. I was more afraid out there in that desert then in the streets of Fallujah; it had nothing to do with getting blown up."

Padric grabbed his hand. "Father, I'll be waiting for you when they finish patching you up; we'll talk…what was done to you, damn it. I'll personally take care of this."

The priest shook his finger. "No, no, John, the Lord has His ways. Now listen to me."

Padric laughed. "Ay, Father, forgive me my sins."

But he wanted to tear things apart when the priest said: "Please come to me, both of you. I know now, I know…" He passed out and was rushed upstairs to surgery. Padric was unable to fix this or erase what had happened. Magdalen had heard every word and urged him to go inside with the priest; she withdrew, spent and weary of soul, missing her sacristy, her convent walls and a normal San Miguel day or would this be the *new* normal?

Padric with Declan and Martinez ducked into an unoccupied room; the EMT understanding the case more than they thought. "It's the one you don't know, Detective; the woman's transparent. We know who and what she's about; the lad's the one flipping the switch and turning the wheels." Kelly joined them and said the same. Before leaving, Brady said: "We need to go, but my da' wants you with us for his birthday next Friday. If no killing's calling us out, would you be joining us for a pint? Bring your partner. We like him…my sister thinks he's a cat."

Padric laughed. Martinez shook his head. "Don't tell Marisol."

They laughed some more. Padric ran up the stairs to check on his wife, but not before eyeing the parking lot. His nun was gone; Tomas had taken her home.

It was near nine when they hurried up the bishop's front steps. Santo Cantera knew Magdalen had initiated the rescue; Steed had explained her gift of knowing to him, but Santo Cantera knew all about it; he'd hoped she would come to him and listened intently to her report. His young priest…*Dios mio*. Steed drove him to Meadow at once.

The nuns were relieved when Duran popped her head in the door. "Come now. I'm walking you home, Sisters." She was a wisp of a woman, yet they felt safe with her and as they walked through the courtyard, they looked up. The elder was waiting; they laughed when she raised her fist in the air. She had vowed not to sleep until they had found the good priest. Duran cried: "Woohoo!"

The two raised their fists in victory. The soldier-priest was alive!

"*Benedicite*…how can we help?"

It was mid-morning the following day. He had the convent number on speed dial. "Sister?"

She was surprised. "Detective?"

"Are you okay? I'm sorry I couldn't stop this one…that's all I can say."

Magdalen was standing in for Gabriela at the front entrance the following day and ignored the apology.

"I am concerned about you. When is the last time you were with your wife?" He said he had seen her when the priest was brought in. "No, Detective, I mean…with your wife?" She stepped into the parlor and shut the door; he too closed his office door and sat down. Was he hearing things? "Go to her; bring her home with you soon or go stay with her at Meadow for a day and a night. You will heal each other…get her out of that place and into your bed."

Who was she? "So you know about such things?"

"It's not for the telling, Detective; this isn't about me."

"And what if I want it to be about you? Who heals you?"

"We've talked about this. I am loved. I have my Lord."

"That can get lonely…at least here on earth."

"Ah, John Padric, one can live on faith and conviction in amazing ways. I'll admit I've had my moments but not been lonely a day since the veil was placed on my head."

"Sister, you're sounding like Ingrid Bergman in *The Bells of Saint Mary's*." It was his mum's favorite movie. "Thanks. We'll speak soon." *Damn, I never expected this conversation.*

Later that afternoon Magdalen and Steed stepped off the elevator; the floor was quiet. Neither knew what to expect since Father Sebastian had asked to see both of them. But they were relieved when they saw his resilience; he was healing already. He smiled weakly as they rushed to his bedside surrounded with tubes and machines; he had sustained some internal injuries, his arm in a sling. He reached for Magdalen.

The rush of words, his coherence, surprised her; she silenced him. He said he was more convinced of her gift now. She glanced at Steed…he shrugged. "I can't keep a secret."

Sebastian pointed to a chair for Steed to sit down and Magdalen understood. She withdrew to a bench in the hall. Occasionally, she glanced at Sebastian's face through the glass, but quickly looked away…he had tears in his eyes and was straining to say what had happened to him. It was too painful to watch.

When Steed emerged from his room, he was ashen…he knew now. Joanna, the woman he had welcomed at night into the place where he lived with her brother, was a degenerate, a killer.

He looked straight ahead. Magdalen stared after him...*get in line, monsignor; we all want a piece of her. Dear God, I'm starting to even think with John Padric's words.*

Sebastian motioned for her to come to him. "Father, how can I help you get through this? You know so much more than I do, our human nature, what we are capable of...please free yourself from your own memories. You tell us to do this...it is you who must."

"Sister, there isn't much time. That nurse, built like a sixteen wheeler, is gonna stick me with some good stuff and I'll be in a place close to heaven for a few hours while they work me over... seems there were a few complications. I'll be quick. It was the bishop's sister, Joanna, and a young man who called her 'Sis'...an odd guy, young, violent, a schizo."

"How could you observe all this with all that was happening?"

"I was eyeballing them, what else? I didn't take notes, but I damn well wanted some good recall especially about him." She pleaded with him to tell her about the male assailant. "He'd go mellow then maniacal in seconds." She asked who was the dominant. "Definitely the male...he had my name-saint's life memorized, wanted me to suffer like him but not like he wanted me personally to suffer...I was a means to an end. It was the act that mattered."

"Their moves seem rehearsed then...a good deal of work put into the preparation."

"There was more." He stopped, put his hands over his eyes and sighed deeply. "I could feel her on me after the last hit; she... my apologies. She was all over me." He stopped.

"So she persisted in doing this in the midst the chaos." He nodded...there were tears in his eyes and she comforted him. "Father, when I saw you, the look on your face...I knew."

He was grateful she'd said it. "Plain and simple, she tried to... do things, opened her blouse, but the kid went ballistic. He said she'd messed up; it had to be his way or nothing at all. It was about keeping it pure; he had no desire to disrespect me but he wanted me dead. His intent was to martyr me. I'm curious, how'd you know about the sex angle?"

"It's the woman's MO She molested both Lara Padric and my Sister Petra."

"Go on." He was saddened…she was more specific, told him how sorry she was. But he could see she was weary of soul and studied her face. "You're suffering…you are carrying too much around. I'll listen whenever you need to speak to a priest. You haven't done that in a while."

She looked away and took a deep breath. "I thought I was looking braver than that, Father." His read on her was scary. "I haven't been to confession since I arrived at San Miguel. I have no spiritual director accept the elder, but she's not a priest and offers me no sacramental grace." She said she had no grave sin on her soul but struggled with her vanity and impatience, wanting to be in control, not relying on God. "I wanted an end to it. John Padric feared I'd go rogue…I did yesterday to save you."

"You understand their concern for your safety, don't you? I'm with them on this." She understood and wanted to say something else. He had waited, given her space.

"Would you be my confessor?" Sebastian said he would be honored; he'd be there, guide her steps…the woman was principled, knew why she'd chosen the Life, but knew the world, too.

He thought for a moment. "The path we have chosen is difficult and most of us seek no reward but only His love and His grace. Many think celibacy, madness; a poor life lived with less, foolish; one can't do this alone. God gives the grace to those He has called; there is freedom in having little." She said nothing. "And your work for the Precinct; it makes you feel things I don't like. I know your heart. I'm here. No worries now."

She stared at him. "I should be cheering *you* on and you are helping me. Thank you." She kissed his cheek. "I must go."

"Can I count on you to do that once and a while?" He chuckled and sounded like Padric.

"I make no promises. Forgive me; I do that. But I must speak to you. Tradition says…"

"Oh, damn tradition, Sister!" *Yes, he did sound like the detective.* He tried to sit up. "Forget that sicko's fantasy. Put them away, lock them up!" A burly nurse appeared in the doorway and asked Magdalen to leave. "Go now; be careful. Not to worry…I'm here."

Sebastian came home later that week, but wheelchair bound. Unable to sleep and knowing Marcus had been assigned to a night watch in the garden, he'd perch himself on the landing of the old brick steps and one night did a wheelie, spinning his wheelchair around and around. They laughed and talked of many things.

The nun sitting behind the drape at her window smiled. Slumber would come easier knowing Marcus was there until, slipping over the wall at dawn, he'd return to the Precinct. Nightly he traversed the terraces, tracing the vine-laced paths, walking about in a garden he'd always wanted to see. But he missed the pair of eyes that would occasionally follow him everywhere...even when he knelt down at the altar to pray. On such nights, a shower of moon glow touched his soul.

But tonight someone else would stand watch a while. Was the nun at her window? He glanced up but looked away; it wouldn't be right. He smiled...Sebastian had graduated from wheelchair to cane and he sat with him under an acacia. They talked Marine, something they rarely did with anyone else; Padric spoke of his youth living through the Troubles in Belfast.

"I'm in law enforcement because of it, though my mum said I should have been teaching Shakespeare somewhere in Europe."

"But what, John?"

"My personal life's close to ruin and I'm turned inside out with this case." He wanted to continue but fell silent, looked away.

"Say it isn't so. Not you, John...you're Batman. Let your men and the nun help you." The nun. He was silent but the priest was an observant man and would say it. "I know you love her, Detective." Silence. Padric stared at him. "Just keep it in perspective. Let Magdalen go...in here." He touched his own heart.

Had he just said that? "And you, do you love her? I see how well you two get along."

"I did once for a little while." No way...never. Padric was curious. "It was short-lived. We were young, early twenties and met in Italy, but she doesn't remember. I was at university; trying to look like Billy Idol, bleached hair, the whole bit; she was working a dig near the school. She and her crew came into a jazz bistro where my boys and I were having some drinks at the bar. The music was hot; we had a good time. Everyone was talking to each other and she and I met. It was one night. We drank wine."

Padric wanted to know what else…he was jealous and fighting it. Again Sebastian told him again…they drank wine. "Come on…you're talking to me, Father." He said they had danced and were good with each other, that he was smitten, in love for a while. "But…" Padric urged him to speak.

"She didn't love me back. She couldn't; her mind wasn't in it. She'd suffered in her heart somewhere else, but she was great to be around, beautiful, respected by her colleagues."

"You kissed her then." He had to know, having imagined doing this more than once, but his thoughts of Lara and how he'd hurt her, kept him from dwelling on it.

"I did…but I trust you'll keep this between us, John. She doesn't remember; the night was hazy for all of us. Wine in Italy does that to you. She can't know, not a word."

"A shot of Jameson can do the same in L'Arroyo. But say anything? I wouldn't do that to either of you…never. What was her name, Father?"

"Brid, you know, one of your saints, Brigid. Brid Williams."

"She's a Celt then. Welsh, maybe…Williams, for God's sake."

"She was into the Troubles in Northern Ireland, had gone to school there. She comes from an academic family…they had money, sent her to Europe."

"You're joking…Belfast is my home, my heart. She knows that. When was she there?"

"It must have been the late eighties. Not sure, but she's taken a walk or two through it gone to school there I think. I'm surprised she never told you."

Padric had gone back; was in Belfast then, too…*what if, no. And she's never said a word about it?* "They're interesting women…reveal very little about themselves, especially her."

"And the Life she lives now is not understood, I mean less of self, more of Christ, especially the Sisters of the Crucified. They're more ascetical, very traditional."

"We had to do a sweep of the convent after Sister Petra's assault; her room…nothing."

"Their ways look old-fashioned to many and even other communities of nuns think they're out of date, radical in reverse. They made a choice to return to the old traditions, dress in full religious attire…they're solid, holy nuns with a purpose and Magdalen's part of that." Padric understood these things, but Magdalen, this Brid; she'd given her all to a life so removed from his. "You can be pretty intense, John; it can overwhelm. Be easy on her."

"I will and thanks for the conversation and some insight into this woman…ah, well."

"That's what I said…ah, well." They smiled at each other and promised their silence. Padric had always been a keeper of secrets even as a boy. He asked the priest if he'd spoken with the bishop about Joanna especially after all that had happened; BOLOs had been issued on her and her cars but as yet there had been no search executed on the Cantera ranch.

"Had the bishop said anything?"

"Nothing…but he's looking worried, not himself. Something's up; she hasn't been around as far as I know. I'm living on the first floor now next to Santo's office; a guard sits outside my door at night…my God. But then you know this." Padric had insisted on it when the priest had chosen not to remain at Meadow.

"But what if he knows, the two of them, did this to me?"

"Then we have obstruction of justice and knowledge after the fact in the bishop's house. The Captain had a chat with the man but it needs to be done properly down at the Precinct. And quite frankly, I'm uncomfortable you're living where a murder suspect is known to come and go…maybe still does. Damn, this woman's the bishop's sister." He reached down and pulled a 9mm out of his ankle holster. "I brought you something…compliments of yours truly. You told me you have a permit. You can register this in your name within the next month. Use it if you have to. I can't ask you to leave, but I'd like to hide you and the monsignor somewhere till we make some arrests. The bishop…I can't go there right now."

"Like I said, he felt bad, was horrified, apologized for even letting the woman into the house, so I think he knows she's the one. I told Steed what happened; I know he went to him. The man's complicated, but I owe him; he helped me return to the priesthood and treats me with respect." He paused, deliberated. Padric wondered if he was the bishop's confessor. "There are issues, private matters; he's shared things…we'll see. Let me snoop a bit."

"Don't even 'do a Magdalen' on me." Both men laughed.

But she had observed the two that night without thankfully hearing a word that was said…it seemed the priest did not sleep well either. But slumber would finally come for the nun and the detective would slip quietly over the wall before dawn.

Martinez was waiting for him at the Precinct. He'd connected with Lupe and threatened her with charges of obstruction of justice if she did not ID Petra's assailants. She tearfully said she'd lawyered up on the advice of her younger sister and walked away. He said he wanted to go Latino on her, whatever that meant.

After chanting the Hour of Lauds at dawn the next day, the Sisters filed into the refectory and ate in silence until Agnes rang the bell for some conversation. The room was filled with nuns' voices until she stunned them with an announcement: "Sisters, the bishop, in an unprecedented move, is again surprising us with something I hope you can bear. With the recent violence and loss of life so close to the school, parents are complaining. He's cutting short the academic school year by a month." This would mean an earlier final exam schedule and graduation bumped up a month? "We'll sort it out…is there anything to add?"

"April Fool?" Dolorosa was half hoping.

"No, it is not. But we'll be feeling like ones if we don't rise to the occasion." They were subdued when they left the refectory, Agnes approached.

"Sister, it has come to my attention you kissed our priest, Father Sebastian." There had been no lead up to the question…this was Agnes. She was annoyingly blunt and Magdalen, irritated…a kiss on the cheek of a man who had almost died was the least of her concerns. Yes, she had done this, but who would be so concerned about this to report the supposed lack of decorum?

The nurse…she would learn she was a member of the parish.

"It was a simple gesture of caring, no more. He had suffered."

"Try caring in other ways; you are often around men in all you are doing. Let us not show too much familiarity…no kissing please."

Men, it would seem, were the great evil and Magdalen had always enjoyed their company, worked well with them…she had loved several. And now she had been indiscreet and "demonstrative", the convent word for showing too much external affection.

But hadn't Petra, the most graceful and dignified among them, often hugged and kissed even strangers maintaining Jesus had done the same? She called her hugs *homeopathic*, her kisses *healing*. Some Sisters laughed, others agreed and still more, like Sister Amata raised their eyebrows; but Magdalen had learned the wisdom of the healing kiss from a hermitess in Egypt…she knew things.

But how could she say this to Agnes? It would stir a debate lasting into Christmas. But she understood; Agnes was trying hard to be Petra.

Upstairs, the elder settled herself on the window seat. "You are wistful, Magdalen."

"I am numb with all that has happened to our priest and the detective…I need God's comfort. They do."

"I know about Father but what else are you talking about?"

"Detective Padric…he recused himself, there was a conflict of interest, almost insurmountable. He had stepped down but was reinstated at the Commander's insistence."

"Yes, I thought that might happen; he works at being a mystery, but isn't." *What did that mean?* "It will be resolved, dear one, watch where you go. Understand what lies beneath."

Should I tell her I don't know what that means either? She withdrew into her room and wove some Saint Brigid's crosses…the gift shop in the Cathedral had asked her for a dozen.

O'Manion said they needed to wind up this case in two weeks or he was handing it off to another detail in homicide. Major Crimes would never allow this; their guts were all over the case.

They'd regroup. Marcus returned to the bishop's garden; he was told Joanna no longer came to her brother's residence but sometimes at night he thought he heard a woman laughing then all was silent. They continued round the clock surveillance on the Cantera ranch...there was no tricked out red Mercedes, no black Escalade or unmarked moving van. But a block from the ranch, Pistasio's tact squad picked off ranch hands as they left for the day, grilling them in the back of a police van then letting them go.

The Canteras were feeling the full court press.

"She's got a new ride, Johnny." Tark had spotted a Sentra close to the Cathedral several nights in a row. Homicide questioned friends and employees; business associates of Arturo Cantera...still nothing. Tark trolled clubs with Marcus, both working the crowd at the bar, on the dance floor, in the parking lot for a Joanna sighting.

Pole-cams offered little. Padric went on forays of his own; he was Batman, climbing staircases and fire escapes to the rooftops of tall buildings overlooking a city that wanted it over.

Things were clearer up here but not enough to give him a lead.

Author's Notes

"Buona sera!" – Italian, for good evening.

"Via con Dios, hermana!" – Spanish, for God with you, Sister!

agatazione – Italian, for worked up, stressed, commotion.

patriarchi – Italian, for the wise ones and elders, the experts.

tradizione – Italian, for tradition.

investigatore – Italian, for detective, inspector.

Nancy Drew – fictional character of a girl detective in a series started in the 1930's.

Miss Marple – fictional character, self-appointed detective named Jane Marple and created by Agatha Christie for her British crime novels.

Law and Order: SVU – refers to L&O: Special Victims Unit series, a spin-off from the original Law and Order created by Dick Wolf; longest running primetime television drama to date.

Martyrologium Usuardi – manuscript from 1350 written in Latin on vellum and said to have been authored earlier by Saint Augustine of Hippo; lists of martyrs, their lives and deaths.

maldita sea – Italian, for damn it.

Arizona territory – land so named from 1863-1912 when the remaining territory was admitted into the Union as the state of Arizona during the Civil War; some still affectionately refer to the state in this manner.

muskatoon – shorter-barreled; similar to a musket or shotgun and commonly associated with naval use and piracy, similar to a carbine used by the cavalry.

grande tristezza – Italian, for great sadness.

'manita – Spanish, for little sister.

Billy Idol – singer, songwriter, actor associated with late seventies punk rock and Generation X into the nineties, noted for his bleached, white hair.

19 LUPE

Two weeks passed. Pistasio informed Padric, Lupe was back; it seemed she'd cut her trip short to family in Sonora. Returning through the side door on Church Street, she stopped to pray before climbing the choir loft steps to her room. Her satchel was heavy; she swung it over her shoulder. Padric wasted no time. In response to his call, Magdalen and Dolorosa were waiting for him; he'd need them if he hoped to get anything out of the woman.

"He must be back on the job." Magdalen had whispered and Dolorosa had smiled.

Impulsively she hugged him, scolded in Spanish: "Never do that again. Now tell me you are with us and you will finish this shit."

He chuckled, familiar now with the saucy-mouthed nun. He liked it. "Just when I thought I was out, they pull me back in…" Did they even know he was doing some Al Pacino? They knew…Magdalen whispered Lucy had shown them the Godfather saga in the artroom on Saturday nights but not during Lent. He had laughed even more. "Yeah, I'm back; my team wanted it. Let's have a go at this, Sisters."

Lupe Rojas. They needed her; by her own admission, she'd often sit in the choir loft through the night in prayer…she'd seen everything. Forget the lawyer and remaining silent. Confused at first, the woman beckoned them into her sitting room. Padric glanced around…a small bedroom; linens on the tables were clean; there were flowers. "We know each other, *señora*, may I call you Lupe?"

She had always admired the detective and was grateful Magdalen and Dolorosa had joined him to soften his presence. Lupe asked them to sit. He told her why he was here; at first she was hesitant…it would take time. Dolorosa insisted she had nothing to fear. But Padric needed to say it. "You understand I'm compelled to make you aware of your rights."

She knew what they were. "Do I speak? What?"

"What do *you* want to do? You're not under arrest. What did you see…tell me, *señora.*

"Terrible things." The nuns moved slightly in their chairs.

"I sit at night in the last row of the choir. It's quiet except when the bishop comes."

"Why do you think he does this?"

"It's his church; he can do whatever he wants, sir."

The nuns were amused but Dolorosa was insistent. "What did you see, Lupe? *Por favor,* you must say it."

Lupe seemed relieved, preferring to address such things to her friend. Padric would allow it…whatever works. "*Mi pobrecito*, my poor one, my Petra, was dragged passed the main altar to the cross and strung up by her feet and duck-taped. The woman was laughing. She climbed on to the altar like an animal and helped the man wind the tape all around Sister. This *demonia* picked at her with a knife with little pricks like a *picador,* but the man stopped her. He told her over and over: 'No, no, no'. He was scolding, saying it wasn't the way it should be. I thought: are there rules for something like this, *Dios mio!*"

"*Sí*, Lupe, tell me. Go on." Dolorosa knelt down beside her.

"She touched…" *Here we go again*, Padric sighed…she looked at him curiously. "What is it, Detective…do you know her ways?"

Do I, dear woman. "What did she do, *por favor?*" He wanted to leave.

"She tore Sister's holy habit open like an old rag. I could not believe it, sir…she was touching her bosoms, biting them, laughing. She wiped the lipstick away with a cloth she put back in her pocket…like she planned not to leave *evidencia.*" She lowered her eyes. "The man was angry." Padric wanted to throw things around. "When they were done, she grabbed the man, kissed him hard on the mouth like she was his lover…and she's not." Padric wanted to…*what did she say?*

Magdalen caught it, too. *Lupe knows.* "You knew both of them."

"Sister, they even tried to put nails in her like they did Jesus."

Padric pushed on. "*Señora*, again…you knew who they were. Their names…who?"

"*Demonia*, she is a *bruja*. I know both…" But she gasped and stared passed him.

"Well, well, well, what do we have here?" The voice was familiar. Without turning around Padric said: "Sister Petra died in your Cathedral. Ms. Rojas could be helpful unless you would obstruct her from doing so…what will it be?"

"This is my house, sir."

"It's the Lord's, a public place and you are its gatekeeper." The nuns were stunned at his assertions. "This Cathedral belongs to the diocese and on loan to you from the Church. Ms. Rojas hasn't sought sanctuary; she lives here and invited us in…we violate nothing." *Rook to Bishop, baby, your move.*

The bishop smiled…*right or wrong, well played, John Padric.* He would control himself. "I suggest you be done with it quickly."

But Lupe was done. "Santo, stop it. Away with you now." *Santo?* The nuns were amused. This was theater; again the bishop insisted the detective leave…Padric glared at him, wouldn't move.

"What are you going to do, call the police?"

The nuns almost laughed. But Lupe was wanting out of the situation, wanting this finished…she was expected somewhere. *Damn, the man has done it again.* "I must think on things, sir." *Ah, the old switcheroo.* Lupe stood up, a signal for them to leave. "A man and a woman hurt my Sister Petra. I will never forget it. I must go."

Padric noted the bishop's dignified smirk. *Son-of-a-bitch.* "Do that again and I'll have you down at the First Precinct for obstruction of justice." He had said it.

Santo Cantera paled. Livid, he whispered: "You will answer for this to your own superiors, Detective."

"Enjoy the rest of your day, bishop, while I try to clean up the mess you have in your diocese. I had hoped for an assist from you."

The bishop had not expected Padric's earnest approach. Uncomfortable, the nuns filed from the room; Lupe disappeared. Santo Cantera stepped back, hoping the three would feel his eyes following them as they returned to the sacristy but they slipped out the front entrance into the afternoon sun and gave him no satisfaction.

It was near rush hour, L'Arroyo Boulevard almost bumper to bumper, the bishop alone in his Cathedral. Their opportunity with Lupe had fizzled. Dolorosa looked heavenward in desperation. "God forgive me, that son-of-a-…" Padric smiled and walked them back to the convent. "Detective, my parent's are your biggest fans."

"And they've solved the case." The nuns smiled…even they knew everyone wanted in; its horror had reached the Border and beyond. There were online blogs dissecting the case. Tark and the FBI were monitoring the social media; they too were listening to that hot new Latina band, *Cilantro Extreme*, five twenty-something beauties from the notorious Fifth Street hood in the *barrio*. Their songs weren't the usual *narcocorridos* but immersed in sadness and mourning for *la luna muerta*. Even young people knew the words and sang them to honor the moondead's remembrance. Padric and the case were making bank.

Dolorosa's mood changed. She said she could have ended it all by telling him things. Padric looked at her kindly. "You may not have been able to do that at all, no matter what you say."

"Monday then; bring Detective Martinez; our families go way back. I'll bring Sister Magdalen." Padric couldn't resist and asked if this was a double date. "No; I just don't want to repeat myself."

They laughed. "Got it…but you had me there for a minute."

The man had been up twenty-four hours and when he arrived at Mairead's, he threw himself on the bed in the loft. Downstairs the chatter was priceless; he rolled over and looked at his girls' toys, their clothes…they grounded him.

After shift, he'd bring Lara her favorite from Cuppa. They'd always untangled their differences and made decisions under the roof of the Irish coffeehouse. He closed his eyes; he'd take her to Cuppa everyday if she wanted.

Author's Notes

Godfather saga – reference to all of the Godfather films but more recently the TV miniseries by the same name. Joanna asked to be spared all of that as her abductor dramatically talks on about gangster life.

mi pobrecito – Spanish, my poor one.

picado – Spanish, for chopped.

evidencia – Spanish, for evidence.

narcocorridos – refers to the present day drug-ballads, a sub-genre of traditional folk music from northern Mexico, popular on both sides of the US–Mexican Border. Produced throughout Latin America, the music uses danceable, accordion-based polka rhythms but its lyrics focus on the cartels and drug smugglers. Early non-narco corridos existed in the 1930s; go back as far as 1910 and the Mexican Revolution, telling the stories of revolutionary fighters. Modern music critics compare the style and lyrics of narcocorrido to gangster and mafioso rap. Corridos singer Chalino Sánchez was murdered in 1992 after a concert in Culiacán. In death, he and his music became a legend and, like other corridos have long described the poor and destitute, bandits and untimely death.

20 AN UNPAID INFORMANT

The search was on for the other one now. BOLOs and pol-cams near the ranch were looking for more than Joanna Cantera, but they gave them nothing unusual. Padric would put some real eyes on it during the day. Martinez. Snapping pics with his iPhone and with earpiece in place, his partner sat in an unmarked car hidden behind a large clump of boulders near the Cantera compound. He was running every vehicle and chatting it up with Tark in front of his screen back at the Precinct. "Got three Sonora plates; cartel in the house, Sosazuta maybe."

"Arturo Cantera isn't into that shit," muttered Tark.

"And lookie here, my brutha, an unmarked moving van approacheth. What the hell?" The van had passed through the Cantera gate and on to the barns...but what he had glimpsed was over in an instant, a flash of red then nothing at all...*a truck inside a truck, very smooth.* Men moved feverishly about like ants; boxes loaded and unloaded.

But a click and cold steel next to his left ear gave him a jolt; he reached for his gun. "Don't even, motherfucker." This wasn't the first time for something like this; he waited, closed his eyes and saw Marisol's face. He heard his kids' laughter. The gun was pushed even harder against his skull. "What are you looking at?"

"What do you want from the Canteras?" asked another voice, older, familiar.

Who are these fools? "Get that fucking piece away from my head or you'll never know anything. Dead men don't talk." Silence.

Martinez waited. The gun was removed from the side of his head.

"Get out of the car and keep your hands where we can see 'em." *Prime time TV. Fuck this…*Martinez was more annoyed than afraid. He studied the two: male, eyes dark and intense; heads wrapped in black bandanas. "Alex, Uncle Alex?"

Relieved but angry, the detective glared at the young man with the gun; he'd changed, taller now. "Any uncle of yours would be ashamed of you." But he needed to hear the voice again.

It was cordial. "Joey, Jose Diaz. Your nephew." Grinning like it was a family reunion, he pulled the scarf from his face and turned to his companion. "No need for a rag, man." The older one didn't move. Martinez knew him, too; had arrested him more than once for burglary and assault, put him away for ten years, made sure he did time. But Jose threw his arms around his uncle.

"Jose, what the…I should slap you right now. Get the fuck off me. Your mother would beat the shit out of you if she saw this." Joey paled, said he was sorry, pleaded with his uncle not to say a word to his mom. But he heard himself sounding like he was twelve and straightened his shoulders. "What are you doing? I'll kick your skinny ass into next week. I could have killed you defending myself, if it came to that." Martinez was dumbfounded…his own, involved with the Canteras.

But the young man was pleased with himself. "We work for them, man."

"I'm not your man, *mijo*." Martinez looked curiously at the other one, who was clearly annoyed at Joey's show of affection for a cop. "I know you."

"Hey, Dondo, lighten up. This is my dad's older bro'. He's my favorite uncle."

"Fuck you, Jose. I'm not ancient and you don't love me that much." Martinez was done with this conversation; he turned to Dondo. "And you. This is just great…Lupe's little brother, once wanted in three states; a *cabron* involved in devil knows what. Daniel Dondo Rojas. Christ, the Canteras are really scraping the barrel. How'd you work that?"

"Charm." Dondo ripped off his bandana. "I've worked for them all my life."

"I put you away and Arturo Cantera hires you back? Christ, I thought he had standards. What do you do for him; give me something to laugh about."

"Everything. Anything."

"Building tunnels back into Mexico? Give me a hint."

The men laughed. "We're the *Momentos*, special forces."

Martinez almost doubled over laughing. "Your scrawny ass is doing a Rambo now? Damn, the Canteras have a militia and, Holy Jesus, you're it? Join the United States Army and go legit, for God's sake. Grow the fuck up and stop playing make-believe."

"It's nothing like that; we're ready at a moment's notice."

"For what? Put that fucking gun down. Dondo, you, too."

He wasn't carrying, but Martinez pulled out his when Dondo started to walk away. "I'll shoot you in the foot if you move. Talk." He called for a squad car.

"We enhance, pick up and deliver; influence a little."

"Is that so…you influence and whatever the hell enhance means. What are you doing, running for Congress?" The Q&A continued. Finally Martinez turned to Joey. "Where's your conscience, *mijo*?" Joey frowned. "A conscience, you little shit."

"What's a conscience?" Joey looked at Dondo.

Even Dondo was shaking his head and cleared his throat. "We do no harm."

"You're not gonna recite the Hippocratic oath, are you?" Dondo got it; Joey did not. "You're the same articulate bastard you were ten years ago." But Joey wanted to chat. "Shut up, Jose. You're dumber than dirt. I oughta slap you where you stand, fool." Martinez handcuffed him; again Dondo started to walk again. "Don't even or I'll send your brains back to Juarez with your old man's." Lupe and her brothers had a father who was infamous on the Border and had been returned to his childhood home in a box. "I mean it. Dondo, you've violated your parole by even standing next to this dipshit holding a gun; working under the radar doing God knows what. We're due for a long conversation." The man had forgotten this one knew his soft spot. "How's Lupe gonna react when I tell her about this, Dondo?"

He hesitated, hadn't expected the question. "We work for the same family."

"And tell me how her job compares in any way to what you're doing?" He nodded to the responding officers who pushed the two into the police van.

Joey glared at Martinez. "I can't believe you're doing this to your blood, man."

"And I can't believe you're hanging out with a shit who has a rap sheet as long as the I-10." Martinez slammed his fist on the roof of the patrol car; it moved slowly away.

He called his partner. "Got two; had a gun shoved into the side of my head. Be there in ten." Padric stood up. *Gun to the head…*he cursed. "Johnny, it's my fucking nephew."

"So, Dondo, *what it is*, man?" Padric threw a thick file on the table and the ducking and weaving began. Magdalen had passed on to Padric a comment Lupe had made concerning some work her brothers were doing for the bishop under the Cathedral…they had been moving things. Dondo would tell him he'd seen Joanna coming and going while they were there.

He'd offered a polite "Good evening, Lieutenant." Lupe's favorite brother had attended community college at her insistence. "Like old times. What do you need?"

"Like I'd come to you if I needed something." Padric glared at him; what did he need…*damn, right about now, my woman, any woman and a few shots of Jameson.* "You're not exactly my go-to guy. Let's keep this succinct. Arturo Cantera."

"Concise, I like that. It's nothing. Joey's a player. He's acts all gangsta; today he did some drama on Detective Martinez and blew the whole thing outta proportion. We deliver."

"To?"

"Nogales, Tijuana, Juarez…even Nuestra Laredo."

"And you're still alive? Good people, great food, but a whole lot of body parts! Arturo Cantera."

"What? I have ethics." Padric laughed. "You mock me?"

"Stuff it. Damn, you're good. Joanna Cantera."

"A nice piece of ass."

"And I'm assuming from the compliment, you've had some."

"I'm not her type." Padric needed to know who was. "She's stylin', likes 'em rough but smooth. Street has it she's into some dark shit and certain guys like that." Padric didn't flinch...*damn, I was all that?* "She can be who you want her to be." *Ah, there it is...out of the mouth of fools;* Dondo had nailed it. But the man wanted to talk: "A prima donna, goes after what she wants, educated, acts entitled but good to those who aren't. House staff and ranch hands have no complaints; she's easy with the franklins, throws them around like they're *pesos.* Her Salsa House workers like her; money keeps 'em loyal; she knows their kids' names, other stuff."

"Sounds like Mother Teresa...what else?"

"She's a dirty girl." *Yeah, oh, yeah...*Padric would let him talk. "I've been her driver a few times. She does the nasty with some big names." He hesitated...he'd seen it. "I caught some chat on her cell; she uses throwaways. Rich old conservative white boys like nasty but they choose wives who don't."

"Sounds like partisan politics, my man...Tea Party, GOP?"

Dondo laughed. "You still got it. Detective. I'm what you call apolitical, anarchist. Shit, I'm leading the charge against the Zionist Government in D.C. But I digress; Ms. Cantera's no escort; she's a respectable man's little secret."

"And that list of names?"

"There's talk, but that's all it is; her boys want to be faceless and nameless. *Yeah, he'd been one of those.* "She likes it that way, would never give up a name, doesn't fuck and tell. But when a *chica* like her is one *jalapeño* short of an *enchilada,* she's dangerous. "

"Cut the Bobby Flay commentary." He needed some meat. "Give me the real deal."

"No drugs. She needs a clear head for some of the shit she does. I've driven her to some hot spots, blood bars...they're big now." *Damn, I'm getting old...do I need this?*

"She goes in alone and comes out hooked on to a suit, judges and shit."

Padric stared at him. "Got any names?"

"No names, faces though. One's pretty high profile; comes from a big family. His courtroom's a circus, but he's fair, you know him." *Whitton.*

"How's she move around when you're not the chauffeur?"

"Bruno's her man. He takes care of Ms. Cantera...won't let her out of his sight."

Bingo...the big guy's facilitating her moves. "Who is he?"

"Her bodyguard. She needs one so she gets out unscathed."

"Unscathed...damn, Dondo, love the vocab'" He thought for a moment. "Are you afraid of her?"

"Nah, I could take her." *Yeah, that's what I thought.* "She can go all crazy on you if you ask the wrong question like when I saw some blood on her pricey Nike Air Maxs."

"What do you think that was?"

"With her, who knows? Cruising around in that hot Mercedes under the radar!"

"We've been looking for that."

Dondo grinned. He knew more than he was saying. "She's got Bruno but there's someone else; don't have a name. Can't say...not sure." He looked down at the table, thought for a moment. "Fuck it...you're looking for a cop."

Martinez and Tark were in front of a monitor. "Damn it, not one of our own...never."

Tark nodded. "And Bruno...he's switching her cars with that damn moving van."

Padric pressed: "Do you know where she goes...other then the clubs, I mean?"

"She's big time in the Edge, and for the past month, she's got something going on at the church in the Plaza." *Bingo again.* "She digs it there...the graveyard. She visits somebody."

So that's where she was going the night Sebastian bumped into her. He'd play along. "You mean the bishop." Dondo clammed up.

"Dondo?"

"Are you charging me, Lieutenant?" He was free to go. They had nothing but new *intel.* "And what about Stupid?"

"Not if he put a gun to my partner's head. Get outta here.

Tell Mr. C. he's minus a soldier for a while. You and me…we'll be chatting it up very soon." Padric walked out. *Damn, Joanna's name is a bad word with these blokes.* Martinez was waiting.

"He gave us something…he goes. Your nephew…book him."

Martinez grinned; his sister was Joey's mother. She would thank him but bail him out later.

Later that night and miles away, another Rojas eyed the Border Patrol van moving slowly down the road on the other side of the river. Isaac had a kind, handsome face; he glanced at the young, dark-haired woman smelling like coconut and sitting beside him. He'd made no moves and was there to protect her; after all, she was bringing in the big *dolares.* She'd been a nun and everyone wanted a look. In his Border town cabaret, Chato aka Constanzio Enraza was promoting her as the Virgin Mary, an ex-nun…she'd teach you how to pray on your knees; Dogg made up that stuff.

It made Isaac uneasy; the music pumping inside didn't help. S*anta Madre de Dios*…they called her, but they'd tagged the wrong lady; nothing good could come of it. Dogg was messing with stuff that would bring down a curse on all of them, on their family. Isaac leaned toward her. "You need to go home, somewhere, any place but here, *chica.* But they love you, even the *madres* and *nanas.*"

She looked up at him; he was a strange man. He'd never touched her though there were times when his eyes said things. Even Dogg hadn't pushed himself on her, though he'd shoved her once for not moving fast enough onto the stage; he apologized later…she couldn't have any bruises or marks. When no one was looking, he'd put out cigarettes on her scalp for not eating the food he put in front of her. She never told but knew her past would keep her alive…she'd been a nun; it had spooked them. Lisa aka Sister Anna had a past; it was her only protection and she was counting on it.

A large woman appeared in the doorway. "Hey, Calderama, get your sweet ass in here. You're on next." She shook her finger at Isaac. "The broad may be making you money but she'll bring down damnation on all of us." She slapped her buttocks. "Move it, holy mama."

Isaac tipped his chair back against the wall. *How do I get her out of here? Fuck, Dogg.*

Back at the Precinct, Padric was watching Martinez at his computer, could hear Tark on the phone hammering an informant. He pushed his reports aside, closed his eyes. *Lara.* He glanced at his watch. His girls…it was late but he knew his mum; it wasn't a school night. "They're watching Scooby Doo on your bed."

"Scooby Doo's on my bed?" His mother laughed.

"Da', wuz up?"

"Where are you getting that kind of talk, Kate?"

"Um…Mikey O'Malley." *What happened to Joey Byrnes? Little Tony Pezelli? Damn.*

"She wants to marry him, papa." Kara.

Padric was feeling uncomfortable. "In your dreams with a mouth like that. What is he, a gangster?"

"What's a gangster, da?"

"We already talked about this and Mikey O'Malley. You don't need to know. Now go to bed when granny tells you; sleep sweet, girl. And no more Mikey what's-his-name."

The runt's an O'Malley…he'd ask around. Years later when the handsome, well-spoken lad would come to the door to escort his Kate to her first high school prom, he'd say the same. Padric didn't trust 'handsome and well spoken'; he'd been all that…still was.

Later, Martinez walked into his office and threw himself into a chair. "I'm wired."

"Then you're coming with me to that invite at Brigid Brady's tonight; it's the old man's birthday." Making your own hours and off the clock was never off duty. "Need to get low to the ground anyway…we may learn something."

Author's Notes

Sosazuta — *fictitious Mexican cartel and criminal organization threatening the peace in L'Arroyo, the lives of people on both sides of the Border; its main operation and money maker, human trafficking and the Arizona desert, the main corridor for transporting the trafficked into other states and the rest of a nation.*

Tijuana, Juarez, Nuestra Laredo — *cities mentioned by Dondo Rojas, ex-felon brought in for questioning. He explains where he delivers goods for his boss, naming three of the most violent cities on the Borde; the detective shakes his head.*

Mother Teresa (1910-1997) — *reference to famed Catholic nun and founder of the Missionaries of Charity, a religious order of over 4,500 sisters, active in 133 countries in hospices, soup kitchens, dispensaries and mobile clinics for HIV/AIDS; children's and family counseling programs, orphanages and schools. Recipient of the 1979 Nobel Peace Prize for her good works, Mother Teresa was beatified with the title of Blessed, paving the way for her canonization to sainthood scheduled for September 2016. A controversial figure in life and death, she challenged the consciences of national leaders and persons of wealth and was both praised and criticized.*

21 BRIGID BRADY'S

Friday, eleven in the evening, April 18

The drive took them north across the I-10 and off road into the White Tanks. They spotted the pub through the grove of mesquite. It wasn't a welcoming landscape. Morte Creek, named by and known only to locals, was a trickle of water, flowing close to the bar; a final resting place occasionally for a few dead unfortunates, revered like a shrine by the inebriated making their way to their cars close to dawn. When Padric was a student at ASU, he'd worked here, stocking the bar and pouring a few. His da' had been a regular and told him Brady's was a place where you learned things; everyone had their ear to the ground.

An upscale décor was lost on the place, but law-types inhabited it at all hours. Maybe it was the old, ragged lithographs of Irish patriots and news clippings on a now fragile peace process in the Six; the establishment was a veritable trove of memorabilia gathered during the Troubles…it covered the walls. No friend of republicans, Margaret Thatcher's face looked out from a wanted poster over toilets and urinals, each sheet of toilet paper printed with three letters…RUC, a left-handed tribute to the Royal Ulster Constabulary; they'd greatly opposed the North's nationalist movement.

Guin Padric had suffered their wrath and he wasn't alone; no one would deny the pub's hardliner republican sympathies. Padric even reminded his partner that, for a time, in the seventies and eighties, the place had been off-limits to law enforcement.

"You know, *kema sabe*, the ban was lifted when we were in the Academy. But the ATF's been running surveillance up here for years, sniffing about, never setting foot in the place."

"Rumors of gunrunning and Armalite under the floorboards, my man, what else?"

"And a little Symtex to boot…this was no place for the faint of heart and it isn't now." They knew O'Manion despised the pub's reputation…it tainted the officers who frequented it. Taint or no taint, rep or no rep, the two opened the door to the familiar sound of the owner tickling the keys and the rollicking lyrics of *Molly Could Ne'r Find Her Britches*.

Martinez laughed. "It's only Tuesday and the place is howling." They sat down at the end of the bar.

"It's like this every night." Padric was feeling better already but he glanced around…who knew what he might discover?

"Detective, you made it!" Brady was delighted, his sister made a fuss over Martinez who didn't understand why, but laughed anyway and allowed her one of his smiles. Soon they were left to themselves and drank in silence, listening to the *craic* all around them. Martinez spoke first: "So, Johnny, Lara…good news?"

Padric pulled his partner from the bar to a table. Patrons called out his name; he waved. "I'm in a world of hurt." His partner wanted to help. "I'm not sure you can."

Not far from the pub, another man was feeling the same. Santo Cantera with much on his soul asked Steed to stop by the side of the desert road. Tonight he would visit an old friend and confidante; he was in need of his wisdom.

"Leave me, Theo. Return in two hours…*gracias.*" Steed watched the bishop walk from the edge of the road into the moonlight. When his silhouette dropped behind a low hill, the monsignor drove away. The desert was cooler tonight; he too was burdened, haunted by how he had been blinded by Joanna…she frightened him now.

His uneasiness lifted as he finally turned up the road where the murky green light of a pub tinted the hood of the bishop's white SUV. It was crowded tonight. *Good*…the monsignor could do with a little distraction.

Back in the cliffs rising out of the desert dwelt a cohort of hermits, men of prayer, members of the holy order of Saint Antony and blessed by the Church. Here they fasted and prayed every day, had a small craft industry of hand-built pots and holy things made from what the desert floor offered. Plans for a small brewery were underway and Padric, in the months ahead, would be called to assist in a small mystery at the humble adobe by the side of the road called Antony's Ale and Prayer.

Here lived, Father Anthony Peña, the pastor who had built the bishop's Cathedral with the newly ordained Father Cantera by his side. Tonight the man, not the bishop, stood humbly in the open door of the hermitage; he was looking at the one who had buried a graveyard under his house, the same who had tried to cast out its demons and was never quite sure he had done it.

Appointed by the Vatican, the holy solitary was one of two exorcists in the remote desert region where evil persisted; the other, Father Santeresa, who had confronted it head-on with scars to prove it. He extended his hands to the tall, serious man who was forced to lower his head as he walked through the door of his hermitage and pointed to the wooden chair near the pot of rice and beans on his hearth.

"Santo, what brings you here on such a dark night?"

"I think the dark night is bringing *me* here, Antonio. I'm in a world of hurt. I fear my own self and the choices I've made. I can't take them back." He settled himself heavily into the chair and stared into the fire.

Peña offered some ale in a cup. "I know, my son."

Santo frowned. "What do you know?"

Antonio threw some chips of mesquite on the fire. The rain in the hills had left an unusual chill in the desert night air; the pungent fragrance, a comfort. "An insidious vainglory lies behind your achievements and holiest acts."

"I admit to this." He studied the floor. Peña urged him to continue. "I've injected my ego into something to shield the Cathedral from those who would ill serve it."

"Is that what you're calling it…shielding it now? No, no, my friend, you have made that house of God your own and it's only on loan to you." *That arrogant Irish detective had said the same.* "In your conceit, you are pleased with the notoriety these so called martyr murders give you; that in your diocese, the blood of martyrs is spilled. It makes you a martyr…you like that."

"I do not deny I am an ambitious, over-confident man."

"And what else don't you deny?"

"I admit…I…it has been a dark, brutal time for my good nuns." But what else…the hermit wanted to know. "These so-called martyrdoms have me perplexed. Demented souls are replicating the deaths of early Christians. I'm torn by this dilemma."

"Your dilemma then is whether to acknowledge something you know or have certain suspicions about; you know then who does these things?"

He nodded. "I'm not sure."

"You nod your head and don't know. Why no certainty?"

"Denial."

The musicians were taking a break from their fiddle and *bodhran*, but laughter and good conversation made up for the lack of it. Padric shared with his partner how his visits with Lara had become more amorous; she was healing, saying all the right words he wanted to hear, but he'd been reading the woman his whole life…something was off. The girls seemed of little interest to her. "There's a brooding in the back of her eyes." He was suffering his own agony with the truth that if tragedy had not spoiled his game, he'd still be with Joanna. Martinez listened, said he wasn't surprised. "Damn, I knew I could count on you to pull it all together."

"What do you want from me?" Martinez was annoyed. "I hate the shit you do and love you like a brother. If Lara hadn't been assaulted by that *bruja*, you'd still be…"

"What would stop me? I have no conscience. It took her near death to…I'm a prick." Martinez drank very little; his partner was downing his Guinness too fast, but he could hold it. "Fucking that woman has sent me to hell for the rest of my life." His partner agreed. "Lara and I have been here before, but if it gets back to her I was with this one, Joanna…" He took a long sip. "I'm a dead man. It's only a matter of time. Anyone else but Joanna Cantera, damn."

"What kept you from and quitting the bitch?"
"Denial."

Steed had sat quietly at the end of the bar unaware the detectives were sitting nearby. He contemplated his draft of cold ale and spoke with Daphne, the woman doing the pouring. She liked it when the good man came to sit. He glanced at his watch and didn't see the detectives until he heard a familiar voice. "Monsignor!"

Quickly whisking him away to their table, the detectives poured out their frustration…he shared his own. But Padric had his own agenda, needing the man to gain access into the cemetery under the bishop's house without a warrant but Steed's cell lit up and he was gone. Detectives from Homicide feeling friendly after their ale surrounded the two; Ducci hugged Padric.

"Damn, you gotta stop doing this, Ducci. Bloody hell!" Everyone laughed.

But the man said he loved him. "The wife wants you and your Lara to come over when she's feeling better. *Pesto* everything, your favorite." Again Ducci hugged him and walked away but someone had taken his place.

Padric leaned back in his chair, said nothing. Dan Mason was sneering down at him; he had lingered with a few cronies, waiting for an opening and sauntered up, his speech slurred; a drink spilled down his shirt. An articulate man from a wealthy family, he was slumming tonight: "Your neighborhood has given up few leads on your wife's assault, John." So this was about Lara.

Padric glared at him, asked him how much time he'd put into her case. Mason cursed; both men locked now in verbal fisticuffs. "You've made zero reports; there's no paper work, nothing. I've heard zipp. I'm her husband…what do you have?"

The has-been detective was once good at his job, but more often of late relieved of his duties, suspended for weeks at a time. The list was long: failure to follow procedure, derelict in the performance of duty and use of a firearm; openly biased with no time for Latinos and blacks on the force or in the streets, his integrity was called into question. Few would partner with him on the job though

O'Manion had said he'd shown promise in the Academy. Mason had always had a good read on people; but knew even better how to manipulate because of it. He broke the rules to solve cases; Padric had done that, too…all of them had, but Mason excelled at it.

Now all eyes in the pub were watching the two; everyone knew Mason had it in for Padric. Envy, plain and simple, they said; he wanted to be Batman and wasn't and the man had a secret. Unknown to anyone, Mason was obsessed with something else Padric had; that's why no one had ever been to his place, never invited. Mason ached for and wanted Lara, his wife, but knew he'd be dead if her husband learned the extent of it: walls in his condo were covered with Lara from photos quickly captured on iPhone. They'd been enlarged and framed, made into posters…a veritable shrine would be discovered later.

"What's it gonna be, Dan…never once have you come to me, asked me a question. Do you just pick and choose what you want to do on a case?"

Mason stepped closer. "I'll ignore that, Lieutenant. Watch your mouth." Padric stood up, tipped over his chair; heads turned. Ducci stepped away from the bar.

Martinez rose from his chair. "Don't talk like that to my partner." He pushed the table aside, stood in between them.

With disdain, Mason looked him up and down. "You always hung with the *chiquitas* and homeboys, didn't you, John?"

But he'd forgotten he was in Colin Brady's house. Declan dived into the fray. "My father's askin' you to leave or I'll be revoking your privilege to even set foot in here. Cease using our place as your pissing court."

"Say please you ignorant mick." Gone was Declan's finesse; he punched Mason squarely in the jaw and dragged him out the backdoor. The man's cronies scattered like roaches; when Declan returned, he was given a cheer. Padric wouldn't condone it; granted he'd easily and more than once, torn up a place when he was younger, but allowing himself and others to be wound up by a fool like Mason was pointless. And now here he was, standing squarely in the center of a smack down in a pub his father had loved. He thanked the young man, but asked him to refrain from popping a man on his account; he could have "ameliorated the situation" on his own. Those around him asked what that meant. Declan said he'd look up the word in his sister's *Thesaurus*.

Everyone laughed, Padric didn't.

Ducci wouldn't back down: "You're not doing anything without me and Alex."

"And I thank you, *El Duce*. My apologies to your da', Declan."

"Ay, we've got your back here." And that was said for his father, Guinness John Padric...Brigid Brady's held the man in special remembrance; his ghost walked the property.

Padric pointed to the door. "We're leaving now, *kema sabe*."

They needed to go...O'Manion would break their heads when he found out what had happened tonight. Martinez strode to the door only to be confronted by Mason. Padric stepped in between them.

Mason liked baiting him: "What...you're not going to kick me around a little?"

"Dan, you'll apologize to my partner now or very soon." Padric would have felt better to go with his gut and not take the high road, wipe his ass up off the floor, as he admitted later, but he walked away. Martinez preferred the low road under the circumstances and was reluctant to leave; he'd been insulted.

But Mason kept pushing, shouting put-downs for all to hear. "Seriously now. John, Lara wanted to end it. She was miserable and this was her out. How unhappy *was* she with a man like you?"

That's the best this dirtbag can do? "Fuck you!" He glanced at Martinez. "I'll lay him out dead on the floor...let's go!"

Martinez looked back at Mason. "We'll talk, you and me... soon." He shoved Padric into the passenger side of the new Chrysler 300 he'd worked hard to give to his wife and slammed the door.

But Mason wouldn't back off. "Damn, where'd you get those wheels, Alejandro? A little skimming off the top or is your cousin's cartel taking care of you?"

"Fuck this, is he looking to die? *Un momento, Juan, por favor.*"

"Don't *Juan* me, Alex...I don't like what happens when you do that. Get back here."

But Martinez was gone. Padric knew his partner could take care of himself, but he jumped back into the fray and would need to extract his man from the scene. Mason retreated…he could never compete with the likes of Alejandro Martinez; he had his own reputation. "I'm going to speak *Inglés* so your pink *gringo* ass gets this. You lack civility, punk, and have shown my partner's *familia* no respect. Do your job."

"And what else, Detective…you're sounding eloquent. Get it all off your chest."

"Don't ever be condescending with me. Twice in one night you cut me down with bias unbecoming an officer…watch yourself. I'm giving you notice. Make a move to hurt my partner or his family and I'll throw your wilted ass in a cage for some dereliction of duty and a little obstruction; hell, just about anything. I'm taking notes and if that's too wetback for you, get out of town 'cause we're staying. *La Raza*, fool. *Buenos noches*."

Pub patrons on the back patio cheered. Two homicide detectives close to Martinez walked him back to his car. They told him Mason and his boys had a nest back in the hills, neo-Nazi, *supremacist shit*, something like that…they'd watch his back.

More cheers followed when Padric opened the door for his partner and bowed; with some moves of his own,

Martinez broke into a Victor Cruz touchdown dance and the patio erupted. There were even more cheers when Padric leaped over the hood of the car like a stunt man and dove through the window, passenger side.

The pub howled, never wanting for some late night entertainment from the First Precinct; tonight, their antics would go viral on YouTube and the squad room send up a hoot. O'Manion would growl for a week; Ramirez, horrified for all of three seconds, had a good chuckle and wished he'd been there, but Precinct Commanders didn't do that. Ben and Danny would show it to Magdalen and Dolorosa several days later and were surprised when the nuns burst into laughter but quickly recovered.

But now Mason was back, yelping like a Rottweiler pup, his face pressed to the window. Martinez sped off, spraying gravel all over him and his cohort; they cursed. Heading south on 85, they drove into the darkness toward home.

Neither spoke until Padric whispered: "Never a dull moment with us, eh? What if he's right…Lara wanting to take her own life?" But they knew better…not Lara. "Dan Mason. Another one I want dead." But he laughed. "Yo, yo, my man, you were preaching, *kema sabe.*"

"The one night I'm driving the family car, he's got to see it…"

"Mason was right about one thing. I always hung with you *vatos, ese.*"

"And we always wanted you with us, white boy."

"You mean *blanquito*…say it!"

"*Blanquito, si, mi amigo!*" Laughter.

Author's Notes

Margaret Thatcher – (1925-2013) known as the Iron Lady, longest-serving British Prime Minister of the 20th century and the first woman to do so. She is known for the tensions between her and a resentful N. Ireland, her dealings with the Irish Republican movement and certain prisoners, hunger strikers seeking to regain their status as political prisoners and not that of criminals, she would not concede, She said: "Crime is crime is a crime; it is not political" They would all die.

RUC – acronym for the Royal Ulster Constabulary, police force of N. Ireland (1922 to 2001). At its peak, it numbered 8,500 officers with 4,500 in the RUC Reserve. During the Troubles, 319 members of the RUC were killed and almost 9,000 injured in paramilitary assassinations or attacks mostly by the Provisional IRA. It transformed the RUC in 1983, became the most dangerous police force in which to serve in the world. During this conflict, the RUC killed 55 people, 28 of whom were civilians and earned a reputation for one-sided policing and discrimination, collusion with loyalist paramilitaries prompting several inquiries. Conversely, it was praised as one of the most professional policing operations in the world by British security forces. The report identified police and Special Branch collusion with loyalist terrorists under 31 separate headings, but no member of the RUC has been charged or convicted of any criminal acts as a result of these inquiries. Ombudsman Dame Nuala O'Loan stated in her conclusions that there was no reason to believe the findings of the investigation were isolated incidents.[The RUC was replaced by the Police Service of Northern Ireland (PSNI) in 2001.

craic – Irish, for fun/enjoyment, good conversation with alcohol and/or music.

hermit – individual who chooses an eremitic life, prayer-focused and in seclusion to bring about a change of heart, to serve God.

holy order of Saint Antony — *fictitious order in religious community of hermit-brothers and priests living in the desert cliffs west of the city though there may be other orders who bear the same name. Saint Antony is remembered as the first desert solitary, the first hermit.*

pesto — *Italian, for a green sauce, often called pesto alla genovese, having originated in Genoa, Italy and common in many Italian dishes with basil, pine nut, Parmesan, garlic, and olive oil.*

un momento — *Spanish, for just a moment.*

La Raza — *Spanish, for a term often mistakenly translated into English meaning "the race"; its meaning however, much closer to "the people", implying pride of ethnicity and lineage. The term became popular in the United States during the 1970's Mexican American Civil Rights Movement.*

Buenos noches — *Spanish, for good night.*

Victor Cruz touchdown dance — *reference to American wide-receiver for the N.Y. Giants, known for his celebratory salsa moves after making a touchdown to honor deceased grandmother who taught him the salsa.*

vatos — *Spanish, for dude or homeboy but also for "man" as one who means business.*

blanquito — *colloquial Spanish for white boy.*

22 BACCALAUREATE

Sunday, Baccalaureate Mass, one in the afternoon, April 20

The day had finally arrived. Baccalaureate Mass would commence at one-thirty. Dressed to the nines, the unit had met for coffee at Cuppa. Padric and Martinez were still living down the notoriety their moves had earned them on YouTube, but they'd already moved on. As long as the killers were out there, a pall still covered the city, their every encounter…it wasn't over.

Marcus said: "We need something big, something that knocks us out of our shoes to break this case wide open."

It would happen sooner than later.

The day was well planned for San Miguel. Distribution of diplomas and awards would be in the school auditorium later that evening; wanting to be pastoral, the bishop had chosen himself to be the keynote speaker, something he did often in matters regarding the school. Steed and the school board were as usual frustrated, the Sisters left shaking their heads. But now the nuns were walking slowly toward the Cathedral, pausing briefly to comfort each other, remembering Petra. Magdalen had been in the sacristy all morning and now stood at the bottom of the sacristy steps watching the families arrive.

"And how are we this afternoon?" Sebastian emerged in white vestment and sporting a cane.

He had startled Magdalen. "My Lord! I am well and you?"

"This is not bonnie England, my lady. I assure you I'm not a lord!" They laughed. "I promised the graduates I'd walk down the aisle with them…see." He waved his cane in the air and pointed to a group of them running toward him in caps and gowns.

"Ah, youth."

"They love you, Father; come I will walk with you!" With students whirling around them, they walked through the colonnade to the portico. Smiling a little, he wondered if she would ever remember him from that night in the street in Italy, but half-hoped she wouldn't.

Two steady hands reached out to guide them up the steps. Padric, in suit and tie, was grinning at both of them. "Well, aren't we looking grand?"

But Magdalen said she was suddenly looking like Cinderella. "Look at both of you!"

"Ah, Sister, you always look like royalty!" The men glanced at each other. From out of nowhere, Marcus and Tark and even Jana, looking like they were dressed for a wedding, approached. With much concern and best wishes for Sebastian, they quickly dispersed. Padric watched Magdalen return to the sacristy door; both unaware of what would befall her within the hour.

Agnes had wisely insisted the nuns be visible at every entrance; the people delighted. It had been a smooth start. The detectives, with eyes everywhere, took their places in the vestibule of the Cathedral, mingling with graduates as they formed their lines. Pistasio's tact squad in dress blues circled the complex in van and on foot, he himself posted on the front steps and never too far from Padric on such occasions, LCAT, L'Arroyo's new criminal apprehension team eyed the crowd.

And there was some good news: Ducci arrived; his nephew, a graduate. He'd just been assigned to Lara's case; both were relieved. *At last…justice for Lara.*

At the bottom of the sacristy steps Magdalen's altar servers, Sam and Ellie with Mario, waited. Larry Whitton was no longer with them…he was graduating and at one point ran toward them for a group hug. When it was time, the bishop and his priestly entourage walked toward the entrance to the Cathedral. Padric and Martinez, now standing like sentinels inside the great doors, watched as Mario, the crucifer holding cross high, led the procession into the Cathedral; he glanced at his father. "*Hola,* poppy."

A smiling Martinez bowed to his son then acknowledged the

bishop. But Padric would not and simply locked eyes on him. He held his gaze until Sister Edwardmary brought the assembled crowd to its feet when she intoned *Pomp and Circumstance*. At Magdalen's request to the bishop, Sister Edwardmary, retired, a stunning composer of liturgical music and former teacher, was playing her heart out. The Bishop was pleased.

The regal march drew the graduates into the Cathedral; they were in a good mood. Marisol had calculated that in this year's graduating class alone, her husband's nieces, nephews and cousins comprised near half of it...he had been invited to celebrations all over the city and laughed when they dodged out of line and hugged him. A few of the boys turned to Padric and fist-pumped their coach from Pop Warner Football. One said his mother still had a crush on him from high school, but the detective would not ask her name...he couldn't deal with another woman.

His throat tightened with memories the music evoked; Friday night lights, AP English and Theater with Helmstone, his own graduation, his father's smile; a time when he was *right with God*. Life was simpler then. This business of policing had taken him down a dark road; he contemplated his present state...he was a jaded man.

But today would be a milestone; he was attending Mass for the first time in years; Lara had always gone alone to Our Lady of Sorrows on Sunday. He found himself praying, needing her, but wanting forgiveness more; inwardly, he was struggling, weary of trying to hold on to his woman and a marriage that might be over.

In the sacristy, Magdalen was enjoying her Sister Edwardmary's best efforts but her smile had faded...she was tired. The nun leaned wearily against the vestry door; the fragrance of incense and linens, a comfort. Gathering up unused vestments, she entered the room and, tripping over a brief case, lost her footing, falling backward into a rack of chasubles and sat there on the floor. Looking up at the velvet and silk draped around her, she almost laughed, but when she tried to stand, Magdalen caught the heel of her shoe in the hem of her robe and fell through the wall...a black shroud seemed to envelop her. She passed out.

Not knowing how long she had laid there, Magdalen came to; realizing an unseen panel in the vestry closet had given way. Now with eyes open wide, she was looking up into the dark all around her. She felt with her hands the wooden landing beneath her and turned slowly; she drew back. The nun was staring down a flight of stairs into a void. She had tumbled into an Edgar Allen Poe novel.

The air was cool, smelling of incense and candlewax from years of Holy Masses and liturgies; it was the same she had found on the rocks where Cecelia's body lay and now scattered here and there on the steps leading into the dark below. She rose to her feet; turning back wasn't an option. The Mass had only just started; her altar servers, well rehearsed. Who would miss her? She could hear the last measures of the Entrance Hymn through the half-open vestry door…there would be time. Almost at once, she had noticed the fresh matches and half-spent candle at the top of stairs.

Magdalen slowly descended, the walls, surprisingly clean, free of cobwebs. It was fresh smelling, air-conditioned. A gate to her left barred her entrance into a dark tunnel that seemed to lead toward the Plaza; she shivered. To her right, a light at the end of a long passageway drew her further into the shadows and the nun was suddenly peering into a large, dimly lit room, draped all about and comfortably furnished with overstuffed chairs and a long leather couch. Money had apparently been no object in making this dark, lonely place comfortable.

She waited and listened then stepped into the room; a study perhaps, full of books and artifacts, antique weapons. Examining closer the leather-bound tomes in old bookcases lining the perimeter, Magdalen noted the large well-polished tables of wood covered with even larger books. Many opened and bookmarked, they were scattered everywhere among parchments and pens, some newly purchased. Partially concealed behind a sideboard covered with lit candles was a small refrigerator…someone lived here. The dim light revealed even more.

On the wall was a large print of Il Sodoma's painting of Saint Sebastian. She had seen the original in the Uffizi. And here was Domenichino's *Saint Agnes,* Veronese's *Martyrdom of Saint George.*

There were more…they covered the walls, holy ones portrayed in the throes of death everywhere. Whoever lived here had wrapped themselves in their obsession. It was beautiful. But like a page from one of the bishop's homilies, here were the martyrs he spoke of, those whose virtue and final demise he praised.

Her small room in the convent was so austere, this looked like heaven or even a movie set; yet beneath all its old world charm, she sensed a more sinister vibe. *Who would live in darkness like this regardless of its beauty?* Open, on a round table, were much older volumes, treasured perhaps for their embossed covers and illuminated pages. Leaning closer, Magdalen's heart skipped a beat: *martyrologies…the bishop's obsession. His study then…yes; this was the bishop's hideaway; absorbed in the ancient texts and always the scholar, he was coming here, a place for his research and where no one would find him. But surely he hadn't crawled through a hidden panel to do so. There had to be a different way in from above…an entrance, a stairway. Interesting that Steed knows nothing about this…or does he? Lately he seemed never to know where the bishop was. Had Petra known of this or had the not-to-be-found Sister Anna discovered it?* She could see Petra keeping this to herself *but what might Anna have done?*

Magdalen fleetingly thought of Padric and how she would need to explain what she'd found; she'd make a case for what she'd done on her own. But she could picture his rage…he would definitely oust her; no longer need an assist from a prying nun. Yet they had both agreed the Cathedral was the beginning and end of the martyr murders; the detectives had told her O'Manion believed this as well. And here she was, but what if the killers were, too?

Was the one looking back at her as he closed the doors to the van the night of Sebastian's abduction watching her now and what of Joanna? Part of her answer lay on the chair, large fashion sunglasses, a beauty magazine and half-empty glass of merlot still on the table. It shattered the mystique; the spell was broken. Apparently Joanna had been comfortable here.

Magdalen was suddenly not feeling that brave. She knew the woman's sick ways…she'd need all the strength she had to fend off her malice. She'd go…now; she'd run back up the stairs and straighten the vestry as if nothing had happened then return later perhaps when she felt more courageous.

Yes, she'd come back. Perhaps CSI Milleau would return with her…certainly not the detective; she'd wait, say nothing until she had a better read on what all this was.

She looked around one last time, loving it all then turned to leave. But something moved in the dark. It was too late.

Author's Notes

Bacculaureate Mass – liturgy of the Eucharist celebrated in Catholic institutions of learning to honor the graduating class.

"Pomp and Circumstance" – Op. 39, one of a series of marches for orchestra composed by Sir Edward Elgar; known in the United States as "The Graduation March", heard at virtually all high school and some college graduation ceremonies. It was first played on 28 June 1905, at Yale University.

Edgar Allan Poe (1809-1849) – editor, and literary critic, best known for his tales of mystery and the macabre; considered the inventor of the detective fiction genre and first well- known American writer to try to earn a living through writing alone, resulting in a financially difficult life and career.

Il Sodoma (1477-1549) – name given to Italian Renaissance painter Giovanni Antonio Bazzi; works reflect the transition from High Renaissance to Mannerist style.

Domenichino (Domenico Zampieri) (1581-1641) – Italian Baroque painter of the Baroque or Carracci School, of painters; nicknamed Domenichino, meaning "little Domenico" in Italian.

Veronese (Paolo Caliari, known as Paolo Veronese) – (1528 – 1588) Italian Renaissance painter, based in Venice, known for large-format history paintings of religion and mythology. Known as a supreme colorist, he developed naturalist style of painting, influenced by Titian. His most famous works are elaborate narrative cycles, biblical feasts, crowded with figures, painted for monasteries in Venice and Verona, the leading Venetian painter of ceilings.

23 THE BOY

S uddenly, from a chair in the shadows, a bundle of brown cloth slowly unraveled into a man. Magdalen stepped back, wanting to flee, but the lamplight caught his stunning features, his flashing dark eyes set deep into a well-sculpted face under a hood. In his early twenties, he looked like the bishop. Fascinated, she stared at him; the nun was in trouble.

It was he she had seen in the garden at night, the one her two boys saw crouched over a dying priest in the street. And those eyes…they had stared at her through the broken door in the garden on Holy Thursday. She turned to leave.

"Magdalen?"

She whirled around; the man had drawn back the hood; he was neither menacing nor threatening and long, black hair covered one eye, one side of his face beginning to heal. It had suffered injury; a scar from eye to jaw…yet he was beautiful, even more handsome than the bishop; there was no mistaking he was a Cantera.

"And your name?" After all, he knew hers.

He stepped slowly toward her and reached out her hand. "Come closer. Allow me."

For reasons she could never explain, she allowed him to lead her to a chair. His hand was cold and thin but strong; she saw the black nail polish. The stranger was unruffled, almost delighted by her intrusion. But the candlelight reflected a hard edge to his jaw; he haunted, sad look in his eyes contradicted his demeanor and smile. He wanted to talk, eager for her to know all about him.

"I think you're wondering if I'm the bishop." He was amused when she said the thought had crossed her mind. "I'm his younger brother, a lot younger. Being down here has aged me. I...I'm sorry you have to see me like this." His words spilled out as if there were no reason to be afraid. "I guess I could leave but my brother says I must stay here for my own good. I really mess up if I'm anywhere else, but I love it here."

She'd play to his better instincts. "It's beautiful."

"I knew you would like it. I wanted you to..." He had given this thought...he had given this thought, was expecting her, assuming she'd find her way here some day. In a sad way, he continued to insist he was a good person, a devoted brother. "My name is Bernardo."

So this is where the bishop disappears, but surely not through a panel close to the floor; she would investigate when she returned...if she returned. *Bernardo. Why could the bishop not speak of him and why hide him here? Most families have a black sheep, but they are loved...and live above ground. Did Monica know he was here?* Though not letting down her defenses, Magdalen would listen to a young man, lonely and grateful for company; he seated himself opposite her. She looked squarely at him. "How did you know my name?"

His face brightened. "I watch you from the crawl space above the sacristy...it makes me feel close to you without really being there." *Mystery solved*...he had been watching her; she was uneasy, not liking his apparent delight in her. "I can go anywhere, hear everything. I watch Lupe too when she works. I like it when the old Sister comes, too. She's the holy one I remember...I loved her."

"You know her then." In the most pathetic manner, he told her that Monica liked him, as if this was unusual for someone to do so, that he and the bishop and Sister had dined several times together when he was younger. "Yes, my brother and me and your elder...I think that's what you call her." But why had not Monica mentioned him to her?

He suddenly said: "You're a good person, Magdalen." She would need to keep up; he was switching lanes, had so much to say as if there was little time. "You are good to my brother."

Would this give me a free ticket out of here? She would thank him; exit quickly. Magdalen rose from the chair. *Now.* But no, she would pace herself then make a run for it. She walked to the table where a pile of very old books lay open and bookmarked with ribbons. "This one…a copy of course, how did you acquire it?" The ancient tome lay silent as if waiting for her. "This is a 17th Century hagiography of the saints."

He was pleased; surprised she knew of it, told her it was his brother's. "He wants me to know everything, as you can see from all this." Magdalen touched the vellum cover of a small martyrology; he liked when she asked: "May I?"

"Yes, yes, please. These are my treasures. Look!" He held up a large gold key he wore like a pendant, moved to a mahogany armoire and threw back the doors; Magdalen was forced to sit down again. She could only stare at its contents as they stared back at her with shiny, cold eyes…*santos,* wood figures of dozens of saints in their traditional attire but with modern-day doll faces. She looked closer…*but these were of martyrs.*

"Do you like them?" She said yes. "I knew you would! I knew you would!" Magdalen desperately tried to read this young man who sounded like a boy with issues and layers of emotional scarring surely never to be healed by living in such isolation. She listened carefully…*a savant maybe, brilliant and restless, overwhelmed with ideas, hypersensitive and perhaps an artistic temperament trying to remake and re-image the world all around him.*

She took note of the canvasses, an easel, brushes and paint tubes, a worktable with fabric, scissors and glue pots. It was frightening to Magdalen: he was showing her too much attention for someone who had invaded his space…obviously he was here in the dark for a reason. He had expressed too much affection for her.

"So you've been expecting me?"

He laughed a little. "I didn't think it was possible but hoped one day I could share this with you for as long as you'd stay." So…she'd be allowed to leave then; she would be careful not to alarm him. Slowly she moved from one artifact to the other then to the armoire.

"You made all these, Bernardo?" He nodded, urging her to come closer.

Shelf after shelf was lined with dolls in period clothing, Roman Empire; *circa* first and second century. Detail and trim; facial expressions rendered to an exact likeness were exquisite; staring eyes, at first sinister, followed her; but they were pleading, telling her things. She drew closer, gazing at his meticulous efforts, but a shadow passed over her soul; name cards lay neatly at the feet of each doll. In rows, all of wood with well-painted features, they were silent and waiting.

Here was a visual, three-dimensional litany...

Saints Donatus, Saturninus, Telesphorus and Cecelia, Eusebius, Fidelis. Their garments were of fabrics familiar to her, the same as those in the holy habits of nuns, the cassocks of priests, the robes of the brothers, all finely stitched onto their wooden bodies and limbs.

Saints Theodore, Dorothy, Bibiana. Her hand gently touched their heads, some hooded, in veils.

Saints Felicitas, Apollonia, Sabina. The hair of still others was smooth, real and soft, woven together framing expressionless faces.

Saints Nicomedes, Evaristus, Prisca. "You think they are beautiful?"

Saints Silverius, John the Baptist, Romanus. Bernardo stood very still.

Saints Lucius, Irenaeus, Venantiu. She had always loved dolls but had been allowed only one. The sight of these made her sad and remembering the dark of her childhood bedroom, its closet, she had played quietly there and alone. Her mother had believed dolls were an aimless pursuit to further feminine weakness and she must be strong.

Without knowing why, she shared this with the young man, his compassion for her so great, she stepped back. "I'm sorry this happened to you," he whispered.

She almost wept. "Thank you, thank you, but your collection, the workmanship, it is priceless." She didn't say how dreadful the eyes were. "Where did you get the materials?"

"Santo, my brother, brought me the small mannequins from a talented woodworker in Mexico. My sister loves painting the faces."

She froze. "Your sister, Bernardo?" *Say any name but Joanna. Don't say it.*

"Her name is Joanna. Her art is all over Arizona and Mexico.

I love her and she paints here with me sometimes." *But was she here now…*she wouldn't ask?

"Joanna, yes, Joanna." *Ah, yes, the Joanna who drives a tricked out red Mercedes; a black Escalade, and God knows what else; the Joanna who maimed and violated how many? My God, this woman is everywhere and I'm looking at the other killer, the one no one knew, the same the detectives are calling architect of the martyr murders, the dominant.*

Magdalen realized she was smiling at Bernardo, not wanting it to be him. Dark thoughts and dreadful imaginings crowded in; this duo had killed her Petra, the same who had brutalized the detective's wife and savagely murdered Cecelia. He never would have tried to stone a priest but she could see him having a meltdown when his sister disrespected the women he martyred. And she had seen him abducting a priest in a moving van.

"I collected the cloth and accessories myself."

"From where?" Her voice must have sounded colder. She would need to play this more carefully. "Even the hair?"

"Sometimes there are those who are willing to give up what is precious to them." *Did he say that?* If he were so eager for her to know all about him and his craft, she'd push a little: how did he get someone to do that? He laughed. "I can be pretty persuasive sometimes." *Persuasive.*

"These are replications of holy ones you have read about in your books?"

"Oh, yes, I research each one." Unaware and unwittingly, this was the bishop's doing; sharing with him his martyrologies, hiding him here, keeping him safe. Even more disturbing was Bernardo's believing he was well cared for by his brother down here in the dark. It was almost heartbreaking to see all that he had done with his time…it was hard to wrap one's mind around the macabre being so beautiful. This was all very sick. Magdalen felt ill but smiled. He was the loveliest psychopath she'd ever met.

She clicked off a long list in her head: *a selective conscience, charming, controlled when he needed to be, desperate for her affection, a planner, taking his time, organized. And his dolls, garments made from what he gleaned from each victim; the armoire, showcasing his pathology, his torment.* She would need to get closer and drew a deep breath.

*Saints Lucy, Cecelia, Sebastian, Stephen, James…*she studied more carefully the name cards. *Stefano. Stefano Villa, Father Stefano Villa. And even Sebastian…*his card was newer, his doll, incomplete. *Lucy…no not Lucy; had he plans for her, too?* The entire collection had been born out of pain, taken on a life of its own. Now she could see it more clearly: *swatches of serge and cotton, touches of linen,* the very same she was wearing now; surely remnants from her Sisters' garments. *Cecelia… yes, but there was no Saint Peter for Petra. Where was she?* Later she would learn he hadn't had time to escape with a momento…her manner of death in his brother's Cathedral would not permit it. Time had been of the essence; the replication too challenging; his sister, Joanna, distracting. This was a killer's trophy case built out of chaos.

Interesting how quirky even gracious he was, welcoming her into his lair with seemingly no ill intent…she had no martyr's name to trigger that need in him. If his sister were here, she'd be dead or dying by now…and other things. Bernardo continued to speak of his research, his love for ancient antiquities. *Had he seen her resume, choosing just the right words?* It wasn't working. She needed to go, wrestling now with the panic of wondering when he would reveal more of his dark side.

*Poor, poor thing…*but on the other side of her mind, she could hear the detective shouting at her: *you mean poor, fucking psycho…get the hell out of there!* But how could she run away graciously? Bernardo stepped away, pointing to one of the tables. She'd use the moment, reach back into the armoire for one of the name cards. The reverse side bore a bloody print. She picked up another and another, the same. Had he carefully impressed a bloody thumbprint of his victims on each? Her host returned to where she was standing and pointed to the other armoire.

"There are others in there as well." *More?*

She could only whisper, her voice nearly gone. "May I come back tomorrow? I must return to the sacristy. Your brother needs me." He said he liked how she cared for him and reached for her hand but she sidestepped Bernardo and thanked him, rushed away, gliding, it seemed, down the passageway.

"So sorry, Bernardo, thank you! You've been so kind…I won't forget you." Of course, she wouldn't.

Making no effort to pursue her, Bernardo slumped down on the couch. "I wasn't going to hurt you, Magdalen, I wouldn't." She half-turned; he was whispering: "You've helped me so much just being here." The voice, its pathos and pain, would haunt her for years into old age.

But, giddy with discovery, she was stumbling and crawling back through the opening. Closing the panel, she remained on her knees and lowered her head to the floor. Slowly she lay down on the crumpled chasubles. The organ music seemed far away, a recessional; the bishop and graduates were leaving the Cathedral. The Baccalaureate Mass was over.

No, she wanted to rest. "You look like you need me." Her eyes opened wide. Sebastian. The priest was grinning down at her. "I knew I'd be of some use to you someday...let's go, Sister." He pulled her quickly to her feet. "Explain later. His grace, as you call him, is here." He was gone; she could hardly stand and sank into the bishop's chair at his table; from her sleeve, she drew the name card she had taken: *Saint Stephen*. On the back there was a bloody thumbprint; this was for CSI Milleau.

But the bishop's laugh at the sacristy door brought her to her feet; she brushed herself off and straightened the linens around her face. Magdalen swept up the vestments strewn on the floor, tidied the vestry as visiting clergy poured into the sacristy to remove their liturgical garments. The bishop was pleased to see Magdalen assisting the priests, but he hadn't seen her in church; their eyes met.

As the priests talked of their invite to the L'Arroyo Grande Country Club, compliments of the Darby Hill graduates and their families, she slipped out the door and stood at the top of the sacristy steps, looking for Sebastian and smiled. Grateful mothers and nanas were kissing him, students hugging him. He had made a good first impression. *Thank God*. The priests thanked her as they left and she returned to the vestry where the bishop confronted her silently in the doorway. They were alone now; her throat tightened. Conflicted, she had been touched by Bernardo, this boy in the dark, his terrible sadness, his delusion, killer or not. Magdalen brushed away tears. Santo Cantera was the last one she wanted to see her looking like this.

Now he was, his eyes full of concern and a weary Magdalen felt herself sinking, growing weaker…she sank heavily into the chair again. He rushed to her, knelt down beside her, reached for her hand."Calmly, Sister. We will talk…not to worry."

"My apologies! I am embarrassed."

"Not a word…you are tired. But what burdens you?" *Did he really want to know?* Did he sense perhaps she had found her way into the dark during Mass?

She smiled a little. "Perhaps not today. You have so much to do…" But he insisted. She would say it. "I know you are burdened by family matters and I could help you."

He surprised her. "Sister, I've wanted to speak with you. I understand why you were in Lupe's room with the detective, working on that horrible case with John Padric, God bless him." *What…but he despised the man.* "He needed to do what he did; terrible things have happened here. I tend to be too territorial; but I will take care of things." *Bernardo. He knows…I've discovered his secret and knows where it lives.*

She would need to deflect his suspicions. "My apologies for showing such weakness; we are all trying to keep our balance. I am sad sometimes." She had never said this to anyone.

He sat down in the other chair. "I am, too." He'd never said that to anyone either.

"You?" She wanted to understand him if he would let her.

"Oh, yes, more often of late, but enough about me; thank you for all you do. Now go and be happy and enjoy the day. We will continue this conversation." His younger brother had said the same. "I hope we can speak like this again." She assured him they would and have all in order by the end of the day.

"Sister, you've put yourself out there, trying to make a difference. You've not had it easy yet bravely carried on. No work now… go mingle." *Mingle…she never had mingled; it wasn't her style.*

They left the sacristy together; his words, a comfort…she'd say nothing, tell no one. Magdalen turned to thank him again but he was no longer there; she turned. He'd retraced his steps and was looking back at her as he disappeared into the sacristy. *Bernardo. In a childlike way, he'd tell him all about me.*

A dull hint of something not right was distracting Padric when the bishop had given the final blessing; he'd thrown his partner a thumbs-up, but hadn't seen Magdalen during Mass. The event had gone off without incident. O'Manion appeared and directed his unit to fall behind as people exited the Cathedral; he watched as parents and graduates gathered for one last goodbye in the high school lobby before the traditional lunch at the Nile Hotel for the graduates and faculty. School doors would close for an extended summer.

Padric walked up the front steps of the high school. Still no Magdalen but suddenly they were face to face. She smiled, looked away, spoke vaguely of things and joined her Sisters. *She's gone and done it, poked her head into something and it scared the hell out of her.*

Their eyes met again. She couldn't hide from him...he was reading her; she'd confirm his suspicions with a look that was code for *I found something.* He shook his head and looked down at the floor but the bishop arrived to say his farewells and thanks to the parents.

The school band struck up a rousing musical send-off and Martinez smiled; his wife was there, looking pleased. Mario was singing his heart out as Mr. Helmstone's musicians blew the roof off the school with the fight song: "Onward, Coyotes, loyal and true, forward forever, through gray skies and blue." Granted, it wasn't Francis Scott Key, but Padric loved it; he was a happy man until he realized their nun was gone again.

She had to remove herself. The delighted voice of a delusional young man in the dark was all Magdalen could hear; she slipped out a side door into the quad. It was a warm afternoon and a breeze lifted her veil as she headed toward the convent; she would hide in the garden before telling Padric everything.

"Sister, may I have a word?" No, he could not but his smile tugged at her. Alejandro Martinez, *yes, he was less complicated than his partner.*

"Please, Detective, can we sit?" In seconds, she was talking too fast about school and the case and Petra...she was missing her terribly, she said, especially today.

Martinez found it maddening; he wanted to tell her Petra was alive, Ramos, too. But their nun had a haunted look. "What is it, Sister?"

"Nothing." She looked away. "Something."

"No, yes…what? It's me, Alex. Your detective's main man."

My detective, again. "He is not mine, Detective. I hope he has never heard you say that."

Martinez smiled and pointed. Padric. "I like it and have called you my nun more than once."

She scolded him though she knew it was useless. "You may not refer to me like that."

Martinez laughed. "And that's an order, *kema sabe.*"

"What do you want to tell me, Sister?"

They had never seen her on edge like this. "I thought I could do this on my own but I need to speak with the police."

They didn't know whether to laugh or not. Padric did and sat down. "We *are* the police, luv."

She straightened. "A pervasive Cantera dysfunction weighs heavily on the bishop."

"And that sounds like a Freud-Shakespeare sandwich."

"Detectives, you might not be happy with me."

"Try us." He was tired of the niceties. "Who did you see?"

"The killer."

The huge bells of the Cathedral tolled four. It was ominous.

They could no longer sit in the quad, hear the voices of young people and cars speeding passed on the boulevard. Magdalen invited them into the convent and asked Dolorosa to join them; she had followed the sacristan everywhere and was angry and horrified when she learned what she'd discovered without her. Finally here was Dolorosa's opportunity to say what she'd promised; but for someone who sat on several boards in the city, she was looking uncomfortable and in the hot seat.

"In lieu of what Sister has told you…I must tell you things; it will change how you look at your suspects, those you are looking for in all this."

Padric could hardly sit still after all Magdalen had said…they needed to go there; pull this freak out of the dark. He alerted Pistasio and LCAT, called O'Manion, put in a call to Ramirez. He'd listen to Dolorosa and sat down. *Damn, this better be good, but what was she saying...she and Joanna were childhood friends, had been close?* Her father had worked for Arturo and she'd spent a lot of time on the ranch. "In eighth grade, she found out she was pregnant. We were thirteen; it scared both of us." *Joanna at thirteen*, Padric could hardly listen. "Her mother insisted I be her companion and study-mate while she was home-schooled and paid well to keep secrets; we de Torro's knew a lot about them; my Dad does. When Joanna went into labor, she was scared and wanted me with her; Lidia, her mother, told me to get out. Arturo insisted I stay and all hell broke loose when he was called away to the phone." Dolorosa could hardly breathe. She said Lidia too left the room and returned with one of Arturo's belts. Like a mad woman, intent on punishing her sinful daughter, she wrapped it around Joanna's legs to block the delivery. The baby's head crested and Dolorosa thought both mother and child would die.

"Lidia cursed and demeaned her, called her a *puta*, a devil, and to this day, I still hear Joanna crying out for her father." Magdalen knelt down beside her. Padric asked if she wished to stop. "No, no, I must speak." She was whispering now. It seemed the midwife stepped up and hit the out-of-control Lidia so hard she fell to the floor unconscious. She rescued Joanna from her misery and a child was born but near death. It was Arturo Cantera who breathed life back into the baby, brought it out on the balcony into the fresh air and sang a sweet song. He said he was grateful to me and looked with great love at the midwife. Dolorosa looked at Martinez.

"The dear, good midwife was your *abuela*."

He had listened to every word and now understood. "So that is the story she'd never tell us...the woman had secrets about the rich she served, things she wouldn't say. She came to the aid of the wealthiest and said nothing, keeping things in her soul."

"Detective, I must tell you, she was a dear *partera*, greatly respected by Arturo Cantera; in fact, my mother thought they were lovers. They were close." He glanced at Padric who was smiling a little. *His nana and Arturo Cantera...ay-ay-ay!*

Magdalen touched her Sister's face, patted her hand. "You suffered so with all this."

Dolorosa held on to her. "I didn't do it with grace, Maggie...
I was scared and knew my parents would kill me if they knew I was
part of all this. I had enough and jumped the woman, but she gave
me a thrashing and to this day, I've not told my parents or brothers.
I ask for your silence in this matter. They will hunt her down and
we'll all be dead. She's connected, you know, lives in the hills below
the Border."

Padric looked at his partner. "What do you know of all this?"

Martinez said one night his *abuela* had come to their house;
sobbing, his own parents, upset by something she'd finally told
them. "They saw me in the doorway and closed the door. Back in
the day, grown ups and kids lived separate lives." To this day, he still
didn't know.

Magdalen smiled. "And this is why you excel in reading lips
and facial expressions."

"Sister, I did it all the time in my house. I only learned about
Joanna Cantera later, how her baby was taken from her and she
sent away for years. Three years ago, she returned to her father's
house with a vengeance. That's when Lidia dropped out of sight,
moved back and forth between her *haciendas* in Sinaloa and El Salvador." He paused and looked at Padric; both knew things they
couldn't say. "Joanna was doing things I can't even talk about here,
earning a rep...but that's another bowl of *menuto*." The nuns did
not look at Padric.

Magdalen was curious, wanted more. "But what you said of
Aruro Cantera is not the picture we have of him, Sister." Dolorosa
explained how she had spent time with him. She said he had promised never to forget her or her family.

"And how has he remembered you, *hermana*?"

She said the man had paid for the college education of every
de Torro who desired it. "My father looks at me and thanks me,
saying his only daughter did this." This had been a wrenching tale;
her voice now only a whisper: "Arturo's reach is wide, and more
powerful than any judge in L'Arroyo."

And that's what the detectives dreaded. Padric wondered...
what did the man have planned for him? He, a married man and

a cop, had been with his daughter in all kinds of ways. Surely he knew of all this. He would be vigilant.

"You know Joanna had once been a good girl, a beautiful young women, living with a nice enough aunt and uncle in California where she attended high school and even USC. She excelled, studied art, ran track for the university and was happy...but she pined for her son and could stand it no longer and came home to take him back...it seems she has done this."

"If Arturo is so good why would he allow Lidia to raise Joanna's baby as her own?"

"She had a hold over him...like Joanna does now over men. Have you ever seen Lidia Cantera? She's a beauty even now, persuasive, knows secrets about Arturo's family in El Salvador and holds it over him. He's given her everything. And she gives him nothing...not even a night in her bed. For years, she's carried on a very public affair with a mayor in a town south of here." The detectives were surprised at her savvy.

But Magdalen wanted to know. "And the baby?"

"This little boy would never grow up a whole person but remained very damaged."

"A boy then. What happened? Did he live? Where is he now?"

"I'm sure he's the one you met, Maggie, that young man living under the sacristy. It's Bernardo...he's Joanna's son."

The bells in the campanile tolled five. Even the detectives were on edge listening to what sounded like a death knoll...they had been silent until there was a knock at the door. They moved in their seats; Dolorosa rose to her feet. "I've asked someone else to join us...you need him, Detectives, you need what he knows. Please listen." A graveyard tale was to be told and who better to spin it than the bishop's long-time gardener, Eduardo Morales, the undisputed but under-acknowledged historian of another time in old L'Arroyo. He and Dolorosa's grandfather had worked side by side as young men on the Cantera ranch. The two were old family friends.

Eduardo and Dolorosa had frequently conversed about many

things, so today when he arrived in the vestibule of the convent, she kissed his cheek and he followed her into the parlor but when he saw the detectives he was more at ease.

He knew that handsome and tough *caballero*, Alex Martinez, and had followed the exploits of the one called Batman. He was even more pleased when Magdalen appeared with some beverage and took her seat beside him with promises of speaking soon. It would be about the basement below the convent or the tunnel within the back wall of the bishop's garden…she was a curious one. Dolorosa wasted no time, explaining to Eduardo how she told the truth about Joanna and Bernardo.

He only said: "This *mijo*, he is a sad one…he must be saved somehow from her." Padric knew this would not be an easy conversation. Anything about Joanna made him uneasy…he would never be done with her; it would be awkward.

Martinez sensed Eduardo's apprehension. "*Calmate*, Mr. Morales. We won't take long. You know the place called Gethsemane."

"And you do not…a boy raised in the Sonoran?"

"Not like you. No worries now."

"I have none, sir." Eduardo's slight frame and humble appearance belied his inner conviction. "Sister Dolorosa knows I have lived through worse than a troubled bishop and his family." The others smiled a little, but for Padric, time was of the essence: "We have knowledge of Bernardo's living in the cemetery under the bishop's residence. We've learned he's lived for some time under the sacristy." Eduardo knew this, too; he nodded. "I need to talk to someone who's part of this place. Never did I think I'd be asking questions about San Miguel."

Martinez added: "We need to know we can rely on your silence."

"What? You think I would tip off the bishop and his boy? I work for him; that is all. I've seen too much and happy to see this day; it's time to put the truth out there. I've waited for this and sometimes been afraid and not sure what I was seeing and hearing. Things have gone terribly wrong here with the bishop's care of his…his relative. If it is Bernardo you want, you'll find him below." He hesitated for a moment, then whispered: "It was once a holy place, but the story is too long for one sitting." He drew from the pouch he always carried, a roll of paper. "I have brought you a map, my map, the one I drew years ago and have changed as it changed." The detectives were delighted and the three men spoke of a cemetery no one knew much about it. It would be easier now. They left, grateful, determined to finish this.

But, damn, this Bernardo, this killer, is Joanna's son. Everything pointed to a Bonnie and Clyde turned mother-and-son team and the detectives would walk away angry, wanting it bad; they'd go down there right now and yank that delusional fool out of the dark. O'Manion wouldn't hear of it...not yet.

Vigilance tightened around the Cathedral but in a forgotten shed next to the house in the alley, a small Sentra waited. Its owner, in jeans and an old Black Sabbath T-shirt, was barely able to lift one of the slanted doors to the basement, but she managed and slipped into the dark.

No longer creeped out by the eeriness, she was glad all those bones wrapped in tarp were gone...it was in all the papers. DNA revealed most were the remains of homeless down on their luck, oddly bearing the names of martyrs like those in the case of the moondead. But when had he done this? He'd acted alone, pulled this off before she'd ever returned to L'Arroyo. Joanna Cantera was angry, remembering how he had torn at his clothes, told her someone had taken them. These were his treasures. The tunnel to the underground graveyard had been barricaded for years, but Bruno had fixed that. Joanna could squeeze through it now and ahead was an oak door the old caretaker had used years ago to come and go. She breathed easier and gave it three taps. *Damn, he's playing that funeral shit again.* The door opened.

Dies irae, dies illa.

Down the street and unaware more was to come, Padric and Martinez, Marcus and Tark worked a plan over *enchiladas* at Casa Mary's, but Padric was hungry for more than a meal or a woman. Dark thoughts consumed him as he slipped away from the others. His contact, the assistant night manager at the Nile, had called him as he had requested he do a month ago.

There was activity on the fourth floor…she was back.

"Our privacy policy requires we look the other way; I'm breaking the rules."

"So you're saying you won't let an officer of the law drag a killer's ass down to the Precinct? Where's your conscience…you've got one of those, right?" It was part of the air he breathed…he was obsessed with the one obsessed; she needed to die.

They found only a bed and a newspaper, some left over Merlot in a wine glass and the scent of Chanel No. 5. But the detective would have more to worry about closer to home.

Author's Notes

partera – Spanish, for midwife.

menudo – Spanish, for traditional Mexican soup, made with beef stomach called tripe in broth with a red chili pepper, lime and chopped onions.

caballero – Spanish, for knight; in the Southwest, a horseman.

calmate – Spanish, for "be calm.

Black Sabbath – late sixties English rock band featuring singer Ozzy Osbourne, Originally a blues band, the group soon adopted occult themes using horror-core lyrics dealing with society's instability, corruption and war.

24 OBSESSION

Sunday, six in the evening, April 20

Gina had taken a day and night off to sit with her aging mother; it had been good to be with *familia*, the gangbanger brothers who loved her. But now, at the beginning of shift when she arrived on the floor, she discovered a man had come calling on one of her high-risk, more fragile patients. With an insidious line of questioning, he had shrewdly planted more doubt; his intention: to ruin a woman for her husband and bring him down as well. She'd never be the same nor would the couple ever come back from it.

The man, in the end, would get what he wanted. Dan Mason hated John Padric, *a low-life Irish immigrant, arrogant and too damn sure of himself*. Without even trying, Padric had made him look bad, nailed suspects he had in mind. Granted, Mason admitted, Padric was quicker, more driven, doing it by the book…well, most of the time. In payback, Mason had destroyed crucial evidence Padric had found; his cases went cold, perps walked. O'Manion had told him he wasn't welcome back at the First Precinct.

Their policing was like night and day; the one all-or-nothing, hardworking and loyal; the other, waiting for leads while he sat on a barstool. He'd been shelved, assigned to the city's premier retirement community, Sunset City; the pace slower, the scene uneventful except for a few women who created some drama. They worked harder to please and Dan Mason liked that, could read the tilt of a lady's head and the look in the eyes of an aging travel agent with maxed-out credit cards and needing a man on her arm for the next cruise.

He dealt mostly in cases involving property crimes and lar-

ceny theft, the stolen golf cart or domestic dispute between two
eighty year olds. No one would work with him; everyone knew he'd
advance his career at a fellow officer's expense. But recently he'd
stepped up, asked for a chance, some forgiveness, said he wanted
to start over. Unaware of the detective's obsession for Padric's wife,
O'Manion, with a reputation for giving everyone a foot up, let him
back in the circle. But Padric had insisted he be given no access
to Lara at Meadow. Flags went up then for the staff when he was
observed recently visiting the patent; Gina alerted O'Manion and
Mason was booted, gone...told not to set foot in the building.

But delusion is obsession's companion...he imagined himself
still on the case. Gina was gone. Today he had timed it well, determined to forge some kind of intimacy with the woman he wanted
all to himself. Mason couldn't get enough of Lara Padric.

In previous visits, Padric had insisted Gina be present, conversations were brief and Lara disinterested; she thought him a fool;
knew of the ongoing tension between him and her husband. Seasoned and callous, Detective Mason had smiled. his plan to knock
Padric's legs out from under him like he wanted to do at Brigid
Brady's that night. He'd been encouraged, urged on, when yesterday he'd acquired a tidbit.

In a bistro at lunch near the school where Lara had taught, he'd
cozied up to the teachers who dropped in after work; he learned
their colleague Lara Padric had complained her husband was never
at home. The comment was said in passing, but Mason would build
a story around it. He remembered how Padric, in his early days on
the force had drawn women like bees to honey but Mason knew
little of Padric these days. He'd lived under the radar.

Today his wife was looking vulnerable in a hospital bed and
wearing only a nightgown and robe. "It's great to see a beautiful
woman like yourself rejoining the land of the living."

She was surprised when he'd walked in the room. Had he been
put back on the case? "What developments have there been in the
investigation? I'm sorry I've been of no help."

Sorry was good. He told her she'd done more than enough.
"What do you remember? Let's try this again...it won't take long.

May I sit?" He didn't wait for an answer.

"We've been through this, Detective."

"How many times have I asked you to call me Danny?" She was uneasy. "Think now." He moved his chair closer. "Had your husband been coming home regularly at end of shift?"

She hesitated. "No, he hadn't done that for the past year."

Lara searched his face; what was he doing? She and her husband had a history of growing apart then coming back to each other stronger than ever. Johnny had always admitted things, his indiscretions; she knew of the women, but would say nothing to this creep about someone he may have been seeing when she was attacked. In the past, she would have waited, let whatever he had for someone, smolder and die...but she had told him she was done with him now; the pregnancy she had hoped to discuss with him, over in her mind.

Mason watched her silently processing her thoughts. This afternoon he was in heaven, doing what he did best, destroying another's world and now he was chinking away at the heart of a shaky marriage. "Mrs. Padric?"

"What? Johnny has been very involved in the deaths of those poor nuns and that priest and the brother; and yes, his hours have been irregular and I understood that." She knew Mason only from the few comments Padric had made; he rarely brought his job home, was close-mouthed about all of it. But Lara remembered now...this one man could set him off; he was not to be trusted. She'd take him down a peg. "You know all this or you think you do. You're looking for something but what do you have to show for your life?"

It caught him off guard. His reputation preceded him: three broken marriages, no kids, bankrupt, and a jacket full of reprimands at the Precinct. Bitch. He'd do some damage.

"Your husband wasn't home at the time of the attack?" His tone had changed.

"No."

"Where was he?"

"I don't know. He was working that night."

"No, he wasn't." He waited, watching the information register on Lara's face. "Didn't he tell you where he'd been?" His subtle suggestions would drip slowly like a leaky faucet into Lara's soul as one question followed the other. "Mrs. Padric…"

"What? No. I didn't ask, didn't care. I was dying that morning…he saved me."

"Barely, it would seem. Do you recall what your assailants looked like? You say it was a man and a woman." She nodded, remembering: she'd waited up…even the next morning, she'd watched for him at the window, even watered the back yard earlier than usual. Her friend had taken the girls to school, she'd wanted to talk, had something to tell him. She was pregnant…this might mean something for both of them, a new start.

"Bright red…her lipstick, Chanel No. 5; she spoke to me." Lara was thinking aloud now. "The woman was laughing." *Good, this is good.* "I had passed out and came to; she kept saying his name… Johnny. She laughed at me. Hurt me." *Ah, yes…go in for the kill.*

"Was she speaking to your husband? She was talking to him, wasn't she? What did he look like?"

What did he mean? Johnny wasn't home. "I don't know…I couldn't see." Her voice was weaker now.

Mason heard it…*doubt.* "You saw him, right?"

"I never saw his face…he never spoke." Lara frowned; *no, he had not said a word.* "He wore a monk's robe, a hood over his eyes; and masks, they both wore them, beautiful, strange, crafted masks, almost elegant…staring at me, no expression. Terrifying." She wanted Johnny to suddenly appear in the doorway.

"What cologne?"

"What? None. I don't know."

"Does your husband wear cologne?"

What? "No. I hate it on men."

Mason was embarrassed; *damn*, he hadn't known that; he wore it like armor. She was tougher than he thought. *Jugular time.* "So you can't ID the male. What if I told you he was your husband?"

Lara was slowly being persuaded. "Why would he want to do this?" She was sounding more vulnerable. "And you think the woman was his lover?"

He would employ the dramatic pause…difficult when he wanted her like he did, but he'd waited for this and would let her fears simmer. "Dear woman, they wanted you out of the picture. Your husband could easily pull off an affair, live a whole other life with a night detective's schedule." He was almost breathless; watching her pain aroused him…this was intimacy, filling a void. Dan Mason loved what he'd done. Bringing her to the edge; he'd wait on the other side.

But Lara was no pushover; the tone in her voice was colder, the glint in her eyes harder; after all, she had practice, sparring with the likes of Johnny Padric. "Are you trying to wind me up, Detective?"

No. Didn't she get it? He couldn't lose her, but he'd overstepped and saw her revulsion. He'd need to act quickly: "Johnny and his lover came to your house to kill you."

Dead silence.

A cop was fingering another cop for attempted murder in his own house where his little ones played; where they might find their mother dead when they cane home from school. Lara's eyes narrowed. *Not Johnny, he wouldn't go to the trouble. If he had enough, he'd just say it and leave. Well, no, he'd have kept on playing the fool for as long as he could. He'd never walk away from his children like his da' did.*

But Mason in a last ditch effort was driving his point home. "If a man is content in his marriage, he does all he can to get home to his family."

"And you know this for a fact."

"Yes, because I didn't do it. It takes one to know one."

"Indeed. But, with no apologies, you're nothing like Johnny Padric, Detective."

What? She's not backing down. "I'll take that as a compliment; your husband's a philanderer and a wannabe murderer. He came to your home with his girlfriend to kill you."

Lara remembered…her attacker had said his name like she knew him, told her things she didn't want to hear. Now she was shaking her head, covering her ears and in no state to be hearing such things even if true. *This needs to stop, damn it;* her voice was louder now: "How they allowed you in here is beyond me. Where is your proof? You're full of conjecture and innuendo. Leave. Please go."

Lara pressed the call button on the device Padric insisted she keep under the blanket. But the detective was not stopping anytime soon. "His prints were everywhere."

"Uh, for God's sake, he lives there. My attackers wore gloves."

"Did you know there have been repeated BOLOs issued for Joanna Cantera in a murder investigation making *mucho* news in this town? Her description fits what you've given us down to the Chanel No. 5."

Wait…he's saying my husband's lover was Joanna Cantera, that Joanna Cantera…anyone else, anyone else, but that maneater. She'd seen her around, eyed her when she made news on the art channel, heard the gossip; every woman in town knew her. Those at work had spoken of her. Lara, for only a moment, had regained control of the conversation; now she was falling apart, getting hammered.

"What other woman would want you dead but your husband's lover? She delivered the blows; she brutalized you. Why didn't her male accomplice join in…he was your husband and couldn't do it. He's a wuss and let his girl do the deed. Johnny Padric stood there and watched and he's going down for this. I'm making sure of…"

The door opened. Gina. "Get out, Mason!" Lara's light was blinking over her door.

"I've just as much right to be here as you do, sweetheart."

"Wrong. You didn't get the memo? We have rules, something you've never been too cool with. Get up!" Gina nodded to an orderly to attend to her patient. "I'll deal with this idiot."

But it was too late…Dan Mason had gotten to Lara, confirming her worse fears. Gina ordered Mason to step into the hall. "Make me. I'll sue your ass."

He stood up, leered down at her. Gina eyed him…*he's soft. I can take him;* she kicked Mason's legs out from under him and threw him onto his stomach. "Hooking you up, fool!" An orderly hoisted him to his feet. "Lara, are you all right? Landen, did you call security?"

"You *are* security, Sarg; you're the man! But I buzzed Agent Watson." And this is why the FBI had an office on the fifth floor.

Bobby responded in seconds. "What the hell is it with this guy? He's been given one free pass after another. Johnny will…"

All Gina could think of was what Padric would do. "Not a word, not a word. He'll tear up the place; I'll make the call. I want something done to this man. Dump him somewhere. And Mason," she stopped the elevator door with her hand. "I'm not your friggin' sweetheart. Fuck you." She quickly walked toward room 355.

Desperation. Mason had left in his wake the usual collateral damage. Lara, for one, had taken a hit, but violence is insidious, whether mental or physical; others on the floor sensed it. They already were victims, wounds still fresh; that's why they were there. Napping or heavily medicated, some stirred in their beds; others cried out when they sensed one of their own was being hurt. Staff moved quickly from one room to the other. Then it was over.

Gina breathed easier when she found Lara quietly waiting for her to return. She was sad but looking very much in control. "How soon can I leave here?"

"I'm afraid not until arrests have been made…they are close and you know we keep you safe here in protective custody. The doctors…they'll know best and exercise caution."

"Caution…dear God. How did this man get in my room then? Stop it…just stop it. I don't want to be saved and I know now what happened. I was a cop's wife."

"*Was?* You still are." Mason had turned her. "What did he say to you?"

Lara laughed. "Gina, for God's sake, stop it with all your secrets…just stop it. I'm a big girl and will be leaving him as soon as I leave here. He let this happen to me, the one who had loved him in his darkest moments. And there's that other thing I've never told him and must be said. He needs to know and I'll enjoy saying it… he's due for some payback." Gina knew well what she meant. The old Lara was gone, had disappeared. "I want nothing, no more, from this man." Mason had achieved what he wanted but there was that other matter.

An incident had occurred, delicate, something unexpected within minutes after being brought up to surgery upon arrival at Meadow. She insisted no one on staff say a word; Gina had not been happy and still in conflict over it all. "Lara, it's time. You must tell him…I've said nothing. Don't keep it from him one more day." Lara smiled an odd, cold smile. But still, Gina wanted answers. "You say you know who your attackers were?"

"Thanks to Dan Mason; it sounds reasonable. Johnny and his latest lover, Miss Come-get-you-some." The quick-witted, often sardonic Lara was back and done with her man. "That son-of-a-bitch is right." She told Gina all Mason had said. "Joanna Cantera. How long do I wait for him to forget that? What is left of a man after she's had him? Tell me, Gina, where does a wife go after that?"

Did she require an answer or were those rhetorical questions? Gina was speechless...even she pondered the possibilities: *damn, she sounds like Lauren Bacall talking smack to Bogie. How fucking good could the divine Ms. Cantera be?* She too wanted her gone. Gina was "street", Martinez had said once as he had said the same about Dolorosa but with more respect and in a whisper. He knew Gina's family and like him, she'd hated the hold this woman had on Padric; she'd contemplated messing her up...she could take her, no problem. She'd figure out something, make it happen. Gina was beyond furious now.

Padric's mind was on other things; he glanced at his watch. Again he and Martinez demanded the chance to go after the Canteras and still, O'Manion wanted a strategy then he'd listen. *A plan...hell, we've outlined it on bar napkins and carried them around in our pockets; now we have a real place to go with it. We need to pounce; Bernardo could be long gone if the nun showing up spooked him.*

"Get me a fucking warrant, Cap'. Our nun knows where he is; this kid has to know he's running out of time and his martyring days over. Our ADA isn't moving on this...never wanted to. She does shit."

O'Manion agreed. He thought for a moment, chewing slowly on his Wendy's pretzel bacon cheeseburger. "Fuck her." He smiled a little. "I've always wondered what that would be like." Silence. "She's a good-looking woman." He took another bite.

"Say it isn't so, Cap', you too entertain impure thoughts concerning the ladies? I'm the only sinner around here and I'd like to hold on to that title. Let's move it along or I'm going in and under and drag that fuck out into the open. Now what'll it be and put that damn pretzel shit down." Martinez stepped away from the conversation and doubled over in laughter.

O'Manion carefully placed his burger again on a paper plate. He spoke: "It's Sunday and I know for a fact, Jay's in chambers with two big trials coming up. The man's a player but he works weekends. He called me an hour ago, asked a favor on one of the cases. I'll put in a call. You're up, lad. Get your ass over there; make nice with your football buddy and go work your magic on the most obnoxious judge in the state. And, son, my sexual musings and exploits are none of your damn business...get out."

Padric grinned and shouted down the hall. "Briefing's pushed back to midnight!" He checked his iPhone. *Gina.* She'd left three or four messages, all vague. *Later.*

It was still light and across the Plaza, parents and friends were gathering for graduation exercises in Cathedral High's auditorium. The courthouse looked empty, entrances locked, but two guards gave him a nod; they knew him. The halls were silent; he took the marble stairs two at a time. At the door of the judge's chambers Padric stopped. He heard conversation, a woman voice and knocked.

"Who is it?" *Whitton.*

"John Padric, Jay. I need your help..."

The door opened at once, some mellow jazz in the background. The judge wore only a towel and was covered in love-sweat. He could be careless like that...they went way back, but Padric didn't like him. He'd always been too attentive to Lara. "Hey, Johnny, not another one."

Padric's eyes narrowed. *The good magistrate's doing his secretary again*; it was common knowledge he had a bevy of paralegals at his bidding, but *harems be damned, this was hallowed ground, for God's sake, a hall of justice and not the venue most judges chose to get it on with someone.* But Jay, as the Cap' said, was a player, standing there looking pleased with himself.

Padric shook his head, but who was he to pass judgment on another man? "Looks like I've come at a bad time." It seemed the most logical and clichéd thing to say. "I need a warrant for the Cathedral and whatever's below it and the graveyard under the bishop's house." He told him about Bernardo and Joanna. "What'll it be?"

Whitton closed his door for a minute. There were words, a woman's voice then silence. He returned in a tee shirt and jeans.

"Damn it. Johnny, you know what we're talking about here? The Canteras, the bishop, for God's sake." *Oh, that.* Padric could see the writing on the wall. "I'm going to need more than probable cause." *Who needs more than probable cause?*

Whitton stepped into the hall and shut the door. One of the best legal minds in the state was struggling with this one, but Padric was adamant. "O'Manion said we've got exigency…the nun, the one you said was sharp, on point with the interpretations she'd given us; you like her. She had an unintended face-to-face with the guy…he liked her, too; didn't harm her. She even held on to some evidence for us. He's our man with Joanna Cantera…we've got her on all this."

What was this? Whitton paled. The mention of her name could do that to certain men. He stared at Padric then at the floor. "Joanna Cantera…okay. Damn. But the other one, the bishop would let someone live under his house?" Padric was watching the ping pong game in the magistrate's head.

He was furious and punched his fist into the wall. "Don't do this to me, damn it. Give me a search warrant if the arrest warrant goes against what you have for the Canteras. I get it, though I'm ashamed of you, Jay, for screwing around with the law like this."

Only he could say something like this to Whitton. "What did you say?"

"About what? Which time?"

"Joanna Cantera. You have Joanna Cantera and this supposed relative for all those murders of nuns and priests?" His eyes grew dark with something he couldn't reveal. Padric was reading him… *ah, Jay, what did you do? Joanna.* Padric felt nauseous…*she was fucking both of us.* But hadn't the Commander implied something like that? He could hardly breathe. Whitton paced back and forth in the hall. He looked out the window then down at the floor then finally stopped in front of Padric.

"You're right."

"Damn straight I am." He frowned. "What am I right about?"

"That thing I have for the Canteras…long story, getting worse as we speak."

"It needs to be done, Jay…what do you say?"

"I'll give you a search warrant...let it take you where it sends you, Johnny. We have our ways in L'Arroyo. Love ya, man. Wait here. But shit, get something on that hand...don't bleed all over my hall." He disappeared. *It's his fucking hall now?* Padric pulled a handkerchief out of his pocket, wiped his hand clean and sat down on a bench at the end of the hall. With elbows on his knees and head in his hands; the lieutenant looked like a schoolboy waiting outside the dean's office.

Moments later he was walking down the front steps of the courthouse. "You need a ride?" Marcus was leaning against his car. Padric grinned. Neither spoke on the way back to the parking garage. He'd pressed Whitton and now here he was walking down the hall toward the Captain's office. His partner called out to him but Padric was moving like luggage down a conveyor belt. He didn't knock, walked into O'Manion's office and threw the warrant down on his desk. "I want to do this in an hour, at the most twenty-four... give me this. Jay says play it as I see it. His words!"

O'Manion picked up the document and glanced at it. "It's your party, son." He was happy now and handed it back. "Guard that scrap of paper like it's the Pope's encyclical. Everyone in the Bog! I assume you're ready."

"Born and raised...and with no papal bull. I assume you know what that is as well."

"Don't go erudite and Vatican Catholic on me, John. I hate it when you show off like you studied at Boston College. The Jesuits would throw you out on your ear."

"No, they wouldn't...they'd love me. They got tossed by everyone." O'Manion wanted to argue the point but Padric continued. "They were suppressed, kicked out of everywhere."

O'Manion ignored him. "You'll pull off your Cirque du Soleil with my blessing, but you need to do some reconnaissance; the bishop may have moved that kid after the nun found him. Don't go in half-cocked. Get your gang of misfits in line then make 'em drop and do fifty."

Padric snatched up the warrant. "Hell, we've been planning this for days, Cap', we're going in sooner than later."

He walked out. Padric handed the warrant to Martinez who let out a howl; the others came running. "It's not going to expire. Hold on to it. I need to see my wife…there's something not right." Again he glanced at his watch. "Briefing at midnight. Your asses are mine. TCB, my friends, take care of shit…see family, pay bills, don't get drunk but try to get laid; be back here with a clear head. We've got uniforms canvassing the neighborhood…again. How many times do we do this at San Miguel? Out with you!" But Martinez lingered. "Alex, go see that beautiful wife of yours."

He spoke to the Commander on the phone and left. Glad to be alone, he threw himself into his car. Even if she were asleep…he'd wake her. He always did this before something big. With flowers and a chamomile tea from Lady Brid's Tearoom, a place Lara loved and open until ten in the evening.

Padric stepped onto the floor. Gina was nowhere in sight or she would have detained him with a warning and up-date. Lara was waiting but oddly, not reaching out for him like she always did; refusing the tea, she tossed the flowers aside. Padric in an instant was reading his wife, not sure where this was going. She was looking more fragile. He didn't have to wait long.

"Johnny, I'm leaving you."

"No, you're not." His voice was steady; unmoved. *But yeah, this time it's different…that edge in her voice. The woman is serious…and why not?* He'd messed up big-time; screwed her over once too often, but this too would pass. She wasn't herself and he'd been consumed with the case; he'd listen, let her talk. He had his ways; she'd mellow out, be okay…but her eyes were holding him at a distance; he dared not move closer. It was inevitable and he'd dreaded it.

Joanna. She knows.

"I was once your Lois Lane." *Don't do this, Lara.* But she didn't hesitate. "You were all I could look at, think about, ache for…it was the same for you, I know that, but then everything changed; you weren't listening or looking at me anymore but I loved your way with me when…" She shook her head. "The doctors say I'm their miracle and for what, for whom and what good is it if I live or die or am well?" Gina appeared in the doorway. "A minute please," Lara said. "He's leaving." *I am?* Padric stood up, closed the door and leaned on it, listening to the lilt of her voice, watching her lower the noose, making sure it was tight.

"Joanna Cantera, Johnny...Joanna fucking Cantera."

He said nothing did nothing, showed no reaction but there it was. Her eyes drilled a hole through his skull.

"I haven't told you everything about my recovery nor have the doctors because I wouldn't let them. The day they informed you I might never have any more babies, you were in agony." *What is she saying?* He frowned. "The day before I was attacked by your lover, I learned I was pregnant and couldn't wait for you to get home but you were with her; Joanna told me all about it, made sure I knew everything, what you did for her, what she did for you. So our little talk never happened. I'd asked Belinda to take the girls to school with her kids that morning. I wanted to tell you; we'd have been alone just the two of us, a game changer for us. We'd be happy again, close. But oops, Joanna Cantera." He slumped into the chair by the door and put his head in his hands. "On the way up to surgery that day, I knew I was losing the baby. I called out, do you remember...my babies, I said, my babies. This child would be our third. They told me I was farther along than I thought; I kept hearing Joanna saying things, talking to me and I told them; dead or alive, I didn't want it, didn't care and still don't. Don't try to save it, I said. Tell me nothing. I hope it's dead."

"It's? That's what you're calling our baby...like the wee one was garbage?" He wanted to leave, walk into traffic; let a truck hit him.

"You had a son." Four words. *Let a truck hit me...traffic.* But Lara wasn't stopping. "I don't want your children; the girls, they are precious, good girls, but no, not even them." He wasn't hearing this; *she was tossing them, too?* "I want nothing that's part of you. Your lover killed me...I'm dead." Lara wouldn't stop talking. "She has you free and clear now, but she doesn't know how really good for nothing you are."

Holy Mother, where was all that sophistication and wisdom and warmth

I married? Well…he'd walked all over that, hadn't he?

But she was still talking. "I hate you."

Her words were terrifying and belied the sound of her voice… it was peaceful and soft like she was telling him she loved him. Lara was having her moment, enjoying what she was doing to him like Mason and Joanna had enjoyed what they'd done to her. Padric could hardly breathe, his tears had turned inward, falling into his soul; with jaw set and eyes on fire, he wanted to curl up like a wee lad in the dark and die.

But Lara was eyeing him…she thought she knew her husband and he wasn't doing any drama, raging, throwing things around then trying to gather her up in his arms. But maybe that's all she really wanted and perhaps she'd played it too cold.

The man was contemplating his hell, his hypocrisy: *if a woman wants to get even, this is the way to do it, throwing a child into the mix…nice touch.* Padric hated her for keeping this from him, her choice of words when she told him, the timing. He was a cop, had an eye for the human response, a woman's way with her words; *but damn, she's really thought this through. And worse, she swore everyone into secrecy even Gina.*

His mind went into Precinct mode. "Where would they bury his remains if he were dead?" His voice was hard and cold. A cop question…it made Lara hesitate. "Answer, Lara."

His eyes were full of pain now. She glared back at him and murmured something about someone taking care of things.

"Things: who the bloody hell are you? Dead or alive, he has to be somewhere." Padric turned his back on her and opened the door, but not before picking up the flowers she'd tossed on the foot of the bed. They were the most beautiful red roses he'd ever given her. "I'm putting these on the grave of my son if he's in one. I'm sorry you suffered all that alone and I'll make sure you're taken care of for the rest of your life. When I married you, I promised that to your parents, God rest their souls…but, woman, the girls and that wee lad you just tossed away are mine and I'm guarding them with my life." He left.

The door closed. Lara stared at it.

Gina in the nurses' station looked up as he approached, smiling, wanting to talk. *The woman's actually smiling after betraying me, damn her…is she on something?* Padric glared back and kept walking…he could have stayed, pounded his fist on her desk, torn up the place, demanded to speak to the doctors. He had questions: *was it a miscarriage or delivery? Have i no rights or do my sins not allow me any?*

He disappeared down the backstairs. Gina stared after him… *Dios mio.* Lara has told him. She heard a crash and ran to her room. John Padric's wife had swept everything off her bedstand; her sobs so agonizing, Gina had to sedate her.

Padric slipped into his car near the back gate and stared up at the trees. The grounds at Meadow set the building apart from all others; they were lush and well tended, the sinking sun turning the palms overhead into gold. He was tired. Sleep…later, not now, too much to do.

His son, his boy…he dreaded telling his mum the details. Padric drove slowly to the crest of a hill where he ran when he was younger and sat for a long time staring into the early nightglow of the city. Things were looking better for the case; they had more answers, could put a face on each killer. They had exigency, a warrant; the moondead were calling him, but the up-feelings he'd had were short-lived. Lara's eyes, hollow with pain, made him sick with regret; perhaps that's why he was here in the middle of nowhere instead of going after Dan Mason with the long gun he kept under his seat. But…a son, his boy and what had she said?

He was dead, maybe not and she didn't care either way. But how cold and insulting was it that the staff he knew so well at Meadow had stood silent as he came and went from the building…they'd told him nothing about his boy. What had Lara said for God's sake, to make them commit to such a promise like that? *She painted the worst possible picture of me…damn, I'm not like this.* He had enjoyed an outstanding professional reputation; his private life was a another story and not to be aired. Staff knew then of his infidelity, his crass disregard…their patient in Room 355 was proof of it. Though numbed by it all, he'd keep it together; his son was waiting somewhere and had been for over a month. He was surely alive.

Fuck walking into traffic, getting hit by a truck; he'd stay sane, throw himself into the next day and the next and play it for all it was

worth. He'd put an end to the Canteras; he'd divide them and con-
quer, turn one on the other. Arrest son and mother separately; keep
those sick, obsessed Canteras apart. He'd finish the case; stay fo-
cused. Forget Lara; he was weary of trying to make things right;
what he feared the most had happened anyway.

But his son...how strong could he be if he survived the trauma
done to his mother? How does a four-month-old fetus live outside
his mother? Some did. He returned to the Precinct and spoke briefly to O'Manion and Martinez, who saw at once, he wasn't with
them...he withdrew, wrote up his reports, reached for the phone.

"Johnny, I'm so glad you called...what can I do?"

"Where's my son buried, Gina; they buried him, right?"
Silence. He waited then suddenly shouted into the phone: "Talk,
woman! Forget your misguided loyalty to my wife. I'm his father.
Where is he?" She'd stand firm; block his rage but what to say to a
man with the reputation he had for getting what he wanted?.

Slowly she said: "We need to talk about this."

"Talk? Damn, when did you decide to that?"

"Lara told you one thing and it's something else."

"And I assume you'll speak clearly with words I can understand. Talk."

"Lara's in a deep depression and has been for over a year; her
near death only exasperated and prolonged it. You, Johnny, have
done a little violence of your own on this woman, abused her heart,
mocked the girl with your nocturnal activities." *What...she's waxing
eloquent now?* "Is that articulate enough for your educated ass?"

"Keep it coming."

"I'm just getting started, but I'll let you off easy. Only this past
week have the doctors realized her medications aren't working...
we're turning to naturopathy and we'll see." He told her to answer
his question. "She...we wanted to tell you regardless of what she
had asked, but waited, hoping she'd do it herself." Gina paused.
"She's depressed."

"Yeah, me, too; the whole fucking world is...we're full of
original sin." *What? Sister Moira.*"Where's my son? While all your
high-minded, big car owning, just back from a cruise medical experts are piddling around with some kind of "opathy", my son's

where? I could give a shit about the state of things with Lara. I can list with footnotes my sins. I want my son! You, Gina, for Christ's sake, I loved you more than I should have once. Talk to me, damn it, or I'll come over there and tear up that whole fucking unit."

"He was so tiny…she was four months pregnant not three; he weighed less than two pounds. She's thin, didn't show; Lara wanted out of the marriage and motherhood. Despite what she suffered, your son is alive." *Silence. Your son is alive…my boy.* Padric could hardly stand still. "Though the assault on his mother has damaged him, he will make it with all the new research and therapies. But Lara believes this is on you and especially Joanna Cantera; she did this. Lara wants nothing to do with a baby touched by that woman or you." There…she had said it and dreaded the response. His woman had written him off, plain and simple.

"Where is he, damn it?" *My son.*

"She thought…"

"Where is he, Gina?" *My boy.*

"The baby was taken by special conveyance to…to the… Father Seamus at Saint Aidan's took care of all this. Go to him."

The dial tone was deafening…she held on to the phone like Lara had done. He was gone. Gina too had loved him more than she should. But she was feeling even more guilty now…she too had done violence to Lara. Betrayal was deadly; she left the floor.

Elsewhere in the hospital, Marcus had arrived as he'd done every week since Good Friday evening. Padric had asked him to spend time with Petra; "representing the unit", he called it, but Marcus was doing it more for himself; he'd looked forward to their conversations. But as always, the lieutenant had his reasons; his youngest detective, the one he called "priest', might get the nun to speak of her assailants, nudge her memory a bit.

Petra had slept most of the day and was eager to see him. He'd even taken some notes so he could remember all he wanted to tell her; this delighted her and they spoke of this evening's graduation; he'd timed it well. Perhaps this would be the night she'd tell him what she'd seen. To date she had said nothing.

"Who are you looking for in my attack?"

His heart skipped a beat. "We have a suspect." He'd give her an opening. "But there were two." She said nothing. "We are frustrated, Sister, it's imperative we stop them before they kill or hurt one more person. I don't want anyone else to suffer the way you have." He waited…still nothing. "I'm sure you agree with me. But all in good time."

Petra changed the subject, but more reluctantly this time; something he'd said had obviously made her hesitate and he caught it. She was frustrated and said she missed Magdalen and longed to speak with the elder. Marcus smiled. He'd become attached to Petra; in the quiet of the early evening, it was easy to listen to her wisdom. A man between two worlds, he was living a little in each. She would be forever his confidante; he turned to leave.

"My attackers were the bishop's sister and a young man who I met a very long time ago when I first came to San Miguel. I was the bishop's sacristan like Sister Magdalen is now."

Marcus returned to the chair by the bed of the nun with the large frightened eyes.

⊕

Sunday, after eleven in the evening, April 20

Padric closed the door quietly and walked down the dark hall, but there was a light in his mother's room; Mairead was with her and they turned when he paused by the half open door.

"Mum, what are you doing up?" She told him to sit. It didn't sound good; he didn't care…what else could happen? He threw himself into an overstuffed chair and looked from one to the other.

"Your Lara, she's spoken with us and is leaving you and I'm wanting' details. She said you'd be giving them to me…our Mairead knows something, but this daughter of mine has always been so loyal to ya', for God only knows what reason, and I'm waiting for an explanation. Explain away then." He was speechless. "Stop actin' like you're feckin' twelve! No more squirmin' around in that chair, lad. Speak, John James Connelly Padric, or I swear I'll upside you." His middle name honored the 1916 Irish patriot and his brother, Liam's, Michael Collins. So what honored name would the newest male in the family inherit?

And "upside", that was street; where did mum pick that up? At any other time, Mairead and her brother would have rolled on the floor laughing, but his day of reckoning was here; no one more fearsome than his mother was demanding he confess his sins.

He wasn't intimidated much by his mum or anyone else any more; but tonight he'd put it out there. "I did things, dishonored my woman and she still loved me."

"Dishonored is it…don't go all Yeats on me. You've been feckin' everything coming your way like your da'." Her children looked at her…even she was shocked at herself for saying such a thing and fell silent, her eyes suddenly fierce and unforgiving. Their mother had never spoken of any of this until now. Mairead's eyes blurred with tears; Padric was hearing what he knew already.

He'd have to say something and quick. "It was *who* I was fuckin', mum…I've been havin' a go with one of our prime suspects and didn't know it; it's on for tomorrow with or without the First Precinct and I'm doing the take down. When she was ID'd, I recused myself."

"You what?" Mairead gasped.

"Let me finish. They asked me to reconsider…I'm back in. But the woman, she was different, I guess, and I couldn't stay away. And now I can't get rid of her; turns out, she wanted all of me, still does, but wanted Lara out of the way more and that's why my lass is in protective custody and healing at Meadow. I'm in danger and so are my girls and even you; does the Precinct posted outside our door tell you anything?"

Darragh cursed him, asking how all this could have happened but made it clear: "No one's in danger in this house…I'm here now." Padric women were formidable.

"My woman sat at home waiting for me night after night; my wee girls never saw me. And now I can't leave them for more than a few hours; I never knew they loved me so much."

Mairead sobbed. Darragh glared at her. "Oh, Jaysus, girl, get some intestines! Stop it. Go on, John, I'm listening." She wanted to rush to him, hold him, but believed it a moral imperative for a mum to play Ice Queen.

"They're keeping me sane. I watch them sleep at night and gave them my word I'd be good to their mum. I didn't know I was fucking a killer until one of my men put it to me; I tried every which way to keep it from Lara, not add to her pain. The woman has a rep…"

Darragh was listening; there was a new glint in her eyes, more understanding. She silenced Padric. "And no woman wants her man gettin' the kind of loving she's known for." Again her children stared at her…whence all this knowledge?

Mairead was frantic. "So what happened, Johnny? How did she…"

He was crying out to her with his eyes. "Dan Mason, a detective who has wanted my badge and my life, dropped a story on her, saying this woman and I wanted her dead, that it was I who accompanied her to our house to kill her."

Darragh was shaking her head. "Only in Arizona. Write all this down, Mairead lass, we could make money on this. Ron Howard…Neil Jordan, send it to them. Better yet, that one I like, Michael Mann." Padric closed his eyes…*sufferin' Jesus*. He was being dragged down more by his mother's asides than the truth of the matter. "So then, your Lara…"

"She's got a mind like a steel trap and had followed the case."

Mairead stared at him in disbelief: "She put two and two together then."

"She did, girl. It got her thinking, analyzing later what she saw during the attack and what she'd been hearing; she was asking me questions. And now the woman wants nothing to do with me because of *who* it was more than what I was doing with her. Even when the woman was hurting my Lara she used my name, said things no wife should hear. Lara wants no part of me or my girls; she has no like for them."

Mairead cursed. "This is impossible…why she loved them more than herself. A perfect mother she was and I'm angry, Johnny, that you'd be saying this about dear Lara."

But Darragh raised her hand for silence. "The girl's in a world of hurt; a haunting's inside her; Americans call it depressions and such. She's in a deep one. But you, John James, were always my *Cuchuliann*, the greatest among 'em. This woman, she is *Mal*, come

to have you whether you want her or not. And what did *Mal* do...
she chased *Cul* all over Ireland but couldn't keep up; he so intent
on riddin' himself of the woman. What happened then...she
misstepped while scrambling after him and was dashed to pieces
against the rocks of Mather."

"Mum, are you done?"

"Do what he did...lead her into harm's way, lad, and kill her."

Silence. Her children looked at each other; their faces blank,
but liking it. *Ay, mum was IRA as I've known all along.*

But hadn't he had the same thoughts? Padric needed to finish
this. He sighed deeply; a sign more was coming. "It gets even more
complicated. At the time of the assault, Lara was pregnant, four
months maybe, and never said. I learned only after the fact there
was a baby. And that's all I'll say, mum."

"A wee baby, you say, *my* grandbaby?"

"You'll get nothing else from me."

"You will if I'm asking."

"Mum, for God's sake, let him be." Mairead was in anguish.
"Can't ya' see he can hardly speak as it is? But Johnny, the baby, it's
alive, isn't it...a boy, a girl?" Her voice was full of hope. A boy, he
said, but what was his mother doing now?

Darragh had pulled out her cell phone and punched in a number. Sister and brother glanced at each other. "How are you, dear?"
Padric frowned. The two waited. "That's nice, my luv...good. And
I'll be seeing you soon, but no, Liam. Liam, listen to your mum
now. Your fecking' sinner of a brother, has unzipped his breeches
once too often and Lara's had enough...she's leaving him when
she's released from the hospital. My oldest son, your older brother,
the grand Poopah of our kin, is in need of God's mercy, so get your
arse down here and give it to him. You must hear his confession."

Brother and sister were livid now, but could hear the priest,
their brother, clarifying a few issues for his mother in a loud, firm
voice. Her face grew somber, gone was the venom...she was hurt
now. Liam, missioned in the Tenderloin section of San Francisco,
was a practical man and knew about sinning and breeches unzipped. It would take only minutes for him to settle his mother.

Tears rolled down her face.

Padric could stand it no longer. "Bloody hell…give me the fuck-ing phone and don't ever do that again, mum. Liam, lad!" He was full of apologies to his brother and withdrew into the hall. When he returned, he handed the phone to his mother and left the room. "I'm leaving and won't be back for a day and a night; we're going in. That's all I can say and not a word to a bloody soul…nothing. You know the drill. And on another matter, bottom line: I live now for my girls and my son and I'll be seeing him before morning. And thanks for taking good care of my lasses." The two women looked sadly at him. "Pray for me; this Mal, you so eloquently told us about, will be in a jail cell by suppertime and so help me, mum, if you ever go playing judge and jury with me again, I'll…you don't own my soul."

The women stared after him as he ran up to the loft and kissed his girls. Mairead rushed into the hall; he kissed her forehead. The two held onto each other with not a word…they'd been looking after each other since they were kids. Mairead had a flashback of Belfast nights when her six-year-old brother, his little face hard as granite, stood in their narrow hallway holding her tight as Brit Land Rovers rolled passed the house. Sometimes they banged on the door and pulled their da' into the street. They'd clung to each other; he shielding her with fear in his eyes. She was three and five-year-old Liam, always with a rosary in one hand, would squeeze his big brother's, looking to him for answers. They had relied on him, still did; always would.

She was weeping now and he said: "When it's over…in your newspaper, tell a good story for us down at the First Precinct. The boy, my son, I must go to him now." He left. She sobbed and slowly slid down the wall to the floor…she would tell a good story.

Darragh turned out the light and shut her door.

They needed to finalize a plan with Ramirez and O'Manion forced him to return to the Precinct. He drove away from Mairead's wanting a drink and a woman, his woman, but she was dead to him now. There was another though…*that luv of a nun, Magdalen, and I'm damned to hell for even thinking it. Wish I could take her away for a while.*

But he'd behave and not do a John Garfield; his Mum's words had delivered brimstone and condemnation.

He was his da' all over again.

Author's Notes

gangbanger – *member of a street gang.*

TCB – *acronym for "Takin' Care of Business" meaning get the job done and written in '67 by Randy Bachman, even later sung by Elvis Presley. The phrase would be forever used by athletes, performers even Hilary Clinton during her 2008 presidential campaign. Consisting in the same chords C, B flat, and F played over and over with no hook.*

Jaysus – *Irish slang interjection and alternative name for Jesus of Nazareth.*

The Tenderloin – *older neighborhood in downtown San Francisco, California; 50 square blocks, since the thirties, notorious for its gambling, pool halls, boxing gyms, speakeasies and dive bars depicted in the crime fiction of Dashiell Hammett and where, at the corner of Hyde and Post, he wrote The Maltese Falcon in an apartment he allows his character Sam Spade to live; both movie and book were set here. The area has a long history, some of it folklore; its name said to refer to the "loins" of prostitutes. Most of the original buildings were destroyed in the 1906 earthquake but for years has been home to the transgender/gay community, historically known for "gay riots", raids and confrontations with police; one in the mid-sixties, resulting in police lining up and photographing 600 participants and arresting several prominent citizens. Some historic gay bars and clubs still exist. Though it has recently been designated an historic district on the National Register of Historic Places it still maintains its criminality and poor living conditions, its homeless, illegal drug trade and prostitution, liquor stores and strip clubs. In any given month, there are reports of human feces found in the streets. Known for its violent street crime, it is said it is here the notorious Filipino gang Bahala Na Gang or BNG with its murder for hire extortion, and drug sales originated. However, there has been a revival of the arts and a thriving theater district thrives among many bars and speakeasies dating back to prohibition. Today it serves as magnet for artists and musicians. The Tenderloin's heart however is its social services network of non-profit agencies, soup kitchens, homeless shelters and religious rescue missions where the detective's brother, a priest, ministers to the poor and immigrant population.*

25 UNDER SIEGE

Sunday, near midnight, April 20

Elsewhere an anticipated evening had ended on a subdued tone; even the cheers of the graduates half-hearted and not one mortarboard thrown in the air. Cathedral students in solidarity respectfully kept their caps on and in one strong voice shouted: "Sister Petra! Sister Petra! We are Cathedral!" It was stunning, chilling for most. Magdalen would later weep when she was alone. The auditorium emptied out quickly. With the nun's death fresh in their minds, families chose to party closer to home; the Darby Hill crowd however, allowing little to mar their pleasures, headed for the country club nearest their mansions. In the streets, there was tension; Martinez, alone and with a foreboding he couldn't shake, cruised the Plaza. He slowed down to talk with uniforms posted around the Cathedral and school. He rarely rode without Padric, but the man had been busy, something about family and "personal shit"…they'd talk later, he said.

In the convent of San Miguel, Magdalen had moved to the window seat in the hall; the elder, asleep in her room. Below in the courtyard, officers standing post didn't make her feel any safer. When would the detectives move on what she had found?

Returning to her room, she scanned the garden…the priest with head bowed in prayer was seated on a bench; he'd managed to climb down the old brick stairs and up the terrace. But her thoughts were clamoring with images of her earlier discovery under the sacristy; Bernardo was all she could wonder about.

She didn't want him to be the killer.

Duran would be at her desk in the vestibule…they had become friends since Petra's death. Restless and wrapping herself in a shawl and night veil, she would talk with her for a few minutes. She slipped into the hall and walked to the landing. Duran.

She was gone.

Magdalen flew down the stairs…*the convent garden; she'd be there.* She entered the downstairs hallway; it was dark and too quiet. Should she be doing this? She stopped. Above on the second floor, she heard it…a thud, muffled noises, sounds of a struggle. *Not here, not tonight, not in the elder's fortress protected by angels; it's untouchable.*

Hoping a dispatcher would hear what was happening, she punched in 9-1-1 on the vestibule phone and left it dangling, Shouting again for Duran, she planted her feet on the bottom step of the staircase, half-knowing what to expect. She looked up.

Grotesque and in a sinister black vulture mask, a hooded figure in monk's robes had appeared on the landing; one became two, the second wearing a like mask in red…the contrast between them, macabre. All they had done to prepare and premeditate was over the top. But now there were suddenly three: one of her Sisters, unveiled, limp in their arms. In some sick way, they were struggling to steady the nun, in defiance propping her up so she could see what they'd done. Their prey was near dead.

She gasped…it was terrifying; the voice she knew. "*Magdalena…cara mia.*" *Lucy!*

Her face was bloody, mutilated, an eye missing…she swayed, fainting away, but the duo stood poised, silently taunting her with the dying woman then, in a quick, careless gesture, they let the nun drop, slump to the floor. Magdalen cried out, took the stairs two at a time; woke the house with her shouts. Sisters appeared in their doorways but were unable to move…horrified.

Magdalen threw a punch at one of the assailants and cried out: "Take care of Lucy…do something!"

At the end of the hall, the elder emerged from her room in her wheelchair and raced toward her at a clip. The older nuns joined her; Patrice and Edwardmary pulled the battered Lucy away with the help of the dear sage of a nun, old Sister Maryjohn. The three half carried, half dragged the battered nun into a four-bed infirmary. Like angels they hovered over her, shocked at the brutality, her face, contorted and blue. There had been an enucleation, an eye surgically removed...they were more angry than shocked.

But the intruders were stunned, too...they hadn't expected a fight-back. Another nun suddenly tore down the hall. Dolorosa... or was it Melissa de Torro? She was on top of them, cursing in a tirade of Spanish. Small and tough, she was all over them, her punching and gouging taking them off-guard. But one slammed her head so hard into the wall she fell to the floor, unconscious.

Monica at the sight of it, whirled her wheelchair around and shot into the circle; surprising everyone; using the wheels as a weapon, she rolled forward and back, slamming into the intruders.

One snarled and went after Magdalen, tearing the veil from her head. "You bitch!" *A woman. Joanna.*

No matter...Magdalen managed a tackle. Joanna hissed like a snake as she slid down the wall but she'd make this nun hurt, end her life once and for all. In a sweeping move, she slapped Magdalen hard...she went down. It was then her accomplice turned, oddly horrified. He pushed her aside. "Not this way...we did what we came to do!"

Blurry eyed, Magdalen watched the interaction between them; they were arguing, the man furious. He turned and knelt down, leaning close to her face; behind the mask, his eyes desperate, his long hair falling from under his hood, practically touching her face. She should have known. *Bernardo.*

Impulsively she reached for him, wanting him to go home, but the mask so close to her face was hypnotic...it was terrifying, sinister. A vulture symbolized only one thing in the Sonoran...slow death. She didn't want him to be the killer, but saw the blood on his robe. The two were wearing cloth booties and gloves. *Sadly brilliant*, Magdalen thought, *they'd come prepared.*

But Joanna's direct hit to her face was blinding her now...the world was receding or was she leaving it, this time for good? Far away, she could hear the elder calling her name.

"Up! Up, Magdalen!"

She struggled to her feet in time to see Bernardo nearing an open door opposite the chapel, odd…she'd never noticed and now here it was, their way up onto the second floor, it hid a narrow staircase. But Joanna was back…this time for the elder, raising her hand and ready to strike. Magdalen cried out, again knocking her into the wall…but how had Dolorosa described her childhood friend earlier today? She was hard, didn't go down easy and Joanna was up on her feet again. Magdalen glanced quickly around looking for help and saw only Agnes, frozen, unable to move, on the stairs.

"Move it, Sister, get help. Do it…now!" At the sound of Magdalen's voice, Agnes regained her bearings and ran from the convent and out into the night, shouting for anyone within earshot. She too again called 9-1-1. In seconds Marcus and Martinez, spotting the nun in the moonlight, alerted dispatch, calling for backup and sprinted toward her. Uniforms flooded the courtyard.

But Padric, too, alone in his office, heard the scanner and jumped to his feet. Tark shouted his name. In yet another one of his classic moves, the lead night detective rushed into the street like a rodeo bull out of the shoot; he rounded the corner at an all-night Cuppa and every patron within stood up and cheered him on. They knew who he was.

The 9-1-1's had called out half the Precinct and Firehouse No. 4; both were now clogging the Plaza. Hell, he'd get there faster. Only Johnny, muttered Martinez, when he was told his partner was approaching on foot with the speed of light. He and Marcus burst through the door in time to see Joanna launch a kick to Magdalen's face, a final blow that sent her sliding to the edge of the stairs.

He shouted to Marcus: "The other one's getting away. Grab the *bruja*…damn, our nun's down." *Come on, Johnny, get here*…he pulled Magdalen carefully away and down the hall.

Shouting for the nuns to clear the landing, Marcus went after Joanna, hood off, mask gone; he pulled her by her hair to the floor but there were nuns everywhere. He was surrounded with veils and, for a moment, distracted. Joanna, laughing, struggled free and stumbled away. Quickly she followed Bernardo down the staircase into the dark but not before slamming the door so hard, the lock jammed, blocking Marcus' pursuit. He turned…Martinez and Maryjohn were huddled on the floor beside Magdalen. The elder, somberly, stoically, staring down at her from her wheelchair. Their nun was drifting away, whispering the name of Jesus, asking her Lord to forgive her sins.

Marcus rushed to her side. He and Martinez had heard this before on the lips of the dying. "Have mercy, Lord…" She reached for Martinez. "You two…so kind, such good men."

Furious, desperate, Martinez gathered her up in his arms. He knew Joanna Cantera had done what she came to do, *but no, not their nun; this isn't happening.* "Where's Johnny?" he whispered, looking at Marcus. Both men were frantic.

Magdalen closed her eyes. "Just let me go…I'm so tired."

Padric, having stopped briefly to speak with some first-responders, finally reached the front door of the convent; inside, it was quiet but for the weeping of nuns. Directing the coming and going, Duran, ambushed earlier by the Canteras, stood at her post with a black eye and bruises. The duo had been here…he'd just missed them, she said. He looked up; nuns, old ones, staring down at him, pointed. "Come, please…you are needed."

His nun! He knew she would have been in the thick of things but a chill passed through his soul. Whatever Bernardo may have come to do, the hag had her own agenda; he knew she was looking for Magdalen. *Holy Mary, don't let…*"Duran, where's my partner… where's J?"

"Upstairs, sir. A nun's near dead in the infirmary…Sister Magdalen's down." He paled. "She took a few hits, not sure how bad. Get up there and fix it."

He bound up the stairs in time to hear his nun say to Martinez: "Let me go, Alejandro…am so grateful to you and that partner of yours." Martinez looked up at Padric who fell on his knees beside them. "Tell that dear man I loved him, you know, in the right way, of course." Unable to see clearly, she reached out for Monica and Maryjohn; called out to Dolorosa. "Jesus, help me. Jesus, Savior."

She sighed deeply and lay very still. Padric was stricken, unable to move though there was much to be done. He wanted the nun who "loved him in the right way" to come back...it was astounding to him that someone even loved him like that.

"You're not leaving...I won't allow it, woman. Magdalen! Sister Magdalen!"

But a hand gently gripped his shoulder. He looked up. Mary-john slowly knelt down beside them and kissed Magdalen's forehead. "She's too feisty to leave us just yet. An angel like Magdalen doesn't vanish that easily." *Angels*...he'd wondered once if she was one; *didn't some walk among them, appear to be human, bring a blessing, work a good thing? Sister Moira.* She'd said that. Besides, hadn't he seen one at every crime scene, another, strong like a warrior on the campanile of the Cathedral? He could no longer understand this Life, these nuns, their ways.

"Magdalen! Sister Magdalen, damn it! Get up now...come back to me!"

Hadn't he shouted this at his wife a month ago to the date? Now both men were shouting her name, checking her pulse...*but wait, what was her other name, the one Sebastian had mentioned, her birth name.* "Brid, luv! Brid Williams!"

Magdalen's eyes opened wide, her gasp so sudden, even the detectives drew back. She looked from one to another, her eyes finally resting on Padric, her look strange, unforgettable. "I couldn't make all this right...what do you need, Detective?"

What do I need; damn, and you're asking me that in public? He needed her in ways he could never say. But now here she was back on the job. He didn't care who thought what...he pulled her to him and, rocking her back and forth in his arms, apologized to her and the Sisters for what the Precinct, Major Crimes, he himself, had been unable to stop. He rose with the nun in his arms and carried her into the infirmary.

But she insisted on being laid down beside Lucy. "Lucy... Lucy!" She could see no one else, pulling her Sister close, praying, whispering; Padric helplessly watched as she wept, pleading with Lucy to fight. Already Patrice had attempted to wipe the blood from Lucy's face, apply gauze to her wounds, swath her head in towels. Again Padric shouted for a medic. "I need Brady...where the hell is he?"

Bloodied and battered, the two nuns remained wrapped in each other; no one could pull them apart. A hush fell over the room except for Magdalen's whispers. He glanced at Martinez and Marcus; there were uniforms everywhere. His rage would come within moments; he had two nuns, his nun, both lying very still on a bed and one appeared gone. *What a mess.*

When Magdalen still would not let anyone near Lucy, Padric intervened and carefully pried them apart. "Let me help, Sister." But in the midst of the chaos, he for a moment wondered if her profession of loving him in the right way was one of those last dying declarations he could cherish for the rest of his life. But that would mean she'd be gone and no one was ready just yet to live without Magdalen.

Oddly, she would never remember saying she'd love him but her words would keep him going for days, in the dark ones ahead. He'd never speak of it to his partner and Martinez wouldn't touch it nor did Maryjohn or Monica; they were old souls and understood. Marcus got it. Padric turned his attention to the wounds inflicted on the beautiful Italian nun to whom he'd spoken so often. *What had they done to her?*

"Where's Declan, damn it?" He could see Magdalen's strength ebbing away.

But she could feel Padric's eyes and turned; she could see clearly now. "I couldn't wait for you any longer and got myself into some trouble." Padric again pulled her close; the nuns only grateful for what he could do and thankful Agnes was nowhere in sight. He listened…she was whispering, doing her job. "My Sister, my Lucy! It was two of them, the Canteras again; another martyrdom, Santa Lucia, my Sister's eyes; they took one or both; I can't tell. No more…I'll kill them. It's the right thing to do, but now I'm sounding like him. Bernardo. I saw him." She was murmuring things, drifting off.

Then Maryjohn whispered to him the martyr's tale of Lucia, how the saint's eyes had been gouged out. She was finally killed with a sword, but her devotees always remembered her eyes, gone, yet she could miraculously see. "The blind pray to her, son. Be a brave boy now." *Boy. Mijo. Little one.* Old women and nuns were calling him this lately. He looked at the nun with tears in his eyes; he'd heard the Gaelic in her…from the south, Kildare, Kerry maybe, and half her name was his; they'd talk.

She blessed him with the sign of the cross. "Go be Cuchulain now, lad."

He stared after her as she withdrew. Magdalen was smiling a little. "I love her. She's our mythologist-mystic, our *seanchai*…" Storyteller…how well he knew the word. "I call her wizard…she loves the old lore like you." *Old lore…the convent of San Miguel was creating some of its own.* "They gained access through that door by the chapel. Do what you must. Below…go below." Martinez and Marcus heard what she said…Padric looked at them.

He kissed her forehead. "Shhhh, girl." He laid her down gently. "Stay put now."

Martinez was waiting. "We need to get into the graveyard… they're down there."

"It ends now."

At Padric's nod, he and Marcus kicked in the locked door near the chapel and disappeared into the dark. Padric shouted for uniforms to guide the nuns down the stairs to a quiet place to be cared for and questioned. A voice made him turn. "It didn't start here, John…the real crime took place in there." The elder in her wheelchair had been waiting for a word. She pointed to the chapel. "Our Lucy was attacked while she prayed…you'll see." But she hesitated…he urged her to continue. "The woman who hates my Magdalen spat on her."

It needed to be said; she regretted it though when she saw the detective's reaction, a Johnny Padric rage building inside him. He returned to the infirmary, knelt down…spittle still clung to her hair and he apologized for the effrontery then turned to Monica, staring at him from the doorway. "Sister, show me your chapel."

He shouted for Duran; she was to gather what she could for Milleau from Magdalen's hair. It would be the first DNA evidence from either killer left at the scene; swabs from Joanna's bite marks had yielded nothing. Evidently she'd always taken the time to wipe away what she'd done; her dental records, too, unavailable and with some unknown dentist in Sonora. He stepped into the chapel.

Blood. Lucy had put up the fight of her life. Statues were toppled, pictures askew, there was castoff on walls and pews. "*Che macella!*" Sebastian. Padric knew enough Italian to know the priest had called the chapel a slaughterhouse. "*Una profanazione!*"

The two stood in the doorway. "Another near dead, Father, and one down. So about Saint Lucy?"

"Santa Lucia, *mi Dio!* Not Sister Lucy!"

"Go to her…give her Last Rites, the anointing you do; look in on our nun. She's hurting inside and out. I need to find my partner."

Sebastian pushed his fist into Padric's shoulder. "Do this, John! I'm coming with you when I'm done here."

Padric tried to smile; he explained who and what Magdalen had discovered below the sacristy, how she'd fallen through a panel hidden behind some vestments. Sebastian understood then why she lay on the floor in the vestry where he found her earlier that day. He was horrified. In the darkness beneath where he lived was a killer. Padric needed him. "Take care of the nuns first with Last Rites then try to find me. You've got an arrow on your head already, Father, but come if you want…I've got a bad feeling. The bishop should be here soon."

And it was so.

Santo Cantera was suddenly in the house, looking aghast and astounded, as he'd done in the Cathedral; this time even more horrified, if not a little afraid. Padric studied his demeanor. *He'd been looking aghast and astounded a lot lately. Does he know or wonder if his own blood did this? When will he get it or has he already?*

He'd be going downtown very soon for a chat…the detective would see to it. And so would O'Manion who also walked in the door with none other then the Commander himself looking grave. Still others converged on the vestibule: CSI Milleau and Miller spotted Padric and charged up the stairs, but the detective couldn't resist and called down to the other men in the doorway. "Bloody hell…you finally show up and leave the cavalry behind?"

Ramirez smiled a little, but a glaring bishop ignored him; he moved on and found most of the nuns in the downstairs chapel; they were not happy to see him. Freaks, bearing his name, had violated them, Patrice would say later.

Declan and Kelly appeared and called out with a wink: "So, Chief Inspector, sir, who would be needin' us?"

"Upstairs, in the infirmary, lads! It's two nuns this time."

Ramirez took the stairs three at a time. "Talk to me."

Padric pointed. "The Canteras…no question. Our nun ID'd them; hell, all of them did. We know where they are; hold up in the graveyard or maybe on their way to the Border by now. My boys are already checking it out. The chapel's the primary. Give it a look."

Ramirez had the reputation of being stone faced…his officers called him *la Roca*. His dark eyes scanned the chapel slowly; he spoke briefly to Milleau and Miller…he was concerned about body count. "And the good Sisters?"

"We've got two down; one injured the other dying if not dead already. My officer, Duran, was beaten up pretty bad…she's hanging in."

"And the broken door, John, you and your crew have a habit of doing that."

"Hey, it'll be on the Precinct's dime. We do what we do."

"That's a poor try at an excuse, not an answer…we'll talk."

Declan gave a shout. "*Bhoyo,* I thought you said there were two!" Padric stepped into the hall. "There's only one and I need to be leaving with her STAT!"

One. Damn. Woman, where are you? Padric frantically looked about then shouted at uniforms for an answer…they hadn't seen Magdalen in the hallway or anywhere. The blood left his face. "Our nun's gone and done it again." He cursed.

Ramirez eyed his lieutenant. "Done what, John? Where is she? My wife will kill me if anything happens to her…she loves the woman. Find her." Padric would remember the Commander said this and laugh later. "Where did she go, John?"

"Down the rabbit hole when we weren't looking." Padric fought the panic inside him. "I've got Alice in fucking Wonderland! She took some hits, passed out and we thought we lost her; but she was talking, weak though, I have no idea how she got up and walked away."

He spotted Cunningham in the vestibule; beside him *the beast*, Major Crimes' new name for Nevel. "I need your pup, Sargeant. Get the lad up here."

The dog heard Padric's voice and pulled at his leash…it meant something exciting was happening. At his partner's command, he bound up the stairs. But Monica hadn't taken her eyes off the detective. He asked for something of Magdalen's. "Take the dog to her room, Detective; a pillowcase, yes, get her pillowcase then have dear Nevel sniff out the spot where she lay on the floor…must I do everything, lad?"

Padric leaned down and kissed her cheek. The men smiled. Ramirez himself had come prepared and wired them up, Tark would have eyes wherever they went. Padric with Cunningham and Nevel were gone. Anointing Lucy and giving Last Rites, Sebastian too had wondered where Magdalen was and returned to the Commander. "Is it true…did she follow them in? Sir, I think I can help."

"Do you now, Father, well then, take God with you and bring them back to me…and find Sister Magdalen." He threw him his own night goggles.

The priest shook his hand and vanished. Padric looked back as he hit the bottom step of the staircase and grinned. "Come on, *padre*, I need you to scold the nun for me. Give her hell." But she was already walking into one of her own.

Twenty years ago in some passage tomb, she wouldn't have blinked. Magdalen had never been afraid of the dark, still wasn't, but her wounds, that old pain in her shoulders, the hits she'd taken and the one she'd tried to give back, had left her disoriented. Hadn't she passed out and now here she was, wanting to settle this, no longer able to wait for the First Precinct? But what did she think she could do? She'd know when she got there.

For now, Magdalen would become part of the darkness around her; no worries…she'd find the detectives, tag along, try to assist. After all, they'd brought her on board, though this was not what they had in mind. The convent basement was what she'd expected, nothing mysterious; but she knew those bones the elder had buried long ago were on the other side of the wall where the garden pressed up against it. She stopped, placed her hand on it reverently then whispered a prayer and kept moving. She entered the tunnel and there it was, beyond a half open door, the cemetery under the bishop's house. But something was very wrong, an altercation, an out and out battle; men pounding each other.

She kept close to the wall, moving closer, the black and gray of her holy habit, a blessing and blending into the dark stone around her. She'd cleaned up, her veil in place and now wondering if the white linen around her face would give her away. What she saw ahead made her more angry than fearful. Martinez had been struck down then snatched up by a hulk of a man who held him over his head before tossing him aside. There was a thud. She watched the same man drag Marcus' body passed the open door and deeper into the graveyard…*officers down, officers down. Angels, help us. Holy Saint Michael, San Miguel…I need you.* Even a furious Padric would be a welcome sight.

Magdalen by now was halfway into the tunnel and had reached the door she supposed would take her through the shed under the altar and into the garden. She had a choice; she could hardly bear to lay eyes again on the Canteras, their sinister masks, hellish. She'd not have to face them if she ducked into the garden where her marble angels were waiting.

But ahead, the door was still open revealing another world too tempting for her to ignore; besides the detectives would need her. But the dark beyond was like nothing she'd seen; did she want to go there? There would be no angels beside her here unless she brought her own, those she believed walked beside her. Or she'd be on her own.

But it was too late for choices; someone emerged from the shadows. "You made it, sweetie. Had a feeling you'd join us."

Magdalen had forgotten the killers were wearing dark hooded robes; unseen, they could easily approach.

The voice was bitter: "You're not getting my son." Joanna. This thing with her son; it had turned her…she'd not always been this way. Dolorosa had said as much. Now they were face to face; the woman no longer masked. She stepped closer. The two studied each other, thinking how beautiful the other one was.

But Joanna's eyes, hungry and sick, needed to hurt her, hell-bent on ridding herself of the nun, who had nowhere to hide. The detectives were lost to her now; where was her backup? It would begin. Again and again, Joanna lunged at her; each time Magdalen side-stepped her efforts, turning the woman's rage into some macabre dance.

Something quite unexpected would occur and suddenly force Joanna to shrink into the shadows. It was the nun who was suddenly center stage; she had changed, was transforming into a…no. Magdalen herself was fighting it, trying to ignore what she realized might be a calling she feared. That pain in her shoulders, the one she bore daily, was now disappearing, an undefined courage taking hold of her. She'd let it happen…perhaps it was time. It would last for several minutes, Joanna the only witness, staring helplessly at the nun.

Even Magdalen herself glanced back and beheld wings of light emerging from her upper back. *So be it then. Your will be done, my Savior.* Magdalen advanced. "Let me help you, Joanna." She lowered her head like a wolf; eyes, penetrating the darkness inside the woman… *my Lord, let me bring her back into the light.*

But it was not to be in the struggle between good and evil; Joanna had ventured so far to the dark side, she couldn't leave. It seemed the powers of hell stood with her against a nun who, for the first time, was experiencing a holy self-revelation. It was not of this world. But why now and in the presence of such a woman, a soul lost. Magdalen knew… if this side of her was to mean anything it would be used for service…the world was in need of her.

Joanna, sobbing and breathless, collapsed into a heap. The nun knelt down and extended her arms, embracing her like a mother would her child; how many times the abandoned Joanna had longed for this. Light enveloped them and then it was gone.

No word was spoken until Joanna whispered: "I'm so unhappy,

so sad and so want forgiveness. I'll never be free of my demons."
Oddly she didn't question what she had seen though it had been
extraordinary; she appeared almost grateful, accepting that such
things could happen.

But a shout rang out from the far end of the tunnel. "Joanna
Cantera, get the fuck off our nun!"

The women looked back at the three rushing toward them.
On his partner's command, Nevel took off. But gone was the grace
of the moment: Joanna was a connoisseur in the art of escape and
struck an unprepared Magdalen hard in the face, dragging her,
stunned and disoriented, into the cemetery. There was only darkness; the angel in her, gone or at least hidden for now. Terrorized by
the sight of the animal, Joanna howled like a demon and kicked the
metal door shut in time to deny Nevel entrance. Yanking the nun's
limp body into the shadows, she dropped her like garbage by the
edge of a deep, open grave.

But having seen the presence of light all around Magdalen,
she hesitated. Anything supernatural frightened Joanna; it was her
enemy, the dark her only companion. Since her return to the city
three years ago, she'd suffered her own transformation, falling in
with those of like mind; drawing closer to real evil…her home in
the Edge was proof of this. But she'd always been superstitious,
knew all the mystery and spirit lore of her Mexican heritage. What
she'd just witnessed had spooked her; the woman she despised was
not whom she thought. She was more than a nun; Joanna knew…
she'd messed with something she shouldn't.

Killing the nuns and priests, well, that was on Berno; damn, I need to be
careful with this one, an empty grave waiting will suit this one fine, let her rot…
let them find her. She'd tie her up, not think about her too much. If
she haunted her in her dreams…so be it; they were after all, only
dreams. The woman was feeling out of control. Joanna was going
crazy and afraid she was turning into her son.

Dazed, Magdalen stared up at her attacker standing over her.
She was no longer mocking and arrogant but looked somehow compelled to do what she did next. With her foot, she pushed Magdalen
over the edge and into a shadowy grave then disappeared into the

dark. Padric and the others however were beating the door down to no avail. Nevel pawed at it, whined…his friend, on the other side.

"My men are inside, damn it!" Padric could shoot off the lock but there was none, no doorknob, nothing. Sebastian shouted for them to follow him through the door under the altar; in seconds, they were looking up at the stars.

"Come with me: I found something last night and was too tired to check it out."

A narrow door under the moon garden rocks opened onto a long corridor below the Cathedral. They were standing under the sacristy, the very place Magdalen had described. Nothing. Not one piece of furniture; no sign of life, Bernardo gone.

Sebastian drew them further into the dark toward the cemetery beneath the bishop's residence. "This is it…we need to get passed this." They were confronted by a massive, wooden door carved with the ominous crest of Cantera, a cross with a raven perched on the crossbar. It wouldn't budge. They knew beyond was the Garden of Gethsemane cemetery.

Padric needed more than a priest or a dog and his partner on this one. Joanna had her. *But what was that back there at the far end of the tunnel?* Later he'd need to address this with Father Sebastian…a light so blinding the men had not been able to take one more step. And now here he was wanting in. "Tark…give me something."

"On your right in the wall, some kind of mechanism built in or embedded."

Padric and Sebastian were thinking the same; examining the unusual, almost carved surface they frantically patted the wall. Nevel started to fuss, sniffing and whining low to the floor. Padric pushed on the spot, a section of wall moved. "What the…we've got the fucking, Tower of London here." With shoulders to the stone, the men pushed harder as a kind of crude turnstile revolved on its axis; crunching forward, it gave way.

Before them lay a graveyard, frozen in time, as if waiting for them. They slipped noiselessly through the opening and planted their feet on the earthen floor. They gazed upward. Huge pillars rose from among the tombs to the ceiling. Everywhere were sarcophagi and funerary sculptures, Celtic and Spanish crosses, many crumbling but beautiful. A sound made them turn; dropping down through the opening, Pistasio, ready to shadow Padric, winked at him; others in full gear followed.

"La Roca thought you might need us…he's on his way. We're wired up."

Two more fell in behind him. "Say hello to two of L'Arroyo's new Criminal Apprehension Team." Padric knew both. "LCAT! Woodson, am I glad it's you and, bloody hell, Lady Kate Morrow. Welcome to not a better class of men."

She rolled her eyes. Morrow was one of only two women on special units in the city and like Padric, a transplant from Ireland. "I'm impressed…now don't go all Belfast on me, Johnny. What are you needin'?" The men chuckled.

One more squeezed through the opening. Ducci, never too far from whatever Padric encountered, nodded. "I gotcha', man. What are we doing…where's Martinez and Marcus?"

"That's what I'm asking and I got a nun?"

"You got a nun…you?"

"Strike that…she's unfortunately married to God and I can't have her." Sebastian smiled and Nevel, impatient for the fun to begin, eyed Cunningham.

Like a dome lowered over their heads, they turned into stone as Padric laid out what they faced. He looked at Morrow. "Our nun's somewhere down here and in a world of hurt if Joanna Cantera has anything to do with it. I may be needing some help with her and dreading the state she'll be in when we find her…you will assist, Lieutenant." She understood and they broke from their huddle.

He had vowed never to say: "let's do this", "game on" or "bring it"; these were clichéd and too Hollywood for the man. No one would utter these words in his presence; rookies warned never to say them. He nodded. Tark muttered some last minute *intel*.

Author's Notes

seanchai – Irish, for traditional storyteller/historian; also spelled shanachie.

Che macella! – Italian, for "what a mess" literally, "what a slaughterhouse!"

Una profanazione! – Italian, for "A desecration!"

mi Dio – Italian, for my God.

STAT – from the Latin, statim meaning "at once!" Used often in medical speak.

Tower of London – built by William the Conqueror in 1078, a symbol to the English of oppression inflicted upon London by the new ruling elite though early history simply saw it as a grand palace and the royal residence. Infamously, it was used as a prison from 1100 until as late as 1952 where notably, famous British crime figures, the Kray twins, were residents. Though this was not the Towers primary purpose, it maintained the reputation as a place of torture and death, popularized by 19th-century writers. In all its history, only seven people were executed within the Tower before the World Wars of the 20th century. In a period of 400 years however, 112 executions occurred in Tower Hill, north of the castle; thus, the origin of the phrase, "Sent to the Tower." John Padric mentions the Tower of London when he discovers an old entry mechanism to gain access into a graveyard under the bishop's house.

26 EXHUMATION

Woodson and Morrow moved up the path toward the mausoleum then Padric and Ducci; Pistasio followed. Sebastian fell back moving from one open grave to the other. Cunningham and Nevel would stay put until called upon, but what lay before them took their breath away. It was something out of the Middle Kingdom. Extending the full length of the bishop's house overhead was a murky expanse of standing stones and monuments, the ceiling twenty feet high. The first L'Arroyo had been built within a deep depression in the desert floor surrounded by low-lying hills and arroyos running haphazardly through it.

The city's first founders and pioneers had gradually built over it, leaving another world underneath. Here was only part of it: museum-like with lit candles in broken and blackened bits of glass, their soft light brushing the graves; among them, sarcophagi left half-closed, some with no covers at all. At the base of most tombstones were stone boxes full of the dead's personal things, old photographs, oddly never removed by the families when the bodies were disinterred and buried elsewhere.

Ahead stood the Cantera mausoleum.

Larger than Padric expected, a marble pediment over the entrance displayed the Cantera family name carved in classic Palatino font, A jagged crack in its surface had ominously severed the name from top to bottom; the letters C-A-N-T glared back, the rest obliterated. *Can't* enter, *can't* bring us down…was it prophetic? It had been beautiful once.

Elsewhere in an open grave waiting, its occupant wondered if perhaps she was dead, but if this was so...*where was God? And what had happened back there? Who was she?* Her affinity for those angels back in the garden had done something to her, made her delusional perhaps; had she not formed a nightly solidarity with them...was she perhaps one of them? Had what she felt in the tunnel been only a dream...she was remembering, that pain in her shoulders gone but wings of light were not for the likes of Brid Williams, the sinner, now called Magdalen. Like Joanna she too feared she was losing her mind. She shuttered and summoned what courage she had and tried to move; she looked up.

Joanna was gone...she was alone. *I surely am dying. Here lies the soul of...in nomine Patri et Filio et Spiritui Santo.*

Magdalen, watched as the sides of the grave began to give way, soil sifting slowly, silently down soon to cover her. She leaned back...she could die here. *Give me wings.*

Required under guard to remain in the convent parlor, the bishop gave them nothing. The Commander would force him to give up where Bernardo was and where he had moved him. He finally condescended to speak and explained: due to unforeseen circumstances, a new arrangement had been made for his nephew in old Gethsemane. He's been planning this for a while, he said. "The boy is unusual, different; it's important he be contained, live apart for his own sake and everyone else's." He said he'd spent time there growing up, had played there when he was child...*he'd played there.*

He'd played there? Ramirez could hardly contain O'Manion when the bishop, seemingly pleased with his own ideas and sounding delusional, said he'd accessorized the mausoleum, made it livable. The Captain finally exploded...accessorize this!

Ramirez took a more steeled approach, demanding he say what he knew of his sister and nephew, their criminal activity, their comings and goings at night. Santo Cantera was horrified, not sure with whom he should be angrier. But the Commander had no concern for the bishop's power and became even more adamant. He threatened the man, said he would be taking him in for questioning on charges of possible obstruction of justice. Santo Cantera wilted under the hard glint in his eyes, but that's why he was the Commander. The bishop insisted: Joanna…this was her doing; the boy blameless. He demanded he be permitted to go to Bernardo; he was told that wasn't happening.

Many had said an evil lived in the graveyard under his house…urban legend maybe. But it wasn't Padric's thing to argue the battle between good and evil though at the moment, he was having second thoughts. *Sister Moira.* She'd told him evil was the absence of good…*ay, Thomas Aquinas. But damn, here in L'Arroyo, I've come face to face with evil and some people are absolutely no good at all.*

Deepening shadows concealed them as they drew close to the Cantera tomb. Odd, how cool it was, but air vents tucked into the walls answered why…this was a must if someone was living down here. Pistasio eyed Padric…how many times he had followed his friend into the dark. He'd made it his mission not to leave Padric anywhere alone for too long. O'Manion had told him he was Padric's insurance policy, so when he nodded for him to move forward, Padric smiled. "You're given me your permission now?"

"Damned straight." Pistasio had come upon countless crime scenes but this mystified him. *Leave it to Johnny to be in the middle of something like this.* But all were caught off guard when they came upon a compelling, life-size sculpture of a kneeling Jesus blocking their path. The Savior was looking up at an angel, sad faced and offering Him the chalice of suffering. Padric remembered. *Again, Sister Moira. What had this Christ of stone witnessed here?* It wasn't of God… broken wine glasses and empty bottles of Patron Reposado, Patron Silver, were proof enough the Canteras, or at least one of them with her friends, had enjoyed themselves here. Even more curious were newly dug graves.

Ducci muttered: "These are for new kills, your next victims." They walked passed them and later, would wish they'd examined them closer.

When Martinez and Marcus had rushed into the tunnel and

spotted the door at the far end half-open, they had cautiously entered but were slammed by an almost superhuman attacker, someone they'd never seen before. He'd punched Martinez hard in the face then threw him against one of the armoires removed from Bernardo's old quarters. Marcus had immediately leaped on the man but was brought down from behind by a shovel in the hands of none other than Bernardo himself. Moments later, a dazed Martinez, almost out cold, awoke on the marble floor of the mausoleum.

*J-Dog, where is he…*silence. *Damn, who is this?*

Staring down at him, a hooded figure in sinister black vulture mask, muttered: "First one on the right next to the other one, Bruno…please do it now; I'm done with these men getting in my way; I must do God's work for Santo."

*Ay, Dios mio, here he is…he's the one…*darkness. The two detectives were to be buried alive but the one shoveling dirt onto their bodies had been spooked when he heard Padric and the others moving the turnstile in the wall; he'd taken Bernardo below and into the tunnel. Now Martinez lay there alone in the last place he wanted to be.

Johnny, find me. The two men had promised: they'd never leave the other behind. His man wouldn't do that. He'd…*kema sabe, rescatarme.* Had he not loved God his whole life? *Save me for my children? Marisol.* He didn't know she'd learned only moments ago he was missing; that Padric was looking for her husband in the graveyard under the bishop's house…it was all over the street, on the news. She knew the drill; they'd planned for something like this; there were close calls before and they had survived. Both had vowed to each other from the first night they fell in love they'd mentally, in their souls, talk the other one out of a bad situation, mind to mind, heart to heart. They'd laughed when they said it. And now…

Alejandro, come back to me. She slipped into the gathering crowd, her son beside her; Mario, taller now looking more like his father. *Alejandro, come back to me.*

Marisol, please, no goodbyes.

At the Precinct, Tark was cursing and swearing; his equipment down and no longer able to make contact with Padric. L'Arroyo PD won no awards for its resources. Woodson and Morrow looked at each other; they'd entered first, cleared the mausoleum. *This is what all the hype was about…no fun at all. And what the hell was all this…a place for the dead flipped into a live-in studio?* LCAT wasn't happy.

Padric stepped inside the tomb and scanned the accommodations, a re-dux in process. The surface of a marble sarcophagus was now a table for dining; already two place settings visible. A comfortable couch with expensive pillows and luxurious throws looked ridiculous in such a setting; there was too much wrong with all this. Scattered everywhere, books and artifacts seemed like they'd been there awhile.

No Bernardo, no Joanna; the team knew nothing of Bruno. Padric backed out of the tomb…was he not the Hound of Ulster? Nevel. One dog knows another. Their beast, tail pounding on the earthen floor, was eager to get on with it when he caught sight of the detective returning.

He knelt down and told Nevel about Magdalen: "They're here…she's here and I don't like what I'm imaginin'!" The dog whined. "I need her back, *bhoyo*. Damn it, lad, you have to do this."

Nevel nodded his head, yipped and pawed at the soil…*let me get to it; let me find her.* He nuzzled the nun's pillowcase Cunningham had been holding like some kind of sacred sacristy linen.

Padric grinned. "Let him go." The dog took off but not before glancing back one last time at Padric…he'd do this. The men followed, zigzagging among the graves, even passing those where Marcus and Martinez lay waiting and covered in dirt. Rounding the mausoleum, men and dog entered the darkest part of Gethsemane; more graves, new ones open and waiting…*what had these two planned to do, genocide?*

Padric cursed. Nevel moved from one to the other. Where the shadows were deepest at the end of the row, he went off, crazy with discovery. He sat down, scolding Cunningham with his whine to move faster. Then they heard it…muffled, a cry, someone in agony. Padric peered into the dark. Eyes. They were hers, no longer green and peaceful, full of pain.

"Sufferin' Jesus." Nevel, given the go-ahead, dived in, whining and pushing the dirt away with his nose from Magdalen's face; his paws pulling the soil away from the rest of her.

"Fuck this!" Padric slid down the side of the grave, the last thing in the world he wanted to do; he hated cemeteries. "Magdalen, lass!" Her face was visible now. "Your main man, Nevel, found you. We've got you. I...I've got you."

Both man and dog pushed the soil away, but her eyes were screaming...he kept whispering to her, only understanding her desperation when he realized her bodice was gone, shredded and torn when Joanna dragged her across the hard stone floor of the tunnel. Magdalen could not hide her nakedness and the other Johnny, saw what he saw and diverted his eyes, but later and sometimes at night, he'd recall the sight of her and feel guilty...*she's beautiful, damn.* He tore off the shirt he wore over his bulletproof vest and covered her, quickly removing the tape from her mouth and the zip ties.

He pressed her close. "I'm sorry...but saying this here in a grave doesn't speak much to my sincerity." Magdalen leaned her head on his shoulder, holding onto him. Cunningham called off the dog; Nevel turned to obey but licked the nun's face and was gone... she wept. "Damn, what a Romeo...wish I'd thought of that."

"I'm so glad you found me, so happy and sorry I did this...I just wanted it done, ended. They'd hurt my Lucy." But she suddenly remembered Joanna and drew back. "Where is she?"

"Not far...I know where she went, almost certain. But damn, come 'ere, lass. Never again are you doing this." He was holding a nun in his arms in a grave. "Hollywood doesn't write this stuff." He was grateful when Morrow slid down beside him. "Kate, luv, take care of our nun!" He climbed up and out of the darkness, but not before kissing Magdalen on the forehead.

Morrow brushed the dirt from her face. "I'll be takin' you out o' here, Sister."

Dumbfounded, three first-responders appeared; they'd entered through the front door of the bishop's house and descended into the graveyard by means of a foldout metal stairs the monsignor showed them. But Magdalen refused to go to the ER at Meadow and insisted she be with her Sisters. Carefully paramedics lifted her onto a gurney and delivered her to the rectory of Our Lady of Sorrows. Father Santeresa had invited the nuns to stay under his roof until CSI said they could return; the convent of San Miguel was a crime scene and the body of Sister Lucy Genova had been taken away in a coroner's van.

In the Garden of Gethsemane, there was even more discovery: Sebastian cried out; he had found the two men. Padric, cursing in Gaelic, leaped over graves to get to them. Unable to send his men into a subterranean graveyard without him, Ramirez could stand it no longer and left the convent with an unhappy bishop under guard. With O'Manion, the Commander lowered himself through the revolving stone door and was now extricating an unconscious Martinez up and out of the dirt. He shouted for Padric: "Get down here, John. Your *amigo* isn't responding."

Padric jumped in beside them. "Alex, damn it…get your ass up or I'll…" Martinez blinked. "That's all you got? You were leavin' me? Fuck you, fool…we talked about this."

Alejandro Martinez opened his eyes as Petra had done on the way to the morgue; he looked around and slowly made the sign of the cross. But realizing his situation, he became agitated, wanted up and out of the dark…*and what the hell was Johnny yelling about?*

"I'd need to get a new partner? Fuck you!"

Martinez was horrified. "Shhhh, *kema sabe*…quiet; this is a cemetery." He was whispering now.

Ramirez and Padric laughed. "You're in a damn grave telling me this?" Padric hugged him and wouldn't let go.

Martinez stiffened, pushed him away. "Marisol!" He'd learn soon enough she and Mario were standing unseen in the crowd outside the bishop's house. But across town at Meadow, another woman waited to catch a glimpse of the husband she didn't want anymore.

Lara was glued to the television after hearing some talk between two orderlies…an arrest had been made in the case of the moondead. Crowds had gathered outside; rumors of officers down and detectives missing filled her with fear.

Johnny, you son-of-a-bitch…come on, let me see you…where are you?

While the drama of finding the living among the dead was underway, Ducci hadn't liked what he'd seen; the freshly tossed dirt, open graves. With Woodson, he'd entered the mausoleum again; some carpet had been pushed back and both spotted the hatch door and plunged into the dark, shouting for Padric who glanced one more time at Martinez and Marcus, both being treated now; they'd be back in the game soon enough and his nun was safe with her Sisters. Life was good again or at least for a moment.

He tumbled down the ladder after the men into the once barricaded tunnel leading to the house in the alley. Tark was back, muttering about heat sensors ahead.

"Bloody hell!" Padric took off. Ahead shafts of light from the street above gave them a glimpse of Bruno, guiding the young man, a wanted killer now, through the dark. The men could hear him insisting Bernardo go to his grandfather's ranch. He balked, would go no further...*no way, out of the dark and into the light? Never!* He liked being buried, wasn't ready for his own exhumation. Anxious and half way to freedom, the young man ran back toward the graveyard only to be snatched up by Woodson.

Ducci and Padric pushed on...they heard footsteps behind them. Martinez, patched up and dusted, wanted in. "That bastard tried to bury my ass."

Padric chuckled. "Get the fuck outta here, Alex." He was glad to see him. "Come on."

Bruno had reached the cellar under the house but not wanting to leave without Joanna, hesitated, the detectives almost on top of him. He clumsily pulled himself up through the same hole in the floor where the detectives had fallen into a makeshift morgue weeks ago. They scrambled after him. Bruno was out the door, his Land Rover a short distance away, but Martinez wanting a piece. Lighter and faster, he hurled himself off the edge of the porch onto the man, but barely holding on as he whirled him around, slamming him into the alley wall to rid himself of this idiot cop.

Padric winced...it looked painful; his partner was suffering some serious damage; he stepped in front of the man as Ducci restrained him. But the Irish detective would need to exercise some diplomacy. "Bruno Hill Letterly?" He'd done his research...CODIS was his friend. The man froze, Martinez still on his back. But

Ducci gave Padric a look...*what the hell. Why the discussion...why stop now?*

Padric however was assessing the man, his thought process skewed, mental reflexes off...he followed orders, never gave them. Joanna Cantera pushed his buttons and she wasn't here.

He would settle him: "Ms. Cantera's in some trouble...she'd probably like to see you." Padric recalled Ramos had said Bruno rarely spoke and now the man was letting them know he'd like to speak. Ducci wanted bad things for the man but Padric wouldn't allow it. He laughed instead...Martinez was still hanging like a koala bear onto Bruno's neck.

"Alex, get the fuck off him and come with us. Lt. D., stand down, if you would."

Bruno and Padric seated themselves on the edge of the porch while Martinez still glared at the man who had buried him in a grave. No one was more surprised than the two when they finally heard a refined British accent. "I've been in the employ of Arturo Cantera for years and cannot leave his service, due to a family debt owed." Had Dolorosa not intimated the same in regard to her family? "Ms. Joanna is my charge and I do what is required."

The men were stunned. It was Padric's move. "Is this what you really want...I'm hearing something else."

Bruno lowered his head, frowned, his eyes to the ground, how to answer...he'd never spoken this long with anyone other than the Canteras. "Her son...I need to be there if you're arresting him; he'll panic, get crazy. You saw him back there...I was trying to save him, no offense."

The men had been studying his demeanor. Padric said: "You see and do only what they want, is that correct? You have no life." Bruno sighed and said it was so. Padric pondered what he must do with this character out of a graphic novel. "Sir, you've been obstructing justice big time for the Canteras, facilitating their escapes from the law, helping both disappear when we were in minutes of apprehending them. You did damage to two of my men. But your record shows you have taken no lives, yet you carry that AK. You've never killed anyone."

"I refused...it was negotiated in my contract." *He'd negotiated,*

had a contract? That sounds like Arturo Cantera. The man hesitated…
how to say this, would it mean worse punishment? "I have thwarted your efforts, but there is another, one of your own who aids and
abets in the disappearing, sir, and does it better than I do. I'll leave
it at that."

Padric's hair stood on end; he glanced at Martinez, his eyes
dark and angry at the thought of betrayal not heard of in the First
Precinct. "You won't be leaving anything we've discussed, Mr. Letterly. What else do I need to know about this individual? You will
give an assist." But now Bruno was suddenly holding his throat.
"What is it…what's ailing you?"

"This happens, sir, when I speak for more than five minutes."

Martinez, weary and weak, was done with civility and cursed
in Spanish. "That's fucking convenient when the lieutenant's putting it to you. Speak or I'll…Christ, Johnny, haul his ass in. This
isn't the Treaty of Hidalgo-Guadalupe."

Padric laughed. "You know what I must do, Mr. Letterly."

"I do…but I need to be with Ms. Cantera; check on the boy."

"And I'll be doing the checking." Padric nodded to Ducci.
"But…how did you arrive at your disability, this condition?"

Bruno lowered his head. "My mother called me Pig when I
was a boy…she tried to butcher me like one and slit my throat.
By God's grace, I live." *By God's grace*…the mother's cold act of
violence stunned the detectives; pathology breeding pathology.
Strangely, here was a man who could speak of God's grace after all
he had done at Joanna's bidding. Padric could only imagine what
he had witnessed, there was an apparent disconnect in his thinking.
Like linebackers walking off the field after a game, Ducci led Bruno
to a waiting police van.

From a narrow side alley, two faces peered from a hole in the
fence. "Papa?" Mario then Marisol stepped into view then broke
into a run. *Familia.* Padric would take it from here after Marisol
kissed his cheek and promised a prayer. Lara…he'd blocked her
out of his thinking. He'd given his shirt to Magdalen and with only
a tee-shirt beneath his vest, he walked back through the tunnel,
pondering the theology of choices and consequences…the great

disconnect between God and all that makes us less human. *Sister Moira*. But throughout the day, his thoughts returned to the son he must find. He must see his face, have a sit-down with his boy-child but the graveyard was calling. Too many things still stood in his way. He'd make short work of it; bring the Canteras to their knees. But Ramirez had suggested Padric take a back seat in the interrogations…the less he was seen the better. He was relieved. But that would change.

Bernardo was waiting to be exhumed, brought up and out into the light, like it or not. Moments before, the others like monsters had stood in a circle pointing assault rifles in his face; he'd stared at them, looking curiously at their gear, the pepper spray canisters and grenade pouches. With all his pathology, he was wide-eyed and non-aggressive, giving not the slightest resistance, gazing into the faces of those who would snatch him up and out of his lair. He wondered why they were asking him questions; why wasn't the man he thought was his brother there to send them away?

No one had told him Santo Cantera was his uncle, Joanna, his mother. Padric had insisted; knowledge of such things would throw him into a tailspin; they'd get nothing from him.

The detective climbed back up the ladder and into the mausoleum. Thin shafts of morning light pushed their way through slits of glass high on the wall in the cemetery. Padric eyed him…a handsome lad, neither suspicious-looking nor afraid. *So this was her son, same eyes, but he was different and brilliant, a young man full of knowledge and wit though daft and delusional.* Bernardo was tall like the bishop, bore a resemblance, but this Cantera, with shoulder-length hair, black and disheveled, was wired, looking too fragile and pale to be the strategist in a series of murder plots. Bernardo was fixed in his own reality now, detached from the violence he'd perpetrated just hours ago.

"Bernardo Cantera?"

He raised his hand like a student. *Delusion, an expanded version.* Marcus stepped into the tomb. At the sight of him, face bruised but clothing brushed clean, Bernardo straightened. Another *persona*, older, and more sociable, emerged. The two men could have been brothers, their features quite similar.

He eyed him curiously. "You're precious."

"I assure you, sir, I am not."

"Sir? My...aren't we formal?"

Padric glared at him. "Bernardo Cantera, we're arresting you on multiple counts. We'll explain down at the Precinct." He read him his rights as Woodson had already done but this time, the young man crumbled before them; his face like chalk, pupils dilated. Cat-like, he eluded their grasp and leaped onto the marble sarcophagus; dinnerware crashed to the floor. He shrieked like a child then collapsed, sobbing, folding himself into a fetal position, clawing with long painted black nails at his face.

Marcus settled him. "Mr. Cantera. Calmly now."

Bernardo rolled over and looked at him. "I've never been called that before."

"We're not here to hurt you." Padric disagreed...he would have liked to do that and was tempted, but said nothing; the up-heaval subsided; their 'priest' had stepped up.

"I've seen you before in the garden at night. Please, could you help me?"

Marcus looked at Padric. "Lieutenant, what would you like to say to this man?"

For Padric, this was Shakespearean: the lonely, haunted prince of Cantera, obsessed. In an uncommon gesture, Padric placed his hand on Bernardo's shoulder; the others looked at each other. "Son, I need to understand...explain your surroundings."

"You're not my father...I'm not your son."

"Make believe." Padric almost toppled him.

Bernardo was up for some show-and-tell. "Would you like to see something?"

O'Manion had joined them...they listened and watched as the unfortunate man moved from one antechamber to the other, one swathed in black drapes looking like something out of a goth-ic chronicle. But most eerie and unexpected for Padric were the armoires when Bernardo flung them open and the round, glassy, all-seeing eyes of the dolls looked back at him. He noted their garments and wrappings of cloth, the fibers and human hair. He knew...this was a trophy case.

Padric stepped closer, studying each name card, noting even fingernails, harvested from victims then cut, snipped and shaped into what was required. Over the following months, the ME and Milleau would compile an astounding report on just this one piece of evidence.

Bernardo was now lost in his craft as he had been with Magdalen, eager to show them another chamber...a well-appointed kitchen, refrigerator overflowing with food. Behind an embroidered drape, a luxurious bathroom with shower and spa, footed tub. Apparently preparations for this had been going on for some time and a misstep by their nun had moved up the date for him to take occupancy. "My brother has given me everything."

In a brief rush of pity, Padric wanted to tell him this wasn't everything. That the bishop had gone to such lengths to transform a place for the dead into something like this was astounding and sick. But it had a woman's touch...Joanna. Later the question would become which Cantera was more in need of intervention and a sanitarium.

Padric smiled a little. *Milleau will have a field day with this.* He'd get their archaeologist-nun in on this, too. Bernardo pointed to shelves cluttered with miniature coffins, brimming with strands of braided hair tied in ribbon. There were crosses and amulets, bones, the skulls of small animals piled high on shelves...the move-in had evidently been hurried.

Marcus whispered: "Santeria maybe." He had returned but would rethink what he had said...*no, not this time. This was Bernardo being Bernardo.*

But Padric was looking for something. "What did you do with the nun's hand you removed?" This startled Bernardo...the mood suddenly changed. The detective could not know of this, Bernardo whispered. It was his secret, his treasure. "I want Sister Magdalen. You will get her for me."

Padric lost it. "Don't ever order me around, you little shit?" Onlookers relaxed. *Ah, there's Johnny...*he'd been too polite, too contained in the face of a killer, let alone a Cantera.

Bernardo shrank back and tore at his clothing. "I want Magdalen." *Yeah, so do I...*Padric wondered what this pathetic soul might do if he knew what Joanna had done to the nun; he'd use this to separate them. "Your friend, Sister Magdalen was hurt and is resting quietly…you and your sister beat up the nuns pretty badly back in the convent. But what Joanna did to her later was worse…throwing her in a grave with plans to disrespect her and do all that shit you don't like. Where is your sister?" Silence…no reaction. "Seems she left you to take the rap, buddy." God knows what Joanna was doing. Bernardo was pale now, another *persona* emerging, a child, frightened and anxious; he was shaking, no longer able to stand.

He sobbed: "No, not Magdalen!" He shouted threats at Joanna and kicked the walls of the tomb.

Mission accomplished. It's a cold business…this. Padric felt lousy but not that much and nodded. Marcus would guide the young man from the tomb, but not before whispering a word. "Well, you worked that out nicely, sir. Looks like we may need our nun down at the Precinct; we're not getting anything out of him and she's all he wants at the moment."

Padric knew the feeling. "Precisely, lad. Get him up top; let's get this hapless wonder down to our house for a big Cantera group hug. The bishop will follow and I'm going after his sister." Ramirez had told him to drag Joanna in by the hair and he'd do that, but for now he studied a compliant Bernardo, who saw none of this as part of his reality…why was he being arrested? What could he have done wrong and why all the alarm? They needed to move.

Pistasio and his tact squad had left; they were supposedly looking for Joanna…a BOLO in effect once again. The rectory of Our Lady of Sorrows was surrounded by uniforms, the Cathedral complex looking like a militarized zone. The convent, once a peaceful retreat, now a fortress breached.

"Upheaval is the operative word here, a*migos*," muttered Padric when he heard crowds outside in the street. Below in the Garden of Gethsemane, they could hear them as Marcus and Martinez hoisted the killer up the set of foldout metal stairs. Old statues, still standing tall, looked relieved. But there was one lighter moment for Padric, standing there in the graveyard; he'd noticed two rookies looking more than interested in being part of the takedown.

He would only realize after today how they and their academy mates "just out of the shoot" would be vital to all he would undertake in the months ahead. These two had been especially on point today. He asked their names.

"Officer Joe Maselli, sir."

"Officer Morna Maclone of the clan Maclone."

"You jest, lass…and I'm assuming you've read your countryman Arthur Conan Doyle; it's a must in this business." She said she had, but wished to speak further; more seasoned officers within earshot rolled their eyes.

"Sir, another good read is *The Private Memoirs and Confessions of a Justified Sinner*…I'm sure you're familiar." He smiled a little and would give it some play.

"James Hogg, Officer…nineteenth century; and for what reason should I be reading him or does such a title suit me?"

Had her comment offended…she froze. "My apologies, sir, for taking the liberty."

Padric smiled a little…*there is a God. She's articulate; the young ones coming up have some education and a love of the book.* But the two rookies looked at each other; in the academy, they had argued the case over and over. "Please, sir, can we assist…anything, we'll do anything."

He eyed them carefully. "How are you with graveyards?" They loved them. Again there was bliss…*to be young and born in America, a country with no apparent mythology to haunt them except for a Headless Horseman. Forget "Twilight" and vampires. Here in L'Arroyo, 'a bump in the night' would easily become urban legend within weeks and now these two were excited.*

Padric nodded. They'd shadow the detectives until the Canteras were in lock up then return to stand post in the cemetery with CSI.

For the rest of his life, Padric would depend on the two, even now forming a plan; he and his partner would take them along later. They proceeded down the path toward the rear of the cemetery and Maselli pointed to the metal stairs as if guiding him out of the mess. "I'll help you." Padric, for one brief moment, took some comfort in this; he was feeling suddenly old and said he'd be up in a moment.

When he and O'Manion were alone, the detective slowly seated himself on a sarcophagus. "I should have been a priest like my brother…help the poor, teach the ignorant; no women, no fucking around. I'd give a good homily; chant some Latin." He stood up.

The voices were louder now outside in the street and O'Manion grunted: "Let's go face our public." They climbed up the stairs, through the kitchen and into the bishop's vestibule. Ramirez, now back at the Precinct, was on the phone. "I heard things from Bishop Cantera I didn't like; get him down here. And John, he is the bishop. I rely on your discretion. You will use the smoothest of words for which you are famous."

Padric was a happy man but Steed and Sebastian stood nearby observing and listening to all that took place. What must they be thinking? The young priest was disturbed that so much trouble should surround his bishop, his mentor. Padric approached. "Father, we will use some finesse…I have the right man for this." He was not. "Sgt. Marcus will accompany His grace to the Precinct."

A look passed between him and the young man he called *priest*. But Marcus had been watching Bernardo…it was painful. He stood very still, smiling. Rarely had he been upstairs in his brother's house and now gazed with great pleasure at the pictures and photos on the vestibule wall. In the most touching manner and oblivious of what was about to befall him, he whispered: "I am so happy just to be standing here."

No one moved at first, so stunned were they; some glancing suddenly at him with pity, others looking at Padric, his face grim; his eyes seeing more than a criminal. Sebastian would quietly explain to a baffled monsignor where he'd been living.

Padric spoke quietly to his men and the rookies then nodded. They understood…extricating a killer and the bishop from his own house would take some strategy. They'd talked about this and the lieutenant opened the door unprepared for the sea of upturned faces. He had forgotten it was almost noon and business as usual in downtown L'Arroyo, but now a scandalous takedown at the Cathedral had flooded Church Street and the Plaza with people.

He stood in the doorway. *Ordered chaos*. "Christ, don't these people have jobs. Go back to work, for God's sake!" Pistasio's tact squad and dozens of uniforms were everywhere. The Canteras were finally getting some comeuppance and the crowd not sure why. But they had picked up on something they heard…the killers had been found in the infamous graveyard below the bishop's house. What were they doing down there? And who was that handsome young man with the pale face and monk's garb? Confusion and rumor traveled quickly from one to the other. When he appeared on the portico, they fell silent.

"Get these fucking Canteras out of here." Padric glanced back at the priest. "My apologies." But the priest said he knew what they'd done to his family and asked what he could do. Padric thought for a moment: "Baptize my son for me."

"And I assume you'll tell me more about this wonderful news."

"You wouldn't believe it if I told you but I will very soon, Father. He and I are in a world of hurt and it's on me."

"It's in our DNA, John…we do more damage to ourselves than most others would. You'll find your way back to your lady." *My lady…the guy's a friggin' romantic.* "The healing will begin for the child and you…I mean it."

Padric searched the priest's face. "In what lifetime?"

It would begin. Bernardo, unshackled, stared at the faces then hid his face with his arm but not out of shame…the daylight was too intense. "But where is Magdalen?"

"She will speak with you soon. Go with the officers now."

"Okay." *That was it?* Would there be no resistance, no drama from this pathological killer? But then…he wasn't his mother or uncle. Bernardo was simply Bernardo in all his complexity. Padric touched his elbow and, without incident, walked with him down the stairs to a waiting police van; the driver none other than the Commander himself…he nodded to Padric. But the crowd realized this one must be the killer; low murmurs turned into a roar as the van pulled away from the curb, sirens popped and downtown was abuzz. *He'd been living below alone in the dark? And the bishop knew; oh, yes, he did. Shame on His grace!* They had forgotten Bernardo was one of the killers and they pitied him. He was their Quasimodo.

Marcus suddenly emerged on the portico with Santo Cantera. The sight of him drew a collective gasp from a crowd who was turning to leave; they regrouped. More uniforms converged, forming a shield around Padric who remained at the bottom step. The crowd was eerily silent…*what was this? A supposed killer had been removed without handcuffs and the bishop was wearing them?*

Santo Cantera wasn't going down easy…he'd resisted. Cameras rolled. Swooping in with her news crew, Betty Branston pelted the bishop with questions. Padric cut her off.

Marcus, beside the bishop, was as usual calm and half-smiled at Padric. "Good afternoon, Lieutenant. We've told the bishop he is simply being brought in for questioning."

"I said low key…what's this?" Padric pointed to the handcuffs.

"The bishop was combative and we found it necessary."

The bishop glared at Padric. "You know not what you do."

His stone-cold eyes met those of the bishop. "Ay, but I do. Bishop. The high regard others hold of you is of little concern to me. You're squarely in the middle of this and I'm sure you will kindly assist us with all of it." He nodded to Marcus.

The bishop's face softened: "Spoken with elegance by the golden-tongued Celt." He slowly seated himself in the back of the police van. Marcus brushed passed Padric. "If 'tinez was doing this, he'd be calling you a sweet-talking fool."

"Indeed I am. And you're the only one who can do what is required…I'd kill him. Get his holy arse down to the Precinct with the speed of light, *mi hombre*. We can hold him for forty eight in this town." He quickly walked up the bishop's front steps but not before barking: "Take off those bracelets."

Marcus slid into the van and looked back at the bishop rubbing his wrists. "Lt. Zalconi will be our chauffeur, Your grace." An irony…Jana was behind the wheel this time; her family and the bishop's were among the Big Five in L'Arroyo.

"*Si*, Sgt. Marcus…I am honored and it is you who stand guard in my garden. And the fine lieutenant beside you…this I suppose is not the best time to give your father my regards." He had regained his dignity but neither made any reply. "Ah, yes…protocol, best to say nothing; everything as it should be. I will rely on your prayers."

But Marcus was praying for himself…who hooks up a bishop and brings him down to the Precinct in the back seat of a police van? Jana was thinking her own thoughts. Called "road warrior" by Major Crimes, she could drive through a firestorm. Moving away from the curb, she headed straight for a gaggle of overzealous reporters milling about at the end of the street. They threw themselves onto the sidewalk cursing and swearing…she winked and popped the sirens. Like the Red Sea, a crowd of onlookers parted. Santo Cantera made the sign of the cross.

In a condominium down the street, Darragh Padric leaned back in her chair and smiled. Today L'Arroyo was more exciting than Belfast with her son in the thick of it…the small TV in her bedroom was her constant companion. America was a strange and wonderful place, she observed, but it frightened her.

The whole city had been glued to iPhones and televisions. Near the Plaza, the lunch crowd in pubs and eateries craned their necks. They'd even gathered in front of Levell's, L'Arroyo's largest appliance store; its windows with twenty screens in HD, streaming live breaking news. Marisol and Mario now safe at home, watched, as the drama played out on the screen. But Martinez' *abuela*, sitting beside them, had seen something else; the baby she'd delivered so long ago, now tall and pale and a killer…*Dios mio. Bernardo. But the mother…where is she? What had life done to them…and the bishop? Ay-ay-ay, that was another plate of rice and beans.* She wondered aloud how Arturo was taking all this.

At Meadow, Petra with her parents looked in disbelief at the screen. "Mercy, Lord," Petra whispered.

Her Sisters, taken quickly in the dark in police vans to Father Santeresa's rectory for safety, now gathered in his sitting room to view the ongoing saga of L'Arroyo v. Cantera. Some hurried off to the rectory chapel. Monica, mourning the pain her Magdalen suffered, was seated beside her now lying silent and still in the room they would share at Magdalen's insistence. She vowed not to let the elder out of her sight with Dolorosa close by; she too was their roommate, an avenging angel allowing very few entry.

For several days, Monica would have a new window from which to look out on the city, this one facing the Cathedral three blocks away. She could look down now at Our Lady of Sorrow's parish cemetery, shaded by countless mesquite and acacia. She prayed without ceasing and when sitting with the others would urge them to stand tall and be at peace in the Lord. Maryjohn was her constant companion; two holy sages whispering things, often touching the arm of their stricken Sister, kissing her forehead, blessing her.

Finally brought down and no longer the warrior, Magdalen, with head wrapped in gauze, her body covered in bruises, had allowed Gina to treat her…they had talked quietly when she came to the rectory at Padric's request, but now Dolorosa was fighting back tears, her Sister lay silent and trembling, remembering the darkness, the grave and worse. And there was her own failure to change things, make a difference; this too was hard to admit. But there was a comfort.

It was over…well, almost. Joanna was still on the run; it would only be a matter of time.

On her laptop, Dolorosa and Magdalen, when she could sit up, had watched with surprise the news coverage of Padric standing at the top of the bishop's steps. The crowd too was pleased when the lieutenant called Batman, brashly whistled through his teeth for silence; they wanted someone to talk to them and why not that immigrant lieutenant with a bit of a brogue and some mystery about him…good-looking, too. It was said he liked a good pint; that ladies of the evening, on their corners at night, would call out his name as he passed in his hummer; they'd promise him things and he'd shake his finger. They'd laugh and he'd disappear into the night. They didn't know about Joanna Cantera. But this afternoon he wasn't smiling. He'd keep it short…they'd seen enough Cantera drama.

"I'm Lieutenant John Padric." They cheered. He silenced them, sending them back to their homes and workplace with a reminder. "If you're looking for some quick Wild West justice, forget it; the First Precinct can't promise you that. For now, *mi amigos*…go in peace; let us fix what has happened here, *por favor.*"

At first, no one moved as if waiting for a blessing; after all, he was standing on the bishop's front steps. But someone had joined him. They smiled…the new priest. Padric turned. "Damn, Father, preach!" Padric stepped aside and with one sweeping gesture, Sebastian made the sign of the cross over their heads, appealing to them with kind words in Spanish, his Italian accent charming them as he spoke of forgiveness, asking them to believe again in a God who loves them. They would sleep better tonight; the darkness lifted; he had mesmerized them. Steed smiled from behind his office curtain…show biz wasn't his thing.

From her hospital room, Lara had watched with tears in her eyes. There was the strong, tired face of her husband. Reluctantly she smiled when his voice rang out; her complicated, absent, Cantera-screwing husband was in charge. How in command of himself he had looked, but she knew…he was suffering and she'd done it to him. Lara Padric had her moment; she'd gotten even. It felt good… for at least ten seconds. Staring at the man she had loved once or still or never, she followed him with her eyes as he withdrew and was gone. When the priest had concluded, Padric suggested: "You and me, Father…we'll go on the road. We'd knock 'em dead, no pun intended."

But Sebastian had only smiled and hoped the detective would visit him later. He had many questions, much to discuss. Ramirez, now in his office, had observed on a monitor Padric's remarks and the people's response…*when had this ever happened?*

Martinez was waiting in the vestibule of the bishop's house, fired up. "Joanna Cantera. Where is she…I'm not going back to the Precinct without her."

They returned to the graveyard below. Padric looked at Martinez, disheveled, clothes mussed and dirty. "You look like crap."

"Knew I could count on you for that; *gracias.* I'm not going dancing, fool."

"I gotta say…that rugged, unkempt, dirty look becomes you."

"Rugged, *si.* Dirty, hell, yeah, but unkempt…what kind of word is that?" Padric grinned…*like old times.*

Author's Notes

exhumation – to dig out of the earth or disinter a dead body.

Underworld – reference to a series of dark, murky 2003 action horror films depicting conflict between vampires and werewolves.

Palatino font – form of lettering perhaps based in Italian Renaissance typography; in the present day, the work of designer Hermann Zapf, calligrapher.

In nomine Patris et Filii et Spiritus Sancti – Latin, for in the name of the Father and of the Son and of the Holy Spirit, words often spoken when making the sign of the Cross.

Rescatarme – Spanish, for rescue me, save me.

Hound of Ulster – refers to Cú Chulainn, an Irish mythological hero who appears in the series of the Ulster Cycle as well as in Scottish and Manx folklore. As a child, he killed Culann's fierce guard-dog in self-defense then offered to take its place until a replacement could be reared. At seventeen, he defended Ulster single-handedly. Known for his terrifying battle frenzy or ríastrad, translated to mean "warp spasm" by writer Thomas Kinsella, he would turn (like the Incredible Hulk) into a monster. He is often referred to as the "Hound of Ulster." During the literary/art Celtic Revival, Augusta, Lady Gregory records many of the legends of the hero in her 1902 book Cuchulain of Muirthemne, romanticizing some, omitting the more violent. Friend, William Butler Yeats, wrote several pieces based on the legend, including plays On Baile's Strand (1904), The Green Helmet (1910), At the Hawk's Well (1917), The Only Jealousy of Emer (1919), The Death of Cuchulain (1939), and a poem, Cuchulain's Fight with the Sea (1892).

The Private Memoirs and Confessions of a Justified Sinner – novel by Scottish author, James Hogg, and published acronymously in the early 1800's; thought to be an early example of modern crime fiction told from the viewpoint of its criminal anti-hero though also part-gothic/psychological. Set in Scotland, it describes a pseudo-Christian world of angels and devils.

Headless Horseman – fictional character from American author Washington Irving's short story "The Legend of Sleepy Hollow", published in 1819 with 34 of his essays. The story is set in New York, within a 1790s Dutch settlement that residents nicknamed "Sleepy Hollow"; its protagonist, a schoolteacher named Ichabod Crane, terrorized by the ghost of Hessian horseman, allegedly decapitated by a cannonball during the American Revolutionary War and roaming Sleepy Hollow with his severed head resting on the pommel of his saddle. Linked perhaps to the belief that ghosts cannot cross water, he is unable to cross the bridge into town. His target, schoolmaster, Ichabod Crane, will disappear, fate unknown, but a shattered pumpkin found beside Ichabod's abandoned hat, seems to point to an abduction by the Horseman himself. The townspeople are left to conjecture and there will be sightings.

"Twilight" – reference to four vampire-themed fantasy romance novels by American author Stephenie Meyer and a series of films released between 2005 through 2008.

27 COMEUPPANCE

"**Y**ou and I have some searching to do…fuck protocol." He asked where the "runts" were; on cue, Maselli and Maclone tumbled down the metal stairs after the men. "Am working a hunch and need you to cover us. You two are up. Pistasio does this, but he's God knows where."

Hiding their excitement, the rookies slipped through the open revolving stone door and pulled the two into the dark. Before them lay a network of tunnels…it was part of the famed urban legend of L'Arroyo. In minutes they were under the Plaza en route to the Nile Hotel. "Hell, she couldn't have gone too far," Padric muttered. *The bitch is in the last place the LPD would ever suspect.*

With the exception of her father and as far as he knew, Padric had been her only visitor; she'd swept her in to her personal hideaway tucked into the Cantera suite even existed. She'd vacated it after the crimes of two Canteras made nightly news and BOLOs for both had been issued; but he'd recently learned there were signs she'd returned. Would she risk it so close to where she'd escaped arrest?

The four made their way through the dim light of tunnels skirting the underground operations of every large building surrounding the Plaza. For Padric, this was new, things had changed… he hadn't been below in a while. And now, he had no idea how to access the Nile from here. This was a goose chase.

He and his partner laughed when Maselli told him he knew all about *it*. "In high school, we'd come down here on Friday nights after football and check stuff out. It was a blast, like Jason and Freddy all rolled into one; we partied hardy. We had a few scares but now no one comes here anymore; they say a tall guy in a hood and mask walks these tunnels at night…he's a slasher; killed a few people."

But he didn't know about Ben and Danny and some of their classmates; this was their playground on weekends. "I wanted to tell you about this, but I think we nailed him already. This Bernardo, he's the one that was trollin' people down here. I'm sure of it."

So were the two detectives. "We'll talk. But for now…the Nile, take me there, lad."

Maselli nodded. "Follow me."

Padric sensed he was walking the same route Bernardo had walked many times. Eerie passageways trailed off into a dark that was fearful.

Maselli pointed to a broken electrical grid and a dimly lit stairwell. "At the end of those cinder blocks; a few steps will bring you up to the parking garage levels under the Nile."

From a dark, forgotten corner, they emerged into the underground parking garage. It was then Padric told Maselli and Maclone he had knowledge of Joanna Cantera's possible whereabouts; they would stand fast by the less frequented back entrance to the lobby in the Nile hotel.

To say more would reveal what he could not admit. He was ashamed. With heart pounding out of his chest, he took the familiar backstairs two at a time; here for a different reason today and with his best friend, like a shadow not letting him out of his sight. The hallway as usual was silent. With back to the wall, Martinez stood to one side; he was wary, fearing what Padric might do to a woman he wanted dead. He knocked his knock. They heard something; a wine glass perhaps, fall to the tile floor then there was silence until the hood on the peephole was raised.

Martinez didn't see a topless Joanna fling back the door. "Johnny! I waited…I knew you couldn't stay away. Come in, baby… please Johnny!" She threw herself into his arms, legs straddling his waist. Pure delusion…had she forgotten the past twenty-four? The detective had no want in him for the woman though they both knew each other in ways no one else could imagine or he could deny. He pushed her off him; how could she assume it would be like old times. He was furious...he'd end her. But he should have known Joanna Cantera didn't take rejection well. She laughed and, pushing him into the wall, tried to kiss him. Her lips, he was remembering and angry for doing it. Her breasts pressed against him but all he could see were the bite marks on those of her victims, the hurt in their eyes, Lara's eyes hating him.

He cursed her, shouting the names of her victims. She screamed when he flipped her around and slammed her into the wall. But Alex Martinez knew Johnny Padric and, fearing his partner might kill his ex-lover, stepped into the room; even he was horrified. Padric, with his hands across Joanna's face was in seconds of snapping her neck but he locked eyes with his friend of so many years. It seemed like forever. Time stopped, a lifetime suspended in mid-air. Martinez could see Padric eating his gun after all of this ended... *silence eternal.* He cried out.

John Padric backed off, raised his hands, walked away; let the woman drop to the floor. Today his partner had saved him. She lay now in a heap on the floor and knew now why he'd come. Sobbing and pleading, she clung to his legs; her words, gibberish, trying to tell them what she had seen. "Your fucking nun is an angel...watch yourself. She's not like us...she's..."

"Shut up!" Padric unmoved began his recitation: "Joanna Cantera, you're under arrest, you have the right..." Martinez threw some clothes at her; she covered herself. Padric kicked open the door and dragged the woman uncuffed into the hall and down the backstairs. Slamming her into the wall over and over, he shouted aloud her crimes. "My kids, my kids, those nuns, damn it...my wife. You come into my home. I want you dead and that's gonna fuckin' happen!" She screamed; they reached the ground floor and he pushed her into the lobby for all to see. "Get away from me, bitch!"

But as only a Shakespearean actor could do, Lieutenant John Padric transformed himself in an instant into a proper cop and calmly cuffed Joanna Cantera; the Nile Hotel, in an uproar, scrambling for damage control and attempting to placate their guests. He nodded to Martinez who had followed him down the stairs, he just as angry, not caring how Johnny handled himself this time.

At the back entrance, the rookies spotted them and stepped forward. With a confused and defeated Joanna still talking about angels, Martinez walked her out the door and into the back courtyard. It looked quiet enough; the detective grateful there were no media present, no crowd to greet them; a patrol car rolled up as Padric had requested. He'd timed it well. But it was the end of the tourist season with eyes everywhere; in the strip mall of boutiques and eateries facing the Nile back entrance, onlookers were already gathering. Establishments emptied; cell phones lit up. Joanna's arrest went viral and her appearance drew shouts of disdain. But she threw back her head, eyeing the crowd; her subjects were becoming unruly and she was minus her entourage.

Martinez gripped her arm: "Cut the diva act…move it!"

But bad news traveled fast in L'Arroyo; the city fed off it and hecklers pushed forward, enthralled by a scandal in one of the Sonoran's most exotic hotels. This was Joanna Cantera's perp walk but she saw it differently. The woman could pump up a crowd every time she walked into a club, but this time she wasn't wearing her little red dress and no longer passing out Franklins. Despite jeering and catcalls, she breathed in the attention, unaware everyone knew she and that odd looking boy were the killers…forget allegedly.

From the hotel doorway, Padric watched reality set in. Joanna was suddenly fearful, struggling; her last name not fixing things. The crowd's pity for Bernardo didn't extend to her; she had misread them; wrenching herself away from Martinez, she ran back to Padric. What she thought might be a safe haven turned into a nightmare; he grabbed her by the hair and brought her, cursing, back to the van. It wasn't one of his finer moments and he regretted the rookies had seen it. The detective was even more embarrassed when the crowd cheered him on. But if only for a moment, it felt good and his boss had his back; hadn't Ramirez given him orders to do this?

Maclone stepped forward. "Ms. Cantera, these people aren't your friends. Cut the crap."

Joanna lowered her head. "Then save me, for God's sake!"

By now, some were throwing things, even their lunches. Even a huge pail of garbage near the Nile service entrance was tossed into the fray; falling short of her, it knocked Martinez off balance. But nothing could take him down; had he not been raised from a grave? He glared at those nearest him. "*Silencio, por favor!*" Martinez was one of them; they fell silent. "*Vamonos, mi amigos,* go home or go back to work!" As if choreographed, they stepped back.

Joanna glanced back at Padric; there was nothing for her in his eyes. She'd gone after his children's mother, damaged his son who he was aching to see. She'd laid a threat on the elder, blackened his nun's eyes and abused her; the bitch had spit on her. And had she not watched as her demented son mutilated another? Mercy was for priests and nuns to give; Padric had none.

Maselli and Maclone pushed Joanna into the van. Martinez slid into the passenger side; Duran was behind the wheel.

"So what's your pleasure, Detective? It's you and me now."

Martinez cackled. "Take me to paradise, *mija*...step on it." She popped the sirens and he looked back at Padric. "This is on you, my brutha. The cleaning bill's first."

Padric wasn't smiling. Joanna. *Hell's waiting, babe.*

He'd help her get there.

It was six in the evening and Ramirez glanced at his watch. Where was John Padric? *Come on...get back to me, mijo.* His cell lit up. "John Padric here, sir."

"Joanna Cantera, Lieutenant."

"As we speak, she's signed, sealed, delivered and en route to you via Martinez and Duran." The Commander was grateful. "I went in with no plan and some reliable *intel*; enough with the tip-toeing around. She was arrested without incident." He didn't tell him he'd thrown her around, almost broken her neck. Ramirez, watching his monitor, would learn more momentarily on breaking news. "There's something else...I dragged her by the hair to the van as you requested, but I need CSI over here now...the suite is a gold mine I'm thinking." But would they find any evidence of him having been there on other occasions? He broke out in a sweat. "IA will go after my ass on this one."

Considering a city's desperation, Ramirez reassured him the powers-that-be would overlook just about anything at this point. But Padric was seething, struggling with what all of them did, the same age-old dilemma: *why does an ID'd killer need the courtesy of the law?* They spoke further but both men knew it wasn't over and Padric again returned to the Cathedral, more for *his* soul than for their reassurance. He spoke for more than an hour to Sebastian and Steed and, seeing his inner agony, they ministered to him.

But when he took leave of the men, he couldn't take leave of the graveyard below. Padric was curious; it was still in his head... that fleeting sight of something or someone among the tombs. If Ramirez or O'Manion called, he'd ignore it; say later he was waiting for CSI to arrive.

Still on a high from the arrests; he returned to the dark and the flickering light of the candles. At the far end, the mausoleum still glowed from a lamp within; he moved slowly among the graves. More sure now of his footing and the shadows around him, he was able to see better. All too soon, CSI would be bringing its own light show. Milleau had called, asking a thousand questions; he was leaving the convent, letting others take over and anxious to get into the graveyard. But the call was suddenly dropped.

"Lieutenant? What's up?" Nothing.

Padric was suddenly facing his own mystery. There was movement along the wall. "Who goes there?" He almost laughed. They said that in old black and white movies. His voice had bounced off the tombstones. Nothing. More curious than spooked, he eyed the perimeter. Padric was up for this and feared very little except his own demons...*bloody hell, I could go a few rounds.*

There! He peered into the dark; almost amused, half-thinking it was his mind playing tricks. He'd play it out; besides, he needed a good ghost story to tell his kids when they were older. Not for a moment ignoring his sense of a curious presence, he walked slowly up one path and down the next, reading a gravestone, brushing away silt from another. He'd string it along; draw it out but not before revisiting the mausoleum. *Fuck it...come and get me.*

Padric's unease in graveyards left him mystified with the thought that someone would have been living here...*who does this?* It was a cold and unholy place now; here, Bernardo would have been entombed alive for safekeeping by his uncle and the mother he thought was his sister. Unable to fight off his demons, the young Cantera might have ended his life in some macabre way. Padric's thoughts raced with the possibilities.

The detective scanned the interior more carefully now. There were no urns for ashes since an abhorrence of cremation among many in L'Arroyo was bound to the lingering belief it was unacceptable by former Church standards...they liked bones. Padric smiled. *No fire for me. Let my good-looking bones be wrapped in the Tri-color, laid to rest in a fine, satin-lined box, something beautiful, an American flag draped over it. Semper fi.*

With gloved hands, Padric paged through a worn journal. Bernardo's penmanship, jagged but legible, shouted out to him...this was a movie script pointing to motive and premeditation. In his latest entry, he had painstakingly copied word for word the hagiography of the martyr Saint Agatha, who had suffered interrogation and torture, breasts crudely removed and other humiliations. *Leave it to Bernardo to discover the most gruesome to replicate.* But eerily, scrawled in the margin, was the name Agatha Locke. *Sister Agatha, nice lady, tough, had a sweet smile.* Gina had introduced her, a triage nurse in the ER. He read on. *Christ Jesus...according to this, she'd have been next,* her death another copycat tragedy lifted from early Church history.

He felt sick...their nun was right. Hadn't she said they wouldn't stop, choosing more challenging martyrdoms to re-create? On another page was a list of prospective victims, dates and times, martyr's names linked to priests and nuns, monks and brothers; all were potential targets. These were real people living out ministries all over southwest Arizona. Perhaps it had happened already.

The two would never have stopped.

Wanting to leave, he stepped into a cemetery plot overcrowded with tombstones; the graveyard was darker now. *Where the hell are Milleau, CSI?* Padric needed them now; lightheaded, he tried to steady himself. Two shots of booze at the Dirty Rice before takedown, no food all day and spending most of it in an underground graveyard hadn't helped. Within seconds, he'd need to step up. Coming toward him at an unusual speed was a phantasm. Gone was the panic. Padric stood fast, reading it. "Come on, freak... gimme something!"

Had he gone mad? *Who is this?* Swathed in rags and loose bindings, it stopped within feet of him. He could reach out, grab its throat but saw it more clearly, a man once. It was no ghost at all and swayed back and forth, as if deliberating what to do next. Poised and waiting, with bony bare feet, it planted itself on the earthen floor, regarding him now with dull eyes deep in their sockets. The creature tilted its head, measuring his mindset, analyzing him. Or was he seeking his help...*was he a she?*

Padric wanted to give him a little "ghost" of his own, something from Hamlet and fitting for the occasion, like revenging *"a most unnatural murder"* or *"murder most foul, as in the best it is..."* But oddly the detective could say nothing, unable to utter a word.

The unknown backed away. It stretched out its hand, uttering a miserable, unhappy rasp of words, pleading for Padric to take care of something or someone then it was gone. The chance to engage in some conversation and fisticuffs had escaped him. He had always been up for something like this; too much so, his partner would say. The thought of some barebones fight to the finish strangely quieted his nerves. "Get back here. Damn it; show me something!"

A familiar voice called out: "Are you sure you want me to do that?" Milleau.

"Where the hell have you been, *bhoyo*...so you think you can show me something?'

"I played some third-string football in school. Wasn't very good, but I could hit."

"Where...now that we're having a chat?"

"Brophy in Phoenix, of course. But wanted to go to Saint Mary's."

"Ah, Saint Mary's football, the Knights and '87, my senior year at Cathedral. They beat the crap out of us. But that's for another night by the camp fire."

"You camp?"

"Hell, no. Too spooky, waking up with bears or a warlock."

The irony of two men standing in an underground graveyard where one had just seen a ghost and now admitting to a fear of camping was not lost on the men. They laughed. With some relief, Padric sat down on a gravestone. "Christ, am I glad to see you."

"The arrests and the climate down here have improved your appearance, sir. You're looking better."

"Compared to what? Damn, how bad was I looking before?"

Milleau looked around. "Were you talking to someone?"

"I don't do twilight zone, lad, but I'm seeing things."

The young man showed no surprise. "Color, shape?"

"It was brownish, gray…rags, dressed in them, moving this way and that."

"A face?"

"Not much of one…empty eyes maybe, skull like." And what about odor? "Come to think of it, decomp, but no, not the same, dry flesh…I don't know. His skin looked bad, patched, some gone." Milleau asked if where they were standing had been used for anything else except hiding these graves. "You and the nun will be looking into that. Say when."

"When…I mean now. I can start after I get this processed."

"I'm holding you to it. What were your first thoughts about what I just told you?"

"Zombies." The lad was serious. "They're real, don't let anybody debunk that for you; they won't be the ones depicted in your old Boris Karloff flicks or "The Walking Dead", but I'm thinking something creepier?" But as Padric pointed out, what could be creepier than a zombie?

"Twenty of them…no. I'm messin' with you, Lieutenant."

"Do not mess, lad, do not mess."

"That tunnel you said you took to the Nile under the Plaza extends to my dad's museum and beyond; what if something unwanted was accidentally or deliberately shipped to the museum or someone stowed away and got loose…just saying."

"Something…something like what? You jest." But Milleau rarely did that and reminded him of his father's latest acquisition of treasures from Egypt for an upcoming exhibit.

"You may have seen your first one."

"My first one what?"

"Your first zombie." He grinned then sobered. "But there are more credible possibilities."

"And you'll tell me what the fuck you're talking about sooner than later."

"You described what might be a leper, a lost one maybe"

"What the fuck is a lost leper?"

"Let me know if this happens again."

"Thank you, Doctor. For Christ's sake, I'm not talking about the common cold here. Lepers and zombies…we could have an epidemic, a fucking apocalypse."

"You're reading too many graphic novels. I'll do some more thinking on this."

"And that's it?" Padric was not pleased but then, *if he's not freaked either am I.* "First things first then, come with me." He explained how the arrests had gone down and opened the armoires for Milleau to see. Could they get these, just as they are, down to the lab? Milleau would take care of it.

But the young man was stuck in what Padric had seen.

"Are you going to report what you saw?"

"No…who'd believe me?"

"I do."

"Then it's your mystery…uncover anything you can find, but don't get yourself killed. I might have Detective Marcus help you with it…"

"Sister Magdalen. This is Egypt stuff…we just got a new shipment from Cairo."

She'd eat this up, but…"Nothing, I mean, nothing can happen to her."

Milleau searched his face. "You're not crushing on her, are you…I mean, I could see why and all that, but, you know, she's a nun and…"

"Don't even say that shit, Jon-Gabriel." *What had he said…crushing on her? Case closed, but yeah, I've been doing that since I laid eyes on her, just a little maybe, but who loves a nun, for God's sake? It's complicated.*

Milleau was pleased. "You called me by my first name."

"Hey, it's not Valentine's Day. I swear I'll…"

"Okay, okay…just saying." But they turned around when they heard a commotion at the top of the metal stairs; the CSI team, carrying huge lights and tripods and strange looking objects, were tumbling into the graveyard and laughing about it.

Padric shook his head. "Christ, it looks like fuckin' film school." As spooked as he was, he knew he stood on holy ground, disrespected over and over again by the Canteras, but the arrival of those who would probe and peer into every crevice, seemed just as invasive. The place would be lit up like a dance hall. He'd leave Milleau to his work and come back later to rout out what he'd seen; he'd say nothing about what this sad thing had uttered.

That he was taking this seriously bothered Padric; he was worried about leaving CSI with what he'd encountered. He'd post some uniforms here, convinced it would do them no harm or even make itself known. Padric reached the top of the metal stairs and looked back. Already CSI was setting up their equipment and abuzz. Milleau was thrilled with his surroundings and shouted: "Way cool here. Give me a necropolis any day, but for now I'm a happy man."

"Those armoires are trophy cases of the dark kind, lad!"

The entire team turned and stared at Padric then like ants moved in the same direction to look at them. Padric would throw out more bait for Milleau. "You need to know, lad, I'm looking for some bones, female, over sixty." Patti Devlin and her disappearance here in this cemetery had come to mind several times…only last week, O'Manion had said this was to be his next case.

"Yikes, that's even better."

"I'll even up you one. That garden out there's a burial field. Your Sister Magdalen said a mass grave of bones is somewhere near the convent wall. We got nuns buried there and need DNA on this."

He didn't know what Magdalen had just learned from Eduardo; her Sisters were buried beneath the angels that stood in the garden. Wide-eyed, Maselli and Maclone suddenly appeared at the top of the manhole. Padric was preparing to pull himself through and they gave an assist. But they'd heard every word that he said.

Coming off the excitement of bagging Joanna Cantera, the two hadn't counted on spooky when assigned to the First Precinct; the academy hadn't covered that. They were ecstatic.

"I need you two. Shadow the team down there. If anything unusual occurs, anyone enters the perimeter, Pistasio's men are in the street."

The two literally slid down the ladder into the graveyard. His cell phone lit up. He laughed. "Damn, son, are you finished already?" Milleau was insisting he wouldn't do it without Sister Magdalen. "You got it…get busy." He smiled when the young CSI let out a hoot. He had entered the mausoleum.

The sun was doing its last dance on the edge of the mountains; the night sky still holding onto some light…it was dusk. A hush fell over the city and, like a woman waiting for her lover, the Sonoran desert watched for the moon to come into view. Leaving the bishop's house, Padric would slip into the Cathedral for one last look around…two female uniforms were posted within and they nodded. He walked through the nave of the church and genuflected but remained on one knee with head bowed. He was broken inside and uttered no words to the Lord.

The detective's presence did not go unnoticed: Lupe, allowed to return to her home in the campanile, followed him with her eyes; she made the sign of the cross…*Dios mio!*

Here was her chance; she cried out, her voice echoing through the Cathedral. "*Teniente, por favor!*" He turned. "I must say it."

Padric walked toward her slowly. "Well then, Ms. Rojas, should I come to you or will you come down for a chat?" She rushed down the narrow staircase and ran to him; he knew what she'd do and stepped back but it was too late…she'd thrown herself into his arms.

The rookies stepped forward; Padric raised his hand and carefully extricated himself from the woman. "Officers…would you bear witness to this good woman's words to me then take a proper statement after we're done?" They were young and thrilled to do whatever he wanted, assisting her into a pew.

Padric sat down. "I've needed your help for a very long time, Lupe; you've already admitted you witnessed a death in this church but we were interrupted. I need more, the smallest thing, a word, a name; it would assist me in knowing who did this and I'd be grateful." He also knew what might move her. "It might help the bishop."

She eyed the detective...he had spoken so humbly; she saw the pain in the back of his eyes. Lupe was good at finding that in a person; something weighed heavily on his soul, but Padric was reading her, too. She looked away and he reached for her hand. "*No preocupa, no tiene miedo.* No worries now."

She patted his face and blurted out all he had hoped to hear: "*Vi Joanna y Bernardo de matanza a Hermana*...I did. I saw what happened to my Petra. You've arrested them...the boy and his mother, this Joanna woman. But still there is danger; be careful, little one." *Little one.* He was two feet taller than she; Padric glanced at the uniforms, warning them with his eyes not to laugh. She was the witness he needed. "We'll meet again soon and thank you."

"*Via con Dios.*" She traced on his forehead the sign of the cross. "You will need God...careful, *mijo.*" *Mijo*...Alex would be laughing for a week. But after he left, one of the officers asked Lupe: "What should the detective fear, *señora*?"

"Why, *bonita*...the demons living inside that poor boy and his mother." She wept.

Before climbing into his hummer, he glanced up at the empty convent. The elder was gone; no warm lights in the windows, but it was well guarded. Duran had resumed her post in the vestibule; uniforms everywhere. Among them were two female rookies walking the quad. "What is this, ladies night at the Cathedral? What are your names?"

"Tarkington, sir...Officer Rhea Tarkington." *Tark.* He eyed her curiously. "He's my uncle, sir." He asked if she'd like to tell him anything about one of his finest detectives. "He taught me how to ride my two-wheeler and play a mean trumpet."

"Good enough...and you, Tate, is it? What do you play?"

"Basketball, sir." They laughed. As always, he thanked them for their service, said they would talk again soon. The sky had grown darker, more brooding; the outline of a moon had emerged;

he smiled. This was that "once in a blue one", Marcus had mentioned. It had been in all the news, something about happening every twenty-seven years.

But he was looking for something else, almost hoping for it... then he saw the winged figure perched high on the campanile of the Cathedral; he glanced back at the officers...they seemed not to notice. Dignified, mystical, it looked out over the city.

Padric needed more than ever to believe in something; gazing one more time at this winged being. Hair parted and flowing down his shoulders, it turned and looked at him; a chill passed through his soul. Too much graveyard, too much everything...he needed more than a drink. Sanctus watched as the detective sped away then took his leave, bowing to the empty window where the nun usually sat. She'd been allowed to do battle on her own today and was one of them now. He would need to explain about living in two dimensions with purpose...but she knew; she always knew she had lived half in this world and half in the next.

Oddly, her shoulders no longer hurt; what they had hidden within had appeared. They would return but she hoped it would not happen too often. Magdalen looked up at a blue moon still in the sky...there was yet time for its glow to make everything right, if only once. Padric had wanted to check in with his nun but there was someone else waiting for him.

Author's Notes

comeuppance - a punishment or fate that someone deserves.

Boris Karloff flicks - William Henry Pratt, better known by his stage name Boris Karloff, was an English actor and widely known for his roles in horror films, particularly for his portrayal of Frankenstein's monster.

"The Walking Dead" – reference to an American horror TV series developed by Frank Darabont and based on the comic book series of the same name. The lead character awakens from a months-long coma to confront a post-apocalyptic world overrun by zombies.[4] Grimes and his family struggle to survive in and adapt to a world filled with zombies and humans who are more dangerous than the zombies themselves.

Teniente - Spanish, for lieutenant.

28 WARRIOR

Monday, mid-evening, April 21

He sped into the dark and soon saw the church spires against the night sky. Saint Aidan's was thirty minutes northwest on the edge of the city; its property bordered the desert. Beyond, one could see the cliffs and mesas where the hermits and Father Antonio dwelled. A light in the rectory window told Padric Father Seamus hadn't retired. He was praying his breviary and Padric hesitated; it was too late and he, undeserving. None of this would be happening if he hadn't sinned. His request would probably be a strange one, but Irish-born Father Seamus was his countryman; he'd chance it and knocked on the door.

"Ah, John, lad...if you hadn't come to me tonight I'd have been seeking you out in the morning, though I know you've been busy. Come in."

"You know why I'm here then, Father."

The priest drew him to a cold fireplace and prodded the still glowing ashes into a blaze; though it was mid-April in the Sonoran, it had been exceptionally cold at night and it was his custom; they sat down before it.

There was no dead child.

An hour would pass and the light in Padric's eyes returned, the pint in his hand finished. "This is a miracle." He leaned back. "I must see him...now."

Father Seamus left the room and made several phone calls; Padric stared into the fire, putting the pieces together. He'd wronged his wife terribly but the hurt she'd delivered on him had flattened him; he'd never fully recover, never fully trust her again…such things didn't happen to him. And if by chance, they would find their way back to each other, he knew she would never trust him; they would simply live for their children.

The priest tried to enlighten him: his wife had apparently blocked it out: a supposed miscarriage had indeed been a very premature birth. Her state of mind kept the doctors at a distance and, right or wrong, they'd left the matter alone, trusting she'd heal with a few medications and better nutrition. Padric pondered these things, more saddened than angry.

Father explained: "You must know, it was Gina Chavez who initially asked for my help…she does this in certain cases. Your son has a wee heart but that of a warrior; I baptized him as little as he was. Meadow has no neo-natal facilities and, with the Canteras at large, we couldn't risk placing him in the general population at Good Shepherd."

Padric was hurt and offended, outraged at the silence all involved had maintained. They'd been his colleagues; he'd bumped shoulders with many of them in serving the city. He would trust no one again accept his partner, his team, Pistasio. He'd…but Father Seamus was telling him something; it would bring comfort.

"I serve as chaplain to the cloistered order of the nuns at Saint Uriel's Abbey. They have several small infirmaries for cases in need of privacy and under grave circumstances. Considerable sums are offered for special attention. But babies are welcome free of charge or by donation in certain cases. They have private donors, some corporate, who cover the costs for others. I was present when Gina and Agent Watson brought your son there." *Gina and Bobby.* Were they not his friends? He'd been left in the dark about his own flesh and blood.

Padric wept uncontrollably. "I must go to him…I'll give them whatever they want, money. I want my boy. I must see him now and if I must go alone, so be it."

"Your wife has said nothing then, never asked for your child?"

"Father, she said if he's alive she wants nothing to do with him because he's part of me. She was assaulted, disrespected, left for dead by an ex-lover, the woman I sinned with. His life is in my hands now. There'll be no more back and forth with Lara. It's only this lad and my girls I'm living for now…maybe then I'll see things fall into place."

"You'll go alone then with me." Through the dark roads and rocky terrain, Padric in his hummer followed the priest to the abbey. In no time, he saw the cross, raised in the hands of the Archangel Uriel, affixed to the belfry rising over the walls of the cloister.

A nun unseen at her post on the other side of the turnstile, used to pass things back and forth from visitors, came round to the gate. They drove through and up to the cloister door. Though familiar with the convent of San Miguel, this was a cloister, more otherworldly than Padric expected.

Mother Mary Rose greeted the men warmly; hastily reassuring Padric his baby was holding on to life with a will of iron and waiting for him. His heart was once more beating out of his chest. "Please take me to him. My apologies for the hour." She reassured him it was no inconvenience; they followed the nun through a colonnade of great beauty. Even the detective was overwhelmed by the fragrance of a garden lush with roses in the heart of the abbey; but a small *casita* attached to the building and standing alone in the far corner caught his attention. The nun explained it too was a small, private infirmary; she turned down a long hall and pointed.

The door was ajar. An unusual and sudden peace enveloped him as he stepped into an almost heavenly setting; two nuns in white looked up and smiled, around them a small infirmary full of soft light; three incubators with babies, resting and still, were before him. He eyed each one and instantly knew. Here was his son. He pointed; the young nun standing nearby delighted.

Like an angel, she beckoned him forward. Mary Rose introduced her as his son's private nurse. "Sister Rosemaeve has been your son's caregiver and personal nurse since he arrived." His eyes filled with tears; his boy's guardian angel was indeed a lass…her eyes green as the glens of Antrim; he heard the twist in her tongue and Ballymurphy when she murmured a welcome. But how could this be? Had Magdalen's prayers brought him these blessings?

Father Seamus would clarify: "I requested a Celt remain by his side for a proper start and you were in need of such comfort. Now be grateful and a gentlemen." Padric smiled a little. He approached and thanked the nun, kissing her cheek, which he'd been doing lately to women of God. When he learned later the cloister had not seen the likes of this toward one of their nuns, he smiled a little. They'd need to get use to Batman/Johnny Padric.

He fell to his knees, his hands pressed to the glass of the incubator. In small print, the name on his son's chart read Baby Boy Padric. *Bloody hell…the lad has no name.* He'd been in this world for a month without one; he'd fix that at once. But first Sister Rosemaeve sat him down and described the baby's condition. "Detective, you must know he may not make it, but what a fighter he is and now that I've met his father, I know where he gets it."

"Am I that transparent or was it that wee kiss I placed on your cheek? Apologies."

She smiled. "It was a happy surprise, but we'll say no more." She sounded like Magdalen. "And no, you are a bottomless pit to decipher, sir." *But that was a good thing for a cop, right?* He'd listen. "That sadness and fire in your eyes, the fight in your step, tells me you are determined to save your son despite your own burdens. He is your priority, I'm thinking, but you may wish to let people help you. We understand here; Father Seamus has explained." He had not taken his eyes off his son while she spoke.

"He must live; I will care for him. I have family here; they will help. Their mother, she suffers and I bear the guilt of it. But this isn't about me. He needs a miracle."

"He needs to hear your voice telling him this…"

"I will stay…I can stay."

"For a while then." She offered him a comfortable "papa" chair, as she called it. "You will assist me by speaking with him." She was in charge now. "Your being here is a blessing for him." When had he ever heard that…*I'm a blessing?* "Just sitting here, being here; he senses you. You can rest, close your eyes; sleep if you must. I will allow you to hold him. He has had no one."

This infuriated Padric all over again; his son had been waiting for him, for anyone to come, and here he was, holding on. Padric gazed at him, pondering the future for both of them. "He can be held…I can hold him? Please, Sister, now." With the greatest care, the boy was placed on his shoulder.

Padric leaned back, barely able to feel the child resting on him and he wept, closing his eyes; in the months to come they two would begin a lifetime of never being too far from each other; Padric spoke of this to his son. He whispered, introducing himself, bestowing on him his new name: *Finn, it will be Finn, the very same who was the great Celt hunter-warrior Fionn mac Cumhaill, the glorious and rollicking Finn McCool.*

"Lad, you are Finn Shakespeare Alejandro Padric." Again he wept for the boy who would become mythical in his own right. "You are Shakespadric." Boom.

He remained at the abbey all night and through the next day, sleeping beside his son, speaking with him, the Irish nun bringing him tea and at lunch, a bowl of lamb stew. But then would come the inevitable: Ramirez was calling him back to the Precinct; they'd reached a stalemate: the Canteras, refusing to talk.

Padric drove through the streets; the past forty-eight had been mind-bending but now the Precinct had only twenty-four to get what they needed. His partner grinned when he saw him but had nothing but bad news: "The bishop got physical and tried to level a punch at anyone within arms-length. He and O'Manion had words, lots of them. "He wanted to speak to someone important. We didn't do it for him."

For his own good, the bishop had been placed in the only available cell facing a holding tank brimming over with the drunk and disorderly. They called out to the prelate who attempted to say a few words; it did little to quell them though Santo Cantera was known far and wide for his eloquence. Joanna had demanded a conversation with Johnny; Bernardo, with Magdalen. He was curled up like an armadillo on the floor in an interview room.

Padric half-listened, was somewhere else. *Finn, lad, you will never set foot in the life I chose. You will be different, a whole new star in the sky.*

Author's Notes

*"No preocupa, no tiene miedo Vi Joanna y Bernardo de matanza a Hermana." – Spanish,
loosely for "No worries, I am not afraid. I saw Joanna and Bernardo slaughter Sister
Petra."*

Via con Dios. – Spanish, for "Go with God."

*Fionn mac Cumhaill or Finn McCool – refers to Fionn mac Cumhaill transcribed into En-
glish as Finn MacCool or Finn MacCoul, a mythical hunter-warrior of Irish mythology;
occurring also in the mythologies of Scotland and the Isle of Man. "Fionn" means "blond",
"fair", "white", or "bright" and John Padric's baby son will notably have very light hair
throughout his life. The 19th-century Irish revolutionary organization known as the Fenian
Brotherhood took its name from his legends. The Scottish form of his name, Fingal comes
from a retelling of the legends in epic form by the 18th-century poet, James Macpherson.*

29 THE CANTERAS

Tuesday, near six in the evening, April 22

"**B**ernardo Cantera?" Marcus was standing over him. The young man rolled over.

"Help me." He'd been sobbing and wanted Magdalen.

"You'll need to sit up for that, Mr. Cantera." Bernardo scrambled into a chair; he knew how to act psychotic until he got what he wanted.

Padric and Martinez eyed both on the monitor. But Martinez could see a change in his partner. "What is it, Johnny? What's up?"

"Something's gotta be up? Come with me. Let them marinate, think on their sins."

Padric pushed his partner into his office and closed the blinds. Martinez threw himself into a chair. "What's got you going this time?" But the story of a newborn fighting for his life and a mother, filled with delusions and pain, both amazed and horrified him. He was joyous for his partner...a son. *Ay-ay-ay*, and he'd given this precious child his name; he was to be his godfather.

"Christ, Alex, he needed a Christian name with the two I gave him and who better than you, *kema sabe*. There are a few Alexanders."

"Those martyrologies really got to you, man...look at you." Martinez watched the light, for a while lost in his friend's eyes, return as he talked about Alexander of Jerusalem...*say what?* Hungry lions had kissed the saint's feet when he was brought into the arena to die and Padric wanted that for his son. They laughed.

But the saint, he explained, had created one of the first libraries. "How many guys had one of those back then?" Books...he wanted his son to read books. Martinez shook his head…*the poor kid, having a firestorm for a father like Johnny.* "And you'll be his defender if anything happens to me."

Martinez grinned. "And that sounds like something out of *The 300.*" They stood up and hugged then left to face what they must. Padric checked in with Tark; O'Manion and Ramirez were waiting. They knew he had the art of the interview down, alternating sledgehammer and feather. It had always been Padric who had warmed suspects up for the other detectives. But they were in for the ride of their life; he would not be on top of his game tonight and his past with Joanna would prove awkward and even more of a firestorm with the bishop. He'd leave Bernardo to someone else…to their "priest", Marcus, and the nun perhaps. They had less than a day.

Both sides would play each other and, at one point, Marcus would ask: "Will anything Bernardo Cantera says be admissible?"

Padric snapped: "He's a loon with all the law allows, but a shrewd one. The kid's brilliant. I could give a crap what he *is*; I know what he *did* and he needs to tell us he did it.

He described Bernardo's odd leather journal, its annotations and planning, proving premeditation. He admitted he wanted to slip it into his jacket but CSI had first dibs. Milleau had already tucked it away for their perusal. Padric half-glared at Ramirez and O'Manion. "And you think pulling me back in to speak to that woman will help?" They both nodded their heads; she'd messed with all of them…he was their last shot at the truth.

They left and with Tark in front of his screen, Padric eyed the monitor as Joanna entered the interview room. She sank into a chair, pouting; a female officer stood silently glaring at her. Joanna had hit on every male in the Precinct, but she was silent now.

"This needs to be over." He was silent for several long minutes. "That woman's not the beautiful, intelligent, cultured Joanna I knew; the one I remember was smooth as a slow sip of Johnny Walker Double Black Label." He twirled a pencil in the air, caught it and left the room.

Tark leaned back in his chair. "The man still has her inside him whether he wants it or not. Curtain up."

It was quiet now in the Precinct. Padric had a lot on his mind as he walked down the hall. It was part of First Precinct lore: the detective never entered an interview room without a legal pad and an old college law book from which he'd occasionally cite some obscurity. Tucked inside and seldom revealed was a Batman comic for luck; if a suspect refused to cooperate, he'd spread it out on the table and flip through the pages, smoothing down each one like some sacred treatise. It was said his quirkiness had broken some of the most hardened.

They'd expected Joanna to rush Padric when he entered the room; she didn't. Cool and contained, she eyed her man who wasn't that. The detective said nothing at first, arranging his materials carefully and only then did he lean back in his chair. They locked eyes; hers hungry for him, wondering what he knew, what he would do; his, giving her nothing.

"The priest in the street in front of San Paolo." He'd put it out there but she wanted his eyes all over her, she'd waited all night and all day for this and it wasn't happening. Joanna knew what she had to do; if she talked, told him every last thing, he'd stay in the room.

He threw down his first card. "You and your son…"

She flipped upside down and wailed like a cat. Suddenly he'd pushed the right button; Padric folded his arms…he'd reel her back in on his own terms. Opening the law book, he flipped through some pages but there was an echo; Bernardo was howling like a wolf in the interview room next to Joanna's. The bishop from his cell looked up; O'Manion stepped into the hall. After Padric slammed his fist down on the table, there was silence. But Joanna would go for some drama and lowered her head to her knees; she sobbed with no tears.

"He can't find out…he must never find out." She raised her head slowly and went for the sultry eyed thing, but Joanna's 'here-I-am, take me' look wasn't working.

"Bernardo and the priest…what happened?"

He was surprised when there was no hesitation. The woman would detail one martyr murder after another, dulling the sensitivities of her listeners when, with each admission of guilt, she ended with the same: "He's doing it for Santo." She maintained she was only a bystander. But an odd back and forth was taking place through the walls. Though not in the same room, the son in his conversation with Marcus would pick up where his mother left off.

An eerie symbiosis played out for those at the monitors watching, as if both Canteras were attached in mind, in sync and echoing each other. Joanna would continue to explain away her son's actions. "On the way home, he'd flip on that Latin crap." But there was always the same question from Padric: what did her brother, the bishop, know and when? "That's all you're going to say to me?"

"Answer."

"He knew nothing…it was us, Berno's project, his mission. We did it." Bingo. She flounced about in her chair, looking bored. "How many ways do you want this? Move on, for God's sake. It got him excited; he put his own twist on it, you know."

No, he did not. But Padric was getting what he wanted; he would give her the pleasure of his company and she'd sing like a bird. After consulting with Padric and Martinez, Ramirez put in a request to the convent of San Miguel. Magdalen arrived at the First Precinct with Dolorosa, veils swirling around them; heads turned when they passed. They looked straight ahead, the small, fiery nun, the other tall, with green eyes. Noting the bruises mostly hidden by the linens around her face, Jana expressed her concern then gave them an assessment of what had transpired thus far…it wasn't pretty, she said.

Meanwhile in front of the monitors, O'Manion put down his slice of anchovy pizza. Joanna was old news; he was eyeing Bernardo who wanted Magdalen. The nun finally entered the room, he was ecstatic to the point of embarrassing her, but the details he gave would prove to be cruel and unusual punishment for Magdalen.

Padric was more than concerned when at one point he observed her clenched fists; Bernardo's naive pleasure in telling her everything, terrifying. But she understood the man-child's thinking, his delusion. She remained until finally, exhausted, Bernardo himself, wrote down on a legal pad all he had done. He repeated over and over his martyring was a gift for his brother, the bishop.

"I chose nuns and priests because they were good and worthy to die for Christ. My brother said it was good to do this…it's a surprise."

In the next room, there were moments of empathy when Joanna described Cecelia's last words: "She cried for her poppy and mommy and the nuns…she called them her Sisters." Joanna had tears in her eyes. "She asked Jesus to forgive her sins…what sins did she have? And she asked God to forgive ours, mine." She fell silent than blurted out: "I didn't want this but did it for him, my son, and am sad that it happened." When Padric didn't respond she continued: "He's sick, obsessive-compulsive, OCD, full of ritual. It was the script this, the story line that, for God's sake; who the hell is he, Jerry Bruckheimer?"

Padric would let her unravel but when she caught herself showing some emotion, her eyes hardened. She straightened and coldly explained how Bernardo insisted the nun's head stay attached. "What the hell that was about, who knows." Coldly, she described how Bernardo cut off the nun's hand. "Did you find the ring? I wanted that ring."

Bernardo said later they cleaned themselves up with bottles of water they had in the truck and drove down the I-10 into Phoenix. "Sis took me to Donny's All Nighter. I ordered my favorite with extra everything." But they had slipped up. Full of swagger, Joanna would confess to "offing a very good-looking hot *tomatella* who gave premium lap dances at Chato's bar." It seemed the unfortunate girl had seen a nun being slashed on the other side of the canal. Later at Chato's bar, she dropped this on all who would listen. She said she'd seen a *muchacho* cut off a nun's head, claimed a woman was with him; both wearing hoods and robes like the *padres*. They wore masks, she said."

This was new; Padric and his friends in Homicide had not known who the girl was; they'd found the body through an anonymous tip and had little to go on. Now Joanna wanted to unburden herself. Chato's, she said, had been crazy that Friday with the usual long, loud party, a lot of illegal this and that, high-stake card games in the back and dog fights below in the pits.

"I needed to get her out of there and offed the bitch." When a fight broke out, as it usually did, she saw her chance and pulled the girl into the back parking lot and out to her truck. "She was stupid and drunk and the Edge is full of dead things and roads going nowhere and ending in piles of rocks. Most don't know they cover the graves of poor, dead fools." She rattled on. "Bags of lime are a must-have in the Edge. If you find rocks, you'll find dead people or what's left of them."

She said her father, Arturo, had told her there'd been sightings of huge, wild dogs, "some red; others purple, who knows, *chupacabra* maybe, roaming the desert near Chato's. He has dogs too, the ones he lets loose into the fields when they're too banged up to fight anymore...we call them *Hambrientos*." *We*...the woman sounded like she was in deep. "But those other ones eat his dogs for lunch."

She admitted to stabbing the girl repeatedly in the left breast so anything out there would tear out her heart. "Hey, it wouldn't be the first meal they'd had out there. I kicked her sorry, dumb ass into the ditch." Her brutality was shocking even to Padric...*was she on drugs? Who is she?*

Joanna waited for a reaction. Nothing.

But she'd give Padric something he didn't know about the Cathedral; she said she cleaned up with some rags in the back of her truck and burned them in the incinerator under the Cathedral."

Under the Cathedral...damn. He'd put Milleau on it. But Joanna was smiling; it had been indispensable to her and Berno, she said, their way to get rid of things. Satisfied and untroubled, Joanna leaned back in her chair.

"Write it down." He stood up. But...where was he going? He addressed nothing she had said and walked out. Disappointed, furious, Joanna had wanted to go a few rounds with her man; it was like sex. She rested her head on the table and wept. "I was nice once...I was a good girl."

Padric returned to the monitors contemplating the woman; his eyes, sad and dark. He'd return but said he was close to killing her. Martinez reminded him. "She talked, Johnny...hadn't done that, wouldn't." This made him nauseous; his skills in the interview room hadn't accomplished this; he'd slept with her...that's why she talked.

He'd used what he had with her to get what they needed. "We're looking at one of the most adolescent, full-blown sociopaths to ever set foot in this Precinct and certainly one of the worst I've seen in my time as a cop and, bloody hell, that includes gangbangers. She's done, over." He walked to the window and looked down at the street. *"God has given you one face, and you make yourself another,* damn it."

"And I'm assuming that's your boy, Shakes, minus the curse," said Tark. Padric said it was so and retreated to the Bog. Later when he pushed the woman on how much the bishop knew of her nocturnal activities; it would blow up in his face.

She asked where he was going with this. "You prick!"

She shouted accusations at him and the First Precinct; they were trying to nail the bishop for "some obstruction of justice and knowledge after the fact." She stood up. "You bastard, I'll kill your kids; go after your *gringa* wife's ass again. She's dead."

And that was the confession they needed. Padric torched her soul with his eyes and she knew…she'd said too much. Martinez almost punched his fist through the monitor.

Tark muttered: "Johnny will handle it, chill."

O'Manion had been waiting for this. He'd do something he rarely did and walked into the interview room; he'd pull his man out. "Lieutenant, you're needed elsewhere; I'll take this."

He had his own style and "hated messy." With no flair for the dramatic, books or ritual, he sat down. "Ms. Cantera, you've been advised of your rights and signed papers accordingly. Is this correct?" She nodded and rolled her eyes. "Well then, here it is: did you unlawfully enter a police officer's home with intent to murder his wife?" Nothing. "You will answer."

She lowered her head. "Yes." But Joanna suddenly stood up and pounded her fists on the table. "No one gets between me and my man."

"Sit." She sat.

There was silence; the two glared at each other until Joanna looked away. "Listen up, *princessa.* You have no man, at least anyone we know around here. Said person to whom you refer actually saved Lara Padric because he was *her* man. That woman you tried to off was the mother of his kids and his wife and you were never any of that." Joanna was white-knuckled now, gripping the table.

He took his time; he liked serving up hard, cold reality. "You did a job on his woman. She was with child…it lives, holding on just to spite you. Now settle your disrespectful, entitled ass down and do what he said…write all of it, everything. If you wiped your nose during a criminal act, I want to know about it. You will behave under my roof and stop acting like this place is City South High School. You and your son are being charged with malice murder and if you don't know what that means, get a lawyer…you'll need one. See you in hell." It was a boom moment. He left.

The detectives were in disbelief and shook his hand when he returned, but he was hungry, said he needed a bratz and asked them to save him a root beer. They asked nothing about his mention of Padric's baby…they'd leave it alone. Besides, they had more drama to watch; Joanna was falling apart; she had slumped to the floor mumbling something about "the bitch!"

"I wanted that…he was supposed to be my baby-daddy."

Cursing under his breath in Gaelic, Padric could hardly stand still; no one looked at him. Tark muttered: "You're up, Alex!" They were triple-teaming it; they needed more. Martinez liked jamming up perps with his own brand of *caliente;* and this one was screaming: "I want Johnny!"

"That ship has sailed." He slammed the door and leaned against it. He'd try to play nice and had promised Ramirez he wouldn't use the word *puta*. But after staring at the door for five minutes and refusing to speak, Joanna, true to form, slowly looked up at him. "God, you're good-looking."

Padric winked at Tark. "Easy come, easy go."

Tark laughed. "You've been scratched, homeboy."

Joanna was purring now. "I think you know about me. Say something nice." She thought Martinez would be easy; she could turn him. He glared back at her.

She's telling me to say something?

"Enough with the small talk!" He sat down.

"Oh, you're gonna talk big now?" He'd let her sputter. But

when she mentioned the nun who got between me and my Johnny, he pounced.

"There was no you and Johnny; what are you, fifteen? Don't even try pushing that hockey puck around."

But Joanna would take it further, admitting she'd wanted to "off" her. "Yeah, I wanted it bad, getting rid of that Magdalen *chica.*"

Their nun was a *chica?* Martinez had all he could do not to slap her, but she said her son and her brother, the bishop, loved the nun and she decided to do something else. She moved her head side to side with some swagger. "Did what I do…delivered some damage."

"Shut up, woman, those gangbanger moves and looking ridiculous don't cut it here. You do every L'Arroyo homegirl an injustice."

She smirked like a teenager. "Nothing comes between my man and me, never…"

"Looks like that's happened…oh, well."

She didn't like that. But her arrogance was suddenly gone; she was remembering. Joanna blurted out what she'd seen in the tunnel like she had when arrested. The nun was an angel. Padric had thought she was crazy; Martinez, could see it; why not, why couldn't she be? That Magdalen was indeed a supernatural filled his devout soul with wonder. *Dios mio…un santo ángel?*

He listened; a winged vision and a moment of light had spooked her. Her voice softened when she said the nun had offered to help. "Can you believe it…she wanted to help me. I'm not the type to be saved by all her shit." The edge in her tone returned: "After that, I knocked her around and will be cursed forever for doing it. It's what I do; this bitch-girl you're looking at, hurt her."

She said the nun put up a pretty good fight, but she gave it back and pushed her into a grave. "Did you find her…is she dead? Dang…I hope so. Johnny liked her. But I know he was banging her, he…"

Martinez could hardly contain himself at the disrespect. He shut her down, said not to go there.

Padric was devastated Magdalen's name had been brought into the conversation; it was inevitable…he'd done this to her. The nun's association with him had sullied her name. He disappeared into the Bog again.

But Joanna realized playing the Johnny card wasn't working; she eyed his partner, someone new to work over. Wanting to keep him around, she'd repeat all she'd said to Padric with even more details concerning the deaths of Father Villa, Brother James Hardy, the nuns. She glossed over what she had done to Father Sebastian.

Ramirez had insisted they get it in writing. She'd given them nothing, scrawling only hip-hop horror-core lyrics from Gravediggaz all over a legal pad. She was out-of-control, pulling out all the stops, as Tark would describe later. Joanna had moved from one *persona* to another: small girl to teen, seductress to reflective woman, sad mother, rejected lover.

Aching and weary, Padric was filled with all kinds of emotion, sad yet joyous over his son and longing to hold his wee girls, he stretched out on the conference table and looked up at the ceiling stained with cigarette smoke from back in the day. But old habits don't die and on impulse he called his wife like he'd always done after a difficult arrest or hard interview.

Her cell phone rang several times...she picked up. "Johnny?" Silence. "You've just questioned Joanna Cantera, haven't you?" He sat up...*damn*. "Well? Answer my question? Have you had enough of her yet? Obviously you'll be with her all night but that's nothing new, is it?" More silence. He sighed...*what is the point?*

Padric didn't play word games with women, not even with Lara, not even when he was wrong. He was angry all over again at the woman who'd kept him and his son apart, allowed a wee boy to lay in an incubator without name or parent beside him and worse...a father and son, not knowing the other existed. He was done. The dial tone buzzed like a hornet.

Later, Lara couldn't remember how long she'd held the phone to her ear. There was a crash in Room 355; she'd swept everything off her nightstand and Gina found her sobbing and clawing her bed sheets. Johnny Padric could do that to a woman.

Santo Cantera would be a challenge not only for the First Precinct, but also for Magdalen; he had requested her presence while he was questioned; neither she nor the Commander understood why. But the man had simmered too long and was not in the mood when finally "that smart-ass with a shield" entered the interview room. The bishop was in fact devoid of all mood when Padric put it to him: "We have enough from your sister's statements alone to charge both of them with multiple counts of murder. They knew their rights, asked for no counsel and signed papers stating as much. Your sister reminded us she's a Cantera."

The bishop frowned; they knew then Bernardo was Joanna's son. "We are Canteras, yes." He fingered the pages of his breviary. "And what does this have to do with me and your case?" They had reason to believe the bishop knew about the criminal activity of his sister and nephew and never came forward. They locked eyes. "Young man, I don't like your tone."

But Padric said he didn't care. "I'm not young and you'll call me detective."

The bishop would go for the jugular: "And did my sister call you detective?"

The son-of-a-bitch knows. Padric didn't blink. "Does thinking about something like that turn you on?" O'Manion cursed at the monitor. "Again…what did you know and when did you know it?"

"My sister was part of this; my nephew the instigator?"

"Big time. She tagged along, did things. You wanted martyrs; you got 'em."

The bishop leaned forward. "Do you know who I am?"

Tark chuckled: "He's asked this a lot…listen to his answer."

"We don't discriminate in the First Precinct. There's nothing like lock-up and interrogation to level the playing field. Jail is the great equalizer and an arraignment for something like obstruction of justice, that's even better." He sat down and glared at the man. "If you get in our face, we'll be in yours in ways you won't like. The martyr murders, what did you know and when?"

Once more ignoring the question, the bishop would attempt to make a case for his nephew, a young man eager to live in a tomb; the boy was brilliant, a savant. He saw the world differently, sensed beauty where most wouldn't. His voice grew louder, more accusatory, blaming the First Precinct for an unprecedented home invasion on his residence to which the detective retorted they had a warrant and that so-called wonder boy was the architect of one of the worst serial killings in L'Arroyo history or even the state.

Now the bishop was furious; they had sullied his family name with their defamation, committed sacrilege in his precious grave-yard; it was sinful.

Padric countered: did His grace know of the good times Joanna had hosted there with her friends?

The bishop blocked him with a question: and what of the detective and the state of his soul? In a tirade, he went off on Padric about his "illicit, sordid affair" with his sister; he said he would hear his confession immediately, now. He must pray to Saint Michael the Archangel, patron of all those in law enforcement, the great…

There was a knock and just in time…Padric had wanted to shout in the bishop's face: "Who gives a fuck!" But O'Manion was back and again sent Padric away.

He'd close the deal: "Do you really want to talk home invasions, Bishop? The Padric residence was in shambles after your sister got done with it. We know now, your nephew stood back…it was her party; she left Mrs. Padric for dead, badly beaten, a victim of Ms. Cantera's signature move; she bites the breasts of her female victims. Should I go on?" The bishop was silent.

When O'Manion asked why he allowed Bernardo to live in a graveyard, the bishop explained with great pathos, how much the boy loved his books, the tombstones and funerary art. He need-ed containment "because he was sometimes inappropriate; spoke out of turn, appeared delusional, was not well-received in polite society."

"Polite…is that what you're calling it? Does L'Arroyo have one of those?"

"The cemetery plays to my nephew's artistic nature, he enjoyed it there as a child." *What*? "Bernardo has a vivid imagination."

"We got that from the crime scenes and what he did to his victims." Silence. Crumbling inside, Santo Cantera had nowhere to hide; again he went on the attack, accusing the Precinct of victimizing him and his family, grasping at straws in a desperate attempt to close a case it couldn't solve.

O'Manion stood up. "Give us fifteen more minutes of your time then you'll walk out of here knowing things you refused to give up and we can't prove. Rarely can we get inside a man's mind, but sir, the truth will come out."

The bishop was horrified and paled when told Magdalen was in an interview room with his nephew. "My God, is someone in there with her?" And there it was, he knew what Bernardo could do and had done and now feared for his sacristan.

Magdalen had finally entered the room where Bernardo lay curled up in a ball; he unraveled and quickly stood up. Two hours of verbal cat and mouse would ensue. Magdalen would say later, criminologists would use his psychopathy in their textbooks for ages to come. His absolute joy at seeing her made it easy to tell her everything regardless of what she might suffer in hearing it. It was clear he viewed this time with her as a social occasion. Evidently, Bernardo didn't have many of those. He even drew Marcus, standing behind him, into the conversation. "I saw you in the garden one night, when my sister and I were good and stayed home."

Magdalen saw her lead in. "But what do you do when you're *not* good?"

"I martyr."

His directness stunned even Padric now in front of a monitor. Bernardo explained what they already surmised: he charted his kills based on the moon cycle. Each was scripted on what he read in his brother's martyrologies. It had to be right.

But he digressed: "It wasn't all good though. Sis kissed me like…like I was her lover."

"And you are her brother." *But what would he do if he knew she was his mother?*

"You understand then."

"I do and I'm sorry." She urged him to continue: would he "martyr" again; he said yes…it was the right thing to do though he'd tried to stop. He turned pale, became confused when Magdalen inquired: "But if it's right, then why do you want to stop?"

"It hurts not to, when I know I must." Startled by his words, she asked if he wanted to rest for a moment. "Oh, no, you are my rest, Magdalen."

Padric frowned…the lad was dangerous and sick; it made him uneasy. Magdalen remained stoic, unmoved, though Marcus stepped closer. Unprompted, he rattled on, admitting to screaming sometimes at night because it felt good; sharing with her his murderous plans, but gave no names of potential targets. When he put his head down on the table; Magdalen quickly glanced into the camera lens high on the wall. She knew Padric was watching, her eyes speaking to him. She was in pain, finished here.

But suddenly the young man straightened…he'd seen her two nights ago when he'd "visited" the convent, he said. "Your hand is bandaged; your face bruised. Did I do that?"

"You were violent, did horrible things, but your sister is the one who did this to me?" He flew into a rage like he had in the graveyard when Padric told him the same. "I must kill her."

"Bernardo, that's not the way. I will speak with her soon."

"She's…I don't want you talking to her. I can't picture you doing anything with Joanna." Padric couldn't either. But Bernardo was fixated now on what he'd done in the convent.

Magdalen took a deep breath; preparing herself for what was to come…her painkillers were wearing off. Slowly, methodically, he explained every detail and how excited he'd been about this one, the unusually heinous martyrdom of Saint Lucy, how eager he'd been to replicate it in a nun who happened to bear her name.

Marcus glanced up at the camera. Padric saw it…something was happening. *Magdalen. If this fool continues, she'll be reliving the whole thing.* He'd get her out of there but stopped when he heard her say: "You may tell me about this if you like, Bernardo. I imagine breaching the convent was a high point for you in what you were trying to do for the bishop."

"Yes…you understand then…it was perfect, you know, among all those lilies of the field Jesus talks about in the Bible." Detectives at the monitors winced.

Magdalen visualized how she might kill him.

Bernardo spoke as if in a trance. Entry into the convent had been complicated. The door at the top of the stairs had slowed them down and then, there had been all those nuns getting in the middle of it and fussing about. Marcus and Magdalen glanced at each other; he, speaking to her with his wise-for-his-years eyes, trying to comfort her, she nodding ever so slightly. She'd let Bernardo's grave inner sickness shout to the world, seal the case against him and his mother. He was more animated now; talking about the set of tools he had used in the lock to gain access when they finally reached the second floor. A practiced master of locksport, he could open any door closed to him and had pulled from a narrow leather fold, a bump key; trying it then choosing a hook-pick and snake-rake as well. He had worked at it slowly with hardly a sound and the double round pick, after one or two tries, finally allowed them to slip silently into the upstairs hall.

He described the assault. With hoods drawn over their faces, they checked the knives in their cinctures and stepped into the upstairs chapel; it was smaller than he remembered.

"And how did you know Sister would be there that night?"

His answer was as she suspected. The schedule of those who held nightly prayer vigils had been innocently posted on a bulletin board in the sacristy; as he roamed about in the Cathedral at night, his obsession made him take note of the nuns with martyrs' names. In his mind, he was back in the crime scene and described the smallest detail, the sanctuary lamp burning quietly on the chapel altar; a nun with head bowed in prayer and seated quite close to the altar. They had swooped down on her but she was quick and eluded them down the side aisle.

Leaping over the pews, Bernardo caught up with her; Joanna grabbed her veil. Both pulled her down. Stunned but not unconscious, Lucy knew and felt all that happened her; he described the crudely performed enucleation he had rehearsed over and over, the removal of just the one eye but wanting both. When Bernardo unceremoniously announced he consumed the nun's eye like the Eucharist, Marcus moved slightly. Magdalen did not; though sickened, she begged God to save this forgotten, lost soul. She could not rescue him. Even O'Manion gasped and again Padric cursed; he was beside himself that the nun should be hearing such things. Tark rarely ruffled by anything stared at the monitor; the confession had been brutally graphic and wore on even the most seasoned.

And then it was over; Bernardo, himself emotionally drained from the telling, could no longer look at the nun, her green eyes, sad. He was oddly detached and even more shocking were his words to Magdalen: "You can go now."

Padric punched the wall; with fist bleeding he left the room. Magdalen rose from her chair and opened the door with a few parting words: "There is a world beyond the small one you live in, Bernardo. You will come face to face with it very soon. God help you."

Silence.

Bernardo finally turned to Marcus. "So what's next?" He was done with her.

Trembling and feeling violated, she stepped into the hall, not knowing which way to turn. Marcus would watch Bernardo write his statement in the most painstaking manner, careful to leave nothing unsaid. Still outside the door, Magdalen pressed her back to the wall leaning like Padric had done more than once after an interview.

He was suddenly there, his hand wrapped in gauze holding hers. She looked like she'd seen a ghost. Padric pointed toward his office and thanked her, but she was troubled. "How do you do this?"

"Just like you did...you were terrific and got that sicko to talk."

"Then why am I not feeling better?" Had she tricked him?

"Wait a minute. You think you pulled one over on him?" She looked down at the floor. "Think what he did to the victims, your Sisters, those good men."

But in another interview room and in sync with her son, Joanna had given her take on Lucy's demise to Martinez. She spoke in a loud careless drone not caring if anyone heard her or not: "I felt suicidal and wanted to end it; blamed myself for what he'd done to this nun and the others. I blamed my mother; she's a crazy woman, took him from me, sent me away." Suddenly changed, her voice fell to a whisper. She sobbed but quickly regained control of herself.

"There in that chapel, I even thought of…of telling him to slit my throat quickly with that precision he has about things. Where better to leave this fucked-up world than in such a beautiful place…the nuns, I had hurt them."

Her mood changed again. She reverted back to what she had seen in the tunnel. "The nun…the one I told you I hate, this Magdalen, I need to tell you…she tried to help me, put her arm around me like a mother; I should have…I didn't…" She had tears in her eyes. "But it scared me, the wings, the light. She's an angel, you know. I'm not sure what kind…they can be evil." Her words drifted off and returned. "She might have been there for me if I'd let her." Her face had softened, the look in her eyes somewhere else. The admissions of guilt ended.

Martinez frowned, told her to write down her statement and left the room…from this day, the detective would look at the nun differently; she was more than a dedicated, good woman. He joined the two as they stood in the office door. In whispers, they discussed what they had learned and turned when another door opened.

Two uniforms were leading Bernardo away to his cell. He glanced back without expression as though he knew none of them. Marcus approached. "He and his mother are being formally charged. It's late now; they'll be arraigned in the morning but we made it and came in under the wire. And get this, Bernardo asked for a lawyer."

They were flabbergasted; the one they thought who had no common sense had gone over the head of his grandfather. Padric nodded: "An interesting move considering all we've heard from the lot of them. He may not be as daft as we think."

But Magdalen wondered who the attorney might be. They were equally stunned when Marcus said Bernardo had written his victims would go to heaven; this was their reward…he just gave it to them faster. Padric told Magdalen the bishop had asked for her as well. He was uneasy, not happy about it; the man could wait.

"Let him sizzle."

"What are these words you use to describe this interrogation process?" She smiled. "When you question your suspects you *grill* them. If you leave them to sit and think, you want them to *marinate*; you let them *stew*. If they're found worthy of death, they *burn* or *fry*. We make them *eat* their words. As an advocate, I've had my share of courtrooms before I came to L'Arroyo; judges scold when attorneys *regurgitate* their facts or reach their *boiling point*. Does all this sound familiar?" They chuckled. Padric said he wished he had said it.

But now Magdalen and Padric were suddenly alone and she admitted she found it troubling that not one but two Cantera men had asked for her. "I don't know what I did to deserve this."

"I don't like it but why not…I'd want you with me, too. You're good to be around."

She glanced at him, looked away. "Thank you for saying that."

"It was inappropriate. I do that with you." But feeling the need for some comfort in all this chaos, she had to admit he was good to be around, too. She smiled a little and shared something else; it had haunted her from the moment she'd arrived at the Precinct.

"This day belongs to my Sister Petra…I cannot get her out of my mind. She was so full of life; I wish she was here with us now to speak for herself."

"She is…she can do that." It was time…*it's over*. He could say it…*the Canteras are in custody, their victims could come out of hiding*.

Magdalen's eyes widened. *What had he said? She is…Petra exists; she lives…where? Is this what he was saying?*

He told her how Tark and Marcus had found Ramos and that he, too, with Petra was recovering at Meadow. The news was too sudden, too much, with all she had endured that day and she swayed, almost losing her balance, reaching for anything to steady her. Padric offered his hand and drew her into his office; she leaned on him for a moment. "I'm good; I'm okay…my God, is it true?"

"Sister, she made it…fought her way back; the EMT and your friend, Father Sebastian, were there in the van with me on the way to the morgue when she opened her eyes…it scared the hell out of me. She even scolded me; told me I must behave. But we were all bound by silence. If the Canteras knew, they'd have been looking to finish her. We know now she saw their faces; she finally ID'd them. It took her a while but she finally told us. Our Detective Marcus spent a lot of time with her...I assigned him to her." Magdalen smiled. But her parents, she wanted to know. "They're good people...they've wanted to speak with all of you, but they did as we asked and are living at Meadow in a guest suite on the top floor."

"How perfect. Sister told me they are retired physicians. And of course, of course, you were right keeping this quiet." She stepped back and looked down at the floor.

"But?"

"Damn you!" *What?* "Damn you, Detective." *She better not take a swing at me. I'm not in the mood.* "Forgive me, but you kept this from me! I was working with you." *She's yelling at me in a whisper. Sister Moira used to do this to me when I acted up in church.* "You, you, my friend, putting me through this; you could not have told me?" With head down, the nun slowly paced back and forth. His wife had often done this; he knew the drill. He'd wait.

She stopped, apologized and he smiled, then told her the nuns had scolded him often, but not with her style. She didn't care. "I wouldn't have pushed you so to resolve her case. You trusted me so little...the one you have..." *Come on, woman, finish the sentence.* She hesitated. "I...I...the one you have cared for so much. My God, I shouldn't be saying this, but you've said it a thousand different ways, how much you..."

John Garfield would have grabbed her and kissed her by now. "How much what?"

"Perhaps I read more into the things you were saying, little things, the innuendo...the..."

"I don't do innuendo." *There, damn it...that sounded like John Garfield.*

Author's Notes

The 300 – refers to a 2006 American epic fantasy war film based on 1998 comic series of the same name; it is a fictionalized retelling of the Battle of Thermopylae during the Persian Wars and filmed mostly with a super-imposition chroma key technique to replicate the imagery of the original comic book. King Leonidas leads 300 Spartans into battle against the "god-king" Xerxes and a 300,000-man army. A voice-over narrative by a Spartan soldier and a crowd of fantasy creatures places 300 in the genre of historical fantasy.

Johnny Walker Double Black Label – *Padric backtracks for a moment and compares in a moment of weakness, his ex-lover to "the intense blend and iconic flavors" of Johnnie Walker Black Label, as claimed in its ads,"heavily charred with a greater emphasis on smoke while keeping true to the sophisticated whiskey of unprecedented boldness." Does this sound like the inimical Joanna?*

Muchacho – *Spanish, for young man.*

chupacabra – *reference to literally a "goat-sucker" and legendary creature of Latin America thought first sighted in Puerto Rico; not scientifically recorded, an animal said to kill animals in Puerto Rico, Miami, Nicaragua, Chile, and Mexico. The origin of its name draws on the supposed discovery of puncture wounds in their necks of dead goats, their blood drained from their bodies. According to UFO Magazine (March/April 1996) there have been more than 2,000 reported cases of animal mutilations in Puerto Rico by chupacabra. Researchers believe the chupacabra may be an imagining based on the alien/human hybrid creature in 1995 film Species.*

un santo ángel – *Spanish, for a holy angel.*

John Garfield (1913-1952) – *American actor known for his roles playing brooding, rebellious, working-class characters; he was spontaneous, his acting, full of abandon. Someone said he didn't recite dialogue...he attacked it. Garfield was quite animated, agile on screen; his appearance, powerful, sensual. He loved the ladies, they him. He is John Padric's favorite actor; the detective, a devotee of film noir, old crime dramas in black and white.*

30 A SMALL CONVERSATION

Magdalen glanced at her watch…she would have to end this but how does one explain something like this? "I meant you are so…so forthright." *Forthright, is it. Alex calls it pushy.* "You are spontaneous." *But that's good, isn't it?* "You speak from your heart, and are so sincere. I know you don't wish to make me uncomfortable and I wasn't, but it has been frustrating…a little. Detective, you know I cannot respond to your feelings."

She was struggling…there were tears in her eyes. He had not meant to do this. "I'm sorry, Sister…damn, I shouldn't be saying this. Bloody hell! I work night and day and there you were walking into my life. You're a nun, for God's sake, a good woman and I'm not a good man and, damn it, I love you." *Shit.*

She was horrified but for only a moment, allowing herself the comfort of his words but then came the guilt…*what did I do to encourage him?* Surely she was at fault though she'd not lost her way or her focus on the Life, never carried on a flirtation. But she'd been distracted by the case, its mystery, her association with the detectives, relying on them…on him.

As usual, Padric was reading her; he'd put her here and would need to help her out of an awkward conversation. "I've done wrong here; I've made you uneasy but this thing I've got for you is on me. You did nothing to encourage this and I'm thinking that worries you. You were being you; it was beautiful." He paused. "I needed to be around someone like you and, damn it, you'll always be brand new to me every time I see you." *What the…what?*

"You must stop this. Your Lara, think of Lara…"

"I love Lara even when I'm hating her and she's hating me now. The woman despises me. But you…." He sighed and looked down at the floor…he'd need to close. "In some other lifetime, I'd…I'd never let anything hurt you. All this shit I let happen to you will haunt me the rest of my life. If I'd met you somewhere else at some other time, I'd have fallen all over myself loving you. I'd taken care of you." *Damn, this isn't right.*

She placed her finger on his lips. "Thank you, John Padric…I'll cherish all this in my heart; please know your words are not wasted on me." He knew this was all she could say and could never fully respond. He listened. "You have a wife. I have my Lord. We will move on now and walk away from all this." But she wasn't herself and so tired, her resistance low; she wished she could stay for a while here, wanting to feel his embrace and be loved by this man.

He would try to be appropriate…*whatever.* He heard himself saying: "Absolutely, we'll move on, yes." *Like hell…I want the world to stop, keep her here. Close the door for five hours.* "I'll take you to see Sister Petra now that we have the Canteras in custody. The charges will stick; we're making sure of that." He guided her to a chair and sat down beside her.

She thanked him but would defer to the elder and Sister Agnes. "They must see her first…though I want to drag Sister Dolorosa out of here and run right over to Meadow." They laughed but she looked away. "I should have known. I felt her touch my face one night as I was falling asleep."

He was grateful she'd changed the subject. "You see things that I can't, Sister. I'm sorry you've suffered. But for now, not a word to anyone." He kissed her cheek, knowing she'd not require an apology.

But she was frowning now, searching his face. "What aren't you saying? Tell me…you are sad."

His heart was bursting with his own story. "You want the low down version, Sister?"

"I can take low down if it helps you make your point."

"She's leaving me, wants nothing to do with me…it's over. My Lara knows it was Joanna Cantera I was fucking; no wife in the city can handle that kind of news. I was fucking her in the Nile before I saw Brother James fall to his death and again, before I went home and found my wife almost dead. Joanna left the room first that night and got there ahead of me with her freak son. She did a job on my woman. A low-life detective, who shouldn't have been working her case, dropped his own interpretation of all this on my wife. It put me in the middle and she flipped. He said Joanna and I wanted her dead and came to the house to kill her…it was the last straw."

"Johnny, you must get her back."

"Ah, Sister, I'm weary of working on it; how do I do it?"

"I will be low down with you." *I'm liking the sound of that… hit me.* "I've said this before: when is the last time you made love to your wife?"

He gave her one of his slow smiles. "Damn, Sister,"

"Answer please." She was serious; it was academic, a reasonable question.

"I don't remember…January; it was months ago maybe at Christmas, I think. I'd met Joanna." He took a deep breath. "We rarely spoke after that, saw her even less. Never knew she was pregnant…as far as I know, she gave birth prematurely while in surgery after the assault. She blocked everything out, doesn't know if she delivered or miscarried…or so she says. Then she lays on me she wouldn't let anyone on staff tell me about it. This alone killed me; I know these people well and they said nothing; her state so fragile they didn't push it and called Father Seamus. He took care of things, she said. Things, damn it!"

Padric stood up, stared at the floor but was suddenly calm, his voice softer; there was a look in his eyes like she'd seen moments ago when he told her he loved her. "Last night I saw him…my son. The nuns at the Abbey are caring for him, keeping him alive for me. He's safe with them."

"He's with the Sisters of Saint Uriel? How blessed you are; you have a baby, a boy?" She was ecstatic. Padric was grateful but surprised at how happy she was. "There is a baby," she whispered. Her eyes filled with tears. "But how perfect!!"

Ah, lass, if you only knew…things are not perfect. "You think so."

"Oh, yes…your boy is being cared for by those beautiful nuns." She had always wanted to make a private retreat there, as was the Sisters' custom twice a year. "Tell me everything." He loved her soft voice.

Padric sat down. "He had no name…my son had no name for a whole month and I didn't know it. Finn, Finn Shakespeare will be his name. He's a fighter." He said how he'd spent time with the boy and would be spending every waking hour with him when not with his girls or down at the Precinct. "When Lara told me she was leaving, she used the lad, the fact that I had a son and he was gone. I'd never see him. Payback's a bitch when you're on the receiving end."

"But surely Lara and you…"

"She's not coming back…she's been grieving alone; says it's on me and obsessed with the thought of me and Joanna Cantera together. But I have my boy. He's alive and beautiful. Finn. Finn Shakespeare Alejandro Padric, he is. We talked…he and I."

This time it was Magdalen who impulsively pulled Padric to her…he had tears in his eyes and she kissed them away, pressing her lips to his face, whispering her care and concern for him. She promised her prayers for his child. Having so often visualized what it might be like to feel her lips, just one of her kisses, he drew her to him; both were holding on to more than each other…this world they were in was pulling them under.

"Detective, you are blessed and must go now again to your boy." She drew from her pocket a clean, white handkerchief and wiped new tears that flowed down his cheeks…*nuns, they always had those back in Belfast. Sister Moira.* "Can you not see Lara is in a deep depression…how much can she endure, you, lost to her and a baby damaged by the woman who took her husband?"

But Padric could only think of Magdalen's lips, her soft ways with him…he'd live for years with the memory of it. A nun, a real nun, an angel maybe, had kissed him…were Joanna's ravings about Magdalen more right than wrong?

He needed to know. "Are you an angel, luv?" He explained.

She was stunned when she learned what Joanna had said to him and his partner; she couldn't tell him she was questioning it, too. But yes, she had been graced by something sacred she still didn't trust…was it all an unholy delusion? She believed in evil, the personification of it in Satan, understood it to be a real entity especially here in the desert where the supernatural took many forms.

Was this a deeper calling for her? She could hardly speak. "Some of us, more than others, are placed here to work a little redemption in others. What do you think?" *How the hell would I know and what had she said…did she ever answer my question? Was that a yes or a no?* "No more tears now." She kissed his cheek. "If well-intentioned, the kiss can be a healing thing. I want that for you." He wanted more kisses, to stay with her here.

He'd chance it: "Could we do this once and a while?"

She shook her head. The priest had jokingly said the same when she'd kissed his forehead in the hospital. These men were dear to her but she'd end this. "Come we must go now. Perhaps I could speak with Lara."

"And you will kiss her and heal her? My wife lives with hatreds she never had. I'm in mourning for her, but hating her for what she did to my boy though I deserve worse."

"This is not Lara…it's the side effects of her medications coupled with the trauma of her attack. But something else needs to be said: your choice of a lover, dear man. What in God's name were you thinking? You feed on danger and I get it, but this must stop in your personal life. You are meant to be with Lara…go to her." But within, Magdalen was questioning everything…was he really? How could she know such things, but she'd say it. "You must heal her with your own kisses and she will do this for you. Couples must do this. She starves for you."

"And what do you starve for?"

"This isn't about me. You worry too much, wanting some kind of better life for me. I'm not alone, Johnny, ever. I live with Christ and am happy, frustrated by things sometimes, but really quite at peace. In another place, years ago, I to was loved and loved back, perhaps more than I should." She looked away; he waited. "A place like Egypt can do that to a woman." He wished he had been there and been the one she had loved too much. "You will be my friend always…your son will be, too." *My son*…and this would prove to be true.

"I'll take you to him…you must bless him, kiss his face."

But she said there was something she wanted. Anything, he said; she could ask anything. It was said humbly…could she hold his son; perhaps sit with him if Lara would allow it. She would go to the abbey until he was strong enough to come home.

"Lara has nothing to say in the matter. You must kiss his face… he's been alone without family and will suffer for it. I knew it when I laid eyes on him…he was waiting for me. I'll take you there after I bring my sister to see him; she's aching inside and suffers her own pain. My mum is beside herself, furious at me yet wanting this child beside her to take care of forever. You will meet them. But tell me; there's something you don't say; someone has hurt you."

Not today, dear friend, don't go there…someday I'll tell you everything, maybe; no. Never. He took her hands in his, kissed them. "Tell me, if not now, some day tell me what's hurting you so I can fix it. I can't patch up my own life but I do this for just about everyone else in this fucking town."

But, dear man, you can't fix this ever; you can't make it better. "And what else, John Padric?"

Now what…I don't like it when the personal turns in on me. Should I say it…ah, fuck it. "Let me hold you once and a while." *Don't tempt me…beautiful, intense, terrifying man.* "A woman like you needs to be taken care of." *Taken care of…by him? I'd be in serious trouble and he would be, too. I'd want to keep him forever. And what's that he said? A woman like me…back in the day, I heard this more than once. Stay the course, Magdalen.* He realized what he had said. She was smiling a little but shaking her head…*thank God she's smiling.* "I'm sorry…you've got me saying things to a nun I thought I never would." *Sister Moira…she'd knock my ass into a corner.*

"You want to hold me…" She looked away. She could hear Dolorosa saying: *Get out of this, sistah-girl…Dolorosa called her this. I wonder what she'd have to say about this?* But with all that had happened since she arrived in L'Arroyo, Magdalen wanted to sit here forever with him. She thought for a moment. "That would be lovely but not in the cards for either of us. I've been indiscreet with you, a man who has seen and done everything."

He was all that and liked indiscreet. *But my nun, when was she indiscreet?* "Never say that, Sister…you're a good woman and I don't make it easy for you, my apologies."

She suddenly covered her face with her hands and shook her head slowly. "I thought I could never say this but you…you have seen me, shall we say, compromised, undressed. It has bothered me so…" Her voice trailed off.

He would ease her discomfort and looked down at the floor. "Oh, that…not another word, lass. I've seen many a woman in the state of undress, dead or alive, for better or worse, up close because I wanted it or not. You know my sins, but what happened down there in that grave is between us and a dog named Nevel…we are friends and you're a luv…no worries. We'll think no more about it." But the gentleman had lied: he would remember her there more than he should.

After a conversation he'd never forget, he'd do what it takes. He'd make his life better; but he felt like he was fifteen. He kissed her hand again and later at home in the loft, while his girls slept beside him, he closed his eyes, felt her lips on his face and didn't feel guilty at all.

But in pouring his heart out to her, he'd unwittingly burdened the woman. Magdalen was left to struggle sometimes as she worked alone in the sacristy, hearing his words of affection; words men say, words that shouldn't be there to distract a nun, but he'd never know that and she'd never say and move on. Magdalen would struggle to forget his embrace and the passion she heard in his voice; the nun asked God for His understanding and knew He was listening.

Waiting in an interview room at the end of the hall, they would be shaken quickly into reality; Bishop Cantera rose from his seat when he saw her; he pointed to a chair, obviously seeing time spent at the First Precinct as an opportunity to hold court. Magdalen was embarrassed. "Your grace, please sit. You asked for me?"

"I did. We must speak of these unfortunate deaths."

"The deaths of my Sisters were more than unfortunate."

He sipped his coffee. "And why is my being here so important to you?" Silence.

He saw the bruises and frowned. "You are well then despite what befell you?"

"Your grace, I have not come for tea." The bishop was treating her presence too lightly; was she simply here for a chat? The nun wasn't finished: "I've suffered at the hands of your sister; I will heal. Others too suffered." Cold words.

He did not know she, too, had been a victim; the bishop had been given few details; she'd give him an update and describe in hard, jagged, well-chosen words, Joanna's relentless obsessions; the insidious pathology destroying the heart of his nephew.

She would punctuate her remarks: "And what is this about a home you have prepared for him in a mausoleum?"

She expected an answer.

31 HIS GRACE

The bishop was known for his wisdom and kindness when counseling a soul, he was a man of unusual insight. This conversation would be disturbing at best; the nuns question could wait. "Ah, in due time, I will explain all...you will have lunch at my residence. We will talk. But for now, this man wishes me to say I have knowledge of something. I wanted you here."

"And I am; so what is it then?" The nun no longer had time for the niceties.

"Sister?"

"Your grace, what did you know and when?"

"I see. Detective Padric has asked me the same."

"And how did you answer?"

Padric wanted to throw things. "You asked for the nun and she's here. Answer."

"You ask what I knew..." Now they both wanted to scream; whether intentional or not, he would play them for over an hour, telling them nothing, sounding pastoral at times then full of rage.

Magdalen would stir the pot. "Joanna is a great discomfort to you, isn't she?"

Discomfort. The bishop buried his head in his hands. "Joanna then...she has no morals, and has squandered the gold in her soul." Sounding like one of his homilies, he insisted Joanna had no viciousness in her but simply fell in love and in bed with men, lots of them. For an instant he looked at Padric who glared back at him.

"In truth, she is a magnanimous woman, known in the city as

generous and kind despite all her fooling around at night and those clubs, *Dios mio,* the places she goes. But no, this is not our Joanna; the death of these so-called martyrs just isn't her style." He was separating her from the crimes. "She wouldn't put in the time, do the research to pull off things of this magnitude." The detectives had said the same. "These foul deeds were murderous acts, too well thought through…the symbolism alone too intricate. There is no one else I can think of and certainly it wasn't the boy. He is an innocent. Never. I will never…" He was growing more agitated. "I know my sister and nephew have admitted to things, but it is all rubbish and fantasy. They love the drama."

He's not getting it. I need to hurt him. Padric was livid. "They never invoked, asked for no counsel. Court-appointed attorneys, big names, some you know, the best defense in the state, came forward and were told to get lost."

"My father will not allow it. We are Canteras. It is our tradition to stand alone. I am here; that is enough."

Magdalen leaned forward, hoping to reach him. Had they not spoken together in a personal way two days ago after the Baccalaureate Mass. "Apparently not, Your grace. Bernardo and Joanna have been charged and you are sitting here being questioned."

Hard realities and a face-off with the First Precinct did not rest easy with the bishop; seemingly, all he had done for years to rescue these two had been for naught. "I've served L'Arroyo for years and am part of its civic life, a shepherd of souls. The name Cantera carries weight in this town."

He claimed they too were martyrs, persecuted by the First Precinct. But even his parishioners, his devotees, were asking how much he knew. He turned to Padric. "Your captain has informed me it was Joanna who attacked your wife and left her for dead. Sir, I cannot apologize enough to you and your children."

"Why would you feel the need if your family is innocent?"

The bishop was being backed into a corner but he would not disappoint: "Surely if she did all this, she had you in mind."

The ungracious remark was not lost on Magdalen.

The bishop would cast attention away from himself and Bernardo; he'd slam this arrogant detective who had sinned with his sister. Before Padric could respond, the man raised his hand.

"No need, no need…things happen and by saying that, you are not excused. But know I can no longer dissuade her from what she may do to you, Detective. Once she has sunk her teeth into you, you are hers." *No worries, bishop…I'll kill her. I almost did in the Nile and within seconds of snapping her neck but my man and my heart, Alex, stepped in; he does that. You can thank him.* "There are others, men in high places still under her spell. My father knows…I know."

Another homily rendered, but he'd pointed to where the Cantera power lay: the bishop, in the confessional, sacred or not, and his father, the silent partner of anyone making moves on the chess board in L'Arroyo; they knew things. And *what* they knew exacted a silent blackmail without uttering a threat. Had the bishop not made it clear to Padric he knew of his sins with his sister and she, a prime suspect? He could ruin the case; but what he was doing could also be construed as intimidation. The bishop wasn't finished. "Pay heed…she is a hauntress." *Hauntress.*

Padric, unamused turned into stone; Magdalen's face, white with rage. She would scold him for deflecting the focus from the crimes of his family by casting the detective in a bad light. Again she asked: "If you had the slightest suspicion about your nephew or sister, why did you not share this with the police?"

"I could not wrap my mind around it and really had no suspicions. You have hurt me."

"And you disappoint me." Silence. She wondered how much this might change her life at San Miguel. *He will not let my comments rest, God help me.*

He now spoke with the last crumb of authority he could muster: "I'm finished here and hope this is satisfactory. I'm not being charged and should never have been subjected to this."

Oddly, he could have left if he wished and had not; now he would bring up another issue. "And what of my sister's activity in the Edge, these death-sex films? *Dios mio,* the work of Satan. Stop her. You must do this for all of our sakes."

"That's for another day. But how did you learn of this?"

"A priest." Padric's eyes gave away some surprise. "Ah, there is something about which the lieutenant has no knowledge. It is one of the most powerful networks in the Sonoran. Priests…they have knowledge of many things; we are a brotherhood. The poor, the rich, angels and demons under human guise, speak to us. We hear things; NORAD has nothing on us."

Magdalen wondered if now she was among them. "You say, with other priests, you are in the know about many things, then why did none of you step forward to assist with this investigation? Or is all this hidden comfortably under the usual confidentiality that allows bad things to continue? You abhor these deaths; so I ask: what kept you from stopping this?"

"You speak against the Church?"

"Only out of frustration." Magdalen despite some passing suspicions had never thought the bishop to be a dangerous man; in fact, he was generally quite down to earth and well meaning; the mystery she saw swirling around him lay in his attempts to care for and keep afloat a family imploding into itself; even his father with all his dealings on either side of the Border worried him. Later she would observe with the elder that Santo Cantera apparently operated on two moral playing fields; ministering first and foremost to his people with integrity and the other, within the code of Cantera, acting in desperation to keep his family afloat, a burden far greater than overseeing a diocese.

Padric would again ignite a smoldering issue. "We will further investigate the living conditions under which we found your nephew. Don't leave town."

The bishop went off on the detective…those listening were numb. "And they were getting along so well," muttered Martinez. Tark laughed but he was studying Santo Cantera.

He had turned his venom on Magdalen. "And you, these law enforcement types have rubbed off on you. You sound like one of them." Padric wanted to up end him. "I will suggest to your superiors you have no further contact with the First Precinct."

Could this overblown cleric do this? He couldn't bear losing her nor could Martinez, who walked away from the monitors, cursing in Spanish. Tark remained calm. "Steady, he's pulling her chain."

Or was the man something else…not overblown, but humiliated and in a very bad spot. Deep inside, Padric had admired his love for the poor and if he wanted to be honest about it, understood his outrage at what he had done with his sister. *Familia*…he got it. But Magdalen had expected something like this might happen once she stepped into the public arena.

The Captain was grunting. "This is over. He goes; the nun stays." It sounded eerily like Clemenza's "leave the gun…take the *connoli*" which, according to Jana Zalconi, was incorrectly spoken. "He should have said take the *cannola*, using the plural. There was more than one pastry." Nothing got passed her; they had laughed.

Magdalen turned to Padric. "The bishop is not being charged. Is there anything else?"

"You first, Sister."

"I am compelled to say this." Padric smiled a little; the bishop had set her off. "You were horrified by the deaths of the first three victims, a priest, a brother, my Sister; but when another, Sister Petra, was murdered so near to where Bernardo lived below, you may have considered this might be his work yet you remained silent. And Joanna, she is such a kind, generous girl…how could she?"

"Sister…"

"*Silencio.*" Padric was uneasy…*could she say this to him?* "We now know that in fact, it *was* Bernardo who called the plays, sadly deluded into thinking he would surprise you with dead martyrs."

"Again, Sister, my nephew and his mother did not do these things; Joanna has drawn her son into her drama and…"

"And she is a kind, generous woman…I know."

"Your tone, the sarcasm…you are sounding like this obnoxious lieutenant who has had an illicit, sordid affair with my insufferable, depraved sister. He is a degenerate as is she."

"But she is a kind, generous woman." Magdalen wished she had a seat belt when the bishop suddenly stood up to make a point.

He said she had proved to be a huge disappointment. "Sister, shame on you for allowing these people to see me in such a poor light. You were devoted to me and an integral part of San Miguel." *Past tense*. Padric was a stickler for grammar. *Was the bishop dismissing their nun, sending her packing?* "You knew the intent of my homilies, yet you allowed these detectives to believe I encouraged Bernardo and Joanna to create martyrs for some delusional cause they thought I had. You were no help, none at all."

O'Manion was muttering things. "Son-of-a-bitch, we sent her into the lion's den." Tark assured him she could handle herself but Padric was glaring up at the camera.

"Our boy's pissed though...watch out."

The bishop was on a roll. "I will consider having you reassigned, Sister." *Could he do that?* "You have busied yourself in things unbecoming and vowed religious." Padric's mind drifted back to his office...*well, yes, the nun had kissed him a few times; it had been most becoming and beautiful but that's something my man Shakes' might have said.*

All eyes were on Magdalen when she responded: "The Cantera loyalty is fierce but your stepping forward may have given these men no need to have me on board. I did so with Sister Petra's blessing; the detectives witnessed her telling me to accompany them, to consult with them on the case. I was impulsive wanting to put an end to this madness after our convent fell under attack. I followed the detectives below into your graveyard. that's what it is, isn't it? I had done this without their knowledge to confront those who murdered my Sister Lucy. I came face to face with your sister, Joanna, and ended up looking like this." She stood up. "But did you not say she was a kind, generous woman?"

What was she doing? Even Padric was unnerved. Silently and with tears in her eyes, Magdalen slowly removed her veil revealing more serious bruises as she drew back her linens. She had been here at the Precinct too long; her face pale. *A beautiful lass, but damn, I need to save her from this.* Padric was suddenly helpless; her green eyes were filled with pain now. He could stand it no longer and rose to his feet, reaching out to her.

She raised her hand. "Thank you, Detective...let me finish." She sighed deeply. The two men waited. "I am embarrassed but, Your grace, what more can I do to show you your family's misdeeds...will you at some point accept Joanna's part in all this or have you known and in a hard place at the moment? She did this to me. It is difficult to be in denial…you are no different than us. We suffer this, too."

The bishop lowered his eyes not to offend and told her he understood. Again she said: "Your sister did this to me."

He finally nodded. Padric looked down at the floor. His ex-lover had done this to her. Those at the monitors were uneasy. Ramirez would give this some closure. He had never allowed his Precinct to be turned upside down by anyone. The Canteras had attempted to do this. He stepped into the hall and walked toward the interview room but not before opening the door to Padric's office and asking Dolorosa to join him. She had been watching a monitor Padric had failed to turn off on his desk and had seen everything.

Frantic for Magdalen, she scolded the Commander in Spanish, cursing the system, wanting to settle the Cantera's collective ass.

The man called *La Roca* smiled. "Follow me, *buena hermanita.*"

She glared up at him. "Commander, I am not little."

He looked down at her. "But you are good, *si?*"

"At most things."

"Ah, then I *am* right."

Dolorosa would have the last word; "This time."

Ramirez chuckled. She followed, not smiling at all; he didn't knock; both entered the interview room. He approached Magdalen slowly. "*Hermana, por favor*, may I be of help here?" He was whispering. Magdalen did not turn her head…she knew his voice. She'd always liked it when men whispered…a man needed to think before he did such a thing; he'd need a good reason or why speak softly at all?

Here she stood in their midst like Joan of Arc or more like Cosette in *Les Miserables* and feeling like she'd been over-dramatic. "You are most kind, sir, but you will allow me to finish, *por favor.*" She had not taken her eyes off the bishop. "Your grace, look at me." The bishop would not. "I said look at me."

Santo Cantera reluctantly raised his eyes. "My God, Sister, what is it, what else?"

"I am your sacristan, a Sister assigned to your parish and serve at your request and you are a good man. But your attempt to distract is troubling, Your grace. You have invited me here to validate your publicly shredding a man for his personal morality or lack thereof, I refuse. And now you are vowing to rid yourself of me as soon as you return to your house. You know all this is recorded; nothing is *sacro-sanct* here."

Sacro-sanct. The wordsmith in Padric liked the word; he would need to borrow her material. But suddenly he was in the thick of it again and the bishop was changing lanes, removing himself from an uncomfortable conversation. "Damn it, man, you irritate me to no end."

"Yeah, I get that a lot." But Magdalen asked if he had heard anything she had said.

"Sister, I am talking to the detective." He turned again to Padric. "You have had the consummate nerve to bring this nun in here when this is how she acts?"

He's burying her…I'll drop him. "Stop talking about our nun like she's not here."

"*Your* nun." This would be a game changer. "I see."

"You see shit. You requested her presence; I'm not her da'."

"I have no interest in your thoughts on all this…what a waste."

"There! You're doing it again."

Ramirez had been silent, "John."

"Sir, allow me to finish…too much has been said here."

"Wrap it up, Lieutenant."

"You have the irritating habit of manipulating the narrative to suit your whim, bishop." What? O'Manion groaned.

Tark loved it. "Come on, Cap', we see it all the time…a fool's in the hot seat and he doesn't like what we're asking then tries to shut us down by taking the talking points sideways."

The bishop hissed: "I will not forget that you sinned with a member of my family! You are a miscreant from the Tower of Babel. Be gone, Satan…now!"

Pure theater, Old Testament maybe but definitely Sister Moira; fuck this! Padric slammed his fist on the table. "You're in my house now and I'm staying."

The Captain grunted again. "Now it's his house?" Tark laughed. But O'Manion was livid. "She's hurting, damn it. Get her out of there."

"Bishop?" *La Roca* sent Padric a look…he was done.

"Commander Ramirez…the voice of reason I hope. I have a nun undressing herself and a lieutenant who plays at his job and shows me no respect. How will you handle this?"

The Commander drew Magdalen aside where Dolorosa was waiting. "Thank you for your assist and my apologies for all you and your Sisters have suffered. You are a good and brave woman and we hope your superiors at San Miguel will allow us to offer you a paid consulting position…we know the convent of San Miguel could use the financial assistance." Padric was jubilant.

Another knock on the door brought Jana into the room. "Lt. Zalconi will assist you and your sister." Padric and Magdalen looked at each other, his eyes full of compassion, hers unafraid. Dolorosa gathered up her garments; Magdalen, her bandages. She took the arm Padric offered. With dignity, she walked to the door.

He leaned toward her: "Sister, methinks you should be gone from this place of demons." She liked when men whispered; she wanted to laugh and refused to look back at the bishop but she was pale now, weaker; Jana hustled her from the room and, within seconds, was re-dressing Magdalen's wounds in Padric's office while Dolorosa scolded her and put her back together again. "Maggie, you must behave…we're leaving."

Down the hall, Ramirez and Padric had remained in the room with a not too happy bishop. "And this recalcitrant detective of yours…what is your take on him?"

"He is indeed truculent and an obstreperous man."

The bishop glared at him. "You mock me?"

"Bishop, I took the liberty to call your assistant, Father Michelantonio. You and I both know there is knowledge in you about certain things…we discussed this in the convent before the arrests. But still you resist and we have no evidence to prove what you know. We run a tight ship here and need to move on; I refuse to give one more second to the Canteras. Your nephew and sister have been charged with a long list of crimes. Their vivid descriptions of depraved acts made us ill; their confessions negate a trial. They stay... you go."

There was another knock; this, too, on cue. Padric smiled a little...he'd kick back and watch when a grave young priest entered the room. Sebastian glanced at Padric and nodded to the Commander. "Santo, I'm here to take you home." Santo.

"I am not leaving until I have..." He looked at Ramirez. "You will apologize to me at some point for this effrontery, Commander, and do something with him." He glared at Padric.

Ramirez grimly stared him down. "As a rule, I never apologize and will only encourage my detective to be even more zealous." The bishop was not ready to back down, insisting on further discussion.

Sebastian interrupted: "Santo, please listen. We've talked about this...you can't win them all and you're not always right. Come. You're fortunate they're letting you leave; quietly then...we're going now." Who had the authority here? Padric was in disbelief... *nothing but class with this guy.* Ramirez as usual showed no reaction but thanked the priest. The bishop scooped up his breviary and left.

Sebastian paused in the doorway and looked at the two. "Thank you, gentlemen. It will be Zalconi's soon for some conversation and *calamari.* I've not had the pleasure of dining there." The two grinned.

"Soon then," Padric said. "It's on me...thank you, Father."

The camera was off; no more monitors. Ramirez eyed his lieutenant who had done battle for days on so many levels, yet he knew the man was hurting and said so.

Padric's usual thick skin had prevailed and he sighed: *"If you prick us, do we not bleed...if you wrong us, shall we not revenge?"*

"Well said, *caballero,* but you're not Shylock and this isn't Venice." He too knew Shakespeare, maintaining for years that crimes in this town had been lifted straight out of his playbook. "Your soul is bleeding, John, and you're wanting payback. Guard yourself." Ramirez left. Padric sat down and looked at the floor for a while.

When he exited the room, he slammed the door so hard the hallway shook. He adjusted a picture gone askew and was face to face with a faded photo of L'Arroyo's first three-man police force.

They were proud men and he gave them a nod. "If I had a glass, I'd raise it, *bhoyos.*" He walked down the hall.

It wasn't over and Alejandro Martinez, a thoughtful man and given to pondering the Divine, observed all that had transpired in the past forty-eight. He wondered if this would be the end of his partner professionally and, well, otherwise. Would he learn one dark night that the man had suffered and died before his time? Could already a curse be laid on Padric for disrespecting the likes of a bishop in the person of Santo Cantera, but then…the man had disrespected him, too. As there were angels among them, so were there rattlesnakes here in the Sonoran.

Without a word, Sebastian and Santo Cantera drove away but not to their residence. Arturo Cantera was waiting for his oldest son at the ranch and minutes later, both were speeding east into the mountains to an off-road where a two-story tower house of granite and quartz, reminiscent more of Ireland than Spain or Mexico, stood silent behind stone walls and a gate manned by the Cantera's own small militia called the *Momentos*. The two men would sit for several days in one of its huge rooms, their faces lit only by torches protruding from the walls, candelabra on the tables.

Santo didn't ask why his father had not come to the Precinct, why he had not hired legal counsel…he knew the Cantera way. But Arturo was grieving. No kin of his would be caged, not his Joanna. He would strategize to change all this.

And the boy…the baby into whom he'd breathed life, he would not allow him to be buried alive with the criminally insane; he was sickened beyond words at all his son said at the Precinct.

There were Joanna's and Bernardo's graphic admissions of guilt. It would be from this time, he spoke less or not at all except to do business. But someone had caught his attention and would continue to be of great interest to him; hated perhaps by one Cantera and loved almost to obsession by another…this nun, what was her name?

Ah, *si…Magdalena.*

Author's Notes

buena hermanita – Spanish, for good little Sister.

Joan of Arc – saint in the Catholic Church; peasant girl of medieval France, who believed she was chosen by God to lead France to victory in its long-running war with England. With the blessing of crown prince Charles of Valois, she with his army achieved a momentous victory over the English and allies, the Burgundians at Orléans, but, at age 19, she is put on trial for witchcraft and heresy by certain Church officials and burned at the stake in 1431. Known as the Maid of Orléans, she was officially canonized by the Church in 1920, an symbol of French nationalism.

Cosette – fictional character in Les Misérables a French historical novel by Victor Hugo, first published in 1862 and considered one of the greatest novels of the 19th century; an exploited and victimized child, rescued by Jean Valjean, raising her as his own during the French Revolution. It is a novel full of metaphor, she, throughout, is beauty and hope against the backdrop of a turbulent world as the oppressed and abused rise up during a very dark time.

Sacro-sanct – place or situation, too important and valued, to upset or disturb; hallowed, special, respected.

"If you prick us, do we not bleed…if you wrong us, shall we not revenge?" – Padric quotes Shylock from The Merchant of Venice, Act 1, Scene 1.

32 FLIGHT OF THE VULTURE

Tuesday, five in the evening, April 22

With the departure of the bishop and imminent removal of mother and son to the County Jail, Martinez would honor the Commander's wishes. Joanna, though charged, had given them nothing in writing. He turned to Dolorosa. "Would you talk with the woman?" Marcus and Jana would accompany her but Joanna was pouting, glaring down at a blank legal pad, wanting Johnny. The nun entered the room.

Magdalen meanwhile had retreated to Padric's office and called the convent. They would be home within the hour, she promised, but Ramos had been found; might she visit him very soon? She said nothing of Petra, that the nun was alive. She would wait for a final nod from the detective. But she had her *own* agenda…she would slip into Petra's room, and then there was Lara…she had promised to visit with her and not looking forward to it. She said none of this.

Agnes was elated to hear of Ramos' return. "Of course." She was for it. "I want you anywhere but that horrible place. But there is someone eager to speak with you."

Magdalen was comforted by the elder's voice. "My dear, you sound like you are far off in Egypt again…stay the course." *She knows what is happening here.* Magdalen wished she were sitting in the window seat next to her. She needed a waterfall. "Are you all right, Sister? I will be home very soon." She had neglected her.

"Then and only then will I be all right…you and your warrior-sister must finish this." What did the elder sense that she didn't? They spoke for a while and she was renewed, but said nothing of her own radical move to undress in a roomful of men; already Dolorosa had been sworn into secrecy. She would need some private time with Monica to tell her a man had told her he loved her. Magdalen wondered if she would scold her but didn't know that when old Jack Whitton came to call on the elder the other night, he'd said the same.

She put down the phone and leaned back in Padric's old chair, remembering the cool of his forehead when she had kissed him, the taste of his tears on her lips…she closed her eyes but opened them quickly. Her sense of things told her something was off. She stood up and opened the office door.

The hallway exploded, a shout and doors slamming! A cadre of uniforms rushed passed her. Ahead Dolorosa lay sprawled on the floor near the door to the parking garage. From nowhere Padric appeared… he was running, the Commander behind him, pushing her back into the office, but Magdalen rushed after them to her Sister.

Joanna Cantera was gone…she had escaped.

What had happened…how could it? Marcus had accompanied Dolorosa into the interview room; Jana had joined them. Joanna, surprised to see her childhood friend, was at first confrontational then mellowed; they had their memories. Feeling comfortable, Joanna admitted things, horrible things. When Dolorosa told her to write it down, she did, like a student might do at her desk.

Later Joanna carefully laid down the pen. "I wrote this for you, Issa…I love you."

Without warning, she stood up. "And I'm sorry!" She pushed back her chair and kicked Marcus in the groin. It slowed him down but he recovered yet not quickly enough. Joanna was pulling Dolorosa out the door. "I need you, *mija*, you're taking me outta here!"

Using the nun as a shield, she slammed her small frame into Jana as she fled down the hall. Ducking and weaving, she headed for the parking garage. When Martinez lunged at her, she shoved Dolorosa into him; they tumbled over each other leaving the nun unconscious. Martinez regained his footing, stumbling forward and shouted for someone to help the *manita*.

Lights and beepers went off, those in their cells howled and hooted. Under a bench nailed into the wall, Bernardo hid, cringing in his cage like a hurt animal. The one on whom he depended had left him behind to suffer alone. He cried out.

Half crawling, half running, Joanna heard her son's voice full of terror. She shouted to him, saying she'd return very soon. "*Lobito*, you must be strong," she screamed over the chaos. "No fear, what have I told you?"

Tark was measuring the woman's moves and stepped in between her and the exit; he whirled her around, pushed her into the wall. "Hey, *chica*, enough with the parenting tips for your baby boy...I'm gonna vomit. Hands on your head; get your ass down on the floor."

She laughed. "Here's some sugah, handsome." She pushed her face into his and bit his lip...he stepped back. It took only an instant...she was gone, out the door, into the parking garage with Tark on her heels and Padric on his.

He pulled a 9mm off his ankle. "Fuck this shit, shoot her!" It would have been easier...done, over. But Joanna had slipped through the compound gate as a patrol car was leaving. She darted into an alley, dead-ending into the delivery entrance of one of her family's Salsa Houses. She managed this one; everyone knew her.

Putting her finger to her lips, she stepped into the kitchen. Her staff knew the drill; her ways not foreign to them. Yet there were some who looked up from cutting their chilies. Joanna glared at those who gave her affectionate smiles and waves. They quickly looked down and stared at their work. One started to sing without missing a beat.

A dishwasher pushed her into a produce room and shoved crates of squash and mangos in front of the door. She'd done this before; she'd hid her employees from ICE in the crawl spaces under the floor, in the walls...they were all over. Now she slipped into one of them while more workers pushed crates and containers against it. Padric questioned the guard at the Precinct gate.

Tark had moved on with Martinez. Both walked into the bistro's back entrance with guns drawn. "Joanna Cantera! Give us Joanna Cantera. Where is she?"

They knew better and stared at him with well-rehearsed faces. "*No Inglés.*" Martinez rolled his eyes, yelling and cursing in Spanish; *nada*. Tark kicked away the boxes in front of the storage room, threw the squash down the hall, the mangos in every direction.

He opened the door. A bare light bulb hung from the ceiling; there were very few places to hide but boxes and more crates were stacked deep, scattered everywhere. Tark scanned the room slowly; he cursed and yelled: "Clear!" He was generally right about something that felt wrong…and he was right. Uneasy, he walked away.

Martinez studied the women's faces. Still nothing. Putting their guns away, they left the kitchen and walked through the dining room, leaving patrons shaken and wide-eyed. When they stepped into the street, Padric was standing in front of them. "You've got to be kidding me. What the fuck happened?"

"She sprung herself loose."

"You mean we let her. And where the fuck is Jana?"

"I'm here." Her face was bloodied. Jana had whirled around when Joanna slammed the door into her face. "I want her ass like yesterday…fuck this."

"A good Catholic girl like yourself using the f-word!" He smiled wearily. He thought of his daughters. "Fuck, who knew? We had this wrapped up…and now we don't; she's out there and may go for our nun or the priest again. She knows he's not dead and it'll eat her alive. Sister Dynamite's down, people. Take care of her…go."

Tark, his lip bloodied, punched the chain link fence. "We'll never put this to rest."

"Get our medic to look at that…you'll need a shot. The woman is rabid, *amigo*." No one laughed least of all Padric…Tark disappeared to get clean, repulsed, not liking any of this.

Marcus was hurting, but standing tall. "We've got her statement but I wasn't quick enough."

Padric told him to forget the *mea culpas* and put his arm around him. "You worked your ass off on this. It happens. But ouch, man, ice it." Marcus winced…that would be worse. "Let uniforms continue the search. LCAT is on this…I can see Woodson and Morrow wanting this bad. Pistasio's out there for us; return to the Precinct."

They headed back.

Martinez said: "What the fuck is a *mea culpa*?"

Joanna waited but was curious; she slipped from her hiding space and peered through a slit in the shed wall. Tears rolled down her face…would she ever see him again? She watched Padric disappear behind one of the buildings.

"So that blonde cop wants my ass. Lots o' luck, Zalconi." She rotated her hips, danced a little. "My Pilates paid off big time…" but she stopped, sobbed aloud and slumped to the floor. She'd given up her son and herself in all she had said. She was breaking down, talking in circles. *I'm sorry, Daddy, I'm sorry.* She'd wait; try to survive…*Daddy, find me, take me to Mexico; hide me forever. And my new cop with his tight ass and thinking he could take Johnny's place. The fool was a pushover, stupid in love. But he'll be nice for a while and my poppy will work this out for me very soon…they got this bitch's back.*

Later at closing, three women stole quietly into the shed. "We live where cops never go. Come on, *bonita*, we got your back." An old Monte Carlo pulled up to the back entrance then moved away silently into the night. She'd get more anonymity than she wanted.

In the squad room, surrounded by three female uniforms, Dolorosa was getting too much attention; she thanked them and pushed them away. The linens around her face were askew and her veil torn. She wanted to rip it off, but Magdalen put her back together in minutes and asked for some privacy. They held each other, Dolorosa wept; she was furious. "I should have fought harder, kicked some ass, rolled all over that bitch."

Magdalen would not let her go. "I'll take care of you now. Paramedics are on the way."

The pain in her head was almost unbearable, but Dolorosa could only think of Joanna. "She's the most damaged woman I've ever encountered and she's gone God knows where; she's a master at this…she's been escaping from things all her life. She won't be caged. Joanna is like nothing no one has reckoned with…there's only one Joanna." Tark had said this, too. "Lashing out soothes the dark in a soul. You may throw her behind bars and think you can hold her down for the rest of her life, but she'll not be contained. I know it, I know it." The Precinct was suddenly quiet as if they were the only two in the building; they remained huddled together. Paramedics arrived; the detectives concerned.

The First Precinct was embarrassed.

Wednesday, mid-morning, April 23

Cactus wrens hopped back and forth on her windowsill. She sat up. Outside the desert was drenched in sunlight. She heard strains of music, *narcocorridos*, praising a drug lord and his dead lover. Joanna sank into the pillows; they smelled clean. She rolled over, sat up; with heart racing, she went to the window. The old Monte Carlo was parked under a wooden lean-to.

I'm not chained up, not feeling high and don't think I had sex. I'm so good I'm bad, motherfucker. Need to get my pretty bitch ass out of here...but where the fuck is my purse? She looked in the mirror, adjusted her clothing, but noticed clean jeans and a sweatshirt on a chair; she quickly slipped into them. Joanna opened the bedroom door. Men, playing cards at a table, didn't look up like this happened often. A woman beckoned to her.

"*Señorita*, you know me, Rosalinda. I work at the Salsa House near the police station." Joanna was relieved. She had no idea where she was, but recognized her employee. Several other women motioned for her to come into the kitchen. She sat down, but why would they help her...*I'm rich and I'm kidnapped. Fuck. They're using my bitch self for a hostage? Gotta go...get away.* Something wasn't right; they pushed her purse into her hands. She'd know soon enough.

The beep of a horn brought the women to the window. They turned and looked at Joanna. She looked from one to the other. "What is it? What now?" They didn't answer.

Finally one said: "Well, you can't stay here." This one had blown smoke in her face when they took her away from the shed. "They're looking for you. They're harassing all of us; the po-po are even walking into your employees' *casas* without knocking or anything. You got to go now; we did what we could."

"Yeah, we did," said a younger woman; the others laughed. Joanna would remember; she'd be sorry, all of them would. They had changed; had heard things perhaps, knew what she'd done, killing nuns, doing things to a priest. The warmth they had offered each time she'd stopped by her restaurant and handed out Grants had disappeared; their eyes anxious now, wanting her gone. They were all business; a deal had been made. She looked out the window, *damn, a '64 Impala, gangsta-ride low to the ground...not good.*

The women sensed possible flight; they grabbed her. Cursing in Spanish, she struggled as they brought her out to the waiting car; the driver punched her in the face several times. She picked herself up but he dragged her away and threw her into the back seat of his car. Joanna slowly sat up and looked through the rear window; the man was counting a stack of bills for Rosalinda. "I wanted small ones, what do I do with a bunch of Benjamins?"

They had sold her. And now they were watching her as the man drove away into the desert. *I'm going to die;* she remembered the nun she and her son had taken out to the middle of nowhere and under a blood red moon, had severed her head... almost; she had wanted to vomit then and did now, all over the back seat. The driver turned around in his seat, struck her again in the face but this time with the butt of a 9mm. She slumped onto the seat, her whole head covered in blood and yesterday's meal at the Precinct.

Yet another twist in the ongoing Cantera saga was all over the news; there was excitement down at the courthouse. Padric sank into the chair in his office and was watching the news on his iPhone. In the rectory, Father Santeresa had turned on the television and alerted his guests who were settling in; the nuns were curious. Dolorosa and Magdalen sat very close to each other, watching the drama unfold, both feeling relieved at last to be safe with their Sisters. But Magdalen gasped. Bernardo Cantera was showing up for arraignment and beside him his court-appointed attorney. He'd asked for one against family wishes and now the lawyer was accompanying him into the courthouse. His looks were striking, a handsome man with a decided mystical air about him.

Magdalen's eyes narrowed; she knew him, eyes intense, jaw set; his shoulder length hair, light in color, parted in the middle and pulled back in a ponytail like Padric's. At one point, he looked directly into the camera; *yes, there you are and a blessing to all of us.* He was the same who had visited her several times in the garden. *Sanctus.* Magdalen whispered his name.

Padric knew him, too, and smiled; he'd contacted him. With Ramirez' okay, he'd asked him to step in and now here he was, his old law professor from ASU, Dr. Conor O'Connor, Esq. But when the defense attorney looked directly into the camera at him, a chill passed through his soul. He was one and the same...*the watcher*, the one who stands on the campanile late at night, looking out over the city. All of L'Arroyo however was now watching this undercover celestial calmly and swiftly as if on wings, guiding his client up the steps of the courthouse.

Magdalen. Her soft lips and voice came to mind...had she not made some reference to angels walking among them when he asked her if she was one? "Some are called to walk between heaven and earth, doing good," she had said. *No way, not here in Sin City, this dust bucket, ass-kicking town called L'Arroyo.* There was a bit of the Celt mystic about her, walking to the beat of a higher calling. *Ay, maybe...I could believe it.*

Bernardo, an object of much conjecture by all of L'Arroyo, had peacefully entered the courthouse. But what was this...*my God, he's dressed in a suit, the first perhaps he's worn in a very long time and with hair neatly combed and pulled back in a ponytail like his lawyer...well done, bhoyo, but you know the lad is a killer, I'm hoping.*

Conor O'Connor had carefully choreographed everything down to Bernardo's head lowered and calm. How decent and polished he looked. Magdalen glanced at the elder...she was smiling a little. But they would learn, once inside the courtroom, the defendant had dissolved into a panic and cried out for Santo and Magdalen. No longer was he clinging to any thought of Joanna. The judge knew who Santo was but *who, in God's name, was Magda-something?* The district attorney himself, Jimmy Devlin, was there to put him away and in strident tones, made his demands. Bernardo, though silent, was terrified by the voices and urgency; why were they talking about him?

With the deepest concern and compassion, his attorney had gazed steadily into his eyes. Calm returned to the courtroom and was duly noted by the presiding judge. Seeing the psychopathy of the young man before her, she hastily remanded him to the County Jail psych ward, refusing bail to be set.

Waiting in the back of the courtroom and hardly noticed, his grandfather had come back from the tower house just to be there. This time Cantera money would get no respect. Arturo watched as a befuddled Bernardo was taken away. He locked eyes with the DA who froze momentarily then left. The older Cantera returned to his lair in the mountains and found his son, the bishop, silently staring into nowhere with an unopened breviary on the table beside him.

Later in the day, with their families around them, both detectives slept for the first time in days. Padric alone in his bed awakened to the aroma of brown bread and lamb. He tumbled down the stairs and his mum threw her arms around him...no words were necessary. He noticed her rosary beads lay on the windowsill next to her reading glasses. He glanced up...he knew her small ivory handled pistol was tucked into the folds of the drapes above her chair.

Mairead mentioned the condo above them would either be up for sale or rent by the end of the week. Was he interested? Without Lara...he thought for a moment. That house in the old part of the city he had wanted for her, it too was for sale. She had loved it, even lived in it once, when she was a child. But things were different now.

Fuck it, yes, he and his girls and their little brother would live upstairs from their granny and aunties. His younger sisters, Fiona and Mary, were arriving soon and eager to help. Mairead hugged him, both holding on to each other; Darragh glanced at them and remarked their da' always said they should have been twins.

This was a sad, wrenching business he had brought on himself and his loved ones. The little ones squealed when they realized he was awake and there was no rest for him. He wanted to hear every word they said; it would cleanse his soul of all that was wrong inside it. Padric listened, healed by the sound of their voices; once again, he remembered a nun's soft kiss leaving him strangely at peace. There was no more Lara…they spoke seldom of her. Her girls had moved on with their little lives, silent about it. Now Padric must go to his son. There was good news; the wee lad was showing signs of improvement; he'd met his da'. His da' had found him.

    Later, with a woman-hunt still on for Joanna, Major Crimes broke down what had happened and what they had now; it had taken its toll. Padric said very little as all was picked at and poured over. When Joanna's name was mentioned, so much pointed to him in lurid ways. There was no way around it, no way to hide what the woman had said for the whole unit to hear. He felt foolish and guilty. As good as Ramirez and O'Manion were, they'd used him to get what they wanted.

    Martinez, too, felt beaten up by the woman; this *bruja* had brought out the worst in him. They needed to breathe some fresh air and stopped by Father Santeresa's rectory with roses for the nuns.

    "We put both of you through a lot yesterday." Magdalen and Dolorosa, still looked gaunt, but brightened when they saw the two and ushered them into a visiting room. The men were full of concern and apologies.

    Both nuns asked about Bernardo. "He's not going to make it. My God, what will happen to him? I have a bad feeling."

    Padric was done with the Canteras. "Sister, let this one go."

    "You don't understand my thinking on this. I know very well I am only an object of comfort for him; he has chosen me to obsess over. I am not disillusioned…he could turn on me in an instant as I saw at the end of the interview when I was no longer of any use to him but…"

    "And there's always a but…"

    "And for good reason…he lives, is a human being with a soul and for several moments I saw it…that light, a flicker of reality and awareness that shone through in his eyes then it was gone. All of us have a real self inside us…his is so buried within from his childhood trauma, the real Bernardo will never return. He will never know he was wrong, think his deeds evil." The detectives understood, but had been there, done this for years in ways they could not mention. They rose to leave.

Dolorosa continued: "But, Detective, how is your Lara?"

She did not know of their troubles, the new baby. Padric smiled a little. "Thanks for asking; she'll be coming home next week but not to me."

"To whom then? Are you going somewhere?"

"Why, no. She is…and I'm not sure where that is; she's making her own plans and has said no more about it. You know what I've done and I ask for your prayers. Joanna Cantera…there's no wife in L'Arroyo who would forgive that. When she's caught and nailed into a cell, my wife is safe and free to go wherever she wants."

Dolorosa was adamant. "Then go after her."

Magdalen would try to take care of things tomorrow at Meadow and whispered to Padric: "Rest and go to your son."

He wanted to hold her again; that brief encounter had been the closest he'd been to a woman in weeks and this was too long for the likes of John Padric, but he whispered he would.

The night air cooled Padric's face as they walked to the car. "Fuck rest. I need a drink."

Somewhere else, a woman he knew was staring at all the liquor John Padric would want…boxes and boxes of liquor; barrels and kegs, stacked high, waiting. The air was cool; the ceiling trembled with the throb of a bass guitar and she could hear people laughing. In a storage basement under a club, her ankle was chained to a wall by a heavy iron cuff. High overhead, stars blinked through a window. The pain in her head was unbearable; she'd taken multiple hits to her face in the last twenty-four hours. She tried to stand but once on her feet, quickly slumped to the floor, pretending to sleep; someone was on the stairs, the cigar smoke, familiar. She didn't move.

"Hey, bitch." Constanzio. He pulled up a chair.

She sat up slowly. "Whatta' you want with me, Stanzio?"

Smiling, he watched her. "Nothing."

"Then what the hell am I doing here?"

"You…I loved you, then you did something I can't forgive."

"What are you talking about? Spare me the Godfather movie."

"Chana, that girl in the bar, my niece, you hurt her bad, did something punk-ass like you do, slitting her throat, tearing her heart up in the fucking middle of nowhere. Animals tore out her guts, all of her. Red ants had a party on her, eating her dead. She was a beautiful girl, precious."

"So why was she treated like meat in that cesspool upstairs?"

"Hey, she was my niece, my brother's little girl."

"Why all the love now? You were letting her slut in your bar?"

"That's what she does, bitch; she was good at it, liked it; my brother made money off her and we were okay with that."

"So her old man was pimping her and you're both mad at me because you lost your golden hen?"

The comment was lost on Constanzio. Metaphors, he didn't get. "You're gonna pay big-time. At first, I thought I would make you pay on your back, but I'm not. We had something once and I won't disrespect that."

"Hey, *cabron*, what do you call this then? Are you doing right by me now in chains and having the driver punch me out? Look at my face." She acted tough but had tears in her eyes.

"I didn't tell him to do that, *puta*, but you're gonna suffer."

Joanna's bravado was wearing thin. Hadn't her mother said the same when she was in labor with Bernardo? She could still hear her screaming: "I'm going to make you suffer!" Everything bad or painful would always come back to that moment; she'd gone through life making her own party because of it. "I have my eye on that immigrant mick, Detective Juan Padric; his picture's been in the paper with his good-lookin' *amigo*, Alejandro what-his-name…a home boy, nice. They're tight, he and that *gringo*…"

"Oh, for Christ's sake, what's your point?"

"You were doing him I think…just saying, just wondering. You and that dumb-ass brother of yours had something to do with killing the nun. And that other one doing nothing about it, the bishop, Santo the sanctified or whatever…out here, we call him *Diablo*."

Joanna was in pain from the hits she had taken but laughed.

"You...you're calling *him Diablo*? What are *you* then?"

"It takes one to know one. You will suffer and I won't lay a hand on you. I'm sending you back to the po-po, *mija*." He rose quickly, tipping over the chair. He picked it up and threw it at the wall over her head; it shattered in pieces on top of her head, making her bleed...she screamed.

Chato noticed he'd soiled the hem of his white dress pants and cursed. "Chuy, get the van. She's outta here, *ese*." Joanna could tell the young man was afraid...if she had a chance, she'd work him a little. "Get, Fatboy, to pick her up. Gordo! He knows what to do." He chuckled as one of his bouncers, huge like Bruno, tore the chain out of the wall. Leaving the cuff on Joanna's ankle, he threw her over his shoulder like a sack of flour. She cried out, but Constanzio yanked her hair, wrenched back her head, almost breaking her neck. "You killed nuns and priests. Rot in hell. You killed our Chana. Rot in two hells, *bruja*."

She passed out.

It was one in the morning. Zalconi's had been busy but was quiet now when Padric and his crew slipped into the back room... they felt guilty even being there with all that had happened, but no one was looking for a good time, just good food and some quiet. The Captain had joined them; they ate in silence. Ramirez had told them to back down, let others run with the ball.

But two men on their cell phones did not go unnoticed by Padric. They looked out of place when they entered the restaurant and scanned the place; when their eyes rested on him they left. Martinez saw it. "Front window...they're eyeballin' you. Check out those fools."

Tark wasn't hungry; he'd needed his music and was wailing on his sax to an empty room but he stopped in the middle of a note and Padric looked up. He'd jumped off the stage. With his sax under his arm, he was walking toward the front door. Padric tipped over his chair when he stood. "Want some kick-ass, *bhoyos*?" Like a cat, he moved through the main dining room with Martinez behind him.

Tires squealed to a halt in the street. From the back of a huge black van with no windows, a body, wrapped up like a burrito in an old dirty rug, had been tossed onto the sidewalk. It rolled eerily up to Zalconi's front door and unraveled, revealing a woman, hands and feet bound, disheveled and bloody. The valets ran toward her as Padric burst through the door. Tark and Marcus sprinted after the van to ID it, but it disappeared onto the main road; squad cars peeled out in pursuit.

Joanna. Martinez looked down at her. "Karma's a bitch, isn't it, *chica?*" A metal cuff still clung to one ankle; it had rattled across the pavement. A note was taped to her mouth: *Take the bitch. She kills good people. Fry her ass.* The men looked at each other; this was *film noir*, forties and fifties Hollywood, John Garfield.

Padric shouted: "Call for a bus! We need a medic! Thank God there were no customers in the house." *Damn…old Angus Zalconi will have a fit.* Uniforms and more squad cars arrived.

Enzio Falconi, Jana's oldest brother, emerged from the restaurant. "A Cantera…*madone,* they'll be the death of us." He and Padric were friends; he threw his hands in the air, cursing in Italian. "I know, I know. I'll go inside. Take care of this please, Giovanni."

Padric muttered: "Take her to the ER at Good Shepherd." Meadow was no place for this woman; she had no right being there with her victims even though Arturo Cantera had paid for most of its construction. "Joanna, can you hear me?"

She was conscious. "Baby, you're here…I knew you'd come."

"Shut the fuck up!" He lost it. "Get her away from me." With head down, Padric walked away…*again, talking love.* But what bitter irony: Joanna and her son had duct taped and rolled Petra into a cocoon; she now bound and wrapped in a carpet.

Life comes full circle. Mercy and forgiveness were for the nuns; Padric had none. The men gathered round him. "They're not coming back…this isn't their playground; they're already back in the Edge." He barked orders and shouted: "And to the fool who wrote this, *gracias.* The Precinct thanks you." He handed it off to a CSI who had just arrived.

Martinez was a happy man…the *bruja* would be under armed guard in a hospital room. He once again did his Victor Cruz Salsa moves and rendered some Motown: "Signed, sealed, delivered…

She's ours." No one smiled.

Padric sat down at a table and threw down a shot of Jameson. Wise in the ways of the world and women, Enzio joined him.

Johnny Padric could use some old world wisdom tonight.

Author's Notes

Lobito – Spanish, for little wolf.

mea culpa – Latin, for through my fault; loosely used when referring to one's sins and faults, apologizing, saying one is sorry, admitting to wrong.

Pilates Piltes – routine of physical exercise using special apparatus, designed to improve physical and mental strength; named after German physical fitness specialist Joseph Pilates (1880–1967), who devised the system.

gangsta-ride – type of car favored by gang members. Joanna knows all of them; described best by Snoop Dog: "It's a gangsta, gangsta ride On the nutty danger side As we ride, dip and slippin' Take your mind, on a high…"

Grants – fifty dollar bill with Ulysses Grant image.

Benjamins – one hundred dollar bill with Benjamin Franklin image.

33 RETURN OF THE DOVES

Wednesday, two-thirty in the morning, April 23

The nuns swooped down and fluttered about the convent of San Miguel...it was like new. Walls had been painted where the assault on the landing took place; the upstairs chapel immaculate and the Archangel Raphael restored to his pedestal. They were home and immediately set to work. *Viva*...they would move on but with hearts heavy. Joanna Cantera was out there. Magdalen and Dolorosa had smiled at each other as they moved about the sacristy with a uniform on the landing and Tarkington and Tate posted nearby. How good it was to do ordinary things regardless of threat...they would take care of each other.

At Padric's bidding, Marcus came with the news...a phone call wouldn't do it; he'd sent *their priest*. The two nuns were leaving the sacristy when they saw him. He drew Magdalen aside under the trees in the quad; Dolorosa moved on.

"It's a go." he said, "Tell your Sisters!" He told her what Petra had shared and Magdalen wept...her Sister would come home very soon. Later at dusk, lights twinkled warmly from behind convent drapes and a detective in his hummer slowed down and for several minutes watched the house...their nun was safe. He drove away.

With Marcus' news, Magdalen had burst through the door like another Magdalen on Easter morning when she found her Risen Lord in the garden, a tomb empty. She rushed up the stairs to the elder...their Sister had been raised from the dead! Though Patrice had carefully seen to her needs, the old nun was overjoyed with the news. Monica said she had known. Now all was confirmed. Agnes "lost it", Dolorosa said later; she shouted aloud from the vestibule and the convent erupted. The following days would be glorious and plans underway for the elder to visit Petra. They would make preparations for their director's return.

But, there would be no perfect joy for Magdalen when the elder whispered: "And now, dear, you must find Lucy." Something was afoot and yes, she agreed. Lucy was somewhere waiting to be found. Magdalen wondered if a possessive father had snatched her away and brought her, dead or alive, back home to Tuscany…*what else could it be? But how had he managed the logistics?* "Where do I begin?"

"She has suffered great injury," said the elder. "We all saw that…where would our Lucy be taken and by whom? She is not in the morgue where everyone thinks she is."

"And how do you know this?" The woman had her sources… leave it at that.

"You must hurry, Magdalen."

There was no rest for her…just when she thought she could sit unburdened and still, she was back. "I will, I will." *But how… how?* She was weary and withdrew to ponder a plan but Dolorosa found her curled up on her bed. She smiled and knew she would not need to bunk with Magdalen after all, as Padric had suggested. The woman they sought was at last in custody, shackled to a bed at Good Shepherd hospital; Pistasio himself, posted outside her door.

That night, Sanctus, his long hair lifted by an evening breeze, took leave of the garden. But the Sisters of the Crucified didn't trust the sudden peace.

Neither did Padric.

Thursday, mid-morning, April 24

Duran would remain inside the convent, the rookies again at their posts: Tate and Tarkington walked the courtyard perimeter, scanning the shadows inside the Cathedral; Maselli and Maclone were with CSI Milleau in a graveyard; a curious Sebastian frequently joining them. Magdalen was not cleared to do so though she'd occupied one of its graves for over an hour.

Padric would have no down time and would do something he dreaded; it was mid-afternoon in Boston. Mother Thérèse was relieved to hear the voice of someone close to the case. He'd choose his words carefully, not knowing what to expect on the other end. But the woman was calm and collected and she too dropped a bombshell after Padric dropped his. She had sensed Petra was alive; Padric smiled…another one who knows things. But he would not like what he heard. Thérèse told him Lucy was not in the morgue, never had died. When they die her sisters visit her before moving into the light…Lucy hadn't done this.

Twilight zone…damn, here we go. He'd check it out, he said, but for another ten minutes and with a preciseness unequaled, the good woman gave him his orders: "Detective, you will watch over my Sisters, especially our Sister Magdalen…no more black eyes, goodness." She hung up.

Padric would not remember how long he sat staring at the wall in his office; he'd been side-slammed. Martinez and Marcus were waiting for him in the squad room. "Gentlemen, start your engines…we're paying the dead a visit."

It would be business as usual. With showers and fresh clothes, the three headed for double shot espressos at Cuppa then on to the morgue. Dr. Rubin was upset. "I just got back from my daughter's graduation and what a mess."

"Congrats on your lass, Doc, but I'm not liking this."

"I know, I know. Thanks…follow me."

Padric was somber. *Stainless steel. Cold, easy to clean, hose it down. Bodies with toe tags cooling in the dark. Rest in peace.* "How do you do this, Doc?"

"Ah, I note some repulsion. What…not fragrant enough?"

"Something like that…too antiseptic. What am I looking at?"

"Nothing." Rubin pulled open a body drawer. Empty.

"Note the name on this one."

Sister Lucy Genova. "Where the fuck is she?" Padric felt cold; he needed the sun, his little girls' smiles, his son's eyes looking at him. Cursing in Spanish…again, Martinez stepped away. Marcus made the sign of the cross. Rubin was quiet for once but whispered some impossible ripped-from-the-headlines story about Lucy, mutilated beyond recognition, suddenly crying out after Declan and Kelly had delivered her body and left. If they'd stayed five more minutes, they could have whisked her away to Meadow. But this was all hearsay. As Rubin's stand-in reported, he was alone, when a knock at the door turned the case upside down. The presiding doctor could say nothing else. Rubin was almost in tears. This would never have happened on his watch. "It's telepathy between you and me, John. I was calling you when you walked in five minutes ago."

Padric was in disbelief. "So let me get this straight: a private party, male and female, claiming to be family from Italy, demanded she be given to them. They had ID, a medical van, two more men in scrubs; the whole *enchilada*. The doc, who is he?"

"Darby D. Darbeau…don't ask, he let them have her if you can believe it; the man is suspended. He'll never practice again. The paper work for the body release is on my desk with a slew of redactions." The usually upbeat ME fell silent.

"I want whatever you have on this woman and we'll be rousting out Darby whats-his-name momentarily." He turned to his men. "Find him. Get Tark to work voodoo on a computer search." Rubin had no words for what had occurred in his otherwise pristine facility. When he was alone, he pounded his fists on the counter and kicked over a laundry cart.

The night air was warm and no comfort; Padric pulled out his cell phone. "Declan, lad…are you sittin' in front of a stiff whiskey?"

⊕

It was close to eleven at night and Alejandro Martinez, the man who loved Padric was wild with excitement; his partner had called during shift, insisting he must see his boy, come to the Abbey. Padric was there, his son asleep on his shoulder. Quietly Martinez slipped into the parking garage…he was off to see a baby named Finn. He'd soon be his god-child. A quick phone call to the convent brought Agnes to Magdalen's door. "It's late but I think you should do this…someone needs our presence tonight. Go!"

A detective would be taking her to Saint Uriel's Abbey. Magdalen smiled and rushed down the stairs, adjusting her veil as she hurried out into the moonlight.

Martinez grinned and bowing, opened the car door with a flourish. "You wanna ride shotgun?" She laughed.

He would explain. Padric had insisted his partner bring the nun who said she had *loved him the right way*. They'd found the slightest of blips in his boy's heartbeat and they had laid his small body on his father's heart, trusting their rhythms would blend into one. It was one of Rosemaeve's Celtic remedies. He needed his nun and her healing kiss on his boy's face if permitted. Father Seamus had been there already and left. He needed an angel now, but didn't say that.

The cross on the belfry rose high over the walls of the cloister against the night sky and a nun unseen at her post on the other side of the turnstile greeted the two who passed through the gate and up to the abbey. Mother Mary Rose greeted them…so this was the archaeology-nun hired to serve at the First Precinct. *Delightful.*

Magdalen was immediately drawn in and swept up by the roses she saw in the inner quadrangle, the garth, the cloister itself. At last she was here in this place she had wanted to visit, but she was quickly directed to a half-open door at the end of a hall. Mother Mary Rose beckoned her forward and pointed.

Padric with eyes closed was holding his son over his heart. Magdalen gazed at him from the doorway…had anyone seen the detective like this? She smiled with tears in her eyes.

Gently Sister Rosemaeve took the child from him and looked into his eyes. "Someone has come to see you."

"Detective?" Magdalen.

"Sister?" Padric rushed to her…when he embraced her, she held him close and whispered, reassurances. He needed this…it was something he wanted from no one else.

He hugged Martinez and drew them into the quiet and peace of Rosemaeve's gentle world. The nuns exchanged kind words and Magdalen immediately knelt down beside the bed where Finn had been laid. She asked if she might hold him close. Padric smiled, prayed she would kiss his small head. What a sight it was for the two men to see their nun holding this little one with her angel prayers. She kissed Baby Finn. Padric knew then…he knew why she was sad sometimes. He would wait…she would tell him someday.

But the baby's appearance had suddenly changed. He was pinker; his heart rate was normal. Magdalen whispered: "I will help…my Sisters will help with your girls, anything to make this child welcome and safe. A boy…such a beautiful boy, such a precious child! Babies…they are wonderful. I pray for your wife, your Lara…we will care for her, too." Silence.

"Right now, her thoughts are not my concern…I've a lot to think about." He motioned to Alex.

A good father himself, he was thrilled to see this miracle child and said so. "*Ay, ay, ay…Dios mio.* A *caballero,* look at him, Johnny. He's a mini-you." Rosemaeve and Mary Rose were not sure what that meant but smiled and asked that only one remain for the sake of the infants; the other two, little girls, older than Finn and sleeping peacefully.

Magdalen rose to her feet. "When you or your family cannot be here…I will stay and talk with your boy. We will take turns, you and I and your sister Mairead, of course. Will you tell her now? Please you must?"

"I've done that. Let me speak with these good Sisters; then you can return." Martinez and Magdalen withdrew and spoke of nothing but Padric and the future of the fragile infant they'd seen. "Sister, you are upset about more than seeing this child. Tell me." Martinez too had a heart for Magdalen; she had grown on him. He was reading a pain she would not reveal. She only smiled and said perhaps at another time. The heart of the abbey was suddenly before them, the rose garden, silent and beautiful, edged on all sides by a colonnade. It seemed to be waiting for them.

Martinez sat down at one of the tables on the edge of the garden…he smiled. Food. The nuns had prepared a small repast for them. But Magdalen was mesmerized by much more; they were surrounded by every imaginable color.

"Do you like our roses, Sister?" Magdalen turned. A beautiful nun offered to walk with her. "I'm Sister Rosetta and you are the archaeologist-nun, Sister Magdalen."

"I am...but how do you know this?"

"I think I heard someone mention it recently in regard to your helping the police with these martyr murders."

"And how blessed are you to live in this wonderland apart from the world. But how do you keep the roses so beautiful?"

"We pray...all the time; it is our calling. It is our contemplation, our heart-cry to God."

"And you are saying..."

"My Sisters are holy ones who far surpass my attempts at living our life...many are older and have given their whole lives to His service. I cannot explain. Perhaps you too can find peace here."

She guided her further into the garden, but Martinez called out to her. Padric and he had received a call from O'Manion, but Magdalen was not ready to go...something or someone was tugging at her like Petra had done from the body bag when they left the Cathedral that Good Friday night. Her eyes scanned the rose garden; for a moment, she studied the small *casita* joined to it. Nothing.

"Would you like me to return...I mean, I will be coming here more over the next month or so to look in on Finn Padric...perhaps we can talk."

"Go...it is the will of God. Come back to us soon."

She suddenly turned with dread in her eyes. A nun was calling her name, demanding she come at once. Her accent...Magdalen turned; *Italia, Tuscan. Interesting.* Magdalen studied her; she looked out of place. Rosetta whispered: "Save us and you will find what you seek."

The following day Dolorosa accompanied Magdalen to visit Ramos at Meadow...there was joy; Sebastian, making his rounds as part of his weekly schedule, popped his head in the door. There was much conversation and Magdalen was overjoyed when the priest asked the young man if he would like to return to Cathedral and play football next fall. It was settled.

But Lara would be more of a challenge. Surprised to see Magdalen in the doorway, she asked her to leave if her husband had sent her. "You're kicking me out of your house then?"

"Well, no…you just got here." They laughed. One word led to another; Lara sometimes in tears, sometimes smiling, on a rant; every sentence beginning and ending with the name: *Joanna Cantera*. Magdalen studied her: an intelligent, beautiful woman, but…if all she could think of, speak of, and weep over was her, then John Padric's ex-lover had achieved what she wanted. Ms. Cantera had won leaving Lara on the side of road to suffer the rest of her days. Lara was her prisoner.

And now, the frustrated woman wondered what a sweet innocent nun would have to offer her. "So poor Johnny, is it?" She went on the offensive. "You think you know my pain…you've not been his wife for fifteen years of not so wedded bliss." She spoke bitterly of the First Precinct's "boys' club" on and off the clock; even the female officers were all manned up and on point. He's all Batman and adrenaline." Lara didn't care whether Magdalen spoke or not, insisting she and her girls made him look good; she was the one who waited each early morning for him to come home. She wondered aloud if when he made love to his women or when he was fucking Joanna Cantera had he thought of her for even one second? The detective's wife held nothing back, not caring who heard or how shocked they might be at the venom she poured onto her husband.

But Magdalen found an opening: "You know very well the machinery inside a man often lets him fuck, say the right words and not love at all." Lara was stopped cold. Magdalen continued: "Forgive my language. I was making a point."

"Oh, no, it was just unexpected." She laughed. "Point taken."

"So you will not be returning to him when you leave Meadow."

"I will not…so now what shall we talk about? Why are you here?"

"I wanted to see you, not on behalf of your husband, but for the sake of love itself, that perhaps two people who have never stopped loving each other might take a leap of faith and try one more time." She could feel Lara thinking on what she had said. "He believes all you suffered at the hands of this woman is on him.

He recused himself from the case so nothing would stand in the way that you and the others victims might get justice." Silence.

Lara stared at her. "My God! Johnny recused himself…no, no, he can't do that."

"He did this when he realized who he'd foolishly chosen to be with, thinking all his unit's hard work would be lost; the killers allowed to go free if he remained on the case."

"Of course. But why then is he still working it? I saw the arrests on TV. I saw him."

"He was forgiven." More silence. *Forgiven.*

Lara frowned when Magdalen explained. But she was fixated. "He interviewed her face to face; how did that go?"

"I was told by the book and in a most disciplined manner; he was unwavering and professional though very brief; she laid threats on him, lashed out and said things." She could not tell her what Joanna had said she would do to her and her children. "Captain O'Manion walked into the room and shut her down. Your husband left; I'm not sure what he did then."

Stunned, she fell back on her pillows. "I do. My God…I know what he did. Oh, Sister, he called me. It was our thing…he would call me after a difficult arrest or interrogation just to…to hear my voice. I was always there; this time I wasn't. I'd told him things earlier, something horrible that I had done." Magdalen listened, knowing already all she would say. "I'd used poor judgment, wanted to hurt him. I wanted nothing but pain for him…yet he tried to reach out one last time even after all I had said. I was a bitch, cold…he hung up." She wept.

"I cannot describe to you what this woman put them through… but they got what they wanted. Her own words buried her."

"And you assisted with the interview process as well? With whom did you speak?"

"Not Joanna Cantera…at least in the interview room." She sat up, curious. "She wishes me dead, Lara. She attacked me in the cemetery when I attempted to assist in finding them…it was foolish on my part, but I did it; she found me and…" She drew back her veil exposing the bruises. Lara was horrified, regretting her own anger, her words, and impulsively drew the nun to her, empathizing, telling her how sorry she was. "She has put you through hell…you and your beautiful Sisters. I have had the comfort of Sister Petra while here. We have spoken often and I'm afraid I've shocked her at times with my anger…my sadness." Silence.

The nun allowed Lara to sift through all she had said. She was frowning. *So Batman/Supercop has been forthright enough to recuse himself at the loss of his own good name.* Lara then spoke of the past, her marriage. Her mood changed; she softened when she said they loved Shakespeare, the arts and books, continually debated and argued the state of the universe and the ways of the powerful *ad infinitum.*

And oddly in her husband's defense she whispered: "What you see on the job is not who he is." So…the woman who hated him, wanted him and his children out of her life, was telling the nun all these good things about him? Magdalen was hopeful. But Lara was curious…whom had she interviewed?

Bernardo…her eyes widened; she was concerned. "He is obsessed with you then." Magdalen calmly said yes, that she thought so. "And refusing to talk to anyone else, he talked to you." Magdalen nodded. "And you listened." Magdalen said yes, the pain of remembering apparent to Lara. "I'm sorry, Sister, so sorry, but shame on Johnny for placing a woman, especially a nun, in this position…I will speak with him." She realized what she had said. They slowly smiled at each other.

But Magdalen said she had been willingly to do what she did. Lara was adamant. "Regardless…he should not have put you in harm's way."

She assured her she felt safe at all times, that Sergeant Marcus had been with her and Padric, quite anxious for everyone's feelings and safety throughout the process. "It was terrifying though to watch what the detectives went through to make the charges stick." Lara was silent. "But you must be weary of me…I will go."

Magdalen however had made an impasse; Lara's demeanor softened. "Stay…you wanted to say something else, I think."

Magdalen thought for a moment. "You know your husband's job puts him out there; he makes an impact wherever he goes with his attitude, his appearance and flash, his European ways. He can fill a room with his intensity and when he leaves there's a void, but he knows that doesn't impress you...that's not why you chose him. You love him for the other John Padric you know. You are his standard and he's messed up, lost everything, has no rudder."

"I'm not his mother; I hate that in a woman."

"God forbid, Lara...I cannot visualize him wanting that."

Unwittingly Magdalen was revealing some of her own feelings for Padric; she realized how all this must have sounded and fell silent. Lara smiled a little. "And you...are you impressed, do you want to rescue him?"

"If I was, in the way I think you infer, I wouldn't be sitting here pleading a case for your marriage. Impressed, no...overwhelmed a little, yes. He's complicated and the Life I have chosen doesn't allow me to dwell on such things." She could never tell her of this intense man's all-or-nothing concern for her well being or how passionately he had spoken to her at the Precinct. "With John Padric, it's difficult to keep up."

Lara laughed. Gina looked up from the nurses' station. It was a warm friendly sound...something she had not heard from her patient in weeks. But Joanna Cantera was still in the room when Lara whispered in a faraway voice: "This woman who hurt me was all over him. She is known for certain things with men."

Magdalen stroked her hair. "Do not over-think this, Lara...our dear Lord is with you."

"I know this, but I am so weary of needing God." Magdalen had never heard anyone say this before, but how true...had she not thought the same in recent days? "Look what she did to me." Lara pulled back her gown, revealing the scar from the bite mark.

Had Magdalen not said the same to the bishop, shown him her wounds? She touched Lara's face and asked if she could whisper a prayer; she comforted her then kissed her cheek. "I pray your memory be healed, this reminder gone, that you be whole again. Nothing, the very least, a scar, will keep your husband away or hinder your care for each other. But I understand all you feel about this... you are the one with the scar."

Lara gripped Magdalen's hand. "Woman to woman, you are more than you seem."

"Ah, I was not always dressed up like this, Lara."

"But it's complicated?" They laughed quietly.

"I simply wish to bring two lovers together again; your husband's every free moment is spent with your little girls now because they are part of you...they are your heart. Can you not join them again?" Her girls. She said she had not wanted them near her.

She was desperate and torn. "I have gone mad, fighting back in the only way I knew how to hurt him." She hesitated as if wanting to tell Magdalen something important. Magdalen wondered... *would she speak of the baby she bore and discarded?* "My God, my beautiful girls, I miss them so...more than anyone, anything, more than him. I want to die and live at the same time." It was then Magdalen realized...*this is shocking: no one has told her, her baby boy lives and is fighting for his life somewhere. What had she thought happened?*

Magdalen could hardly breathe; she could say nothing; it wasn't her place. She would say other things. "Detective Padric says your pain is on him, but we know now the only two in your house that awful day were Joanna Cantera and her son, who wanted nothing to do with what *she* was doing...he wouldn't just kill."

Lara said she knew of him and was oddly touched by his story despite all he had done. Magdalen realized this woman had seen Bernardo up close, asked several more questions. She was trying to remember, wanting to help. "I think...yes, he was there but did nothing, never touched me; he acted like he wanted to leave but was silent, said not a word, looking frustrated." She paused.

Magdalen asked her to continue. "And that is why I thought it could be my husband after Dan Mason suggested it; that he had simply watched, unable to control his woman, this Joanna, that he simple let her do to me what she did. But that boy, that son of hers; I forgive him."

Silence...the women stared at each other. This was profound.

"How generous of you...so few would say this. This Bernardo is wired differently."

"I know...I know. I was played. I've watched and read everything I could on the case, thought it through on my own. I do that with every case Johnny has worked, discussing it with him. A detective, who has envied my husband forever, spun a tale. We were at our lowest; our marriage…" She was unable to continue and wondered if Magdalen understood. "His work made him invisible; we weren't speaking and my husband has…has needs." The nun could only imagine. "She, this Joanna, is a sociopath with a dark side. She's a collector…she made it hard for him to walk away."

Her insight was uncanny.

But Magdalen would refrain from offering her own assessment of Joanna Cantera, a soul defeated and broken, someone in need of a friend…a woman condemned by everyone. She had no idea she would be meeting her again under different circumstances.

But it was time to withdraw, and Magdalen hoped she'd not overstayed. Grateful for the conversation and all it had done for her spirit, Lara embraced her. "You are my blessing, Sister." But she said something that sent chills through Magdalen. "When you are most in need, I will be there for you." Were her words a foreboding?

Magdalen slipped from the room. But alone in the hall, she was suddenly tearful. John Padric would be less in her life now; she'd done this for him regardless of what she told Lara. But the baby…*he must tell her.* She would insist Padric do this. Dolorosa was waiting at the end of the hall. Within seconds, two nuns, holding hands, ran up the stairs. On the fourth floor, Gina was waiting for them.

"Gently now." But Petra cried out not gently at all; her Sisters rushed to her. *Familia.*

Gina envied their joy. She walked quietly down the hall and sat by herself for longer than she intended. How like a chessboard these last days had been, moving her patients and visitors about and making things right. Returning to the floor, she moved quietly from one patient to the next. Her cell phone lit up. "Johnny?" Silence. "Where are you, downtown?"

"Downstairs."

"Are you bringing someone in? Is it bad?"

"I'm bringing myself in and yeah, I'd say it's bad…I'm here to take back my woman."

"Well, you're right on cue. Your nun just spoke with Lara for almost an hour and left her over thirty minutes ago. In fact, your wife is asleep for the first time in a month without being sedated."

Silence. "I'm there."

She never heard them enter the room. Gina noiselessly drew the blinds, dimmed the lights. She hooked a Do Not Disturb sign on the knob. Padric winked. "Damn, you're good."

Lara lay with eyes closed…she was smiling, asleep; He watched her and wondered if his nun had touched her with one of her healing kisses. Did he believe this stuff…damn, *how desperate was am I?* He wasn't even sure he wanted to be here but knew it was right; it had to be done. *Isn't this what you do if you want redemption?* He wondered if Jesus had thought the same thing before he walked into the garden and got slammed by Judas and those uppity Pharisees. But then…Sister Moira would be telling him he wasn't Jesus.

John Padric sat down on the chair by the door as he'd done full of pain several nights ago. Lara stirred, but still with eyes closed turned on her side. He said nothing, still watching her…not sure of his own feelings since their last conversation, but he had no time to change his mind.

Lara suddenly opened her eyes; she sat up. "Johnny?"

They studied each other…both complicated, proud, each with their own issues, wanting it settled one way or the other and it had to be now. They both spoke at once…she stopped. He nodded. He'd let her "have at him"…he looked down at the floor, listening. But oddly there was no condemnation, grief and pain maybe, but she'd said all she wanted to say the other night. Now in one last ditch effort, she was crying out, pleading for understanding; he countered her every word with his own list of *mea culpas.*

And then he said it, told her the truth: "The baby, luv, our son is alive." She was near broken, remembering, struggling to put things together, not understanding her own feelings and desperate at the thought he was so far away and she not beside him.

At one point, he thought he might have to call Gina for something to calm her. But she became peaceful, listening to all he would say. Right or wrong, Padric would make it clear: if she held the slightest repugnance for the boy, he'd walk away with him and the girls, raise the three on his own with family. Bluntly put, he told her she'd done it to him by keeping the boy from him; "there were a thousand other ways you could have put it to me."

He would go even further regardless of outcome: "Despite my guilt in all this, I'm not sure I can ever come back with my whole heart after not knowing I had a son and he was with strangers when I could have been there."

She lay down again on the pillows and closed her eyes. Both knew things would never quite be the same; they'd make a life together again with the children. As for Johnny Padric, he'd always be restless, his heart full of discontent, dutifully loving the woman he married but loving more the one he could never have. Martinez would say later in life: you don't mess with Johnny when it comes to some things. He never forgets. But...Lara wouldn't forget either.

Neither had reached out to touch each other for over an hour but he could stand it no longer. She knew her husband and opened her arms; he pulled her to him and kissed her; but her gown fell away and she froze, remembering. He stopped, reassuring her of his love, his sorrow. He sat back "Lara, I can wait."

"No, you can't. After all this time and all we have suffered."

"It's fine but what is it then; tell me, luv?"

"My breast, the scar, her mark on me...I cannot." She pointed; he frowned and asked where it was, what was she talking about; he knew well the scar, the bruising and bite marks; he'd agonized over it. But now there was nothing...they were gone.

Padric was too realistic for miracles, thing happening for no reason weren't part of his world but still...he gently showed her. "Look...you're beautiful; what are you seeing?" Lara looked down with tears in her eye...his nun had been here. "There's nothing." He held her close. "You are free, we are. Come on, lass; let me show you how sorry I am. Let me do what I do..."

This wasn't the first time the two had found each other again. But this time, it had been terrifying for both of them. She smiled a little and whispered the last line in James Joyce's *Ulysses*...they'd read it aloud together in pubs on Bloomsday, a yearly remembrance for the book and the poet among the Irish in L'Arroyo.

"And his heart was going like mad and yes I said, yes, I will, yes."

"Ah, Molly Bloom now, you're quotin'…I love you, lass."

Leaving Lara was difficult. He said he needed to speak with the doctors and forced himself from the room; he'd be back to take her home within days. In their white jackets, they stood at the end of the hall; he walked toward them. John Padric, an observer of human behavior, noted how they'd glanced at each other when they saw him. They could do nothing else but invite him into their working space behind the glass in the nurses' station.

The doctors would tell him "next week…she could go home." But Padric had questions about the drugs his wife had been given; they said she unfortunately exhibited the side effects often linked with her medications…they would research it further. But he questioned as well their ethics in colluding with his wife in keeping from him that he had a son.

When one of the braver doctors, who knew little about the detective, suggested his actions had almost sent her over the edge, he agreed and after informing the man it wasn't his judgment to make, he laid out the *Padric law* for all within earshot: *Thou shalt not screw him over*…he'd done enough of that to his wife. But she and they had done wrong as well and they as professionals more culpable. Whether this was right in the court of public opinion, was something else. The man had a point.

To the doctors, it was apples and oranges. Padric however insisted that to refrain from telling a man he had a son because an unwell, depressed, sadly scorned woman told them to do it was absurd…just how often, to put it bluntly, did they allow themselves to be pussy-whipped by a woman. He wasn't a criminal; he's the one who went looking for bad guys at night all over this fucking city.

Granted, he'd broken his marriage vows "not unlike some of you standing in front of me." He knew the habits of two of them; both notorious womanizers and they knew he knew. They paled.

"And you punish me, pass judgment on me? *Is hell empty and all the devils are here?*" They stared at him.

But Sebastian finishing his rounds suddenly appeared on the floor and recognized a familiar voice. "My God, he's quoting Shakespeare." He quietly checked in on Lara who urged him to stop whatever her husband was doing...but she was smiling a little. The priest was relieved but hurried back to the nurses' station and beheld a not too content John Padric; the doctors' faces, quite somber. He approached.

"And it will not be next week...enough! My wife needs family; we need her. She wasn't herself when she made those requests; the woman is brilliant and would have acted differently had you monitored her intake of medications more closely. She's far from a weak person. In two days you will release her."

Sebastian stepped forward. "I think you can do that for the detective...he has just come off a demanding case as you know, Doctors; you are caring for more than one of its victims. You will assist him in every way."

They acquiesced, but said Padric would need to proceed with Lara slowly to which he retorted he never "proceeded" nor did he ever do anything "slowly"; he wanted her home and had been too long without her...to put it bluntly again.

"John. Come with me, John." Padric smiled...the young priest had said the same to a feisty bishop two days ago. They walked down the hall and entered Lara's room; now it was she who was calm and at peace and worried at what he might say and already shaking her finger at him.

But she smiled and pleaded. "Yes, in two days then please." And she would go every day to the abbey no matter how many months it would take for her baby to be whole and happy; if permitted she'd sleep there, bring her girls if allowed...they'd help the Sisters.

To his surprise, Lara insisted: "Sister Magdalen must bless him, kiss his head and his hands. She did this for me. I must see my Finn...a perfect name. Take me to him. Take me home...my girls." She stopped, looking desperately from one to the other. She reached out to her husband. "And you...I must come home with you now."

Padric glanced at Sebastian…he was smiling and sat down with the two and they talked for some time; the first in several marriage counseling sessions for Mr. and Mrs. Padric had begun. What she'd done, what he'd done…they'd fix it; they'd talk to each other, kiss more like a nun had told Padric to do…a nun, but he would never reveal that to either of them. Father left and they continued to speak until Padric said he must go.

He glanced at Gina; he was grateful but she mentioned the Sisters were still in the building. His nun. "She's here? Where?"

"Now Johnny let her be…she's with Sister Petra."

He smiled a little; she went to see her without me; *the hell with it…the woman can do whatever she wants.* Lara's kisses had been balm to his wounds. He'd go…leave the nuns to their happiness. He'd go to the abbey, have a sit-down with his son; tell him about his beautiful mother and some problems he'd had.

Saturday morning, April 26

Anxious and awaiting his wife's return, he'd fitfully tossed and turned in the new bed but his mind constantly returned to his son…his thoughts were never far from him. Off-duty for two days and the first time in ages, his head was still at the Precinct. He'd let the women fuss over Lara's homecoming and, with Tark and Martinez, emptied the storage pod. His condo upstairs at last looked like home; more importantly, the bookcases were up; his books out of their boxes and ready to sort; Lara would laugh.

Kara and Kate were delighted with everything and Padric sighed as he watched them run from one room to the other…at last their mother would hold them again, read stories and fix their hair, paint their toe nails and make them paint his turquoise blue while he slept. She'd play ragtime and songs from the Sound of Music and all of Granny's old Irish tunes on the piano at night before bedtime…she'd cook; she was a good cook.

Meadow was releasing Lara after eleven this morning and when he arrived, he thought it odd the guards at the gate only nodded without the usual banter. Gina looked up and the nurses looked down at their charts when he stepped off the elevator; *am I paranoid?* It was hard living a cop's life, scanning the smallest detail, not letting anything pass. He kept walking but turned when Gina called out: "Johnny, wait!"

He knew her…the edge in her voice flipped on a switch. "Gina, what's going on? I'm here to pick up my girl."

"Johnny." Gently she guided him into Lara's old room. "You must promise me you will listen." It was serious when Gina said this; he looked around, nothing but a well-made bed with fresh linens; no Lara, her books gone…machines and equipment removed.

Had she changed her mind about starting over and simply left? "Where is she?"

Agent Bobby Watson had been alerted when Padric entered the building; he was on the floor in seconds, now in the doorway. "Johnny. Sit down."

"And now you're gonna tell me we've got a situation. Where the fuck is she?" His eyes were empty. "Where is she, damn it!"

"Johnny, Dan Mason escaped two hours ago from federal custody; the guards said he was on his way here. They found papers, some notes, in his cell…he was coming for Lara. But Judge Whitton was here visiting those two wounded officers from that bank shootout. He took Lara to an undisclosed location; he said he'd contact you."

"Did he now…how fucking undisclosed do you think that might be? Son-of-a-bitch, that dickless wonder, walks off with my Lara and no heads up? Fuck you. Where's Mason?"

"We don't know."

"Who's on him?"

"Our people and a fugitive retrieval team, everybody…drones are in the air."

Damn it. "He's dead when I see him; the fool's dead. What the fuck is the Bureau running over there? Jay Whitton…he always wanted my Lara." Padric paler, still wanted details.

"Johnny, she's safe and…."

"In an undisclosed location…I know. Last Sunday you caught the tail end of a theory Mason was selling my wife. A nun had to come in here and work a miracle. Do you know how much conversation it took to bring my girl back from what he said to her?"

"Do I know? You're kidding!" Gina wasn't happy…she'd put hours into Lara Padric. "What do you think I've been doing here? For reasons that maybe you should think about, Lara believed you and this *puta* wanted her gone. I'll be frank, Johnny…any woman who knows Joanna Cantera had a piece of her man will suffer." Gina looked at Watson. "Talk to him, Bobby, before I kick his ass. Fuck me…fuck us? Fuck you, Johnny, get a grip."

He'd been given an attitude adjustment by the best in the business. But there was Jay Whitton. "Of all the bastards, he's the one who comes to the rescue? He's never gotten over it that Lara loved me, not him; married me and not him." He pounded his fist on the arm of the chair. "I thought he was bigger than this. I never…"

Gina would give it another shot. "We had to insure her safety. He was trying to help. It isn't even about us and the feelings we're dealing with." He wasn't seeing the whole picture.

Johnny looked at her for a long time; his cell lit up. "What?"

"Johnny, don't be answering your mum on the phone like that." Padric rolled his eyes and put it on speaker. Watson closed the door…*this should be good.*

"Mum, I lost Lara."

"I know you did."

"I'm dyin' here. Whatta ya' know?"

"Laddy, she's sittin' here with her Kara and Kate and with…"

"Jay Whitton."

"Judge Whitton, where's your respect?" *Respect.*

"Get him the fuck out of there now?"

"Shame on ya, Johnny. I'll get crazy on you and you won't like it." Gina and Watson smiled…here was someone in the universe who could shut him down. He was silent.

"Johnny?" Mairead.

"Readie?" He relaxed…his sister could do that to him.

"Judge Whitton wants a word. There was a reason why he did what he did."

"Fuck him."

"Now you listen to him, *bhoyo,* and don't go all Johnny on him."
Watson laughed; he and Padric had walked a beat together years
ago...he knew about Johnny going all Johnny.

"I don't have to do any such thing. I want him out of there now."

"Johnny, this is Jay."

"Fuck you, Jay. Get the fuck out of my sister's house, you son-
of-a-bitch. I'll cut you down where you stand." Gina looked worried. "You'll have two broken knees when I'm done with ya"...we
do that where I'm from." Again Watson laughed. Gina glared.

"I imagine you would. You're in better shape than I am...let
me meet you somewhere."

"Fuck you. I want to talk to my wife."

"Johnny?" Lara. Her voice.

But he couldn't respond; his heart rate was suddenly soaring
through the roof; his face chalky; his eyes, staring at Gina. He was
pointing to his heart. "Lara, what the fuck are you doing?" He was
gasping now.

"Johnny, come home. Come to your mum's. You're upset."

"Honey, I'm beyond upset. I..." He was perspiring now...he
stood up, his knees buckled under him. "I'm not doing so good..."
His cell phone dropped to the floor.

Lara cried out: "Johnny, my God. I can't lose him! Gina!" But
all she could hear was a code blue and shouting. Quickly the two
pulled Padric onto the bed and hooked him up to a monitor. He
grabbed a small pillbox from his pocket and handed it to Gina. She
slipped one under his tongue and wondered why he was carrying it.
The room was suddenly brimming over with staff. "Is he having a
heart attack?"

"Pretty close. He's been under unbelievable pressure, no wonder." It would be twenty minutes before he was stabilized and his
color returned. With eyes closed, he'd give in to her care and drifted off. They would not leave his side until he finally opened his
eyes. Gina kissed his forehead. "Thank God, Johnny! What are you
doing to me? I thought we had lost you. How long have you been
carrying these around?"

"Doc's orders...was feeling some pressure, shortness of breath.
This case with the nuns and the priests really got to me. That thing

with my Lara and what I did to her and then what those sick, miserable fucks did to her, and then there's my nun…"

She smiled. "The one who visited Lara; she's your nun?"

"Yeah, she's a beauty but off-limits, my nun. I just call her that. I love her…"

"And you love Lara."

"Yeah, most of all, I love Lara…but the nun, I need to take care of her…" Watson and Gina winked at each other. "Yeah, I love Lara, my lass…" He drifted off but came back. "Those pills…I was feeling things. It's what I did to Lara and my girls; it's wee Kara and Kate. They're so small…and my boy now." His voice trailed off. Padric squeezed Gina's hand. "Probably the only lad in Belfast who never touched a cig; was a good lad once, never smoked…" He was so tired. "Did everything else wrong…did it all badly."

Only John Padric would end a sentence with an adverb.

He woke up to rays of sunshine dusting the bed covers.

Padric was not sure how long he'd been sleeping or where he was. He blinked…his wife was beside him, watching him. He could hear his girls laughing…Nick Jr. or Disney. He tried to roll over to pull her close and fell back in pain. "What did I do to myself?"

She laughed; "You threw out your shoulder when you took a swing at Jay Whitton"

"Damn, where'd I do that?"

"At the bottom of the stairs when he was leaving."

"Did the girls see it?"

"Oh, no. They were with us at Mairead's."

"When did I do that? Damn…did I take it into the street?"

"Almost. Bobby stopped you. You didn't come home until late with him and Gina. After you hit Jay, they brought you upstairs and she gave you a sedative."

"Christ, what's mum thinkin'?"

"She was proud of you. She doesn't like him anymore."

"And why's that?"

"She offered him a glass of sherry and he wouldn't take it."

"That's it?"

"It was her best sherry." They laughed.

Having nowhere to go and his wife in his arms; to hear his girls in the other room playing dress-up…had he walked through the looking glass into some kind of Wonderland?

She whispered to him: "Look, Johnny, this was left this morning. A runner from Jay's law office dropped it off." She pointed to a bottle of Jameson next to the bed. "Read the card."

"When you're up for some racquetball, I'll get even. Cheers, Jay. We need to talk ASAP. See me tomorrow after my morning in court." Padric flipped the card in the air.

"ASAP? Fuck him!" Their laughter brought Kara and Kate squealing into the room and a knock at the door brought breakfast in bed from downstairs. Mairead assured them this would not be "a daily service they'd be gettin'."

Padric hated to admit it: watching Jay Whitton at work was like watching a bloodsport. Everyone knew he had a penchant for going after the lawyers; even the defendants liked being in court. But Whitton was fair and meted out an equitable justice. Like the other men in his family, he lived flamboyantly, had a broad view of things, but kept his clarity on the bench. Today the prosecution was haranguing on charts the jury had seen once too often. Jay had been silent long enough. "Your visuals are growing a beard and I'm getting bald here. Move it along, Counselor."

Some in the courtroom laughed. When he finally said: "Court is adjourned until nine tomorrow morning" he looked back at Padric and motioned him into his chambers.

Martinez said he'd wait in the hall.

Though the invite he'd sent with the Jameson was lighthearted, the judge was not looking forward to a face-to-face with the man; Padric, with an ax to grind, could be formidable. He pointed to a chair; the detective ignored it and walked to the window staring down at the Plaza. "What the fuck were you thinking, Jay? Why'd you do it?"

"To protect you and Lara."

"And now you're Batman?"

"That's *your* alter-ego. You were both in hot water."

"Hot water's new? Answer this: a month ago, I'm waiting for the elevator down the hall and I see you and that punk-ass Mason backslapping each other, yuckin' it up; who was working who?"

"Always on the job. You don't miss a thing."

"Shut up, your Honor! What did I see?"

"Mason's a rat-bastard ferret, always working an angle to stick it to someone and deluding himself into thinking I give a shit. I remember...because I never saw him again after that; this fuck-up laid out a "what-if", what if you tried to kill your wife. He had no interest in solving the case; he was obsessing over your Lara and I couldn't tell you."

"Why the fuck not?"

"Would you tell someone like you that kind of *intel*? You're a volcano walking." Silence...but Padric went off on Jay all over again. Jay shut him down. "I can't tell you the number of times he's come to me with shit...he's a dangerous man. You had enough on your mind; we decided to work it from our end. Two months ago, we searched his place, his desk and locker at the station in Sunset City."

"Probable cause?"

"He talked too much, had designs on people, you included; his weapon of choice defamation of character, slander, ruining lives. I had no idea of his thing for Lara. It gets darker...his place, what he's done with it."

"And I assume, you'll give me the name of his interior decorator. Hurry this up. If he's out there, I need to check on my wife...I need to go."

"And very well you should; when we're finished here, go to his condo. It's under heavy guard now. He'll need to go back there; he's got...you need to see it. Take your partner; everyone knows you. They'll let you in."

"I need to bury him for what he did to my Lara. It was mind-rape."

"He was killing two birds with one stone, ruining you and

destroying whatever you had in your marriage. His reward: Lara. About those interviews with the Canteras…watched the tapes. Who'd believe it…you with the likes of Joanna Cantera and all she was spouting? She's a wack job." Padric looked down at the floor… *so he doesn't know. He's watched tapes of the interviews, in a hurry maybe, thought it was garbage. Damn. Martinez said this would happen…the Commander knew this, so did the Cap'. They said no one would believe it.*

Padric's eyes narrowed. "She's who Mason put me with at my house." He felt like a hypocrite with all his outrage. "Did you believe it?"

"Of course not, absolutely not, but I have people." *I bet he does;* Padric wanted to hear this. "Mason likes pillow talk and took some broad he was banging into his confidence. He told her he planned to scare the hell out of a detective, stash his wife somewhere, enjoy her for a while." Padric could hardly breathe; this was more than he had imagined. "His gal-pal that night was an escort and paid informant." *Wonder who laid out the bucks for that?* "When Mason was questioned about what he'd said, he put two and two together; my people found her body behind the Dragoon. His day will come."

Padric slumped into a chair. "Your people…Christ, you sound like a gangster! Who's taking responsibility for that woman losing her life, putting her there? This is bad business. Damn, you knew he was after Lara; that he'd get to her. Do you know what he did to her?" *But damn, what am I saying…I drove her crazy for months.* "Gina Chavez picked up the pieces." Johnny Padric felt like a phony…it was his mess.

"Tell me what you'd have done if you knew?"

There was silence for a moment: "I'd have killed him."

Jay didn't flinch. "I rest my case. You're a crazy, good cop with a risky jacket, a file full of trouble with authority and the way you deal with shit in the streets. But I hear how victims love you; even perps want to see you after I put them away. You follow up with the families on both sides, for God's sake. You're Batman with flaws."

He heard about my stash of comic books…that I know the way to the rooftop of every building edging the Plaza. "My wife says I should thank you but I won't."

Whitton didn't care. "I was there and was asked to step up."

"So what does my lass do now, hide for the rest of her life, live with the First Precinct outside her door just because she's my wife and this fool has a hard-on for my ass? She'll never be safe as long as that son-of-a-bitch is out there." He pulled out his cell phone then paced up and down like a cat. It had been done already: Cunningham and Nevel had been pulled off Mairead's door and ordered upstairs to guard Lara; besides, his girls missed the dog. "How'd you get Lara to go with you?"

"Are you kidding me? When I explained it to Lara, well, some of it, she got it. I saw her eyes light up when she walked through your sister's door."

"And you don't get it, Jay. I wanted to see that, to watch her face when our girls hugged her and my mum kissed her. Damn you...you're not family." Whitton was silent; his face changed. He knew something and wasn't saying.

"Mairead and she are good friends I see...they hooked on to each other like glue with your girls crawling all over her." And he'd taken that moment away from him, too.

"Thanks for that." Padric was unrelenting. "Do you know what it's been like for me and my girls? I want to lay you out cold." But in all his posturing, he knew. *I'm one miserable son-of-a-bitch; my woman would never have taken a hit if I hadn't fucked her assailant.*

Whitton looked out the window. "Okay, okay...I get it. Bobby Watson asked for an assist. I thought you'd be glad. I didn't hang out with your family or sit down with them. I stood outside the door with Cunningham if that makes you feel any better. What a good-looker your sister is though, Johnny?"

"Don't even go there. I've warned her about all you married Darby Hill boys."

"Married? Not anymore...she left me, found out I was spending my time with someone else?" He looked away. "It was Joanna Cantera...got caught up, did wrong." *And there it is. Hadn't the Commander said the man was very conflicted?* "I couldn't get enough of her." *Yeah, I know the feeling.* Padric listened to the man's regrets...rarely did anyone hear this coming from the Honorable Jay Whitton.

But now he needed to leave; remembering Martinez was waiting for him, he found him asleep on a bench in the hall. He roused him but looked back at Whitton. "Dan Mason's done."

"Amen." A look passed between them. "Do what you must if it comes to that." According to Whitton, when he landed under the FBI's microscope, "Shit hit the fan with a lot of complaints. Bad stuff. Foul, a full jacket of misdemeanors and conduct unbecoming. There's something else you need to know: he lives dangerously, flipping back and forth between a neo-Nazi white group north of the I-10 and, get this, some *familia* connected big time to human trafficking back and forth over the Border into Cali and Az, baby...the list goes on. His case is coming up soon if we can find him, but Judge Jane Ellis...she's a pistol; the duchess will stick a needle in his arm."

"I want only one reward when I find him, and I will."

"God, what is that?"

"If he's not dead after I'm finished with him, than let me watch him hang publicly. I'll be doing some damage on this one." Silence. That he would openly say this to a judge terrified Martinez, but Whitton smiled a little; Johnny boy would never get caught.

"Tell me this, whatever possessed O'Manion to assign that fool to your wife's case?"

The men didn't appreciate the innuendo against their Captain and Martinez jumped in: "The Cap' was giving that *cabron* a chance to redeem himself and be a better man for it."

Whitton grinned. "You're a good man, Alex; Johnny doesn't deserve you. Loyalty. But that was a risk for a stellar cop like O'Manion to take; he and I need to talk."

"And you'll keep your hands off O'Manion." Padric was adamant. "He's first-class. I swear, I'll..." Martinez stopped him.

Whitton grinned. "Ah, true blue, both of you. I'm surprised you didn't file a law suit on Mason with all you and Lara have been through." Had he not thought of it already? But not with his luck, it would blow up in his face. Besides...the guilt in the end was his.

"Suing someone isn't my style." Martinez shook his head.

Whitton laughed. "Yeah, I forgot...but self-anointed, self-appointed vigilante is. Watch yourself."

This fool is telling me to watch myself? Kettle black. "Fuck you, Jay."
He kept walking. "Racquetball, Thursday, your ass is mine."

They took a ride, talked, Martinez concerned...his man feeling the stress had needed medical attention. He turned down the street slowly. "There...at the end of the block; that ten story, second floor." It was an impressive high-rise of condominiums in an upscale neighborhood. "That shit bag lives here?"

Two vans, unmarked with dark tinted windows, were parked down the street. Padric and Martinez smiled...FBI. No one acknowledged each other. The doorman was an agent, who recognized the detectives but said nothing; he talked with his eyes...law enforcement all over the city knew Padric's wife was in danger.

Upstairs two uniforms stepped aside. Dan Mason had impeccable taste...minimalist, black and white. Martinez moved down the hall, waited for Padric then pointed. They stepped into a master bedroom. Lara was smiling at him.

It was a shrine like no other; here was his wife immortalized in poster and print, some larger than life, wall to wall candles, some burned to their wick. A huge, well-made bed against one wall made Padric ill; from here, this sick freak had contemplated his wife.

He'd abducted her in his own mind and made her his own...
it was his sanctuary. Padric's eyes scanned the room and knew if he stayed one second longer, he'd tear the whole place apart.

"Get me the fuck out of here, *kema sabe.*"

His wife would be waiting for him this time. He sped home.

Padric could smell his favorite mesquite chicken through the door...she was back and he was hungry but spoke for several long minutes with Cunningham; Nevel was excited to see him.

At last inside, he called out to Lara. She'd taken a shower and was wrapped in a towel. "Where are the girls, luv?"

"Downstairs with their granny."

He smiled his slow smile and unbuttoned his shirt.

It was twilight. Bobby Watson gazed at the reflection of the city lights in his new lady's eyes. She was beautiful; it had been one

of the best nights of his life. They were seated by a window at a ma-
hogany-wrapped bar in the Drambuie. Gina had been here years
ago and never returned; back then she'd sat in a corner with a lover
named Johnny.

"Are you trying to impress me, Agent Watson?"

"Oh, yeah." She was surprised when he had brought her here.
They'd been meeting for lunch, a drink after work; it was more than
comfortable for both of them.

"I was impressed already. You know that." He said he hadn't
been sure. "I wouldn't have spent as much time with you. I have so
little of it with my schedule."

"I'm feeling it, too. When's your next day off?" They talked
about schedules, the patients, Dan Mason…and Johnny. Both knew
him well. "How's Lara Padric doing?"

"It's delicate. But she's tough and at home with family…the
same with the nun, Sister Petra. I miss her. I miss Lara, but her
situation was starting to wear on me."

"Johnny gave his wife a run for her money…he'd been playing
around, right?"

"He's been known to do that, yes." She looked away; it didn't
go unnoticed by an observant FBI agent. He'd let it go. "Johnny's
complicated and doesn't think he is; he has his own demons…we all
do. What are yours, Bobby? Tell me everything."

He grinned. "Hang with me more and I'll show you. Are you
up for that, Sarg?"

"Yes, sir." He asked if she'd like to go and hang out. She smiled.

He put his arm around her. "Come on, you can meet some of
my demons."

Monday, noon, May 19

Justice takes time in the Sonoran but a blue moon high in the
sky on the night of the Cantera arrests was said to have changed
that…for once. It didn't take long; weighing the scales of justice
Whitton-style was swift.

Media coverage and the sacrilegious nature of the crimes had
so burdened the public mind, there was no will to prolong the pro-

cess; the statewide obsession over the case, so pervasive. It was impossible to find an untainted jury for sentencing. It was left to the judge, but there was talk in the streets of plotting vengeance against the Canteras…vigilante justice was common.

Today the courtroom overflowed with family and friends of the victims; one victim on the arm of Magdalen appeared in the courtroom; Petra was here with her parents. No one from the Genova family as yet had responded either to convent or Precinct in regard to Lucy; Major Crimes and the coroner maintained their silence but Magdalen would say in open court she represented her Sister Lucy today. Though they'd never discussed it, Padric knew Magdalen sensed Lucy was gone from the morgue. He waited and wondered what she might do. The nun would uncover a ruse so bazaar, it would only continue the drama of all that had happened. Lucy's story was for another day in late summer.

It was High Noon in L'Arroyo.

Joanna was there; Bernardo was not. When it was time for family and friends to speak for the victims, they unleashed their resentment and outrage not only on Joanna but her father, who was present; they berated him and his parenting, his misplaced love for his daughter. Her reckless life of entitlement had made her hard and cold, a horrible mother…she was a joke.

Privacy would not be safe in the courtroom today. Arturo Cantera was seemingly there to be sentenced as well. His eyes flickered with anger, but not a muscle moved in his face when Cecelia's parents belittled him for his weakness in not controlling his iron-willed wife. The judge would allow it. They claimed Lidia Cantera was the reason for Joanna's delinquency, her son's depravity, but unwittingly, provided some mitigating circumstances for the defendant. Others turned on the man, too caught up in his deals on either side of the Border to rein in Joanna or to speak for a grandson living alone in a graveyard. And the bishop…he should be here, his absence cowardly.

Stoically, Petra and Magdalen, eyes down, gripped each other's hand, listening as father and daughter were flayed in public with nowhere to hide. They wondered why a judge would allow it but Whitton knew what he was doing. *Let others condemn them and save me the trouble…*he was reluctant to lash out at the Canteras for many reasons; after all, he slept with one of the killers.

He asked if anyone else wished to speak and a nun rose to her feet. In the back of the courtroom, the detective's heart skipped a beat…*their nun, his lass, Holy Mary.* John Padric and his team had slipped quietly into the back during the ruckus and were now standing together like gargoyles. The crew would let no one touch him… they were on recoil and ready to pounce. He had not seen the nuns, one a victim, the other her advocate; he groaned inside that it had come to this. There was silence now…dead silence.

"Sister Magdalen, is it? We thank the Sisters of San Miguel for their commitment and dedication to our city." Whitton was curious…*this is Padric's girl; well, she's his friend.* Major Crimes had spoken good things of her. He knew why she was here.

"Your honor, I speak as an advocate on behalf of my Sister, our Sister Petra…she was a victim and still is. But it seems two are condemned here today, only one to be sentenced. I will address both very briefly."

Joanna was breathless…*the angel-nun, is this some kind of omen?*

Whitton was ecstatic…a nun in his courtroom. She walked slowly to the table where Joanna sat, eyes straight ahead. Here standing before her was the woman she'd hated, the one who had taken her man. *But what is she saying now?*

"Ms. Cantera, my Sister, was one of your victims, she survived your attack, your desecration of her, but where are the others… Sisters Cecelia and Lucy? I loved them and miss them. Sister Petra and I mourn the loss of good Father Villa and our Brother James. I found the Cathedral's new priest, Father Sebastian, near death in the desert beyond the Edge. He survived…he lives like my Sister still with the pain of it but says very little about what you and your son did. And there is another, a beautiful woman, the wife of a police officer, a detective…Lara, what a lovely name. She lives."

Padric had tears in his eyes. *Damn…She's taking a chance.*

But Magdalen had trusted her sense of things. Joanna might blurt out her mantra: *No one gets between me and my man*...and that could ruin him. But she didn't. Padric wouldn't have cared, not anymore, but where would he go after such a public admission by one condemned? Only angels could hear him sob aloud in his soul.

Martinez touched his arm; he knew. "Hold, *kema sabe*, hold."

But suddenly Joanna reached out to the nun. "And I hurt you, *angél de Dios*...forgive me. I'm sorry." She laid her head on the table. The courtroom gasped; *what angel is this that she speaks of?* Whitton was happy. Her defense lawyer, grateful...*the nun knows what she's doing, showing mercy when no one else will.*

Joanna had shown little remorse but Magdalen placed her hand on her head. "My Sister wishes me to say she forgives you, forgives your son...wishes you mercy and the presence of Jesus." Silence.

She turned. Arturo had stood silent by the podium from which family could speak. Whitton wanted him there. During his years on the bench, he'd not only watched, he'd choreographed this kind of drama every day. But now something else was happening; with players larger than life, all of them passionate; a city looking for justice was rising from the ashes on their words and emotions.

The nun approached. The older Cantera bowed his head. "Sir, my Sister wishes to express her sympathies to you in your present predicament in facing the crimes of your family. But we are saddened that you are condemned as well, appalled at the demand for bloodletting in your regard. We..."

He raised his hand and was grateful. "*Gracias*, much respect, but no, *hermana*, not *we*, you...I want to know *your* thoughts."

"His honor has no desire to hear my personal take on this case and I will withdraw."

And she was right...Whitton would call for a thirty minute recess to deliberate in chambers; the prisoner removed from the courtroom. All were permitted to remain in their seats but oddly no one spoke, the venom gone. Someone whispered the nun, the bishop's sacristan, had put out the fire; the momentum they'd built in the streets. The parents of Sister Cecelia however were angry, hurt that she'd shown the condemned mercy, but then…perhaps they should behave. Those around them were quiet, now understood; others murmured her name. Magdalen attempted to speak with them…they turned away.

Major Crimes stepped into the hall, spoke to no one, circled Padric; they didn't see an officer invite the Sisters through the door they had used to remove Joanna. Her defense lawyer, the very same Conor O'Connor, was waiting, graciously guiding Petra into a softly lit waiting area. Quickly a paralegal was bringing her tea and offering her comfort. He turned to Magdalen, requesting she might have a last word with his client; his eyes so intense, so unusual, she knew at that moment, they were connected in a most holy way.

He opened a door. Joanna was waiting. "Oh, Sister…" She reached for her, shackles weighing her down.

"What is it, Ms. Cantera?"

"No, no, I am Joanna. I wanted to remember your angel-face and be blessed again."

"Joanna, please…my face? I am not what you think."

"Yes, you are. I don't have much time. Whatever happens, knowing you will pray for me will be all that keeps me whole. I'm going to hell." Magdalen stepped closer.

Her lawyer asked. "What is she talking about, Sister, is this legit?" But he knew.

She shook her head, said it was nothing, perhaps something Ms. Cantera had hoped she might find in her. "If she is cuffed and unable to leave where she sits, could we not have a moment alone?" She had noticed there were no cameras; she'd take her chances. A killer, a woman sick and bewitched and now loathed, needed to speak to a nun, a woman she'd hated.

The guards left the room; the lawyer remained on the other side of the glass. "When there are so many you may have asked for, why me, Ms. Cantera?"

Joanna lowered her head. "Please, I wanted the light of your wings to cover me just one more time. I'm going into the dark and will never feel human kindness again. I'll fight back with everything I have, be obnoxious, mouth off, knock someone around and have the same thing happen to me. I'll land in one of those holes at Ravenswell and never come out until put to death unless…" She looked down at the floor.

"Unless what?" No answer. "So how can I help…I'm powerless to change any of this for you unless you try to comply with the rules there and make something better out of it all. And those wings…I have no control over it and apologize if you are misled."

"In the tunnel…it was the first time in years, I was held like a child. I am hated and my name will be linked to evil forever. If only for a moment, you were like a mother to me though we are probably close in age. I wanted to ask that you look after my son… he loves you more than me and has no idea I'm his mother. And this is as it should be…I have no soul."

Here was the articulate, educated Joanna, Padric had known once. The two women conversed quietly for more than ten minutes. But the door opened; her words left dangling in Magdalen's head. Two guards stepped into the room.

"It's time…we have to move this along. Leave." *No finesse here… may God help us all.* They guided her from the room. The lawyer joined her; he took her breath away, she, not believing how close he was…yes, it was he; the same she had met in the garden. Here was the angel, Sanctus, walking among them, serving them. A strange and sudden peace filled these harsh surroundings; it was a cold place, full of decisions and final judgments.

Tall, with long, sun-streaked hair tied back at the neck, the man had a noble brow, good eyes; the tone of his voice unusual, full of assurances. "Thanks, Sister, your coming here today calmed her. As you see, Ms. Cantera finally asked for an attorney, as did her son; I offered my services. I work *pro bono* for those who no one wants anymore."

"But how can you afford to do this, forgive me for asking."

"I've been blessed." *Yes, I imagine you have, good spirit.* "My father's wealth allows me to do this. *His Father, his heavenly Father, yes.* "He has a large estate far from here, but he has been a judge for years and oversees all that I do. It's our way of giving back. He insists on it."

Magdalen almost wept. *His Father.*

He extended his hand; his grip so compelling, she felt dizzy. "Call me Conor, Conor O'Connor."

Her head was spinning. "I…excuse me," Magdalen whispered; she stepped back. 'Yes, I am Magdalen, from the convent of San Miguel where we have…have been under siege lately." She would venture to say it. "But you know all about this…don't you?"

"Indeed…are you all right, Sister? Here…sit for a moment." The guard nodded and opened the door to a small room for conferencing. They spoke for fifteen minutes or more discussing the twists and turns of the case, her perceptions in regard to the Canteras, what she had personally endured though it was her intention to say nothing about herself. He knew of her encounter with Bernardo, was aware of his obsessions, her anguish. But they avoided what was most on Magdalen's mind…*who am I, am I one of you?*

When it was announced, Joanna should return to court, she withdrew. This time the nuns stepped into the back of the courtroom. Padric was immediately at Magdalen's side, his hand pressed to her back as if to protect her; he felt her relax not move from his touch. His eyes were full of concern; she grateful to see him. Together they stood silent. He had no mercy in him for Joanna but his nun had shown mercy.

There was a murmur in the courtroom when before sentencing the defendant was asked if she wished to speak. Joanna stood up.

"Your honor. Jay." She had addressed him by his first name. Whitton paled; she had fascinated him once; he could think of nothing else after he'd been with her. He saw her several more times until he came to his senses; she would never allude to this. "I am guilty as charged and done terrible things. Sentence me." Her attorney urged her to sit…she whispered something to him; he nodded.

"Ms. Cantera?" Whitton's eyes scanned the courtroom and, for one brief moment, locked on to Padric.

"I knew what I was doing, but my son was out of his mind…I ask you to have mercy on him. I understand he'll be sentenced this afternoon. I beg you. Give his sentence to me. Do this…enough with this circus. Do it now." She would get what she asked for… annoyed that she'd called his courtroom a circus.

Whitton would pontificate on the aggravating circumstances outweighing anything mitigating; Joanna Cantera had killed with malice aforethought, he said. He explained precisely the heinous, cruel and depraved nature of each of the martyr murders; Whitton was forced to draw only one conclusion: death by lethal injection.

Silence. Time stopped…later someone remembered the second hand on the clock pause then resume its rotation when a collective gasp grew to a roar. They could contain themselves no longer.

Padric stared straight ahead as shouts of approval broke out all around him; the thud of the gavel brought silence. He watched her; long black hair in a ponytail; her attire, a business suit, Joanna stood very alone with head down; more than one guard moved in to lead her away. Discarded like the victims she'd tossed aside, she was pulled from the room. The nuns quickly exited the courtroom and disappeared.

A victory for Major Crimes…Padric had wanted her dead and he got it. So why was he feeling so lousy? But then…he caught a small, nuanced exchange between father and daughter. Joanna had turned to look one last time at her father; a glance, something telling, passing between them and she was gone. *The old man is planning something.* A high-security vehicle waited in the underground tunnel below to remove her to death row at Ravenswell Prison; Arturo slipped from the courtroom.

Jana and the others hustled their friend into the hall. "We're getting you as far away from here as we can."

"Get off me. I've work to do." But he let them pile him into the Precinct hummer and Martinez drove slowly away from the courthouse. They circled the Plaza. He asked where Pistasio was…no one had seen him. He was part of a six-vehicle convoy transporting the prisoner; they were taking no chances.

But Padric's thoughts raced…*money buys anything.* "*Mi amigos,* this isn't over…mark my word. We have trouble ahead with this one." He knew her father had resources from Mexico to Vancouver's Grouse Mountain…he and Joanna and even the bishop skied there each year. But waiting for the light to change, Padric observed its approach in the right side mirror, a silver hummer; Arturo's 'signature-ride'. He was alone; unusual, considering the import of what had just happened. Padric side-eyed him, noting how proudly he sat at the wheel, but suddenly the old man turned his head and looked at him.

The sadness in his eyes was apparent and he read something in Padric's…was it regret, an apology, condemnation? Oddly he nodded respectfully; the detective did the same; the light changed.

Later that day, a special team transported Bernardo to Whitton's chambers for sentencing…if open to the public it would have been chaos, since he'd been marked by the media as the mastermind behind the macabre killings. Before sentencing, he had been housed in the forensic hospital on the campus of a state mental institution. Though the staff was heroic, they were working each day in a run-down institution built in the late 1800's; the buildings rampant with asbestos and sunken floors.

Arturo had been furious knowing his grandson could barely handle the light of day let alone the screams and horrors of a decrepit facility. He'd laid curled up in ball in a padded cell flooded with light twentyfourseven; yet at times, he refused to sit or lie down at all and stood for long intervals, repeating Magdalen's name, until, near catatonic, he collapsed. It was one of the first times Arturo felt helpless…he would change things. But who was this Magdalen who had placed her hand with a blessing on the head of his precious daughter, whose name was continually on his nephew's lips?

In judge's chambers, family and friends of victims would not have the opportunity to vent; there were none present, but Arturo was there. O'Manion and Padric stood silent beside their Commander when the young man, unable to hold up his head, was assisted into the room by his attorney; the same who had appeared for Joanna. O'Connor saw Padric…they acknowledged each other with a nod, teacher to student…but Padric noted he was more striking now; he had not appeared to age but his manner was more serene. Angels did walk the earth.

In a strange twist, Bernardo looked slowly around.

"But where is Sister Magdalen?" Arturo again heard her name. Whatever his attorney said, it had a calming effect and the young man was suddenly transformed. Later Whitton asked Padric if the nun might consider taking an ongoing interest in the young man. He had smiled a little. Bernardo was remanded to an institution for the criminally insane and sentenced to life without the possibility of parole even if deemed rehabilitated.

Arturo imploded within but called in some markers: he knew important men's secrets and had brokered too many deals to line the pockets of those in courts of law and high places. Within hours, he'd used his influence to remove his grandson to a private facility, its location so embedded in a rocky ravine it was known only to law enforcement and the Benedictine monks who built it. Saint Dysmas was a home for the banished; its patron, the penitent thief who died beside Jesus. Here, the monastery overlooked the prison where Father Sebastian had prepared for his ordination. Following the armored van transporting the serial killer, Arturo turned to his bishop-son who had remained at the ranch during the sentencing. He asked again: "The nun...my Joanna asked for her; the one who is loved by the boy...her name?"

"Magdalena...Sister Magdalen, father." Santo Cantera looked out the window.

In the early dawn of the following day, Santo Cantera realized he was finally home in his bed when he heard the birds in the acacias below; he closed his eyes, wishing he could hide in his suite and never emerge. He would sit in his garden, fix things, weed the upper terrace and deadhead the roses...a Cardinal from the Vatican suggested he take a sabbatical.

He would not. Under cover of darkness, he had returned home on the same day Joanna was processed into Ravenswell. Combative and not in the mood, she had already racked up four violations against inmates and staff and had been instantly thrown in the hole. No one listened when she cried out for her son and screamed for her father and her brother, the bishop, who was deeply humbled before all of L'Arroyo by his family's misdeeds, ridiculed for his blindness, intentional or not.

As it had been for his nephew, the dark streets were a comfort as he returned to San Miguel. He was pleased...how heroic the young priest, Michelantonio, and Steed had been, carrying the weight of his parish and diocese when he vanished. The people would not forget...new loyalties were formed; more than a few, from this moment on, would look to Father Sebastian for answers.

It was mid-afternoon in the Cathedral. Magdalen asked if he'd be hearing confessions. "Yes, if the penitents come, I will minister to them. Monsignor will assist as well; a new priest will be joining us briefly until he takes up his new post, an amazing young man with a fine intellect and good sense of humor. For a few days he will assist Father Sebastian...he arrived last night; they are like brothers already. There is laughter again in my house."

"This is good news," she whispered and knew not a few priests had withdrawn their services to the Cathedral, claiming other more pressing commitments and hoped the bishop would understand; he did...perfectly. Interesting how fear of being tainted by association can clear a room, he had said to his father. But he was smiling now at Magdalen.

"This new priest...his name is Father Liam, Liam Padric."

She masked her utter surprise with a simple "How nice!" and made no reference to the detective nor did he. She wondered if he had heard of her final encounter with a sorrowful, broken Joanna...she wouldn't ask. But he knew; Joanna herself had told him and he was grateful. He had heard she had spoken kindly to his father in court. She was a blessing.

Magdalen was feeling better. Petra had been right. Forgiveness without judgment eases the heart; it was a godly act even though some did not approve of her words in the courtroom. Cecelia's family would arrive at the convent door to scold her...what was she thinking? Dolorosa was at her side in an instant. "I've got this!" She told them in a flurry of Spanish of the convent's sympathies but there was a larger picture, every soul precious no matter how mired in evil. They would sadly never speak again, the de Torro and Redondo friendship forever severed.

It troubled Magdalen but now she turned to the bishop.

"Is there anything else?"

"No and yes. I pray Sister Petra will receive me at some point. I am glad she is with us."

"I am sure of it, Your grace."

He sighed. "There will be changes here. It is important that both of you are pleased."

"And why…it isn't necessary, no need."

"What do the young ones say: it is what it is. I have no desire to tax anyone any further. There is much to be done and God's work goes on. Thank you for being so gracious today in the courtroom. I am sure Christ's Holy Face shone in yours. God embrace you." He had not said this in a very long time…an expression he had frequently used when departing.

Santo Cantera quietly withdrew from the sacristy and walked through the afternoon shadows into the nave of the Cathedral. She heard the confessional door open and close; it was early. Confessions would not begin for another hour; the bishop would sit in the dark weeping. Her tasks completed, Magdalen walked down the sacristy steps, but she hesitated and returned…she could not leave, sensing the man's desperation.

Though he knew nothing of her decision to stay, she set to work mending a vestment. But contemplation and silence vanished, when the door suddenly opened and the Padric brothers, laughing and conversing in Gaelic, burst into the sacristy; they grinned at her. "Say it isn't so…what am I seeing?" The men laughed. They were almost identical.

"My brother the priest needed an escort to his first duties here in L'Arroyo, God help us, and here we are…here he is and God help you, too, Sister."

"A police escort I'm getting. Good afternoon, Sister, I'm Liam and I'm in need of a stole so I can hear confessions. It's you, I'm assuming, who put up with the likes of John."

"And you're not twins?"

"Close enough…we're ten months apart and our mum won't discuss it."

"That's too much information already. I'm so glad to meet you at last. It's your turn now; I'm done with him. Please make him behave." The men laughed out loud.

Ay, John, you know how to pick 'em. So this was the nun and there's a bit of the mystic in her, she had the sight; ah, Johnny bhoyo, you better be behaving with this one. We'll have a wee chat, you and me.

Padric would leave them to their duties. He sighed as he closed the door. His brother was home, but his brother and the bishop? He needed a drink, but not before reentering the Cathedral through the side door to kneel in the shadows debating whether to enter his brother's confessional. Though he couldn't bring himself to it, he thanked God over and over; his brother was home, his wife in his bed, a son growing stronger each day in an abbey and his girls surrounded by family.

But today, a Jameson sounded better than a lengthy examination of conscience and saying his sins. He stepped into the early evening…he'd spend the night again by his bassinet at the abbey. In between shifts and, whether his wife was with him or not, he'd sped out to the edge of the desert just to be with Finn Shakespeare Alejandro Padric.

It was easier now; the case, officially closed. Lara's first visit to her son had been so emotional the nuns had urged her to stay for the night; a bed for her, placed by his side. In silence the next day, Padric drove home with his wife…they had been through so much. He would take care of things.

But for now, he was needed…there was a party soon to begin for his brother Liam when he returned from the Cathedral. Padric glanced up at the campanile. A figure, seraphic and noble, stood looking down at him…a gust of wind lifted his long hair from his shoulders and, bowing to Padric, he disappeared into the night.

Padric knew now; Magdalen was right. Angels walked the streets of L'Arroyo like demons did. He thought briefly of the entity, the unknown he hadn't pursued below the Cathedral…where was it? Milleau. Leave it to him. He sensed he would have more to contend with soon enough. He watched his nun as she walked with head bowed back to the convent, Tarkington and Tate observing her every move. They nodded to him and he smiled. In the convent of San Miguel, a nun, once nearly crucified upside down, drew her Sisters around her and told them how much she had missed them.

Next week the moondead would be memorialized, their bodies in coffins laying in remembrance for two days and two nights in the Cathedral...Bishop Cantera's orders.

But one would be empty. Lucy.

Padric sighed...it would never end, but he had been closer to solving a mystery than he thought. A nun with a patch on her eye in the abbey on the edge of the desert entered the nursery-infirmary to peek at the baby called Finn Padric; she'd done so every night since his arrival. His nurse, occupied elsewhere, knew of her visits and smiled and tonight she sat down and spoke to the boy in a whisper how she wished her Sister, who loved a good mystery, would rescue them all from the grips of someone who was holding her here and had taken control of the cloister.

But not to worry, dear Finn, sweet bambino, you are safe; no one will hurt you here. God's angels surround you. Later, she returned to her own infirmary bed in the casita where she could look into the quadrangle brimming with roses. She whispered her night prayers and wept.

Come for me soon, cara mia; find me, Magdalena.

Author's Notes

The Twilight Zone — refers to 1960's TV series created by Rod Serling, presenting each week three tales drawing viewers into a different dimension of horror, suspense even humor, there is always a surprise twist at the end.

James Joyce's Ulysses — novel by first serialized in American journal *The Little Review* from March 1918 to December 1920, and then published in its entirety by Sylvia Beach in February 1922, in Paris; chronicles one day in the life of protagonist, Leopold Bloom, in Dublin on 16 June 1904. Joyce creates a series of parallels between the characters in the Greek poem and those of the novel. Approximately 265,000 words in length, it is divided into eighteen episodes, the book has attracted controversy and scrutiny, including early obscenity trials especially regarding the final episode titled Molly's Soliloquy written with no punctuation and revealing her sexual fantasies and comments regarded the male anatomy and…her own. But the last pages are considered to be some of the most breathtaking prose in the English language.

Kettle black — Padric's version of a common phrase "The pot calling the kettle black", an idiom claiming a person guilty of the very thing of which they accuse another.

High Noon — reference to a deadly meeting and a town's dread in the 1952 American Western film classic, High Noon, starring Gary Cooper. As the well-publicized dreaded encounter for revenge in New Mexican territory draws near, so does a similar event, the sentencing of the Canteras, in the fictitious city of L'Arroyo, Arizona.

angel de Dios — Spanish, for angel of God.

Conor O'Connor — the earthly name of angelic-human, Sanctus, whom Magdalen has encountered in the bishop's garden; he is indeed an angel, a watcher, and will shadow the nun in subsequent narratives.

EXITUS

A Friday near midnight in early June

Beneath a Strawberry Moon and the razor wire of Ravenswell Prison, a police van slowly circled the prison; the driver was looking for something. He slowed down. The delivery gate was busy tonight with produce and food trucks coming and going. Every Friday it was the same; he pulled up behind the last one in line, words were quickly exchanged. Later when Gellantano's Produce left through the gate, it followed the police van. Company trucks always asked for an escort. But once outside the gate, instead of remaining behind, it followed the truck down a two-lane road until both made a turn into a bridal path covered with trees. There were farms for miles.

The officer handed the other an envelope stuffed with cash. The men grinned and the back door of the truck opened, a woman laughed. "Baby, you didn't forget me."

"Never, but we need to move, get out of here. Let's go."

"First things first. Show me how happy you are to see you...get over here." She pulled him into the van and the two took their time making love then half-dressed, drove slowly away. The woman with the long black hair and shining dark eyes whispered and purred, snuggled close to the man who had been there for her. "My father's waiting for us, right?"

"In Poco, babe...then we'll keep going."

Joanna laughed. "It's been you and me and nobody knew it."

"Who would a thought?" He laughed but kept his eyes on the rear view mirror.

Six hours later back at the Precinct and near end of shift, Padric looked up from his paper work. O'Manion and the Commander appeared in the doorway and he stood up; they closed the door. Marcus thought it odd…they'd drawn the blinds; there was silence then a roar, so full of pain, it caused other detectives to turn in their seats; some rose and walked toward Padric's office.

It was a chilling sound. Ramirez stepped into the hall and motioned to the young detective. Jana flew from her desk and descended on Padric like a mother bird; the two threw their arms around him, not letting him go. O'Manion spoke to him like a father and he turned to Ramirez. "Get his brother the priest on the phone. He's pastor at Our Lady of Sorrows now."

Finally wrestled into his old worn chair, Padric immediately regained his composure, apologized; his face like stone. "I need to go to him. Where is he?"

"He's gone, John," whispered Ramirez.

"He needs me…"

"Johnny…he's dead." Jana turned to O'Manion. "Right?"

"They found what's left of him just south of Poco…it's bad."

Marcus knelt down beside him…Maselli and Maclone appeared in the doorway; they would not leave the room. Marcus had an idea. "Come, I'll take you to him; you and me, we'll bring him home. I know the way." He knew every inch of the Sonoran, north and south. His nana lived just over the Border.

They waited for Ramirez' nod. "Take him with you." He pointed to Maselli and Padric was grateful…he was calm now.

They left. It would be a two-hour drive to the Border.

Dies irae, dies illa.

Author's Notes

Strawberry Moon – from the Latin solstitium, from sol (sun) and stitium (to stop), a June moon known as Strawberry Moon to early Native American tribes, who measured time by things like the moon; this one marks the season of strawberries and aligns sometimes with the North American summer solstice when the sun stands still at its northernmost point as seen from Earth. It marks the day with the most sunlight and a visit from a Strawberry Moon every seventy years.

ADDENDUM

THE PLAYERS

THE FIRST PRECINCT
Commander Oliver Ramirez
Captain Brendan O'Manion, Major Crimes
Lt. John Padric, *protagonist*, lead night detective, Major Crimes
Lt. Alejandro Martinez, night detective, Padric's partner
Lt. Jace Tarkington, crime tech, night detective, Major Crimes
Lt. Jana Zalconi, undercover night detective, Major Crimes/VICE
Sgt. Jesus Marcus, night detective, Major Crimes
Sgt. Joe Pistasio, head of tact squad. LPD; Padric's main back-up
Sgt. Anzo Ducci, Homicide, Padric's close friend
Sgt. Ian Cunningham, Canine Division, Padric's countryman
Nevel, K-9, police dog, Cunningham's partner
Officer Amanda Duran, patrol, assigned to convent surveillance
Sgt. Patrick Mahoney, backup for undercover Lt. Jana Zalconi
Sgt. Leo Garcia, backup for undercover Lt. Jana Zalconi
Sgt. Woodson, LCAT, criminal apprehension team
Sgt. Morrow, LCAT, criminal apprehension team
Rookie officers: Maselli, Maclone, Tarkington, Tate
Sister Magdalen, *protagonist*, consultant in the case of the moondead
CSI Jon-Gabriel Milleau
CSI Mike Miller
Declan Brady, EMT, LFD
Billy Kelly, ambulance driver, EMT, LFD
Dr. Rubin, medical examiner/coroner, LPD

FAMILY MEMBERS OF THE FIRST PRECINCT
Lara, John's wife; children, Kate and Kara Padric
Darragh Padric, John's mother
Guinness "Guin" Padric, John's father believed to be dead
Liam Padric, newly ordained priest, John's brother
Mairead, Mary and Fiona Padric, John's sisters
Marisol, wife of Alex Martinez; Children, Mario, Manny, and Lisa
Deanna C. Ramirez, wife of Oliver Ramirez

SUNSET CITY POLICE DEPARTMENT
Sgt. Dan Mason, detective, Sundowner City, John Padric's *nemesis*

MEADOW: HIGH-SECURITY MEDICAL FACILITY
where most staff are law enforcement
FBI Agent Bobby Watson, friend of John Padric
Physician's asst./Sgt. Gina Chavez, friend of John Padric

THE CATHEDRAL
Bishop Santo Cantera, Church leader in western Arizona
Monsignor Theophilos Steed, Vicar General, assistant to bishop
Father Michelantonio Sebastiano, newly ordained
Sister Magdalen, sacristan
Lupe/Guadalupe Rojas, aging caretaker of the Cathedral
Eduardo Morales, bishop's gardener/manager of the Cathedral
Altar servers: Larry Whitton, Mario Martinez, Ellie Thomas

THE CONVENT OF SAN MIGUEL
Sister Magdalen, the former Brid Williams, *protagonist*, archaeologist-
    turned-nun, second assistant to Sister Petra, caretaker of the
    elder, Sister Monica, and other retired nuns
Sister Dolorosa, the former Melissa de Torro, Dean of Students
    Cathedral High, frequent companion of Magdalen
Sister Petra, director-superior of the convent of San Miguel
Sister Monica, revered elder and mystic, only living member of the
    Sisters of the Crucified from "the first days" in early L'Arroyo
Sister Lucy, art teacher/artisan, confidante, friend of Magdalen
Sister Amata, retired, Magdalen's former novice mistress
Sister Edwardmary, retired, musician and convent gardener
Sister Patrice, manager of the house and chef
Sister Johnmary, retired professor, sage-storyteller, called "wizard"
Sister Agnes, first assistant to convent director
Sister Barbara, genius/scientist/teacher, friend of Magdalen
Sister Cecelia, charge nurse, chaplain, Meadow Medical

Cathedral High School

Sister Petra, Principal
Sister Dolorosa, Dean of Students
Sister Lucy, Art Dept. Chair,teacher of painting and ceramics
Sister Magdalen, teacher of art history
Sister Patrice, teacher of Life Education in baking and sewing
Sister Barbara, Science Dept. Chair, teacher of physics/chemistry
Dr. Dave Helmstone, Theater Studies and Band Advisor
Students: Ramos Robles, Carlos Guerrero, Ben, Danny, Julie

The Diocese of L'Arroyo

Bishop Santo Cantera, Bishop
Monsignor Theophilos Steed, Vicar General
Father Santeresa, exorcist, pastor of Our Lady of Sorrows
Father Stefano Villa, pastor, San Paulo Mission Church
Father Seamus , pastor, Saint Aidan's Church of the Desert
Brother James Hardy, director, Holy Cross Homeless Shelter
Father Liam Padric, John's brother
Sister Mary Rose, Abbess, Cloistered Order of Saint Uriel

The Edge

Constanzio Edraza, owner of Chato's in the Edge, Chato II in Poco
     on Mexican Border
Ruth Ruthless, co-owner of a "no-name" in the Edge
Joanna Cantera, owner of a business in the Edge…and other things

GLOSSARY

Benedicite. Ancient greeting used by the Friars literally meaning "Good word!", the modern usage meaning "Good day!" or more loosely "A blessing!" The convent of San Miguel uses the greeting when answering the phone.

Breviary is book of liturgical prayers to be prayed at certain times throughout the day and night. It consists of psalms and antiphons, responsories and the reading of certain lessons to inspire and appropriate for the holy day of a saint, Our Lady or Christ. After the reforms of Pope Paul VI it has been called the Liturgy of the Hours. Some may refer to it as a Psalter or Antiphonary. Priests pray the breviary daily: nuns pray a shorter version.

Brigid's Cross is a cruciform made of rushes and sometimes straw. It is woven into a square with four long wisps extended and tied at the ends. They are traditionally woven in Ireland on February 1, known as *Lá Fhéile Bhríde*, when Saint Brigid of Kildare is venerated. Also known as Mary of the Gael, she was not only an abbess/founder of many monasteries, but a bishop and revered as patron of Ireland with Saint Patrick, who was her friend. It is believed the cross protects the house from evil and is hung over doors and in Irish kitchens to guard it from fire. Sister Magdalen's birth name was Brid Williams, a common derivative of Brigid or Bridget.

Book of Hours was a medieval manuscript of devotional prayer consisting mainly in psalms and lessons and illuminated pages. There are thousands in many varieties, one of which is the Little Office of the Blessed Virgin Mary often prayed by the members of religious communities. The Sisters of San Miguel pray this daily. At night, they chant aloud Compline, the evening prayer of the Church.

Cathedral. Derived from *cathdrale* in French and *cathedra* in Latin meaning "seat", it is the central church in a diocese and the seat of the bishopric. It is imposing and often larger than any building around it. Many cathedrals are built east/west; the Cathedral of San Miguel, north/south allowing many to believe it was, from the beginning, destined for dark times as we discover in The Moondead. Its floor plan is *cruciform*; the main body of the building called the *nave*, derived from the Latin word for *ship*. The transepts make up the cross bar and contain small chapels. The Cathedral in our story contains the chapel of Our Lady of the Desert and the chapel of the Cathedral's patron saint, Saint Michael or Miguel. *Sanctuary* meaning "holy place" is the focal point of the building consisting of the main altar and tabernacle where the Blessed Sacrament or Eucharist is retained; in the Cathedral of San Miguel there is a side altar over which hangs a simple wooden cross to the right of the main altar. A *sanctuary lamp* is perpetually lit not as decoration but as a sign of eternal worship…this is observed in both Christian and Jewish tradition. Many Cathedrals are listed among the UNESCO World Heritage sites and are huge repositories for art and historical treasures…they are cultural museums. They often have domes and spires symbolically lifting us heavenward. The Cathedral of San Miguel has a *campanile*, a bell tower with seven bells. The caretaker, an old woman, lives in a space next to the choir loft under the belfry. The bells commence at seven in the morning and cease at seven at night. The Cathedral's architecture was modeled on the bishop's favorite church in Sonora, Mexico: The Church of Santa Maria Magdalena in the town of Magdalena de Kino. As a young priest he assisted in the planning and construction of what would become his Cathedral when he later became a bishop.

Confessionals. Private enclosures for the Sacrament of Peñance may be found on either side of the nave of the church. Here the penitent may approach the priest to confess their sins. He forgives and makes things new in Christ's name for the soul

Convent. In general terms, a community of nuns, vowed to God and living together for reasons of Christian fellowship and devotion to works of charity, living in service. It also refers to the house or residence itself in which the nuns live.

Hagiography. Hagiographers wrote lives of the saints, their good deeds, sometimes exaggerated, descriptions of their *passio* or manner of death. They embraced the local traditions and customs, the devotional cults surrounding the holy ones. Their stories were the genre of a medieval times.

Hiermonymian Martyrology. *The Martyrology of Jerome* is a book containing a list of Christian martyrs compiled from the 6th C. and considered the most influential martyrology, an ultimate source for such matters. Amendments and edits, additions and rearranging of pages in the 9th C. give us today's text, preserved in the *Bibliotheque nationale* in Paris.

Holy habit. Distinctive garb generally worn by nuns, monks, priests and brothers according to the custom of the Order they have chosen. It can be tunic-like or fitted with a *scapular* or broad cloth worn from neck to feet. A veil generally covers a *coif* or head covering of white linen. Canon law is not particular about the design of the garb, but that it is definable, a witness to the values of Christ to whom they have vowed their lives.

Holy vows. A public commitment to the evangelical counsels: poverty, chastity and obedience, principles derived from the words of Christ in His Gospel and to which some are called to a greater observance, a consecrated life lived in His service. The terms *vocation* and *calling* are used to describe the attraction to such a life of detachment from material things, to give one's heart and one's love wholly to God, to live humbly in obedience to the wishes of the order one chooses to join.

Lectionary refers to an ordered collection of the Scriptures to be read during Mass and other liturgies. It contains those passages to be read from the Old and New Testament during the Lessons and those from the New Testament for the Gospel reading. There are many types of lectionaries in both the Roman and Eastern Orthodox Churches. These can be found in every sacristy. Interestingly, Rembrandt painted his mother reading one; his depiction of it, quite detailed, *circa* 1630 A.D.

Lent. A six-week or forty day religious observance from Ash Wednesday to Holy Saturday, the day before Easter. In both Catholic and Protestant traditions, the penitential season is honored with fasting and prayer, a deeper devotion to Christ. *Passiontide* refers to the last two weeks in Lent and still, in many Catholic churches, all statues and crosses are covered in purple; *Holy Week,* the last week in Lent. Holy Thursday, Good Friday, and Holy Saturday are often called the Holy Week Triduum. Holy Thursday is set aside for the *Supper of the Lord*, during which the pastor or bishop wash the feet of random individuals from the congregation in remembrance of the Lord washing the feet of his apostles at the Last Supper; on Good Friday from noon until three o'clock, the devout observe the *Tre Ore*, the three hours' agony of Christ on the cross before He gives up His spirit.

Martyr. One who witnesses to Christ in his/her dying for Him. The term is derived from the Latin *martus* meaning witness, but it grew to mean more than simply living a Christian life. Those who refused to deny their faith in Christ publicly were put to death during what is called the Age of Martyrs. Many are honored as saints in the Church.

Martyrology. A cataloged list of martyrs and saints records their lives and deaths. In terms of scholarship, there are difficulties discerning historical truths due to the number of disparate characters and the inclusion of local histories.

Nun or Sister. Terms often used interchangeably as in The Sacristan Mysteries; however, a *nun* is generally one who lives a cloistered, vowed life of prayer, the *sister*, a member of an active mission community also living a vowed life but serving the world in teaching, nursing and other external works. Though some retain their baptismal name, others choose to take the name of a holy one, a saint, a reference to Our Lady

Order or religious congregation/community refers to religious institutes of men and women vowed to God and His service. Orders of the Church formerly referred to the Franciscans, Dominicans, Benedictines Augustinians and others; the newer orders, religious communities. Today the terms *order* or *religious community* may be used interchangeably but this was not always so…there was a distinction between solemn vows made in the ancient orders and the simple vows made by those in religious congregations.

Ossuary is a reliquary or chest, also a building and place of rest for skeletal remains. It might contain the remains of those known as the Incorruptibles, certain individuals whose bodies did not decompose but have stayed intact, considered by some, a sign of favor from God.

Sacristy. A room usually next to the sanctuary in the church protects and cares for the sacred vessels and linens, objects for the liturgy and parish records may be kept here. A sacristan is responsible for the care of it. The *chalice* is a gold cup used during Mass by the priest to hold wine and, through the act of transubstantiation, changed into the Blood of Christ. The *paten* is a gold, flat plate used to hold the bread or Body of Christ. The *cruets* are glass containers holding the bread and wine before Consecration during Mass. A *finger bowl* is used for the washing of the priest's hands. *Incense* is generally a form of tree resin emitting smoke and a fragrance when lit in a *thurible* or *incense boat* containing charcoal and which can be swung back and forth to incense a coffin or the people or the main altar as a sign of devotion. *The apergillam* is a kind of hand sprinkler dipped in a container of holy water. The priest blesses the people with it. The *pyx* is a small round metal container by which the Sacred Host may be carried to the sick and dying. Church linens serve different purposes: the *corporal* is a square linen cloth placed on the altar during the Consecration of the bread and wine into the Body and Blood of Christ. A *purificator* is also a square linen cloth with a cross in the center and used to wipe and purify the chalice. The pall is cloth used to cover the casket during a funeral Mass.

Vestry. A room generally attached to the sacristy houses the vestments worn by the bishop and priests for Mass and other liturgies: *alb* - long, white robe worn under the outer garments of the priest's vestments worn during Mass; *chasuable* - meaning "little house", a decorative outer vestment of specific color for one of the six seasons of the liturgical year, i.e.; purple for Lent and Advent, white for the feasts of Jesus and Mary, red for Pentecost and the feast of martyrs. The *cincture* is a rope-like belt worn round the *alb*; *stole*, black or purple scarf worn by the priest during the Sacrament of Peñance like the prayer cloth Jesus wore as a Jew during prayer.

THE AUTHOR

Wordsmith L. A. Mascone is a native of New Jersey
and lives in the Arizona Sonoran; holds masters degrees in
Urban Education and Systematic Theology.
Was a high-school teacher of history, political science,
theology, English and art; is a veteran of the Armed Forces.

With a penchant for the dark side of a telling,
Mascone is a listener and sometimes hears things others do not,
especially when souls speak of their troubles
or the ones they fear lie ahead.

*"I'm hooked on the characters who slip and fall
and try to get up; how they might run to God or maybe not.
I've done that a lot; at times messed up badly and
been in the dark…so I get it when others are there."*
~L.A. Mascone

The Moondead's protagonist, Sister Magdalen, frequently
whispers: "Everyone's looking for a little redemption"
and so is Mascone.

The green bushes bowed, as though they had been visited by archangels…
Katherine Mansfield (1888-1923)

Also by L.A. Mascone

The Tomb Woman
A Sacristan Mystery - Book Two

The Church of Bones
A Sacristan Mystery - Book Three

llyndragonpublishing.com